THE
AX

By Donald E. Westlake

NOVELS
The Ax • Humans • Sacred Monster • A Likely Story
Kahawa • Brothers Keepers • I Gave at the Office
Adios, Scheherazade • Up Your Banners

COMIC CRIME NOVELS
Baby, Would I Lie? •Trust Me on This • High Adventure
Castle in the Air • Enough • Dancing Aztecs
Two Much! • *Help* I Am Being Held Prisoner
Cops and Robbers • Somebody Owes Me Money
Who Stole Sassi Manoon? • God Save the Mark
The Spy in the Ointment • The Busy Body
The Fugitive Pigeon • Smoke

THE DORTMUNDER SERIES
What's the Worst That Could Happen?
Don't Ask • Drowned Hopes • Good Behavior
Why Me • Nobody's Perfect
Jimmy the Kid • Bank Shot • The Hot Rock

CRIME NOVELS
Pity Him Afterwards • Killy • 361
Killing Time • The Mercenaries

JUVENILE
Philip

WESTERN
Gangway (with Brian Garfield)

REPORTAGE
Under the English Heaven

SHORT STORIES
Tomorrow's Crimes • Levine
The Curious Facts Preceding My Execution and Other Fictions

ANTHOLOGY
Once Against the Law (coedited by William Tenn)

"*THE AX* IS A TIGHTLY CHARTED SUSPENSE STORY, FULL OF SURPRISES. . . . This story has all the euphemisms of life in the 90s."
—*USA Today*

"A CHILLING PORTRAIT of a downsized middle manager turned serial killer. . . . This cold, clever novel is bolstered by Westlake's inventive plotting, his meticulous use of abundant, credible details, and his burning anger over corporate tactics."
—*Booklist*

"A DARK SATIRE. . . . It's hard to sympathize with a killer, but . . . readers will root for him to succeed."
—*Albuquerque Sunday Journal*

"Westlake knows precisely how to grab a reader, draw him or her into the story, and then slowly tighten his grip until escape is impossible. . . . *THE AX* FILTERS EVERYTHING THROUGH THE CONSCIOUSNESS OF AN OUT-OF-SHAPE RASKOLNIKOV WITH BIFOCALS. BURKE DEVORE COULD BE THE UNEMPLOYED GUY NEXT DOOR. . . . HIS STORY WILL MAKE MANY READERS PAST FORTY DEEPLY UNEASY."
—*Washington Post Book World*

"A CHILLING LOOK AT THE DISINTEGRATION OF THE MIDDLE CLASS, *THE AX* IS AS SATISFYING AS A CLEVER MYSTERY AS IT IS A SOCIAL COMMENTARY."
—*Ft. Lauderdale Sun-Sentinel*

more . . .

"[*THE AX*] SEDUCES READERS INTO CHEERING THE SNUFFING OUT OF INNOCENT MIDDLE-AGED MEN. IT MAKES A PLAUSIBLE CASE THAT MURDER IS A RATIONAL RESPONSE TO CEOS WHO FIRE LEGIONS OF LOYAL EMPLOYEES TO PERK UP STOCK PRICES. IT SPINDLES ONE'S SENSE OF RIGHT AND WRONG."
—*Washington Post*

"A humane novel. . . . Hitchcock-style . . . Westlake does manage to question . . . both the wisdom of deriving one's identity from a job and the white middle-class man's right to unchallenged prosperity."
—*Worth*

"ACERBIC HUMOR, BITING SATIRE, AND DEAD-PAN DELIVERY . . . a biting satire of our stressed-out, speed-driven time."
—*Milwaukee Journal Sentinel*

DONALD E. WESTLAKE

THE AX

WARNER
VISION
BOOKS

A Time Warner Company

WARNER BOOKS EDITION

Warner Vision is a registered trademark of Warner Books, Inc.

Cover design by Tony Greco

Warner Books, Inc.
1271 Avenue of the Americas
New York, NY 10020

Visit our Web site at
http://warnerbooks.com

🅦 A Time Warner Company

Printed in the United States of America

Originally published in hardcover by The Mysterious Press.
First Paperback Printing: May, 1998

10 9 8 7 6 5 4 3 2 1

This is for my father, Albert Joseph Westlake, 1896—1953

The old superstition about fiction being "wicked" has doubtless died out in England, but the spirit of it lingers in a certain oblique regard directed toward any story which does not more or less admit that it is only a joke. Even the most jocular novel feels in some degree the weight of the proscription that was formerly directed against literary levity: the jocularity does not always succeed in passing for orthodoxy. It is still expected, though perhaps people are ashamed to say it, that a production which is after all only a 'make-believe' (for what else is a 'story'?) shall be in some degree apologetic— shall renounce the pretension of attempting really to represent life. This, of course, any sensible, wide-awake story declines to do, for it quickly perceives that the tolerance granted to it on such a condition is only an attempt to stifle it disguised in the form of generosity. The old evangelical hostility to the novel, which was as explicit as it was narrow, and which regarded it as little less favourable to our immortal part than a stage-play, was in reality far less insulting. The only reason for the existence of a novel is that it does attempt to represent life.

Henry James, *The Art of Fiction*, 1888

If you're doing what you think is right for everyone involved, then you're fine. So I'm fine.

Thomas G. Labrecque, CEO
Chase Manhattan Bank

1

I've never actually killed anybody before, murdered another person, snuffed out another human being. In a way, oddly enough, I wish I could talk to my father about this, since he did have the experience, had what we in the corporate world call the background in that area of expertise, he having been an infantryman in the Second World War, having seen "action" in the final march across France into Germany in '44–'45, having shot at and certainly wounded and more than likely killed any number of men in dark gray wool, and having been quite calm about it all in retrospect. How do you know beforehand that you can do it? That's the question.

Well, of course, I couldn't ask my father that, discuss it with him, not even if he were still alive, which he isn't, the cigarettes and the lung cancer having caught up with him in his sixty-third year, putting him down as surely if not as efficiently as if he had been a distant enemy in dark gray wool.

The question, in any case, will answer itself, won't it? I mean, this is the sticking point. Either I can do it, or I can't. If I can't, then all the preparation, all the planning, the files I've maintained, the expense I've put myself to (when God knows I can't afford it), have been in vain, and I might as well throw it all away, run no more ads, do no more scheming, simply allow myself to fall back into the herd of steer mindlessly lurching toward the big dark barn where the mooing stops.

Today decides it. Three days ago, Monday, I told Marjorie I had another appointment, this one at a small plant in Harrisburg, Pennsylvania, that my appointment was for Friday morning, and that my plan was to drive to Albany Thursday, take a late afternoon flight to Harrisburg, stay over in a motel, taxi to the plant Friday morning, and then fly back to Albany Friday afternoon. Looking a bit worried, she said, "Would that mean we'd have to relocate? Move to Pennsylvania?"

"If that's the worst of our problems," I told her, "I'll be grateful."

After all this time, Marjorie still doesn't understand just how severe our problems are. Of course, I've done my best to hide the extent of the calamity from her, so I shouldn't blame Marjorie if I'm successful in keeping her more or less worry-free. Still, I do feel alone sometimes.

This has to work. I have to get out of this morass,

and *soon*. Which means I'd better be capable of murder.

The Luger went into my overnight bag, in the same plastic bag as my black shoes. The Luger had been my father's, his one souvenir from the war, a sidearm he'd taken from a dead German officer that either he or someone else had shot, earlier that day, from the other side of the hedgerow. My father had removed the clip full of bullets from the Luger and transported it in a sock, with the gun itself traveling in a small dirty pillowcase he'd taken from a half-wrecked house somewhere in muddy France.

My father never fired that gun, so far as I know. It was simply his trophy, his version of the scalp you take from your defeated enemy. Everybody shot at everybody and he was still standing at the end, so he took a gun from one of the fallen.

I too had never fired that gun, nor any other. It frightened me, in fact. For all I knew, if I were to pull the trigger with the clip in place in the butt, the thing would blow up in my hands. Still, it was a weapon, and the only one to which I had ready access. And there was certainly no record of its existence, at least not in America.

After my father died his old trunk was moved from his spare room to my basement, the trunk containing his army uniform and folded duffel bag and a sheaf of the orders that had moved him from place to place, way back then, in the unimaginable time before I was born. A time I like to think of as simpler and cleaner than ours. A time in which you knew with clarity who your enemies were, and *they* were who you killed.

The Luger, in its pillowcase, was at the bottom of the trunk, beneath the musty-smelling olive-drab uniform, its clip lying beside it, no longer concealed in that long-ago sock. I found it down there, the day I made my decision, and brought it out, and carried gun and clip up to my "office," the small spare room we used to call the guest room before I was at home all the time and in need of an office. I closed the door, and sat at the small wood table I used as a desk—bought last year at a lawn sale offered by some particularly desperate householder about ten miles from here—and studied the gun, and it seemed to me clean and efficient-looking, without rust or obvious injury. The clip, this small sharp metal machine, felt surprisingly heavy. There was a slit up the rear of it, through which could be seen the bases of the eight bullets it contained, each with its little round blind eye. Touch that eye with the firing mechanism of the gun, and the bullet leaps off on its only journey.

Could I just insert clip into gun, point, and pull the trigger? Was there risk involved? Afraid of the unknown, I drove to the nearest bookstore, one of the chains, in a mall, and found a little manual on handguns, and bought it (another expense!). This book suggested I oil various parts, and so I did, with Three-in-One oil. The book suggested I try dry-firing the gun—pull the trigger without the clip or any bullets in place—and I did, and the click sounded authoritative and efficient. It seemed that I did have a weapon.

The book also suggested that fifty-year-old bullets might not be entirely trustworthy, and told me how to empty and reload the clip, so I went to a sporting goods store across the state line in Massachusetts and with no trouble at all bought a little heavy box of 9-millimeter bullets and brought them home, where I thumbed eight of them into the clip, pressing each sleek torpedo down against the force of the spring, then sliding the clip up into the open butt of the gun: *click*.

Fifty years this tool had lain in darkness, under brown wool, wrapped in a French pillowcase, waiting for its moment. Its moment is now.

❦

I practiced with the Luger, driving away from home one sunny midweek day last month, April, driving thirty-some miles westward, across the state line into New York, until I found a deserted field next to a minor winding two-lane blacktop road. Hilly woods stretched upward, dark and tangled, beyond the field. There I parked the car on the weedy verge and walked out across the field with the gun a heavy weight in the inside pocket of my windbreaker.

When I was very close to the trees, I looked back and saw no one driving past on the road. So I took out the Luger and pointed it at a nearby tree and—moving quickly so as not to give myself time to be afraid—I squeezed the trigger the way the little book had told me, and it *shot*.

What an experience. Not expecting the recoil, or not remembering having read about the recoil, I wasn't prepared for how violently the Luger jumped upward and back, taking my hand with it, so that I almost hit myself in the face with the thing.

On the other hand, the noise wasn't as loud as I'd expected, not a great bang at all, but flatter, like an automobile tire blowout.

I did not, of course, hit the tree I was pointing at, but I did hit the tree next to it, making a tiny puff of dust as though the tree had exhaled. So the second time, now at least knowing the Luger was operational and wouldn't explode on me, I took more careful aim, with the standing stance the book had recommended, knees bent, body angled forward, both hands gripping the gun at arms' length as I sighted down the top of its barrel, and that time I hit *exactly* the spot on the tree I was aiming at.

Which was nice, but was somewhat spoiled by the fact that my concentration on aiming had made me again pay too little attention to recoil. This time, the Luger jumped out of my hands entirely and fell onto the ground. I retrieved it, wiped it carefully, and decided I had to conquer this matter of recoil if I were going to make use of the damn machine. For instance, what if I ever had to fire twice in a row? Not so good, if the gun is on the ground or, worse, up in my own face.

So once again I took the standing stance, this time aiming at a tree farther off. I clenched the grip of the Luger *hard*, and when I fired I let the recoil move my arm and then my whole body, so that I never really lost control of the gun. Its power trembled and shivered through my body, like a wave, and made me feel stronger. I liked it.

Of course, I was well aware that in giving all this attention to the physical details, I was not only providing proper weight to the preparation but was also avoiding, for as long as possible, any thought of the actual object of the exercise, the end result of all this groundwork. The death of a man. Though that would be faced soon enough. I knew it then, and I know it now.

Three shots; that was all. I drove back home, and cleaned the Luger, and oiled it again, and replaced the three missing bullets in the clip, and stored gun and clip separately in the bottom drawer of my filing cabinet, and didn't touch them again until I was ready to go out and see if I were actually capable of killing one Herbert Coleman Everly. Then I brought it out and put it into my overnight bag. And the other thing I packed, in addition to the usual clothing and toiletries, was Mr. Everly's resumé.

Herbert C. Everly
835 Churchwarden Lane
Fall City, CT 06198
(203) 240-3677

MAJOR WORK *Management*
EXPERIENCE Responsible for in-flow of pulp paper
from Canadian subsidiary. Coordi-
nated functions of polymer manufacturing arm, Oak Crest Paper Mills,
with Laurentian Resources (Can).
Maintained delivery schedules for
finished product to aerospace, auto,
lighting and other industries. Oversaw 82-person manufacturing
department, coordinated with 23-
person delivery department.
Administration and Personnel
Interviewed and hired for department. Wrote employee analyses,
recommended raises and bonuses,
counseled employees where necessary.
Industrial
23 years' experience, paper mills,
paper products sales, with two corporations.
EDUCATION BBA, Housatonic Business College,
1969
REFERENCE Human Resources Division
Kriegel-Ontario Paper Products
PO Box 9000
Don Mills, Ontario
Canada

There's an entire new occupation these days in our land, a growth industry of "specialists" whose function is to train the freshly unemployed in job-hunting, and specifically how to prepare that all-important resumé, how to put that best foot forward in the increasingly competitive struggle to get a new job, another job, the next job, a *job*.

HCE has taken such an expert's advice, his resumé reeks of it. For instance, no photo. For those applicants over forty, one popular theory holds that it is best not to include a photo of oneself, in fact not to include anything at all that points specifically to the applicant's age. HCE doesn't even give the years of his employment, limiting himself only to two unavoidable clues: "23 years" and his college graduation in 1969.

Also, HCE is, or at least he wants to appear to be, impersonal and efficient and businesslike. He says nothing of his marital status, or his children, or his outside interests (fishing, bowling, what you will). He limits himself to the issues at hand.

It is not the best resumé I've seen, but it's far from the worst; about middling, I would say. About good enough to get him an interview, if some paper manufacturer should be interested in hiring a manager-level employee with an intense history in the production and sales of specialized polymer paper products. Good enough to get him in the door, I would say. Which is why he must die.

The point in all this is to be absolutely anonymous. Never to be suspected, not for a second. That's why I'm being so very cautious, why in fact I'm driving a good twenty-five miles toward Albany, actually crossing into New York State, before turning south to make my way circuitously back into Connecticut.

Why? Why such extreme care? My gray Plymouth Voyager is not after all particularly noticeable. I'd say it looks rather like one vehicle in five on the road these days. But what if, by some remote chance, some friend of ours, some neighbor of ours, some parent of a schoolmate of Betsy or Bill, happened to see me, this morning, eastbound in Connecticut, when Marjorie has been told I'll be westbound in New York or even airborne by now, toward Pennsylvania? How would I explain it?

Marjorie would think at first I was having an affair. Although—except for that one time eleven years ago that she knows about—I have always been a faithful husband, and she knows that, too. But if she thought I were seeing another woman, if she had any reason to question my movements and my explanations, wouldn't I eventually have to tell her the truth? If only to relieve her mind?

"I was off on a private mission," I would finally have to say, "to kill a man named Herbert Coleman Everly. For us, sweetheart."

But a secret shared is no longer a secret. And in any event, why burden Marjorie with these problems? There's nothing she can do beyond what she's doing, the little household economies she put into place the instant the word came I'd be laid off.

Yes, she did. She didn't even wait for my last day on the job, and she certainly wouldn't have waited until my severance pay was gone. The *instant* I came home with the notification (the slip was yellow, not pink) that I was to be part of the next reduction in force, Marjorie started the belt-tightening. She'd seen it happen to friends of ours, neighbors of ours, and she knew what to expect and how—within her limits—to deal with it.

The exercise class was cancelled, and so was the gardening workshop. She cut off HBO and Showtime, leaving only basic cable; antenna TV reception is virtually impossible in our hilly corner of Connecticut. Lamb and fish left our table, replaced by chicken and pasta. Magazine subscriptions were not renewed. Shopping mall trips ceased, and so did those wandering slow journeys pushing a grocery cart through Stew Leonard's.

No, Marjorie is doing her job, I couldn't ask for more. So why ask her to become part of *this*? Particularly when I still can't be sure, after all the planning, all the preparation, that I can do it. Shoot this person. This other person.

I have to, that's all.

Having driven back into Connecticut, well south of our neighborhood, I stop at a convenience store/gas station to fill the tank and to take the Luger out of my suitcase, putting it under the raincoat artfully folded on the passenger seat beside me. There's no one around at the station except the Pakistani nestled behind the counter inside, surrounded by girly magazines and candy, and for one giddy second I see *this* as the solution to my problem: banditry. Simply walk into the building there with the Luger in my hand and make the Pakistani give me the cash in his till, and then leave.

Why not? I could do that once or twice a week for the rest of my days—or at least until Social Security kicks in—and continue to pay the mortgage, continue to pay for Betsy and Bill's education, and even put lamb chops back on the dinner table. Just leave home from time to time, drive to some other neighborhood, and rob a convenience store. Now *that's* convenient.

I chuckle to myself as I walk into the station with the twenty-dollar bill in my hand and exchange it with the surly unshaven fellow in there for a one-dollar bill. The absurdity of the idea. Me, an armed robber. Killer is easier to imagine.

I continue to drive east and a bit south, Fall City being on the Connecticut River not far north of where that minor waterway enters Long Island Sound. My state road atlas has shown me that Churchwarden Lane is a winding black line that moves westward out of the town, away from the riverside. I can come to it, according to the map, from the north, on a back road called William Way, thus avoiding the town itself.

The houses in the hills northwest of Fall City are

mostly large and subdued, light with dark shutters, very New England, on large parcels of well-treed land. Four-acre zoning is my guess. I wind slowly along the narrow road, seeing the affluent houses, none of the affluent people or their affluent children visible at the moment, but their signs are everywhere. Basketball hoops. Two or three cars in wide driveways. Swimming pools, not yet uncovered for the summer. Gazebos, woods walks, lovingly reconstructed stone walls. Extensive gardens. Here and there a tennis court.

I wonder, as I drive along, how many of these people are going through what I'm going through these days. I wonder how many of them now realize just how thin the ground really is, beneath those close-cropped lawns. Miss a payday, and you'll feel that flutter of panic. Miss every payday, and see how *that* feels.

I realize I'm concentrating on all this, these houses, these signs of security and contentment, not only to distract myself from what I'm planning, but to make me firm in my intention. I'm *supposed* to have this life, just as much as any of these damn people on this damn winding road, with their names on their designer mailboxes and rustic wooden signs.

The Windhull's.

Cabett.

Marsdon.

The Elyot Family.

William Way does T at Churchwarden Lane, as the map shows. I turn left. The mailboxes are all on the left side of the road, and the first one I see is numbered

1117. The next three have names instead of numbers, and then there's 1112, so I know I'm moving in the right direction.

I'm also coming closer to the town. The road is mostly downhill now, the houses becoming less grand, the indicators now more middle class than upper middle. More appropriate for Herbert and me, after all. What neither of us wants to lose, because it's all we've got.

The nine hundreds, and at last the eight hundreds, and there's 835, identified only by number, HCE apparently being the modest sort, who doesn't flaunt his name at the brim of his property. The mailboxes are still all on the left, but Everly's house is surely that one on the right, with an arbor vitae hedge along the verge of the road, a blacktop driveway, a neat lawn with two graceful trees on it, and a modest white clapboard house surrounded by low evergreen plantings and set well back; probably late-nineteenth century, with the attached two-car garage and the enclosed wraparound porch added later.

A red Jeep is behind me. I continue on, not too fast, not too slow, and about a quarter mile farther down the road I see the mailman coming up. Mail woman, actually, in a small white station wagon plastered with US MAIL decals. She sits in the middle of the front seat, so she can steer and drive with left hand and foot, and still lean over to reach out the right side window to the mailboxes along her route.

These days, I am almost always home when the mail is delivered, because these days I have a more than casual interest in the possibility of good news. Had there been good news in my mailbox last month or last week or even yesterday, I wouldn't be here now, on Churchwarden Lane, in pursuit of Herbert Coleman Everly.

Isn't he likely to be at home as well, watching out the front window, waiting for the mail? Not good news today, I'm afraid. Bad news today.

The reason I've given this full overnight trip to the Everly project is because I had no idea how long it would take me to find and identify him, what opportunities I might have to get at him, how much time would be spent tracking him, waiting for him, pursuing him, before the chance of action would present itself. But now, it seems to me, the likelihood is very good that I'll be able to deal with Everly almost at once.

That's good. The waiting, the tension, the second thoughts; I hadn't been looking forward to all that.

I turn in at a driveway to let the Jeep go by, then back out onto the road and head uphill once more, back the way I'd come. I pass the mailperson, and continue on. I pass 835, and continue on. I come to an intersection and turn right, and then make a U-turn, and come back to the Stop sign at Churchwarden. There I open my road atlas, lean it against the steering wheel, and consult it while watching for the appearance of the mailperson's white station wagon. There is almost no traffic on Churchwarden, and none on this side road.

The dirty white car; coming this way, with stops and starts. I close the road atlas and put it on the seat behind me, then make the left turn onto Churchwarden.

My heart is pounding. I feel rattled, as though all my nerves are unstrung. Simple movements like acceleration, braking, small adjustments of the steering wheel, are suddenly very hard to do. I keep overcompensating, I can't fine-tune my movements.

Ahead, a man crosses the road from right to left.

I'm panting, like a dog. The other symptoms I don't object to, I half expect them, but to pant? I'm disgusting myself. Animal behavior . . .

The man reaches the mailbox marked 835. I tap the brakes. There's no traffic visible, either ahead or behind. I depress the button, and my driver's side window silently rolls down. I angle across the empty road, hearing the crunch of tire on roadway now that the window is open, feeling the cool spring air on my cheek and temple and hollowly inside my ear.

The man has withdrawn letters, bills, catalogues, magazines; the usual handful. As he's closing the front lid of the mailbox, he becomes aware of my approach and turns, eyebrows lifted in query.

I know him to be forty-nine years old, but to me he looks older. These past two years of unemployment, perhaps, have taken their toll. His mustache, too bushy for my taste, is pepper and salt with too much salt. His skin is pale and drab, without highlights, though he has a high forehead that should reflect the sky. His hair is black, receding, thin, straight, limp, gray at the sides. He wears glasses with dark rims—tortoise?—that look too large for his face. Or maybe his face is too small for the glasses. He wears one of his office shirts, a blue and white stripe, under a gray cardigan with the buttons open. His khaki pants are baggy, with grass stains, so he's perhaps a gardener, or helps his wife around the place, now that he has so much free time. The hands holding his mail are surprisingly thick, big-knuckled, as though he's a farmer and not a white-collar worker after all. Is this the wrong man?

I pull to a stop next to him, smiling out of the open window. I say, "Mr. Everly?"

"Yes?"

I want to be sure; this could be a brother, a cousin: "Herbert Everly?"

"Yes? I'm sorry, I—"

. . . don't know me, I think, finishing the sentence for him in my mind. No, you don't know me, and you never will. And I will never know you, either, because if I knew you I might not be able to kill you, and I'm sorry, but I really do need to kill you. I mean, one or the other of us must die, and I'm the one who thought of it first, so that leaves you.

I slide the Luger out from under the raincoat and extend it partway through the open window, saying, "You see this?"

He looks at it, expecting no doubt that I want to sell it to him or tell him I just found it and ask if it's his, or whatever happens to be the last thought that crosses his brain. He looks at it, and I squeeze the trigger, and the Luger jumps up in the window space and the left lens of his glasses shatters and his left eye becomes a mineshaft, running deep into the center of the earth.

He drops backward. Just down and back, no fuss, no lunging, just down and back. His mail frets away from him in the breeze.

I make a sound in the back of my throat like someone trying to pronounce that Vietnamese name. You know the one: Ng. I put the Luger on top of the raincoat and drive on down Churchwarden, my trembling finger on the window button until the window completely shuts. I turn left, and then left again, and two miles later I finally think to put the Luger under the raincoat.

My route is now planned out. A few miles farther on, I'll find Interstate 91, which I'll take north through Hartford and on up into Massachusetts at Springfield. A little north of that I'll turn west on the Massachusetts Turnpike, heading once again for New York State. Tonight I'll stay in an inexpensive motel near Albany, paying cash, and tomorrow afternoon I will return home jobless from my interview in Harrisburg, Pennsylvania.

Well. It seems I can do it.

2

I did it their way for eleven months. Or sixteen, if
you count the final five months at the mill, after I got
the yellow slip but before my job, as they said, ceased
to go forward, the period of time when the counseling
was done, and the training in resumé writing and the
"consideration" of "options." This entire charade as
though we were all, the company and its representatives and the specialists and the counselors and yours
truly, as though we were all working together on some
difficult but worthy task, the end result of which was
supposed to be my personal contentment. Sense of ful-
fillment. Happiness.

Don't go away mad; just go away.

Earlier, for a year or two, there had been rumors of
the downsizing to come, and in fact two smaller win-
nowings of staff had taken place, but they'd merely
been the preliminaries, and everyone knew it. So,
when the yellow slip was presented to me with my

paycheck in October of 1995, I wasn't as shocked as I might have been, and I wasn't even at first all that unhappy. Everything seemed so businesslike, so well-thought-out, so professional, that it was more like being nurtured than weaned. But I was being weaned.

And I had plenty of company, God knows. The twenty-one hundred people at the Belial mill of Halcyon Mills was reduced to fifteen hundred seventy-five; a reduction of about one-fourth. My product line was dropped entirely, good old Machine No. 11 sold for scrap, the work absorbed by the company's Canadian affiliate. And the long lead-time—or so it seemed, then—of five months not only gave me plenty of time to look for another job but meant I would still be on salary through the Christmas season; nice of them.

The severance package was certainly generous enough, I suppose, within what is considered generous and rational at the moment. We discontinued employees received a lump sum equal to one month of salary for every two years of employment, at the present wage for that employment. In my case, since I'd been with the company twenty years, four as sales director and sixteen as product manager, I received ten months' pay, two of them at a somewhat lower rate. In addition, the company offered to maintain our medical insurance—we pay twenty percent of our medical costs, but no insurance premiums—for one year for every five years of employment, which means four years in my case. Full coverage for Marjorie and me, plus coverage for Billy for two and a half years until he's nineteen; Betsy's already nineteen, and so is uninsured, another worry. Then, five months from now, with Billy's nineteenth birthday, he's also without insurance.

But that isn't all we got when we were severed. There was also a single flat payment to cover vacation time, sick time and who knows what; it was figured out using a madly complex formula that I'm sure was scrupulously fair, and my check came to four thousand, seven hundred sixteen dollars and twenty-two cents. To tell the truth, if it had been nineteen cents, I doubt I would have known the difference.

I think most of us, when we get the chop, see our coming unemployment as merely an unexpected vacation, and assume we'll be back at work with some other company almost immediately. But that isn't how it happens now. The layoffs are too extensive, and are in every industry across the board, and the number of companies firing is much larger than the number of companies hiring. More and more of us are out here now, another thousand or so every day, and we're chasing fewer and fewer jobs.

You put together your resumé, your education and job history, your life, on a page. You buy manila folders and a roll of first-class postage stamps. You carry your resumé down to the drugstore with the copying machine, and run off thirty copies at a nickel each. You start circling in red ink the likeliest help wanted ads in the *New York Times*.

You also subscribe on your own to your trade journals, the magazines your employer used to subscribe to for you. But the magazine subscriptions are not part of the severance package. *Pulp* and *The Paperman*; those are the journals of my trade, both of them monthly, both rather expensive. When they were free, I rarely read them, but now I study them cover to cover. After all, I have to keep up. I can't let the industry move on without me.

Both of these magazines carry help wanted ads, and both carry position wanted ads. In both of them, more positions than help are wanted.

At least I was never fool enough to spend money on a position wanted ad.

Over the years of my employment, I became quite specialized in one kind of paper and one method of manufacture. That was a subject I really knew—and still know—all about. But back at the beginning, twenty-five years ago, when I started out as a salesman for Green Valley, before I switched over to Halcyon, I was marketing all kinds of industrial paper, and I learned them all. I learned *paper*; the whole wild complex subject.

I know many people think paper is boring, so I

won't go on about it, but in fact paper is far from boring. The way it's made, the million uses . . .

We even eat paper, did you know that? A special kind of paper-source cardboard is used in many commercial ice creams, as a binder.

The point is, I do know paper, and I could take over almost any managerial job within the paper industry, with only minimal training in a particular specialty. But there's so many of us out here, the companies don't feel the need to do even the slightest training. They don't have to hire somebody who's merely good, and then fine-tune him to their requirements. They can find somebody who already knows their precise function, was trained in it by some other employer, and is eager to come to work for *you*, at lower pay and fewer benefits, just so it's a *job*.

I studied the ads, I sent out my resumés, and most of the time nothing at all happened. No response. No answer to all the questions you naturally ask: Is my salary request too high? Did I phrase something poorly in the resumé? Did I leave something out I should have mentioned?

Here's my own resumé. I decided to go for absolute simplicity and truth and clarity. No fudging my age, and no unnecessary crowing about my skills and training. But I included my college interests, because I think it's good to suggest you're well rounded. I think so. Who knows?

BURKE DEVORE
62 Pennery Woods Road
Fairbourne, CT 06668
(203) 567-9491

WORK HISTORY

1980–present	Product Manager, Halcyon Mills
	Responsible for manufacture and sales, polymer paper specialty products.
1975–1979	Sales director, Halcyon Mills
	Coordinated sales force in areas of specialized paper applications.
1971–1975	Salesman, Green Valley Paper & Pulp. Learned and described complete product line. Top salesman 19 of 45 months.
1969–1971	Bus driver, city of Hartford, CT.
1967–1969	US Army, Information Specialist, learned typing, radio skills.

EDUCATION

BA, Northwest Connecticut State University, 1967. American history major. Debate team. Track.

Occasionally, that resumé draws a response, and briefly my heart lifts. I get a phone call or a letter, usually a phone call, and an appointment is made. It's usually somewhere in the northeast, though once it was Wisconsin and once it was Kentucky. Wherever it is, you pay your own transportation costs. You want to get to that meeting.

You shower thoroughly, you dress carefully, you try to find the balance between self-assurance and easy geniality. You don't want to be full of yourself, but you don't want to be a toady either. You meet and chat and discuss. You might even tour the plant with the interviewer, showing your familiarity with the machine, the line, the work. Then you go home, and you never hear another word.

From time to time there would be a small news item in *Pulp* or *The Paperman*, when a mill announced hiring so-and-so for such and such a management position; with that usual smirking headshot of the lucky bastard. And I'd read it, and realize it was a position I'd interviewed for, and I couldn't help it, I'd have to study and study that guy's face, his eyes, his smile, the tie he wore. Why him? Why not me?

Sometimes it would be a woman's picture there, or a black man's picture, and I'd decide it was quota time, they were hiring politically and not commercially, and in a strange way that would make me feel better. Because it wasn't *my* failure then. If it was a woman or a black man they wanted, and they were just going through the motions with people like me, there was nothing I could do about it, was there? No blame, then.

But other times I did feel the blame. Why him, why that guy with the sloppy grin or the huge ears or the rotten haircut? Why not me? What did he do or say? What was on his resumé, that wasn't on mine?

That was what started me, that was the first question. What do they have on those resumés? What edge do they have? That's what led me to take out my ad.

3

Yesterday I killed Herbert Coleman Everly, and today I come home from my interview in Harrisburg, Pennsylvania, and when I walk into my house at four in the afternoon Marjorie is waiting for me in the living room. She's pretending to read a novel—she borrows novels from the library, now that we have fewer magazines and less television—but she's really waiting for me. It's true she doesn't know the full extent of our trouble, but she does know there's trouble, and she realizes I'm worried.

Before she can ask, I shake my head. "Not a chance," I say.

"Burke?" She gets to her feet, dropping the novel behind her in the chair. "You can't be sure," she says, to encourage me.

"Oh, yes, I can," I say, and shrug. I don't like lying to Marjorie, but there's no other choice. "I'm getting to know the interviewers by now," I tell her. "This one just didn't like me."

"Oh, Burke." She puts her arms around me, and we kiss. I feel a certain stirring, but it doesn't last, it's like an underwater echo. Not a submarine, but a submarine's refraction.

I said, "Any mail?" Thinking of Everly.

"Nothing . . . nothing that mattered," she says.

"Well."

There are a lot of men now, in my position, who take out their frustrations on their families, particularly on their wives. A lot of wife-beating going on these days, among the middle-class unemployed. I admit I've felt that nasty urge myself, the urge to destroy, to release the frustration by just lashing out at the nearest target.

But I love Marjorie, and she loves me, and we've always had a good marriage, so why should I let this external thing tear us apart? If I'm going to lash out, if I'm going to destroy, I should make my violence more productive than that. And I will.

In doing what I did yesterday, apart from any other benefits to be derived (I hope, in time), I made it even more certain that I would never attack my girl. Never.

"Well," I say again, and we share a companionable and rueful smile, and I carry my suitcase away to the bedroom, as Marjorie returns to her novel.

Knowing she'll stay put in the living room with her book, I carry the Luger and Everly's resumé to my office and stow them in my filing cabinet. Then I go back to the bedroom, unpack, strip and take a long shower, my second of the day. In the shower, I permit myself at last to think about Herbert Everly.

A man, a decent man, a nice man, rather like me. Except he's unlikely to have killed anyone. I feel terrible about him, and about his family. I had trouble sleeping last night, I was racked with guilt much of the day, I thought seriously about giving the whole thing up, abandoning the entire project with it barely begun.

But what choice do I have? I stand in the hot water, clean and cleaner, and go over it all again in my mind. The equation is hard and real and ruthless. We're running out of money, Marjorie and I and the kids, and we're running out of time. I have to be employed, that's all. I'm no self-starter, I'm not going to invent a new widget, I'm not going to found my own paper mill on a shoestring. I need a job.

There are too many of us out here, and I have to face the fact that I am never going to be anybody's first choice. If it were just the job, just the knowledge and experience, just the capacity and the expertise, just the willingness and the proficiency, no problem. But there are too many of us going after too few jobs, and there are other guys out there just as experienced and willing and capable as I am, and then it comes down to the nuances, the ineffables.

Amiability. Sound of voice. Smile. Whether or not you and your interviewer are fans of the same sport. What he thinks of your choice of necktie.

There is always always *always* going to be somebody just that tiny bit closer to the ideal than I am. In this job market, they don't have to take second best, and I have to either accept that fact or I'm going to be very unhappy for a very long time, and drag my family down with me. So I have to accept it, and I have to learn to work within it.

I finish my shower, and dress, and go into my office. I look at my list, and I think it would probably be best not to kill two people in the same state within just a few days of each other. I don't want the authorities to start looking for patterns.

On the other hand, I don't have much time. I've started the operation now, and I have to move briskly to the end of it, before something happens to spoil it all.

Here's one, in Massachusetts. Next Monday, I'll drive north.

4

Technically the computer belongs to the whole family, but it's really Billy's, and a year ago it moved into his room in acknowledgment of that truth. I'd made it a gift to the family at Christmas, 1994, the year before I was downsized, when we were still financially okay. The money was going out, in mortgage and taxes and schooling and food and gasoline and clothing, plus all of those things we hardly thought about but no longer spend money on, like rental tapes of movies, but the money was also coming in, adequately to cover expenses, the ebb and flow nicely attuned, like the inhale and exhale of a healthy body. So buying a computer for the family was extravagant, but not *that* extravagant.

Charles Dickens said it, in *David Copperfield*: "Annual income twenty pounds, annual expenditure nineteen nineteen six, result happiness. Annual income twenty pounds, annual expenditure twenty pounds ought and six, result misery." He didn't say what the result was when you dropped annual income to zero, but he didn't have to.

The point is, the computer entered our lives when we thought we could afford our lives, and is still with us, in Billy's room, on the wheeled metal table purchased for it at the same time. His room is small, and crammed chock-a-block, as teenage boys' rooms tend to be, but oddly enough it's neater now that the computer and its table have been inserted there. Or maybe he just hasn't been able to buy so many things recently, hasn't been able to add to the pile of his possessions.

Well. When all this began, in February, almost three months ago, my second step, even before I had any idea what the plan was or that there would be a plan, was to go into Billy's room and sit down in front of the family computer and, from the wealth of available typefaces and sizes, create letterhead stationery. (My first step had been to take a post office box in a town twenty-some miles from home.)

B. D. INDUSTRIAL PAPERS
P.O. BOX 2900
WILDBURY, CT 06899

The post office box was actually 29, but I added the zeroes to make both the local post office and, by extension, B. D. Industrial Papers, seem more imposing. I made a joke of it with the clerk in the post office, who found the idea amusing and said she'd have no trouble putting 2900 mail into box 29, since in fact there were only sixty-eight boxes in the entire branch.

My next step was to write my ad, basing it on the ads I'd been circling in the help wanted sections for over a year:

> MANUFACTURING
> LINE MANAGER
> Northeast paper mill w/specialty in polymers, capacitor tissue & film require individual w/strong specialty paper bkgrnd to head new product line mnfctring on rebuilt electrolytic capacitor paper machine. Minimum 5 yrs mill exp. Competitive salary, benefits. Send resume & salary history to Box 2900, Wildbury, CT 06899

Then I phoned the classified ad department of *The Paperman*, which it seemed to me usually carried more such advertising than *Pulp*, and arranged for them to run my ad, which would cost forty-five dollars to appear in three consecutive monthly issues. The woman I spoke to said there would be no problem if I paid with a money order rather than a company check, after I explained we were a small mill with little experience of hiring outside our own geographic area and would be paying for this ad from petty cash.

Then I went back to the Wildbury post office and bought the money order and signed it Benj Dockery

III, with a very sloppy handwriting unlike my own.
The copy machine at the drugstore gave me fine letterhead stationery from the original I'd put together at the
computer, and I used it to send the wording of the ad
plus the money order to *The Paperman*. Benj Dockery
III signed the letter as well.

The ad ran first in the March issue, out the last week
in February, and by the first Monday in March, when I
drove up to check, box 2900 had received ninety-seven
replies. "Those zeroes sure attract a lot of mail!" the
postal clerk said, and we laughed about it together, and
I explained that I was trying to start up a trade journal
about trade journals. This was the response to an ad I'd
run in selected magazines.

(I didn't want anyone to suspect I might be engaged
in some sort of mail fraud, and start an inspector after
me. What I was doing was probably not illegal, but it
could be extremely embarrassing, and harmful to my
employment chances, if it got out.)

"Well, I wish you luck with it," she said, and I
thanked her, and she said, "More and more people are
becoming their own boss these days, have you noticed?" and I agreed.

That first flush of mail soon dropped off to a steady
trickle, kicking up again in the few days after each
issue of *The Paperman* was published. The May issue,
the last one with my ad, is still current, and I've had
two hundred thirty-one responses so far. I'm guessing
there'll be another ten to fifteen, and that will be the
end of it.

It was fascinating to study those resumés, to see how much fear was in them, and how much gallantry, and how much grim determination. And also how much cocksure bloated self-important ignorance; *those* people are not competition, not for anybody, not until they've been roughened up by life a bit more.

Back in the transition period at Halcyon, when part of my workday was to sit through ongoing training in how to be unemployed, one of our advisors, a stern but hearty woman whose job it was to give us pep talks laced with harsh reality, told us a story, which she swore was true. "Some years ago," she said, "there was a downturn in the aerospace industry, and a lot of bright engineers found themselves unemployed. A group of five of them in Seattle decided to come up with some innovation of their own, something marketable, and after a lot of brainstorming and memos they did create a new variant on a kind of game, something that had real potential. But the idea needed seed money, and they didn't have any. Already in Seattle they'd learned that, when everybody is trying to sell the second car, nobody wants to buy one. They tried every contact they could think of, relatives, friends, former co-workers, and finally they were put together with a group of venture capitalists based in Germany. These financiers liked the engineers' idea, and were very close to agreement on funding them. All that was left was a face-to-face meeting. The financiers, three of them, flew from Munich to New York, and the engineers flew from

Seattle to New York, and they met in a hotel suite there, where everyone got along very well. It looked as though the engineers were going to get the money and start their company and be saved. And then one of the financiers said, 'Let me just get the schedule clear. When we give you this money, what are you going to do to begin with?' And one of the engineers said, 'Well, the *first* thing we're going to do is pay our back salary.' And that was the end of it. The engineers went back to Seattle empty-handed, as well as empty-headed. Because," this counselor told us, "they didn't know the one thing you have to know if you're going to survive and prosper. And that one thing is: Nobody invited you. Nobody owes you a thing. A job and a salary and a nice middle-class life are not a *right*, they're a prize, and you have to fight for them. You have to keep reminding yourself, 'They don't need me, I need them.' You have no demands. You have your skills, and you have your willingness to work, and you have the brains and the talents and the personality God gave you, and it's up to *you* to make it happen."

I have taken that message to heart, perhaps more than she intended. And I have seen the resumés written by the people who did not have the benefit of her breed of advice, the people who still think like that benighted engineer: The world owes me a salary.

Maybe a quarter of the resumés stink of that self-importance, that aggrieved sense that things *ought* to work out right. But the problem with most of the resumés is a simpler one that that; their aim is wrong.

I wrote an ad that *I* could respond to, that was absolutely appropriate to my experience, without being overly specific and narrow. There is such desperation out there, however, that people don't limit themselves to the job openings where they might stand some chance. Clearly, they're sending out the resumés wholesale, in hopes that lightning will strike. And maybe sometimes it does.

But not in the paper business. Not in the specialized kind of industrial use of paper in which *I'm* the expert. These people are amateurs, when it comes to my field, and they don't worry me.

But some of the others do. People whose qualifications are very like mine, perhaps even a touch better than mine. People with a background like mine, but an education that looks in the resumé just a little more distinguished. The people that I would be second best to, if my ad had been real and I'd sent my own resumé in response.

People like Edward George Ricks.

TO WHOM IT MAY CONCERN

My name is Edward G. Ricks. I was born in Bridgeport, Conn., on April 17, 1946. I was educated in Bridgeport schools and took a degree in Chemical Engineering at Henley Technical College, Broome, Conn., in 1967.

In my Navy service—1968 to 1971—I performed as a printing technician on the fleet aircraft carrier *Wilkes-Barre*, where I was responsible for putting out the ship's daily newspaper as well as producing all orders and other printed material on the ship, and where I first combined my chemical background with an interest in specialized forms of paper.

Subsequent to the Navy, I was hired by Northern Pine Pulp Mills, where I worked in product development from 1971 until 1978. When Northern Pine merged with Graylock Paper, I was promoted to management, where I held responsibility for a number of product lines.

From 1991 until spring of 1996, I was in charge of the polymer paper film product line at Graylock, where the customers were almost entirely defense contractors. With the recent military cutbacks, Graylock dropped that product line.

I am now at liberty to present my experience and expertise to another forward-looking company in the specialized paper industry. I have been based in Massachusetts since 1978, but have no objection to relocation. I am married, and my three daughters are at this writing (1997) all at university.

Edward G. Ricks
7911 Berkshire Way, Longholme, MA 05889
413 555-2699

5

I would hire him, before I hired me. That degree in chemical engineering is a real bone in my throat.

And the self-assurance of the man. *And* he was twenty-five years with the same employer, so he must be a good and faithful employee (just as they, of course, are a bad and faithless employer, which doesn't matter).

The form of his resumé is the only thing against him, and it isn't enough. That to-whom-it-may-concern business is just too artificial, and so's the restrained chattiness. The pomposity grates, his being "at liberty to present" himself, and having three daughters "at university," as though they're all at Oxford and not some community college. The man is undoubtedly a prig and a bore, but he's perfect for any job that I would be very good for, and because of that I hate him.

Monday, May 12th. Over breakfast I tell Marjorie I'll be doing library research today, a thing I actually do spend time at occasionally, searching through recent magazines and newspapers for leads to jobs that might be opening up but that aren't yet in the help wanted columns.

Mondays and Wednesdays are when Marjorie has one of her two part-time jobs. We sold the Honda Civic last year, so I'll have to drive her to Dr. Carney's office and then pick her up again at the end of the day. She is our dentist's receptionist now, two days a week, and is paid a hundred dollars a week off the books. On Saturday afternoons she's cashier at the New Variety, our local movie house, her other part-time job, where she's paid minimum wage on the books, taxes are deducted, and she brings home nothing. But she feels better getting out of the house, doing something, and the perk is that we get to go to the movies for free.

Today, though, is Dr. Carney. I drive Marjorie to the mall where his office is located, and leave her there at ten. Now I have eight hours to drive to Massachusetts, see what the situation is with EGR, and get back to the mall to pick up Marjorie at six.

But first I have to return to the house, since I didn't dare carry the Luger with me while Marjorie was in the car. At home, I put the gun in a plastic bag from the drugstore, carry it out to the car, and put it on the passenger seat beside me. Then I drive north.

It's forty-five minutes northbound, up into Massachusetts, then a right turn at Great Barrington, and another thirty minute drive to Longholme. Along the way, I keep remembering last week's event with

Everly, which now seems to me about as clean and perfect as such an experience could ever be. Will I be that lucky again today? Can I merely once again follow the mail carrier, and have EGR delivered into my lap?

(I have no idea, of course, what happened after I left Everly last week, and I think it would be dangerous to try to find out. The shooting was not important enough to be written up in the *New York Times*, and the only other paper I normally read, the *Journal*, our local weekly, does not extend its reach as far as Fall City. Our cable service doesn't carry local channels, but I doubt Everly made the TV news.)

My Massachusetts road atlas shows Longholme about twenty miles west of Springfield and north of the Massachusetts Turnpike. Berkshire Way is another wiggly black line—suggesting hills again—extending out of the town proper, this time northward. It's a long sweep around for me to avoid the town and stay on country roads, but I think it's worth the time and trouble. Still, it's almost twelve o'clock when I finally make the turn onto Berkshire Way.

This is decidedly more rural, with a few actual farms along the way. The private homes are mostly large but unpretentious, as though the residents don't feel they have anything to prove to their neighbors. The countryside is more open, with cleared fields and wide valleys rather than the tumbled woodsiness of Connecticut. It doesn't feel suburban, probably because it's just a little too far from New York and Boston and Albany and every other northeastern urban center.

7911 Berkshire Way turns out to be a modern house on a traditional plan, on the right side of the road as I come along. Probably built after World War II, when the boys came home to create us baby boomers, so that fifty years later we could all be shunted off the social order.

I'm a bit surprised at the house and disappointed with EGR, with his daughters "at university," which does not imply yellow aluminum siding and green fake shutters and a TV satellite dish as prominent as an erection right next to the house. There are scrubby plantings around the base of the building and a few small specimen fruit trees haphazardly placed, but nothing has been planted along the line between scraggly lawn and roadside.

The wide door of the two-car garage is lifted open as I drive by, and there are no cars in there. Nobody home. Damn.

I drive on. A quarter mile farther, a convent school provides a handy parking area in which to turn around. I drive back, looking for an inconspicuous place to park. Unlike the last time, the mailbox is on the same side of the road as the house, so I'll have less warning when EGR comes out to get his mail. If he's home. If he comes out to get his mail. If the mail hasn't already been delivered.

Next beyond the Ricks house, back the way I'm now going, is an empty field, strewn with shrubs and low pines, with a For Sale sign—white letters on red, phone number added in black Magic Marker—on a post near the road. Next beyond that is another house similar to EGR's, built around the same time, probably by the same builder, onto which a few additional rooms were pasted over the years. Stucco was applied at some point, instead of aluminum, and painted the color of squash. A large metal For Sale sign from a local real estate agent stands on the unmowed lawn, and the place has an abandoned air to it, as though the family has gone away to live somewhere smaller, less expensive, closer to the Welfare office.

I turn at this decamped home, enter the driveway, stop, and back turning out of it, so that I'm parked off the road in front of the house, with a clear view beyond the offered field to the front of EGR's place. I've been careful not to block the view of the For Sale sign with my Voyager, because I want the occasional passerby to assume I'm waiting for the agent.

I'm getting hungry, but I don't want to give up my vigil, lose my opportunity to finish the day's work. In my mind's eye, a car pulls in at the driveway over there, a man gets out of it, he crosses to the mailbox, I drive forward, and it's all over.

Does he get his mail while still in his car? And then does he drive into the garage before getting out of the car? And does he close the garage door immediately? And do I follow him, the Luger in my hand, or under my jacket?

I can only guess at any of these things. I can only wait to see what happens, and see what I do in response.

Three hours go by, and nothing happens, and I'm getting very hungry indeed. I may be out of work and desperate, but I'm still not used to missing meals. Still, the thought remains, that if I leave my post, EGR will appear immediately, and will be safely inside his house before I return.

Twenty past three. A Windstar minivan, gray, very like my Voyager, drives slowly past me, and what attracts my attention is that the heavyset middle-aged woman at the wheel of it is glaring at me. Glaring. I blink at her, not understanding her hostility. She drives on by, and then she stops at that mailbox just up ahead, in front of EGR's place. Would this be Mrs. Ricks?

Apparently. I see her slide over to the right side of the Windstar, open the mailbox, pull out the mail. Then she drives on into the garage, and the door slides down.

So. It could be that she wasn't exactly showing hostility, after all, but merely close observation. If she did make the assumption I'm hoping for, that I'm a prospective buyer waiting for the Realtor, maybe she was just frowning at me, studying me, as a potential neighbor.

But the question is, where's her husband? She closed the garage door, so she's not expecting him to drive in any time soon. Was he at home all this time? Maybe he's sick today, got a spring cold.

Or maybe he's out on a job interview, won't be back for a couple of days.

It's getting late. I'm very hungry, and I also have to get back to the mall to pick up Marjorie at six. I can see now that nothing is going to happen here today. A wasted day.

I can't have too many wasted days. This whole operation has to be done as quickly and cleanly as possible, without sloppiness or unnecessary risk, to get it over with before the equations change. Still, nothing is going to happen here today.

Now what? Tomorrow, oddly enough, I have a job interview of my own, in Albany, with a man from a package and label manufacturer, an outfit that specializes in the labels that wrap around tin cans. I don't have much hope, since labels are really some distance out of my line, and surely there are label experts who've been downsized in the last few years, but you never know. Lightning might strike.

Well, if it does, I won't be back here on Berkshire Way any more, will I? And EGR will never know what a lucky man he is.

But if lightning doesn't strike, what then? I can't come back up here on Wednesday, that's Marjorie's other day with Dr. Carney, and the next time I come here I'd better leave home a lot earlier. Clearly the mail had already been delivered when I first got here today.

Thursday, then. I'll be back here Thursday. Unless, of course, by Thursday I'm becoming an expert in tin can labels.

6

When I first got my hands on that great pile of resumés, with more coming in, and still more, what I
felt, I now realize, looking back on it, was a kind of
gleeful power. I'd put something over on these people,
the competition, I'd learned their secrets and they didn't
even know I was there, in the darkness, in the shadows,
in the corner, in the box number, watching them. I was
like a miser with his gold, hunched over the file folders of resumés in my office, secret even from Marjorie,
no one knowing the power I had, no one knowing the
coup I'd accomplished.

But that first euphoria had to wear off, and it did,
leaving only questions in its wake. What would I *do*
with these things? How, after all, could the resumés
help me? Or would they merely serve to discourage
me, as when I would look at this sheet or that sheet and
see someone just slightly better-looking for the job
than I am. *Look* at all these people out here, all of them

worthy, all of them accomplished, all of them willing. Look how many there are, and look how few the berths they're all steering toward.

So I went from secret pleasure at my cleverness in amassing this hoard of resumés to just as secret depression. I might have given up then, given up everything—this is before my current plan, of course—I might have given up all hope of finding a new job and maintaining my claw-hold on my life, this life, I might have given in completely to despair, if only there had been any other choice.

But there wasn't. There wasn't, and there isn't. I kept going then, only because there was nothing else to do. And who knows how many of these people in these resumés are in the same state? Going forward with no hope, but only because there's nothing else to do. We're like sharks, in that way; if we don't keep swimming, we'll merely sink.

Suicide is not an option, I wouldn't consider it for a second, though I know some of these people have considered it and some of them will do it. (This world we live in began fifteen years ago, when the air traffic controllers were all given the chop, and suicide ran briskly through that group, probably because they felt more alone than we do now.) But I don't want to kill myself, I don't want to *stop*. I want to go on, even when there's no way to go on. That's the point.

In any event, I was feeling just about as low as I've ever felt, I was having real difficulty just to rouse my energy enough to send out my own resumés. But just then an article in *Pulp* caught my eye and got my brain working once more.

It was one of those inside-a-corner-of-our-fascinating-industry pieces, the sort that used to make my eyes glaze over when I was working for Halcyon, but which now I read slowly and carefully, even underlining certain trenchant sentences, because I need to keep up with the industry. Don't ever permit yourself to become yesterday's man, that's one of the basic rules.

Well, this particular piece in *Pulp* was about a new process at a plant over in New York State, at a town called Arcadia. The company, Arcadia Processing, was a wholly owned subsidiary of one of the biggest paper companies in America, one of the outfits that make their millions in toilet paper and tissues. But Arcadia was a success story in itself, so the owners were leaving it alone.

For much of this century, Arcadia had specialized in turning out cigarette paper made from tobacco leavings, the shreds and stems that are left over after the manufacture of cigarettes. Early in the twentieth century, a couple of different processes were developed to make paper out of that stuff—it's hard to do, because tobacco fibers are so short—and this tobacco-paper was initially used to strengthen the end of cigars, to make them chewable. Later, a variant on that paper was bleached and aerated so it could be used as the paper around ordinary cigarettes, and this is the product Arcadia produced.

A few years ago, it seems, Arcadia's management

came to the conclusion it was no longer a good idea to be tied so closely to the fortunes of the tobacco industry, and so they looked for another area in which to diversify. The area they found, I read to my astonishment, was just the polymer paper specialty that I'd been working on the last sixteen years!

The article writer went on to say that, rather than compete with mills that had already been in that business, and feeling they had a superior product with a new manufacturing method (wrong about that; it was precisely the system we'd installed at Halcyon back in '91), they'd gone offshore for their customers. Aided by NAFTA, they'd found Mexican manufacturers who were delighted by their products and could afford to buy them. With Mexican customers already in hand, they'd spread their sales force farther south, and now had customers all through South America as well.

It was a true success story, one of the few around these days, and there was something very bittersweet about reading it. But one part of the piece really snagged my attention, and that was the brief description of and interview with one Upton Fallon, production line manager. Fallon, who was known by his middle name, Ralph, answered questions from the writer about the production process and about his own background; he'd been there all along, starting almost thirty years ago on the tobacco-paper machine, apparently straight from high school.

Upton "Ralph" Fallon had my job. I read the piece, and I read it again, and there was no doubt in my mind.

He had my job, and in a fair contest *I'd* get it, not him. Of course, there wasn't as much information about him in the article as there would be in his resumé—he didn't *need* a resumé, the bastard, he already had my job— but there was enough stated and implied so I could get a good solid reading on the guy, and I was better than him. I knew I was. It was obvious. And yet, he had my job.

I couldn't help it, I couldn't help daydreaming about it. If he were to be fired, for getting drunk or having an adulterous affair with a girl on the shop floor, say. If he were to come down sick, with some wasting disease like multiple sclerosis, and have to leave the job. If he were to die . . .

Yes, why not? People die all the time. Automobile accidents, heart attacks, kerosene heater fires, strokes . . .

What if he were to die, then, or just become too sick to stay on the job? Wouldn't they be glad to see *me*, so much more qualified for exactly the same position?

I could kill him, if that's what it took.

I thought that, mostly as hyperbole, in the day-dream. But then I thought it again, and I wondered if I meant it. I mean, really meant it. I knew how bad my situation was, I knew how unlikely things were to improve, I knew how surely things were going to get even more desperate, I knew how expensive Betsy was in college and Billy would be, graduating this year from high school. I knew what my expenses were, my outgo, and I knew my income had stopped, and now I saw the one man who stood between me and safety. Upton "Ralph" Fallon.

Couldn't I kill him? I mean, seriously. In self-defense, really, in defense of my family, my life, my mortgage, my future, myself, my *life*. That's self-defense. I don't know this man, he's nothing to me. He sounds like a jerk, to tell the truth, in this interview here. If the alternative is despair and defeat and grinding misery and growing horror for Marjorie and Betsy and Billy and me, why *shouldn't* I kill him, the son of a bitch? How could I *not* kill him, given what's at stake here?

Arcadia. Arcadia, New York. I looked it up in the road atlas, and it was so *close*. It was like an omen. Arcadia was probably no more than fifty miles from here, just across the state line, barely in New York at all, maybe ten miles in. *Commuting* distance, I wouldn't even have to relocate.

Pulp magazine and the road atlas open on my desk. Silence in the house, the kids at school and that being a day when Marjorie was at Dr. Carney's office. Daydreaming.

That's when I thought first of the Luger, remembered it at the bottom of my father's trunk. That's when I first imagined myself pointing that gun at a human being, pulling the trigger.

Could I do it? Could I kill a man? But people do that, too, every day, for far less. Why wouldn't I be able to, with the stakes so high? My *life*; the stakes don't get higher than that.

Daydream. I'd drive over to Arcadia, New York, the Luger beside me in the car. Find the mill, find Fallon—don't have his picture, not printed in *Pulp*, but that can be solved somehow, we're only daydreaming here—find him, and follow him, and wait for the opportunity, and *kill him.* And apply for his job.

Which is where the daydream broke down, and came crashing down at my feet. That's where I went again from pleasure to misery. Because I knew what would happen next, if reality were to follow my daydream this far, if Upton "Ralph" Fallon were actually gone from that job, through his own actions or mine.

Of course I'm better than he is, in any contest between us for that job it would be *my* job, no question. But the contest isn't between us, and never can be. The contest, once Fallon is out of the way, is between me and that stack of resumés over there.

Somebody else would get my job.

I went down through the stack again, winnowing them, picking out the ones I feared, and that first time I was so pessimistic that I pulled out over fifty resumés as being people with a better shot at that job than I had. Which was wrong, of course, overstating them and underestimating me, that was merely the despondency doing my thinking for me. But the problem was still overwhelming. And real.

I was so blue by then I couldn't stand to be in the office any more. I left the room, and killed some time cleaning out some old trash in the garage—once we'd sold the Civic, the space it used to take up began immediately to fill with junk—and my mind kept circling back to Upton "Ralph" Fallon, fat and happy, smug and secure. In *my* job.

I couldn't sleep that night. I lay in bed, beside Marjorie, thinking, mourning, frustrated, miserable, and it wasn't till first light outlined the bedroom windows that I at last fell into fitful sleep, full of troubled dreams, nightmares out of Hieronymus Bosch. I'm glad I don't remember my dreams; their echoes are bad enough.

But I finally did fall away into that restless sleep, and when I rose to cold consciousness three hours later, I knew what to do.

7

Thursday. I'm on the road by eight-fifteen A.M., telling Marjorie I have some follow-up to do on Tuesday's job interview in Albany, and that I might be late this evening, coming home.

The interview. Well, of course I didn't get that job, I won't be learning the intricacies of tin can labels after all, so here I am once again, on the way to Longholme.

I didn't get that job, and I didn't expect to get it. Just another failed interview. But this time, there was a bit more to it. This was the first interview I've gone on since I've added this second string to my bow, the plan (if I can make it work, make the whole complicated thing work, and not lose my determination), and as a result of that, I guess, I somehow saw Tuesday's interview differently from the ones before it. I saw it more dispassionately, is what it was. I saw it from outside.

And what I saw only increased my desperation. I

saw that Burke Devore, *this* Burke Devore, this man I've become in half a century of life, is not friendly.

I don't mean I'm unfriendly, I don't mean I'm some snarling sort of misanthrope. I simply mean not friendly *enough*. Back in my young days, in school and then in the Army, I could always build up enough enthusiasm to be a part of the gang, part of the group, but it was never really natural to me. The four years I spent as a salesman, on the road for Green Valley, selling their industrial papers, I did learn how to be a salesman, grinning, cheery, shaking hands, slapping backs, making people feel I was glad to see them, but it was always hard.

Hard. I'm not a natural glad-hander, hail-fellow-well-met, I never was. Studiously, in those salesman days, I would collect new jokes and memorize them and retail them around to my contacts. Earnestly I would have a vodka or two with lunch, to loosen me up for my afternoon calls. I was drinking much too much in those days, and if I'd gone on being a salesman I'd probably be dead of cirrhosis by now.

That's what made the line so perfect for me, the product line, me the manager. Running that, in charge of that, I was expected to be amiable but a little aloof, friendly but always in command, and that suited me right down to the ground.

What I'm supposed to do now, I realized on Tuesday, is be a salesman once again. The resumé merely gets me in the door, if it even does that much. My whole work history, my entire life till now, is simply the sales tool to get me in the door. And the interview is my sales pitch, and what I'm there to sell is me.

I'm not good enough at it. Whatever salesman skills I laboriously developed in the old days are gone now, atrophied. An ill-fitting suit, long ago given away.

Am I going to start memorizing stupid jokes again, telling them to the interviewers? Kidding with the secretaries? Giving people hearty compliments about their watch, their desk, their shoes? I just don't know how to get *back* to that person.

Those resumés in the filing cabinet in my office; a lot of *those* people are salesmen. You bet they are.

I'll do it once, when the time comes. I'll do it with the interviewer for Arcadia Processing, after the unfortunate demise of Upton "Ralph" Fallon. I'll tell that fellow jokes, you know I will. I'll praise his necktie, compliment his secretary and turn beautifully sentimental over the family photos on his desk. I'll *sell*, by God.

But not yet. That is then, and this is now, and now is the road to Longholme. I know that road better than I did on Monday, and traffic is light, so it's quite early, just quarter to ten, when I stop the Voyager in that same spot in front of the squash-colored stucco house for sale.

And the first thing I see is that the flag is up on EGR's mailbox, which means he has put letters in there to be picked up, which means the mail hasn't been delivered yet today. I didn't bother to drive past the house before coming to rest here, and from this angle I can't see whether the garage door is open or closed, but I do see the mailflag up, and I know it means the mail is yet to be delivered, so there's a chance, a hope, that today EGR himself will come out to get it. The Luger is on the seat beside me, under the folded raincoat, waiting. The both of us wait.

For twenty minutes, nothing happens. There's very little traffic along Berkshire Way, mostly delivery vans and pickup trucks. I see them out ahead, or in my rearview mirror, and they pass, and they're gone.

And then all at once there's a vehicle braking to a stop right behind me, abruptly large in my mirror, gray, familiar. I stare at it, afraid, with that awful immediate certainty that I've been caught, disaster has struck, exposure, condemnation, Marjorie and the kids staring at me in shock—"We never knew you!"—and a woman in an open gray zippered jacket leaps out of that vehicle and runs toward me.

The woman is the one who glared at me Monday: Mrs. Ricks! What on earth is she doing? Is she a mind reader?

It's a cool day, cloudy, and the Voyager's windows are shut. The woman runs up next to me, yelling, gesticulating, hugely angry and upset about something. But what? I can hear her yelling, but I can't make out the words. I stare at her through the glass, afraid of her, afraid of the whole situation, afraid to open the window.

She shakes her fist at me. She screams in rage. She suddenly cuts away, and runs around the front of the van, and yanks open the passenger door, and thrusts her head in at me, blotchy red face, tear-streaked cheeks, and she yells, "Leave her alone!"

I gape at her. "What?"

"She's only eighteen! How can you take advan— Don't you have any *shame*?"

"I'm not—" She's mistaken me, she's got me mixed up with somebody, it's just wrong, but I'm too flustered to correct her: "I'm not, you've got the, this isn't—" Then what am I doing here, if not stalking her daughter?

"*Listen* to me!" she screams, drowning me out. "Don't you think I could talk to your *wife*, whatever Junie says? Don't you have any self-respect? Can't you, can't you, can't you just *leave her alone*?"

"I'm not the man you—"

"You're killing her father!"

Oh, God. Oh, let me out of this, let me away from here.

My silence is a mistake. She's going to reason with me now, she's going to convince this married middle-aged swine to stay away from her eighteen-year-old daughter. "There are doctors," she says, trying to be calm, supportive. "You could talk with—" And now she's going to sit beside me in the van, and she sweeps the raincoat off the seat, out of her way, and we both stare at the gun.

Now we both experience true horror. She stares at me, and in her eyes I see the entire tabloid scenario.

The lust-crazed older lover is here to slaughter his nymphet's parents.

I lift a hand. "I—" But what can I say?

She *screams*. The sound caroms inside the car, and the force of it seems to drive her backward, out of the vehicle and away. She turns, and runs along the road, toward her house, screaming.

No no no no no. She's seen me, she knows my face, she saw the Luger, none of this is happening, none of this can happen, everything's destroyed if this happens. I grab the Luger and jump out of the Voyager (at least, unlike her, I think to slam the door on my way), and I run after her.

I'm a sedentary man, I've been a manager for sixteen years, sitting at my desk, walking along the line, riding my car to and from work. Even more sedentary since I was chopped. I'm healthy enough, but I'm no athlete, and running uses me up right away. Long before I get to that yellow aluminum house, I'm gasping for breath.

But so is she. She's also out of shape, and she's trying to run and scream at the same time. *And* flail her arms. She had a good lead on me, but I'm catching up, I'm catching up, I'm not so far behind her when we veer to run angling across her unlovely lawn toward the front door of her house, and she's screaming, "Ed! Ed!" and before she gets to the house I catch up with her, and I hold the Luger directly behind her head, bobbing as we both run, and I fire once, and she drops straight down onto the lawn, like a bundle, like a duffel bag, and the momentum flings her jacket halfway up over her head, covering the hole the bullet made.

Exhausted, spent, I sink to one knee beside her, and look up to see the front door opening, the astonished face of what must be her husband, Ed, EGR, my EGR, his astonished face is in the doorway, staring out, and I raise the gun and shoot, and the bullet punches into the aluminum beside the doorframe with a muted twang.

He slams the door, already turning, running away into the house.

Reeling, almost fainting, I force myself to my feet, I lunge forward to the door, I yank the handle, but it's locked.

He'll be in there right now, dialing 911. Oh, God, this is terrible, this is a mess, this is a disaster, how did I ever think I could do these things, that poor woman, *she* wasn't supposed to—

I can't let this happen. He can't telephone, he can't, I won't permit it, I have to get to him, I just have to get to him.

The garage door is open. Around that way, through the house, find him, *find* him. I stagger like a drunk as I run along the front of the house and through the gaping open broad doorway. There, to my right, is the closed door to the house. *That* won't be locked. I hurry to it, the Luger dangling at the end of my right arm, and just as I reach the door it opens and *he runs out*!

What was he doing? What did he have in mind? Was he going to try to drive away from here, was he so rattled he never thought of the telephone? We stare at one another, and I shoot him in the face.

Much sloppier, this one, blood everywhere, face ruined, body a tangled unknotted mess on the garage floor, one arm flung backward through the open doorway into the house.

No one else at home? Daughters all at university? Or with their unacceptable lovers? How I *hate* them for making this confusion, driving that woman to mistake me for someone else, attack me, harangue me, discover the gun. Where's the neatness this time, the efficiency, the impersonality?

I'm shaking all over. I'm sweating, and I'm cold. I can barely hold on to the Luger, which I now put away in the inside pocket of my windbreaker, then trot along holding it in place with my left forearm.

I don't know if there's traffic, I don't know if a thousand people are watching me or no one. I only know there's the lawn, with that terrible dead sack on it, and there's the empty field, and there's the Plymouth Voyager.

I drive away, gripping the wheel hard because my hands are shaking. My whole body is shaking. I force myself to drive for ten minutes away from there, away from that neighborhood, staying within the speed limit, obeying all the traffic rules. Then at last I allow myself to pull off onto a dirt road and there, out of view, let the shaking have me. The shaking and the fear.

The sight of that woman's face. The memory of her running, and my hand holding up the gun, and then she falls. Her husband, goggle-eyed, made stupid by terror and grief.

This is horrible. Horrible. But what could I have done? From the instant she pulled away that raincoat, what could I have done differently?

What have I started here? What road am I on?

8

Once I knew what I had to do, after that sleepless and despairing night, I went back through the resumés three times more, and each time I was increasingly cold and critical and realistic. *This* person? Competition for *me*? Education excellent, work record outstanding, but not in my field. A real find for some employer, but not for Arcadia Processing. Not for *my* job.

And so gradually I whittled the people down to six. Six resumés from people who, because of their work history and their education and their geographical location, were my true competition. I had to count location because I knew most employers would. They don't like to pay moving expenses unless they absolutely cannot find a qualified individual who already lives within commuting distance. So the bright stars in Indiana and Tennessee I decided not to worry about. Their competition was closer to home.

I realized from the beginning the irony in what I planned to do. These people, these six management experts, Herbert Coleman Everly and Edward George Ricks and the others, were not my enemy. Even Upton "Ralph" Fallon was not my enemy, I knew that. The enemy is the corporate bosses. The enemy is the stockholders.

These are all publicly held corporations, and it is the stockholders' drive for return on investment that pushes every one of them. Not the product, not the expertise, certainly not the reputation of the company. The stockholders care about nothing but return on investment, and that leads to their supporting executives who are formed in their image, men (and women, too, lately) who run companies they care nothing about, lead work forces whose human reality never enters their minds, make decisions not on the basis of what's good for the company or the staff or the product or (hah!) the customer, or even the greater good of the society, but only on the basis of stockholders' return on investment.

Democracy at its most base, supporting leaders only in return for their sating of greed. The ever-present nipple. That's why healthy companies, firmly in the black, lush in dividends to stockholders, nevertheless lay off workers in their thousands; to squeeze out just a little more, look just a little better for that thousand-mouthed beast out there that keeps the executives in power, with their million-dollar, ten-million-dollar, twenty-million-dollar compensation package.

Oh, I knew all that when I started, I knew who the enemy was. But what good does that do me? If I were to kill a thousand stockholders and get away with it clean, what would I gain? What's in it for me? If I were to kill seven chief executives, each of whom had ordered the firing of at least two thousand good workers in healthy industries, what would *I* get out of it?

Nothing.

What it comes down to is, the CEOs, and the stockholders who put them there, are the enemy, but they are not the problem. They are society's problem, but they are not my personal problem.

These six resumés. These are my personal problem.

9

The murders of the Rickses make the TV news, of course, being so much more dramatic than the death of Herbert Everly. Nine hours after I killed them, I sit in my living room with Marjorie, and we watch my crimes described by a solemnly excited blonde woman in a good green suit. Betsy and Billy are not with us. They never watch the news, not being interested in anything much beyond their immediate lives. At this moment, before dinner, I believe Betsy is on the phone, as she often is, and Billy is on the computer, as *he* usually is, while Marjorie and I watch my murders on the news, and Marjorie says, "Oh, Burke, that's horrible."

"Horrible," I agree.

It's strange, but someway or other I don't entirely recognize my actions from the blonde woman's recountal. The facts are essentially right; I did chase the wife across the lawn and shoot her there, and I did intercept the husband in the garage and shoot him there, and I did leave without a trace, without witnesses, without clues in my wake.

But somehow the tone is all wrong, the sense of it, the feeling of it. These words she uses—"brutal" "savage" "cold-hearted"—give completely the wrong impression. They leave out the error that caused it all. They leave out the panic and confusion. They leave out the trembling, the sweating, the icy fear.

But there's more to the story, all at once. They have a suspect! The police are questioning him, even now, at this very minute.

He's seen being led from an office building on a community college campus. He's a tweedy slope-shouldered middle-aged man with a gray widow's peak and large bifocals. He isn't handcuffed, but he's closely surrounded by beefy state troopers, one of whom puts his hand atop the suspect's head as he's urged into the backseat of a white state police car.

His name is Lewis Ringer, and he's a professor of literature at that community college. He is also the unacceptable lover of June Ricks, eighteen-year-old youngest child of the murdered couple. He is the man her mother thought I was, and I look more closely at that quick glimpse of him from building to police car, the second and third times they show it. I too wear large bifocals, and I too have a gray widow's peak, but other than that I don't see the similarity at all. Mrs. Ricks was a very stupid woman. I try not to think that she got what she deserved, but that thought does hover around the boundaries of my brain.

We also see the daughter, and what a piece of work *she* is. Not at all like our Betsy. June—or Junie, as her mother had called her when yelling mistakenly at me—is a sly, sullen, secretive girl, pretty in a foxlike way, full of sidelong glances and flickering smiles. Clearly, she's delighted to have caused such emotional upheaval in a man as to lead him to murder her parents, though just as clearly she can't admit to either the delight or the belief that in fact Ringer did it. The camera leaves her as fast as it decently can.

And then we see Lew Ringer's wife, tear-stained and stunned, briefly in the doorway of a modest house on a modest town street. She stares at the media on her lawn, and slams the door, and that's the end of the item. We move on to northern Ireland, where the murders are much more frequent, with far less reason.

After the news, and before dinner, while Marjorie goes to the kitchen, I retire as usual to my office. It is time to decide which of my resumés is next. I have four to go, and then Mr. Fallon.

But somehow I can't think about any of that. I can't even open the file drawer and take out the folder with those resumés. There's a great discouragement holding me down.

I try to talk myself out of this inertia. I tell myself I've gotten away with everything so far, I'm not suspected by anybody, or even thought about. I tell myself this is a good beginning, even if the second expedition was so much sloppier and more emotionally exhausting than the first. But why couldn't it turn out at the end that that one had been the worst of them, and that from then on they'd all been easy, as easy as Everly?

But it doesn't work. I am discouraged, and nothing will bring me out of it. I can't stop now, I know that, or everything till this point will have been in vain. I *have* to go on, now that I've come this far. And I have to do it all soon, and I remind myself *why* I have to do it all soon.

The fact is, these vast waves of dismissal move through industries, one after another. A swath is cut through the auto industry, and then everything is calm there for a while. A bloodletting among the phone companies is followed by peace. The computer industry will sacrifice its thousands, and then rest.

Well, the paper industry had its most recent downsizing two years ago, when I got the chop. All of these resumés in my files come from people laid off at just around the same time, in a period from six or seven months before me to a period six or seven months after me. This is the group, this is the labor pool, these are the people I have to concern myself with.

But the reductions are cyclical, and eventually return. If I don't move ahead briskly, rid myself of the competition, rid myself of Fallon, and get established in that job, I may suddenly find a whole new wave of resumés flooding the mails. And there they'll be, a whole new batch of people after my job, and some of *them* will be real competition, too. Fresh competition.

Six is a lot, but six I think I can handle. Seven, if you count Fallon. But a dozen? Two dozen? Impossible.

No, I have to do it *now*, move forward, choose the next one, go out there, *get* him, keep the momentum alive.

And here's another thought. What if Fallon dies ahead of time, without my help, before I'm ready? If that happens, and one of these four still on my list gets that job, what then?

And yet, I remain immobile. Discouraged. I just sit here, at my desk, not even looking at the file cabinet. I keep seeing, in my mind's eye, that woman struggle ahead of me, across the lawn, the two of us plodding like a couple of cows, the Luger bobbing in the air behind her head, at the end of my arm.

Marjorie calls, "Dinner!"

I turn off the light, and leave the office, and shut the door.

10

For a while, before the beginning, even when I knew absolutely and positively what I should do, I did nothing. For a while, even though I theoretically and intellectually understood that my plan was my only possible hope, I did nothing. I thought it, I planned it, I prepared for it, but I didn't yet believe it.

I did the make-work stuff instead. I studied the Luger. I bought a book to help me understand it, and I read the book cover to cover. I cleaned and oiled the gun. I bought it bullets. I took it into a field and shot trees.

I even saw Ralph Fallon one time, though I don't believe he would have noticed me. What I did, back before I was actually in motion on this thing, as a part of my make-work, my fakery, my stalling, I drove one day over to Arcadia, just to look it over. That's how it happened.

There are no large highways between our part of Connecticut and that part of New York. I took my time,

studying the road atlas, wanting to find the best route
because I intended this someday to be my commute to
work. The roads went through little suburban towns
and even smaller farm villages, past dairy herds graz-
ing and cornfields being plowed for this spring's crop,
and I thought how nice it would be to make this drive,
routinely, roundtrip, five times a week. Not much traffic, beautiful countryside. And at the far end, a job I
could love.

Arcadia itself turned out to be a sweet old town,
very small, a cluster of twenty or so clapboard homes
on the slopes flanking a small but lively stream called
the Jandrow, a tributary of the Hudson. Mills are built
along streams, because they need a lot of water, and
the bustling Jandrow clearly provided all the water this
mill could want. There was a dam, just upriver from
the mill buildings. The main road through town, east-
west, dipping down one slope on its way in, crossed
over that dam and then climbed up the far slope and
away.

Other than the mill, there was little commercial activity in Arcadia. Up the western slope, overlooking
the mill, there was a luncheonette where you could
also buy newspapers and cigarettes and a few minor
grocery items. Farther up the slope, at the edge of
town, was a Getty gas station. That was it.

I got to Arcadia around noon, and decided to eat
something in Betty's, the luncheonette. It was only
after I was seated at the counter, the only person there
not with others at a table, and after I'd ordered a BLT

and coffee, that I realized from the conversations behind me that the twenty or so people at the tables were all from the mill.

Had I made a stupid mistake coming here? Would these people remember me, much later, after everything was finished and I had Upton "Ralph" Fallon's job? Would they suspect what I'd done? Had I ruined my chance to put the plan into effect, even before I'd started?

(I think, during this period of time, I was probably unconsciously trying to find some excuse not to go forward with the plan, even though *there was no other plan*. There was no other plan, and there still is no other plan.)

But there I was, I'd already placed my order, and the one sure way to be conspicuous was to run out now, before my food arrived. So I sat hunched between my shoulders, looking at nothing but the array of items on the counter along the wall ahead of me, and from time to time I heard bits of conversation from the tables behind me. Shoptalk, some of it, shoptalk I recognized. Shoptalk I could easily, gladly, have joined. I hadn't realized until that moment just how much I'd missed being around that world. Oh, how I would have liked to sit at one of those tables and just let the shoptalk wash over me.

Well, I couldn't. I sat where I was, at the counter, and the buxom waitress brought my BLT, and doggedly I ate. While behind me, from time to time, people would call in a joshing way to somebody called

Ralph, and Ralph would answer, with that kind of hill-billy cracker voice that's more rural than regional. Not an accent, exactly, but something twanging in the mouth that makes them sound as though they have false teeth even if they don't.

I snuck a look around my shoulder at one point, and this Ralph was at a table by the window, and he was a rawboned rangy guy of about my age, but thinner. He looked like that oldtime singer/songwriter, Hoagy Carmichael. His voice, though, with that cracker twang, wasn't as musical.

Their lunch break was finished. All at once they all needed their checks, and the waitress was very busy for a few minutes, writing out the checks, ringing up totals on the cash register. The groups all left, and walked in little clumps downhill, and I turned to watch them through the windows, talking together, having a last cigarette (there wouldn't be smoking allowed inside the mill).

The waitress moved around between me and the windows, clearing tables, and I said to her, "That fellow that was sitting over there. Was that Ralph Fallon?"

"Oh, sure," she said.

"I thought so," I said. "I met him years ago, but I just wasn't sure. Doesn't matter. I'll take my check, when you've got the chance."

Driving home that day, through the pretty countryside, the memory of those lunchtime conversations circling in my head, I knew I had to do it. I had to go forward. I couldn't live without my life any longer.

That was the day, when I got home, I took out Herbert Everly's resumé, and looked at his address, and turned to my road atlas.

11

Lew Ringer has killed himself! Who would have guessed?

It's Monday now, four days since my terrible experience at the Ricks house, and Marjorie and I are watching the six o'clock news, and this has just been announced. Lew Ringer hanged himself in his garage, sometime last night. Lew Ringer is dead.

The police are saying this pretty well wraps up the case. They'd been just about certain Lew Ringer was their man, right from the beginning, but they hadn't had enough solid physical evidence to pin it on him, and without that solid physical evidence they'd had no choice but to let Ringer go on Saturday afternoon, when his lawyer demanded it.

The principal piece of physical evidence they still didn't have was the gun Ringer had used. It was a nine millimeter, they knew that much, but they hadn't yet found the gun nor the dealer from whom Ringer must have bought it. The assumption now among the authorities was that he'd picked it up some time ago, probably in some southern state using false identification, and that he'd thrown it away, after he'd done the double killing, in a nearby river or lake.

In any event, without the gun or any other evidence tying Ringer to the crime, and with Ringer's lawyer making such a fuss, eventually on Saturday the police had had to let him go, though they did keep a very close eye on him, including a police car parked twenty-four hours a day in front of his house. (That was partly also to keep at bay the crowds of the curious.)

His empty house, as it turned out. When Ringer got there Saturday afternoon, his wife had already left that morning, having announced to the media in a tearful press conference Friday evening that she was returning to her parents in Ohio, where she would begin divorce proceedings.

The police theory was that, with the departure of his wife, with June Ricks having so clearly turned against him (she'd told several reporters that she thought Ringer had killed her parents for love of her, and that she believed he really did love her but had gone too far), with the police so strongly on his trail, and with the awful knowledge of the crimes he'd committed, he simply had not been able to face the world any longer, and that's why he'd hanged himself, in his garage, in the space where his wife's car used to be, sometime last night.

Watching this news item, looking at the faces, listening to the words, it seems to me nobody's sorry Lew Ringer is dead. Everybody's pleased it ended this way, I think, because it makes less work for everybody and less doubt in anybody's mind. He was accused of killing Mr. and Mrs. Ricks, his inamorata's parents, and then he killed himself. QED.

The last four days, I've continued to do nothing, not even to *think* about anything. My despondency and discouragement have held me in a tight and smothering grip. Here I've come this far, and yet I just haven't been able to take one single step farther. The wind has been knocked out of me.

But there's something about Ringer's suicide that's making a change in me, I can feel it. Something about the glee and relief of everybody connected with that case, from the police spokesman to the blonde woman reporter, from the furtive and cunning Junie to the anchorman at his desk. The Ricks case is over, and everybody is pleased. No investigation any more, no search for the gun, no hunt for witnesses, no consideration of any other motive. Turns out, I didn't kill them!

After the news, while Marjorie goes to the kitchen to ready dinner, I return to my office for the first time since Thursday. I sit at my desk, I open the file drawer, I take out the folder with the remaining resumés. I study them, and it seems to me the best thing for me to do now is move my activity as far away physically as possible from the first two incidents.

Here he is, in north central New York State. Good, a

different state again, though I won't be able to do that every time.

Lichgate, New York, according to my road atlas, is north of Utica, probably three hundred miles from here. That would put him two hundred fifty miles from Arcadia, too far to commute, but a relocation within New York State wouldn't be complex. He remains a threat.

I could drive there this Thursday morning. Five or six hours to get there. Stay overnight. See what happens.

12

When I was a boy, I was for a while a science fiction fan. A lot of us were, until Sputnik. I was twelve when Sputnik flew. All the science fiction magazines I'd read before then, and the movies and TV shows I saw, assumed that outer space belonged by natural right to Americans. Explorers and settlers and daredevils of space were all Americans, in story after story. And then, out of nowhere, the Russians launched Sputnik, the first space vehicle. The Russians!

We all stopped reading science fiction, then, and turned away from science fiction movies and TV shows. I don't know about anybody else, but, as I remember it, I turned my interest after that to the western. In the western, there was never any doubt who would win.

But before Sputnik turned my whole generation away from science fiction, we had read a lot of stories that talked about something called "automation." Automation was going to take the place of unintelligent labor, though I don't think it was ever phrased quite like that. But simple assembly line stuff is what they meant, the kind of dull deadening repetitive labor that everybody agreed was bad for the human brain and paralyzing to the human spirit. All that work would be taken over by machines.

This automated future was always presented as a good thing, a boon to mankind, but I remember, even as a child, wondering what was supposed to happen to the people who didn't work at the dull stupefying jobs any more. They'd have to work somewhere, wouldn't they? Or how would they eat? If the machines took all their jobs, what would they do to support themselves?

I remember the first time I saw news footage of a robot assembly line in a Japanese auto factory, a machine that looked like the X-ray machine in the dentist's office, jerking around all by itself, this way and that, welding automobile pieces together. This was automation. It was fast, and although it looked clumsy the announcer said it was much more precise and efficient than any human being.

So automation did arrive, and it did have a hard effect on the workers. In the fifties and sixties, blue-collar workers were laid off in their thousands, all because of automation. But most of those workers were unionized, and most of the unions had grown strong over the previous thirty years, and so there were great long strikes, in the steel mills, and in the mines, and in the auto factories, and at the end of it all the pain of the transition was somewhat eased.

Well, that was long ago, and the toll that automation was going to take on the American worker has long since been absorbed. These days, the factory workers are only hit sporadically, when a company moves to Asia or somewhere, looking for cheaper labor and easier environment laws. These days, it's the child of automation that has risen among us, and the child of automation hits higher in the work force.

The child of automation is the computer, and the computer is taking the place of the white-collar worker, the manager, the supervisor, just as surely as those assembly line robots took the place of the lunch-bucket crowd. Middle management, that's what's being winnowed now. And none of us are unionized.

In any large company, there are three levels of staff. At the top are the bosses, the executives, the representatives of the stockholders, who count the numbers and issue the orders and make the decisions. At the bottom are the workers on the line, the people who actually make whatever is being made. And between the two, until now, has been middle management.

It is middle management's job to interpret the bosses for the workers and the workers for the bosses. The middle manager passes information: downward, he passes the orders and requirements, while upward he passes the record of accomplishment, of what has actually happened. To the suppliers he passes the information of what raw material is needed, and to the

distributors he passes the information of what finished product is available. He's the conduit, and until now he has been an absolutely necessary part of the process.

Once you bring in the computer, you no longer need middle management. Of course, you still need a *few* people at that level, to serve the computer, to run specific tasks, but you no longer need the hundreds and thousands of managers that were still needed only yesterday.

People like me.

As the computer takes our jobs, most people don't even seem to realize why it's happening. Why was I fired, they want to know, when the company's in the black and doing better than ever? And the answer is, we were fired because the computer made us unnecessary and made mergers possible and our absence makes the company even stronger, and the dividends even larger, the return on investment even more generous.

They still need some of us. This is a transition we're in now, where middle management will shrink like a slug when you pour salt on it, but middle management won't completely disappear. There will just be fewer jobs, that's all, far fewer jobs.

But *my* job, the one Upton "Ralph" Fallon is holding for me, that one still exists. A human being or two is still needed to run the production line, to be above the working stiffs but capable of communication with them, so the bosses won't have to deal directly with people who play country music on their car radios.

Fallon is my competition, all right. And the six resumés I've pulled out of the stack are my competition. But this is a sea change taking place in our civilization right now, and *all* of middle management is my competition. A million hungry faces will be at the window soon, peering in. Well educated, middle-aged, middle class.

I have to be firmly in place, before the flood becomes overwhelming. So I have to be strong, and I have to be determined, and I have to be quick. Thursday, I have to drive into New York State and find Everett Boyd Dynes.

EVERETT B. DYNES
264 Nether St.
Lichgate, NY 14597
315 890-7711

EDUCATION: BA (Hist) Champlain College, Plattsburgh, NY

WORK HISTORY

I have worked in the paper industry for 22 years, in sales, design, customer relations and management. I have worked in the area of polymer paper specialized applications for 9 years, during which time I have dealt with customers and designers, and have also run a product line, where my responsibilities have included interfacing with design and production teams and being in charge of a 27-person production line crew.

EMPLOYMENT HISTORY

1986–present—Production line manager, Patriot Paper Corp.

1982–1986—Customer relations and some design, Green Valley Paper

1977–1982—Salesman, all product lines, Whitaker Paper Specialties

1973–1977—Salesman, industrial product lines, Patriot Paper Corp.

1971–1973—Salesman, Northeast Beverage Corp, Syracuse, NY

1968–1971—Infantryman, US Army, one tour in Vietnam

PERSONAL HISTORY

I am married, with three nearly-grown children. My wife and I are active in our church and our community. I have been a Boy Scout scoutmaster, when my son was of the appropriate age.

INTENTION

It is my hope to join a forward-looking paper company that can fully utilize my training and skills in all areas of paper production and sale.

13

The New York State Thruway is an expensive toll road. It goes north from New York City to Albany, then turns west toward Buffalo. In that western part, it runs along just to the south of the Mohawk River and the Erie Canal. Just to the north of river and canal is a state road, Route 5, which is smaller and curvier, but doesn't cost anything. I am on Route 5.

I was never in Vietnam. Until I shot Herbert Everly, I'd never seen a human being dead because of violence. It irritates me that Dynes, old EBD, has to put right there, in his resumé, that he was in Vietnam. So what? Is the world supposed to owe him a living, a quarter of a century later? Is this special pleading?

I was stationed in Germany, in the Army, after I got out of boot camp. We were in a communications platoon in a small base east of Munich, on top of a tall pine-covered hill. A foothill of the Alps, I suppose it must have been. We didn't have much to do except keep our radio equipment in working order, just in case the Russians ever attacked, which most of us believed wasn't going to happen. So my eighteen months in the Army in Germany was spent mostly in a beer haze, down in Mootown, which some of us called Munich, I have no idea why.

Mootown. And while the guys in Vietnam called the kilometer a click—"We're ten clicks from the border"—we in Germany were still calling them Ks— "We're ten Ks from that nice gasthaus"—though the Vietnamese influence was getting to us, and Ks were becoming clicks in Europe as well. Nobody wanted to be in Vietnam, but everybody wanted to be thought of as having *been* in Vietnam.

Like this son of a bitch, EBD. Twenty-five years later, and he's still playing that violin.

On a midmorning Thursday in May, there isn't that much traffic on Route 5, and I'm making pretty good time. Not quite as good as the big trucks I can see from time to time across the river on the thruway, but good enough. The little towns along the way—Fort Johnson, Fonda, Palatine Bridge—slow me some, but not for long. And the scenery is beautiful, the river winding through the hills, gleaming in spring sun. It's a nice day.

Mostly it's just river, there to my left, but some of it is clearly manmade, or man altered, and that would be remnants of the old Erie Canal. New York State is bigger than most people realize, being a good three hundred miles across from Albany to Buffalo, and in the

early days of our country this body of water to my left
was the main access to the interior of the nation. Back
before there was much by way of roads.

In those days, the big ships from Europe could come
into New York Harbor, and steam up the Hudson as far
as Albany, and off-load there. Then the riverboats and
barges would take over, carrying goods and people on
the Mohawk River and the Erie Canal over to Buffalo,
where they could enter Lake Erie, and then travel
across the Great Lakes all the way to Chicago or
Michigan, and even take rivers southward and wind up
on the Mississippi.

Some years ago, I was watching some special on
TV, and the announcer described something as being a
"transitional technology." It was the railroads I think
he was talking about. Something. And the idea seemed
to be, a transitional technology was the cumbersome
old way people used to do things before they got to the
easy sensible way they do things now. And the further
idea was, look how much time and effort and expense
was put into something that was just a temporary stop-
gap; railroad bridges, canals.

But everything is a transitional technology, that's
what I'm beginning to figure out. Maybe that's what
makes it impossible sometimes. Two hundred years
ago, people knew for certain they would die in the
same world they were born into, and it had always
been that way. But not any more. The world doesn't
just *change* these days, it upheaves, constantly. We're

like fleas living on a Dr. Jekyll who's always in the middle of becoming Mr. Hyde.

I can't change the circumstances of the world I live in. This is the hand I've been dealt, and there's nothing I can do about it. All I can hope to do is play that hand better than anybody else. Whatever it takes.

At Utica, I take Route 8 north. It goes all the way to Watertown and the Canadian border, but I don't. I stop at Lichgate.

A factory town on the Black River. Prosperity, and the factory, left this town a long time ago; more transitional technology. Who knows what used to be manufactured in that great brick pile of a building that molders now beside the river. The river itself is narrow but deep, and very black, and is crossed by a dozen small bridges, all of them at least sixty years old.

Bits of the ground floor of the old factory have been kept more or less alive, converted to shops—antique, coffee, card—and a county museum. People making believe they're at work, now that there is no work.

My road atlas doesn't include a town map of Lichgate. It's after one when I get to town, so first I have lunch in the Red Brick Cafe, tucked into a corner of the old factory building, and then I buy a map of the area in the card shop down the block.

(I know it would be easier simply to ask directions to Nether Street, but what's the chance I would be remembered, as the stranger who asked the way to Nether Street just before the murder on Nether Street? Very strong chance, I should think. The idea of seeing myself on TV in an artist's rendition from eyewitness accounts is not appealing.)

From the name, I would have guessed Nether Street would run along beside the river, that being the lowest part of town, but on the map I see it's a street that borders the southern city line eastward over to the river. When I drive over there, I see that the hill the town is built on slopes down to the south, this way, and Nether Street got its name because it runs along the base of that hill.

This area is neither suburban nor rural, but an actual town, and this a residential area, old and substantial, the houses mostly a hundred years old, built back when the factory was still turning out whatever it was. They are wide two-story houses on small plots, made mostly of native stone, with generous porches and steep A roofs because of the very snowy winters.

When these houses were built, the managers would have lived here, middle management from the factory, although I don't think they called it middle management back then. But that's who they would have been, along with the shop owners and the dentists. A solid comfortable life in a stable neighborhood. None of those people would have believed for a second that the world they lived in was transitional.

264 is like its neighbors, wide and solid and stone. There are no mailboxes out by the roadside here, but mail slots in front doors or small iron mailboxes hung beside the door. The mailman will walk. And the roadside isn't a roadside, but a curb.

There's a sidewalk as well, and when I first drive down the block a father is using that sidewalk to teach his scared but game daughter how to ride a two-wheeler. I see them, and I think, Don't let that be EBD. But in the resumé he described himself as having "three nearly-grown children."

Most of these houses have garages that were added decades after the houses were built, and most of them are free-standing, beside or behind the house and not attached to it, though here and there, because of those rough winters, people have built enclosed passageways to connect house with garage.

264 has a detached garage, an old-fashioned one with two large doors that open outward, though right now they're closed. It's on the right side of the house, and just behind it, with a blacktop driveway that's crumbling here and there, overdue for a touchup. In the driveway is an orange Toyota Camry, a few years old. No one is visible anywhere around the house.

Three blocks farther on, closer to the river, Nether Street crosses a main north-south road, and there's a gas station. I stop there, fill the tank, and use the pay phone to call EBD.

A male voice answers, on the third ring: "Hello?"

Trying to sound very cheerful and friendly, I say, "Hi, Everett?"

"Yes, hello," he says.

"This is Chuck," I say. "By golly, Everett, I didn't think I'd ever track you down."

"I'm sorry," he says. "Who?"

"Chuck," I say. "Everett? This *is* Everett Jackson."

"No, I'm sorry," he says. "You've got the wrong number."

"Oh, *damn*," I say. "I'm sorry, I beg your pardon."

"That's all right. Good luck," he says.

I hang up, and go back to the Voyager.

There's no trouble parking in this neighborhood. Parked cars take up about half the curb space on the westbound side, facing away from the river, as I am now. There's no parking at all on the other side, where EBD's house is, the street not being that wide. It would have been laid out before there were cars.

The horse: a transitional technology.

I park almost a block away from 264, in front of a house with a For Sale sign on the lawn and no curtains in the windows. Today I'm not trying to pretend I'm a potential buyer, I simply don't want a housewife peering out at me from behind her blinds, wondering who that is, just sitting there in his car in front of her house.

EBD is home. Sooner or later he'll come out. The Luger is under the raincoat on the passenger seat. If he drives off in the Camry, I'll pull up beside him at a red light and shoot him from the car. If he comes out to mow his lawn, I'll walk across the street and shoot him there. One way or another, when he comes out, I'll shoot him.

On the drive, all the long time coming up, I never thought about EBD or what I had to do here. I just thought about historical forces and all that stuff. But now, seated in the Voyager, watching the front of that house, all I think about is EBD. Quick and clean, and get it over with. Get the bad taste of the Ricks experience out of my mouth. Make this one simple, like Everly.

Quarter to four. The father and daughter and bicycle have long gone. The mailman has walked down the block, pushing his three-wheeled cart with the long handle. Clouds have come in from the west, and it's getting cool inside the Voyager.

I am patient. I am a leopard in the shadow of a boulder. I can stay here, without moving, until the night comes. And then, when it's dark, if he still hasn't emerged from his house, I will go in after him.

That is, I will circle the house on foot, I will look in the windows, I will find him and shoot him. I won't actually go indoors unless it's absolutely necessary, and even then with extreme caution. I have no desire to meet the wife, or the three almost-grown children.

I'll adapt myself to circumstance, but I am determined . . .

Movement, at 264. The door is opening, obscured by the shadow of the wide porch roof. A man comes out, pauses to call to someone inside, pulls the door shut, comes down off the porch. He stops there, on the slate walk that makes a part in his lawn, and looks up. Will it rain? He adjusts his windbreaker collar, pulls his cloth cap down more firmly on his head. He continues to the street, turns, and walks this way.

It's my man, EBD. The right age, coming from the right house. He's walking toward me, on the far side of the street. I can pick up the Luger, hold it against my leg, walk across the street, ask directions. He will turn aside, pointing, head raised. I will shoot him in the near eye.

My left hand is on the door handle, my right reaches under the raincoat for the Luger. Half a block away, EBD pauses and waves at a house. He stops. He speaks.

I frown and peer, and now I can see a couple seated on the porch there. I'd never noticed them before. Have they been there all along? This light is difficult, with the sun gone.

I can't do it, not in front of witnesses. My left hand leaves the handle, my right comes empty out from under the raincoat.

Across the way, EBD touches his cap and walks on. He walks past me, on the other side of the street, no parked cars over there to block my vision. He's a tall man, gaunt, with rounded shoulders. His head is thrust forward and down, so that when he walks he looks at the sidewalk directly in front of himself. His hands are in his windbreaker pockets.

Those people on the porch; a couple, I think. Still there. When I start my car, they'll notice me. I have to wait here as long as possible, I have to try to minimize any connection between the passing of EBD and this car driving away.

I see EBD in my outside mirror, walking steadily away. He's more than a block off by now, and still moving steadily on. I can risk losing sight of him for a minute or two.

I start the Voyager. Without looking at the people on the porch, I drive forward, away from EBD. I drive briskly but not crazily down to the corner, where I turn right. I drive rapidly down that block and turn right again, and then a third right, which brings me back to Nether Street.

Only a few major streets go through here, north to south; the rest, including the street I'm now on, end at Nether. I stop at the Stop sign there, then make the left turn onto Nether, and EBD is perfectly plain, still walking along, out ahead.

Where I got the gasoline and made the phone call, up ahead on the right, is the intersection with Route 8, my road up. Diagonally across Route 8 from the gas station there is a diner. I can park in its lot, and trail EBD from there. How far can he be going, on foot?

I drive slowly by him, and he simply walks methodically along, a man with a destination but in no real hurry to get there. I continue on.

The diner, called SnowBird, faces Route 8, with its blacktop parking lot in front of it and spreading around to its left side, away from Nether Street. There's a traffic light at the intersection, and it's red against me when I arrive. I stop and wait.

In my mirror, EBD walks diagonally across Nether Street behind me, and keeps coming.

The light turns green. I turn left onto Route 8 and then right into the diner's parking area. I drive on around to the side, and take a space near the front corner, where I can watch the intersection. The parking area's almost empty.

I switch off the ignition, and look up, as again the light turns red for Route 8, and EBD comes walking across the road. He almost looks as though he's coming to *me*.

No. He's coming to the diner. He crosses the parking lot, goes up the three brick steps to the entrance, goes into the glass-enclosed vestibule—the severe winters up here have surely caused that to be built there—and I can see him as he pushes open the inner door and goes inside.

All right, this is easy. He's here for a late lunch or a mid-afternoon snack. When he's finished, I'll see him as he comes out to the vestibule. I'll have time to start the engine, lower the window, pick up the Luger. As he comes down those brick steps, I'll drive by and stop in front of him. I'll call his name, and when he looks at me, I will shoot him.

There are exits from the parking lot both onto Nether Street and Route 8. Depending which way the traffic light is green, after I shoot EBD I'll take one or the other of those exits, and head straight down Route 8. No witness will have any idea what was going on.

I'll be home for the eleven o'clock news.

Four-fifty. He's been in there almost an hour. Does he have a girlfriend in there? How much longer do I have to wait? How long can you spend in a diner, in the middle of the afternoon? He wasn't carrying a newspaper, but I suppose he could have a paperback book in a pocket of his windbreaker. Maybe his wife is doing the housecleaning, and he's agreed to stay away from home for a few hours.

I have to find out what's going on. I make sure the Luger is completely concealed by the raincoat, and then I get out of the Voyager to find that the day has become raw, with a sharp wind rushing down Nether Street from the west. I lock the car, and walk into the diner, and he isn't there.

I have a mad instant of dislocation, something out of a melodrama. He's snuck out a back entrance and into a waiting car and he's off . . .

Doing what? An assignation with that girlfriend I'd given him earlier? Is he robbing banks while waiting for a new job to come through? (I'd thought of that.)

Is he after *me*?

All of which is ridiculous. He's undoubtedly in the restroom, and I see the sign for it down to the left, so I go to the right, find a place at the counter, take the menu out of the metal rack that sticks up there.

There's only five people in the place, three solitaries drinking coffee along the counter, and an elderly couple having dinner in a booth. I think, when he comes out of the bathroom, why not just shoot him here? Who would be able to identify me, in the shock and suddenness of it? I'll have to go back to the Voyager, get the Luger, wear the raincoat—it's chilly enough for that, anyway—and then come back and wait till he comes out of the men's room, and do it right then.

No. Wait. Wait until he's seated again, wherever he's sitting, that would be best.

He comes out of the swing door behind the counter. He's wearing a green apron and he's carrying a plate of fish and chips, which he places in front of a customer down to my left.

He works here.

I'm so stunned I'm still sitting there when he comes over to me. "Afternoon," he says. He has a pleasant smile. He looks like a nice guy, with an honest glance and an easygoing manner.

Middle management, and he's working the counter in a diner. It won't pay his mortgage on that house three blocks from here. I'm sure it helps, the way Marjorie's days at Dr. Carney's office help, but not enough. And it isn't the same thing as your own real life back.

I'm still stunned. I don't know what to do, what to think, what to say, where to look. He keeps smiling at me: "Know what you want?"

"Not yet," I say. I'm stammering. "Give me a minute."

"Sure," he says, and goes on down the counter to

ask somebody else if he'd like a refill. The answer's yes, and he reaches for the glass coffee pot.

Don't get to know them. That's what I told myself when I started this. *Before* I started this. Don't get to know them, it'll be that much harder to do what you have to do. It will be impossible to do what you have to do.

He's a counterman in a diner. That's all he is. I don't know him, I don't have to know him, I'm not going to know him.

He's back. "Decided?"

"I'll, uh, I'll have the BLT. And french fries."

He grins. "Comes with fries," he says. "We're top drawer here. Comes with fries and cole slaw, little slice of pickle. Okay?"

"Sounds good," I say.

"And coffee?"

"Yes. Forgot that. Right. Coffee."

He goes away to the kitchen, and I struggle to control myself. He hasn't noticed anything yet, or at least nothing he can't put down to highway daze, the result of somebody traveling alone for hours in a car.

But what am I going to do now? How long does he work here? Am I going to have to sit in the Voyager in that parking lot for eight hours? Six hours? Twelve hours?

He comes out through the swing door, goes to get a cup and saucer and spoon and the glass coffee pot, brings them all over to me, pours me a cup of coffee. "Milk and sugar on the counter there."

"Thanks."

He puts the pot back on its electric burner while I add milk to my coffee. Then he comes back, leans against the work counter behind him, folds his arms, gives me a friendly smile, says, "Passing through?"

I hate having to look at him, talk to him, but what else can I do? "Yeah," I say. "Pretty much." And then, because I'm beginning to realize this isn't going to be as quick as I'd hoped, I say, "Is there a motel anywhere around here?"

"None of the chains," he says. "Not close, anyway."

"I don't need a chain. I don't much like chains."

"Neither do I," he says. "You have that feeling, there's no human touch to it."

By God, I don't want a human touch between *us*, but what can I do? "That's right," I say, just hoping to cut the conversation short.

He unfolds his arms, points away to my right, lifting his head. I look at his near eye. I wish I had the Luger with me now, wish I could get this over with now. "About a mile and a quarter south," he says, "on Route 8, there's a place called Dawson's. I've never stayed there myself, of course, you know, I'm local, but I'm told it isn't bad."

"Dawson's," I say. "Thanks."

I look away, but I can feel him considering me, thinking me over. He says, "You looking for a job?"

Surprised, I look back at him, and he's so naturally sympathetic that I tell him the truth: "Yes, I am. How'd you know?"

"I've been there," he says, and shrugs. "Still am, really. I can see it in a fella."

"Isn't easy," I say.

"Not around here, anyway," he says. "I'm sorry to have to tell you that, but there just isn't much of anything happening around here." He gestures at his own territory, his side of the counter. "I was lucky to get this."

This is an opportunity to get my question answered. I say, "You work a full shift?"

"Almost," he says. "Eight hours a day, four days a week. Four to midnight."

Eight hours. Four to midnight. He'll be coming out at midnight. In the dark, I won't see his face, he could be just anybody. In the dark, I'll shoot him. "Well, it's something, anyway," I say, referring to the job.

He grins, but shakes his head. "Not my regular line of work," he says. "I was twenty-five years in the paper business."

Being ignorant, I say, "Newspaper?"

"No no," he says, amused, shaking his head. "Paper manufacturing."

"Oh."

"I was a salesman, and then a manager," he says. "Years in a white shirt and necktie. And then one day, I got the boot."

"It happens," I say, and there's a ding from the kitchen. "It happened to me, too," I find myself saying, though I shouldn't prolong this conversation, I really shouldn't do it.

"That'll be yours," he says, meaning the ding from the kitchen, and he goes away, and I take the minute of respite to tell myself I can't relax into this thing, I can't let us be just a couple of regular guys talking over the news of the world together. I've got to keep that distance, for my own sanity I've got to keep that distance. For my future. For everything.

And aside from all the other considerations, I've already lied to him, pretended I didn't know anything about the paper industry, because I didn't want him thinking about the coincidence of me being here, a guy with the same work history as his. But that means I *can't* let the conversation go on. What am I going to do, invent some whole new life story, in a whole new industry?

He comes back, with my BLT and all the extras on a thick white oval china plate, and puts it down in front of me. "Refill on that?"

My coffee cup's half full. "Not yet," I say. "Thanks."

"Any time."

He goes away to deal with other customers, and I gnaw at my BLT. I'm not hungry, partly because I just ate four hours ago, but mostly because of the situation. I want to be out of here, on my way home. But I *need* this to be *over*, and then I'm out of here, and on my way home.

He's back, taking that stance again, arms folded, back against the work counter. "What line were you in?" he asks.

I panic for just a second, but then I say, "Office supplies," because I do remember something about that industry, from my first years as a salesman for Green Valley Paper & Pulp. "Memo pads, order sheets, accountancy forms, things like that. I was middle management, ran the production line." Then I force a chuckle, and say, "For all I know, we bought from you folk."

"Not from us," he says. "We did specialized papers, industrial uses." Another grin, another headshake. "Very boring, for anybody outside the business."

"You probably miss it," I say, because I know he does, and I can't help saying it.

"I do," he agrees, but then shrugs. "It's a crime," he says, "what's happening these days."

"The layoffs, you mean?"

"The downsizing, the reductions in staff. All those rotten euphemisms they use."

"They told me," I say, "my job wasn't going forward."

"That's a good one," he agrees.

"Made me feel better," I say. I'm holding the sandwich, one triangular quarter of the sandwich, but I'm not eating.

"You know, I've been thinking about it," he says. "I haven't had much to do, the last couple years, except think about it, and I think this society's gone nuts."

"The whole society?" I shrug and say, "I thought it was just the bosses."

"To let the bosses do it," he says. "You know, there's been societies, like primitive peoples in Asia and like that, they expose newborn babies on hillsides to kill them, so they won't have to feed them and take care of them. And there's been societies, like the early Eskimos, that put their real old folk out on icebergs to float away and die, because they couldn't take care of them any more. But this is the first society ever that takes its most productive people, at their prime, at the peak of their powers, and throws them away. I call that crazy."

"I think you're right," I say.

"I think about it all the time," he says. "But what do you do about it? Beats me."

"Go crazy, too, I guess," I say.

He gives me a broad grin at that. "You show me how," he says, "and I'll do it."

We chuckle together, and he goes off to run up the elderly couple's check on the cash register.

While he's gone, I force myself to eat most of the food and drink the rest of the coffee. I can't have more of this conversation, I just can't.

When I see him coming back down the counter, headed toward me, I make that squiggle in the air that means I want my check, so he about-turns, goes to where he keeps the book, and adds it up.

He has a couple more things to say, just chatting, but I barely answer him. Let him think I'm suddenly in a hurry. I pay the check, and I leave him too big a tip, even though it's stupid to do that, I mean, really stupid any way you look at it.

When I'm going out the first door, he calls, "See you around." I smile, and wave.

At least he didn't offer to put me up.

"Good Vibrations" is playing; the old Beach Boys song. "Good Vibrations," and I'm floating in a glass boat on a luminous yellow-green sea, it looks like dish detergent, it's terribly sad, I'm very sad all the time, and then I'm awake and I'm in Dawson's Motel, and the radio came on at 11:30 P.M., just the way I programmed it. I get up and switch off the radio and go into the bathroom, to pee and brush my teeth and wash my face and prepare to kill EBD.

Dawson's Motel is a pleasant old-fashioned place with knotty pine walls and ruffled amber shades on the lamps and a dark wood floor that squeaks as I move around. The closet has a green paisley curtain instead of a door, and many metal hangers on the pipe rod inside. The plumbing fixtures are old-fashioned and make a lot of noise.

There was a rack of skiing brochures in the office, when I went in there this afternoon, but at this time of year they don't do much business. The old man in the office was pleased at the sight of a customer, and even more pleased at the sight of cash. "I don't much like those credit cards," he told me, "but I suppose they're here to stay."

Cash: a transitional technology.

I realize I'm hearing rain on the motel roof. When I come out of the bathroom I go over to open the door, and it's a steady rainfall out there, without much wind, coming mostly straight down, washing road dirt into patterns on the Voyager.

I shut the door, and get dressed, but I don't pack, because I expect to come back here after I do it. 11:47 say the red numbers on the clock-radio. I put on my raincoat and the cloth cap that's very much like EBD's. I take the Luger out of my overnight bag and put it in the pocket of the raincoat.

The motel door is old-fashioned enough that I have to lock it with the key when I go outside. Fortunately, there's a roof overhang here, so I don't get wet while I'm doing it. I've left the lights on in the room, and the glow against the window curtains gives it a warm and homey look. I'll be glad to get back here.

There are only two other vehicles parked along the front of the motel, both facing in toward the rooms where their owners sleep. One is a pickup with Pennsylvania plates; I'm guessing he's a blue-collar guy, a carpenter or something like that, looking for construction work. I don't know why I think that; I guess it's just comforting to make up a story about the people around you. Invent a tribe.

The other vehicle is a big van that's been converted to a small camper. The license plate is Florida, and I'm guessing this is a retired couple. No more shocks to the system for them; winter in Florida, drive north when Florida weather turns muggy and miserable. Not bad.

But not for me, not yet, not even if I could afford it. Which I cannot. God knows if I'll ever be able to afford that kind of retirement life.

I drive north, back toward Lichgate. There's no traffic at all, and very few lights to be seen. The rain is steady and pretty heavy, once you're out driving in it. It slows me down, but it's still only five minutes to twelve when I get to the traffic light at Nether Street. It turns red just before I get there, of course.

The gas station on my left is closed, but the diner ahead to my right is open. And crossing the street in front of me, on the far side of the intersection, shoulders hunched against the rain, inadequately dressed in his windbreaker and cloth cap, is EBD!

Damn! Damn it to hell, he's leaving early! *I'm* on time, dammit!

It was going to be so easy. I would switch off my headlights as I drove into the parking lot. I would wait near the entrance, I would see him come out into the vestibule, I would drive forward, and as he came down the brick steps I would reach the Luger out the window and shoot him. And that's it.

But now he's walking, he's well away from the diner, he's already across the intersection and walking down Nether Street away from me, hands in windbreaker pockets, walking briskly because of the rain, moving along on the right side of the street past the parked cars, three blocks to walk to his house on the left.

And this damn light is still red in my face. It's going to change now; I can see the amber light come on, facing Nether Street. There's still no traffic anywhere, nobody to be seen, nobody at all out in this rain.

I switch off my headlights. Now I'm as black as the night, and when the green light switches on in front of me I turn left.

He's moving briskly. This is going to be a difficult shot, out to the right from the left side of the car, me at the steering wheel, past parked cars, at a man in the dark, walking in the rain. It would be horrible to miss, to alert him, to have him running, to have him escape and at once get on the phone to the local police. (EBD would remember the phone, wouldn't get rattled like Ricks, I can tell that much for sure about him.)

Up ahead, with only the briefest glance over his shoulder, EBD comes out from between parked cars and walks at an angle, crossing the street. And now I know what I must do.

I hit the accelerator hard. The Voyager leaps forward. EBD is a dark mass against the dark masses of the night, everything vaguely glittery from the rain, everything except his wet windbreaker and wet cloth cap. The Voyager leaps at him like a fox after a mole.

He senses me. He looks over his shoulder. It's too dark to see his face, but I can imagine his expression, and then he jumps, trying to launch himself all the way over to the left curb, and the Voyager smashes into him. But he was jumping, his weight was going upward, so his body doesn't go under the car, but pastes against it, right in front of me, almost hitting the windshield, draped there like a dead deer being brought home by a triumphant sportsman.

I slam on the brakes, and he slides down the front of

the car. I see his hands clutching, scrabbling for some hold, but there is none. The car is still moving, though more slowly, and he goes under it, and I feel the heavy bumps as we drive over him.

Now I brake to a stop. Now I turn on the headlights, and switch into reverse gear, so the backup lights will come on, and I see him three times, in all three mirrors, the inside mirror, the one outside to my left, the one all the way over there outside to my right, I see him three times, and in all three mirrors he's moving.

Oh, God, no. He has to stop. We can't go on like this. He's rolling over, he's trying to rise.

I'm already in reverse. Now I accelerate, and I close my eyes, and I feel the *thump* and the *thump*, and I slam on the brakes and skid, and think no, please, I'm going to hit a parked car, but I don't.

I open my eyes. I look out front, and he's there in the glare of my headlights, in the rain, one arm moving on the pavement, fingers scratching on the pavement. His hat is gone. He's crumpled, mostly facedown, and his forehead is against the pavement, his head twitching in slow fits back and forth.

This has to stop *now*. I shift into Drive, I drive slowly forward, I aim at that head. Ba-*thump*, the front left tire, yes. Ba-*thump*, the rear left tire, yes.

I stop. I shift into reverse, and the backup lights come on. In three mirrors, he doesn't move.

I'm weeping when I get back to the motel, still weeping. I feel so weak I can barely steer, hardly press my foot against the accelerator and, at last, the brake.

The Luger is still in my pocket. It weighs me down on the right side, dragging down on me so that I stumble as I move from the Voyager to the door to my room. Then the Luger bangs against my hand, interfering with me, while I try to get into my pants pocket for the key, the key to the room.

At last. I have the key, I get it into the lock, I open the door. All of this is mostly by feel, because I'm sobbing, my eyes are full of tears, everything swims. I push the door open, and the room that was going to be warm and homey is underwater, afloat, cold and wet because of my tears. I pull the key out of the door, push the door closed, stagger across the room. I'm stripping off my clothes, just leaving them anywhere on the floor.

The sobs have been with me since I made the U-turn on Nether Street and drove carefully around the body in the middle of the pavement. The sobs hurt my throat, they constrict my chest. The tears sting my eyes. My nose is full, I can barely breathe. My arms and legs are heavy, they ache, as though I'd been pummeled for a long time with soft clubs.

A shower, won't that help? A shower always helps. Here in Dawson's Motel, the bathroom contains an old-fashioned clawfoot tub. Above it, sometime later, a shower nozzle was added to protrude from the wall, and a small ring to hang a shower curtain. When you step in there and turn on the water, if you move an inch in any direction you touch the cold wet shower curtain.

But I'm not moving. I stand in the flow of hot water, eyes closed, tears still streaming, throat and chest still in pain, but the hot water slowly does its work. It cleanses me, and it soothes me, and at last I turn off the water, push the too-close shower curtain aside, step out, and use all the thin towels to dry myself.

I've stopped weeping now. Now I'm merely exhausted. The bedside clock-radio says 12:47. Exactly one hour ago I left this room, to go kill Everett Dynes, and now I'm back, and I've done it. And I'm exhausted, I could sleep for a thousand years.

I get into bed, and switch off the light, and I don't sleep. I'm so weary I could start crying all over again, but I don't sleep. The scene on Nether Street, in the dark, in the rain, in the lights of my Voyager, keeps replaying in my head.

I try to remember the last time I cried, and I cannot; sometime when I was a child, I suppose. I'm not good at it, my throat and chest still ache, my head feels clogged.

I try not to move around in the bed, I try to do things that will help me get to sleep. I count to one hundred, then back to one. I try to bring up pleasant memories. I try to shut down entirely.

But I cannot sleep. And I keep seeing the event on Nether Street. And every time I turn my head, the clock-radio shows some later time, in red numbers, just there, to my right.

I must have been crazy, out of my mind. How could I have done these things? Herbert Everly. Edward Ricks, and his poor wife. And now Everett Dynes. He was like me, he should be my friend, my ally, we should work together against our common enemies. We shouldn't claw each other, down here in the pit, fight each other for scraps, while they laugh up above. Or, even worse; while they don't even bother to notice us, up above.

When the clock says 5:19, I come to my decision. It has to end now. I have to make a clean breast of everything, atone for what I've done, do no more.

I get out of bed. My exhaustion has left me, I'm awake and alert. I'm calm. I turn on the lights and look around for writing paper, but Dawson's Motel does not equip its rooms with stationery, and I've brought no paper with me.

Paper lines the dresser drawers, white lengths of paper, in the old-fashioned dark wood dresser. I take out the paper from the bottom drawer, and find it stiff, rather thick, smoother on one side than the other. A very simple level of manufacture, this paper. (I could cry all over again, just for a second, when I notice myself noticing that detail.)

The rougher side is better for writing on. I sit at the table, I smooth the paper in front of me, I pick up my pen, and I write:

My name is Burke Devore. I am 51 years old and I live
at 62 Pennery Woods Rd., Fairbourne, CT. I have been
unemployed for close to 2 years, through no fault of my
own. Since my army service, I have at all times been employed, until now.

This period of unemployment has had a very bad effect on me, and has made me do things I would never
have thought possible. Through placing a false ad in a
trade journal, I got the resumés of many other people
who are unemployed, as I am, in my field of expertise. I
then determined to kill those people who I feared were
better qualified than I was for one certain job. I wanted
that job, I wanted to be employed again, and that desire
made me do crazy things.

I wish to confess now to four murders. The first was
two weeks ago, on Thursday, May 8th. My victim was a
man named Herbert C. Everly. I shot him in front of his
house on Churchwarden Lane, in Fall City, CT.

My second victim was Edward G. Ricks. I only meant
to kill him, but his wife mistook me for an older man
who'd been having an affair with her young daughter,
and in the confusion I had to kill her, too. I shot both of
them last Thursday at their home in Longholme, MA.

My final victim was last night, in Lichgate, NY. His
name was Everett Dynes, and I deliberately ran him
down with my automobile.

I am truly sorry for these crimes. I don't know how I
could have done them. I feel so sorry for the families. I
feel so sorry for the people I killed. I hate myself. I don't
know how I can go on. This is my confession.

My last resumé.

When I finish it, I sign it, but I don't date it. There's no need.

I'm not sure yet what I'll do tomorrow. Either I'll shoot myself with that Luger in my raincoat pocket hanging from the pipe rod in the closet over there, or I'll drive back to Lichgate, find the police station, and show my confession to a policeman there.

I just don't think I can kill myself. I think I have to atone. I think I have to pay for my crimes. And I think I'm just not somebody who commits suicide. So I think I'll turn myself in to the police tomorrow morning.

I leave the confession on the table, turn off the lights, get back into bed. I feel very calm. I know I'll sleep now.

14

I sleep like a log. I wake up refreshed, comfortable, hungry as a bear. I left no morning call, so I've slept until I was finished sleeping, and the clock-radio reads 9:27. I'm usually out of bed by seven-thirty, so this is really coddling myself. I always had to get up at seven-thirty to get to my job, when I had a job, and I did that for so many years that the habit has stayed with me.

I shower with the curtain only half closed, which is much more comfortable for me, but leaves the floor very wet. I'm sure that's not the first time that's happened.

It's still raining outside, a steady rain out of a low grayish white sky. It won't stop today. I put my overnight bag, with the Luger in the bottom, into the car, then hunker down in the protection of the roof overhang to look at the front of the Voyager.

The glass over the left parking light is gone, and so is the chrome rim around the headlight, but the headlight seems to be intact. There are dents on the body-work in the left front. If there was ever any blood any-where on the car, the rain has washed it away.

I go back into the room one last time, to see if I've left anything, and that's when I see the sheet of paper on the table. I'd completely forgotten about that, done in the woozy hysterics of the night. Wow, and I almost left it behind.

I sit at the table, and read what I wrote last night, and that awful dread begins to creep over me again. How terrible I felt last night. Tense, anxious, terrified, unable to sleep. I'm glad writing this made it possible at last for me to lose consciousness for a while.

I meant all of this last night, I know I did. Every-thing seemed so hopeless. The first one, Everly, went so smoothly, but both of them since have been absolute disasters. I'm not used to this sort of thing, it would be hard enough to do even if they all went smoothly and cleanly, but to have two horror shows in a row really ground me down.

From now on, I have to be more careful and more patient. I have to be sure the circumstances are right before I make my move.

I sympathize with the me from last night, who felt such despair, and wrote these words, and apologized to his victims. I too would apologize to them, if I could. I'd leave them alone, if I could.

I take the confession with me, folded in my pocket. I'll burn it later, somewhere else.

I don't have to go back through Lichgate, which is good. I head south toward Utica on Route 8, and as I drive I think about the damage to the car. I have to get it repaired. I have to fill out a report for the insurance company, though I'm not sure the damage will exceed the deductible. I have to give Marjorie an explanation.

And at the same time, of course, I have to remember the police will be looking for this car. Even if they don't call it a murder back there—and I have no idea if they can tell the body was driven over more than once—but even if they don't call it murder, even if it's merely a hit-and-run, that's still manslaughter, and they'll be looking for the car.

What do they have? Probably tread marks. The glass from the parking light. The rim from the headlight. One or all of those things will tell them the make and model of the car. They'll know they're looking for a Plymouth Voyager with these specific injuries to the left front. I didn't see any paint chipped off, so they probably don't have the color.

There are a lot of these cars on the road, but there won't be many with these particular scars. Fortunately, the headlight still works, and the headlights are switched on because of the rain. With that rain falling, and with the light glaringly on, it will be very hard for any passing cop to see the small dings around the front of the car. I should be safe, until I can get it fixed, and I think I know how to do that.

I told Marjorie I was going to a job interview in Binghamton, so I have to wait until I'm far enough south to be on a route that makes sense for that to be where I'm coming from. Then, with the help of the rain, I'll take care of this problem.

My chance doesn't come until early afternoon, just short of Kingston, New York, where I will cross the Hudson River. For my route back, I continue south after Utica, and although I'm starving I wait a good long time, until almost noon, before I stop at a diner to eat what they would call lunch but I would call breakfast. While I'm in there, I make sure to put the Voyager where no one can casually see the front end of it.

After breaking my fast with lunch, I drive on down through Oneonta, where I turn southwest on State Route 28 through the Catskill Mountains, a winding hilly road, mostly only two lanes wide. It's in a little town along in there that my opportunity knocks.

There's a lumberyard up ahead on the left side of the road, with several vehicles along its front, parked facing in. A pickup truck suddenly backs out from there, too fast and too far, without the driver paying sufficient attention. I could avoid him, if I tromp on the brake, or if I drive briefly onto the shoulder to steer around him, but I do neither. I tromp on the accelerator and ram him, my left front against his left side by his rear wheel.

The pickup skids away sidewise on the wet road, taking my hooked bumper with him, and winding up just off the road in front of the lumberyard. I fight the wheel, roll to the right shoulder, and stop. I turn off the ignition, and get out of the car.

Three men in mackinaws come out of the lumberyard, staring at the destruction. The driver of the pickup truck, a skinny kid in his early twenties wearing a New York Giants warmup jacket and a baseball cap on backwards, sits in the truck, stupefied with shock. His engine has stalled, and his right hand is still high on the steering wheel, holding tight, and country music is blaring loudly from his radio. A dozen planks and a big can of joint compound are in the back of the pickup.

I cross the road and meet the three men in mackinaws. I say, sounding as dazed as that kid over there looks, "Did you see that?"

"I heard it," one of them says. "That was good enough for me."

"He came," I say, and shake my head, and point this way and that, and start again. "He came out, all of a sudden all the way across the road. I was going *that* way, I was way over *there*."

One of the men in mackinaws goes over to tell the kid to turn off his ignition, and he does, and the music stops. Another of them says to me, "We better call the cops."

"He came *right out*," I say.

Everybody agrees I am not at fault. Even the kid knows he's to blame, jumping way out into the road like that, not looking both ways, playing his radio too loud.

The state police treat me with the calm courtesy reserved for the innocent victim, and they treat the kid with the cold efficiency reserved for assholes. They take down everybody's particulars, get names and phone numbers from the three men in mackinaws in case witnesses are ever needed, and assure me they'll send me a copy of the accident report for me to give my insurance company.

I thank them all for their help, and at last I get back into the car, which still runs, though it has some new rattles, and I drive on, and when I reach Kingston I stop in a little neighborhood bar, nearly empty at this time of day, to have a beer, to quiet my nerves.

When I come back out, a Kingston city cop is looking at the damage to the front of my car, parked at the curb by the door to the bar. This damage is now considerably more severe than it was. He asks me if it's my car, and I say yes. He asks to see a driver's license, and I show it to him. Still holding my license, he says, "Do you mind telling me when you got that?"

"About half an hour ago," I tell him, "maybe ten miles back up Route 28. I was just calming myself with a beer in there."

He asks me the particulars of the accident, and then asks if I mind waiting while he calls in, and I tell him in that case I think I'll have another beer.

"Don't drink too much," he says, but he smiles, and I assure him I won't. He walks off to his own car, carrying my license.

I'm still in the bar, a warm and dark and comforting place, five minutes later, halfway down this second draft beer, when the cop comes in and says, "Just wanted you to know, it checked out." He hands me my license. "Thanks for the cooperation."

"Sure," I say.

15

We still treat Sunday as something different, Marjorie and I, although there's no reason to any more. I don't mean we go to church. We don't, though we did years ago, when the kids were young and we were trying to be a good influence. Since I was chopped, Marjorie's mentioned the idea once or twice, going to church some Sunday, but she hasn't made a real point of it, and we don't have a church in particular here in Fairbourne, don't really know any churchgoers, so it hasn't happened yet. I don't suppose it will.

No, what I mean by our treating Sunday as something different, I mean we still act as though it's the day I don't go to work. (The *other* day. Saturdays I get up early and do chores, still maintaining that fiction as well.) We sleep an hour later, not getting up till eight-thirty or nine, and we dawdle over a long breakfast, and we don't dress until lunchtime, and we spend most of the daylight hours with the Sunday *New York Times*.

Of course, these Sundays I turn first to the help wanted section, so that's a change.

So today, this Sunday, is a true time-out. After my experiences last Thursday and Friday up in Lichgate, I'm ready for some time out. Tomorrow I'll take the Voyager to a body shop for an estimate on the damage, which I hope I can get taken care of very soon. I mean, urgently.

Originally, I thought I'd spend part of this afternoon in the office, to decide which of the three remaining resumés I should deal with next, and how to deal with him with less chance of the kind of disaster I've been having. But then it occurred to me, with that damage on it, the Voyager is a lot more identifiable than it used to be. I probably shouldn't use it to go after the others until it's been made anonymous again.

Which I don't like. I want to do it now, I want to get it over with, I really want to get this whole thing over and done with. While I was burning that confession in the backyard yesterday, during the time Marjorie was away at her movie-house job, I realized the tension of this situation could get to me again, that I could have more weak moments, and that some time, in dread and despair, I might even actually make a phone call to the authorities, blurt it all out, destroy myself. So the sooner I get this over with, the better.

"Burke! Burke!"

We're in the living room, Marjorie and I, in our robes, with the sections of the Sunday *Times* and our cooling coffee. I'm in my regular chair, with its view slightly leftward to the TV set on the far side wall and its view slightly rightward through the picture window to the front of our yard and the plantings that partly shield us from the road and our neighbors. Marjorie is, as usual, on the sofa to my left, feet curled up under her, newspaper spread all across the sofa beyond her.

And now I realize she's calling to me. I start, the paper rattling, and look at her. "What? Something wrong?" Something in the paper, I mean.

"You haven't heard a word I said."

She looks surprisingly tense, agitated. I hadn't noticed that before. Is this about something that *isn't* in the paper?

I'm a pretty big guy, now going to seed a bit, and Marjorie's what they call petite, with very curly brown hair and wide bright brown eyes and a wholehearted way of laughing that I love, as though she's about to blow herself over. Though I haven't heard that laugh for a while, really.

When we first started going together in '71, back in Hartford, we had to put up with a lot of not-very-witty jokes from our friends because I was so big and tall and she was so skinny and short. I was still a bus driver, then, for the city, and in fact I first met Marjorie when she got on my bus one morning. She was a college student, twenty years old, and I was an Army vet and a bus driver, twenty-five, and she had no intention of getting involved with somebody like me, and yet that's what happened. And even though I was a college graduate myself, she took a lot of ribbing from her friends at school when she started going out with a bus driver, and I suppose it was that as much as anything that led me to apply to Green Valley, and get the job selling paper, and find my life's work, that's now been temporarily lost.

And now she's telling me I haven't heard a word she's said, and it's true. "I'm sorry, sweet," I say. "I was distracted, I was a million miles away."

"You've *been* a million miles away, Burke," she says. There are little white blotches under her eyes, high on her cheekbones. She almost looks as though she might cry. What *is* this?

I say, "It's the job, sweet, I just can't—"

"I *know* it's the job," she says. "Burke, honey, I *know* what the problem is, I know how much this has been weighing on your mind, driving you crazy, but—"

"Well, not entirely crazy, I hope."

"—but I *can't stand it*," she insists, not letting me interrupt or make a joke. "Burke, it's driving *me* crazy."

"Sweet, I don't know what I can—"

"I want us to go into counseling," she says, with that abrupt matter-of-factness people use when they finally say something they've been thinking about for a long time.

I automatically reject this, for a thousand reasons. I start with the most explainable of those reasons, saying, "Marjorie, we can't afford—"

"We can," she says, "if it's important. And it *is* important."

"Sweet, this can't go on forever," I tell her. "I'll find another job before you know it, a good job, and—"

"It'll be too late, Burke." Her eyes are bigger and brighter than I've ever seen them. She's so *serious* about this, and so *worried*. "We're being torn apart *now*," she says. "It's been too long, the damage is being done. Burke, I love you, and I want our marriage to survive."

"It *will* survive. We love each other, we're strong in—"

"We're not strong enough," she insists. "*I'm* not strong enough. It's wearing me down, it's grinding me down, it's making me miserable, it's making me desperate, I feel like a . . . I feel like a woodchuck in a Hav-a-Hart trap!"

What an image. She must have been thinking about all this for quite a long while, and I haven't even noticed. She's been unhappy, and keeping it to herself, trying to be brave and silent and wait it out, and I haven't noticed. I should have noticed, but I was distracted by this other thing, concentrating on this other thing.

If only I could tell her about all that, tell her what I'm doing, how I'm making sure everything will be all right. But I can't, I don't dare. She wouldn't understand, she couldn't possibly understand. And if she knew what I was doing, what I've already done, what I'm going to do, she'd never be able to look at me in the same way again. I understand that, all at once, right now, sitting here in the living room, looking at her, in our robes, the both of us covered like bums in the park with sections of the *New York Times*. I can never tell her what I've done, what I'm doing, to save our marriage, to save our lives, to save us.

I say, "Sweet, I know what you're feeling, I really do. And you know I'm feeling the same frustration, I'm having to deal with it every second of every—"

"I can't do it," she says. "I'm not as strong as you are, Burke, I never was. I can't deal with this awful situation as well as you can. I can't just, just *hunker down* and wait."

"But there's nothing else to do," I say. "That's the bitch of it, sweet, there's nothing else to do. We *both* have to just hunker down and wait. But believe me. Please. I have a feeling, I just have a feeling, it won't be that much longer. This summer, sometime this summer, we'll—"

"Burke, we need counseling!"

How she stares at me, almost in terror. For God's sake, does she *know*? Is that what she's trying to say?

No, it can't be. It isn't possible. I say, "Marjorie, we don't need any third party, we can talk things out together, we've always been able to do that, even that bad time when I was . . . You know."

"When you were going to leave me," she says.

"No! I was never going to leave you, you know that. I never for a second thought or said or planned that I could ever leave you, not *you*, sweet, my God. We talked all that—"

"You were living with her."

I sit back. I put one hand over my eyes. With everything that's going on, to have to deal now with something like this. But it's important, I know it is, I have to pay attention to this. Marjorie is my other half, I learned that eleven years ago, the time we're talking about now. Everything I do is as much for her as for me, because I can't live without her.

Still shielding my eyes with my hand, I say, "We talked that out then, and that was the worst thing that ever happened. We talked it out—"

"It wasn't the worst."

I lower my hand and look at her, and I want her to see in my eyes how much I love her. "Oh, but it was," I say. "This job business is terrible, but it isn't as bad as that was. And we talked that out."

"We had help."

"Yes, that's true."

A friend of Marjorie's from her college days had been her confidante, back then, and the friend was a churchgoer, and she took Marjorie along to meet this Episcopalian priest, Father Susten, and then Marjorie brought me along, and he actually was a help, he gave us somebody to pretend to talk to when we were saying things we couldn't say directly to one another. Father Susten's church was down in Bridgeport, he probably isn't even there any more, he wasn't a young man eleven years ago.

Besides, that was a marital difficulty, that was my infidelity, the stupid mistake of a man who had to go for just one last hurrah, no matter how much it hurt. Our problem now is a job and an income; what could he say about that? What could he do to help? Give us something out of the alms box?

And what would I have to say to him about *this* problem? Discuss what I'm doing with the resumés? I say, "Marjorie, Father Susten couldn't—"

"He isn't there any more. I phoned."

So she's very serious about this. But I want to head it off, I don't want to entangle my mind with *counseling* when I have this hard, tense, frightening work to do. I say, "Marjorie, we can talk it out together, all this stuff about the job."

"I can't talk to you," she says. She looks over at the picture window. She's calmer now. "That's the problem, I really can't talk to you."

"I know I've been inattentive," I say, "but I *can* pay attention, and I *will* pay attention."

"That's not what I mean." She continues to look at the picture window. Now that she knows I'm listening, she's become very quiet, draining all the passion out of what she says. "I mean I can't talk to you about the current situation."

I simply don't understand. "Why not?" I ask her. "We both know the situation isn't—"

"No, we don't both know," she says, and turns her head, and looks at me again. "You don't know the situation at all," she says, "and that's why we need counseling."

I don't want to know what she's telling me. It's too late not to know, but I don't want to know. I feel myself trembling. I say, "Marjorie, you haven't . . . made any . . . *done* any . . . you're worried about . . . you think you might . . ."

She's looking at me. She's waiting for me to stop. But when I stop, I'll have to know. I take a long painful breath, a deep inhale, and when that breath comes out I say, "Who is he?"

She shakes her head. I'll kill him, I think. I know how, I didn't used to know how, but now I do, and I know I can do it, and I know it's easy. It's easy. With this one, a pleasure.

"Just tell me who he is," I say. I try to sound very gentle, like someone who doesn't kill people.

She says, "Burke, I called some state social services offices. There's counseling we can go to, it isn't terribly expensive, we can—"

"Who is he, Marjorie?"

How many people could he be? How many places does she go? Not many, not since we sold the Civic. Could it be the dentist, Dr. Carney, that white-coated wimp with his Coke bottle glasses, endlessly washing his hands? Or that fellow at the New Variety, the movie house, what's his name, balding, harried, slovenly,

Fountain, that's it. Could it be Fountain? Somebody at one of those places.

I'll follow her, I'll trail her, I know how to do these things now, she won't know I'm there, I'll find him, and then I'll kill him.

She's still talking, while my mind races around like a dog that's lost the scent, and what she's saying is, "Burke, either we go into counseling together, or I'm going to have to move out."

That stops the questing dog in his tracks. I give her my full attention. I say, "Marjorie, no, you can't go— How could you? Where could you live? You don't have any money!"

"I have *some*," she says, and I realize I'm the one who doesn't have any money, not since the unemployment insurance ran out a few months ago. (That was so humiliating, taking the unemployment insurance, going down there, signing the forms, standing on the lines with *those people*. It was shaming and degrading, but it wasn't as bad as when it stopped.)

And if Marjorie goes away? We can't afford *one* household, how could we afford two?

She says, "I have my part-time jobs, and I can get another one, part-time, at Hurley's."

Hurley's is a liquor store, in the same mall as Dr. Carney's office. Could it be *Hurley* she's shacked up with, stinking of stale cigarettes?

I'm feeling desperate, scared, trapped. I say, "Marjorie, none of this would be happening if I hadn't lost my job."

"I *know* that, Burke," she says, as desperate and trapped as I am. "Don't you think I know that? That's what I'm saying, the strain of this, it isn't *fair*, it isn't fair for any of us, but it's getting to us, it's making you silent and secretive, I have no idea what you do in that office all the time, all those papers you're constantly going over and marking up with your pencils, all those trips you take—"

"Interviews," I say, quickly. "Job interviews. I'm *trying* to get work."

"I know you are, honey," she says. "I know you're doing your best, but it's driving us apart, it's making me feel I want to *laugh* again sometimes, I want to stop being so miserable, feeling so weighed down all the time."

"All right," I say. I have to speed up the operation, I have to finish it all very soon. Her . . . person . . . whoever he is, I'll get to him later. I have to finish the other first. "All right," I say.

She cocks her head, watching me. "All right?"

"I'll go along with you, to . . . counseling," I say, and even as I say it I feel lighter, happier. It won't be easy, I know. I'll have to hide so much from this person, and this is a person you're supposed to be seeing so you can have somebody to be *open* with. But I can't be open, not with anybody, not till this is over, and even then never about this. I'll never be able to tell anyone in the world about this, about this awful period in my life, not a single human being ever. Not Marjorie, not a counselor, not a thousand counselors sworn to secrecy.

But still, we'll be able to talk about some of it, the desperation, the resentment, the feelings of inadequacy, the shame, the feeling that somehow it is all my fault even when I know it isn't.

"All right," I say again. "Counseling. I'm sure it's a good idea anyway."

"Thank you, Burke," she says.

I say, "Marjorie . . ."

"No," she says. She's very firm. "Don't say anything about it."

I was going to say to her, don't see him any more. But I know she's right, I can't say that, I don't have the right to say it. "All right," I say.

16

Three hours later I am in my office. This time, I'll go after the nearest one, to make it simple and easy, and so I can make more than one trip, reconnoiter, be sure I know what I'm going to do and how I'm going to do it, and how I'm going to *keep* it simple and easy. *Then* I'll do it.

The road atlas. Here he is, in Dyer's Eddy, a dot of a town right here in Connecticut, not thirty miles from this spot.

Marjorie is reading a novel in the living room. I say to her, "I'm going for a drive, I have to think," and she nods, not looking up from the book. We're extremely awkward together.

I don't carry the Luger, this is just reconnaissance. I carry the resumé.

KANE B. ASCHE
11 Footbridge Road
Dyer's Eddy, CT 06687
telephone 203 482-5581
fax 203 482-9431

EMPLOYMENT HISTORY: Most recently, (1991-present) Product Manager, Green Valley Paper & Pulp, introduced the new product line of industrial polymer paper applications.

1984-1991, assistant plant supervisor, Green Valley Paper & Pulp, responsible for paperwork for OSHA and other Federal regulators as well as state regulators. Additionally, oversaw second shift, home products line.

1984, oversaw the dissolution of Champion Pulpwood after bankruptcy. Dismantled machinery, negotiated with purchasers, maintained records of dispersal of machinery, money, materiel.

1971-1984, various responsibilities with Champion Pulpwood, beginning on factory floor as sludge operator, moving up through various jobs to night shift supervisor, then to assistant to the manager during the period when Champion was being purchased and dismantled by Kai Wen Holding Corp.

EDUCATION HISTORY: High school diploma, 1962. Received bachelor's degree in business administration from West Texas University Extension while serving as an enlisted man in the United States Army (two tours, 1963-1971). Received master's degree, Connecticut Tech (night school) 1985. Am pursuing doctorate part-time.

I am still under 50 years of age, eager to share my experience and give a long-term commitment to a solid reliable employer.

Still under 50. The bastard. He doesn't know it, but he's going to be under 50 forever.

It's all back roads between Fairbourne and Dyer's Eddy. Last week's rainstorm has finally drifted out to sea, leaving a clean-scrubbed world behind, glistening under pale spring sunshine. There are a number of Sunday drivers out, looking at the fresh greens of spring, the colors of the tulips people plant beside their porches and around their birdfeeders. I'm in no hurry, I drive along in their wake and I think about Kane Bagley Asche.

(In my research, in that stalling period after I knew what I had to do but hadn't yet steeled my mind to do it, I used our family computer and its modem—we're online, though we can't really afford it, and I have to keep warning Billy not to spend too much time there—to access public records on my six resumés. Birth certificates, wedding licenses, property ownership. You can learn a lot about other people, though none of it did me much good. No good at all, really, except that when you know things about other people, and they don't know you know those things, you feel a sense of power over them. That's a help, if you ever intend to deal with them in some way. And one extra result of it all was that I now know everybody's middle name, and that's pleasurable in a strange way. I know their secret name, the one they don't usually tell people. That's probably the same sense of power the police feel, because they always use the middle name, you notice, when they announce a manhunt or an arrest.)

The eddy that's been named after Dyer is a small seasonal whirlpool in a little stream called the Pocochaug, a tributary of the Housatonic River. There are a lot of Indian names around this part of the country, some of them worse than Pocochaug.

This is the eddy's season, springtime, with snowmelt and the spring rains. New Haven Road, the town's main street, almost its only street, runs along the west bank of the Pocochaug, then angles right where the stream angles left, and that's where the town is. Just above that, at the north end of town and just within the town limits, is the eddy, considered such a local attraction that there's even a small parking area there, between road and stream. At the moment, midafternoon on a May Sunday, there are about seven cars there. I make it eight.

There's a footbridge across the stream here, over the eddy, which is simply water behaving, in a somewhat larger fashion, the way it behaves when you empty your sink. Half a dozen people lean on the stripped-bark log railing there, looking down at the eddy, I have no idea why. Beyond them, the footbridge, which is wooden planks over a solid iron structure, curves down to the far side of the Pocochaug, where there's a little park, some boulders sticking out of the ground, a few picnic benches, and a seasonal (like the eddy) snack shop.

It's open. I don't buy anything, but I walk around the little rustic building and the general area of the park. It's so pleasant here, as though there are no problems in the world, as though there was nothing difficult I had to do, as though Marjorie had not delivered earlier today her terrible news. Walking here, among the trees, in the neat park, I am feeling relaxed. How long has it been since I felt relaxed?

I stand in the middle of the park and look back toward the stream, where people still lean on the railing to watch the water eddy. It looks to me as though some of them are the same people as when I first got here. Beyond them is the gravel parking area, and beyond that the lightly traveled road, and beyond that a couple of white houses and a road winding away uphill.

Footbridge. KBA's address is Footbridge Road. That must be Footbridge Road right there.

A few houses are visible, uphill, through pine trees. Can I see KBA's house from here? I've forgotten the number.

Tensing up, feeling excitement grow, I walk back across the footbridge. KBA's house. Is he home? Can he be one of these people down here, looking at the eddy? Unlikely; the eddy will be old news to him.

Why don't I walk up there? It can't be far, and people are walking today, it's a nice day. And it would be good not to drive the car past KBA's house in its present condition.

I go to the Voyager and look at the resumé, to remind myself of the house number, and it's eleven. I leave my cap on the car seat, and open my windbreaker, and start to walk.

It's a little farther than I expected, and certainly not

visible from that park back there, but the road is a gradual slope, an easy climb, past well-cared-for New England houses, all of them cleverly fitted into the slant of the hill. Many retaining walls, the older ones of stone, the newer ones of railroad ties.

Number eleven uses railroad ties, and a lot of plantings. The house is on the left as I walk up, well set back from the road, the blacktop driveway walled on one side by the railroad ties, the mailbox built into the wooden post constructed at the road end of the ties.

I walk past, on the other side of the road, and as I get a little higher I can see them. Husband and wife. Digging in the garden.

Planting season. They have several gardens, all around the house, including this elaborate one on the uphill side, with a tall wire fence all around it. I look more closely, and see small green clumps growing in there, and realize those are different kinds of lettuce. A vegetable garden. They're growing their own vegetables.

They're both in blue jeans. His T-shirt is dusty rose, with words on it I can't read from here, while hers is wordless and pale blue. They both wear sweatbands around their foreheads, his white, hers the same blue as her T-shirt. She's wearing gloves, he isn't.

They're absorbed in their work, digging with trowels, inserting little plastic markers to show what they've planted. I look at him, as I walk by. It's probably only the dirt streaks on his face, but to me he looks more than 50. If they think he's lying at interviews . . .

No. That's a powerful resumé. If there were jobs to be had, in our shared industry, he would have one. Before me, he would have one. He's the most recent arrival among our group of unemployed, and even without my intercession he wouldn't be with us long.

I know him now, know what he looks like. I walk on up the slope, and a while farther on it begins to get steeper, so I stop to sit on a stub of stone wall and look back down the way I've come, and think things over.

It's just as well I didn't bring the Luger today. I am *not* going to do anything while the wife's around, period.

Rested, I walk back down the slope. I wonder, on the way down, should I start a conversation? Ask directions, something like that? But what's the point? In fact, I'm much better off if I don't talk to him. It was doubly horrible with Everett Dynes, having talked with him, gotten to know him, like him. I'm not going to let that happen again.

They're still at work, struggling toward vegetable self-sufficiency. A black Honda Accord is in their driveway; I memorize the license number.

I continue on down to New Haven Road, and cross it to the parking lot, and a state trooper's car is parked behind mine. When I get closer, a young trooper with cold eyes rises from inspecting the damage to the front of the Voyager and looks at me. "Sir? This your car?"

This far away, the alert has gone out. I'm surprised, but of course I don't show it. "Yes, it is."

"Could you tell me how you got banged up here?"

"I was just asked that question last week," I say. "Over in Kingston, New York. What the heck is going on?"

"Sir," he says, "I'd like to know what happened here."

"Okay," I say, and shrug, and tell him the story; the pickup truck backs out of the lumberyard in the rain, unavoidable collision.

He listens, watching various parts of my face, then says, "Sir, may I see your license and registration?"

"Sure," I say. While I'm getting them out, I say, "I sure wish I knew what was going on."

He thanks me for the documents, and goes away to his car, which is blocking mine. I take off my windbreaker, feeling warm from the walk, and toss it on top of the resumé on the passenger seat, with my cap. Then I sit behind the wheel, lower my window, and listen to the burbly rush of the water in the eddy. It's soothing, and the air is sweet and not too warm, and I'm actually about to fall asleep right here when the trooper comes back, trying to be less cold and formal, which is rather like watching an I-beam try to curtsey.

"Thank you, sir," he says, and gives me back my license and registration.

He's about to go away, without another word, but I say, "Officer, give me a break, will you? What's going on? This is twice now."

He considers me. This is a need-to-know guy if there ever lived one. But he decides to relent. "A few days ago there was a hit-and-run," he tells me, "upstate

New York. This type of vehicle. We expect it's got some damage on the front left."

"Upstate," I say. "No, I was in Binghamton. But thanks for telling me."

Nodding at the front of the Voyager, he says, "You ought to get that fixed."

"I'm taking it in tomorrow," I promise. "Thank you, officer."

17

For some reason, I seem to do all these things on Thursdays. I didn't plan it this way, but with Marjorie working Mondays and Wednesdays, and only one car in the family, this is the way it's been happening. I dealt with the first three resumés on Thursdays, and now here it is Thursday again, and I'm on my way back to Dyer's Eddy.

Will I deal with KBA today? I hope so. Get it over with. Now that the car is anonymous again.

It wasn't possible before this. Monday, after I took Marjorie to Dr. Carney's office (I kept the radio on in the car, tuned to WQXR, the *New York Times*'s classical music station, to hide the silence in there with us), I went to the dealer where I'd bought the Voyager, five years ago, back when I was replacing my cars every three years, and I talked with Jerry in the service department. I've had the car serviced there every time since I bought it, because I have to keep it going for who knows how long, so Jerry and I know one another, and he has some idea of my financial situation. He looked at the car, and he looked at me, and he said, "Your insurance covers this?" This is the first time we've dealt with damage.

I'd brought along my policy, which I handed to him, saying, "Two-hundred-fifty-dollar deductible."

He frowned over the policy. When he handed it back, he said, "Uh huh." Giving nothing away.

"Jerry," I said, "you know my situation. I can't afford two hundred and fifty dollars."

"This is a rough time, Mr. Devore," he said, and he sounded sympathetic. "They just let my wife go at the hospital."

I didn't follow. I said, "What? She was in the hospital?"

"She *worked* at the hospital. X-ray technician. She was there eleven years."

"Oh."

"Some big health care company from Ohio bought them up," he said, "and they're cutting back. All the problems about health costs, you know?"

Funny; I don't think of hospitals as being commercial institutions, bought and sold, belonging to corporations. But of course they are. I think of them as being like churches or firehouses, but they're just stores, after all. I said, "So they let her go? After eleven years?"

"Boom, like that," he said, and poked at his thick moustache with a knuckle. "They had nine X-ray technicians, now they'll get along with six. To do the job nine did before."

"Still," I said, "that's a skill, isn't it? X-ray technician?"

He shook his head. "They're all cutting back," he said. "She thought it'd be easy, find another job, but the placement people told her they got more people with her training than they know what to do with."

"Jesus, Jerry," I said. "I am sorry. Believe me, I know how rough it can get."

"I know you do, Mr. Devore," he said, and looked around. "For all I know," he said, "in some office somewhere, right this minute, they're deciding this place only needs two service managers, not three."

"They won't let *you* go, Jerry," I said, though of course they might. They might do anything.

He knew it, too. "Nobody's safe, Mr. Devore," he said. Then he lowered his voice and said, "We know each other, I can take a chance with you, help you out a little. There's likely to be two different estimates, you know? One for you, one for the insurance company."

"God, that'd be a help, Jerry," I said.

"Take a seat in the waiting room," he told me, "I'll see what I can do here."

I thanked him, and forty-five minutes later he gave me the two estimates, and grinned and said, "Make sure you send the right one."

"Oh, I will," I promised, and on the drive home I thought, I could have returned that favor by telling Jerry how to keep his job, if the crunch ever came. Just kill one of the other service managers. And if his wife had chopped three X-ray technicians before *she* got the chop, she'd still be working at that hospital.

But that's not a thing you could say to anybody.

An hour after I got home, the mail arrived. I can't help feeling a little queasy these days, every time I go out to the mailbox. I can't help looking around for parked cars. I know it's silly.

The mail included the accident report from the state police; very good. I phoned Bill Martin, my insurance guy, and he said to bring my paperwork right over, and I did, and we met in the office that used to be part of the built-in garage in his home. I gave him the police report and the estimate, the one for the insurance company, and he whistled and said, "Boy, you really banged it up, huh?"

"It wasn't fun," I told him.

"I'm sure it wasn't." He peered at me. "How are *you*, Burke? You okay? You didn't get hurt?"

I laughed and said, "Should I claim whiplash, Bill?"

"No, for God's sake," he said, in mock terror. "They're cracking down on fraud these days," he told me, "and looking for it harder, too. Everybody's squeezing a dollar."

"I know it."

"Where is the car? At the shop?"

"It's the only car I've got, Bill," I said. "It's right outside."

"Let's look at it."

"Okay."

We went out, and he looked at it, and looked at the estimate again, and then he looked at me, and casually he said, "You get a new position yet?"

"Not yet," I said.

He nodded, and we went back inside, and he said, "I'll fax these things off to the company today. There shouldn't be any problem."

"Great," I said. "When will it be okay to get it fixed? It looks kind of ugly now."

"Tomorrow, I hope," he said. "I'll give you a call, when they fax the approval."

"Thanks, Bill."

We shook hands, and I left, and drove home.

It's a wide-ranging conspiracy.

Tuesday was our first meeting with the counselor. Marjorie had arranged it, not through any of the state agencies, after all, but through that church where we'd met Father Susten eleven years ago. "His name is Longus Quinlan," she told me, as we drove south toward Marshal, where the office was.

I was surprised to hear it was a man we were on our way to see, expected Marjorie to have preferred a woman, but I covered whatever surprise I might have showed by saying, "Longus. That's a weird name."

"Maybe it's a family name," she said.

Our appointment was in a newish redbrick building four stories high on the edge of Marshal, called Midway Medical Services Complex, midway between what two points I don't know. Life and death? Sanity and lunacy? Yesterday and tomorrow? Hope and despair?

Columbia Family Services was on the top floor. We rode up uncomfortably together in the elevator, and found a receptionist at the top, who took our names and asked us to wait in the reception area there, a simple pastel space with simple pastel furniture, clearly designed to keep everybody calm until we can get this trouble sorted out.

We only waited a minute or two in this well-meaning but very boring place before the receptionist said, "Mr. and Mrs. Devore?"

We were the only people waiting. We stood, and she pointed down the hall to our right and said, "Room four."

We thanked her, and walked down to room four, where the door stood open. We stepped in, and a heavyset black man of about forty, wearing white shirt and dark tie, got to his feet from behind his desk, smiled at us, and said, "Mr. and Mrs. Devore. Come on in. Why not close that door there."

Had Marjorie known he was black? I shot her a quick look as I shut the door, but her profile was blank, unreadable. She didn't look in my direction at all, but went straight over to sit in the chair Longus Quinlan gestured to. I came over, then, and took the remaining chair, and now we made a triangle.

It was a small office, with venetian blinds over the wide window at the back. The desk faced the door from under that window, with the other two chairs angled to face it from the side walls, closer to the door, so that people in those chairs faced the person at the desk directly but still had a good clear view of each other.

Once we were all seated, he gave us an amiable smile and said, "I'm Longus Quinlan, as you probably guessed. Father Enver told me he didn't really know much about you two, your connection with the church was before his time. Father Susten, was it?"

We agreed it was, and he nodded and said, "Before my time, too, but I've heard good things about him." Drawing a printed form toward himself, picking up a pen, he said, "Let's just get the boilerplate out of the way to begin with, okay?"

Well, the boilerplate, as he called it, took the whole first hour. I was sitting there waiting to hear how Marjorie would describe her affair to this counselor—waiting also to hear if there would be any clues to the guy's identity—but we never got to that. We got to all the normal personal information, and we got as far as bringing up the fact that our difficulties—unstated difficulties, as yet—seemed to be caused by my having been out of work for almost two years.

Then the time was up, that fifty-minute hour, and he put his hands together on top of the form on his desk and smiled at us and said, "I'm glad you've come to me, not because it means you've got a problem, but because it means you've got the desire to *solve* that problem. And what I'm here for, as I guess you already know, is not to solve the problem for you, because I can't do that. It can only come from inside yourselves. A Band-Aid from me isn't gonna help. My job is to help you look inside yourselves and see what strengths are there, see what you really want from each other and from life, and help you find the way that's already there inside you to rise above your problems and make things come out right. But one thing."

He held up a hand and raised a finger and smiled past it at us. "We don't yet know what it is you want," he said. "You *think* you know what you want. What you probably think is, what you want is what you used to have. But it may turn out, that isn't what you want, after all. That's one of the things we'll have to discover along the way."

What he's saying, I realized, is that we may wind up ending the marriage when this is all over, and then that'll turn out to have been what we wanted all along, and he'll have turned out to have done his job. Pretty good. How do I get into this line of work?

It was agreed we'd come to see him every Tuesday at this same hour, and he'd bill the insurance company—we're still covered, for a while longer—and after he was paid by them we'd make up the differ-

ence, the twenty percent deductible that was our responsibility.

Then we left, shaking his hand and thanking him,
and in the elevator going down, I said, "I've had a lot
of job interviews went just like that."

"Oh, Burke," Marjorie said, and put her arms
around me, and we kissed very warmly. But that was
it, just that one instant. I pulled back, and so did she.

We listened to WQXR in the car again, going home.
Along the way, I decided I didn't think much of
Longus Quinlan, but I'd go along with the program,
because maybe it could help after all, some, along the
way. And eventually I'd find out who the man is.

And if these sessions are the price to keep Marjorie
in the marriage, I'm more than willing to pay. After
I've killed her boyfriend, and after I've got my new
job, things will be all right again.

Then, on Wednesday, Bill Martin rang up in the
morning to say I could go ahead and get the car fixed,
and when I phoned Jerry at the dealer he said he'd expected the call and had the necessary parts waiting, so
after I dropped Marjorie at Dr. Carney's office I drove
on over to the dealership and they gave the Voyager its
plastic surgery, to make it look like everybody else.

And now it's Thursday again, and I'm on my way to
KBA.

18

That's where I sat the other day, the first time I came
here, and walked up Footbridge Road. Now I sit in the
Voyager, parked by the side of the road, next to that
stub of stone wall where I caught my breath, last Sunday, after the climb. I sit in here, unnoticed, and I
watch KBA and his wife put stakes in the ground,
bring out flats of seedlings, dig and plant and fill. How
they garden.

How they believe in togetherness, in fact. From this
vantage, from the height of the Voyager, I can see
down over the slope, the uncleared land above their
house, and I can see them moving around together,
working together, handing each other things, talking
and sometimes laughing together. They're goddam irritating.

I got here a little before nine this morning, and they
weren't yet out, but the Honda Accord was in the driveway, just as it had been last Sunday. I waited, sitting

here, and at about nine-thirty out they came, dressed for gardening again, and they've been down there ever since, as the morning has slowly passed.

It's like watching a Japanese art movie, seeing those two in the distance, putting in their crops, not knowing the bandit is in the hill above them, watching. This time, he isn't waiting for the harvest, to steal it. This time, he's waiting for them to separate, just for a few minutes. That's all I need.

But it doesn't happen. They brought a cordless phone out with them, and twice this morning I've watched the wife answer it. Once it was for her, and once she handed it on to him, but neither call made one of them go off alone into the house.

That's what I need, for *her* to go in. If she does, and if it looks as though she'll stay indoors for a while, I'll get out of the Voyager and take the Luger from under the raincoat on the passenger seat, and I'll walk down there and shoot him.

Or why doesn't one of them take the car, and go on an errand? If he leaves, I'll follow him and shoot him. If she leaves, I'll walk down to him in his garden and shoot him.

But neither happens. They keep working, and I suppose they're taking advantage of the cool and cloudy day to get all this hard laborious donkey labor done.

At twenty to twelve the mail delivery arrives, a youngish man in a small green station wagon with US MAIL posters in the windows. I suppose this is a second or third job, these days, for a lot of those people.

At work most of their waking hours, and only sliding backward a little more every day.

Isn't there something in *Alice in Wonderland* about that?

They put down their tools and walk down to the mailbox *together*. What are they, Siamese twins?

I could almost do it, shoot them both, but the memory of Mr. and Mrs. Ricks holds me back. How horrible that was. It's enough I'm going to take this woman's husband, I can't take her life as well. I have to wait it out.

I'm very visible, parked just up the road, when they come out to the mailbox, but neither of them looks up in my direction at all. They're very involved in one another. He opens the mailbox, pulls out the little messy stack, distributes some to her, keeps some for himself. I see her ask the question, I see him shake his head in response; no job today. Then they go up to the house, together, put their mail on the table on the side porch, and walk back out to their garden.

Twelve-thirty. They compare watches, and go inside, hand in hand. Lunchtime; of course.

I'm hungry, too. Just north of town, I noticed this morning, there's a small mall, with an extensive garden nursery and an Italian restaurant. I wait two minutes after they disappear into the house, just in case he has to go to the store for something, but when he doesn't emerge I drive on down to New Haven Road and turn left, and have a not very good spaghetti carbonara in the Italian restaurant, with coffee.

When I drive back up Footbridge Road, they're in the garden again, still together. I'm reluctant to park in the same place as this morning, because sooner or later they're bound to notice me, or neighbors farther up the hill will notice me. I drive another quarter mile, and pull off the road to consult my road atlas, and I see that this road is no use to me at all in this direction. It merely curves around and heads south, away from home. So I make a U-turn and drive slowly back down Footbridge Road.

Yes; there they are. There's no point watching them any more today. They'll simply keep on doing what they're doing, and then they'll go indoors together, and that will be the end of it.

Not a Thursday this time, then. Maybe Friday.

I drive on down to New Haven Road and turn left, and drive past the place where I had the not very good lunch—tomorrow, if I'm still on watch, I'll have to find somewhere else to eat—and I head home.

One strange advantage to this miserable experience with Marjorie is that I no longer have to tell her where I'm going. We aren't talking to one another that much any more. This morning, after breakfast, I simply got into the Voyager and drove away.

Not having to make up destinations and job interviews and library research is a great burden lifted. Not the greatest burden, of course.

Driving homeward, I can't help but contrast KBA and his wife with Marjorie and me. It's true he hasn't been out of work as long as I, and he could have a much thicker financial cushion. His resumé didn't mention children, and I saw no sign of children around the house, and come to think of it, that togetherness of theirs is something I associate with childless couples.

Children are the great expense in life, or one of the great expenses. If KBA and his wife have no children, and if they have a bigger nest egg, and I know he hasn't been jobless as long as I have (and he's still under fifty, the son of a bitch, as he likes to tell us), then naturally he'll be calmer about his situation than I can be, he'll be more patient, less worried. It won't affect his marriage as much, not yet. But wait till he's out of work for two or three years, *then* see how much togetherness they show.

Well. We won't be testing that, will we?

19

I can't sleep, at first, tonight. Marjorie and I are polite with one another now, even concerned about one another, but neither of us has much to say. We watched television together this evening, and at ten o'clock there was some sort of talking-heads special on about the millennium, which we watched by unspoken mutual agreement, but neither of us made any comments during the program, as we always used to do.

I missed that, the little disrespectful remarks about the TV show in front of us, and I'm sure Marjorie missed it, too, but there was no hope that either of us could break through.

Being in bed together is grim. We don't touch. We don't acknowledge each other's presence. The lights are off, and because today's cloud cover has continued, the night is very dark, and we lie here next to one another like parcels to be delivered, and for a while I can't sleep. I don't know if Marjorie's dropped off or not, I only know that I am awake, and my mind turns this way and that.

I think about many things. I think about the job to come, in Arcadia. I think about killing the boyfriend, when I find out who he is. I think about the circumstances that have led me here, to this thorny place. And I think about the millennium.

Strange, that. I'd never thought about it before, that the simple arbitrary numbering of years could have an effect on us, but it turns out to be so. Having the number of the year change from 1 to 2, which will happen just two and a half years from now, has a great effect, it seems, on people's minds and actions, and on society itself.

It's ridiculous, of course. There couldn't be a more arbitrary number in life than the number of the year. The one we use is dated from the birth of somebody who possibly existed, and if he did exist his birthday was either four years or six years earlier than the date chosen when the year was being worked out. So even if you go along with Jesus Christ—yes, he's God, yes, he was born, yes, we number our years from his birth—even then this can't be 1997, the way we think it is. No, it has to be either 2001 or 2003, and the millennium's already gone past, so it's too late to worry.

The Chinese think the year's a different number from us, and the Jews go with yet another number. But none of that matters. The generally accepted idea in *our* society is, the world is going to reach the magic number two thousand very soon now, and therefore people are going a little nuts.

It happened last time, a thousand years ago, as the program explained. Strange religions came along, mass suicides, strange migrations, all kinds of milling around, pushing and shoving, all because the year 1000 was on its way.

Even the hundred-year anniversaries have an effect, the same way the full moon is supposed to. But the thousand-year marker is the big one.

One reason, the program said, is that it seems that many people, even intelligent, educated, sophisticated people, believe way down inside themselves, down at some instinctive level, that the millennium is the end of the world. They believe somehow the world is going to blow up or vanish or melt or spin out of the solar system or do *something* cataclysmic. That's why there's more and more religious fanaticism at the moment, and more and more strange cults, and more and more group suicides. The millennium is shaking us up, the way a high-pitched tone shakes up a dog.

Lying here, unable to sleep, in the darkness, I find myself wondering if that's why I'm out of a job. They didn't suggest this on the program, it's my own idea, which I'd never thought of before, but what if that's what's happened? All these hard-nosed executives, all these tough businessmen, making their brutal decisions, firing people from healthy companies, stripping everything down, ignoring the human cost, ignoring their own humanity, what if, without their knowing it, without their even being able to accept the idea, what if they're doing it because they believe the world is coming to an end?

2000; and it all stops.

Maybe that is what they're doing. It's as good an explanation as anything *they've* offered. They're trying to make everything neat and perfect for the end of the world. When the hammer crashes down, when everything comes to a dead stop, they want to be in the very best position possible.

This kind of business management that has never been seen in the world before, trashing productive people from productive careers in productive companies, is happening because of the millennium. Because of the year 2000. I'm out of work because the human race has gone mad.

On that thought, I fall asleep. It's only later that I wake up to terror.

20

I get a late start, having had trouble rousing myself this morning, after last night. But I'm on the road finally a little after nine, and make the turnoff to Footbridge Road at quarter to ten.

Last night. After the trouble I had getting to sleep, with all those thoughts circling, suddenly I woke up in the middle of the night, in pitch-black darkness because of that cloud cover—which is still here today, but not as though it's going to rain—and I woke up into that blackness with a sudden feeling of terror.

At first I couldn't imagine what it was that had me so terrified, and I lay there rigid, on my back, staring up at black emptiness, listening to the tiny inhabited silences of the house, while my brain tried to find its way back from panic, tried to sort out what the problem was. And when at last it did, and I figured out what it was that had so frightened me that it had driven me up out of sleep, what I was afraid of was me.

The boyfriend. Somehow, in my sleeping mind, the boyfriend had appeared, or I mean the *idea* of the boyfriend; I still don't know who he is. But that thought, the idea of the boyfriend, was circling in my sleeping brain, along with the idea that I was going to kill him when I found out who he was, and how easy that idea was, how unlike the angry way that people say, "I could kill him!" or "I'll kill that guy!"

Mine hadn't been like that. What I had said, in my mind, calmly, was, "Oh, okay, he's a problem, so I'll kill him," and I had absolutely meant it. Absolutely.

And that's why I woke up in terror, thinking, What am I becoming? What have I become?

I'm not a killer. I'm not a murderer, I never was, I don't want to be such a thing, soulless and ruthless and empty. That's not me. What I'm doing now I was forced into, by the logic of events; the shareholders' logic, and the executives' logic, and the logic of the marketplace, and the logic of the workforce, and the logic of the millennium, and finally by my own logic.

Show me an alternative, and I'll take it. What I'm doing now is horrible, difficult, frightening, but I have to do it to save my own life.

If I kill the boyfriend, it will be something else. Not exactly casual, but *normal*. As though killing has become a normal response for me, one of the ways I deal with a problem. Simple; I murder a human being.

The untroubled *ease* with which I'd thought that thought—kill him, why not—is what's frightening, what scares me. I'm harboring an armed and dangerous man, a merciless killer, a monster, and he's inside me.

That's another reason why I have to get through this process very soon, I can't let it drag on. It's changing me, and I don't like the change. The sooner this business is *done*, and the sooner I'm in that job in Arcadia, then the sooner this new change can start to bleach away, like the most recent fat melting off when you first go on a diet.

Which is why I just can't accommodate the Asches' togetherness forever. They're going to have to move apart from one another soon, or else. I have a horror of killing the wife, very like the horror of that decision to kill the boyfriend, but my greater horror is in staying in this swamp too long, being changed permanently by it, becoming forever somebody I wouldn't be able to stand to be around.

So I've come to that decision this morning, as I drive toward Dyer's Eddy. It wasn't an easy decision, a blithe decision, like deciding to kill the boyfriend, but it's solid, and it's unswerving. If those two insist on living together, every second of every day, they'll just have to die together.

Footbridge Road. I make the right turn, and drive slowly up the easy slope, and the first thing I notice when I reach their property is that the Accord is gone from the driveway. Have they driven off somewhere together? Will they be out all day? Damn; I should have got an earlier start.

I continue to drive upward, slowly, and there she is, the wife, in the garden, in a pale yellow T-shirt and white headband. She has a clipboard and seems to be doing a drawing. A chart of the garden, I suppose, to show where everything is.

She's there. The Accord is gone. He's in it. Damn, damn, and double damn, if only I'd been here earlier, when he left.

The nursery. It comes to me in a sudden leap, an immediate understanding. The garden nursery down there in the mall, across the parking lot from the Italian restaurant where I ate yesterday. He's there, I know he is.

I make my U-turn at the same place as yesterday. I drive more rapidly down the hill. It won't do me any good to meet him coming back. If I'm ever to come across him on the road, it will have to be when we're both traveling in the same direction, so I can pull up next to him and shoot him. Not to meet him head-on.

I certainly can't do what I did to Everett Dynes in Lichgate, with the car, if KBA is in a car.

Traffic delays me at the turn into New Haven Road. Why does it have to be a left? Cars come from one direction, then cars come from the other direction, then back to the first direction. There's never quite enough space in between for me to get out there, and I expect at any second one of those cars coming down the main road from the left will be a black Honda Accord.

No. A space at last, and I take it, jerking out into New Haven Road, swinging to the left, then running along in convoy with all these other cars. What is it about Friday around here?

It's another left turn into the mall with the nursery, and again I have to wait. I'm punching the steering wheel with my right fist. I *know* he's in there, I know it as surely as if I'd seen him drive in. And now, in my mind's eye, I can see him paying for his purchases, coming out to the car, getting in, driving out, making that easy right turn over there while I sit *here*, stuck.

Another break; I lunge through it, make the turn, drive into the mall.

It seems as though most of this mall is parking lot, fringed with a collar of low buildings. The nursery is at the front left, so I drive over there, slowly cruise the aisles. I know his license number.

And there it is. The black Honda Accord, sitting there, waiting, not far from the entrance to the nursery. I knew I was right, I knew it.

There isn't another parking spot near his, but I see a heavyset woman stuffing packages into a green Ford Taurus, one row over from KBA and about three slots to the right. I drive around there, and now she's being a good citizen, slowly waddling her shopping cart back to one of the collection points. Most people don't do that, lady. Most people leave the goddam cart where it is, and get into their goddam automobile, and drive *away*.

I can see the Accord over there, just the top of it. Still there. KBA isn't near it. Not yet, he isn't.

She comes back to her car, and for a second our eyes meet. I nod and smile, to let her know I'm waiting for her space, and she continues ponderously on, with no reaction, in no hurry. I wait while she finds her car keys in that great horse's feedbag she has dangling from her shoulder. I wait while she arranges herself behind the wheel just *so*, and the feedbag on the seat beside her just *so*, and the rearview mirror just *so*, and by now I'm ready to shoot *her* and come back to get KBA tomorrow.

I have plenty of time to think about this, waiting for her to get the hell away from here. What if I were to do such a thing, kill a few of the more obnoxious people one comes across? Then, when I kill KBA, it will just seem like more of the same. And if they draw any connection between KBA and my first resumé, Herbert Everly, it's just the work of a random killer. The famous serial killer.

People believe in serial killers these days. Movies and novels have come out populated almost entirely by serial killers, as though it's a tribe, or a fraternal organization, like the Elks. The great thing about serial killers, I guess, for the people who make up those stories, is that they never have to worry about motivation. *Why* did that person kill that person? It's unfair to ask that, in such a story, because the answer always is, he did it because that's what he does.

I have a motive. I have a motive, and a very specific category of person I have to get rid of. Which means, unless I'm very careful, I could be vulnerable. A clever detective might begin to get me in his sights. But if Everly and KBA, my only two gunshot victims in

Connecticut, were merely part of the pattern of a serial killer, wouldn't that make me safe?

And does this woman in the green Ford Taurus deserve to live, any longer?

She backs out of the parking space. She doesn't bother to look at me, or acknowledge me. She drives away, and she will never know just how close a call that was.

I ease the Voyager into the space, and stop. Still in the car, I put on the raincoat, then transfer the Luger to its right pocket. This is the kind of raincoat that in college we called the shoplifter's special, because the pockets are open at the top inside, to give access from both the inside and the outside of the raincoat, which means you can put your hand in the pocket and *through* the pocket. And that's what I do, and hold the Luger waiting in my lap, as I keep my eye on the Honda Accord.

Serial killer. That had been a strange thought. It was never serious, though.

I wait ten minutes, and then I see him. He's pushing a shopping cart, laden with small boxes and white plastic shopping bags, with a big sack of peat moss lying over everything else. The Accord is parked facing in, so he stops at the back of it and opens the trunk, while I climb out of the Voyager, holding the Luger against my right leg, and walk forward between the cars until I'm on the same row as he is, just three cars to my left.

He's wrestled the peat moss bag into the trunk, and now he's surrounding it with the rest of his purchases.

He's bent forward, head partly under the open trunk lid, as he moves his new boxes and bags.

I stop behind him. I say, "Are you Mr. Kane Asche?"

He turns, with a questioning smile. "Yes?"

"I know you are," I say, and bring the Luger up past the right flap of my raincoat, the raincoat bunching up around my right wrist, and I shoot him.

The bullet doesn't hit his eye, it hits his right cheek and makes a mess there. The raincoat pulled my arm down, just that little bit. His eyes stare, as he falls backward, half in the trunk, half sagging down across the rear bumper.

This is no good. This is messy, bloody, awful. *And* he's alive. I lean closer, put the barrel of the Luger almost against that staring terrified right eye, and I shoot again, and his head snaps back, and now he lies there, mostly on his back, sprawled, mouth wide open, one eye wide open.

I walk, not briskly, back to the Voyager. I get in, leaving the Luger in my lap, covered by the flap of my raincoat. I start the Voyager, shift into reverse, back out of there, drive away.

There's very little traffic, all the way home.

21

Well, that wasn't so bad.

And I got a good night's sleep, dreamless—at least, nothing I remember or that bothered me in any way— and woke up refreshed this morning, feeling positive about things for the first time in a while.

I think what it is, in addition to the business with Asche being simpler and cleaner than the two before it, almost as clear-cut as the very first one, I think there's the knowledge that finally I'm more than halfway through this thing. At the beginning, I had to do the six resumés, and I have to do Upton "Ralph" Fallon, but then that's it, that's the end of it, forever and ever.

(I'll know how to handle the situation ahead of time, if anything like this ever looms again.)

But now I've done four of them, so there are only three to go, and that lifts my spirits considerably. It's like realizing you've finally made it past the midway mile marker in a long and grueling race.

Also, there's some sort of early indication that there might be a thaw between me and Marjorie. Nothing tangible, really, no words said on the subject, merely a difference in the quality of the air inside the house. A little conversation between us, casual, about minor things. Not like normal life exactly, but closer.

This change may have happened because she'd finally come out with it, told the truth, or at least partly, and doesn't have to keep her burdensome secret any more. (If only it could be that easy for me.) And also probably because I'd agreed to the idea of counseling, and because the first session has happened, however little might have been accomplished so far, and because it looks as though the counseling can continue.

And maybe, just maybe, even more than all of that, it could be there's been a change in me as well. Maybe, when I was determined to kill the boyfriend, when I wasn't even turning it over in my mind but just accepting it as a fixed and certain thing to be done, maybe during that time I was clenched and tense around Marjorie, stalking her, watching her, searching for a trail to my prey. And now that I've caught on to myself, stopped myself, now that I've realized how awful that idea was and given it up completely, maybe she can sense a new ease in me, and my relaxation helps her to relax.

Long-term joblessness, it hurts everything. Not just the discarded worker, but everything. Maybe it's wrong of me, snobbish or something, to think this hits the middle class more than other people, because I'm middle class (and trying to stay middle class), but I do think it does, it hurts us more. The people at the extremes, the poor and the very rich, are used to the idea that life has great swings, now you're doing well, now you're doing badly. But the middle class is used to a smooth progress through life. We give up the highs, and in return we're supposed to be protected from the lows. We give our loyalty to a company, and in return they're supposed to give us a smooth ride through life. And now it isn't happening, and we feel betrayed.

We were supposed to be protected and safe, here in the middle, and something's gone wrong. When a poor person loses some lousy little job that had no future anyway, and has to go back on welfare, that's an expected part of life. When a millionaire shoots the works on a new venture that falls flat and all of a sudden he's broke, he knew all along that was a possibility. But when *we* slip back, just a little bit, and it goes on for month after month, and it goes on for year after year, and maybe we're never going to get back to that particular level of solvency and protection and self-esteem we used to enjoy, it throws us. It throws us.

And what's happening is, because we're family people, it's throwing the families, too. Children turn bad, in a number of ways. (Thank God we don't have that problem.) Marriages end.

Do I want my marriage to end? No. So I have to realize that what's happening to us now is only happening because I've been out of work for so long. If I were still at Halcyon Mills, Marjorie wouldn't be running around with somebody else. She wouldn't be working two stupid jobs. I wouldn't be killing people.

I didn't play the radio in the Voyager when I drove Marjorie to the New Variety just after lunch, for her afternoon cashier job, and that's because we were talking, we were in an actual conversation. It felt good. We talked about whether or not we might want to go see the movie that's at the New Variety now, and that she'd try to get a sense of whether or not the movie's any good while she was there this afternoon. And we talked about dinner, what to have, should I stop at a store after dropping her off or should we shop together later when I pick her up again. We didn't talk about anything that matters—money, jobs, the kids, marriage, counseling—but just *talking* was enough.

And now I've come home, and I'm in my office, and I'm planning my next move. Only two resumés to go. What an astonishment. What a relief.

Three weeks ago, I wasn't even sure I could do it. I was afraid I wasn't up to it. Three weeks ago. It feels like a thousand years.

I study them, my two remaining resumés, trying to decide which to go after first, which to go after second. I'll start on it tomorrow, drive to that resumé's address, check it out, see how it's going to go.

One of the remaining resumés is here in Connecticut, the other over in New York State. And of course Upton "Ralph" Fallon is in New York State, too.

The easiest ones have been in Connecticut. It was in Massachusetts that Mrs. Ricks complicated the situation and made it all so much worse, and it was in New York that I'd had to hit that poor man with the car.

Maybe it's just superstition, but I think the way for me to go is to finish Connecticut first. Do that next, then the last two are both in New York. And then it's over.

22

The phone rarely rings when we're asleep, maybe
once or twice a year, and that's usually some drunk
with a wrong number. But there's been a change in
us, in Marjorie and me and our relationship to the
late-night telephone call, and I never realized it before.

I come slowly awake, in the dark middle of the
night, very beclouded by sleep. I can hear Marjorie
murmuring into the telephone, and then she turns the
light on, and I squint, not wanting to be awake, and the
clock says 1:46. (We deliberately got a bedroom
alarm-clock-radio *without* illuminated clock numbers,
because we like to sleep in darkness. I'm always aware
of those floating numbers at the level of my sleeping
head whenever I spend a night in a motel.)

Slowly I focus on Marjorie and her conversation,
and it's something troubling to her that's keeping her
responses very down and quiet. "Yes, I understand,"

she says, and "We'll get there as soon as we can," and, "I appreciate that, thank you."

Sometime in through there, during the course of the conversation, failing to understand who she can possibly be talking to or what possible subject it could be about, I suddenly have my realization about us and late-night phone calls, and it is this: I didn't hear the phone ring.

We have phones on both sides of the bed, but it's only the phone on my side that rings, quietly. It used to be, whenever the phone rang at night, I would immediately wake up and deal with it—the drunk, the wrong number—and Marjorie would sleep right through the whole thing. I think in every marriage, that's one of the unconscious items that's worked out early on, who will wake up when the phone rings. In our marriage, it was always me, and now it isn't me any more.

Since I lost my job, Marjorie is the one who wakes up when the phone rings. She can't count on me any more; she has to be alert for herself.

I sit there, while Marjorie continues to talk into the phone and listen to the phone, and I turn this new understanding over and over in my head, to study it. I don't know if it makes me mostly angry or mostly sad or mostly ashamed. All three, I guess.

Marjorie hangs up, and looks at me. She's very solemn. "It's Billy," she says.

I think, an accident! At the same instant, I think, but he's in bed in this house, in his room, asleep. Stupid, still clearing cobwebs, I say, "Billy?"

"He was arrested," she says, astoundingly. "He and another boy."

"Arrested? *Arrested?*" I sit up, almost falling over. *I'm* the one who's supposed to be arrested! "Why would he—? Why would they—? For God's sake, what *for?*"

"They broke into a store," she says. "The police found them, and they tried to run away. They're at the state police barracks in Raskill."

I'm already struggling out from under the covers. The sheet and blanket cling to my legs, not wanting to release me into this terrible unknown. "Poor Billy," I say. A store? What store? "It's all my fault," I say, and go into the bathroom to brush my teeth.

The CID detective at the state police barracks, a sympathetic soft-voiced man in a rumpled brown suit, talks to us first, in a small square office painted pale yellow. Three walls are smooth shiny plastic, the fourth, an exterior wall, is bare rough concrete block. The floor is a different kind of smooth shiny plastic, black, and the ceiling is plastic soundproofing panels, off-white. Since the canary yellow paint on the concrete block was certainly put there as a very good sealer, it occurs to me that, if anything really horrible were to happen in this room, they could hose it clean in two or three minutes. From my position, in this green plastic chair facing the gray metal desk, I can't see a drain in the floor, but I wouldn't be surprised if there is one.

Did the architect plan the room this way? Do architects think in such terms, when they design police stations? Does it bother them? Or are they pleased at their professional skill?

Am *I* pleased, at my professional skill? My new skill, I mean. I've never thought about that before, and I don't want to think about it now.

It's very hard for me to concentrate on the detective, here in this deniable room. I can't even retain his name. I want to see Billy, that's all I know.

Marjorie is much better at dealing with this than I am. She asks questions. She takes notes. She's as quiet and calm and sympathetic as the detective himself. And, through their conversation, that I tune into and tune out of, over and over, I finally understand what happened.

It took place in the same mall where Marjorie works for Dr. Carney. There's a small computer store there, that sells business software and computer games and things like that. Apparently, Billy and this friend of his from school went there this afternoon—yesterday afternoon, I guess, by now—and found a moment to sneak unobserved into the back and rig the back door, the door that opens to the wide alley in back and that's used for deliveries and trash removal. They rigged that door so it would seem locked but wasn't. Then, tonight, long after we thought Billy was asleep in his bed, he snuck out of the house, was picked up by his friend—the friend has a car—and they drove to the mall, and slipped into the store from the back.

What they didn't know was, the store had already been robbed in exactly the same way three times before, and as a result they'd added a new burglar alarm, a silent alarm that alerted the state police barracks here, so that when Billy and his friend went in, the state police knew it at once, and four police cars converged on the place, two each from the state trooper barracks and the local town police.

The boys were leaving, with canvas tote bags full of software, when the police arrived. They abandoned the bags and ran, and were immediately, as the detective kept saying, apprehended.

The police have everything, or almost everything. They have an admission from the friend. They have absolute proof the robbery was planned and the door rigged, so they can demonstrate it was a planned crime and not a spur of the moment thing. They have police eyewitnesses who saw the boys carrying the stolen goods. They have the attempted flight.

What they don't have yet, and what they want, is proof that these two boys committed the three previous burglaries.

I hear the detective, and I hear how sympathetic he sounds, and I hear him say they're just trying to wrap this all up, get all this paperwork out of their hair, get it all behind them, and I can see Marjorie nodding and being sympathetic in return, ready to help this honest unassuming civil servant, and finally I rouse myself to speak, and I say, "This is the first time."

The detective gives me his slow sad smile, happy I've joined the group, sorry we have to meet this way. "We can't be sure of that yet, I'm afraid, Mr. Devore," he says.

"We can be sure," I say. "This is the first time for Billy. I don't know about the other boy, or what he might say about Billy, but this is Billy's first time."

Marjorie says, "Burke, we're all just trying to—"

"I know what we're trying to do," I say. I look flat and level at the detective. I say, "If this is Billy's first time, the judge will give him probation. If this is Billy's fourth time, the judge will put him in jail, and my son doesn't belong in jail. This is Billy's first time."

He nods his head slightly, but says, "Mr. Devore, we can't be sure what a judge will do."

"We can guess," I say. "This is Billy's first time. I'd like to speak to him now."

"Mr. Devore," he says, "this has been a shock to you, I know, but please believe me, I've been around this sort of thing a lot, and nobody wants to persecute your son, or make life tougher than it already is for anybody. We just want to clear this all up, that's all."

"I'd like to speak to my son," I say.

"Very soon," he promises, and turns back to Marjorie, more fertile ground than I am, he thinks, and says, "I hope you'll urge Billy to come clean on this.

Just get it off his chest, get it all behind him, and then the whole family can get back to normal life."

I watch him, and I listen to him, and I know him now. He's my enemy. Billy isn't a human being to him, none of us are human beings to his kind, we're all just paperwork, irritating paperwork, and they don't care a pin what happens to the people involved, so long as their paperwork is neat and tidy. He is my enemy, and he is Billy's enemy, and we know now what to do about enemies. We do not accommodate our enemies.

I always believed that I and my family and my home and my possessions and my neighborhood and my world were exactly what the police were here to safeguard. Everybody I know believes that, it's another part of living this life in the middle. But now I understand, they aren't here for *us* at all, they're here for themselves. That's their agenda. They're the same as the rest of us, they're here for themselves, and they are not to be trusted.

Marjorie has understood what I was saying, and she gives the detective less sympathy than before, and he quickly realizes he's lost her, so he brings out the forms. The inevitable forms. Before he gets to fill them out, though, Marjorie says, "Can we take Billy home with us?"

"Not tonight, I'm afraid," he says, and the son of a bitch does a wonderful imitation of sincerity. "In the morning," he says, "Billy will appear before the judge, and your lawyer can ask for his release in your custody, and I'm sure the judge will go along with it."

"But not tonight," Marjorie says.

Looking at his watch, the detective tries a smile, saying, "Mrs. Devore, tonight's almost gone, anyway."

"He's never been in jail before," Marjorie says.

Oh, please; what does this creature care? He's in jail all the time. I say, "You have some forms there? Before I get to see my son?"

"This won't take a minute," he says.

It's all the same questions, all the usual crap. Of course, it has the one zinger question in it: "And, Mr. Devore, where are you employed?"

"I'm unemployed," I say.

He lifts his eyes from the form. "For how long, Mr. Devore?"

"Approximately two years."

"And where did you work before that?"

"I was a product line manager at Halcyon Mills, up in Reed."

"Oh, is that the company that went bust?"

"They didn't go bust," I say. "They merged, two companies merged. Our operation was moved to the Canadian branch. They didn't take any U.S. employees with them."

"How long were you there?" Now his sympathy almost does seem real.

"With the firm, twenty years."

"You were downsized, eh?"

"That's right."

"A lot of that going around," he suggests.

I say, "Not in your business, I think."

He laughs, a little self-consciously. "Oh, well, crime," he says. "A growing industry."

"I wonder why," I say.

"I don't think I've ever seen them before," Marjorie whispers to me, as we follow the detective down a concrete block corridor toward whatever space now holds Billy.

I'm irritable, holding myself in. I give Marjorie an angry frown, not wanting confusion at this point, wanting clarity, and I say, "You never saw *who* before?"

"The parents," she says, and gives me her own surprised look. "Burke, they were *sitting* back there in the big room, when we came through. Didn't you see them? They have to be the other boy's parents."

"I didn't notice them," I say. I'm focused, Billy is my concern.

"They looked frightened," she says.

"They should," I say.

There's a uniformed trooper at a desk in the hall. He sees us coming, and stands to unlock a yellow metal door. Everything is yellow, pale yellow. It's supposed to be spring, I suppose.

The detective says, "If you could keep it to five, ten minutes, okay? He'll be home in the morning, you can do most of your talking then."

"Thank you," Marjorie says.

The trooper holds the door open. We go in, Marjorie

first, and as I go by the trooper says, "Knock when you want to come out."

"All right," I say, thinking, it isn't that easy.

This is the cell; my God. I'd thought it would be a visiting room or something, but I suppose a small state trooper barracks like this couldn't be expected to have very elaborate arrangements. Still, it's a shock. This is a cell, and we're in it with Billy.

He was sitting on the cot, but now he stands. There's only the cot, attached to the wall, and a chair, attached to the floor, and a toilet without a seat. That's all there is.

Billy is in his socks, and his belt is gone. From the puffiness of his face, I would say he's been crying, but he isn't crying now. He has a closed, bruised, defensive, sullen look to him. He's shut himself down inside himself, and I can't say I blame him.

I let Marjorie go first, asking him how he is, assuring him she loves him, assuring him everything will be all right. She doesn't talk about the burglary, thank God.

I let her go on a while, and then I say, "Billy."

He looks at me, ducking his head, pathetically abashed and defiant, almost standing up to me. Marjorie steps back, white-faced, watching me, not knowing what I mean to do.

I say, "Billy, we are not alone." I point to my ear, and then I point around at the walls. I keep my face deadpan.

He blinks, having expected almost anything else from me; recrimination, accusation, tears, perhaps self-pity. He looks around at the walls, and then I can see him trying to gather himself together, trying to be receptive and alert instead of closed-down and mulish, and he nods at me, and waits.

I say, "Billy, this is the first time you ever did anything like this. This is the first time you ever went along with anybody at all to break into that store."

I raise an eyebrow, and point at him, to let him know it's his turn to speak. "Yes," he says, looking at my finger.

"That's right," I say. "I don't know this friend of yours, I don't know what he's likely to say, how much he's likely to want to spread the blame, but *whatever* he says, Billy, don't you ever change from the truth, and the truth is, that is the first time you ever broke into that store, or any other store, or any place at all."

"Yes," he says. He's looking now like a drowner seeing the man with the rope.

"That's all you have to remember," I say, and then I spread my arms, and I say, "Billy, come here."

He comes over and I embrace him hard, feeling my heart well up into my throat. "We'll get through this, Billy," I murmur against his ear. He's as tall as I am, but not as husky. I say, "We'll get through it, and we'll come out the other side, and we'll be okay. We'll all be okay, my darling. It'll be okay, my love. It'll be okay, my sweetheart."

Then he cries. Well, we all do.

We're driving home, and it's not long after three in the morning, but I'm not finished yet tonight. Beside me, Marjorie says how good I was, how strong I was, and I say, "It isn't over. It's just starting. There's more to be done."

"In the morning, we have to call a lawyer."

"Before the morning," I say. "There's more to be done tonight. But there is that, too, in the morning. The lawyer. Who was the lawyer, when we bought the house? Do you remember his name?"

"Amgott," she says. "I'll call him, if you want."

"That might be better," I agree. "To hear from the mother."

I leave the car out, don't put it in the garage, because I'm not finished tonight. "What is it, Burke?" Marjorie asks.

"Some clean-up," I say.

She follows me through the house into Billy's room, the room that has been so much neater lately, and I thought it was because he couldn't afford to buy things any more. I open his closet door, and push the clothing to one side, and there it is. He's built a bookcase in there, or a software case, three shelves of the stuff. There must be thousands of dollars there, far more than they'd need to move the charge up from petty larceny to grand larceny.

"Oh, Billy," Marjorie says, as though she might faint.

"We have to get rid of it all," I say. "Right now, before they come around in the morning with a search warrant." I smile at her, trying to get her spirits up. "Finally," I say, "a use for all those plastic bags from the supermarket you keep saving."

We get her bag of bags from the kitchen, we load them up with the bright-colored little boxes, and we carry the full bags through the house to the side door. Neither of us is at all sleepy.

Billy *should* have these things, he should know about them and have experience of them, if he's going to make it in the new world coming. I should be providing them, I should be making it possible for him to keep up with what he has to learn. This is my failure. Billy wasn't wrong to do what he did, he was right. He was wrong to go to the well too often, though.

I'll never say anything like that to him, of course. A father has responsibilities. Get him out of this mess, but don't condone, and certainly don't encourage.

Six shopping bags; they fill up the backseat of the Voyager. I thought I'd drive alone, but Marjorie wants to come with me, and I'm happy for the companionship.

I drive nearly thirty miles through the dark and empty land. We meet only two other cars the whole way. Almost every house is black dark. Every business is shut down tight.

My goal is a different shopping mall, a bigger one, that I noticed once on my drive to Fall City, weeks ago, when I was after Herbert Everly. This place also is shut tight, dark, deserted. I drive around the back of it, then circle the whole complex, to be certain there are no police cars or private security cars tucked away in the shadows, waiting. There are none.

Along the way, I've observed the dumpsters, the big green truck-sized trash receivers, out behind the various stores, and I choose the supermarket's dumpster to stop next to. A faint unpleasant aroma rises from it, which is why I chose it. Boxes, bags, heads of ancient lettuce; so much stuff in there, not picked up on a Saturday night.

I throw the bags in, one after the other. They disappear, anonymous trash. No software shows.

When we drive back homeward, alone in the world, Marjorie holds my hand.

23

They're waiting for us when we finally get to the house, the police. I'd thought they would be.

It's three in the afternoon by now, the whole day is shot. It was impossible to find a lawyer this morning, a Sunday morning, so finally, at around ten o'clock, I called the state police to ask them where the court was, and they gave me an address and a phone number, and I called the court, and spoke with a woman who was determined to be nothing but efficient, not to permit the slightest vestige of individuality or personality to peek through. That might be a good strategy, I suppose, if you answer the phone at the courthouse for your living.

I kept explaining my problem to this woman, and she kept offering me no help at all, no guidance, nothing, and then all at once she asked me if by any chance either I or the defendant qualified to be taken on by the public defender.

That hadn't even occurred to me. Such things don't occur to people like me. I said, "I've been out of work for two years. I've used up my unemployment insurance. I have no income."

"You should have said so before," she said, being snippy.

I didn't bother to tell her I'm not used to offering my failure as an asset, and she went on to give me another number to call.

Which I did, and this was answered by somebody who sounded like, and possibly was, a teenage girl. I told her the situation, and that the court had given me this number to call, and she took down a lot of information—or at least asked me for a lot of information—and said someone would call me soon.

Then an hour went by, in which nothing happened. Billy was supposed to be arraigned this morning, that strange word. Arraigned. It sounds like a torture. It is a torture. But they wouldn't perform the torture until Billy was represented by counsel, so until I could find a lawyer he would remain in that pale yellow cell, or perhaps some worse cell somewhere else.

So after an hour I phoned that last number again, and this time the teenage girl calmly pointed out that it was difficult to find an attorney on a Sunday, and I said I knew that, and she said someone would call. Chastened, I hung up.

At twelve-fifteen, the phone rang. Marjorie and I were both in a state by then, not knowing what else to do, who else to call, how to get help, how to get this process *started*. We were both pacing the house, like starving lions. But then the phone did ring, at twelve-fifteen, and this was an older man, who slurred. I thought he was probably drunk.

"I've talked to the judge," he said. "Do you have anything to put up as collateral for bail?"

"The house," I told him.

"Bring the deed," he said, "the mortgage, whatever papers you can lay your hands on. I realize it's difficult, on a Sunday."

"I'll find something," I promised.

"I'll meet you at the courthouse," he said. "My name's Porculey. I'll be in a maroon suit."

A maroon suit? He slurs as though he's drunk, and he'll be in a maroon suit, and this is to be my son's lawyer.

On the other hand, he'd already talked to the judge, and it was clear from what he'd said that bail would be set, so that was good.

There's a folder in my filing cabinet marked HOUSE, and I just brought the whole thing with me, along with Billy's birth certificate and Marjorie's and my passports for identification. I didn't want to be one piece of paper shy.

When it did happen at last, it happened with great speed. First we met with Porculey, who turned out to be a much older man than he'd sounded on the phone, at least seventy, and who, from the drooping eyelid and sagging cheek, I suspected of having suffered one or more strokes, which was why he sounded drunk. It's true he was in a maroon suit, a horrible thing, with pin-stripes, but nevertheless, while this was a wreck, it was a wreck of a once-good lawyer. And what was left was good enough for the job at hand; to get Billy out of there, out of their clutches, back home with his mother and father, where he belonged.

It was mostly like going to church, somebody else's church. You watch the other congregants, do what they do, go along with the ritual as best you can, without understanding a bit of it, but keeping in mind always that *they* take it seriously. *They* believe in it.

Oddly, Billy looked better than he had last night, when we finally saw him, in the sunny courtroom with the pale maple wood benches and altar. I know they don't call it the altar, where the judge and his vergers perform their sacraments, but that's what it is.

Billy wasn't there at first. Porculey led us to a pew near the front to wait, and then he went out, through a side door, with all our papers, to do whatever. After a while he came back into the courtroom, nodded reassuringly at us, and sat at the lawyer's table up front, with a few other people as unprepossessing as he was.

Then Billy was brought in, unshaved, wrinkled, exhausted, but looking less destroyed, less distraught. I watched him as he was led to his place up front, saw him try to scan the room without turning his head, saw him see us, and I smiled in encouragement, and he gave me a quick scared smile back.

The ritual was mostly in English, but didn't seem to have much literal meaning. It was all in the code of this church. Porculey and Billy briefly stood together before the judge, as though they were there to be married to one another. The judge, a disgruntled bald man whose head seemed too heavy for him to hold upright, listened and spoke and looked at papers and passed papers on to the verger at the little desk down to his right.

Then Marjorie and I were brought forward, and Marjorie wept a little, and so did Billy, which pleased the judge, who remanded our son to us in our custody, and actually did do the thing of hitting the block of wood with the gavel. Religious to the core.

Of course we weren't done yet. Over at a side desk, I had to sign a lot of forms, and at one point I had to raise my hand and swear an oath, I'm not sure why.

Billy was no longer with us at that point, but Porculey stayed by our side. He seemed to know most of the court employees, including the judge. I would say they all liked him and were happy to see him, but didn't take him seriously. And I would say he knew that and didn't care, just so he could go on playing the game.

I suppose he lives for Sundays, really, when lawyers are hard to find.

When they were at last done with us, Porculey shook Marjorie's hand and then my hand and told us which corridor to go down to collect our son—"You'll have to show them that paper"—and promised to be in touch with us about the court date. Then he went away, carrying a very new brown briefcase that I could imagine some proud grandchild giving him for Christmas last year, and we walked down the corridor to a coldfaced man in a brown uniform who looked at our piece of paper with contempt, went away, and some time later came back to contemptuously give us our son.

Billy was silent on the drive, abashed and ashamed and afraid. We got about halfway home, all of us silent, and then I said, "Billy, it won't surprise me if the police come around, very soon, with a search warrant."

He was riding in the backseat, Marjorie beside me in front. His startled eyes focused on my reflection in the rearview mirror. "Warrant? Why?"

"They'd like to be able to close all those other burglaries," I said. "They'd like to find something to show that you broke into that store before."

Now he looked really frightened. He knuckled his head, and said, "Dad. Dad, I—listen—"

"It's all right," I told him. I don't want to condone, and I don't want to encourage, but he had to know this much. "Everything's all right," I told him.

"Dad, no, listen—"

He still didn't understand, so Marjorie turned in the passenger seat and said, "Billy, it's been taken care of. Your father took care of things."

Then he got it, and the look he gave me was humbled and ashamed, and he said, "I'm sorry, I'm really sorry. It was so stupid, I'll never do anything like that again, I *swear* I won't."

Marjorie said, "Of course you won't. Everybody gets to make a mistake, Billy, it's all right. It won't happen again."

"I know you can't afford," he said, and stopped, and looked away, out of the car. He was starting to cry again.

Well, that's true. I can't afford any of this. The lawyer will cost us *something*. This whole thing will cost money we don't have. And time. Time I don't have either. But you do what you have to do.

"We'll just get through this, Billy," I said, "and then it will be over and done with and forgotten."

He nodded, but he didn't try to speak, and he kept looking out the side window at the neighborhoods going by, and a little later we turned in at our driveway, and there was the police van out front. When they saw us, five uniformed policemen got out of it. Local cops, in blue.

Well, there's nothing for them to find. I did a lot of clean-up last night, even more than Marjorie knows. When we got back from that distant mall, she helped me pull the bookcase out of Billy's closet—back in there, empty, it was too suggestive—and we lugged it into the garage, where I piled it with some paint cans and old rags, so it looks as though it's been there for years. Then, while Marjorie was in the bathroom before going back to bed, I got the Luger out from the bottom drawer of my filing cabinet and put it under the backseat in the Voyager; that is, inside the seat. Under Billy, as we drove home.

And now we wait, in our living room, as the taciturn police go through our house. There's nothing for them to find. They can even paw through the folder of resumés in my office, if they want. What could it tell them? Nothing.

Sitting here, waiting, I start to think about this downsizing business again, how it affects the families, and how smug and blind I was to assume it would never affect *my* family. First Marjorie, and now Billy; it's bending our lives out of shape.

Betsy isn't with us, and now for the first time I have to think about her, too. She seems like such a good kid, so normal, so accepting of the change in our lives, so unaltered by it; but is that so?

We told her this morning, of course, what had happened to Billy, and she wanted to stay with us, come with us to the court, but I didn't want her along. I didn't want her to have that kind of memory of Billy in her mind, the rest of her life.

Betsy attends a community college about forty miles from here. She should drive there, but we can't afford a second car, so another student, a girl she's known since elementary school, gives her a lift every day. She'd been scheduled to go with that girl to a Drama Society meeting this afternoon. She wanted to beg off, but Marjorie and I insisted she go, and I'm glad we did. She shouldn't be here to see the police pawing through her possessions, looking for stolen goods.

All at once I remember Edward Ricks, my resumé from Massachusetts. I remember how his daughter,

Junie, had taken up with a much older man, a professor at her college, and how that had caused the confusion that led to me having to kill her mother as well. I felt so superior to those people at the time, with *their* daughter in such contrast to *my* daughter. I'd simply taken Junie to be an ordinary tramp, sly and vixenish.

But now I wonder. Was Junie a victim, too? If Daddy hadn't lost his job, would Junie have taken up with that other fellow, that unacceptable father substitute? What was his name . . . Ringer.

Was Ringer a victim, too, of downsizing?

How it spreads. And now the police, without a word, depart. May they rot in hell.

24

It's after dinner, Sunday evening, the very first of June. Billy is definitely at home, in the living room, watching television with Marjorie and Betsy, while I am here in my office. It's time to get back to the operation, lose no more days. But I'm sitting here instead, for a minute, to look at a little 3x5 card I push-pinned to the wall over the desk a few months ago, when I first began to realize that doing it their way wasn't going to get me anywhere.

The card refers to a bit of history, in the Scottish Highlands. Until the late eighteenth century, the Highlands were populated mainly by tenant farmers, poor families in little stone huts eking out a small living from the soil and paying a small rent to the landlord. Then the landlord—or whoever acted as the landlord's accountant, in those days—discovered there was more money to be made if the human beings on all that land were replaced by sheep.

So, for the next seventy years, more or less, there was in the Highlands what came to be called the Clearances, in which families, clans, villages, everything was cleared from the land, which was then given to the sheep. The tenant farmers had lived there for generations, built the houses and barns and corrals, worked the soil; but it wasn't theirs. No one had lived on it but them, but it wasn't theirs, so what were they to do?

They left, not willingly. Some went to Ireland, some went to North America, some went to hell. Some died of cold or starvation. Some resisted, and were given the chop right there, on their own land. Well, no; not their own land.

I learned about the Clearances in college. I always enjoyed the history courses, because they were simply stories, so I did well in them, bringing my whole grade average up.

One year, another guy and I did a term paper on the Clearances, and in the course of it my partner looked up the word in the *Oxford English Dictionary*, the big one. I so loved the definition that I never forgot it, and after I got the chop, during one of my days of legitimate library research, I looked it up again, to be sure I had the phrasing exactly right. I wrote it on this 3x5 card and put it up on the wall here, in front of me.

> Clearance 2. *spec*. The clearing
> (of land) by the removal of wood,
> old houses, inhabitants, etc.

You'll never see a clearer proof that history is written by the winners. Just think; one comma less, and the inhabitants would have fallen into the etc.

It's the descendants of those landlords that are doing the clearances called downsizing now. The literal descendants, sometimes, and the spiritual descendants always.

You like that desk where you are? You say you've given the company your life, your loyalty, your best efforts, and you think the company owes you something in return? You say all you really want is to stay at your desk?

Well, it isn't your desk. Clear it. The owner has realized he can make more money if he replaces you with another sheep.

Here's the resumé I want. The address. I'll visit Mr. Garrett Roger Blackstone tomorrow, after I drop off Marjorie at Dr. Carney's office.

Garrett Blackstone
PO Box 217, Scantic River Rd.
Erebus, CT 06397
Tel: 203 522-1201

Born Marysville, NJ August 18, 1947

Loyola Elementary School, Marysville, NJ - St. Ignatius Combined Middle School, Smithers, NJ - St. Ignatius High School, Smithers, NJ - Rutgers University, New Brunswick, NJ, receiving BA, art history 1968

United States Army, 1968-1971 - stationed in Texas, Vietnam, Okinawa

Married 1971, Louise Magnusson - four sons

Salesman, Rutherford Paper Box Co., Rutherford, MN 1971-1978

Manager, product line, Rutherford Paper Box Co., 1978-1983

Manager, product line, Patriot Paper Corp., Nashua, NH 1983-1984

Plant Manager, Green Valley Paper, Housatonic, CT 1984-present

Twenty-six years' experience in the paper industry.

Eighteen years' experience with a broad variety of paper manufacture as manager in charge of all product lines for a broadbase papermaker.

Experience includes consumer paper products, industrial paper products (including polymer paper applications) and defense-related paper products.

I am a willing worker, and am prepared to devote whatever part of my experience and expertise is of use in the new work situation.

25

At the mall, I stop in front of the entrance to Dr. Carney's office. Before she gets out of the Voyager, Marjorie leans over and kisses me, lightly, on the cheek. I look at her in surprise, and her eyes are shining. "It's over," she whispers. Then, seeming to be embarrassed, she slides out of the car, waves behind herself without looking back, and hurries into the building.

I know what she means, of course. The other man, the guy, the boyfriend, that's what's over. She won't be unfaithful to me any more.

As I drive east across northern Connecticut toward Erebus, I think about what she said, and what it means, and why she said it. I've believed the affair happened in the first place because of the general despondency around our house as my unemployment has lengthened from months into years, and I've believed that she finally told me about it *because* she wanted it to end, but she also wanted me to know what she'd been going through, what had made it necessary. And she wanted somebody neutral around, a counselor, our Longus Quinlan, to help us find our way out of this morass. If there is a way.

So the affair was a battering ram, that's all. And now the door is open, and she doesn't need the battering ram any more. And she wants me to know that, too.

But now, driving along on these little roads from little town to little town, I wonder if there isn't a second reason as well. Maybe I'm just trying to make myself feel better, make myself believe that *I* had something to do with it, too, but I can't help wonder if another factor in her change toward me is the way I handled the Billy emergency.

I handled it well, I know I did. But I also handled it differently from the way I would have a couple of years ago, back when I was a regularly employed person in what I thought of as a normal and changeless life. In that time, when I was the person I was before I got the chop, I would have been much more passive in this situation. I would have trusted the law, or society, or somebody, to do right by Billy. And the result would have been, they'd have gotten him for four burglaries instead of one, and he'd be looking at jail time. They might not even have set bail.

I did the right thing with Billy, and the reason I did the right thing, and could even *think* about the problem the right way, is because I don't trust them anymore. None of them. Now I know it; nobody will take care of me and mine but me.

Erebus is a village in the hills of north central Connecticut, between Bald Mountain and Rattlesnake Hill, just across the state line from Springfield, Massachusetts. Scantic River Road doesn't go through the actual village itself, but wanders the nearby hills, southward from the state line. I actually drive up into Massachusetts briefly, to pick up Scantic River Road at its northern end, and then I drive slowly southward, looking for PO Box 217.

This is suburbia along in through here, but a more relaxed suburbia than the areas closer to New York City. This country around here is a bedroom for Hartford and Springfield, so there's less visible money thrown around and less visible effort at high style. The basketball hoops above the garage doors look as though they're actually used from time to time. There are more pools above the ground than in it. The cars are less showy, and so are the gardens.

217 is a bit of a problem, being in the middle of a blind curve, with signs in both directions warning of their hidden driveway. It's on the west side of the road, on the right as I drive south, and while the road itself is mostly level along here the land climbs steeply to the right and falls away to a fast narrow stream on the left. A stone wall retains GRB's land around this curve, with a narrow driveway chopped into it, leading upward toward a house I can barely glimpse.

This is going to be a very difficult place to watch. Can I do the mailbox again? It's on the same side of the road as the house, built into the stone retaining wall next to the driveway. I haven't seen a mail deliverer in my travels today, so I decide to head on south, just to see if luck is with me.

It isn't. I take Scantic River Road all the way south to the Wilbur Cross Parkway, by which time I'm surely in some other mail delivery route, so I turn around at the Parkway and drive north again, and when I'm near Erebus here comes the mail delivery, southbound.

Damn! GRB's house is still north of me, the mail's already been delivered. Is he out there now, picking up his mail?

The Luger is still inside the backseat. I keep driving, not too fast, reaching behind myself, trying to find that slit in the bottom front of the seat cover, trying to extend my arm way back and down inside there to get hold of the Luger by touch alone.

Metal, metal . . . Got it. I pull it out by the barrel, put it on top of the raincoat, then turn it so it doesn't point toward me.

The curve. HIDDEN DRIVEWAY. And here it is, on the left, with a person at the mailbox, head bowed, studying the mail. For just a second I'm very excited, staring at GRB, not looking away from him as my right hand claws for the Luger—but then I realize it isn't him. It's a woman. It's the wife, no doubt, in corduroy pants and a dark green cardigan and a dark blue billed cap with writing on the front.

I drive slowly past, trying to see up the driveway. Is he up there, waiting for the mail? Doesn't he care about the mail? He has to. Or is he ill? There's a lot of psychosomatic illness among us, we who've gotten the chop. Maybe he's in bed and won't get up until his wife finally brings him some good news. That would make him very tough to get at.

About two miles farther north, there's a parking area for a scenic view, pine-covered mountains with a valley between, stretching away to the west, full of peaceful villages. I pull off the road there, put the Luger under the raincoat at last, and study my road atlas, but it doesn't do me any good. It doesn't show any roads that might run along above and behind GRB's property. This road he's on just makes that elbow at that particular point, because of a hill, and their house is built on the slope above the road, with what looks like nothing but undeveloped hillside above them. And I already know, from looking at it, that there's nothing downhill in front of the house but scruffy woods, because of that stream.

There must be a way. I feel like a cat circling a mousehole. I know he's in there, and I know there has to be a way to get at him. But what?

Finally I decide to just drive by the place yet again, see if there's *anything* to be done. So I leave the turnoff, headed south once more, and drive along, the road atlas now on top of the raincoat, and the pressure of other traffic keeps me from going as slowly as I'd like when I go around that curve.

The house, barely seen. No sign of cars or people.

Nearly a mile later, there's a right turn off Scantic River Road. I take it, and am now on a very small residential road marked DEAD END.

There's no other traffic with me now. I drive up as this narrow road twists and turns, with very few houses visible along the way, broad forested spaces between them. Then I come to the dead end, which is clearly marked by a single width of wooden rail fence painted white, with a yellow DEAD END sign on it.

I stop the Voyager and get out to look around. According to the road atlas, this spot where the road has petered out is not that far from the elbow on Scantic River Road containing GRB's house. It should be down that way, to the right, through the woods.

I'm not a woodsman, never have been. It could be both stupid and dangerous to go roaming around in there and get lost, and eventually be found by police or boy scouts or whoever, and have no explanation for why I'm here, with a Luger in my raincoat pocket. Still, I've got to find some way to get at GRB.

I walk around to the far side of the white fence. The woods, out ahead of me, are cool and pleasant. June second; gnats come flying, to study my face. I brush them away, but they won't go. Anyway, they're merely curious. They don't want to bite me, they just want to memorize me. So long as I breathe with my mouth shut, they won't really bother me. They're just an irritation, these tiny fast dots in front of my face.

Looking past them, gradually learning to ignore them, I at last see what seems to be some sort of path, moving away to the right through the trees. Don't deer create paths sometimes, in the woods? But so do people; Marjorie and I have friends, whom we haven't seen for a while, who've made woods walks into the land out behind their houses. (We used to see more people. We used to know more people. When you can't afford to entertain, a certain embarrassment keeps you from maintaining those old friendships.)

So I come to a decision. I'll wear the raincoat, with the Luger in the pocket. I'll walk along that seeming path, which looks to be at least headed in the right general direction. I'll see where it goes, and how far it goes, and the instant it starts to fork or disappear or do anything that might make it hard for me to retrace my steps I'll turn around and come right back here.

It's a pleasant day for walking, with the airy trees protecting me just enough from the rays of the sun. The air is a bit cool, in a refreshing way, like the air near an ice cube. I walk along, following this very clear brown trail in the green woods, and the first time I look back the Voyager is already out of sight.

I stop, then. Is this a good idea? I really don't want to get lost in here.

But so far, this path is very obvious. Also, the land slopes very gently downward here, and the path follows that downward tendency, so if I do get confused at some point, I should merely turn around and head up the slope. That's a theory, anyway.

I walk for about fifteen minutes, and for much of that time I'm not even thinking about why I'm here, what the purpose of all this is, what the function is of that weight dragging down my raincoat on the right. I'm just going for a walk in the woods, led along by this clear path and by gravity. It's nice. No cares, no problems. No hard solutions.

A noise. Up ahead, a sharp cracking noise. Something's coming.

What is it? I look to the sides, and off to my right there's a tumbled mass of boulder sticking out of the ground. It's all tangled brush and weeds between here and there, but it's the only hiding place I see, so I set off toward it at once, trying to be silent. Behind me, I hear that cracking sound again.

If this is a deer, fine, no problem. But if it's a person, I don't want to be seen. I don't want to be the mysterious man wandering in the woods just around the time GRB is done away with.

The boulders. I scramble around them, and the crack rings out again. I crouch low, looking back toward the path, and here she comes.

The wife, it's the wife. The same woman I saw collecting the mail, still dressed in the same cap and cardigan and corduroys. She's walking alone, briskly, and she's carrying a nice thick walking stick, like a shillelagh, and as I watch she uses it to hit a tree as she goes by: *crack.*

Oh, of course. Snakes. She's afraid of snakes, and somebody's told her that if she makes a noise as she goes along they'll stay away from her. *Crack.* On she strides.

Good God, what if she'd had a dog with her? What a mess that would be. The dog would surely know I'm here, would probably come over to investigate. And then I'd *really* be in it. Not just a strange man wandering in the woods, but a strange man *hiding* in the woods.

She's gone; I hear a distant *crack*. I straighten up, behind my boulder. Is he home alone? Do any of the four sons still live with these people? If I follow this path, will I find the house?

One good thing. She announces her presence by hitting trees with that stick, so I'll always know when it's time to get out of her way.

I decide to chance it. I hurry back from the boulders to the path, my raincoat flaps catching on the thorny waving reedy branches of wild roses, and now I set a much brisker pace, walking, I hope, toward GRB's house.

It's another quarter hour, and there it is. Or there something is, some house, visible through the woods where a smaller path branches leftward from the main one. Is it the right place?

I go there to see, and find a two-strand electric fence across my route, to keep the deer out. The other side of it is an expanse of lawn, fringed by plantings of rhododendrons and other things that deer like to eat. Ahead and to the left is a smallish in-ground pool, still covered, even though this is June. But you can't afford to maintain the pool this year, can you? Not without a job.

Beyond the pool and the lawn stands the house, fairly large, stone on the first floor, white clapboard above, several dormers along the top. Yes, that's the house I glimpsed from the road. There's no one in sight.

The gate in the electric fence is just here, at the edge of the lawn. But if I go through, there'll be no cover, and GRB will be able to see me if he looks out any of those windows over there. And what if I'm still on the property when the wife comes back?

No, the thing to do is wait. First, I have to find out for sure where GRB is. There's a stone patio over there, between house and pool, with a table topped by a big umbrella, and several white metal chairs. Maybe they'll have lunch together, right there. Can I do a shot that long? Or can I hope for something to bring him closer to the fence?

Crack. Some distance away behind me. But that means she's coming back. I move away along the fence, careful not to touch it, grateful they've kept the shrubbery cleared along the fence line—for maintenance, I suppose—and as those occasional *cracks* come closer I reach at last the end of the fence, where it attaches to the small pool house. From here I can be very well hidden. And I'm somewhat closer to that patio, which is just beyond the pool, which is just beyond the pool house. Still a longer shot than I've ever tried before, but what if he has to come to the pool house, for ice or something? Then he's mine.

I see her, to my right, as she goes through the fence,

carefully hooking it shut behind her. As she strides to the house, planting that walking stick firmly into the lawn at every second pace, I look at my watch: twelve forty-five. Lunchtime. But I didn't bring any.

Well, I'm getting used to not eating my midday meal. There's a tree stump about five feet back from the fence, a large one. Some big tree was once here, and probably cut down when they put in the pool house. I ease back there, gather my raincoat about myself, sit down. The Luger is in my lap.

Four o'clock. It's getting cooler now, the sun hidden behind higher hills off to the west. I'm stiff and achy, and my back is complaining about this length of time, over three hours, seated here on this stump, with no support.

He never came out. She never appeared again, either, after that walk. I can catch a glimpse of their driveway from here, and neither of them used the car today. I don't know what GRB looks like, and I don't know what his car looks like.

This day wasn't wasted, not entirely wasted. I've learned how to get near the house. But it's frustrating, nevertheless. I want to get this over, over and done with.

Tomorrow I won't be able to come here, because of the counselor, Longus Quinlan. So it's Wednesday, while Marjorie is again working at Dr. Carney's office, that's when I'll be back.

When I stand, bones crack all over my body, enough to scare any snake in the county. I'm tottering, having trouble making my feet work. But it's time to go, get back to the Voyager, drive homeward, get to the mall by six o'clock to pick up Marjorie.

Staggering like Frankenstein's monster, I make my way along the path, back toward the Voyager. In this direction, it's uphill.

26

Yesterday, at the counseling session, Marjorie said, "When Burke first lost his job, I thought it was a kind of opportunity. I thought things were too good for us, we always had whatever we wanted, and so we never had to struggle together for anything, we never had to prove ourselves to each other. I thought this was going to be some little short time, and it wasn't really going to mean anything in the long run, but I could prove myself to Burke, and I guess to myself, too, to be honest about it, just to prove I was the perfect wife, the perfect partner. We're in this together, and this is my chance to prove it. So I immediately started all these little economies and showed how we could save money here and save money there, like I was Mrs. Noah on the Ark, going around finding little leaks, plugging them up, keeping the water out. I never thought it was going to go on this long. I don't think Burke did, either. I think at first he took it a little more seriously than I did, because he knew a little more about what the real situation was, but I don't think he took it really really really seriously then, at first. I think after a while he did, and instead of turning to me and saying, 'Marjorie, we're in a jam, this is a tougher situation than I thought,' he just closed down inside himself, more and more. I thought for a while he was blaming *me* for what was going on, that he thought it was my fault he still didn't have a job, we didn't have any money, but I've thought about it some more, I've had plenty of time to think about it, and now I think Burke's been doing the same thing I've been doing, trying to prove what a perfect husband he is, perfect provider, keep the little woman safe and happy, don't let her see how bad things are. I mean, I can *see* how bad things are, but we can't talk about how bad things are, or what we're going to do about them, or what's going to happen next, so I never actually *know* what's going to happen next. Burke's gotten more and more secretive, more and more silent, more and more cold, and sometimes when he's looking at me it's almost as though he hates me, just for being there and seeing the situation he's in, it looks in his eyes as though he could kill me for being there, just because he feels like he can't protect me the way he's supposed to, and I don't *want* to be protected like that, but how can I say anything? He keeps that wall up. The wall is supposed to be his strength, I guess, but I never thought that was why he was strong. When I met him, I was still in college, I was a completely useless Liberal Arts major, but

I also took typing and shorthand, and summer vacations I did temp jobs to help out, make some money for myself, and I always thought I'd work in industry someplace, as a secretary, something like that. I actually did work for an insurance company for about six months after I graduated, and got one promotion and raise, and I could have stayed, but Burke wanted to get married right away, and then he wanted a family right away, so I dropped out of the job market. The magazines I used to read were always full of pieces about women dropping out of the job market, and then what happens when you get divorced or widowed, and I was never afraid of that. *This* they didn't talk about. This is worse than divorced or widowed, because I'm still with Burke but he's wounded. I'm with a wounded man, and we both have to pretend nothing's wrong. About half the wives I know have jobs or careers, one's a speech therapist, one's a librarian, a lot of them I know, but it seems just as normal either way, if the wife works or doesn't work, and I've always thought that was the woman's decision, except with us it's mostly been Burke's decision, and he makes it plain in different ways. Like, a few years ago, at Christmastime, he bought a computer, a personal computer for the home, he said it was for the whole family. It was really for Billy, our son, but I knew why he said it was for the whole family, and why he teased me about learning it and putting the checkbook in it and all. The children were growing up, almost out of high school then, and I'd been talking about looking for a job again after all these years, wanting to do something with myself, and Burke didn't want me to. This was before he was laid off, before anybody thought he *could* be laid off. So he wanted to be the provider, the protector, the same as always, and he brought that computer into the house just to let me know I didn't have the skills any more. When I got out of college, it was typing, but the computer isn't typing, it's something else, and he wanted me to know I'm hopelessly behind. But actually, he doesn't know it, but I'm farther along with the computer than he is, because I've been doing the billing for this dentist we know, Dr. Carney, so I've been using his computer, and his regular nurse showed me what I had to know, and I've taught myself some more on my own, so I'm not so hopeless after all. But I couldn't tell Burke how happy I was and pleased that I was learning the computer, because he wouldn't like that. I had to keep it to myself, and pretend there wasn't *anything* I was happy about, or anything I could possibly be happy about, until he got a new job, and the exact same kind of job again, of course, even though we read in the newspaper every day that people don't *get* the same kind of job back, especially if they're over fifty. We know a man, a neighbor of ours, he was always considerably more wealthy than us, he was a bank executive, he only had to commute in to the office in New York three days a week, he was that important, and there was a merger, and they let him go, it must be three years ago now, and he was out of work for almost two years, wanting to be a bank executive again. And now he works at a Mercedes dealership in Hartford, he sells cars, and he works six days a week and he doesn't make anywhere near as much money, and Burke, did you notice? Their house is for sale. But a lot of houses are for sale, you've probably noticed that, Mr. Quinlan, so I don't know how long they'll have to wait. And I don't know if we'll have to try to sell our house, too, or *what* is going to happen. I can't find a full-time job now, because I was out of the job market too long, I'm too old, I'm not *that* skilled, and nobody knows when Burke will find another job or what kind of job it will be or when he'll agree to settle for it. It isn't fair for the children, but that isn't Burke's fault, even if he does take the blame all on himself, but they have to live with it the same as we do, and usually I think they understand that, though Billy did get himself in trouble. But that's not the point. The point is, it's so hard to be *happy* at home, and you have to have some place in your life where you're happy. And you have to have some person you can talk with, open yourself with, laugh with. Or even cry with, I don't care, just *something*. But Burke's been so— He's like cryogenics, he's frozen himself, he won't thaw out until he gets a job, and in the meantime I'm living with this frozen thing, and finally, four months ago, a man I know acted tender toward me and I responded, and something started between us. Burke's off on his own secret mission all the time, for a while I thought *he* was having an affair, but I don't believe that any more, I believe he's doing strange like *magic* things, like going off and reading entrails or something, I don't know, he has some kind of mysterious *project* with papers in his office and mysterious trips, and lying to me about where he's going, and I wouldn't *dream* of asking him what's going on. Because he wants to shoulder it all himself, shoulder the burden, shoulder everything, the family, the responsibility, and I'm left out here, and I turned to this other man because at least he'd *talk* to me, and he'd let me talk to him. And he has problems, too, but he isn't afraid to talk about them or say he feels weak when he gets up in the morning, he doesn't know what to do next. I could console him, he was somebody I could put my arms around, I could find some way to make him laugh. I can't do anything with Burke, he's like a rock or a dead person, he's like a stone, you can't put your arms around a stone. You can't get anything from a stone. So when I realized that it wasn't this other man I wanted, it was Burke I wanted, but it was Burke when he's alive, when he isn't all shut down and cold and waiting for a miracle, and I thought, I have to use dynamite. So I told him we needed to see somebody like you, and he fought that idea, and I knew he'd fight it, of course he'd fight it. *Talk* about things! When he fought it, I told him about the man, because I thought that would be sink or swim, kill or cure, and I thought, I can't go on like this. I either want Burke back or I want it over with. And thank God he said all right, let's come here, because I couldn't say this to him without you in the room. And he knows I'm not seeing the man any more, but the truth is, I'm not seeing Burke either, and I want to see Burke, I want my husband back, and I don't know what to do."

Quinlan looked at me, with a gentle smile. He's a great absorber, Quinlan. He said, "You'd like to thaw, Burke, wouldn't you? Knock down the wall?"

"I didn't know I was doing that," I said. "I thought I was just trying to hold myself together." But it's true; I'd caught glimpses of myself, here and there in her description.

He went on smiling, and said, "You didn't buy the computer to insult Marjorie, did you?"

"No, of course not," I said. "That never even occurred to me." That had been part of the description where I had not caught sight of myself, and I was grateful to Quinlan for calling attention to it.

His smile now moved over to include Marjorie, who was sitting there looking exhausted. No, not exhausted, not like somebody who's just run a long time, but drained, like somebody who's just had an operation. He said to her, "We're all of us paranoid, Marjorie, you know," and shrugged. "Like right now," he said, "I'm wondering how you feel about taking advice from a black man. Are you just humoring me? Do you laugh behind my back, in your car together?"

"We don't laugh about anything," Marjorie said, which I thought an overstatement, but kept my mouth shut.

Quinlan smiled more broadly; he has a very broad smile, when he wants. "Paranoia is not a good guide," he suggested, then looked back at me and said, "But Marjorie was right about the cryogenics, wasn't she? You're frozen, waiting to be thawed when there's a cure."

"That sounds right," I admitted, "though I'm not sure what to do about it. I mean, it'll be hard to retrain myself." Retrain; retraining. The sick joke of downsizing, and now I've volunteered to try it in my home.

"We're in no hurry," Quinlan told me, and looked at Marjorie again, to say, "Isn't that right? As long as we know the problem's out in the air, and progress is being made, we're in no hurry, are we?"

"I feel much better," Marjorie said. "Just being here, just talking about it."

I couldn't tell them, of course, that the situation is going to change for the better, the much better, pretty soon now, no matter what we do in the counseling. Two resumés and Upton "Ralph" Fallon, that's all that's left. I'm a short-timer now, in cyrogenics.

But I'm glad Marjorie got to say all that, and I'm very glad I got to hear it. I don't want to lose her, any more than I want Billy in jail. I don't want any of the extra bad things that happen to people in our situation, I don't want the fringe banes.

We're at sea, that's my image, not cryogenics. We're lost at sea on a raft, and it's up to me to keep the raft together, ration the supplies, keep us afloat until we find shore. That's my task, my position. If it's made me cold to Marjorie, then I'm wrong, I'm trying too hard. Hurting her can't help me, or anything else. I've been *too* focused, that's what it is. I have to try to relax, even though all I really want to do is keep my guard up twenty-four hours a day.

In any event, now we know who the guy is. James Halstead; always James, never Jim. Banker turned Mercedes salesman. Now we know, and we don't care.

That was yesterday, and today is Wednesday. I've just kissed Marjorie goodbye at Dr. Carney's, warmly, with love. Now I'm on my way to kill GRB.

27

The weight of my raincoat is more balanced today as I walk through the woods, with the Luger in the right pocket and two apples in the left. Today I'm prepared for a long wait.

It's not yet ten in the morning when I reach GRB's house and take up my position, seated on the stump at the edge of the woods, behind the pool house. The house over there beyond the lawn seems shut up tight, as though the owners have gone away forever. But she, at least, was here the day before yesterday, when I saw her hike through the woods, hitting trees with her shillelagh.

I settle down, trying to find a position that's more comfortable for my back, on this stump, and I wait. And after a while, I find myself thinking about this or that part of yesterday's session with Longus Quinlan, and how all of that history just came pouring out of Marjorie. I must be a different person from the one I always thought I was, if she had to keep so silent around me for so long, if she had to create this entire scenario, an affair, counseling, before she could suddenly blurt it all out like that, like a dam bursting.

I remember what I said yesterday about retraining, that word from when I got the chop, bubbling to the surface all at once there, and I think I'm serious about it. I've just been going along, doing my best to take care of my family, but ignoring the effect I was having on Marjorie, taking it for granted she was happy with me.

Retraining. That was part of the separation package at the mill, what *they* called retraining, and what *they* called retraining was so miserable and false that I really ought to find some other word for the reappraisal I want to make in connection with myself. What *they* called retraining was . . .

I don't suppose they actually meant it to be insulting. I think what they were trying to do was keep us all calm and hopeful until we were well out the door, and that's why we had the severance packages and the inspirational meetings and the offers of retraining, all this crap.

At first, I was even hopeful about the idea of retraining. I'd read all the stuff about it, the same stuff we've all read, how it's going to be necessary in the brave new world of tomorrow for people to move on from job to job, learning new skills along the way, and how males older than fifty have the hardest time giving up the old skills in exchange for the new skills, and

I was absolutely prepared to prove that particular generalization false, here's *one* guy can adapt, just try me.

And so they tried me, all right. They offered me air conditioning repair.

Where am I, in a vocational high school or a minimum security prison, which one? Air conditioning repair? How is this a brand new skill to carry anybody into the brave new world of tomorrow? And what does air conditioning repair have at *all* to do with my entire work history? I manage assembly lines, that's what I *do*.

Okay, forget specialized paper processes, just talk about assembly lines, the management thereof, and that's what I do. Retrain me to run a different kind of assembly line, all right? I'm adaptable. The product lines are still out there, the products are still churning out the factory door. I'm happy to retrain, if it connects with *me* in any way at all, if it makes any kind of sense.

Let's say you're the owner of a company that services air conditioning units in large office buildings, and you have an opening for a repairman, and thirty guys apply (and thirty guys will apply) who have had *years* of experience repairing air conditioners, and I show up with a certificate of two months' training in air conditioner repair and a quarter century of experience in manufacturing specialized paper products. Are you gonna hire me? Or are you not that crazy?

Take James Halstead, the banker turned car salesman. Is that *retraining*? He looks like a banker, which means he looks like a Mercedes salesman. He already has the suit. Is he where he is because he actively welcomed retraining, or is he where he is because he failed? Did he seek for solace in Marjorie's arms because he'd made a successful transition to the brave new world of tomorrow, or because he was discarded like last year's computer? Can it be he's unhappy because he just found out the bank didn't need him after all? Those complacent days of plenty, riding the commuter train three days a week to what turned out not to be his actual life, but just a game they were letting him play, for a little while.

When one of his old bosses comes in to buy a Mercedes, using the money they've saved on his salary, do they recognize him? They do not. But he recognizes them. And never lets on. And smiles, and smiles, and sells the car.

That's retraining.

Eleven-fifteen; she appears, in the same hat and cardigan and corduroys, but a different blouse. The last time, the blouse was light blue, this time it's light green. She carries the shillelagh again, and she marches across the lawn like the commander of a prisoner-of-war camp on inspection. She goes through the gate in the electric fence, and strides off up the path: *crack . . . crack . . . crack . . .*

Is he in there? Do I dare try it? I have at least half an hour, probably more, before she gets back, judging by last time. I can't sit here forever, day after day, on this stump, like a leprechaun.

I rise—stiff already—and cross to the gate, and let myself through, carefully hooking it shut behind me. I thought at first I'd slink around to the right, along the fence, past the rhododendron beds and the birdbath, to where the wires of the fence are attached to the right rear corner of the house, but now I realize there's no point hiding. What if he does see me? So what? I'm a respectable looking man in a raincoat, walking across his lawn, probably got lost out there in the woods, looking for directions. He comes to the door, he asks if he can help, and I shoot him.

So I cross the lawn, not exactly boldly, but casually, looking around as though with a normal curiosity about somebody else's home. Nobody appears at a door, nobody appears at a window. I veer to the left, cross the patio, and try one of the sliding patio doors. It glides open, and I step inside.

The central air conditioning is on, discreet but apparent. If anything happened to it, I wouldn't know how to fix it.

This is a dining room, with its view through the glass doors to the patio and pool. I cross it, and now I'm definitely a trespasser, not an innocent man lost in the woods.

I move swiftly and quietly through the house, first downstairs, then up, and it's empty. GRB isn't here. At the very end, I open the door from the kitchen to the attached garage, and there's no car in it.

He's out. Where is he? Does he have a counterman job, like Everett Dynes? Is he selling automobiles? How do I find him? How do I get my hands on him?

I'm crossing back through the kitchen when I glance out the window and see her coming, still marching firmly forward, headed this way across the lawn, mashing it every second step with her stick. A shorter walk today; damn.

I don't want her to find me, because I don't want to have to kill her. For many reasons I don't want to kill her, but the primary reason right now is that her husband isn't home, and if I leave her dead and him alive he'll be alerted, he'll be surrounded by police, I'll never get my hands on him. If I kill her, and then wait for GRB to come home, what happens if he *doesn't* come home? What if he's on an overnight job interview, won't be back till late tomorrow?

I can't stay here, to wait for him. I can't kill this woman, so I can't permit her to know I'm here.

She uses the patio door, or she has in the past, the same door I just came in by. When she enters, which way will she go?

Either the kitchen, I think, or the downstairs bathroom, which means through the dining room and the smaller sitting room and the hall, *not* through the large living room facing the front of the house. So I move into the living room, and crouch behind the sofa that stands in the middle of that large space. It looks toward the stone fireplace, with its back to the large bow window showing front lawn and the driveway that recedes downward toward the invisible main road. Crouched here, behind the sofa, eight feet from that window, I'm fully exposed to anyone out front, but why would anyone be out front?

I hear her enter, as the door glides open, and then shut. I hear the final *click* as she puts the shillelagh down, its tip striking the polished wood floor.

I crouch behind the sofa. My right hand grasps the Luger in my raincoat pocket. I try to remember to keep my finger away from the trigger, afraid I'll spastically shoot when I don't want to, probably wounding myself, certainly alerting her, surely destroying everything I've done so far.

I hear the duller *tocks* of her shoes as she crosses the dining room. This way, or the other?

The other. Across the smaller sitting room, into the hall, and into the bathroom. Yes, a brisk walk in the woods does exercise the bladder, doesn't it, and that's why the walk was cut short. And she shuts the bathroom door, even though she's alone in the house, as her mother taught her.

I rise up, behind the sofa, and take my right hand out of my pocket, away from the Luger. My fingers are stiff, like arthritis. Briskly, I cross the living room and the dining room. As silently as possible, I slide open the door, exit, slide it shut. I trot across the lawn, wanting to be well off her property before she's done in the bathroom, because next she'll surely go on to the kitchen, and from the kitchen windows over the sink she'll have a full view of this entire lawn.

The gate. I unhook it, step through, hook it. Without a backward glance, I stride up the path, almost as purposeful as she is.

On the walk back, I eat both apples.

28

About three miles before the turnoff to Scantic River Road, still inside Connecticut, there's a gas station with an outside pay phone on a stick. That's where I stop to make my call, glad to see this phone has the same exchange as GRB's. Local calls disappear more readily.

I'm phoning GRB's house because I had a sudden revelation last night. So many marriages fall into trouble among the downsized; not just mine and Marjorie's. What if GRB and his wife have split up? What if he's living somewhere else, all the time I'm crouched in the woods behind his house, waiting for him?

Or, another possibility. What if he's taken one of those time-serving jobs, say, assistant manager at the local supermarket, then he'll *never* be home during the day. For whatever reason, and there must be one, he hasn't been home the two days I've watched the place. So it's time to find out what the situation is.

Nine-forty. She won't have left for her walk yet. I dial the number from GRB's resumé, and she answers on the second ring: "Blackstone residence." She sounds efficient but impersonal, as though she's chief of staff there, not the lady of the house.

I say, "Garrett Blackstone, please."

"He's not in at the moment, may I say who's calling?"

"It's an old friend from the papermill days," I say. "Is there any way I can get in touch with him?"

"Well, he's at work right now," she says. She sounds a bit doubtful.

I say, "Could I call him there?" I need to know where the man is, dammit.

"I'm not sure," she says, not wanting to offend an old friend of her husband's, but troubled by something. "He's just started there," she explains, "and he might not want outside calls right now."

"Oh, it's a job he likes?"

"It's a wonderful job," she says, and all at once the restraint gives way, and she bubbles over, saying, "It's *just* the job he wanted!"

Arcadia! The son of a bitch got my job, I'll kill him today, I'll kill him in an hour! Gripping the phone so tight my hand is cramping, but unable to relax, I say, "Oh? Back at a paper mill?"

"Yes! Willis and Kendall, do you know them?"

Five *hundred* pounds drops away from my body. I could dance. I say, "The tin can labels!"

"That's right! That's just the job, do you work there, too?"

"Oh, that's great," I say, and I truly mean it. "That's wonderful. Mrs.—Mrs. Blackstone, please give your husband my, my *strongest* congratulations. Tell him I'm delighted for him. Oh, tell him I'm delighted."

"Who should I say—"

I hang up, and float back to the Voyager. I couldn't be happier if I had a job myself. It's true; well, almost true. But he's at work, he's in a *position*, he's where he wants to be!

By God, I don't have to kill him.

Oh, that's great, that's great. Starting the Voyager, making the U-turn, I'm grinning from ear to ear.

As the miles go by, as I drive closer and closer to home, the weight slowly settles down on top of me. Two to go.

29

Saturday morning. I'm in my office, and I've just taken out of the file drawer the last resumé, I'm just reaching for the road atlas, when Marjorie knocks on the door. I place the road atlas on top of the resumé, and say, "Yes?"

She opens the door. She looks worried, and a bit confused. She says, "Burke, there's a policeman here. He wants to talk to you. A detective."

Terror closes my esophagus. I'm caught, I know it, and everything was in vain. And I was so close. Standing, trying to find a reaction I can share with Marjorie, I say, "Billy? Is it something about Billy?"

"I don't think so," she says. "I don't know what it is, Burke. He's in the living room."

"All right."

I step into the hall. The Voyager is closer the other way than the living room is this way. But there's no point in that. I walk down the hall, while Marjorie goes back to whatever she was doing.

He's in the living room, a slender young guy in a gray suit, on his feet, facing the sofa as he smiles at the framed print that hangs above it. It's a Winslow Homer seascape, very turbulent, and I don't know why we have it. Marjorie saw it for sale years ago, at a frame shop, and bought it, with some embarrassment. "I just love it," she told me. "I don't really like prints, but we'll never have a *real* Winslow Homer. Is it all right, Burke?"

Of course I told her it was all right, and I drove the nail into the wall and hung the framed print, and it reminds me that other people are mysterious, no matter how much we get to know them. I will never understand why that picture spoke to Marjorie, that picture more than any other, but it's all right; that's the lesson. The surface of the print is flat, it can't hide what it is, a print and not a painting, but the subject is this roiling sea, over vast unknowable depths. That's what we all are for one another, flat surfaces on which some turbulence can be seen, but unknowable depths. It doesn't matter that I'll never know Marjorie very deeply; I know her enough to know I love her, and that's enough.

And would I like her to know my depths?

The detective turns, sensing me, and smiles, nodding toward the picture. "I grew up on boats," he says. "My father's a great sailor. Mr. Devore?"

"Yes?"

He extends a hand and we shake, as he says, "Detective Burton, state CID. I hope I'm not interrupting anything?"

"Not at all. Sit down."

He does, on the sofa, twisting around to look at the Homer again, while I sit on the armchair across from him, trying to conceal my worry, reassured a bit by his friendly manner.

He turns away from the picture at last, saying, "You a sailor, Mr. Devore?"

"No," I say, regretfully. I wish I could say yes, so we'd have a kinship. I say, "My wife loved the picture."

"I grew up on Long Island Sound," he says, taking a notebook out of his inside jacket pocket. Chuckling, he says, "And sometimes in it." Opening the notebook, he studies something written in there, then looks seriously at me and says, "Do you know a Herbert Everly?"

It *is* me he's after! How did I ever think I'd get away with it? But what can I do but pretend innocence, ignorance, disconnectedness? "Everly?" I say. "I don't think so."

"How about somebody named Kane Asche?"

"Kane Asche. No, doesn't ring a bell."

He says, "You worked for Halcyon Mills, didn't you, for a long while?"

"Were they *there*?"

"No, no," he says, grinning at the misunderstanding. "But they did work at paper mills. Different ones from you."

I spread my hands. I say, "I'm sorry, I don't know what you want."

"Neither do we, Mr. Devore, to be perfectly frank," he says, with his guileless smile. Can I trust him? He's still holding that notebook. He says, "We got a very strange call the other day from the personnel officer with a paper company called Willis and Kendall."

"I applied for a job there, a few weeks ago."

"That's right," he says. "And you were one of the people they interviewed."

"I didn't get a callback, though, so I guess I didn't get that job."

"There were four people they called for a second interview," Burton tells me, "and turned out, two of them had just been killed. They'd both been shot to death."

"Good God!"

"It's these two, Everly and Asche." Burton taps his notebook. "And *now*," he says, "ballistics tells us they were both killed with the same gun."

I say, "Was it somebody they worked with?"

"They didn't know each other," Burton says, "so far as we can tell. There's no link we can find between these two men except they both applied for the same job."

I say, "Do you mean, you think somebody's going to come shoot *me*?"

"It's probably simple coincidence," Burton says, "those two getting callbacks for the same job. A number of people applied, and so far everybody else is perfectly fine, like yourself. They hired somebody now—"

"I thought they must have."

He grins in sympathy and says, "Sorry to be the bearer of bad news."

"No, you get used to it," I say.

"It can get rough, I know," he says. "My brother was laid off down at Electric Boat, and his wife was laid off one week later from the insurance company. They're going nuts."

"I'm sure they are."

"What we think," Burton says, "is that Everly and Asche must have met somewhere, sometime. Maybe a trade conference, or a job referral outfit, who knows. They met each other, and they met somebody else, and something went wrong. So the Willis and Kendall connection's just a coincidence."

"The man the company hired," I say. "Is *he* all right?"

"He's fine. No threats against him, no mysterious strangers lurking around."

"So it probably doesn't have anything to do with that company," I say.

"That's right. If there's a link, it's somewhere in the past. That's why I'm here, we're canvassing everybody with any connection at all to either of the victims."

"Mine's not much of a connection," I say. "We all applied for the same job."

"But it's the phone call from that employer that got us started on this," he points out. "We don't know what we're looking for, so we've got to look everywhere we can think of. Like, if we could find some place, some time, when people like you in your industry got together, somewhere you all might have been at, a trade fair—"

"I ran a product manufacturing line," I say. "I almost never went to sales conferences, things like that."

"Would you mind," he says, "taking a look at a couple photos, see if they jog your memory? See if you ever met either of these people *anywhere*."

I say, "It's not—they're not pictures of them dead, are they?"

He laughs: "We wouldn't do that to you, Mr. Devore. They're perfectly ordinary photos. All right?"

"Sure," I say.

He has the photos in his notebook, and now he shakes them out and extends them toward me.

Here they are, my resumés one and four, with their faces intact, before I shot the bullets into them. I look at the photos and feel a great sadness swelling up inside me, so that my eyes sting. I feel so sorry for these two men. They seem like decent guys. I shake my head, and when I look toward Burton I'm aware of that stormy Winslow Homer sea above his head. "They just seem like nice guys," I say. "Excuse me, it's making me teary or something. They look so *ordinary*."

"Sure," he says. "You're identifying, I understand that. Things like that aren't supposed to happen to folks like us. Unfortunately, they do."

Handing the photos back, I say, "I really don't think I ever met them. Either of them."

"Okay," he says, and puts the photos in the notebook and the notebook away in his inner jacket pocket.

Is this it? All of it? Am I still free, uncaught, unsuspected? I say, "I'm sorry I couldn't help."

"Oh, you helped," he says, and gets to his feet, and so do I. He says, "We never like coincidence, but sometimes it happens. If it never happened, we wouldn't have a word for it."

"I guess that's true," I say.

From his side trouser pocket he takes a wallet, and from the wallet a card, which he hands me, saying, "If you think of anything, or if anything weird happens around here in the next week or so, call me, okay?"

With a shaky smile, I say, "Weird, like me getting shot?"

"Whatever it was," he says, "two seems to be it. I really don't think we're going to come across a third. I think you're safe, Mr. Devore."

"That's good news," I say.

30

I'm back in my office. Burton has gone, I've described the reason for his visit to Marjorie, I've had more conversation with Marjorie on the subject of the two murders than I wanted but I felt I shouldn't cut it short, and now I'm back in my office, and I'm shaking with the realization of the close call I've had.

These two dead men, and their link to job-hunting, could be a coincidence, that's true. Two might be a coincidence or not a coincidence, and pretty soon they're going to come to the conclusion that coincidence is the only answer that fits these two.

But not three.

If I'd found Garrett Blackstone. If he hadn't been given that tin can label job. If I'd shot him either time this week that I'd been to his house, Detective Burton and the other detectives would now have *three* job-hunting paper mill managerial types shot in the same state with the same gun, and it wouldn't be a coinci-

dence, and they'd start thinking about possible motives, and they wouldn't rest until they found me.

The same gun. I've been incredibly stupid, and incredibly lucky. It never occurred to me that they
could—or would think to—link these separate murders by showing they came from the same gun. (If
Willis & Kendall's personnel man hadn't stuck his oar
in, they might very well not have.)

But I don't know why I didn't think of it. I've seen so
many cop shows on television, and so many movies, too,
where they talk about ballistics and finding the gun that
fired that particular bullet, and all that, but I never once
made the connection. All I thought was, this gun has not
been fired by anybody in over fifty years, it has never
been fired anywhere on the North American continent,
there's no record of its existence, so it's anonymous.

Even an anonymous gun, it seems, can leave a trail.

They could have four victims of that gun now, instead of two, except that the shooting in Massachusetts
has already been solved, so nobody's going to compare
that bullet with some bullets in Connecticut. And of
course I didn't use the gun with Everett Dynes.

And I'm not going to be able to use it with the last
resumé, either.

What am I going to do? I can't use the Luger any
more, not ever again. I don't have any other gun, and I
don't know how I could get one without leaving an
ownership trail. I know that criminals have ways to do
that, but I don't live in their world, and if I tried to
enter their world something bad would happen to me,
I know that much.

A gun is so clean, so impersonal. It separates you, just a bit, from the event.

Can I stab somebody? Strangle? I don't see how I could do such things.

And I can't use the car again. Even apart from the difficulty of rigging another covering accident, and the suspicion I might arouse by having a second accident of that kind, even beyond all that, I know I couldn't do that again. Once was enough. More than enough.

And I certainly can't walk up to a total stranger with a glass in my hand and say, "Here, drink this."

What am I going to do? I've come this far, I can't stop now. Those deaths can't have been in vain. I've been given a warning, and I'll heed it. I have one resumé to go, and then Fallon, and it's all over. One way or another, I'll do it, because I have to do it.

Not today, though. I have to deliver Marjorie to the New Variety this afternoon for her cashier job, and then pick her up this evening. It would be too difficult and too noticeable, now that we're talking to each other again, to alter our Sunday pattern by spending the whole day away; it would certainly come up in Tuesday's session with Longus Quinlan, and what would I say?

Monday. After I drop Marjorie at Dr. Carney's, on Monday, I'll drive over to New York State and study my last resumé, and see what things look like. Monday, the ninth of June; I make a checkmark on the date on my desk calendar. Not to remind myself, I certainly won't need reminding, but to express to myself my determination to see this through.

I have to think of something.

Hauck Exman
27 River Road
Sable Jetty, NY 12598
518 943-3450

1987–present	- Oak Crest Paper Mills - manager, polymer paper applications
1981–1987	- Oak Crest Paper Mills - supervisor, product development
1978–1981	- Oak Crest Paper Mills - sales director
1973–1978	- Oak Crest Paper Mills - salesman
1970–1973	- U.S. Marine Corps, instructor, Fort Bragg
1970	- Graduate degree, Business Administration, Holyoke University, Holyoke, MD

Married, three grown children. Self and current wife prepared to relocate if necessary.

Reference: John Justus, Oak Crest Paper Mills, Dention, CT

31

"Self and current wife." A lot of undercurrents under that "current." A hard-nosed ex-Marine, I wonder how many wives he wore down.

The simple son of a bitch was more faithful to his employer than to any woman. Out of the Marines and straight into Oak Crest and stayed there until they dumped him. How close was he to pension; a year and a half?

Hauck Curtis Exman; my God, it's my second HCE. I started with an HCE and, except for Fallon, I'm ending with an HCE. Here Comes Everybody. Yes, and here comes a candle to light you to bed.

Sable Jetty is south of Kingston, where I had my accident with the pickup truck. It's right on the Hudson River, a little old river town of wood and brick, built up the steep slope, probably two hundred years beyond any economic justification for its existence. These places have become weekend homes for the city well-

to-do because they're so quaint, and they're quaint because the people have been too poor to keep up with
the latest trends. This is the sort of town movie companies use when they're shooting a film set in the
twenties or thirties. Now that the city people are losing
their city jobs, maybe these towns will go on being
quaint.

Sable Jetty spreads up from a small cove on the
Hudson's western bank, where a hillock of land extends into the river, forming a natural calm basin along
the shore just to its south, downstream. The Indians
launched their canoes there, long ago, and the first Eu-
ropean explorers landed there, because it was out of
the river's current. A settlement built up, and then a
ferry was started, and the town prospered, and all of
that eventually disappeared. Today, the old ferry office
is the county historical museum, the old ferry dock is
long gone, and the old brick or wooden houses built up
the teetery hill westward from the river's edge seem
more and more like two-dimensional flat genre paint-
ings and less and less like places where actual human
beings live their lives.

River Road runs from the square in front of the ferry
dock northward, immediately leaving town, arcing
around the long gradual slope of the hillock. It doesn't go
right along by the water, but partway upslope, with more
substantial houses on its upward side, originally meant to
give doctors and aldermen and hardware store owners
good river views, and less substantial shacklike houses
between road and water, originally meant to give the

working class a roof over their heads where they could supplement their poor incomes with fish.

27 is on the uphill side, a big brick sprawl of a house, with a broad curved porch stretching around the front, set off by thick wooden pillars painted a creamy yellow. There must have been plantings around the house and along the roadside at one time, but they're gone now, re-placed by a long narrow ribbon of lawn, flowing down the smooth and gentle slope from the front wall of the house to the low white picket fence—plastic, not wood—that defines the edge of the road. This lawn is flanked on both sides by very black blacktop driveways, the one on the left belonging to 27 and the one on the right belonging to the house next door. Newer smaller houses flank 27 too closely on both sides, so that this must once have been a more gracious and spacious prop-erty, until the side lots were sold off in the fifties.

Monday morning, 11:30. I came here directly from dropping Marjorie off at Dr. Carney's, crossing the Hud-son on the same bridge as when I came back from Everett Dynes. I drive by 27 River Road southbound, looking up at the house on my right. A red-haired woman in a tan sweatshirt and blue jeans sits on a riding mower, grooming the lawn in slow ovals. The detached garage at the top of the driveway is closed, and no car is parked on the blacktop. The mailbox, oversized and silver, with the address stenciled on it in severe black, stands on a white-washed wooden post between the end of the picket fence and the end of the driveway. Its flag is up; ideal for a shooting, if I could use the gun.

I don't even have the Luger with me; what's the point?

I drive on down into town, where half the small dusty shops around the square are hopelessly for rent. I park in front of one of the empty shops to study my road atlas, and there's no comfort there. River Road sweeps out of town and north around the protruding hillock, on the other side of which it angles west to dead-end at State Route 9, the main north-south state road on this side of the river. Route 9 continues south, avoiding the center of Sable Jetty, but with no other turnoffs before it reaches the town. No other road enters or crosses the area of the hillock, which makes a sort of pumpkin stuck onto the shore of the river. A private road, sealed with an electric gate, leads from the town end of River Road up to the mansion that commands the top of the hillock; long ago a lumber baron's or a railroad baron's place, it is now a Buddhist retreat, impenetrably fenced against its neighbors.

I can't get at HCE's house from behind. River Road itself is quite exposed, a long curve with several houses always visible and with no public parking areas. I hadn't noticed any vacant-seeming houses or For Sale signs near HCE's place. Several of the smaller houses on the river side of the road had looked to me to be seasonal, summer places for today's blue-collar people, but this is June and the season has begun; a few boats bob at rickety wooden docks along there, and any or all of those houses could be occupied right now, even on a Monday.

HCE, my ex-Marine, is being harder to get at than any of the others.

The road atlas can't help me. I put it away, and start the Voyager, and drive around the square to head north again up River Road.

HCE's house is now on my left. The woman on the riding mower is making smaller ovals now, her work almost done. And the garage door is open, the interior of the garage empty.

Damn! He came out! While I was in town, he came out and went . . . anywhere. For all I know, he drove right on by me while I was parked down there, frowning at my road atlas.

I don't know what he looks like. I don't know what the car looks like.

I drive on up to the T intersection with Route 9, where there's a diner just to the south and a big covered mall just to the north. It's almost lunchtime now anyway, so I pull in at the diner, and as I have my usual BLT I wonder if he happens to be working here. Hauck Curtis Exman. HCE. Is this where he drove to, from his house? Is his car outside there somewhere, maybe next to mine? There are only female employees visible out front, but could he be in back? A short-order cook?

Or did he just go out to get the newspaper, and is he home again by now?

Finishing my lunch, I drive back down River Road. The flag is down on the mailbox, so the mail has been delivered. The garage door is still open, garage still empty. The woman and the riding mower are both gone. The mower doesn't seem to be in the garage, so they probably have a shed for it around back.

I drive into town, and through it, and several miles farther south I pull over at a parking area for a scenic river view. I sit there and try to think how to get at HCE. How to find him, and then how to kill him, without using a gun.

But find him first. Identify him, so I can follow him, look for my chance.

How long will he be gone from the house? Has he a make-work job somewhere? Has he a *real* job, a paper mill job, one that takes him out of contention? Could I be that lucky twice in a row?

But what real job would have him leave the house between 11;30 in the morning and noon?

When the clock in the Voyager reads 1:30 I drive away from the scenic view, which I'd barely looked at. I go back up through Sable Jetty and up River Road, and there's no change at HCE's house. Garage open and empty. He's still gone.

There's nothing more I can do today. I feel anxious, impatient, this business is so close to being over and done with, but I know there's nothing more to be done, not today. I don't want to be careless, in too much of a rush. I don't want to cause another mess, like a couple I've had, and I certainly don't want to be caught by the police, not at this stage.

When I reach Route 9 I turn north, past the big mall and on toward the bridge and, beyond that, home.

32

I'm crossing the bridge again, in bright sunshine, high over the Hudson River, seeing towns and woodland and factories and onetime mansions along both shores, the bustling but grubby town of Kingston out ahead. Wednesday morning; my second visit to the second HCE.

Yesterday, at our counseling session, there was an uncomfortable silence for a while, partway through, none of us seeming to have much to say, as though whatever the counseling's purpose had been was now completed, but then Quinlan said to me, "When you were laid off from the mill, it wasn't a surprise, was it? Not a complete surprise."

"Not a *complete* surprise," I agreed. "There'd been rumors, and the whole industry was shaking up. But I didn't expect it so soon, and I guess I wasn't ever sure *I'd* be part of it. I was always good at my job, believe me—"

"I'm sure you were," he said, with a small smile and an encouraging nod.

"I didn't know they were going to move the whole thing to Canada," I said. "We trained them, the Canadians, and now they're cheaper than we are."

He said, "How did you feel, when it happened?"

"How did I *feel*?"

"Well, I mean," he said, "were you angry? Frightened? Resentful? Relieved?"

"Not relieved," I said, and laughed. "All the others, I guess."

"Why?"

I looked at him. "Why? Why what?"

"Why feel angry, or frightened, or resentful?"

I couldn't believe we were descending down to this kindergarten level. I said, "Because I was losing my job. It's perfectly natural to—"

"Why?"

He was beginning to annoy me. He was beginning to be one of those inspirers they'd set loose on us at the mill during the last months before the chop. I said, "What am I *supposed* to feel, when I lose my job?"

"There's nothing you're required to feel," he said. "There's not even anything that's perfectly natural to feel. What *you* felt was angry and frightened and bitter and probably perplexed, and you still do. So what I'm wondering is, why did you take it that way?"

"Everybody did!"

"Oh, I don't think so," he said, and sat back in his chair, away from his desk, farther from me. "Do you remember your co-workers? The ones who were let go the same time as you? Did they *all* feel the way you did?"

"There was pretty general depression," I told him. "Some people put a better face on it, that's all."

"You mean some of them took a more positive view," he suggested. "Saw there might be an opportunity here—"

"Mr. Quinlan," I said, "they sent specialists around to us, the last five months on the job, people to help us learn how to write resumés and dress for a job interview and all of that stuff, people to advise us about our finances now that we weren't going to *have* any finances, and people to *inspire* us, give us all this sloganeering and pep talks and feel-good stuff. You're beginning to sound a lot like them."

He laughed and said, "I suppose I am. Well, I suppose I have the same message, that's why."

"The message is crap," I told him.

I hadn't said that to any of the inspirers at the mill. Back then I was polite and receptive and obedient, just the way you're supposed to be, but I didn't think I should have to go through it all over again, so I just told Quinlan what I thought, to get *rid* of this Pollyanna stuff forever. Every day in every way we are *not* getting better and better.

Marjorie looked at me, startled, when I said that, when I told Quinlan he was saying crap, because we'd all been gentle and polite with one another up till now, but Quinlan didn't mind. I'm sure he's heard a lot worse in that office. He grinned at me and shook his head and said, "Mr. Devore, what you're *picking up* as the message *is* crap, I'll go along with that. But what you're picking up is not what I'm sending out, and it's not what those people at the mill were sending out. The real message is, *you are not the job.*"

I looked at him. Was that supposed to mean something?

He saw that I still wasn't receiving whatever it was he was trying to send, so he said, "A lot of people, Mr. Devore, identify themselves with their jobs, as though the person and the job were one and the same. When they lose the job, they lose a sense of themselves, they lose a sense of worth, of being valuable people. They think they're nothing any more."

"That isn't me," I said. "That isn't the way I look at it."

"But you felt depressed and angry," he reminded me. "Didn't you feel they'd taken away part of your self?"

"They took away my life, not my self," I told him. "They took away my ability to pay my mortgage, care for my children, have good times with my wife. A job is a job, it isn't *me*, but it's necessary. And I'll tell you what we all knew, Mr. Quinlan, in those last five months, the hundreds of us there, used to be best friends, *working* together, counting on one another, not even thinking about it, we always knew we could rely on each other right on down the line. But it was the end of the line, and we were enemies now, because we were competitors now, and we all knew it. *That's* the thing we weren't saying to each other, and the counselors weren't saying, and nobody was saying. That the tribe was bust, it wasn't a tribe any more. We wouldn't be watching each other's backs any more."

He leaned forward again, watching me carefully. "Enemies, Mr. Devore? They were your enemies?"

"We were *all* enemies, each other's enemies, and we all knew it. You could see it in the faces. People who always used to have lunch together stopped having lunch together. When somebody said, 'Do you have any leads?' you said no, even if it was a lie. We started lying to each other. Friendships stopped. Relationships stopped."

"You couldn't trust one another any more."

"We weren't a team, we were each other's competition. Everything changed."

Quinlan nodded. He wasn't smiling, he was serious. "Every man for himself," he said.

"That's what it is. Before you get the chop, you don't have to know that, you can pretend we're all buddies here. *That's* the message the inspirers were trying to implant in us, the idea that we're still all together in this, it's still a society, and it is functioning, and we're all a part of it. But after you get the chop, you can't afford that fairy story any more. It *is* every man for himself. The big executives know that. The stockholders know that. And now *we* know it."

"And what does that mean to you, Mr. Devore?"

"It means I have nobody to count on but me." Turning to Marjorie, I said, "That's why I've been so distant, and so focused, because I'm all I've got, and I'm in the fight of my life. I'm *sorry* it's made me so cold to you, I'm sorry, I wish . . . well. You know what I wish."

"You aren't alone, Burke," Marjorie said. "You've got me, you know that."

I shook my head, but I managed a smile as I said, "Have you got a job for me?"

She took that as rejection, of course, I could see it in her hurt reaction, but it wasn't, that's not what it was meant to be. It was just part of seeing clearly. We don't have the luxury of sentiment now, Hallmark cards. At this moment, in this condition, in this situation, we have to see clearly, there's no other choice.

I turned back to Quinlan. I said, "There's nothing out there but me and the competition, and I have to beat the competition. I *have* to. Whatever it takes."

But we were getting too close to reality here, the new reality, my own personal way of *dealing* with the competition. I'd followed the new line of reasoning all the way to the end, and acted on it, but I didn't want anybody else doing that, not around me. Certainly not these two, not Marjorie or Quinlan. So I added, "It's may the best man win, now, and all I can do is hope I'm the best man."

That was the end of the session. Quinlan had let it run on, it seemed, an extra five minutes. And when we left, I thought he looked very closely at me, trying to understand.

Better not to understand, Mr. Q.

Down off the bridge; Kingston. I turn south, toward Sable Jetty.

33

She isn't mowing the lawn today. The garage door is closed, and no one is in sight. He's home, then, and probably she is, too.

How do I get at this man? You cannot approach that house unobserved, you just can't. It's as though he's still a Marine, and placed himself where he has the advantage of the terrain; the slope up to his place, the clear line of fire, the inaccessibility from anywhere except the front.

I drive around the neighborhood, and the next time I pass the house, at 11:50, the garage door is open, the garage empty. He's gone again, and I've missed him again.

This is no good, I'm not accomplishing anything. I drive away, southbound, back to that scenic view from Monday, and I sit there brooding, staring without seeing at the river as it marches endlessly by, like weary soldiers under heavy packs, blue-gray soldiers in blue-gray uniforms bent low under the weight of blue-gray packs, marching in their tight masses downstream.

The resumé. The resumé itself; can I use it? I put my ad in *The Paperman*, I got my responses, I did my winnowing, I used the addresses from the resumés, but that's all. Is there a way to use the ad itself, the fact of the ad? If I can't get at him when he's home, or find him, or follow him from home, can I *send* him somewhere, and *then* follow him?

I begin to see how it could be done. I must go home, get back to the office, think this thing through.

But first I need a restaurant.

B. D. INDUSTRIAL PAPERS
P. O. BOX 2900
WILDBURY, CT 06899

June 11, 1997

Mr. Hauck Exman
27 River Rd.
Sable Jetty, NY 12598

Dear Mr. Exman:

Three months ago, we ran a help wanted ad in The Paperman, to which you responded. At that time, I must admit, you were not our first choice for the position. However, since then, to our chagrin, it has become apparent that our initial decision was in error.

If you have not as yet found other employment, would you be available on Friday, June 20th, to meet with our Personnel Director, Ms. Laurie Kilpatrick, who will be interviewing in the western New York region?

We would suggest lunch at one PM at the Coach House in Regnery, which I believe is not too far from your residence. The reservation will be in Ms. Kilpatrick's name.

Please fill out and return this letter in the enclosed stamped envelope, to let us know your availability. Since the gentleman to be replaced is still on the premises, a phone call might create unnecessary distress.

If we do not hear from you, we will understand that you are no longer interested in the position.

Thank you for your time.

Benj Dockery III

Benj Dockery III, Pres.

☐   I am available.

☐   I am not available.

☐   I must suggest an alternate date. _____

Signature _____

BD/VK

34

This is a very dangerous letter to send. For the first time, I'm leaving a trail—other than the bullets from the Luger, I mean—and for the first time I'm doing something that might warn my resumé that he's in danger.

The phone number, that's the problem. Though contact with prospective employees is often made by this kind of letter, there's *always* a phone number on the letterhead, and almost always the employer asks you to respond by phone. Explaining that the unsatisfactory hire is still there, and a phone call might make trouble in the shop, should—I hope—calm HCE's suspicions before they arise. But what if he notices there's no phone number on the letterhead?

I thought of putting a fake number on it, any number at all, but what if he disobeyed the letter and made the call? That's unlikely, since job hunters don't disobey prospective employers, but what if he did? He would not reach B. D. Industrial Papers. And, no matter what happened in the course of that call, I could be sure his next call would be to the police.

He and they would probably suspect a con game of some sort, and they would follow the trail of the letter to my post office box, where the postmistress would certainly give them a description of me. She's seen me several times, so the description would probably be a good one.

Also, since the letterhead would lead them into Connecticut, how long would it be before it connected them with Detective Burton, the man investigating the coincidental murders of two unemployed paper mill midlevel managers? Come to think of it, what are the odds that HCE applied to Willis & Kendall for that can-label job? Which would mean Detective Burton has already interviewed him.

But the telephone number is the only problem. The meeting I've arranged isn't unheard of, and shouldn't raise suspicion. Personnel directors do sometimes go on the road, to meet with a number of applicants in the same geographical area, and one of the appointments each day will include lunch, or otherwise lunch is a waste of time.

I've made the personnel director a woman, with a name that suggests she's young, and I'm hoping that the prospect of a good meal (the Coach House has a first-rate reputation) with an attractive young woman (he'll naturally assume she's attractive), one that could lead to a prime job, will throw enough dust in his eyes to keep him from thinking about telephones.

Still, it's frightening. At this point, so many things could go wrong. For instance, I've told him to countersign the letter and send it back, so it won't be found among his effects after I kill him, but what if he makes a copy, what if he's that kind of completist? (I reassure myself that, if he's *that* kind of completist, there'll be so much paper bumf stored among his effects that no one will ever look through it all.)

I've also done the best I can with both envelopes, the one I'm mailing to him and the one included for his return. I had a few sheets of my fake letterhead copied onto extra-heavy paper, and then, carefully, with a straight-edge and a razor blade, I cut out the letterheads from three sheets and glued them as the return address on both envelopes and the destination address on the inner envelope. They do look like printed labels.

This whole move scares me. I've been very careful up till now, I've done my best to control the situations, to keep myself anonymous and separate. Now I'm, at least potentially, leaving a trail. But what can I do? I'm so close to the finish, so close. HCE is all that stands between me and Upton "Ralph" Fallon, who will be easy, easy, easy.

Now I'm desperate. I can't use the gun, and I can't get at, or even find, HCE. I have to try something, anything, and this is all I can think of. So I drive up to Wildbury, to the mailbox outside the post office, and I send the letter, and I'm terrified.

B. D. INDUSTRIAL PAPERS
P. O. BOX 2900
WILDBURY, CT 06899

June 11, 1997

Mr. Hauck Exman
27 River Rd.
Sable Jetty, NY 12598

Dear Mr. Exman:

Three months ago, we ran a help wanted ad in The Paperman, to which you responded. At that time, I must admit, you were not our first choice for the position. However, since then, to our chagrin, it has become apparent that our initial decision was in error.

If you have not as yet found other employment, would you be available on Friday, June 20th, to meet with our Personnel Director, Ms. Laurie Kilpatrick, who will be interviewing in the western New York region?

We would suggest lunch at one PM at the Coach House in Regnery, which I believe is not too far from your residence. The reservation will be in Ms. Kilpatrick's name.

Please fill out and return this letter in the enclosed stamped envelope, to let us know your availability. Since the gentleman to be replaced is still on the premises, a phone call might create unnecessary distress.

If we do not hear from you, we will understand that you are no longer interested in the position.

Thank you for your time.

Benj Dockery III

Benj Dockery III, Pres.

☑ I am available.
☐ I am not available.
☐ I must suggest an alternate date. _____

Signature *Hauck Exman*

BD/VK

I look forward to the meeting!

From time to time, the next few days, I'll drive over to Sable Jetty and go past HCE's house. And if I see a police car parked outside, I don't know what I'll do.

I sit in front of the Wildbury post office, Tuesday, the 17th of June, at the wheel of the Voyager, and I hold the letter in my hands. It has orbited back to me. I look at what HCE has written there, along the bottom, and the letter feels warm, heated by his hunger.

He sent it back immediately, the instant he got it. Clearly, he didn't worry about telephone numbers or anything else.

Another possible snag, I'd realized after I sent the letter, was that he might cut off the bottom part of it, the part for him to fill out, and just send that back, retaining the main body of the letter for himself—and the police. But HCE wants this job; he snapped at the bait like a trout.

Now that my gamble seems to be paying off, I can admit the other aspect of this move that I don't like. I have killed people. I've hated doing it, but I had to do it, and I did it. But I haven't been cruel to them, I haven't toyed with them. In a way, I'm toying with HCE, I'm tantalizing him with a nonexistent job interview with a nonexistent attractive woman. I'm sorry to do that, I wish there'd been some other way.

The letter got back to Wildbury yesterday, but I couldn't check the box until this afternoon, because yesterday was Billy's day in court. We had to be there, Marjorie and I, of course. We were scheduled for ten, and we arrived a few minutes early, with Billy, to find Porculey the lawyer waiting for us. His suit this time was not maroon, thank God, but a neutral gray. It was his tie that was maroon, with little white cows jumping over little white moons. He shook our hands, Marjorie's and mine, and said, "We think it will work out here," and took Billy away for a discussion with the judge.

A lot has happened in the two weeks since Billy's arrest. It turned out that Billy's partner in crime, somebody named Jim Bucklin, had been less quick-witted than we, and so had his parents. In the police car after his arrest, he'd said things that might be construed as confessions that he'd robbed that same store several times before, and apparently he'd said similar things to other detectives at the police station, and kept blabbing away until finally, the next day, he met the lawyer his parents had hired (unlike Billy's poor needy folks, the Bucklins didn't qualify for Legal Aid). That lawyer finally got Jim Bucklin to shut up.

The general feeling was that all of Bucklin's earlier loose talk would not be admissible in court, and after the lawyer arrived, Bucklin too started to claim that this burglary was his very first, so that he and Billy were at last telling the same story.

Which broke down when the police searched the Bucklin house (the same time they were searching ours) and found all that computer software.

Of course, they hadn't found any illicit software at our house. So, if finding stolen goods at Bucklin's house meant Bucklin was lying, then *not* finding them at Devore's house must mean Devore was telling the truth, or at least that's what Porculey was maintaining, and why he was doing his best to sever the two cases. Let Bucklin, the long-term master criminal, fend for himself, while Billy, the innocent youngster lured into a life of crime by Bucklin, faced the judge alone.

In chambers. We weren't there for it, having to sit out in the corridor, but apparently it went well. Over the assistant district attorney's ferocious objections—I saw her, from a distance, a hawklike woman in her thirties, thin and sharp-faced and ruthless—the judge did agree to separate the two cases, and to proceed in chambers with Billy's case.

By then, a jail term was no longer at issue. In fact, as Porculey later explained it to us over diner coffee, the issue had become whether or not Billy would have a felony conviction on his record. He had never been in trouble before, he was a good student in school, he had a bright future, and he came from poverty. (Ah, well.) In chambers, Porculey had suggested the possibility of a sealed indictment, and the judge had said he'd think it over.

Over that coffee, as it cooled, all of us too keyed up to add caffeine to our systems, he'd explained what a sealed indictment was, and it's an unexpected bit of mercy in the judicial system. If the defendant would plead guilty, and if the circumstances warrant giving him a second chance, the judge can choose to seal the indictment, keep it unpublished and unacted-upon, in his court, for whatever length of time he decrees; usually a year. If, in that time, the defendant is arrested for *another* crime, the indictment is unsealed and he faces prosecution for both the old crime and the new one. If, however, he stays clean until the term is up, the indictment is quashed as though it had never been. There is no police record; the defendant walks away pure.

Well, that's what we were hoping for, of course, and Porculey expected we'd know before the end of the day, but first the matter of Jim Bucklin had to be dealt with. We stayed away from court during that time, but apparently Bucklin's lawyer joined the assistant district attorney in struggling to keep the two cases together, and the argument was a lengthy one. He wanted his client, of course, to coast along on Billy's cleaner coattails.

But eventually the judge ruled against both the defense lawyer and the assistant district attorney, and Bucklin's case was held over alone for trial—or a plea bargain later on, more likely—and at three in the afternoon we were brought back in. Marjorie and Billy and

I stood before the judge, who was a different one from that original bail hearing, in a different but similar courtroom. And again it was exactly like some religious ritual, full of arcane language, and we the penitents before the high priest.

Porculey had advised us against talking to Bucklin's parents, so we'd avoided them, though they desperately wanted to talk to *us*; to convince us to re-yoke our boy to their doomed son, no doubt. I was aware of them at the back of the courtroom when our session began, remorseful, resentful and reproachful. I didn't look back at them.

The judge sealed the indictment. I thought Marjorie would fall down when she understood what he'd just said, and I held tight to her arm. The judge spoke severely to Billy about his thoughtlessness—lovely word—and Billy kept his head bowed and his responses short and respectful, and soon it was over.

At twenty to four yesterday afternoon, Billy's troubles with the law were done. So long as he stays honest from now on, that is. And there isn't much doubt of that. This experience has frightened him, and he's aware of just how lucky he is. He has the vision of Jim Bucklin right in front of him, to show him how serious it might have been. And he's grateful to us, and doesn't want to let us down.

We shook hands with Porculey, and tried to express our gratitude, and our awareness that we might well have drawn a much worse attorney, and then I took Marjorie and Billy home. What a relief it was, almost as big a relief as if I'd finished all this other business and had my real job back. And what it showed me was, if you just keep going, keep determined, don't *let* the system grind you down, you can prevail.

I will prevail.

Well, that experience used up all of yesterday, and today was another counseling session. Today I kept my mouth shut, since I'm worried I might have exposed myself a little too much last week and I don't want to risk doing that again. Quinlan tried to probe into me two or three times, I could sense his curiosity about the direction we were heading last week, but I gave him flat answers, greeting card answers that he couldn't do a thing with. And Marjorie wanted to steer the conversation toward our roles within the marriage, which was what we were supposed to be there for anyway, so I think I did myself no damage.

When we got home, I did something I've been planning for a while, and now I think the time is right. I prepared seventeen of my resumés, my own resumés, addressed seventeen envelopes to paper mills I'd already approached in the past, plus Arcadia Processing, and I wrote a covering letter to each, saying I'm still here, I'm still available, just in case any job has opened up since you last heard from me. If the timing is right, my resumé will be the most recent one in Arcadia's files, and possibly still fresh in Arcadia's personnel director's memory, when a job over there unexpectedly does become available. And since I'm sending this whole batch out, and it's a week or two before URF's death, there shouldn't be any suspicion raised.

After I mailed those resumés at my local post office, I drove on up here to Wildbury, to find HCE's answer waiting in the box. And now I sit here a minute, in the sunshine, outside the post office, and I smile at how well things are coming along.

Friday. Three days from now, I'll find HCE at last. Will I be able to deal with him immediately? Find him and just *do* it? Then next week URF and it's all over.

I can see the job, the work, the commute. I can *feel* being in that job, like a warm bath.

Friday.

36

I am parked down the block from the Coach House. It is five to one, Friday afternoon; almost time for HCE's lunch with Ms. Laurie Kilpatrick.

Nine days ago, when I realized I couldn't get at HCE directly, and began to think about this other way to do it, I drove all around this part of the state, looking at restaurants, and decided that, for my purposes, the Coach House in Regnery is ideal. It's fairly upscale, the kind of place where the local gentry goes, and it's right on the main street of town, so there's no problem parking or being anonymous. And there are large mullioned windows on the street, Colonial style, through which a pedestrian can easily see the front part of the restaurant, where the maitre d' greets the customers and where there's a small seating area of two benches for people to await their lunch companions.

Will HCE be early? I'm sure of it. At five before the

hour, he's probably in there already; time for my first walk by.

I get out of the Voyager, which I've parked half a block from the restaurant, and stroll down the sidewalk.

Yesterday afternoon, I phoned here, to make a reservation for two in the name Kilpatrick, so he'll be told the reservation does exist but the other party hasn't arrived as yet, and naturally he'll take a seat in the waiting area.

And is that him? I stroll by, and one man is on the bench there, sitting back, looking confident, one leg crossed over the other. A very good dark suit and dark figured tie, close-cropped gray hair, a squarish face; that's all I can see in that first glimpse.

I walk on, pause at an appliance store, study the VCRs and fax machines in the window for a few minutes, then turn and stroll back the way I came. A longer look at him now, and I'm sure this is my man. He has a blunt way of sitting, a square-jawed, take-command expression on his face, and just a hint of excited anticipation. HCE, at last.

I go back to the Voyager, get behind the wheel, sit watching the entrance to the restaurant. It's pretty popular; well-dressed people keep going in, usually in pairs, usually men together or women together, occasionally a mixed couple, but all middle-aged or older. I don't see another singleton who matches my idea of HCE.

1:10. Time to confirm my guess that the military-looking man in the suit is HCE. (The suit, which looks to me very good and very expensive, is the one small cause of doubt here.) Is he still waiting? Or is someone else there in his place, the *real* HCE?

No. Still him. He's still my man. The former Marine instructor who spent his entire working life with one company. He's looking less confident now, slightly distressed, and when I walk back toward the Voyager I see him looking at his watch.

Again I sit behind the wheel. The only question now is how long it will take him to give up.

1:45. He's still in there. He must know by now that Ms. Kilpatrick isn't coming, something's gone wrong. But still he waits, hope against hope, the faithful soldier.

I hate doing this to him, the elation and then the humiliation, the terrible feeling of wretchedness and no way to strike back at the unfairness. If there'd been any other way . . .

Well. This situation has its grim moments.

2:05. Is he *never* going to give up? He can't sleep in that restaurant, he'll have to leave sometime. Did he decide to eat lunch there anyway, pay for it himself?

Unlikely. HCE and I can't afford places like the Coach House any more.

Should I get out of the car, go see if he's still seated there? If somehow he's gone out some back way, left the restaurant, I should know it. But what if I do get out, and I'm halfway there, and he—

There. At last, he comes out into the sunlight. Standing, he's shorter than I expected, but compact, a stocky man in good physical condition. He stops on the sidewalk, at a loss, looking up and down the block, and then he shakes his head and turns to walk in my direction.

My face is turned away, I'm looking at the bank directly across the street, when he walks past me. Then I turn back and watch him recede in the right side mirror, ramrod stiff. When he's a little farther along I watch him in the inside mirror, and remember poor Everett Dynes, and briefly close my eyes. I don't need that memory now.

He's turned, he's stepping between cars, he's turning again, he's unlocking a car door. When he opens it, I see the car is black; I would have expected that from him. I start the Voyager's motor, sit there with it idling.

Now nothing happens. What is he doing in there? Probably, come to think of it, with the relative privacy of the interior of his own car, probably he's allowing himself a minute to be unglued, to be angry and unhappy and frustrated and afraid. But, if I know my man, he won't need long.

No. Here he comes. It's a Ford Taurus; HCE would buy American.

I switch on my left turn signal. His Taurus drives by me, then a gray Chrysler Cirrus drives by me, and then I pull out.

We drive out of town, me keeping at least one other car between us, his black Taurus always clearly visible up ahead. Out of Regnery, this secondary road takes us over to State Route 9, where he turns north toward Sable Jetty, as expected.

There's more traffic on this road, but he's still easy to follow. I'd thought his anger and frustration might make him drive too fast or too aggressively, but he's a law-abider, and we stay respectably just above the speed limit whenever we aren't slowed by trucks.

I expect him to take the right turn that leads into Sable Jetty, but he doesn't; instead, he continues on up Route 9. I follow, keeping well back, wondering where he's going. North of town, he'll meet the other end of River Road, but that would be the long way round to his house.

Here's River Road, with the diner beside it and the big mall just beyond it, on the other side of the road, and *that's* where he's going, the mall. He signals for a left, moving into the special mall lane there, and the three cars between us all go straight ahead, and I too signal for a left as I come to a stop behind him.

There's no traffic light at this spot, but there is one

some distance ahead, and shortly after that one turns red the southbound traffic peters out, and then we can both make our turn, and so can the two cars that have come along behind me.

It's harder to follow him in the parking lot, without being noticeable. I stay well back, seeming indecisive about which lane I want, while he heads confidently forward and then to the right, and parks some distance away from the main building, half a dozen empty spaces from the nearest parked car. Is he afraid of dents and damage from other people getting into their cars next to his? I think that would probably be like him.

I find a slot closer to the building, and stop, and take out my memo pad and pen, as though I've chosen this moment to do my shopping list. I'm aware of him walking this way, then see him clearly first in the right mirror, then the inside mirror, then the left mirror.

Please. Let this one not be as awful as Everett Dynes.

When he's almost to the end of the row of parked cars, I finally get out of the Voyager, lock it, and follow. He's crossing the lanes between the parking area and the mall building, and I'm not very far behind him. Other people are walking here, too, from their cars. We all enter the building.

This is an enclosed mall, with a long broad corridor from these doors, flanked by chain stores of all kinds, and with a three-story Dolmen's at the far end, Dolmen's being a line of suburban department stores, mostly or maybe entirely in malls. In front of Dolmen's, the corridor Ts left and right, with more shops facing the fashion windows of the department store. Only the part of the building containing Dolmen's is more than one story high.

HCE walks briskly down the long corridor. He certainly seems to know where he's going. Could he be planning to buy himself something, some small luxury to soothe his feelings? He doesn't seem the type.

Dolmen's, that's where he's going. The sliding doors open for him, then close, then open for me, and I see him moving just as briskly as ever toward the escalators in the middle of the store.

I keep well back. There are a good number of shoppers in here, but it isn't really crowded, and I wouldn't want him to become aware that he's seeing me every time he looks around.

Not that he does look around, really. He's clearly concentrated on his destination. Up the escalator he goes, and I can tell he would step briskly upward except that the large family in front of him, everybody but Dad, is standing still.

I hang back, and hang back, and don't board the escalator until he's nearly to the top. Then, as I am rising upward, I just glimpse him make the U-turn and march back toward the second flight.

Yes. As I come off the first escalator and turn toward the second, I just spy his hand and part of his dark suit moving up. I follow.

He's at the top when I reach the bottom, and I see him angle left. I walk up the moving steps, gliding rapidly upward, and when I can see the third floor he's nowhere in sight.

That's all right. I saw him go leftward, toward the left rear of the store, and there aren't that many sections up here. I'll spot him any second.

But I don't. I move along that leftward aisle, looking both ways as I go along, as though searching for something to buy, not a man to kill, and he isn't anywhere. The final department up here is menswear, racks of suit jackets and sport coats along two right-angled walls, and he isn't here, either.

Where the hell did he go? I'm not worried yet, because whatever he's come here for will take him at least a few minutes to choose and buy. He's in this quadrant on this level of the store; I'll find him.

I'm still standing in the middle of menswear, frowning one way and another, deciding which route to take first, when HCE himself comes out from a doorway in the very corner, between the racks of suits and coats. He sees me, and smiles, and marches toward me, and I'm bewildered and frightened and ready to run. Then I realize, he's now wearing an oval blue-and-white nametag. It says DOLMEN'S in the upper half, and below that it says "Mr. Exman."

He works here. He's a suit salesman, that's why his own suit is so good. He's a suit salesman and I'm a customer.

"Yes, sir?" he says, hands clasped together, beaming at me in a way I know to be false to his nature and probably abhorrent to his soul.

I can't just stand and stare. I have to be quick-witted, I have to move things along smoothly, I have to not seem astonished, or guilty, or afraid. I have to be nothing at all, a blank customer, in front of a salesman. "Just looking," I say. "Thank you."

"If I can be of help," he says, with that smile, "you'll find me around."

There are no other customers in this section at this moment, and no other salesmen visible. We're alone here, but not usefully. "Yes, yes, thank you," I say. I don't want him to remember me.

Or, wait. Yes, I do. I'm thinking now, I'm seeing the possibilities all at once. I return his smile, I don't turn away, and I say, "It's a sport jacket I need, for summer, but I can't pick it out for myself, my wife has to be with me. So now I'm just looking around."

"Yes, of course," he says, nodding, sharing my male experience. "We always have to listen to the wife."

"She's a teacher," I explain, "so she's working today, but I could come back with her tomorrow."

"Good idea," he says, and slides two fingers into his inner jacket pocket and produces a business card. "I'll be here," he tells me, extending the card. "If you don't see me, ask."

This sort of job is mostly commission, of course. I take his card and look at it, and it's like his nametag, with the store name prominent above and his own name printed below. On the card, on the lower right, it also says, "Sales Representative." I nod at the card, and at HCE. "I'll be back," I promise. Then I switch the card to my left hand, stick out my right, and say, "Hutcheson."

"Mr. Hutcheson," he says, pleased.

We shake hands.

I walk away from him, my mind suddenly full of ideas. I put his card in my pocket, telling myself I must remember to throw it away soon. In the meantime, I have things to do, beginning with a telephone call.

There's a bank of phone booths just inside the main entrance of the store, next to the large sign giving Dolmen's opening hours; on Friday, it's "12 till 9." I throw HCE's card away in the trash barrel there, check my pockets to be sure I have enough change, and step into a booth, where I phone Marjorie, at home. We both say hello, and I say, "Could we eat dinner early tonight?" We usually eat around seven or seven-thirty.

"I suppose so," she says. "How early?"

"Well, I ran into a guy I used to be at Halcyon with. He's got some sort of idea, some business he thinks we could go into."

Sounding dubious—quite rightly—she says, "Do you think it's any good?"

"Don't know yet. He wants to show it to me at his house this evening, the specs he's done and everything."

"Does he want you to invest something?"

"Don't know that yet, either," I say, and laugh, and say, "If he does, he's barking up the wrong dead tree."

"He certainly is," she says. "What time would you want to leave?"

12 till 9. HCE started late, nearly two-thirty, so he'll surely stay till the store closes. "Seven," I say.

"We'll eat at six."

"Thanks, sweet," I say, and hang up.

And now, I have shopping to do. If you want to kill somebody, you can find everything you need for the job down at the mall.

37

Five minutes to nine. I open the driver's door beside me, and the interior light goes on.

I am back at the mall, and this time I am parked only four spaces from HCE's Taurus, where he'll have to walk by me. The left side of the Voyager is toward the mall building, and the long sliding door on the right side, away from the building, is open. The stubby hood is open, too, in front of me, exposing the chunky little engine. The new hammer rests on the depression between windshield and hood, where the windshield wiper lies when not in use; the hammer's business end is pointed downward, and its handle is out toward the side of the car.

My other purchases are all in the vehicle with me. Over there at the main entrance, the last shoppers trickle out. The parking lot is less than a quarter full, and none of the remaining cars are close to HCE and me.

What I'm planning has some risk to it, but without the gun anything I do must include some risk, and this plan has as little as possible, I think. The long June twilight is nearing its end, so, even though darkness hasn't really settled in yet, it's that tricky time of evening light when you're never quite sure what you're seeing. Also, no one but HCE is going to walk out this far across the parking lot, because our two vehicles are the only ones this far from the building. I expect to have the element of surprise on my side, and I have my purchases from the various shops in the mall.

Four minutes to nine. Three minutes to nine. Still three minutes to nine.

I keep looking at my watch, I can't help myself. My hands clench and clench the steering wheel, no matter how hard I try to relax, no matter how much I tell myself I shouldn't exhaust these hands, I'm going to need them soon.

Someone coming. A man, in silhouette against the lights of the mall behind him. In a dark suit, I think, and trudging as though he's tired, or discouraged. Or both.

He's passed every other parked car now, and he's still coming. Is he going to be so caught up in his own gloomy thoughts that he won't even notice me here?

No. He's a man who notices things, and he does see my open car door, the soft yellow interior light shining down on me, the open hood. "Trouble?" he calls.

I sigh, theatrically. "Won't start," I say, and then I

lean partway out of the car, as though I've just recognized him: "Oh, hi!"

He'd still been walking toward his own car, but now he veers in my direction, squinting at me, finally getting it: "Mr. Hutcheson?"

Yes, you'll remember the name, the hot prospect for a sport jacket, going to come back tomorrow with the wife. I say, "Yes, hello. Didn't expect to see you until tomorrow."

"What's wrong?" He frowns at the open hood. I've read him to be a take-charge kind of guy, somebody proud to be there in an emergency, and he's certainly acting the part.

I say, "I hate to admit it, but I don't know a goddam thing about car engines. I called my wife, she's going to have the garage send somebody out. God knows when."

"That'll cost you," he says.

"Don't remind me," I say. "And I really can't afford it, not now." I step out of the car, keeping my right hand down by my side, and gesture at the engine with my other hand. "There goes my new sport jacket."

Now it's personal. "No, no, Mr. Hutcheson," he chides me. "Never say die, that's my motto."

"I wish it was the car's motto," I say.

He laughs and moves toward the front of the Voyager, saying, "Let's just take a look. Do you mind?"

"Not at all," I say. "If you can save me a tow and a repair . . ."

"No promises." He picks up the hammer and raises an eyebrow at me. "Going to fix it with *this*?"

I move my hands, showing helplessness. "I thought I might have to loosen a wing nut."

Shaking his head, he puts the hammer back where I'd placed it, and leans over the engine, his head close to the open hood. "Try to turn it over," he tells me.

"Sure. Do you want a flashlight?"

"You've got one? Perfect," he says, and turns his head toward me, right hand reaching out for the flashlight, and I Mace him in the face. He cries out and slaps both palms to his eyes, as I drop the Mace can on the ground and reach for the hammer. I hit him on the temple as hard as I can, feeling his skull crack. Quickly, I hit him a second time, same spot.

He's falling. I jump forward, dropping the hammer, and throw my arms around him, holding him up. We must look like drunks dancing, but no one is close enough, with a clear enough view, to see anything going on here at all.

I crab-walk forward, carrying him, staggering under the weight, his limp feet dragging along the ground between mine. Moving like that, I hustle him around to the right side of the car and *lunge* him in onto the clear plastic tarp I've spread over the seat and floor. I hunch him up, hunch him up, and he's completely in.

Now I flip the excess tarp over the body, grab the dark green new blanket from the floor behind the seat, shake it out from its manufacturer's creases, and fling it over him. Then I step back and slide shut the door.

Brisk now, but not too fast. I walk around the front of the Voyager, closing the hood, picking up the Mace and hammer. I toss them across onto the passenger seat, climb in behind the wheel, and shut the door. Turn the key. Surprise; the engine works just fine.

I join the other laggard traffic rolling toward the exit, turn left, head up Route 9 toward Kingston and the bridge and home.

The only lights showing at my house are one table lamp in the living room, the reading light in Billy's bedroom, and the light at the head of the stairs. It's a little after eleven and Marjorie, as I'd hoped, has gone to bed. Otherwise, I'd have to drive around until she did retire, which would make me very nervous. Billy's awake, but he won't be coming out of his room.

I don't like it that I still have this body with me, but I was afraid to stop anywhere along the way to do the necessary preparation. You can find a spot that looks perfectly safe, dark and deserted, and be right in the middle of what has to be done when other people show up, or lights go on, or the police drive by. I'm safest at home, in my own garage, with the family safely tucked in for the night.

I thumb the remote control on the visor and the garage door opens, the light switching on in there. I drive in, hit the remote control again, and wait till the door shuts before I climb out and go over to turn on the main garage light. (That first one automatically switches off again three minutes after the garage door closes.)

Now to take care of the body, at least for tonight. I open the box of plastic bags I picked up at the mall, the very large kind called lawn-n-leaf, dark green, with a tie at the top. I then put on the white cotton gloves I also bought at the mall, open the Voyager's sliding side door, and look in at that mound of green blanket.

First I pull the blanket off and stuff it into the plastic bag. The hammer and the Mace I drop in there, too, and then I set aside that bag and pull another one out of the box.

This is the difficult part. I fold the clear tarp away from the body, and am relieved to see there's almost no blood, just a little around his crushed forehead and leaking from his nose and ears. Very little bleeding means he died the instant I hit him, which is better for both of us.

The body is still limber, but it won't be for long. I move his arms down across his body, elbows nearly straight, so his hands, the fingers partly curled, lie just above his crotch. Then I take the roll of heavy-gauge picture wire—another mall purchase—and loop the end of it around his belt, twisting the wire around itself to hold it secure.

The legs are sluggish, they don't want to move, but I press and push and force the knees to bend and the legs to fold up toward the body, until his knees are against his chest, his legs pressing down on his forearms. I cross the picture wire over his legs, snap off that length by bending it quickly backward and forward, and then secure this end also to his belt.

Now he's a compact package, legs and arms and torso all folded together. But I want to be sure nothing goes wrong, so I put my shoulder against his shoes and push upward, to make it possible to slide the next section of wire beneath him, wriggling it up as far as his waist. Then I let the body settle back down, as I snap apart this length of wire by bending it, and twist its ends together over his shins until it's very tight around him, pressing into him and becoming impossible to twist any tighter.

Getting this trussed body into another of the lawn-n-leaf bags isn't nearly as difficult as I'd expected. Of course, I might just be running on adrenaline, I don't know. In any event, in what seems like no time at all I have the second bag standing on the cement floor.

Now I open the first bag again, and stuff the plastic tarp into it. The idea is, the body never touched any part of my car, so if they do find it—which I hope they don't—there will be no fibers or paint or anything else to connect that body with this vehicle. And the parts that did touch the car, like the tarp and the blanket, go into a separate bag.

Also into this bag goes the rest of the roll of picture wire, the box of plastic bags and, at last, the gloves. When I tie this bag, I smear the plastic with my palms. No fingerprints.

It's my own work gloves from the workbench in here that I use when I wrestle the two full plastic trash bags into a corner of the garage, surrounded by the rest of the detritus that just naturally seems to grow there, particularly since we sold the Civic. The bags are both bulky, but one is much heavier than the other.

I look around the garage. Everything is normal. Nothing is amiss. I turn out the light and go in to bed.

38

Driving toward the recycling center, I find myself thinking about the concept of the learning curve, and how far along it I've come. And how very lucky I was that first time out, with the original HCE. What was his name? I'm having trouble remembering it.

Herbert Everly, that was it.

How simple that one was, simple and smooth and fast and clean. It encouraged me, it made everything else possible, because it made me believe the whole thing could be that impeccable. If I'd had the second HCE to do first, none of this would ever have happened. I just wouldn't have been up to it.

The idea of the learning curve is, the first time you do something you aren't very good at it, but you learn something about how the job is done. Then the second time, you're better, but still flawed, and you learn a little more. And so on, until you're perfect. The learning curve is an arc, beginning with a steep upward sweep, because you're learning a *lot* each time in the early days, and then gradually it flattens out to a level, as you learn in smaller and smaller increments the nearer you get to the ideal.

Well, I'm not perfect at this yet, God knows, I haven't attained the ideal, but I've come a long way up that learning curve since Herbert Everly. Of course, the irony in this one is, as the arc of my learning curve flattens toward complete competence, I'll have mastered a skill I'll never use again.

I certainly hope I'll never have to use it again. But it is, I admit, a useful skill to possess.

Earlier today, I took Marjorie to her Saturday job at the New Variety, and when I backed the Voyager out of the garage even I couldn't readily see anything different in there. The dark bulky bags leaned together well in the back, away from daylight, amid birdseed bags and paint cans and winter boots and all the rest of the stuff garages breed when no one is looking.

On the way to the movie house, I told Marjorie the story I'd made up in bed last night, before falling asleep, about the friend's moneymaking scheme that had caused me to go out for several hours after dinner. The story I told her was that my friend reminded me that the United States government shreds its old paper money to destroy it, and it was his idea to talk the government into letting us make fresh paper out of the shredded pulp. We would make paper bags, colored green, with dollar signs on them, and market them under the name Money Bags; they would be both useful and a great novelty item.

I told Marjorie I'd thought it was a clever idea—she seemed less sure—but that I'd asked my friend what were *we* supposed to do with it? We're both knowledgeable about turning pulp into paper, but that's all. His scheme needed a politician, to talk the government into letting us have the paper, and a marketer, to get the Money Bags out there. "I told him," I explained to Marjorie, "if he could find a couple of people like that, and they were serious about it, I'd be happy to join in."

"Not in a million years," she said, and I had to agree.

When I came back home, after dropping Marjorie at the movie house, both Betsy and Billy were out, she at a rehearsal of a play she's doing at college—*Arsenic and Old Lace*; she's one of the aunts, in much makeup—and he off at a friend's house, engrossed in the friend's new computer software (he'll make do that way until life improves around here).

I opened the garage door, drove the Voyager in, shut the garage door, moved the rear seat of the car out of the way, and loaded the two plastic bags. And now I'm on my way to the recycling center.

The recycling center, of course, is what used to be called the dump, and part of it still is that. There's private trash collection in our neighborhood, but it's considerably cheaper to sort the trash yourself and bring it to the recycling center. Glass and tin and paper and cardboard they take for free, and garbage they take for fifty cents per large plastic bag. The bags are tossed into a chute, and from there they go into a compacting garbage truck, and from there they're taken to a landfill operation down on Long Island Sound.

A sea voyage for Hauck Exman. He's a Marine, he'll like that.

39

My friend with the Money Bags idea turns out to be named Ralph Upton, in honor of Upton "Ralph" Fallon, the last obstacle between me and my new job. It became necessary for this friend to have a further existence, I realized, once Hauck Exman was out of the way and it was time to think about dealing with URF.

Here's the thing: URF is employed. He's got my job, which means he's at work at the mill five days a week, which means I won't be able to ever get at him until the evenings. Weekends are complicated by Marjorie's job at the New Variety and by our own fixed weekend rituals, the Sunday *Times* and all that. So it's a work-night or nothing, and it isn't going to be nothing.

And that meant the creator of Money Bags had to go on being a presence in my life. "He has more ideas," I told Marjorie, when I picked her up from Dr. Carney's office at six on Monday, yesterday, three days after I dealt with Exman. "He has a million ideas, and who knows, one of them might turn out to be something. Anyway, he likes to bounce his notions off me and show me the presentations he's done and all that, and to tell the truth, sweet, I'd rather be doing something than nothing."

"I know you would," she said, and gave me a tender smile, and that was that.

This morning, we drove down to Marshal to spend our hour with Longus Quinlan, and to my surprise I'm enjoying these sessions now, finding them more valuable than I would have guessed. I think any marriage, after a while, falls into routines and automatic responses. Time goes by, and you no longer *see* each other clearly, you just act as though the other person's a robot, with machined and well-known responses to everything, and then *you* act like a robot, and all the life has drained out of the relationship.

Now that the awfulness of Marjorie's affair is finished, and now that Quinlan has given up trying to probe into my personal view of the world, we're dealing with what we went there to deal with, the marriage, and I think it's helping. We're becoming surprised by each other again, we're remembering why we liked each other in the first place.

If only I could tell her about this other business . . . but of course I never can. I know better. There are some strains you don't put on a person, no matter what.

Anyway, that was this morning, and this evening we

ate dinner at six-thirty, and now, at quarter past seven, I am on the road, heading west toward Arcadia, NY.

The long days of June, the long bright evenings. I'm driving along, crossing into New York State, and it's still sunny and nice. It occurs to me, as I drive; I'm beginning my commute. My new commute.

40

There's still daylight along the top of the slope, but the road into Arcadia descends into the blackness of night, decorated with neon from the town's two bars (but not from the closed luncheonette), brighter white and red light from the Getty station atop the farther slope, and the glary yellowish worklights around the mill. There are no lights visible inside the mill buildings; they're a success story, but they're only working one shift.

As I drive down the slope toward town and the dam and the quick black stream running through it, a stray thought occurs to me. What if Arcadia's success story isn't quite as glowing as the magazine made it seem? What if, even though they might not have gone all the way to downsizing, they're doing a reduction in staff through attrition, not taking on any new hires when people leave? What if I've gone through all this, and I deal with URF as well, and they don't replace him? The joke would certainly be on me, wouldn't it?

But, no. They're going to need an experienced man to run that line. If they had a night shift, then maybe the night shift man could move to days while he trains an assistant, already on the payroll, to take over at night. But this way, with only one shift, they'll hire.

I know what URF looks like, from having seen him that one time in the luncheonette, so now my first job is to find out where he lives. I don't expect much from this visit, just a little reconnaissance, to get an idea of the situation.

The Voyager's gas gauge shows just under half a tank, so I drive down to the bottom of the slope, cross the bridge on the dam, drive up the other slope, and stop at the Getty station. I fill the tank, pay the stocky woman at the counter inside, and ask if she has a phone book.

Yes, she does, though she doesn't say so. Without a word, she pulls a tattered thin phone book from under the counter, and I move off away from her a bit, as though to keep the counter clear for other customers— there are none—while I leaf through and find FALLON U R Cty Rte 92 Slt.

I don't care about the phone number, at least for now. I look at the map on the back cover of the phone book, to see what town "Slt" might be, and it's probably a place called Slate, that looks to be not very far from here.

I thank the woman as I return the phone book, and ask her where County Route 92 is, and now she has to speak, though minimally. Pointing up the road, out of town, she says, "Six miles. Where you going?"

"Slate."

"Take the left."

I thank her, and go back out to my full vehicle, and take it six miles and a little more to the county road, where green signs with cream letters at the intersection direct me toward various villages. Slate is the third one down on the sign pointing left.

This is a winding hilly road. It's hard to see what's alongside it, except for the occasional lit window of a house and once, well back from the road, the brightly lit interior of a barn.

I may not find URF's house at all tonight, unless his name is on the mailbox. Driving along through this darkness, I try to think of some way to get here on the weekend, in the daytime, either while Marjorie's cashiering at the New Variety on Saturday afternoon, or while we're normally lying around with the news-paper on Sunday. My new friend Ralph Upton may come in handy here.

FALLON.

That was so abrupt I almost missed it. I'm alone on the road, so it doesn't matter that I slam on the brakes. I hadn't seen house lights for a while, so I hadn't ex-pected anything, and I wasn't looking for a mailbox. Then all at once there it was, on the right side of the road, in the shape of a fake log cabin, with a red metal band running along above the roof with the name in white letters.

I back up to take a second look, and that's it, all right, with a blacktop driveway leading in toward darkness next to it. I squint and lean toward the right window, and now I do see a dim light back in there.

How much do I do tonight? Is this the right Fallon? I drive on, looking for a place to stop, and just a bit farther along there's a broad metal cattle-gate leading into a field on the left, with blacktop from the gate out to the road. I turn around and leave the Voyager there, and walk back.

If I'm questioned? I'm lost. I'm looking for Arcadia.

At first the evening seems almost pitch-black, but as my eyes adjust to life without headlights I realize there's a sky full of stars, giving a cool but soft gray light, like a powder over everything. There's no moon, at least not yet. I walk along, completely alone, no traffic, nothing in sight, and here's the mailbox. I turn and walk in along the blacktop driveway, and up ahead I see the house obscurely, through a thick necklace of trees.

This must have been part of a working farm at one time. Whatever woods had been here were long ago cleared, except for those immediately around the house, which looks to be a couple of hundred years old, small but sprawling. One light gleams deep inside, not very brightly.

There's nobody home. You can tell that sort of thing. People leave a light on to discourage break-ins, but they leave too dim a light, too unimportant a light.

On the other hand, many country people have dogs. Has URF a dog? Cautiously, I approach the house. I am still, if need be, the lost traveler seeking directions.

The house has been added to over the years, mostly with rooms attached on the same side as the driveway, making the house increasingly wide. These first rooms I pass are dark, and don't suggest that anybody ever enters through here. The driveway continues on and widens in front of the house, where two vehicles are parked; a tall large pickup truck, its hood as high as my chest, and an old Chevy or Pontiac, very wide and long, that sags in a way to suggest it hasn't been moved in several years.

And here is what is probably the main entrance, at the windowed door of an enclosed porch, through which another windowed door can be seen and, dimly, a kitchen, with the light source somewhere beyond that.

If there were a dog on the premises, wouldn't he have made his presence known by now? Yes; dogs are not shy about announcing themselves. As a further test, I rattle the front door, which is locked but very loose in its frame. No reaction from within.

A professional burglar would, I am sure, get through this locked door in about ten seconds. I would rather try to find some other way in, so I leave that entrance and continue along the front wall, and when I turn the corner at the end I discover that originally *this* was the front of the house. With all the additions, and the driveway and the twentieth century, it has become the back instead, but this is the original section, facing the other way.

It's a standard Colonial center-hall design, a formal entrance door with two large windows on each side, and a second floor above with five windows, directly above the windows and door below. Inside, when it was first built, there would have been a hall and a stairway beyond this door, and four large rooms; to left and right downstairs, and the same upstairs. With the addition of electricity and indoor plumbing and central heating, all of these old places have been changed and changed and changed again, so that by now you never know what you'll find when you open one of these Colonial doors.

Not even if you're an invited guest.

In most of these old farmhouses, though, this original main entrance is no longer much used, and I see the stone landing in front of this door still has some of last fall's leaves mounded on it. I step up there, turn the handle, and push, and it seems to me it isn't locked, just stuck. I don't want to break anything, alert URF that anything is going on here, but I want to get in if I can. With the handle completely turned and my feet braced among the fallen leaves, I lean my weight against the door, not hitting it but just exerting steady pressure.

I feel it give, and I ease off, but it's still stuck. I lean again, and all at once it makes a quick sound like a sheet of paper ripping, and pops open.

Darkness. A musty smell, like laundry. The air inside is a little cooler and a little damper than the air outside. There isn't a sound. I step in.

I push the door closed behind me. It resists the last inch or so, with small compression sounds, this time like paper being crumpled, but I heave against it with my shoulder and finally hear it click shut.

And now the house. The faintest of light shimmers somewhere off to my right, more than one room away. By its hints, I can see the large doorway just here, and then what might be furniture, and then another, slightly more defined, doorway twenty feet or so away.

I move toward the light, cautiously, not wanting to trip over or disturb anything, and my knee does find a sofa arm. I detour around it, touch nothing else, and reach this next doorway.

Which leads to a corridor. The light source is a room on the left, and when I inch forward and look in, it's a bedroom. A quilt has been thrown somewhat carelessly over a double bed. The small lamp on the left bedside table is lit. There's a wide mirrored dresser, a chair piled with clothing, a lot of shoes scattered on the floor.

I'm beginning to think URF isn't married. I was wondering where his family was, thinking they might all have gone out to a movie or something, but this bedroom has the look of a man who lives alone.

When I get to the next doorway on that side, though, from the little I can see into it, it's a children's bedroom, for two kids. Bunk beds, low dressers, posters on the walls, toys on the floor. Is he a widower?

A bit farther along on the opposite side is the kitchen I saw from outside. I enter it, and cross to look out past the enclosed porch at the road. When he comes home, I'll see his headlights. If he's with his family, I'll have time to ease myself out the door I came in, far from the route they'll take. If he's alone, we'll see what happens.

I check the refrigerator, and it contains milk and cold cuts and soft drinks and beer and very little else. It just doesn't look like a family refrigerator.

I open and close kitchen drawers, because I know there'll be a flashlight here somewhere. There's a flashlight in every country kitchen, because country electricity goes off with fair frequency. Yes, here it is.

Now I can explore the rest of the house, and I do, and find several empty rooms, and underfurnished rooms, and it seems to me URF lives in four rooms out of ten, all on the first floor. He lives in the bedroom with its attached bath, and he lives in the kitchen, and he lives in the first room I went through, with the sofa I kneed and a TV set and a coffee table and an end table and a floor lamp and a telephone and nothing else, and he lives in a room beyond the kitchen, originally a guest room, that he's turned into an office, the same as I have at home. In this office he keeps his tax records and work records and all the paperwork of normal life.

I spend some time in this office, using only the flashlight, because I want to learn as much as I can about

URF, and in his case I haven't had the advantage of a resumé, nor did I ever bother to do a public records check. The windows here face the driveway and the road, so I'll know when he comes home.

It takes me half an hour to go through all the stuff in here, or at least to go through it enough to get a reading on the man. He's divorced, that's the first thing, and it looks to me as though he's been divorced three times. He has three grown-up kids who live in California and write him the occasional not-very-personal letter, and he has two younger kids who come to visit him in the summer and at Christmastime. He makes a good living at Arcadia—though not, I notice, quite as good as I used to make at Halcyon—but he's constantly in debt, with an entire manila folder of dunning letters. He's usually behind in his child support, but scrambles to make it up twice a year, just before they arrive for their visit.

The other thing about him, which surprises me a little, is that he's very serious about his job. From that article where I first read about him, I'd thought he was more of a lightweight, but I see that he keeps a file of articles torn from the newspapers and our trade journals, having to do with our line of work, and that he underlines sections and makes mostly sensible remarks in margins, and seems very intent on keeping up with the industry.

Well, that's fine. I'm good at the job, too, and I'd like my new employer to have somebody first-rate to compare me to, so he'll know what a valuable man he's getting.

The other important fact is, those two younger children always seem to start their summer visit just about the first of July, which means a week from now. So that's a deadline; much better to get all this taken care of before they arrive.

There's nothing else for me to look for in the office, and nothing more to learn. When I leave there and return the flashlight to its drawer, I see by the illuminated hands of the kitchen clock that it isn't even ten. Wherever URF is, tomorrow's a workday, so he'll probably be home fairly soon.

And he won't have his family with him.

My guess is that URF's in one of those two bars in Arcadia. That's where he'll spend his evenings after work, having a hamburger or some pizza for dinner. When he gets home, I don't imagine he'll be completely sober.

There's no point my driving to Arcadia to look for him. I'd be halfway there when he would pass me, coming home, and I wouldn't know it.

I go back into the office, from where I get the best view of the driveway and the road. I sit at his desk, in the darkness there, and after a while lean back in his swivel chair and put my feet up on the desk, and I keep an eye on the windows.

From time to time, a vehicle passes along the road out there, but not often. I sit here at URF's desk, with nothing to do but wait and watch and think, and I can't help but go over and over all the things I've had to do the last two months. Some of them were much harder than others. Some were very hard indeed.

On the other hand, some were easy. And I truly think, more recently, I've gained more confidence, and that makes it easier yet.

Oh! I'm falling asleep. No good, no good.

I get to my feet, stamping around in a circle in this dark room. I can't be *asleep* when he gets here.

I leave the office and go down the hall to his bedroom, just to be near some light, to beat off that sleepiness. And now for the first time, as long as I'm in here, and to have something to do, I make a quick search of the bedroom, and the one thing I find of interest is the pistol in his bedside drawer, next to the flashlight and the Tums. Of course I don't know guns, except my father's Luger, but I can tell this is some kind of pistol, with that round cylinder to give it the pregnant look. It's black, and the handle is a bit worn as though it's old. It looks like the starter gun used in a race.

I don't touch it. I close the drawer, and merely remember it's there.

Back in the hall, I glance into and through the kitchen, and out the porch windows, and I see the headlights just as they make the turn into the driveway. Weaving, slow-moving, hesitant.

URF is coming home.

41

He's drunk. I can tell that much before I even see
him, from the way he drives his car, the excess caution
with which he steers this dark-colored Subaru station
wagon around the driveway curve toward his house.

There are half a dozen methods, right in this house,
by which I can finish him off with no trouble, and even
make it look like accidental death. Which would be a
lot better than yet another murder of a paper mill manager.

The Subaru jolts to a stop, out front. I'm not watching from the kitchen, I've moved on to his living room,
his TV room, whatever he might call it. In one of the
windows there, I can stand without any light behind
me, and watch. I was afraid, if I'd stood in the kitchen
doorway, he might see a silhouette.

Everything he does is in slow motion. Some time
after he stops, the lights go off, so I suppose the engine
went off then, too; I'm not sure I can hear it, through

the glass. And then, a little while after that, he opens his door and climbs wearily out. The interior light goes on, but my concentration is on URF—I'm thinking of him now as a kind of dog, named "Urf"—as he slams the car door and makes his way around the front of it.

Come in, come in. Come home, go to bed, rest, sleep. I'll wait here. Or farther back, in the unused room on the other side of the unused entrance, just in case you decide to come on in here and fall asleep in front of the television set.

He makes his way around the front of the car, leaning on the hood, and then he turns right again, and opens the passenger door, and a woman gets out.

Damn! I stare at her, and she's about as drunk as he is. A large woman in sweater and slacks, weaving. I see her stand beside the car, holding on to the open door, and I hear her voice, quite loud: "Where the hell is this?"

"*My* place, Cindy! Damn! *You* know my place!"

She grumbles something, and moves forward. He slams the Su-baru's passenger door and follows her, and in a minute I hear him fumbling with his keys.

Not tonight. He picked her up at the bar, and he's done it before. So not tonight.

But he doesn't pick up a woman *every* night, not Urf. There are nights he sleeps alone.

As the stumbling sounds of them move across the kitchen, I fade back across the TV room into the hall and to the door I used when I came in tonight. I tug on

it, and it opens more easily this time, more quietly. Not
that they'd hear much. I slide outside.

There are more lights on now, in the kitchen and in
the bedroom. I skirt around all three vehicles parked
here, staying out of the lightspill. I walk away down
the driveway. I am not at all discouraged.

42

I park the same place I did on Tuesday, and walk back down the dark country road toward Urf's house. It's nine-thirty, Thursday night, the 26th of June, and I am here to kill him. He could have an entire harem with him tonight, I don't care. Tonight he dies.

I'm feeling such time pressure now. It's not only that I've been at this for nearly two months, though that's part of it. Having to think about these deadly things all the time, do these deadly things, it's wearing me down. I take less pleasure in life, and for that I don't blame the downsizing, the chop, the *adjustment*, whatever you want to call it; I blame this grim hell I'm living through. Food doesn't taste as good as it used to, simple pleasures like music or television or driving or just feeling the sun on my face have all flattened and become drab, and as for sex, well . . .

Though that problem *did* start with the downsizing. Once I'm out of this. Once it's over. Once I'm out of this and safe on the farther shore, with the new job, with my life back. Then the colors will be bright again.

So that's a reason to want it over, but now there's an even more compelling one, and that's Urf's children. If they follow their normal pattern, and why shouldn't they, next week is when they'll arrive for their summer visit with their father. The 4th of July is on Friday this year, so they'll surely want their travel to be finished well before the weekend, which means I have less than a week before they show up to complicate my life beyond imagining.

No time at all. Weekends are impossible. Mondays and Wednesdays are impossible as well, because of Marjorie's job with Dr. Carney. By the time I pick her up at six in the evening and drive her home, with dinner still to come, it's far too late to set out for Slate, New York. So if I don't get him tonight, I won't have another try at him for five days, not until next Tuesday, and by then his children could already be here.

I'm a little later tonight, deliberately, assuming his pattern is never to come home directly from work. And I seem to be right; his house is as dark as it was when I arrived on Tuesday. The nightlight in his bedroom, nothing more.

There's a learning curve with this house, as well. Tonight, I walk past the two parked vehicles and the entrance to the enclosed porch, go directly on down to the end and around the corner, then straight through the original front door. I walk through the TV room without kneeing the sofa, glance in at the lit bedroom and the dim kitchen, and make my way to the dark office, where I sit again at his desk.

Not home yet. Out drinking his dinner. Anesthetizing himself, just for me.

It's a little warm in here, but I keep my windbreaker on. In the pockets are the things I've brought, just in case. The coil of picture wire. The small roll of duct tape. The four-inch length of heavy iron pipe, one end wrapped with electric tape for a better grip. The cotton gloves.

I don't have a particular plan, not yet. It all depends what the circumstances are, when Urf gets here.

I put my feet up on the desk, and cross my ankles. A car drives by, southbound, out there on the road. Then nothing. I sit and wait for Urf to come home.

43

Light. I blink.

"Wake up, you!"

"Oh, my God!" I twitch, and my feet fall off the desk and thud to the floor, jolting me forward in the swivel chair. I stare in the harshness of the overhead light. My eyes are gummy, my mouth sticky.

I fell asleep.

He's in the doorway. His left hand is still across his body, fingers touching the light switch. His right hand holds the revolver I last saw in his bedside table. He stares at me. He weaves left and right in the doorway. Even as I'm realizing the horror of the situation, I can see that he's pretty drunk. "Mister . . ." I say, trying to remember his name. Urf, not Urf. Fallon.

"Don't move!"

My hand has started upward, to wipe my sticky-feeling mouth, but now I freeze, hand in midair. "Fallon," I say. "Mister Fallon."

"What are you doin here?" He's aggressive because he's afraid, and he's afraid because he's bewildered.

What *am* I doing here? I have to have a reason, something I can tell him. "Mister Fallon," I say again, stuck at that part of it.

"You broke into my house!"

"No! No, I didn't." I protest that in full honesty.

"The door was locked!"

"No, it wasn't." Even though he told me not to move, I do move, pointing away to my right as I say, "The big door by the living room. I knocked, and . . . *that* wasn't locked."

He frowns mightily, and I see him trying to think about that door that's never used. *Is* it locked? He doesn't know. He says, "It's trespassing."

Fair enough. Break in or walk in, it is trespassing, he's right about that. I say, "I wanted to wait for you. I'm sorry I fell asleep."

"*I* don't know you," he says. I'm not being particularly threatening or intimidating, so his aggression and fear are becoming less, but he's still as bewildered as I am as to what reason I'm going to give for my being here.

Is it because we're both paper line managers? Polymer paper? I've just come by for some shoptalk, a little chat about our fascinating employment? At this time of night? Unannounced, walking into his empty house?

And then I see it, all at once, and I turn my honest

face up to him, and I say, "Mr. Fallon, I need your help."

He squints at me. The revolver is still pointed in my direction, but he no longer touches the light switch. That other hand is pressed against the doorframe now, to help him keep from weaving. He says, "Did Edna send you, is that what this is?"

I remember, from his tax returns, that Edna is an ex-wife. I say, "I don't know anybody named Edna, Mr. Fallon. My name is Burke Devore, I'm the production line manager for the polymer paper line at Halcyon Mills over in Connecticut, over in Belial."

Again he squints. "Halcyon," he says. He keeps up with the trade journals, but how closely? Will he know it's all over at Halcyon? He says, "Didn't they get merged?"

"Yes," I say. "That's the whole trouble, it looks like they're gonna move the whole goddam thing up to Canada—"

"Cocksuckers," he says.

"I just don't want to lose my job," I say.

"Lotta that goin around," he says.

"Too much of it. Mr. Fallon," I say, "I read about you in *Pulp*, remember that piece a few months ago?"

"They got some stuff wrong in there," he complains, "made me look like a damn fool doesn't know his own job."

"I thought it made you look terrific at your job," I tell him, lying. "That's why I'm here."

He shakes his head, befuddled. "I don't know what the *fuck* you think you're talkin about," he says.

"I'm good at my job, Mr. Fallon, believe me I am," I tell him, with great sincerity, "but these days you can't just be good at the job, you've got to be perfect at it. I don't have much time. They're going to decide pretty soon this summer, do I stay on, does the line stay here or does it get pulled to Canada—"

"Fuckin bastards."

"I thought," I tell him, "if I could talk to Mr. Fallon, if we could just *talk* about the job, I could maybe pick up some pointers, get to where I could— I can *do* the job, Mr. Fallon, but I'm not that good, talking about it, I can't express myself. In that piece in *Pulp*, you could express yourself. I was hoping, my idea was, we could just talk, and then maybe I'd be better at it on the job. There's gonna be an interview, I'm not exactly sure when."

He studies me. The revolver now dangles at his side, pointing at the floor. He says, "You sound desperate."

"I am desperate. I don't want to lose that job. I keep thinking about it and thinking about it, and today I finally made the decision to come here and ask you for help, and after dinner I drove over here from Connecticut."

"Whyn'tcha use the phone?"

I give a wry grin and a little shrug. "Be some nut on the phone? I figured, if I come here, I can explain myself. But then you weren't home."

"So you busted in."

"The door isn't locked, Mr. Fallon," I say. "Honest, it isn't."

He thinks about that, nodding slowly, and then says, "Let's go see."

"All right."

He steps back from the doorway, and makes a waving gesture with the revolver. It's not pointed at the floor any more, but it's not quite pointed at me either. "You first," he says.

I go first, through the house, which now has lights on in every room, all the way to the door beyond the TV room, which I open onto the black night outside. I turn to him and say, "See?"

He glares at the door. "The goddam thing isn't supposed to be open like that." He comes over, switching the revolver to his left hand so he can slam the door, open it, slam it again, and then peer closely at the lock mounted on the inside of it. He tries to turn the lock's little handle, but it won't move. "Damn thing's painted stuck," he says. "Stuck open. Be a son of a bitch."

During this, I could hit him about seven times with the iron pipe in my windbreaker pocket, but I don't. I think things are going to work out better than that.

He slams the door again, turns to me, shakes his head. "I gotta get that fixed," he tells me. "Anyway, you see how it looked, I come home, there's *you* right there, asleep in my den."

"I'm sorry I fell asleep."

"Well, you had a long drive. Wha'd you say your name was?"

"Burke," I tell him. "Burke Devore."

"Burke," he says, "I know you won't mind if I have a look at your wallet."

I say, "You still think there's something wrong with me? All right." And I take out my wallet and hand it to him.

He takes it from me with his left hand, gesturing again with the revolver in his right. "Whyn'tcha have a seat on the sofa in there?" he suggests.

So I do, and he walks across to the other side of the room, weaving a little, to put the revolver on top of the TV set while he looks at all the cards and papers in my wallet, peering owlishly at them, having trouble focusing, I suppose, because he's had too much to drink.

Well, this can only help. Not only will he see I've told him the truth about my name, but I now realize my old employee ID from Halcyon is still in there, I never did find a moment to throw that away. (I probably didn't want to throw it away.)

I see the instant he finds the ID; his brow clears at once, and he's grinning in a much more friendly fashion when he next looks over at me. "Well, Mr. Devore," he says, "it looks like I owe you an apology."

"Not at all," I say. "I'm the one to apologize, walking in here, falling asleep . . ."

"Over and done with," he says, and crosses the room to hand me my wallet. "You want a beer?"

"Very much so," I say, and *that* isn't a lie.

"You want a little something in it?"

"Only if you are."

"Come on to the kitchen," he says, then looks at the revolver on the TV set as though surprised and not pleased to see it still around. Picking it up, pointing it away from me, toward the hall, he says, "Let me get rid of this."

"Fine by me," I tell him, with a shaky smile.

He laughs and starts off, saying, "I'm Ralph, by the way. You're Burke?"

"That's right."

I stand in the hall while he stows the revolver in his bedside table drawer. Coming back out, he says, "Be damned if I know what help I can be, but I'll try. A lot of these owners— Come on along."

We walk toward the kitchen, and he continues, "A lot of these owners are what I would call pricks. I've heard about them. Got no more loyalty than a ferret."

"That's about right," I say.

"Fortunately," he says, slurring the word, "we got good owners at Arcadia."

"That's good to hear."

In the kitchen, he pulls two cans of beer from the refrigerator and hands me one, then opens an upper cabinet door and brings out a bottle of rye. "Sweeten to taste," he suggests, putting the bottle on the counter.

I follow his lead. He opens the beer, takes a deep swig, then fills up the can from the rye bottle. I open and drink, and when he hands me the bottle I do a trick a bartender showed me at a company party years ago. One of the people on my line was getting drunk on vodka and grapefruit juice, and when I had a word with the bartender he told me, "I already cut him off." "But you're still pouring," I objected, and he grinned and said, "Next time, watch." So I did, and if you weren't looking for it you wouldn't see it. He put in the ice cubes and then tipped the vodka bottle over the glass, slipping his thumb over the open top just before it would pour, and pulling the thumb back again as the bottle came upright, all in one easy sliding pouring movement. Then he filled the glass with grapefruit juice and handed it to the drunk, who didn't get any *more* drunk at that party.

So that's what I do now. I drink some of the beer, and then, half turned away from Fallon, I tilt the rye bottle over the hole in the top of the can, keeping the rye in the bottle with my thumb, then stand the bottle on the counter.

Fallon wants to click beer cans, so we do, and he says, "To the bosses, the rotten ones. May we piss on their graves," and we drink. "Come on and sit down," he says, and staggers a bit as he pulls a chair out at the kitchen table.

We sit across from one another at the table, and he says, "Tell me about your line there. What kinda extruder you got? No, wait a second." And he gets up and reels over to the counter to grab the rye bottle and bring it back and plunk it on the table between us. Then he reels to the refrigerator and gets two more beer cans and smacks them down at our places. "For later," he says, and sits down and says, "So? Tell me whatcha got."

44

I'm sorry when, at last, he does fall asleep. I shouldn't be sorry, because it's very late, past midnight by his kitchen clock, but to tell the truth, I enjoyed our conversation. He's okay, Ralph Fallon. More crude than most of the people I know, because he came up from the laborer ranks instead of out of college like most of us, but a bright guy and very knowledgeable about the job. In fact, he told me a couple of things he's done on the line there at Arcadia that are very interesting, methods I'll certainly keep in place when I take over.

And he can definitely drink. He was already drunk when he came home, and since we've been seated together here at his kitchen table he's had eight more beers, each of them well laced with rye. I haven't kept up at all (I don't think he expects people to keep up with him), having only five beers and not adding any whiskey—though I did fake it every time—but I'm feeling it. I'm feeling a lot of things, really; the beer, the lateness of the hour, the knowledge that I'm almost at the end of this series of trials, and a stupid sentimental attachment to Ralph Fallon.

In my wooziness, my weakness, I even try to imagine scenarios in which Fallon lives and yet I get what I want. I talk him into retiring, or I explain my situation and he offers me a job as co-manager on the line, or he suddenly wakes up and tells me Arcadia is going to two shifts and will need a night manager on the line.

But none of that happens, or is going to happen. My long pleasant beery shoptalk session with Ralph Fallon is over; it is time to be serious.

Weary, feeling as though I weigh a thousand pounds, I get to my feet and reach for my windbreaker, on the back of the chair to my right. In the right pocket is the small roll of duct tape. I take it out and look at it, and then look at Fallon, slumped in his chair across the table from me, chin on chest, left hand on the table, right hand in his lap.

I don't want to do this. But there are always things we don't want to do, and we do them.

I walk around the table, go to my knees beside Fallon, and very gently tape his right ankle to the chair leg. Then I crawl around him on all fours—it's too much effort to stand and walk and kneel again—and tape his left ankle to the other chair leg. Then, with a small groan, I do stand.

It would be safer, surer, if I could tape his wrists together, but I'm afraid if I tried to move his arms he would wake up, so instead I run tape around the chair back and his torso, just above the elbows. It's tricky doing this without letting the tape make too much noise when I pull it from the roll, but at last I get it around him twice, snug and secure. He'll be able to move his hands and forearms, but not, I think, effectively.

With what I do next, he's certainly going to wake up, so I'd better do it fast and clean. I pull off two small lengths of tape, stand over him with a piece of duct tape in each hand, then with an abrupt motion slap the first piece against his mouth, pressing it against the flesh.

He does wake up, startled, eyes popping open, all of his limbs jerking. He's still trying to understand what's happening and why he can't move when I press the second piece of duct tape over his nose, squeezing the nostrils shut. Then I step back from him and turn away, to search the kitchen drawers while he dies.

What I need is a candle. Like the flashlight, and for the same reason of unreliable electric service, every country kitchen keeps a stub of candle somewhere.

Yes, here it is, in the drawer with the balls of string and the extra twisties and the spare keys, a short fat candle of the kind people light in church when they want their prayers answered. I take down a saucer from an upper cabinet, put it on the counter near the stove, put the candle on the saucer.

Meantime, Fallon is making terrible noises. Now that I've found the candle, now that there's nothing to distract me, I hate those noises, and so I leave the room, carrying my windbreaker with me.

I put on the windbreaker as I walk through the house. The gloves and the iron pipe are in the other outer pocket. I won't be needing the pipe, but I will take it away with me; in the meantime, I put on the gloves. Starting at the far end of the house, at the front door, I use my gloved hands to wipe everything I can think of that I touched, and I turn off the lights as I go, except that I leave the bedside lamp lit in his bedroom.

Fallon is quiet now, slumped again. I remove the duct tape from his ankles and then his torso, and he falls forward so his head hits the table. I have to lift his head, trying not to see those staring eyes, and when I pull the last two pieces of duct tape away I discover he's thrown up, into his mouth and then into his nose and lungs because it couldn't come out through the tape. So he didn't suffocate, he drowned. A miserable end, either way.

I use one of his small plastic trash bags for the pieces of duct tape, then put the bag in my windbreaker pocket. I use one of his wooden kitchen matches to light the candle.

In New York State, gas stoves don't have pilot lights, they have electric igniters. I switch on the front two burners of his stove, leave them on high, and blow out the flames. I then leave the kitchen, closing its inner door behind me, so there are now no openings from the kitchen.

By the light from the bedroom, I make my way back through the house and out the door that Fallon hadn't known was unlocked. I walk briskly past the front of the house, seeing the low winking light of the candle flame, and the four tall skinny metal bottles of propane gas tucked into the corner of the outside wall where the enclosed porch ends. I continue on out the driveway and down the road to the Voyager.

I have no idea how long it will take. I don't want to be here when it happens, but I want to be close enough to know it did happen. And I assume, when the stove blows, it will set off the propane bottles as well. There shouldn't be too much of Fallon or the kitchen left, but there should be just enough to make it clear what happened. A drunk fell asleep, unaware that he'd miscalculated in turning on the stove. I don't suppose anyone who knows Ralph Fallon will be surprised.

I get into the Voyager and drive slowly past the house and on the few miles to the intersection where I should turn right for Arcadia. I stop there, and look in the rearview mirror, and then make a U-turn in the middle of the intersection. There's no other traffic at all.

I'm about half a mile from the intersection, on the way back to Fallon's house, when the sudden yellow light switches on some distance ahead of me, showing woods and houses in silhouette. It begins to die down, as though someone had switched on a bright light and then smoothly rotated the dimmer, but then it flares brighter than before, with red and white mixed into the yellow, and again dims down, and the double blast rolls over the car like a wave, like a physical thing.

I stop the car. I make another U-turn. I drive home.

45

Every era, and every nation, has its own characteristic morality, its own code of ethics, depending on what the people think is important. There have been times and places when honor was considered the most sacred of qualities, and times and places that gave every concern to grace. The Age of Reason promoted reason to be the highest of values, and some peoples—the Italians, the Irish—have always felt that feeling, emotion, sentiment was the most important. In the early days of America, the work ethic was our greatest expression of morality, and then for a while property values were valued above everything else, but there's been another more recent change. Today, our moral code is based on the idea that the end justifies the means.

There was a time when that was considered improper, the end justifying the means, but that time is over. We not only believe it, we say it. Our government leaders always defend their actions on the basis of their goals. And every single CEO who has commented in public on the blizzard of downsizings sweeping America has explained himself with some variant on the same idea: The end justifies the means.

The end of what I'm doing, the purpose, the goal, is good, clearly good. I want to take care of my family; I want to be a productive part of society; I want to put my skills to use; I want to work and pay my own way and not be a burden to the taxpayers. The means to that end has been difficult, but I've kept my eye on the goal, the purpose. The end justifies the means. Like the CEOs, I have nothing to feel sorry for.

The weekend following the death of Ralph Fallon, I spend in a kind of contented daze, not thinking, not worrying, not making plans. The call will come, I know it will. The position is open, and the call will come.

But the call does not come on Monday, and by midafternoon, alone in the house, Marjorie at Dr. Carney's, me pacing and pacing, listening for the phone that doesn't ring, I'm beginning to picture troubling alternatives. Was there some other resumé I didn't pay close enough attention to, and he got the call instead of me? Are they promoting from within their work force, over there at Arcadia?

Am I going to have to go back over there and kill some other son of a bitch? How much do I have to do before I get my fair chance?

I'm not going to stop, I know I'm not. I'd love to

stop, I want desperately to stop, but I'm not *going* to stop until I've got that job.

I know how to protect myself now. I will not be made a victim, never again. Anyone who tries to make trouble for me, from now on, with what I now know, anyone at all, corporate or personal, is in for a surprise.

It would be better all around if that fucking phone would ring.

46

Tuesday, I'm very distracted during the counseling session. Unless Quinlan or Marjorie speaks to me directly, I don't listen to what they're saying, and I add nothing. Fortunately, they're both involved enough in whatever they're discussing not to notice my absence.

What I'm thinking about is Arcadia. I'm thinking I'll have to go over there tomorrow, find out what's going on. It seems to me the best way is to get to the luncheonette when the workers come in at noontime, and listen to what they have to say.

Of course, the danger there is that I might be recognized later. I'm wondering if there's any theatrical place around where I could buy a mustache that wouldn't look fake. Or should I start growing a mustache, and be clean-shaven tomorrow and mustached when I finally get the job?

I haven't decided, about the mustache or anything else, by the time the counseling session is over. Marjorie and I drive back home in silence, me continuing to brood, only vaguely aware that she's looking at me, wondering about me.

There's a message on the answering machine, in the kitchen. Marjorie pushes the button and I pause in the doorway, disinterested, and the female voice says:

"This is Mr. John Carver's office at Arcadia Processing, calling for Mr. Burke Devore. I'm calling on Tuesday, the first of July. Could Mr. Devore please return Mr. Carver's call no later than Wednesday, the second of July? His number here is five one eight three nine eight four one four two. Thank you."

Marjorie looks at me, and I know I'm smiling so broadly my cheeks should split. She says, "Burke? What is it?"

"My new job," I say.

47

He was very good, on the phone, Mr. John Carver, amiable and interested. He told me they had an unexpected need for a product line manager of just my history and experience. He told me there'd been a tragic accident: "The funeral was yesterday." Which, of course, was why no phone call on Monday.

He said more. He said I was their first choice, that my resumé made it look as though I was just the manager they were looking for, but that their need is immediate, and when I wasn't home at the time of their call—unfortunate, very unfortunate—they couldn't be sure I was still available, and so of course they'd made a few other calls, which meant he was already seeing three applicants on Wednesday, the day after our conversation. But he promised they wouldn't make a decision before talking to me, and we made an appointment for Thursday at eleven in the morning, and today is Thursday, and I am having a very good time deciding what tie to wear.

Marjorie comes in while I'm knotting the tie, a maroon one in honor of the good lawyer Porculey, but without cows jumping over moons. The last two days, Marjorie has been as smiling and elated as I am, believing I really will get this job, believing it only because she sees *I* believe it so thoroughly, but now the smile has been replaced by a confused and questioning look: "Burke," she says, "that detective is here."

I'm blithe, I barely hear her: "Who?"

"The detective who was here before. Burton."

Detective. The one investigating the two mill managers shot by the same gun.

No. Not now. After all this, after all I've been through? To be stopped *now*, as though none of it had ever mattered?

Go through the process. It could be something else, or he could have nothing more than suspicions. All I have to do is remain firm and constant. All I have to do is remember my own advice to Billy; choose the best story available, and stick to it, no matter what.

"Okay," I tell Marjorie, smiling at her in the mirror. Then I finish knotting my tie, and, wearing tie and shirt and trousers and slippers, I walk out to the living room.

He's studying the Winslow Homer again. Are we going to have another discussion of sailing before we get to the subject? He turns when I walk in, nods and smiles, extending his hand. "Mr. Devore. Good to see you again."

Is this friendliness real, or a lie? I smile back, lying, and shake his hand. "Mr. Burton. Or do I say Detective Burton?"

"Either way," he says. "I can see you're on your way somewhere, I won't take a lot of your time. I have another name and another photo to try on you."

Which of my resumés will this be? One of them, that's for certain. I say, "If I can help."

"Sure." He's taking his notebook out of his inner jacket pocket, opening it, finding the color photo he wants. "The name is Hauck Exman."

My Marine, gone on a sea voyage. You could talk sailing with *him*, Detective Burton. I shake my head. "Doesn't ring a bell."

He hands me the photo, and I look at it, and it's a formal shot, him in a tuxedo somewhere, looking mostly like the President's bodyguard. "No," I say. "Tough-looking guy. Who is he?"

"At the moment," he says, as I hand him back the photo, "he's our prime suspect."

I am astonished, and I don't mind showing it. "Suspect! How did that happen?"

He's pleased with his detective work, that's obvious, and he'd like nothing better than to share it. "It took some digging," he says, "but we—"

I say, "Oh, excuse me. Won't you sit down?"

He's willing, but doubtful. "You've got time?"

"Plenty," I tell him.

"Okay, then."

We both sit, in the same positions as the first time,

and he says, "We finally linked up the other two, Everly and Asche. Four five years ago, there was a government contract for some kind of special paper, I apologize, I don't really understand all that stuff—"

"That's okay," I tell him, "most people don't."

"It was the Treasury Department," he says, "but it wasn't money, it was something else. The bidding companies all sent reps to Washington to talk to the Treasury people—"

"I remember that," I say. "Or I think that's the one. It had to do with import forms, and we didn't bid. I mean, the company I was with then. It wasn't quite our line, anti-counterfeit stuff, and we weren't looking for extra business anyway."

"Well, these other companies did," Burton tells me. "And among the company representatives down there, all at the same time, were Everly and Asche and Exman."

"Ahhhh," I say. "And they met."

"We haven't been able to prove that," he says, "but I don't think we have to. I spoke to Exman a couple weeks ago, the same way I spoke to you, and I have to tell you, I didn't like the way he acted."

I can see it. The haughty Exman, so involved in his own problems, feeling so intensely the humiliation of being a suit salesman, and how easy it was to give short shrift to this earnest detective. No, they wouldn't have hit it off. I say, "Did you arrest him?"

"Didn't have the evidence," Burton says, and shrugs. "But now, it looks like, my visit spooked him. He ran away."

"Ran away!"

"Disappeared completely," Burton tells me, with clear satisfaction. "Left his car behind in the parking lot where he worked, didn't say a word to anybody, just took off."

"I can't imagine it," I say. "Didn't he have a family? You say he was working?"

"Not easy for most people to do," he agrees, "suddenly up and leave your entire life behind. But now we're looking into it, and what do we find out? Exman's been having trouble at home. His wife had already seen a lawyer about a divorce, he'd been playing around, she caught him, all the usual stuff. And she's not the first wife, she's the fourth."

"Making trouble in his own life," I suggest.

"And everybody else's." Burton puts his notebook away, the photo inside it. "When we searched the house, it was full of guns. *Full* of guns. Maybe a dozen weapons of all different kinds. We're testing them all now, against the bullets we have, but the feeling is, he probably disposed of the gun that did the killing."

"Where do you think he is?"

"We're talking to his girlfriends," Burton tells me, "both of them, and the place he always seemed to talk about most was Singapore."

"You think he's in Singapore?"

"Well, he didn't take his passport. On the other hand, he just might have another one." Burton gets to his feet. "I shouldn't keep you any longer. We'll track him down, sooner or later."

Standing, I say, "Once again, I haven't been much help."

"Well, your company didn't bid on that contract. Otherwise, you might have met all three of them down there in D.C."

"And been shot by Exman last month," I suggest, with a wry smile.

He chuckles. "Consider yourself lucky," he says.

"Oh, I do."

He gestures at my tie. "You're off somewhere this morning."

"A job interview," I tell him. "This time, I think it's going to work out."

"Very good," he says. "I hope you're right."

"Wish me luck," I say.

"Good luck," he says.

PRIME CRIME FROM DONALD E. WESTLAKE

- ☐ BABY, WOULD I LIE?, 0-446-40342-3, $5.99 US/$6.99 CAN.
- ☐ BANK SHOT, 0-445-40883-9, $5.50 US/$6.99 CAN.
- ☐ BROTHERS KEEPERS, 0-446-40135-8, $4.99 US/$5.99 CAN.
- ☐ COPS AND ROBBERS, 0-446-40133-1, $5.50 US/$6.99 CAN.
- ☐ DANCING AZTECS, 0-445-40717-4, $5.99 US/$6.99 CAN.
- ☐ DON'T ASK, 0-446-40095-5, $5.50 US/$6.99 CAN.
- ☐ DROWNED HOPES, 0-446-40006-8, $5.99 US/$6.99 CAN.
- ☐ THE FUGITIVE PIGEON, 0-446-40132-3, $4.99 US/$5.99 CAN.
- ☐ THE HOT ROCK, 0-445-40608-9, $5.50 US/$6.99 CAN.
- ☐ HUMANS, 0-446-40094-7, $5.99 US/$6.99 CAN.
- ☐ KAHAWA, 0-446-40343-1, $5.99 US/$6.99 CAN.
- ☐ SMOKE, 0-446-40344-X, $6.50 US/$7.99 CAN.
- ☐ TRUST ME ON THIS, 0-445-40807-3, $5.99 US/$6.99 CAN.
- ☐ TWO MUCH!, 0-445-40719-0, $4.99 US/$5.99 CAN.
- ☐ WHAT'S THE WORST THAT COULD HAPPEN?, 0-446-60471-2, $6.50 US/$8.50 CAN.
- ☐ WHY ME, 0-446-40346-6, $5.50 US/$6.99 CAN.

AVAILABLE WHEREVER WARNER BOOKS ARE SOLD

The Comte drew me to him and kissed me as I had never been kissed before and I wanted to stay in his arms for ever.

"Oh, Minelle," he said, "why do you deny your heart?" Then he released me. "One day you will cast aside all wisdom and come to me because nothing, simply nothing, will be strong enough to withstand it. That's what I want. Whatever I am, whatever my sins of the past, you will not care. You will love me—*me*—not for my virtues, which are nonexistent, but for myself alone. One day, Minelle . . . one day . . ."

Then he kissed me again, holding me as though he would never let me go. I knew he was right. I was fast reaching that stage when whatever he had done, whatever he was guilty of, would seem insignificant beside my great need of him.

I turned and left him hastily, afraid of those emotions which such a short time ago I should have believed I could never experience.

VICTORIA HOLT

The
DEVIL ON
HORSEBACK

A FAWCETT CREST BOOK • NEW YORK

THE DEVIL ON HORSEBACK

THIS BOOK CONTAINS THE COMPLETE TEXT OF
THE ORIGINAL HARDCOVER EDITION.

Published by Fawcett Crest Books, a unit of CBS
Publications, the Consumer Publishing division of CBS Inc.,
by arrangement with Doubleday and Company, Inc.

Copyright © 1977 by Victoria Holt

ALL RIGHTS RESERVED

ISBN: 0–449–23625–0

All the characters in this book are fictitious, and any
resemblance to actual persons living or dead is purely
coincidental.

Alternate Selection of the Literary Guild
Selection of the Doubleday Book Club
Selection of Compact Library

Printed in the United States of America

10 9 8 7 6 5 4 3 2 1

DERRINGHAM
MANOR

1

It was a sequence of unfortunate events which brought me to the Château Silvaine. My father was a sea captain who had gone down with his ship when I was five years old and, having lived in moderate comfort all her life, my mother found herself forced to earn a living for herself and her daughter. A penniless woman, said my mother, must either live through her mop or her needle, unless she has some education which can be turned to good purpose. Being a woman in this category, there were two courses open to her; she could teach the young or be a companion to the elderly; she chose the former of these alternatives. She was a woman of strong character, determined to succeed, and, with very little means at her disposal, she rented a small lodge on the estate of Sir John Derringham in Sussex and started a school for young ladies.

For a few years, if it did not exactly flourish, it provided us with the necessities of life. I had been a pupil and had received an excellent education under my mother's tuition— the inference from the beginning being that, in due course, I should join her as a teacher, which for the last three months I had done.

"There should be a good living for you here, Minella," my mother used to say.

She had named me Wilhelmina after herself. The name suited her, but I never felt it fitted me as neatly. I had become Minella as a baby and the name had stayed with me.

I think my mother's main pleasure in the school was the fact that it provided for me. Her deepest concern had always been that we had no family in the background who might have provided me with help in an emergency. She and I were on our own. The Derringham girls, Sybil and Maria, were pupils at the school and that meant that other families sent their children. It saved having a governess in the house they used to say. When visitors came to Derringham Manor and their children were with them, they became temporary pupils. My mother taught manners, deportment, dancing, and French

6

in addition to the three Rs, and this was considered very unusual indeed.

Sir John was a generous and kindly man, eager to help a woman whom he admired as he did my mother. He had extensive lands watered by a small but very beautiful river in which trout flourished. Many rich people—some from the Court—used to come to stay at the Manor for the fishing, pheasant shoots, or to ride and hunt. These seasons were important to us, because the fame of my mother's school had spread through Sir John's circles, and families, who liked to have their children with them, brought them, and as my mother's school was warmly recommended by Sir John, they were delighted to make use of it. These children who came to us for brief periods were, as my mother used to say in her downright way, the preserve on our bread. We could live on the long term pupils, but naturally higher fees were asked for temporary tuition—so they were very welcome. I was sure Sir John knew this and it was why he took such pleasure in bringing them to us.

There came a day which was to prove significant in my life. This was when the French family of Fontaine Delibes came to stay at Derringham Manor. The Comte Fontaine Delibes was a man to whom I took an instant dislike. He seemed not only haughty and arrogant, but to set himself apart from all other human beings on account of his superiority in every way. The Comtesse was different, but one saw very little of her. She must have been beautiful in her youth—not that she was old at this time, but in my immaturity, I thought everyone over thirty old. Margot at this time was sixteen years old. I was eighteen. I heard later that Margot had been born a year after the marriage of the Comte and Comtesse, when the latter was only seventeen years old herself. In fact, I discovered a good deal about the marriage from Margot, who had, of course, been sent to our school through the kindly Sir John.

Margot and I were drawn together from the first. It might have been due to the fact that I had a natural aptitude for languages and could chatter away with her in French with greater ease even than my mother (though she was more grammatical) and than Sybil and Maria, whose progress in that language, said my mother, resembled that of a tortoise rather than a hare.

From our talks emerged the impression that Margot was not sure whether she loved or hated her father. She confessed her fear of him. He ruled his household in France and the

7

neighboring countryside (which he appeared to own) like a feudal lord of the Middle Ages. Everyone appeared to be in considerable awe of him. He could at times be quite merry and generous, too; but his persistent characteristic seemed to be his unpredictability. Margot told me that he would order a servant to be whipped one day and give that servant a purse of money the next. Not that the two incidents would have anything to do with each other. He never regretted any cruelty—or rarely—and his acts of kindness were not done out of remorse. "Only once," said Margot mysteriously, and when I tried to probe would say no more. She added with some pride that her father was referred to as *Le Diable* (behind his back, of course).

He was very handsome in a dark satanic way. His looks fitted what I had heard of him. I saw him for the first time near the schoolhouse; seated on a black horse he really did look like something out of a legend. The Devil on Horseback, I named him on the spot, and I thought of him by that name for a long time. He was magnificently dressed. The French were, of course, exceptionally elegant, and although Sir John was a man who presented an immaculate appearance to the world, he could not compare with the Devil Count. The Devil's cravat was a froth of exquisite lace, as were the frills at his wrists. His jacket was of bottle green and his riding hat of the same color. He wore a wig of smooth white hair and diamonds glittered discreetly in the lace at his neck.

He did not notice me so I was able to stand and stare.

Of course my mother was never a guest at Derringham Manor. Even the liberal-minded Sir John would not dream of inviting a schoolmistress to his house, and although he was always polite and considerate (it being his nature to be so) we were naturally not regarded as equals socially.

In spite of this my friendship with Margot was encouraged because the association was thought to be good for her English, and when her parents returned to France Margot stayed behind to perfect her knowledge of our tongue. This delighted my mother who had one of her better paying pupils for a longer period than usual. Margot's parents—but mostly her father—paid brief visits to the Manor now and then and this was one of those occasions when they were there.

Margot and I were constantly together and one day, as a reward, though not to be considered a precedent, I was invited to the Manor to tea that I might spend an hour or so with our pupils.

My mother was pleased. After school was closed on the day before the party she was washing and ironing the only gown which she considered suitable for the occasion—a blue linen edged with rather fine lace which had belonged to my father's mother. She was purring with pride as she ironed, certain that her daughter could take her place among the mighty with the utmost ease. Was she not aware of all that was expected of her? Had she not been brought up to behave with poise among the exalted? Was she not more soundly educated for her years than any of them? (True.) Was she not as handsome and well dressed? (A mother's fondness, I feared, rather than a fact.)

Armed with my mother's confidence in me and my determination to do her credit, I set out. Walking through the pine woods I could not say that I felt any undue excitement. So often I had been in class with Sybil, Maria, and Margot that I should be in company to which I was well accustomed. It would merely be a different venue. But when I emerged from the woods and saw the house standing back from those gracious lawns, I could not help feeling a great pleasure at the prospect of entering it. Gray stone walls. Mullioned windows. The original house had been reduced to a shell by Cromwell's men and more or less rebuilt after the Restoration. A Daniel Derringham, who had fought in the King's cause, had been rewarded with a baronetcy and lands.

There was a stone path crossing the lawns on which grew some very ancient yews which must have survived the Roundheads, for they were reputed to be two hundred years old. In the center of one of the lawns was a sundial and I could not resist crossing the grass to look at it. There was an inscription on it almost obliterated by time and it was engraved in an elaborate script very difficult to decipher.

"Savor each hour," I could read, but the rest of the writing was covered by greenish moss. I rubbed it with my finger and looked with dismay at the green stain there. My mother would be reproachful. How could I arrive at Derringham Manor less than immaculate!

"It's difficult to read, you find?"

I turned sharply. Joel Derringham was standing behind me. So absorbed had I been in studying the sundial that I had been unaware of his approach on the soft grass.

"There is so much moss covering the words," I replied.

I had rarely spoken before to Joel Derringham. He was

the only son, aged about twenty-one or two. Even now he looked very like Sir John; he would be exactly like him when he reached his age. He had the same light brown hair and pale blue eyes—the rather aquiline nose and kindly mouth. Considering Sir John and his son, the adjective which springs to mind is "pleasant." They were kind and compassionate without being weak, and, when I come to think of it, that is about the greatest compliment one human being can pay another.

He smiled at me. "I can tell you what they are:

> " 'Savor each hour
> Dwell not in the past.
> Live each day fully.
> It may be your last.' "

"Rather a grim warning," I said.

"But sound advice."

"Yes, I suppose so." It occurred to me that I ought to explain my presence. "I'm Wilhelmina Maddox," I went on. "And I have been invited to tea."

"I know who you are, of course," he said. "Let me take you to my sisters."

"Thank you."

"I have seen you near the school," he added, as we walked across the lawn. "My father often says what an asset the school is to the neighborhood."

"It's gratifying to be useful while earning a living."

"Oh I agree, Miss . . . er . . . Wilhelmina. If I may say so, it is a little formal to suit you."

"I am known as Minella."

"That's better. Miss Minella. Much better."

We had come to the house. The heavy door was slightly ajar. He pushed it wide and we went into the hall. Tall windows, flagged floor, wonderfully vaulted roof with hammerbeams—enchanted me. In the center was the great oak refectory table with pewter plates and goblets. Armory hung on the stone walls out of which seats had been cut. The chairs were Carolean and a huge portrait of Charles II dominated the hall. I paused for a few seconds to study that heavy sensuous face which might have been gross but for the twinkling humor in the eyes and a certain kindliness in the curve of the lips.

"The family's benefactor," he said.

"It's a magnificent portrait."

10

"Presented by the Merry Monarch himself after he had visited us."

"You must love your house."

"Well, one does. It has something to do with the family's having lived here over the years. Even though it was almost rebuilt at the Restoration, parts of it go back to the Plantagenet era."

Envy is not one of my faults but I did feel a twinge of it then. To belong to such a house, such a family, must give one a great sense of pride. It sat lightly on Joel Derringham. I doubted he had given the matter much thought. Always he would have accepted the fact that he had been born into this house and would in due course inherit it. After all, he was the only son and therefore the undoubted heir.

"I suppose," I said impulsively, "this is what is called being born with a silver spoon in your mouth."

He looked startled and I realized that I was giving voice to my thoughts in a manner of which I could be sure my mother would not approve.

"All this," I said, "yours . . . from the day you were born . . . simply because you were born here. How lucky you were! Suppose you had been born in one of the cottages on the estate!"

"But I should not be myself with different parents," he pointed out.

"Suppose two babies had been exchanged and one from the cottages brought up as Joel Derringham and you as the cottage child. Would anyone tell the difference when you grew up?"

"I am very like my father, I believe."

"That is because you have been brought up here."

"I do look like him."

"Yes, you do . . ."

"Environment . . . birth . . . what effect does it have? It is a matter which has confounded the doctors for years. It is not something which can be solved in a few moments."

"I'm afraid I have been rather impertinent. I was thinking aloud."

"Certainly you were not. It's an interesting theory."

"I was overwhelmed by the house."

"I'm glad it has that effect on you. You felt its antiquity . . . the spirits of my dead ancestors."

"I can only say I'm sorry."

"I'm not. I liked your frankness. Shall I take you up now? They'll be waiting for you."

There was a staircase leading from the hall. We mounted this and came to a gallery hung with portraits. Then we went up a winding stair and were on a landing faced by several doors. Joel opened one of them and I immediately heard Sybil's voice. "She's here. Come along in, Minella. We're waiting."

The room was what was known as the solarium because it had been built to catch the sun. At one end was a tapestry on a frame at which I discovered Lady Derringham was working. There was a spinning wheel at the other end of the room. I wondered if anyone used that now. In the center was a large table with a piece of needlework on it. I learned later the girls worked at it in this room. There was a harpsichord and a spinet and I could imagine how different the place would look when cleared for dancing, the candles flickering in their sconces and the ladies and gentlemen in their exquisite clothes.

Margot cried in her accented English: "Do not stand there goggle-eyed, Minelle"—she always adapted our names to her own language—"have you never seen a solar before?"

"I expect," said Maria, "that Minella finds this rather different from the schoolhouse."

Maria meant to be kind but I often found a sting in her kindness. She was the more snobbish of the Derringham girls.

Joel said: "Well, I'll leave you girls. Goodbye, Miss Maddox."

As the door shut on him Maria demanded: "Where did you meet Joel?"

"When I was coming to the house. He brought me in."

"Joel always feels he has to help everybody," said Maria. "He'd carry a basket for a kitchen girl if he thought it was too heavy for her. Mama says it's demeaning, and so it is. Joel should know better."

"And look down his aristocratic nose at the schoolmistress," I said sharply, "for after all, since she is so far beneath him it is a wonder he notices her at all."

Margot shrieked with laughter. "Bravo, Minelle!" she cried. "And if Joel should know better, so should you, Marie. Never cross swords . . . is that right?" I nodded. "Never cross swords with Minelle because she will always beat you, and if she is the schoolmistress's daughter and you are the squire's . . . never mind. She is the clever one."

"Oh Margot," I cried, "you are ridiculous." But I knew the tone of my voice thanked her for coming to my aid.

"I shall ring for tea now you are here," said Sybil, remembering her duties as hostess. "It will be served in the schoolroom."

As we talked I looked about me, taking in my surroundings and thinking how pleasant my encounter with Joel Derringham had been and how much more likable he was than his sisters.

Tea was served, as Sybil had said, in the schoolroom. There was thin bread and butter with cherry cake and little round buns flavored with caraway seeds. A servant hovered while Sybil poured the tea. At first we were a little formal but very soon were chattering away as we did at school, for although my rôle was now that of a teacher, not so long ago I had been a pupil with them.

Margot surprised me by suggesting a game of hide-and-seek, for it was rather childish and she prided herself on her worldliness.

"You are always wanting to play that silly game," said Sybil, "and then you disappear and we can never find you."

Margot shrugged her shoulders. "It amuses me," she said.

The Derringham girls were resigned. I supposed they had been told they must humor their guest.

She pointed to the floor. "All of them down there will have finished their afternoon naps and be taking tea in the drawing room. It's fun. Though better at night when there is darkness and the ghosts come out."

"There are no ghosts," said Maria sharply.

"Oh yes, Marie," teased Margot. "There is the one of the housemaid who hanged herself because the pantryman deserted her. Only she does not appear to you. How do you say? She knows her place."

Maria, flushing, muttered: "Margot talks such nonsense."

"Do let us play hide-and-seek," pleaded Margot.

"It's hardly fair to Minella," protested Sybil. "She doesn't know the house."

"Oh, but it's only up here that we play. It would be frowned on if we went below and ran into guests. I shall go and hide now."

Margot's eyes were dancing with anticipation of pleasure, and this astonished me. But the thought of exploring the house even though I was confined to the top floor was so exciting to me that I forgot my surprise in Margot's unexpected childishness. After all, Margot was always unpredictable and I supposed she was not really so very old.

Maria was grumbling. "It's such a silly game. I wonder

why she wants to play it. Guessing games would be so much more suitable. I wonder where she goes. We never find her. And *she* always has to be the one to hide."

"Perhaps we'll find her this time, with Minella's help," said Sybil.

We left the schoolroom and went onto a landing. Maria opened a door; Sybil opened another. I went into the one with Sybil. It was furnished as a bedroom and I realized that this was where Maria and Sybil slept. There were two beds with half canopies in separate corners of the room, as far away from each other as possible.

I stepped back onto the landing. Maria was not there and an irresistible urge to explore by myself came to me. I stepped back into the solarium. It seemed different now that I was there alone. That was how it was with great houses; they changed when people were there. It was as though there was something living in them.

How I longed to wander about the house, exploring it! How I wanted to know all that was happening in it now and what had happened in the past.

Margot might have understood. The Derringham girls never would. They would have thought it was the schoolmistress's daughter being overwhelmed by her surroundings.

I was not interested in Margot's childish games. It was obvious that she was not in the solarium. There was nowhere that I could see for her to hide.

I heard Maria's voice on the landing and I stepped briskly across the room. I had discovered another door in the solarium and I opened it and went through. A spiral staircase faced me. On impulse I descended it. It wound round and round and seemed to go on for a long way before it came to an end. I was in another part of the house. Here the corridor was wide. There were heavy velvet curtains at the windows. I looked through one of them. I could see the lawn with the sundial and I knew that I was in the front of the house.

There were several doors along the corridor. Very cautiously I opened one. The blinds were drawn to shut out the sun and it took a few seconds for my eyes to become accustomed to the dimness. Then I saw the sleeping figure on the chaise longue. It was the Comtesse, Margot's mother. I quickly but very quietly shut the door. Suppose she had been awake and seen me! I should have been in disgrace. My mother would have been hurt and bewildered and I should never have been invited to Derringham Manor again. Perhaps I never should in any case as this was the first time I had been asked. It was the only time most likely. Then I must make the most of it.

My mother often said that when I wanted to do something which was of questionable behavior, I would make excuses why it was right to do it. What excuse could I make for wandering about the house . . . prying . . . for it was nothing more? Joel Derringham had been pleased that I liked the house. I was sure he would not mind. Nor would Sir John. And it might be my only chance.

I went along the corridor. Then to my joy I discovered that one door was slightly ajar. I pushed it further and peeped into the room. It was very like that in which the Comtesse lay on her chaise longue except that there was a four-poster bed in it hung with rich curtains. I noticed the beautiful tapestries which adorned the walls.

I could not resist it. I tiptoed in.

Then my heart leaped in terror, for I heard the door shut behind me. I had never felt so frightened in all my life. Someone had shut the door. My position was unbearably embarrassing. In such situations I was quick at finding excuses and could generally rely on being able to extricate myself from awkward places, but in that moment I was really frightened. We had talked of the supernatural and I felt as though I could be in the presence of it.

Then a voice behind me said in accented English: "Good afternoon. It is a pleasure to meet you."

I turned sharply. The Devil Count was standing against the door, his arms folded; his eyes—very dark, almost black—were boring into me; his mouth curved in a smile which matched the rest of him and which I could only call diabolical.

I stammered: "I'm sorry. I appear to have intruded."

"You seek someone?" he asked. "It is not my wife, I know, for you rejected her after you had looked into her room. Perhaps you search for me?"

I realized then that the two rooms were connected and he had been in that one into which I had peeped on the sleeping Comtesse. He had no doubt hastily come into this room and opened the door to lure me in in order to trap me when I had entered.

"No, no," I said. "It is a game. Margot is hiding."

He nodded. "Perhaps you should sit down."

"No, thanks. I should not have come down here. I should have stayed upstairs."

I walked boldly to the door but he did not move away from it and I stopped short looking at him helplessly and yet fascinated, wondering what he was going to do. What he did do was step forward and take my arm.

"You must not go away so soon," he said. "Now that you have visited me, you must stay awhile."

He was studying me closely and his scrutiny embarrassed me.

"I think I should go," I said as easily as I could. "They will be missing me."

"But it is Margot who is hiding. They will not find her yet. It is a big house for her to hide herself in."

"Oh, but they will. It is only the top floor . . ." I stopped foolishly. I had betrayed myself.

He laughed triumphantly. "Then what are you doing down here, Mademoiselle?"

"It is my first visit to the house. I lost my way."

"And you were looking in these rooms to find it?"

I was silent. He drew me to the window and pulled me down beside him. I was close to him, deeply aware of the linen that smelt faintly of sandalwood and the large signet ring with the crest which he wore on the little finger of his right hand.

"You should tell me your name," he said.

"I am Minella Maddox."

"Minella Maddox," he repeated. "I know well. You are the schoolmistress's daughter."

"I am. But I hope you will tell no one that I came down here."

He nodded gravely. "So you have disobeyed orders . . ."

"I was lost," I said firmly. "I would not like it to be known that I was so foolish."

"So you are asking a favor of me?"

"I merely suggest that you do not mention this trivial matter."

"It is not trivial to me, Mademoiselle."

"I do not understand you, Monsieur le Comte."

"So you know me?"

"Everyone in the neighborhood knows you."

"I wonder how much you know *of* me."

"Only who you are and that you are Margot's father and that you come from France to visit Derringham from time to time."

"My daughter has talked of me, has she?"

"Now and then."

16

"She has told you of my many . . . what is the word?"

"Sins, do you mean? If you would prefer to speak in French . . ."

"I see you have formed an opinion of me. I am a sinner who does not speak your language as well as you speak mine." He was talking in rapid French, hoping, I knew, that I should not understand. but I had had a good grounding and my fear was deserting me; moreover, although I knew that I was in a difficult situation and he was the sort of man who would not be chivalrous enough to help me out of it, I could not suppress a certain exhilaration. I replied in French that I had thought the word he was searching for was the one I had supplied and if he was thinking of something else would he give it to me in French and I was sure I should understand.

"I see." he said, still speaking very quickly, "that you are a spirited young lady. Now let us understand each other. You seek my daughter Marguerite, whom you call Margot. She is hiding on the upper floor of the house. You know this yet you seek her down here. Ah, Mademoiselle, you did not seek Marguerite but to satisfy your curiosity. Come. admit it." He frowned in a manner which was, I was sure, calculated to strike terror in those who observed it. "I do not like people to tell me untruths."

"Well." I said, determined not to be browbeaten, "it is my first visit to a house of this type and I do admit to a certain curiosity."

"Natural, very natural. You have very pretty hair, Mademoiselle. I would say it is the color of the corn in August. Would you agree?"

"You are pleased to flatter me."

He put up a hand and caught a strand of my hair, which my mother had curled carefully and which was tied back with a blue riband to match my dress.

I felt uneasy, yet the exhilaration persisted. I was forced to move closer to him as he pulled at my hair. I could see his face very clearly, the shadow under the luminous dark eyes, the brows thick, yet finely marked. He was the most striking-looking man I had ever seen.

"And now," I said, "I should go."

"You came at your pleasure," he reminded me, "and I think it only courteous that you should leave at mine."

"As we are concerned with courtesy you will not detain me against my will."

"But we are discussing the courtesy *you* owe *me*. I owe you none, remember. You are the intruder. Oh, Mademoiselle, to peep into my bedchamber! To pry so! Shame on you!"

His eyes were sparkling. I remembered Margot's talk of his unpredictability. At the moment he was amused. In a short time he might not be.

I jerked my hair out of his hand and stood up.

"I apologize for my curiosity," I said. "It was most ill-mannered of me. You must do what you think fit about the matter. If you wish to tell Sir John . . ."

"I thank you for your permission," he said. He was beside me, and to my horror he put his arms about me and held me against him. Then his finger was under my chin lifting my face. "When we transgress," he went on, "we must pay for our sins. This is the payment I ask." He took my face in his hands and kissed me on the lips—not once but many times.

I was horrified. I had never been kissed in such a way before. I wrenched myself free and ran.

The thought uppermost in my mind was that he had treated me as a serving girl. I was horrified. Moreover, it was my own fault.

I stumbled out of the room. I found the spiral staircase and as I started up it I heard a movement behind me. For a moment I thought it was the Comte in pursuit and I felt numb with terror.

Margot said: "What are you doing down here, Minelle?"

I turned. She was flushed and her eyes were dancing.

"Where have you been?" I demanded.

"Where have *you?*" She put her fingers to her lips. "Come on. Upstairs."

We went up the staircase. At the top, she turned to me and laughed. We went into the solarium together.

Maria and Sybil were already there.

"Minelle found me," said Margot.

"Where?" demanded Sybil.

"Do you think I'm telling?" retorted Margot. "I might decide to hide there again."

That was the beginning. He had become aware of me and I was certainly not going to forget him in a hurry. During the rest of the afternoon I could not get him out of my mind. As we sat in the solarium and played a guessing game I was expecting him all the time to come to denounce me. More likely, I thought, he had told Sir John. I was most uncomfortable thinking of the way he had kissed me. What interpretation had he put on that?

I knew that it was my mother's constant concern that I should remain virtuous and make a good marriage. She wanted the best possible for me. A doctor would be suitable, she had once said, but the only doctor we knew had remained unmarried for fifty-five years and was hardly likely to take a wife now; and even if he had decided to and offered to bestow the honor on me, I should have declined.

"We are midway between two worlds," said my mother, meaning that the villagers were far beneath us and the occupants of the Big House far above us. It was for this reason that she was so eager to leave me a flourishing school. Though I must say the thought of spending the rest of my· life teaching the offspring of the nobility who were to visit Derringham Manor in the years to come held no great charm for me.

It was the Comte who had set my thoughts in this direction. I realized angrily that he would not have dared kiss a young lady of good family in this way. But would he? Of course he would. He would do whatever his inclination moved him to. Of course, he might have been very angry. He might have told Sir John that I had come peeping into his bedchamber. Instead of which he had treated me like a . . . like a what? How could I know? All I did know was that if my mother were aware of it she would be horrified.

She was eagerly waiting for me when I returned.

"You look flushed," she scolded tenderly, and a little reproachfully. She would have preferred me to look cool as though taking tea at Derringham Manor was an every day occurrence in my life. "Did you enjoy it? What happened?"

I told her what we had had for tea and what the girls were wearing.

"Sybil presided," I said, "and afterwards we played games."

"What games?" she wanted to know.

"Oh, just a childish sort of hide-and-seek and then guessing towns and rivers."

She nodded. Then she frowned. My dress was decidedly grubby. "I should like to get you a new dress," she said. "Something pretty. Velvet, perhaps."

"But, Mamma, when should I wear it?"

"Who knows? You might be asked again."

"I doubt it. Once in a lifetime is enough for such an honor."

I must have sounded bitter, for she looked sad and I was sorry. I went to her and put my arm about her. "Don't worry, Mama," I said. "We're happy here, are we not? And the school does very well." I remembered then what I had forgotten until that moment. "Oh, Mama, when I was going in I met Joel Derringham."

Her eyes lit up. She said: "You didn't tell me."

"I forgot."

"Forgot . . . meeting Joel Derringham! He'll be Sir Joel one day. Everything will be his. How did you meet him?"

I told her, repeating word for word. "He sounds charming," she said.

"He is—and so like Sir John. It's amusing, really. You could say that's Sir John . . . thirty years ago."

"He was certainly very pleasant to you."

"He could not have been more so."

I could see plans forming in her mind.

It was two days later when Sir John came to the school-house and a Sunday so there was no school that day. My mother and I had just dined and we had sat over the table as we often did on Sundays until nearly three o'clock, discussing the next week's lessons.

Although my mother was normally the most prosaic of women, where her heart was involved she could dream as romantically as any young girl. I knew that she had made up her mind that I was to have many invitations to the Manor and there I should meet someone—perhaps he might not be of too exalted a rank—but at least he would be able to offer me more than I could reasonably hope for if I spent my days in a schoolhouse. Previously she had decided that I must have the best possible education to provide for my future as a schoolmistress. Now her thoughts had escaped to wilder dreams of fantasy and, because she was a woman accustomed to succeed, they knew no bounds.

Through the window of our little dining room she saw Sir John tethering his horse to the iron bar which had been put there for that purpose. I felt myself turn cold. It immediately occurred to me that the malicious Comte had decided to complain against me. I had left him abruptly and shown him quite clearly that I deplored his conduct. This might be his revenge.

"Why, it's Sir John," said my mother. "I wonder . . ."

I heard myself say: "Perhaps a new pupil . . ."

He was ushered into our sitting room and I was relieved to see that he was smiling as benignly as ever.

"Good day to you, Mrs. Maddox . . . and Minella. Lady Derringham has a request to make. We are short of a guest for the *soirée* and supper which are to take place this evening. The Comtesse Fontaine Delibes is confined to her room and without her we shall be thirteen. There is, as you know, a superstition that thirteen is unlucky and some of our guests might be uneasy. I was wondering if I could persuade you to allow your daughter to join us."

It was so like one of the dreams my mother had been conjuring up during the last two days that she accepted it calmly as though it were the most natural thing in the world.

"But of course she will join you," she said.

"But Mama," I protested, "I have no suitable dress."

Sir John laughed. "That had occurred to Lady Derringham when the matter was suggested. One of the girls can lend you something. That is a simple matter." He turned to me. "Come to the Manor this afternoon. You can then choose the gown and the seamstress can do any necessary alterations. It is good of you, Mrs. Maddox, to lend us your daughter." He smiled at me. "I shall see you later."

When he had gone my mother seized me in her arms and hugged me.

"I *willed* it to happen," she cried. "Your father always used to say that when I made up my mind I'd get what I wanted because I believed in it so firmly I just created it."

"I shan't much care about parading in borrowed plumes."

"Nonsense. No one will know."

"Sybil and Maria will and Maria will take the first opportunity to remind me that I am there as a stand-in."

"As long as she does not remind anyone else that does not matter."

"Mama, why are you so excited?"

"It's what I always hoped for."

"Did you ill-wish the Comtesse?"

"Perhaps."

"So that your daughter could go to the ball!"

"It's not a ball!" she cried aghast. "You would have to have a proper ball gown for that."

"I was speaking metaphorically."

"How right I was to educate you thoroughly. You will be as musically knowledgeable as any of them there. I think your hair should be piled high on your head. It shows off its color that way." I heard a cynical voice murmuring: "Like corn in August." "Your hair is your best feature, my dear. We must make the most of it. I hope the dress will be blue because that brings out the color of your eyes. That cornflower blue is rather rare . . . as deep as yours, I mean."

"You are making a princess out of your budding school-mistress, Mama."

"Why shouldn't a budding schoolmistress be as beautiful and charming as any lady in the land?"

"Certainly she should be if she is your daughter."

"You must curb your tongue tonight, Minella. You always did say the first thing that came into your head."

"I shall have to be myself and if that does not suit . . ."

"They might not ask you again."

"Why should they ask me again? Are you not attaching too much importance to this? I am asked because they need another guest. It is not the first time someone has asked to be the fourteenth. If the fourteenth decided to come after all, I should politely be assured that my presence was no longer necessary."

The fact was that my mind was as busy as my mother's. Why had this summons (which was how I thought of it) followed so closely on my visit to the Manor? Who had prompted it? And was it not something of a coincidence that it should be the Comte's wife who was indisposed? Could it possibly be that *he* had suggested that I should fill the gap? What an extraordinary idea! Why? Because he wanted to meet me again? He had not reported my ill manners after all. I remembered what he had said of my hair as he tugged it caressingly; and then . . . those kisses. It was insulting. Was he saying: "Bring the girl to the Manor"? That was how men such as he was behaved in their own world. There was something called the *droit de seigneur* which meant that when a girl was going to be married, the lord of the manor, if he liked the look of her, took her to his bed for a night—more than one night if she proved satisfactory—and then she was passed on to her bridegroom. If the lord was generous there was a present of some sort. I could well imagine this Comte exerting such a right.

What was I thinking? I was no bride and Sir John would never permit such conduct on his estate. I was ashamed of myself for harboring such thoughts. That interview with the Comte had had a deeper effect on me than I had imagined.

My mother kept talking about Joel Derringham. I had to repeat what he had said to me. She was thinking romantic thoughts again. Oh, it was too foolish. She was telling herself that the indisposition was a myth and that as Joel had wished to make my further acquaintance, he had prevailed on his parents to ask me for the evening. Oh, Mama, I thought, dear Mama, foolish only where her daughter was concerned. If she could see me satisfactorily settled she would die happily.

But she did indulge in the most preposterous dreams.

Margot came to the schoolhouse to see me. She was excited.

"What fun!" she cried. "So you are coming tonight. My dear Minelle, Marie has found a dress for you, but I won't have it. You are to have one of mine . . . straight from a *couturière* of Paris. Blue for your eyes. Marie's dress was brown. So ugly. I say: No. No. No. Not for Minelle, for if you are not exactly beautiful—as I am—you have something distinguished. Yes, you have, and I shall insist that you wear *my* dress."

"Oh Margot," I said, "you really do want me to come!"

"But of course. It will be fun. Maman will spend the evening in her room. She was crying this afternoon. It was my father again. Oh, he is wicked, but I suppose she loves him. Women do love him. I wonder why?"

"Your mother is not really ill, is she?"

Margot lifted her shoulders. "It is the vapors. That is what Le Diable calls it. There might have been a quarrel. Not that she would dare quarrel with *him*. He does the quarreling. If she weeps he gets more angry than ever. He hates women who weep."

"And does she weep often?"

"I don't know. I expect so. After all, she is married to him."

"Margot, what a dreadful thing to say of your father!"

"If you don't want the truth . . ."

"I do. But I can't see how you can really know. Does she always shut herself away? Is it the same in your own home?"

"I suppose so."

"But you must *know*."

"I don't see much of her, if that's what you mean. Nou Nou guards her and I hear she is not to be disturbed. But why do we talk about *them*. I'm so glad you are coming, Minelle. I think you'll enjoy it. You liked visiting us for tea, didn't you?"

"Yes, it was fun."

"What were you doing on the staircase? You had been exploring. Confess."

"What were *you* doing, Margot?"

She narrowed her eyes and laughed at me.

"Come, tell me," I insisted.

"If I tell you, will you tell me what you were doing? Ah,

but that is not fair exchange. You were just looking at the house."

"Margot, what are you talking about?"

"Never mind."

I was glad to drop the subject, but I kept wondering about the Comte and Comtesse. She was afraid of him. That I could understand. She shut herself away and took refuge in her illness. I was sure it was to escape from him. It was very mysterious.

Margot took me to her room in the Manor. It was beautifully furnished and reminded me of the Comte's bedroom. The bed was a four-poster, though slightly less ornate. The curtains were rich blue velvet and one wall was covered in a fine tapestry of the same tone as the curtains, which was the predominant color throughout the room.

The dress I was to wear was laid out on the bed.

"I am a little plumper," said Margot, "which is good because that makes it easy. You are a little taller, but see, there is a deep hem. I made the seamstress undo that at once. Now you will try it on and she shall come and make the alterations. I will send for her at once."

"Margot," I said, "you are a good friend to me."

"Ah yes," she agreed. "You interest me. Sybil . . . Marie . . . *Pouf!*" She blew with her lips. "They are dull. I know what they will say before they say it. You are different. Besides, you are only the schoolmistress's daughter."

"What has that to do with it?"

She laughed again and would say no more. I put on the dress. It was certainly becoming. She rang the bell and the seamstress arrived with pins and needles. In less than an hour I had my dress.

Maria and Sybil came to inspect me. Maria sniffed slightly.

"Well?" demanded Margot. "What's wrong?"

"It's not really suitable," commented Maria.

"Why not?" cried Margot.

"The brown would have been better."

"Better for you? Are you afraid that she will look more beautiful than you? Ah, that is it."

"What nonsense!" retorted Maria.

Margot grinned at me. "It is so," she said.

And Maria said no more about the unsuitability of the gown.

Margot insisted on dressing my hair. She chatted as she did so. "There, my *chérie*. Is that not beautiful? Oh, yes, it is true, you have an air. You should not be condemned to spending your life teaching stupid children." She studied my reflection. "Corn-colored hair," she commented. "Cornflower-blue eyes and lips like the poppy."

I laughed at her. "You make me sound like a field of wheat."

"Teeth even and white," she went on. "Nose a little . . . how do you say it? . . . aggressive? Lips firm . . . can smile, can be severe. I know what it is, Minelle my friend, that adds up to attractiveness. It is the contrast. The eyes are soft and yielding. Ah, but wait . . . look at that nose. Look at that mouth. Oh yes, they say, I am good-looking . . . I am passionate . . . but wait a bit. No nonsense, please."

"Yes, please," I retorted, "no more of this nonsense. And when I want an analysis of my looks and character I'll ask for it."

"You never would, because that's another thing about you, Minelle, you think you know that little bit more than anyone else and can answer all the questions so much more correctly. Oh, I know you used to beat me in class . . . as you did us all . . . and that is right and fitting for the daughter of the schoolmistress, and now you teach us and tell us when we are right and wrong. But let me tell you this, my clever Minelle, you have much to learn."

I looked at her dark laughing face with the fine almost black sparkling eyes, so like her father's, the heavy brows, the thick dark hair. She was very attractive and there was something secretive about her. I thought of her joining me on the spiral staircase. Where had she been?

"Something *you* have already learned?" I asked.

"Some of us are born with this kind of knowledge," she said.

"And you are one of those so endowed?"

"I am."

The music was playing in the gallery where a small orchestra had been installed.

Lady Derringham, gracious in pale mauve silk, pressed my hand when she saw me and murmured: "It was good of you to help us out, Minella." A remark which, although spoken kindly, reminded me immediately of the reason why I was here.

As soon as the Comte appeared I suspected he was responsible for my being here. He looked about the music

25

room until his eyes alighted on me. He bowed from across the room, and I could see he was taking in every detail of my appearance in a way which I reminded myself was insulting. I returned his gaze haughtily, which seemed to amuse him.

Lady Derringham had arranged that I should sit with her daughters and Margot—as though to remind the company that although we were present we had not yet been formally launched into society. We were not quite children and could be allowed to attend the *soirée* and supper afterwards, but we should be dismissed as soon as that was over.

I found it a tremendously exciting occasion. I loved music, in particular the works of the composer Mozart which figured largely in the concert. As I listened I felt transported and I thought how I should enjoy living graciously as many of my pupils did. It seemed unfair of fate to have set me outside it and yet not far enough away not to be able to glimpse it and realize what I was missing.

During the interval in the concert people moved about the gallery greeting old friends. Joel came over to me.

"I'm glad you came, Miss Maddox," he said.

"Do you really think it would have been noticed if I had not? Would people really count and imagine doom was overtaking them because of unlucky thirteen?"

"We can't know, as the situation was avoided . . . most agreeably, if I may say so. I hope it will be the first of many occasions when you will visit us."

"You can't expect a fourteenth guest to default at the last minute merely to accommodate me."

"I think you attach too much importance to this reason."

"I have to because but for it I shouldn't be here."

"Let's forget that and be glad you are. What did you think of the concert?"

"Superb."

"You are fond of music."

"Extremely."

"We often have concerts like this. You must come again."

"You are very kind."

"This one is for the Comte. He is particularly partial to Mozart."

"Did I hear my name?" asked the Comte.

He took the chair beside me and I was aware of his studying me intently.

"I was telling Miss Maddox, Comte, that you enjoy Mozart and that the concert was being given in your honor. May I present Miss Maddox."

The Comte stood up and bowed. "It is a pleasure to meet you, Mademoiselle." He turned to Joel. "Mademoiselle Maddox and I have met before."

I felt the blood rushing to my face. He was going to expose me. He was going to tell Joel how I had peeped into his bedchamber when I was supposed to be upstairs and imply how unwise it was to bring people of my station into a higher sphere. What a moment to choose! And typical of him, I was sure.

He was regarding me sardonically, reading my thoughts.

"Is that so?" said Joel, surprised.

"By the schoolhouse," said the Comte. "I was passing and I saw Mademoiselle Maddox. I thought: That is the excellent Mademoiselle who has done so much good to my daughter. I am glad to have an opportunity of expressing my gratitude."

He was smiling at me, noting, of course, my flush and he would know that I was thinking of those kisses and my undignified exit.

"My father is constantly singing the praises of Mrs. Maddox's school," said kind Joel. "It has saved our employing governesses."

"Governesses can be tiresome," said the Comte, sitting down beside me. "They are not of us and yet they do not belong with the servants. It is irksome to have people floating in limbo. Not for us. For them. They become so conscious of their status. Class is something to be ignored. Do you agree, Joel? Miss Maddox? When our late King Louis XV was reminded by one of his friends, a duke, that his mistress was the daughter of a cook, he replied: 'Is that so? I did not notice. The fact is that you are all so far beneath me that I cannot tell the difference between a duke and a cook.'"

Joel laughed and I could not stop myself retorting: "Is that so with you, Monsieur le Comte? Could *you* not tell the difference between a cook and a duke?"

"I am not so high as the King, Mademoiselle, but I am high nevertheless and I could not tell the difference between the daughters of Sir John and those of the schoolmistress."

"Then it seems that I am not entirely unacceptable."

His eyes seemed to burn into mine. "Mademoiselle, you are very acceptable, I do assure you."

Joel looked uncomfortable. He found this conversation in bad taste, I was sure, but I could see that the Comte, like myself, could not resist the temptation to indulge in it.

"I think," said Joel, "that the interval is almost over and that we should return to our seats."

The girls were coming back. Margot looked amused; Maria a little sour and Sybil noncommittal.

"You are attracting attention, Minelle," whispered Margot. "Two of the most handsome men in attendance at the same time. You are a siren."

"I did not ask them."

"Sirens never do. They just send out their subtle fascination."

During the rest of the concert I thought of the Comte. I attracted him in some way. I knew which way. He liked women, and although I was immature, I was fast becoming one. That his intentions were strictly dishonorable could be nothing but obvious. But what was so horrifying was that instead of being angry I was fascinated.

As we were about to descend into the dining hall where cold supper had been laid out, one of the footmen—splendid in the Derringham livery—came into the dining room, sought the eye of Sir John and discreetly went to him. I saw him whisper a few words.

Sir John nodded and went to the Comte who, I noticed not without a little chagrin, was talking animatedly to Lady Eggleston, the flighty young wife of a gouty, more-than-middle-aged husband. She was simpering a little and I could imagine the course of their conversation.

Sir John spoke to the Comte and after a while they went out of the room together.

Joel was at my side.

"Come to the buffet," he said. "There you can choose what you would like. After that we'll find a small table."

I was grateful to him. There was such kindliness in him. He believed that I, who knew no one here, might need a protector.

There was fish of all description and a variety of cold meats. I took little. I was not in the least hungry.

We found a table somewhat sheltered by plants, and Joel said to me: "I dare say you found the Comte a little unusual."

"Well . . . he is not English."

"I thought you seemed a little put out by him."

"I think he is a man who is accustomed to getting his own way."

"Undoubtedly. You saw him leave with my father. One of his servants has arrived from France with a message for him. It seems as though it may be important."

"It must be for the servant to travel so far."

"But not entirely unexpected. You will know that affairs in France have been uneasy for some time. I do hope this is nothing disastrous."

"The situation in that country is certainly grim," I said. "One wonders where it will end."

"I visited the Comte two years ago with my father and even then there was a sense of uneasiness throughout the country. They did not seem to be as much aware of it as I was. Living close to something perhaps makes it less obvious."

"I have heard of the extravagance of the Queen."

"She is very unpopular. The French do not like foreigners, and of course she is one."

"But a charming and beautiful woman, I believe."

"Oh yes. We were presented by the Comte. She danced exquisitely, I remember, and was most beautifully gowned. I think the Comte is a little more uneasy than he admits."

"He does not appear to be in the least so . . . But perhaps I speak rashly. I scarcely know him."

"He is not a man to betray his feelings. If there should be trouble he would have a great deal to lose. Among other property he owns the Château Silvaine about forty miles due south of Paris and the Hôtel Delibes, a mansion in the capital. His is a very ancient family, connected with the Capets. He is very much a man of the Court."

"I see. A most important gentleman."

"Indeed, yes. It is obvious from his demeanor, don't you think?"

"He seems determined that everyone shall be aware of it. I am sure he would be very put out if they were not."

"You must not judge him too harshly, Miss Maddox. He is a French aristocrat, and aristocracy is a state of being which is emphasized more definitely in France than here."

"Certainly I must not presume to judge. After all, as I said, I know nothing of him."

"I am sure he is uneasy. Only last night when he was talking to my father he mentioned the riots which had taken place a few years ago when the markets were raided and boats on the Oise which were bringing grain to Paris were boarded and the sacks of grain seized and thrown into the river. He said something which impressed my father deeply. He said it was a 'rehearsal for a revolution.' But I am boring you with this dreary conversation."

"Indeed not. My mother has always insisted that we keep up to date with modern history as well as that of the past. We have the French papers which we read in class. In fact, we keep them and read them again and again. So I have heard of that alarming period. The trouble was averted, however."

"Yes, but I can't forget the Comte's words. 'A rehearsal.' And whenever something like this happens . . . servants coming with a special message . . . I feel uneasy."

"Ah, there is Minella!" It was Maria and Sybil with a young man. They carried plates. "We shall join you," said Maria.

Joel presented the young man to me. "This is Tom Fielding. Miss Maddox, Tom."

Tom Fielding bowed and asked if I had enjoyed the music. I told him that I had immensely.

"The salmon is good," he said. "Have you tried it?"

"Joel," put in Maria, "if you wish to look after our guests, I know Minella will excuse you."

"I am sure she would if I had that wish," replied Joel, smiling at me. "But it happens that I have not."

"Perhaps you think you ought to . . ."

"Tonight I am bent on pleasure."

I warmed towards him. I knew that Maria was reminding him that he need not treat the schoolmistress's daughter as an ordinary guest, which was typical of her. Whether he was aware of her meaning or not, I did not know, but I liked him for his response to it.

The conversation centered on trivialities, and I could see that Joel, who was clearly a serious-minded young man, would have preferred to go on with our discussion.

Sybil said: "Mama says that when you leave, Minella, she will send someone to escort you to the schoolhouse. You must not go back alone."

"That is kind of her," I said.

"I will take Miss Maddox back to the house," said Joel quickly.

"I think you will be needed here, Joel," Maria pointed out.

"You overrate my importance, sister. Everything will run just as smoothly whether I am here or not."

"I think Mama expects . . ."

Joel said: "Tom, do try the marchpane. Our cook is proud of it."

Since Maria had put the idea into my head, I now began to wonder whether it was time for me to leave. It was half past ten and I must certainly not be the last to go.

I turned to Joel. "It is good of you to offer to take me. Thank you."

"It is I who should thank you for allowing me to do so," he replied gallantly.

"Perhaps I should find Lady Derringham and thank her now."

"I'll take you to her," said Joel.

Lady Derringham received my thanks graciously, and Sir John said he thought it was extremely good of me to come at such short notice.

I could not see the Comte anywhere and I wondered whether he had not returned after leaving with Sir John. I did see Margot though. She was clearly enjoying herself in the company of a young man who seemed to be enchanted with her and she with him.

Joel and I walked the half a mile or so from the Manor to the schoolhouse.

There was a half moon in the sky which shed a pale and eerie light on the bushes. I felt as though I were in a dream. Here I was out late at night with Joel Derringham who showed me clearly that he enjoyed my company. It must have been obvious, otherwise Maria would not have been so put out. I wondered what my mother would say for she would be sitting up waiting for me. She would be expecting one of the servants from the Manor to escort me and when she realized it was the son and heir I could imagine her excitement.

It meant nothing . . . simply nothing. It was like the Comte's kisses. I must remember that, and make her realize it too.

Joel said what a pleasant evening it had been. His parents gave these musical *soirées* fairly frequently, but this was one he would always remember.

"I shall certainly remember it," I replied lightly. "For me it is the first and only one."

"The first, perhaps," he suggested. "You do enjoy music, I know. What a sky! It's rarely so clear. The moon dims the stars somewhat, though. Look at the Pleiades over there to the northeast. Did you know that when they appear it's a sign of the end of summer? They are not welcome for that reason. I have always been interested in the stars. Stand still a moment. Look up. Here are we two little people looking into eternity. It's rather overwhelming. Do you find it so?"

As I stood there, looking up with him, I felt quite emotional. It had been such a strange evening—quite different from anything I had known before—and something told me that big events were closing in on me, that I had reached the end of a road, the passing of a phase, and that Joel Derringham and perhaps even the Comte Fontaine Delibes were not merely passing acquaintances but that my future was caught up with theirs in some strange way and it was a beginning.

Joel went on: "They are supposed to be the seven daughters of Atlas and Pleione—virgin companions of Artemis—who were pursued by the hunter Orion. When they appealed to the gods to save them from Orion's lustful embraces, they were changed into doves and placed in the sky."

"A fate presumably preferable than that which is said to be worse than death," I commented.

Joel laughed. "It has been good to meet you," he said. "You are so different from other girls I normally meet." He continued to look up at the sky. "All of the Pleiades married gods, except one, Merope, who married a mortal. For that reason her light was dimmed."

"So social distinction exists in the heavens!"

"That is just the legend."

"It spoils it in my opinion. I should have liked Merope to shine more brightly because she was more adventurous and independent than her sisters. But of course no one would agree with me."

"I do," he assured me.

I felt exhilarated, excited, and the feeling that I was on the threshold of adventure increased.

"You must not be late in returning," I warned him, "or they will wonder what has become of you."

We were silent as we made our way to the schoolhouse.

As I had guessed my mother was waiting up for me. Her eyes widened with delight when she saw my companion.

He declined to come in but handed me to her as though I were some valuable object to be safely deposited. Then he said good night and was gone.

I had to sit up for a long time telling my mother every detail. I did, but I omitted to mention the Comte.

2

The excitement in the schoolhouse continued. My mother went about with a faraway look in her eyes and there was a smile of contentment on her lips. I knew very well what was in her mind and I was mildly appalled at her temerity.

The fact was that Joel Derringham was determined to be friendly. I was eighteen years of age and in spite of a lack of worldly experience appeared to be quite mature. This was probably due to my having a more serious nature than the Derringham girls—and certainly than Margot. I had had it brought home to me that I must acquire the best education available to me with the purpose of earning my living through it; this had been so impressed on me by my mother since the death of my father that I had accepted it as my way of life. I had read extensively anything that came to hand; I had felt it my duty to know something of any subject which might be mentioned; and it was no doubt due to this that Joel found me different. Ever since our meeting, he had sought my company. When I went for my favorite walk across the meadows I would find him seated on a stile over which I had to cross, and he would join me in my walk. He was often riding past the schoolhouse and on several occasions he called in. My mother received him graciously and without fuss, and the only reason why I knew she was inwardly excited was by the faint color in her cheeks. She was delighted. This most prosaic of women was vulnerable only where her daughter was concerned, and it became embarrassingly clear that she had decided that Joel Derringham should marry me. Instead of at the schoolhouse my future was to be at Derringham Manor.

This was the wildest dream, for even if Joel thought it a possibility, his family would never permit it.

Yet in the space of a week we had become very good friends. I enjoyed our meetings, which were never arranged but seemed to come about naturally, though I suspected they were contrived by him. It was amazing how often I would go out and come upon him. I rode Jenny, our little horse which drew the jingle—our only means of transport. She was not young but docile and my mother had been anxious for me to ride well. Several times when I rode out on her I would come upon Joel on one of the fine hunters from the Derringham stables. He would ride beside me and it invariably happened that where I proposed to go was just where he was going also. He was so gracious and charming as well as informative and I found his company interesting. I was flattered, too, that he should seek me out.

Margot told me that her parents had left England because of the way things were going in France; she did not seem to be very perturbed and was delighted to be left alone in England. Vaguely I wondered about Margot, who was very merry and abandonedly gay one day and subdued and serious the next. Her changes of mood were quite unpredictable, but being absorbed in my own affairs, I put them down to her Gallic temperament and forgot her.

It was Joel who told me about the reason for the Comte's sudden departure. I had ridden out on Jenny, for I used to exercise her after school in the evenings, so the time when I would be at liberty to ride was almost certain to be early evening. Invariably I would see the tall figure coming towards me through the trees and it happened so often that I came to expect it.

Joel looked grave when he discussed the Comte's departure.

"There is a great scandal brewing at the Court of France," he told me. "Some members of the nobility seem to be involved in it and the Comte thought it would be wise for him to go back to be on the spot. It involves a diamond necklace which the Queen is said to have acquired with the assistance of a Cardinal and that in exchange for his services he hopes to become her lover . . . might, indeed, have been her lover. Of course it is denied by the Queen, and the Cardinal de Rohan and his accomplices have been arrested. It is going to be a *cause célèbre*."

"And does this concern the Comte Fontaine Delibes?"

"There is a strong feeling that it might concern the whole of France. The royal family cannot afford a scandal at this time. Perhaps I am wrong . . . I hope so. My father thinks I exaggerate, but as I told you I sensed a seething unrest in the country when I was there. There is a great deal of extravagance. The rich are so rich and the poor so poor."

"Is that not the case everywhere?"

"Yes, I suppose so, but there seems to be a growing resentment throughout France. I believe the Comte is very much aware of it. It was for this reason that he decided to return without delay. He made arrangements to leave on the night of the *soirée*."

I thought about his leaving in haste and supposed he had not given me another thought. And that, I told myself, is the last I shall see of the distinguished gentleman, and that is not such a bad thing. Something told me that his acquaintance would bring me no good. I must dismiss him from my mind. That should not be difficult, for at this time I was enjoying a very pleasant friendship with the most eligible young man in the neighborhood.

We did not speak much of the Comte after that. Joel was interested in the country's affairs and was hoping one day to become a Member of Parliament. His family were not eager for this.

"They think that I, being the only son, should give my attention to the estate."

"And you have other ideas."

"Oh, I am interested in the estate, but it is not enough to occupy a man's lifetime. One can delegate to managers. Why should a man not go out and take an interest in the governing of the country?"

"I dare say Mr. Pitt makes a full-time job of his parliamentary career."

"Ah, but he is Prime Minister."

"Surely you should aim for the highest office."

"Perhaps I should."

"And delegate more and more of estate matters to your managers?"

"That could be. Oh, I like the country. I am interested in managing affairs here, but these are uneasy times, Miss Maddox. They are fraught with danger. If there was trouble on the other side of the Channel . . ."

"What trouble?" I asked quickly.

"You remember the 'rehearsal' I mentioned. What if that really should have been a rehearsal with a full-scale performance to come?"

"You mean a kind of civil war?"

"I mean that the needy might rise against the affluent . . . the starving against the extravagant spendthrifts. I think that could be a possibility."

I shivered, picturing the Comte, proud in his *château* and the mob marching . . . the bloodthirsty mob . . .

My mother said that I allowed my imagination to run away with me. "Imagination is like fire," she used to say. "A good friend but a bad enemy. You must learn to direct it in the way it can serve you best."

I asked myself why I should be concerned about what happened to that man. I was sure that if an evil fate overtook him he would deserve it, but I imagined no ill fate would ever overtake him. He would always be the winner.

Joel went on: "My father always reproves me if I talk of these things. He believes there is a good deal of speculation which means nothing. I expect he is right. But in any case the Comte did think he should return."

"Is it significant that he has left his daughter here?"

"Not in the least. He approves of the tuition she is getting in English. He says that since she studied at your school she speaks far better English than he does. He wants her to perfect it. You can rely on her being with you for another year."

"My mother will be pleased."

"And you?" he asked.

"I have a fondness for Margot. She is very amusing."

"She is very . . . young . . ."

"She is growing up fast."

". . . and lighthearted," he added.

Joel was scarcely that, I reflected. He took life somewhat seriously. He loved to talk politics to me as I was aware of what was happening in the country. My mother and I always read any newspaper which came into our hands. Joel warmly admired Mr. Pitt, that youngest of our Prime Ministers, and he talked of him glowingly, how clever he was, how the country had never been better served, and he believed his introduction of the Sinking Fund would gradually reduce the National Debt.

When there was an attempt on the King's life, Joel actually called at the schoolhouse to tell us about it. My mother was delighted to see him and brought out a bottle of her homemade wine—kept for special occasions—and some of the little wine cakes she took such a pride in.

She was almost purring as we sat down at our parlor table and Joel told us about the demented old woman who had waited for the King as he alighted from his post chariot at the garden gate of St. James's on a pretext of handing a petition to him, and had tried to stab him in the chest with a knife she had concealed.

"Thank God," said Joel, "that His Majesty's guards caught her arm in time. The King behaved in a manner one expects of him. His concern was for the poor woman. 'I am not hurt,' he cried. 'See to her.' He said afterwards that she was mad and that she was therefore not responsible for her actions."

"I have heard it said," my mother commented, "that His Majesty would naturally have pity on one so afflicted."

"Oh, you have been hearing rumors about the state of his own health, I'll swear," said Joel.

"You would know," replied my mother, "whether there is any truth in them."

"I know of the rumors but the truth of them is another matter."

"Do you think the woman was acting by herself, or was she the member of some gang intending to harm the King?" I asked.

"It is almost certain to be the former."

Joel sipped his wine, complimenting my mother on it and her wine cakes, and began to tell us anecdotes about the Court which enthralled us who were far removed from it.

It was a pleasant visit and when he had gone my mother glowed with pride and I heard her singing "Heart of Oak" in her endearing out-of-tune voice, and as she always did this when she was particularly pleased with life, I knew what was in her mind.

My birthday was in September—I was nineteen in that year of 1786—and when I went out to our little lean-to which served as a stable in order to saddle Jenny, I saw a lovely chestnut mare waiting for me there.

I stared in astonishment. Then I heard a movement behind me and, turning, saw my mother. I had never seen her looking so happy since before my father's death.

"Well," she said, "now when you go riding with Joel Derringham you'll look just right."

I threw myself into her arms and we hugged each other. There were tears in her eyes when she released me.

"How could you possibly afford it?" I asked.

"Ah!" She nodded sagely. "That's not the thing to say when you get a present."

Then the truth dawned on me. "The Dower!" I cried, appalled. My mother had saved as she said, "for a rainy day," and the money was kept in the old Tudor Dower Chest which had been in the family for years. We always referred to the savings as the Dower.

"Well, I thought, a horse in the stable was better than a few sovereigns tied up in a bag. You haven't finished yet. Come upstairs."

Proudly she took me to her bedroom and there, laid out on the bed, was a complete riding outfit—dark blue skirt and jacket and a tall hat of the same shade.

I couldn't wait to try on everything and of course it fitted perfectly.

"It's becoming," she murmured. "Your father would have been so proud. Now you look as though you really do belong . . ."

"Belong! To whom?"

"You look every bit as grand as the guests up at the Manor."

I felt a twinge of apprehension. I understood absolutely how her thoughts were moving. My friendship with Joel Derringham had robbed her of some of her good sense. She had really made up her mind that he was going to marry me, and it was for this reason that she was ready to take money from the Dower Chest, which had been almost sacred to her for as long as I could remember. I could imagine her convincing herself that the horse and the outfit were no extravagance. They were proclaiming to the world how suited her daughter was to step up into the world of the nobility.

I said nothing, but the joy in my new horse and clothes was considerably subdued.

When I rode out she was watching me from the top window and I felt a great surge of tenderness for her, and with it was the almost certainty that she was going to be disappointed.

For a few weeks life went on as before. October came. The school was less full than that time last year. My mother was always anxious when pupils disappeared. Sybil and Maria were still coming, of course, with Margot, but it was a foregone conclusion that Margot would one day return to her parents, and Sybil and Maria would probably go with her for they would attend a finishing school near Paris.

I could not help enjoying my new mare. Poor Jenny was relieved to be rid of me, and the mare, whom I had called Dower, demanded a great deal of exercise, so I rode often. And Joel was always there to meet me. We had long rides on Saturdays and Sundays when there was no school.

We talked of politics, the stars, the countryside, and any subject, all of which he seemed to know a good deal about. There was a quiet enthusiasm about him which I found endearing, but the fact was that while I liked him very much I found no great exhilaration in his company. I should never have noticed this if it had not been for my encounter with the Comte. Even after all this time the memory of his kisses made me shudder. I had started to dream about him and these dreams could be rather frightening, though when I awoke from them it was always with regret and I wished myself back in them. I would be in embarrassing situations and always the Comte was there, watching me enigmatically so that I could never be sure what he was going to do.

It was all very foolish and ridiculous that a serious-minded young woman of my age should be so naïve. I made excuses for myself. Mine had been a sheltered life. I had never been out in the world. Sometimes I felt my mother shared my naïvety. It must have been so if she thought Joel Derringham was going to marry me.

I was so absorbed in my own affairs that I only vaguely noticed the change in Margot. She was less exuberant. She was even on some occasions subdued. That she was a creature of moods I had always known, but it had never been so apparent as it was now. There were times when she would be almost hysterically gay and others when she was nearly morbid.

She was inattentive at lessons, and I waited until we were alone to reprove her.

"English verbs!" she cried, throwing up her hands. "I find them so boring. Who cares whether I speak English as you do or as I do . . . as long as I am understood."

"I care," I reminded her. "My mother cares and your family care."

"They don't. They won't know the difference in any case."

"Your father has allowed you to stay here because he is pleased with your progress."

"He has allowed me to stay because they want me out of the way."

"I do not believe such nonsense."

"Minelle, you are . . . what is it called . . . a hypocrite? You pretend to be so good. You learned all your verbs, I don't doubt. . . . and twice as quickly as anyone else. And now you go riding on your new horse . . . in your elegant clothes . . . and who is waiting in the woods? Tell me that."

"I asked you here that we might talk seriously, Margot."

"What is more serious than this, eh? Joel likes you, Minelle. He likes you very much. I am glad because . . . shall I tell you something? They meant him for me. Oh, that startles you, yes? My father and Sir John have talked of it. I know because I listened . . . at keyholes. Oh, very naughty! My father would like me to be settled in England. He thinks France is not very safe for a time. So if I married Joel . . . who will give me riches . . . and title . . . that should be considered. Of course, he is not of such an ancient family as ours . . . but we are prepared to forget that. Now you come along with your new horse, your elegant riding clothes, and Joel does not seem to see me. He sees only you."

"I never heard anyone talk such nonsense as you do when you are in the mood."

"It all began, did it not, when you came to tea. You met him on the lawn by the sundial. You looked quite handsome standing there. The sun makes your hair look beautiful, I thought. So did he. Are you in love with him, Minelle?"

"Margot, I do want you to pay more attention to your lessons."

"And I want you to pay attention to me. But you are doing so. You have grown quite pink thinking of Joel Derringham. You can confide in me because you know . . ."

"There is nothing to confide. Now Margot, you *must* work harder at your English, otherwise there is no point in your being here. You might as well be in your father's *château*."

"I am not like you, Minelle. I do not pretend."

"We are not discussing our respective characters but the need for work."

"Oh, Minelle, you are the most maddening creature! I wonder Joel likes you. I do really."

"Who said he does?"

"I do. Marie does, so does Sybil. And I reckon everyone says so. You can't ride out as often as you do with a young man without people's noticing. And they draw their conclusions."

"Then that is extremely impertinent of them."

"They won't let him marry you, Minelle."

I felt cold with fear—and it was not of Joel or myself that I was thinking, but of my mother.

"It's funny really . . ."

She began to laugh. It was one of those occasions when she alarmed me. Her laughter grew uncontrollable and when I took her by the shoulders she started to cry. She leaned against me and clung to me, her slender body shaking with sobs.

"Margot, Margot," I cried. "What's wrong?"

But I could get no sense out of her.

We had snow in November. It was one of the coldest in memory. Maria and Sybil could not come down from the Manor to the schoolhouse and we had very small classes. We were hard put to it to keep the house warm and although we kept log fires burning in every room, the bitter east wind seemed to penetrate every crack. My mother caught what she called "one of her colds." She suffered from them every winter, so at first we took little notice of this one. But it persisted and I made her stay in bed while I kept the school going. So many pupils stayed away that it was not as difficult as it might have been.

She started to cough in the night and as she grew worse I

thought I should call a doctor, but she wouldn't hear of it. It would cost too much, she said.

"But it is necessary," I said. "There's the dower."

She shook her head. So I delayed for several days, but when she grew feverish and delirious I asked the doctor to come. She had congestion of the lungs, he said.

This was a serious illness—by no means one of the winter colds. I shut the school and gave myself up to nursing her.

These were some of the most unhappy days I had yet known. To see her lying there, propped up with pillows, her skin hot and dry, her eyes glazed, watching me with those too-bright eyes, filled me with misery. The terrible realization had come to me that her chances of recovery were not great.

"Dearest Mama," I cried, "tell me what to do. I will do anything . . . anything . . . if only you will get better."

"Is that you, Minella?" she whispered.

I knelt by the bed and took her hand. "I am here, my dearest. I have not left you since you have been ill. I shall always be with you . . ."

"Minella, I am going to your father. I dreamed of him last night. He was standing at the prow of his ship and holding out his hands to me. I said to him, 'I'm coming to you.' Then he smiled and beckoned. I said: 'I have to leave our little girl behind,' and he answered: 'She will be well taken care of. You know she will.' Then a great peace came to me and I knew all would come right."

"Nothing can be right if you are not here."

"Oh yes, my love. You have your life. He is a good man. I have dreamed of it often . . ." Her voice was scarcely audible. "He's kind . . . like his father . . . He'll be good to you. And you'll fit. Never doubt it. You're as good as any of them. No, better . . . Remember that, my child . . ."

"Oh my darling, I only want you to get well. Nothing else matters."

She shook her head. "The time comes for us all, Minella. Mine is now. But I can go . . . happy . . . because he's there."

"Listen," I insisted, "you're going to get well. We'll close the school for a month. We'll go away together . . . just the two of us. We'll raid the Dower Chest."

Her lips twitched. She shook her head. "Well spent," she murmured. "It was money well spent."

"Don't talk, dearest. Save your breath."

She nodded and smiled at me with such a wealth of love in her eyes that I could scarcely restrain my tears.

She closed her eyes and after a while began to murmur under her breath.

I leaned forward to listen. "Worth while," she whispered. "My girl . . . why not? . . . she's as good as any of them . . . fitting that she should take her place among them. What I always wanted. Like an answer to a prayer . . . Thank you, God. I can go happy now . . ."

I sat by the bed, understanding full well her thoughts, which were as they had been since my father's death—all for me. She was dying. I knew that, and I could find no comfort in deceiving myself. But she was happy because she believed that Joel Derringham was in love with me and would ask me to marry him.

Oh beloved, foolish mother! How unworldly she was! Even I, who had lived my sheltered life, was more aware of how the world acted than she was. Or perhaps she was blinded by love. She saw her daughter as a swan among geese . . . demanding to be singled out for attention.

There was only one thing for which I could be thankful. She died happy . . . believing that my future was secure.

She was buried in Derringham churchyard on a bitter December day—two weeks before Christmas. Standing in the cold wind, listening to the clods of earth falling on her coffin, I was completely overcome by my desolation. To represent him, Sir John had sent his butler—a very dignified man held in great esteem by all those who worked for the Derringhams. Mrs. Callan, the housekeeper, also came. There were one or two other mourners from the estate, but I was aware of little but my grief.

I saw Joel as we left the churchyard. He was standing by the gate, his hat in his hand. He did not speak. He just took my hand and held it for a moment. I withdrew it. I could not bear to talk to anyone. All I wanted was to be alone.

The schoolhouse was deathly quiet. I could still smell the oak coffin which had stood on trestles in our sitting room until that morning. The room seemed empty now. There was nothing but emptiness everywhere . . . in the house, and in my heart no less.

I went to my bedroom and lay on my bed and thought of her and how we had laughed and planned together; and how her great relief had been that when she was gone I should have the school—until later when she had made up her mind that Joel Derringham wanted to marry me and had been elated contemplating a brilliant and secure future.

The rest of the day I lay there alone with my grief.

I had slept at length, for I was quite exhausted and the next day when I arose I felt a little rested. The future stared me blankly in the face for I could not imagine it without her. I supposed I should continue with the school as she had always intended that I should until . . .

I shook off thoughts of Joel Derringham. I liked him, of course, but even if he asked me to marry him I was not sure that I wanted to. What had alarmed me about my friendship with Joel was the knowledge that my mother was going to be heartbroken when it would finally be brought home to her that I could not marry him.

The Derringhams would never allow it—even if Joel and I wished it. Margot had told me he had been intended for her and that would be a suitable match. At least my dearest mother would not have to suffer that disappointment.

What should I do? I had to go on with my life. I should therefore continue with the school. I had what was left in the Dower Chest, which was in her bedroom. That chest had belonged to her great-great-great-grandmother and had come down through the eldest daughters of the family. Money was put into it from the day a girl was born so that there would be a good sum by the time she was marriageable. The key was kept on the chain which my mother had worn about her waist and that chatelaine had also been handed down through the women of the household with the chest.

I found the key and opened the chest.

There were but five guineas in it.

I was amazed because I had believed I should find at least a hundred. Of course, the horse and the riding outfit must have cost far more than I had imagined.

Later, I also found lengths of material in her cupboard, and when Jilly Barton came with a velvet gown which she had made for me. I knew what had happened.

The dower had been spent to buy clothes for me so that I might show myself to be a worthy partner for Joel Derringham.

I awoke on the first Christmas Day alone to a sense of great desolation. I lay in bed unwisely remembering other Christmases when my mother had come into my room carrying mysterious parcels calling out: "Merry Christmas, my darling!" and how I would reach out for my gifts to her and the fun we had scattering wrappings over the bed and exclaiming with surprise (often assumed because we were always practical in our choice of gifts). But when we declared, as we often did, "It's exactly what I wanted!" it invariably was, as we knew each other's needs to perfection. Now here I was alone. It had been too sudden. If she had been ill for some time I could have grown accustomed to the knowledge that I had to lose her and perhaps that would have softened the blow. She had not been old. I railed against the cruel fate which had deprived me of the one I loved.

Then I seemed to hear her voice admonishing me. I had to go on living. I had to make a success of my life and I should never do that if I gave myself up to bitterness.

Grief is always so much harder to bear on feast days and the reason is self-pity. That sounded like my mother's reasoning. Because other people were enjoying life that should not make one more miserable.

I arose and dressed. I had been invited to spend the day at the Mansers', who farmed some of the Derringham estates. My mother and I had spent Christmas with them for several years and they had been good friends to us. They had six daughters and they had all been at the school—the two youngest were still there, great strapping girls destined surely to become farmers' wives. There was a son, too— Jim, a few years older than I, who was already his father's right-hand man. The Mansers' farm had always seemed to us a house of plenty. They often sent us joints of lamb and pork and my mother used to say they kept us in milk and butter.

Mrs. Manser could never be grateful enough for the education her children had received. It would have been quite beyond the family's means to send the children away to school—and they were not the kind to employ a governess—and when my mother had opened the school so close at hand, the Mansers said it was like an answer to their prayers. There were several other families who had felt the same and that was why we had had enough pupils to support the school.

I rode to the Mansers' on Dower and was especially warmly received by all, which was touching. I tried to throw off my grief and be as bright as possible in the circumstances. I could scarcely eat any of the goose which

44

Mrs. Manser had prepared with such loving care, but I did try my best not to cast a gloom over the day. I joined them in the games they played afterwards and Mrs. Manser contrived to partner me with Jim, and I could see how her mind was working. It might have been amusing, if I were not in such a sad mood, to see how the people who cared for me were anxious to see me settled.

I could not believe I should make a good farmer's wife, but at least Mrs. Manser's solution might be more possible than the wild dreams in which my mother had indulged.

Mrs. Manser insisted that I stay the night and spend the next day with them, which I did, feeling grateful not to have to go back to the lonely schoolhouse.

It was mid-afternoon of the following day when I returned. School would start at the beginning of the next week and I had to prepare the curriculum. I could scarcely bear the silence of the house, the empty chair, the empty rooms. I longed to get right away.

I had not been in the house an hour when Joel called.

He took my hands and looked into my face with such compassion that I could scarcely restrain my grief.

"I don't know what to say to you, Minella," he told me.

I replied: "Please say nothing. That is best. Talk . . . talk about anything but not . . ."

He nodded, releasing my hands. He told me he had wondered about me during Christmas and had come over on the morning of Christmas Day to find me gone. I explained where I had been and told him of the kindness of the Mansers.

He took a box from his pocket and said he had a little gift for me. I opened it and there was a brooch lying on black velvet—a sapphire surrounded by rose diamonds.

"I was attracted by the sapphire," he said. "I thought it was the color of your eyes."

I was overcome by emotion. Since my mother's death I had been too easily moved by a show of kindness. It was a beautiful brooch—far more valuable than anything I had ever possessed.

"It was good of you to think of me," I said.

"I have thought of you a great deal . . . all the time . . . since . . ."

I nodded and turned away. Then I took out the brooch and he watched me pin it on my dress.

"Thank you," I said. "I shall always treasure it."

"Minella," he said, "I want to talk to you."

45

His voice was gentle and a little apprehensive. In my mind's eye I could see my mother's smiling eyes, the happy curve of her lips. Could it really be?

Panic seized me. I wanted time to think . . . to grow accustomed to my loneliness . . . my unhappiness.

"Sometime," I began.

He said: "I will see you tomorrow. Perhaps we will ride together."

"Yes," I replied. "Please."

He went and I sat for a long time staring ahead of me.

I was aware of a serenity in the house. It was almost as though my mother was there. I could almost hear the strains of "Heart of Oak."

I spent a restless night turning over in my mind what I should say if Joel asked me to marry him. The brooch was perhaps a symbol of his intentions, which I was sure were honorable—with a man like Joel they could not be anything else. I seemed to hear my mother's voice urging me not to hesitate. That would be foolish. I imagined that she was with me and that we discussed the matter together. "I don't love him as one should love a man one marries." I could see her lips pursed as I had seen them so often when she expressed contempt for a point of view. "You don't know anything about love, my child. That'll come. He's a good man. He can give you all I ever wanted for you. Comfort, security, and enough love to do for the two of you . . . for a start. You couldn't help but grow to love a man like that. I see your little ones playing there on those lawns near the sundial where you first really got to know each other. Oh, the joy of little ones. I only had one, but after your father died she was all the world to me." "Dearest of mothers, are you right? You often were but do you know what is best for me?"

I could never have told her of my feelings when the Comte had seized and kissed me. There had been a kind of stirring within me, something rather terrifying and yet irresistible. It had brought with it a realization that there was something I did not understand but which I must before I entered into marriage. The Comte had made me realize that Joel could not have that effect on me. That was all.

I could hear my mother's gentle laugh. "The Comte! A notorious philanderer. A most unpleasant and uncomfortable man! The fact that he behaved as he did shows him to be wicked. And his wife sleeping in the next room! Think of

46

good kind Joel who would never do anything dishonorable and could give you all that I ever wanted for you."

All I ever wanted for you. Those words kept echoing in my mind.

3

It was on the following day that the drama started. It began by Sir John's riding over to the schoolhouse.

"Miss Maddox," he cried, and his distracted looks amazed me, "is she here? Is Margot here?"

"Margot!" I answered. "No. I haven't seen her for several days."

"Oh my God, what can have become of her?"

I stared at him blankly and he went on: "She has not been seen since last night. Her bed has not been slept in. She told the girls that she was going to bed early on account of a headache. That was the last time she was seen. Have you any idea where she can have gone?"

I shook my head and tried to recall my last conversation with Margot. There was nothing to suggest she contemplated flight.

When Sir John went back to the Manor I was very uneasy. I kept telling myself that it was a prank of hers. She would turn up and laugh at us. For some time, though, there had been a certain secrecy about Margot. I should have taken more notice but I had been so absorbed in my own affairs.

I could not settle to anything and in the early afternoon I could not resist going over to the Manor to see if there was any news. I waited in the hall and when Maria and Sybil came down to me their faces were taut with excitement, yet I felt they were reveling in the disturbance.

"I believe she has gone off with someone," said Maria.

"Gone off with someone. With whom?"

"That is what we have to find out. Joel is most upset." Maria was looking at me. "Of course there was to be a match between them."

"She can't have gone off," said Sybil. "There is no one for her to have gone off with. Besides, she knew she was going to marry Joel as soon as she was old enough. That was why they were so anxious for her to learn English and like it here."

"Have you questioned the servants?" I asked.

"Everyone has been questioned," replied Maria, "but they don't know anything. Papa is frantic. So is Mama. He says he will have to send a message to the Comte and Comtesse if she is not found by tomorrow."

"She was under Papa's care," said Sybil. "It is dreadful for him. I do hope nothing is wrong. We thought she might have confided in you. She was always more friendly with you than with us."

"She confided nothing," I said, and I thought of those occasions when I had been sure I had seen secrets in her eyes. I should have asked her what was happening. I believe she might have wanted to tell. Margot was not the sort to keep secrets.

"Is there anything we can do . . ." I began.

"We can only wait," replied Sybil.

As I was about to leave, one of the grooms came into the hall, dragging a young boy from the stables who looked scared out of his wits.

"Miss Maria," said the groom, "I think I should have a word with Sir John and no delay."

"Is it about Mademoiselle Fontaine Delibes?" asked Maria.

"The French young lady yes, Miss Maria."

Sybil ran off at once to search for her father while Maria pulled the bell rope and sent a servant in search of him. Fortunately he was soon found and came hurrying to the hall. I knew that I had no right to stay but I was so concerned about Margot that I stubbornly remained.

The groom burst out: "Tim here have something to say, Sir John. Come, Tim. Tell what you know."

"It's our James, sir," said Tim. "He haven't been 'ome. He have gone off with the French young lady, sir. He said he were going but us didn't believe 'im."

"Oh my God," muttered Sir John under his breath. He half-closed his eyes as though to convince himself that this was not really happening. I remembered James. He was the sort of young man one would remember—tall and startlingly handsome—a rather swaggering, arrogant young man whose outstanding looks appeared to have given him a good opinion of himself.

Sir John became brisk. He looked straight at the stable boy and said: "Tell me everything you know."

"I don't know nothing but that he be gone, sir. I only know he said he were going to marry into society like . . ."

"What!" cried Sir John.

"Yes, sir, he said as he were going to run away to a place in Scotland. He said they'd get married there and he'd be gentry after that."

Sir John said: "There is no time to lose. I must go after them. I must bring her back before it is too late."

I returned to the schoolhouse for there was no reason why I should stay. I fancied that both Maria and Sybil were inclined to think that I had played some part in Margot's wickedness, for they were convinced that she would have confided in me. I should have to assure them that this was not the case, but Margot herself would do that when she was brought back.

I sat in the sitting room and thought about Margot, who had become involved in this foolish adventure. What if she really did marry the groom? What would the reactions of the Comte be to that? He would never forgive us for allowing it. Margot would doubtless be cast off, for could the proud Comte accept a groom as his son-in-law? How could Margot have done this? She was only sixteen years old and she had a passing fancy for a groom! How like her! No doubt she thought it amusing at first. She was quite childish. But what would the outcome of the affair be?

Mrs. Manser came over to see me. She had brought some eggs but the real object of the visit was the desire to gossip. She sat at the table, her eyes round with excitement.

"What a how-do-you-do! That little Madam . . . going off with James Wedder. My goodness gracious me! They'll never get over this at the Manor."

"Sir John will bring her back."

"If he's in time. James Wedder was one for the girls always. He's got a real fancy for himself, that one. Mind you, he's a fine figure of a man. They say that far back he's connected with the Derringhams. Sir John's grandfather was a bit of a rip, I believe. Ladies and serving girls . . . it didn't matter much to him and that meant that there was a good deal of Derringham blood hereabouts . . . though called by other names. There was one of the Wedder girls who had two bastards by him, so the story goes, and that's where James comes in. Always gave himself airs, did James. And now to run off like that."

"They can't have got far," I said.

"They've got a start, you know. They'll bring them back mayhap . . . and what then?" She looked at me intently. "They say it was to have been a match between her and Mr. Joel. That was why she was brought over here . . . least, that's what I heard. What'll happen now . . . who can say?"

"She is very young," I said. "I knew her well . . . through school. I think she would be inclined to act recklessly and regret afterwards. I do hope Sir John is in time."

"They say Mr. Joel is determined to stop the marriage. He's gone off with his father. The pair of them will put an end to this you can be sure. But what a scandal for the Manor."

Anxious as I was to glean all the information I could, I was glad when Mrs. Manser left. I think she was trying to offer me some oblique warning, for it had been noticed that I sometimes rode out with Joel Derringham. Although there was not such a wide gulf between us as there was between Margot and her groom, still the gulf was there.

Mrs. Manser thought I should be wise to encourage the courtship of her son Jim and learn to become a farmer's wife.

A whole day and night passed in anxious speculation and then Sir John and Joel returned bringing Margot with them. I did not see her. She was exhausted and distraught and put straight to bed. No one called from the Manor to give me the news, and once again it was from Mrs. Manser that I gleaned information.

"They found them in time. Traced them, they did. They'd covered more than seventy miles. I heard it from Tom Harris, the groom that went with Sir John. He likes a jug of our home-brew taken in the parlor. He says they were both scared out of their wits and Master James wasn't so bold when he was faced with Sir John. He's been sent off on the spot. That's the last we'll hear of James Wedder, I shouldn't wonder. Not like Sir John to send a man off when he's got nowhere to go to, but this was different, I reckon. This 'ull teach him a lesson."

"Did you hear about Mademoiselle?"

"Tom Harris said she was crying as though her heart was broken, but they brought her back . . . and that's the end of James Wedder for her."

"How could she have been so foolish!" I cried. "She might have known."

"Oh, he's a dashing young fellow and young girls when they

fancy themselves in love don't always give much thought to what's coming of it."

Again I felt she was warning me.

Life was changing rapidly—my mother gone forever and new responsibilities crowding in on me. The school was not the same; it had lost the dignity my mother had given it. I was well educated and could teach, but I seemed so young and I knew there was not the confidence in me which my mother had inspired. I was only nineteen years old. People remembered this. I found taking class more difficult than it had been; there was a certain amount of insubordination. Margot had not come back to school although Maria and Sybil had. Maria told me that at the beginning of the summer she and her sister were going to a finishing school in Switzerland.

My heart sank. Without the Derringham girls, the school would lose the pupils who came from the Manor—the preserve on our bread, as my mother had called them. But it was not so much the preserve I had to worry about as the bread itself.

"There is talk of our brother's going on the Grand Tour," Maria told me maliciously. "Papa thinks it will be a good education for him, and all young men of his station do it. He will be going soon."

It was as though Margot's adventure with the groom had set something in motion, the object of which was to change everything.

I felt a sudden longing for Joel's company—he was always so calm, so reassuring in a way. And if he were going on the Grand Tour that meant that he would be away possibly for two years. What a lot could happen in two years! The once flourishing little school could become bankrupt. Without the Derringhams . . . what should I do? I felt I was being blamed for Margot's indiscretion. It had often been said that Margot and I were good friends. Perhaps it was also being said that I had allowed myself to become too friendly with Joel Derringham—a liaison which could not have an honorable ending and that had been a bad influence on Margot.

When two girls from one of the nearby big country houses announced that they were leaving and going to a finishing school it was like a red light flickering at the end of a tunnel.

I took Dower out for a long ride hoping to meet Joel and hear from his own lips that he was going away. But I did not see him and that in itself was significant.

On a Sunday morning he came to see me. My heart started to beat faster as I watched him tether his horse. As he came into the sitting room he looked very grave.

"I'm going away shortly," he told me.

There was silence broken only by the ticking of the grandfather clock.

"Maria mentioned it," I heard myself say.

"Well, of course it is considered to be part of one's education."

"Where shall you go?"

"Europe . . . Italy, France, Spain . . . the Grand Tour."

"It will be most interesting."

"I would rather not go."

"Then why?"

"My father insists."

"I see, and you must obey him."

"I always have."

"And you couldn't stop doing so now, naturally. But why should you want to?"

"Because . . . There is a reason why I don't want to go." He looked at me steadily. "I have prized our friendship."

"It was good."

"*Is* good. I'll be back, Minella."

"That will be in the future."

"But I shall come back. Then I shall talk to you . . . very seriously."

"If you come back and I am here I shall be interested to hear what you have to say."

He smiled and I said quietly: "When do you leave?"

"In two weeks' time."

I nodded. "Can I get you a glass of wine? My mother's specialty. She was proud of the wines she made. There is sloe gin too. It is very palatable."

"I am sure it is, but I want nothing now. I just came to talk to you."

"You will see some glorious works of art . . . and architecture. You will be able to study the night sky in Italy. You will learn the politics of the countries through which you pass. It will be an education."

He was looking at me almost piteously. I thought that if I made a certain move he might suddenly come to me and put his arms about me and urge me to be as foolish and reckless as Margot and her groom. I thought: No. It is not for me to lead the way. If he wants to enough he must do that. I wondered what the Derringhams would do if Joel told them he

52

wanted to marry me. A second disaster and so similar to the other. A *mésalliance,* they would call it.

Oh my dear mother, how wrong you were!

"I shall see you before I go," he was saying. "I want us to ride out together. There is so much I want to discuss."

After he had gone I sat at the table thinking of him. I knew what he meant. His family, realizing his interest in me, were sending him away. Margot's episode had alerted them to danger.

Over the mantelpiece hung the picture of my mother which my father had had painted during the first year of their marriage. It was wonderfully like her. I gazed at those steady eyes, that resolute mouth. "You dreamed too much," I said. "It was never meant to come to anything."

And I was not sure that I wanted it to. All I knew was that my world was collapsing about me. I could see the pupils drifting away and I felt lonely and a little afraid.

Joel left and the days seemed long. I was glad when school was over, though I dreaded the long evenings when I lighted the lamps and tried to occupy myself with preparations for the next day's lessons. I was grateful for the frequent company of the Mansers, but I was always aware of Jim and their expectations with regard to him and me. I fancied Mrs. Manser was telling her husband that I had come to my senses and stopped thinking of Joel Derringham.

I was deeply regretting the loss of our savings. There were several lengths of expensive material in my mother's bedroom and the cost of keeping Dower had to be considered. I could not get rid of dear Jenny, who had served us so well, so there were two of them to keep.

Maria and Sybil talked constantly of their approaching departure for Switzerland and I was haunted by the fear that I was not going to be able to keep the school going.

When I was alone at night I would imagine my mother was there and I would talk to her. I used to fancy I could hear her voice coming to me over that great void which separates the dead from the living, and I was comforted.

"One door shuts and another opens." She had a stock of such well-worn truisms at her disposal to bring out when they fitted the occasion, and I had often teased her about them. Now I remembered them and rejoiced in them.

There was one thing which alarmed me and that was the new coolness of Sir John and Lady Derringham towards me. They considered I had behaved in a most unbecoming manner by allowing their son to be attracted by me. I should have known better, and they lay the blame on me, seeing me, I was sure, as a scheming adventuress. Even though Joel had been sent away on his Grand Tour, I believe they had decided that I should be given no more chances to practice my wiles, which meant of course a withdrawal of their patronage. This was the most frightening aspect of the situation. My mother had constantly mentioned what great good had come to us through them, and I was wondering how long I could run the school at a loss.

One blustering March day Margot came to say goodbye to me. She looked subdued, but I detected a sparkle of mischief in her eyes.

It was a Sunday—a day when there was no school and I expected she had chosen it for that reason.

"Hello, Minelle," she said. "I am going home next week. I've come to say goodbye."

I felt suddenly wretched. I had been fond of Margot and it meant that everything and everyone I cared about was slipping away from me.

"This little episode"—she spread her hands as though to embrace the schoolhouse, myself, and the whole of England— "it is over."

"Well, it has been an experience for you."

"Sad, yes, and happy . . . and amusing. Nothing is all one of those, is it. There is always some of each. Poor James. I often wonder where he is. Sent away in disgrace. But he will find a new place . . . more girls to love."

"And you?"

"I also."

"It was a foolish thing to do, Margot."

"Yes, was it not? Like most adventures they are so much more fun to plan than to carry out. We used to lie under the hedge in the shrubbery and make plans. That was the best part. It was so dangerous. I used to run and find him at every possible moment."

"When you played hide-and-seek even," I said.

She nodded, laughing at me. "Anyone might have seen us at any time. We both said we did not care."

"But you were afraid of what might happen."

"Oh yes. But I *like* to be afraid. Don't you? Oh no, you are too righteous. Though what about you and Joel, eh? In a way we are in the same position . . . two of a kind, as they say, do they not? We both lost our lovers."

"Joel was not my lover."

"Well, he hoped to be. And you hoped. It made me laugh. You . . . the schoolmistress. Me . . . and the groom. It was a dance . . . the dance of the classes. Funny, do you see?"

"No, I don't."

"You have become a true schoolmistress, Minelle. But we had fun together—and now I am to go back to France. Sir John and Lady Derringham have been longing to be rid of me and now I am going."

"I am sorry. I shall miss you very much."

She stood up and in her impulsive way flung her arms about me.

"And I shall miss you, Minelle. I always liked you the best. I cannot talk to Marie and Sybil. They look down their silly noses at me as though I have the plague . . . and all because I have known something which they have not . . . and never will most likely. Perhaps you will come and see me in France."

"I cannot see how this would be possible."

"I might ask you."

"It is kind of you, Margot."

"Minelle, I am a little worried."

"Worried? What about?"

"I don't know what I should do."

"Perhaps you should explain."

"When James and I lay under the hedge in the shrubbery we did not simply make plans."

"What do you mean?"

"I am going to have a child, Minelle."

"Margot!"

"The ultimate shame," she cried. "It is not so much what one does as being caught in it. You see, James could have been my lover and that would have been a regrettable incident . . . to be hushed up and forgotten. But when there is living evidence of our liaison, what then? Shame. Disaster. Well, that is the story, Minelle. What am I to do?"

"Do Sir John and Lady Derringham know this?"

"No one knows but you . . . and me."

"Margot, what can you do?"

"That is what I want you to advise me on."

"What advice is there? You are going to have a child and there can be no hiding it."

"It will be hidden. People have had illegitimate children in the past and hidden it."

"How will you hide it?"

"That is what I must discover."

"Margot, how can *I* help you in this?"

"That is what I came to talk about." I saw the fear in her eyes then. "I'm afraid to go home . . . like this. Soon all will see it, will they not? And my father . . ."

In my mind's eye I saw him as clearly as I had that first time in Derringham Manor. I could feel his lips hard against mine.

"Perhaps he will understand," I suggested.

Margot laughed rather bitterly. "He will have had his bastards, doubt it not. That is nothing . . . a bagatelle. But what is acceptable for a man like my father is the ultimate disgrace for his daughter."

"It is so unfair."

"Of course it's unfair, Minelle, but what am I going to *do*? When I think of facing my father I feel like going to the top of the tower and throwing myself over."

"Don't talk like that."

"I never would, of course. I am always so interested to know what is coming next. Minelle, let's run away . . . you and I. The school is not going well, is it? I've heard them talk. Joel has gone. The lover who had to obey his parents rather than follow his love! *Pouf!*" She snapped her fingers. "James . . . he was bold. 'We will become gypsies,' he said. 'I will make a fortune and we will live in a castle as grand as your father's . . .' And then Sir John comes and he withers and is then only a frightened boy. I am not weak like that. Nor are you. We are not people to do something because it has always been done. We can make up our minds. We can fight."

"You are talking nonsense, Margot."

"What am I going to do then?"

"There is only one thing you can do. You must go to Sir John and tell him you are expecting a child. He is kind. He will help you and he will know what to do."

"I'd rather tell him than tell my father."

"Perhaps your mother will help."

Margot laughed. "My mother would not dare do anything. She would only tell *him* and I might as well do that."

"What do you think he will do?"

"He will be mad with rage. I am the only child of the marriage. That infuriates him in itself. No son to carry on the great line and my mother too weak and ailing and the doctors insisting that she must have no more children. So I am the hope of the house. I have to make a grand marriage. Although there was talk of Joel for me, I don't think my father thought it was ideal. He was only considering it because of the troubles in France and he thought English estates might be useful in the near future. Well, now the hope of the house is about to bear a bastard and a groom is its father!"

She burst into loud laughter, which alarmed me for it told me that for all her flippant talk she was on the verge of hysteria.

Poor Margot! She was indeed in an unhappy situation and as I saw it there was only one way out. She must tell Sir John and ask for his help.

She was against doing that and continued with wild plans for our running away together, but at length I impressed on her that this would be as futile as her elopement and when she left me she seemed a little calmer and I believe had made up her mind that the only possible action was to confess her plight.

The next day after school when I was putting the books away and trying to fight off the depression which had beset me when two more pupils had told me that morning that they were leaving at the end of the term, Margot arrived.

She had run all the way from the Manor and was breathless. I made her sit down and gave her a glass of my mother's tonic, which she had said was good for depression, and not until Marogt had drunk it would I listen to her.

Then she told me that she had gone to Sir John and told him. "I thought he would *die* of shock. He seemed to think that although we were lovers and had planned to marry it was quite impossible that we could have behaved in what he called 'this irresponsible way.' He didn't believe me at first. He thinks I am quite innocent and believe that babies are found under gooseberry bushes. He kept saying: 'It cannot be so. It is a mistake. My dear Margot, you are such a child . . .' I told him I was old enough to have a baby and to do beforehand that which was necessary to produce one. The way he looked at me! I could have laughed if I had not been a little frightened. Then he said what I knew he would. 'I must tell your parents at once.' So you see, Minelle, what you have done. Through your advice we have brought about the very thing we wanted to avoid."

"It was impossible to avoid it, Margot. How could you keep such a secret from them? It's not as though it is merely a matter of *having* a baby. After its birth the baby will be there. How could you cope with that . . . without their knowing."

She shook her head.

Then she looked at me steadily, her enormous dark eyes like brilliant lamps in her pale face. "I dread facing him," she said.

I could well believe that, and I did my best to comfort her. Her nature was such that she could be in the depth of despair and shortly afterwards sparkle with *joie de vivre*. She laughed a good deal but there was often hysteria in that laughter and I knew she was terrified of her father.

She did not leave for France at the appointed time. She came to the schoolhouse to tell me that her father was coming to England and that she was to stay at the Manor until he arrived. She had now assumed an air of bravado, but I wondered how deep it went. Poor Margot! She was in great trouble.

It was Mrs. Manser who told me that the Comte had arrived at the Manor.

"I reckon," she said, "that he has come to take Mademoiselle home. She'll have a talking-to and no mistake. Imagine the Comte's rage at his daughter going off with a groom!"

"I can well imagine it."

"My word! He's a gentleman who has a high opinion of himself. You've only got to see him riding round to know that. And *his* daughter thinking she was going to marry James Wedder! I never heard the like. It don't do, you know. God put you where you are and that's where you should stay to my mind."

I was in no mood to listen to her homilies and when she invited me back to supper I pleaded too much school work.

"How's the school going, Minella?" Her forehead was creased into lines of anxiety but her mouth betrayed a certain satisfaction. In her opinion it was not right for women to be anything but wives and the less profitable the school was the sooner I should come to my senses. She wanted to see her Jim settled with a wife of her choice (and oddly enough I was that) and little ones running about the farm, learning to milk cows and feed the hens. I smiled, picturing my mother's distaste.

Soon after Mrs. Manser had gone, a messenger came from the Manor. My presence was requested there and Sir John and Lady Derringham would be pleased if I came without delay. It was almost a summons.

I thought it must be something to do with the departure from the school of Maria and Sybil. Perhaps they were not going to see the term through but were leaving at once.

With some trepidation I realized that the Comte would be there. But it seemed hardly likely that I should see him.

I crossed the lawn, passed the sundial, and went into the hall. One of the footmen told me that Sir John was waiting for me in the blue drawing room and he would take me there without delay. He opened the door and announced me, and I saw Sir John standing with his back to the log fire. My heart leaped and started to pound uncomfortably for the Comte was at the window, looking out.

"Ah, Miss Maddox," said Sir John.

The Comte swung round and bowed.

"I dare say you wonder why we have asked you to come here," said Sir John. "It concerns this distressing matter of Marguerite. The Comte has a proposition to make to you, and I am going to leave you with him that he may explain."

He indicated a high-backed chair facing the window and I sat down.

As the door shut on Sir John, the Comte sat down on the window seat and, folding his arms, regarded me steadily.

"Since, Mademoiselle Maddox, you speak my language a little better than I speak yours, it might be well to conduct this conversation in French. I want you fully to understand the nature of my proposal."

"If I should fail to understand, I shall say so," I replied.

A faint smile touched his lips. "You will understand, Mademoiselle, for you are very knowledgeable. Now this distressing affair of my daughter. What a disgrace! What a shame . . . for our noble house."

"It is certainly unfortunate."

He spread his hands and I noticed again the crested signet ring and the exquisite white lace at the sleeve edge.

"I do not intend to allow it to be more unfortunate than it need. I must tell you that I have no son. My daughter is the one who may well have to carry on our noble line. Nothing must prevent that. But first she must produce this . . . bastard . . . this son of a groom. *He* shall not bear our noble name."

I reminded him that the child might be a girl.

"Let us hope it will be so. A daughter would be less trouble. But first we must consider what must be done. This child must be born in obscurity. I can arrange that. Marguerite will go to a place I shall find for her. She will go as Madame . . . This or That . . . and she will have a companion with her. Marguerite will be a widow in some distress because her young husband was killed in an accident.

Her kind cousin is looking after her. The child will be born, put with foster parents, and Marguerite will return to her home and it will be as though this unfortunate matter had never happened."

"It seems an easy solution."

"Not so easy. It will need some planning. I do not like these secrets in families. This is not the end of the matter . . . with a child who will be there for the rest of its life. You see, Mademoiselle, I am very uneasy."

"That I understand, of course."

"You are a very understanding young woman. I knew it from our first meeting." A smile touched his lips and he was silent for a few moments. Then he went on: "You are puzzled, I can see. You wonder where you come into this. Now I will tell you. You will be the cousin."

"What cousin!"

"Marguerite's cousin, naturally. You will accompany her to the place I shall find for you. You will look after her, be with her, make sure she does not act foolishly again—and I shall know that she is in good hands."

I was so astonished that I stammered: "It . . . it's impossible."

"Impossible! That is a word I do not like. When people say to me, 'Impossible,' I then decide that I will show it to be possible."

"I have my school."

"Ah, your school. That saddens me. I hear it is not doing as well as it should."

"What do you mean?"

He spread his hands and somehow managed to convey that he was distressed by my misfortunes, while the curve of his lips showed that he found my plight amusing . . . and a little gratifying. "This is a time for frank speaking," he said. "Mademoiselle Maddox, I have my need. You have yours. What will you do when the school becomes a liability rather than an asset, eh? Tell me that."

"There is no question of that arising."

"Oh come, did I not ask for plain speaking? If you will forgive my bluntness, you are not the mature figure your mother was. People hesitate. Shall I send my daughters to a school where the Principal . . . the only teacher . . . is little more than a girl herself? Look what happens. One pupil runs off with a groom. Would that have happened while your mother was in charge?"

"Your daughter's elopement has nothing to do with the school."

"My daughter spent many hours with you at your school. There she gossiped and told her love secrets, I do not doubt. Then she elopes with the groom. It is a disaster for her . . . for us . . . for you and the school. Particularly when I hear some gossip that the son had to depart on the Grand Tour somewhat hastily on your account."

"You are . . . offensive."

"I know. To tell you the truth, it's part of my charm. I cultivate it. It is so much more attractive than geniality. Particularly when I am speaking the truth, and that is, my dear Mademoiselle, that you are in an uneasy situation . . . and so am I. Let us be friends. Let us help each other. What will you do when the school no longer provides you with a living? You will become a governess, I'll swear, to some hateful children who will make your life a misery. But you might marry. You could become a farmer's wife, perhaps . . . and let me tell you this, that would be the greatest tragedy of all."

"You seem to know a great deal about my private affairs."

"I make a point of learning what interests me."

"But I cannot do what you suggest."

"For such an intelligent young woman you say some foolish things sometimes. But then I know you do not mean them, so it does not alter my opinion of you. I am interested in you, Mademoiselle. Are you not in charge of my daughter and going to take an even closer interest in her? I want you to leave as soon as possible, but I understand that you will have matters to clear up. I am a reasonable man. I would not wish to hurry you too much and fortunately we have a little time."

"You go too fast."

"I always go fast. It is the best way to travel. But you will find it not too fast. Just the right speed. Well, the matter is settled then and we can get down to details."

"The matter is far from settled. Suppose I agreed . . . suppose I stayed with Margot until the child is born, what then?"

"There would be a position for you in my household."

"Position? What position?"

"That we can decide on. You will be Marguerite's cousin during your stay in the house where I shall send you. Perhaps you could continue to be that. I have always found that when practicing deception it is well to be consistent.

61

One should keep as near to the truth as possible and keep the fiction plausible throughout. Fact and fiction must be skillfully woven to give an impression of complete truth, and once having established yourself as a cousin, it may be that it would be well for you to continue in that rôle. Your nationality provides difficulties. We must have it that the daughter of a great-great-great-grandfather married into England and you are from a branch of that family tree, which makes you a cousin, though a remote one. You will be Marguerite's companion and look after her. She will need looking after. This episode has proved that. Is that not a good proposition? It gets you out of your difficulties and me out of mine."

"It seems quite outrageous."

"The best things in life can be just that. I will start making arrangements without delay."

"I have not yet agreed to come."

"But you will, for you are a woman of sound good sense. You make your mistakes like most of us but you will not repeat them. I know that and I want you to endow Marguerite with some of your good sense. She is a wayward child, I fear." He stood up and came to my chair. I also stood and faced him. He laid his hands on my shoulders and I was vividly reminded of that other occasion in his bedroom. I think he was too, for he sensed my shrinking and it amused him.

"It is always a mistake to be afraid of life," he said.

"Who said that I was afraid?"

"I can read your thoughts."

"Then you are very clever."

"You will discover how clever . . . in time, perhaps. Now I am going to be kind as well as clever. This has come as a shock to you. You had no idea of the proposition I was going to put to you and I can see the thoughts turning over and over in your mind. My dear Mademoiselle, face the facts. The school is in decline; this affair of my daughter has shocked members of the gentry. You may say it was none of your affair but Marguerite was at *your* school and you have had the misfortune to attract the heir of Derringham. You cannot help being charming, but these people are not as farseeing as I am. They will say you set out to catch him and the Derringhams found out in time and sent him off. Unfair, you say. You had no intention of trapping this young man. But it is not always what is true that counts. I give your school another six months . . . perhaps eight . . . and then what? Come, be sensible. Be Marguerite's cousin. I will see that you need not be worried with finances again. Get away from the schoolhouse of sad memories. I know of the love between you and your mother. What can you do here but brood? Get away from slander, from gossip. Mademoiselle, this unfortunate state of affairs can bring a new life to you."

So much of what he was saying was true. I heard myself murmur: "I cannot decide immediately."

He gave a little sigh of relief.

"No, no. It asks too much. You shall have today and tomorrow to decide. You will think about this and the plight of my daughter. She is fond of you. When I told her what I proposed she became happy. She loves you, Mademoiselle. Think of her distress. And think of your future, too."

He took my hand and kissed it. I was ashamed of the emotion it aroused in me and I hated myself for being so impressed by such a philanderer, which I was sure he was.

Then he bowed and left me.

Thoughtfully I returned to the schoolhouse.

I sat up late that night going through the books. In any case I knew I could not sleep. The effect that man had on me astonished me. He repelled me and yet attracted me. I could not get him out of my mind. To be in his house . . . to have a position there . . . a sort of cousin! I should be a "poor relation," a sort of companion to Margot. Well, what was I going to do otherwise?

I did not have to be told that the school was in decline. People were going to blame me for Margot's indiscretion, and was it true that they were hinting that I had tried to trap Joel Derringham into marriage? The dressmaker would know of the dresses my mother had had made; she had probably been shown the dress lengths in the cupboard. I had a new horse that I might ride with Joel. Oh, I could guess what these people were saying.

Desperately I longed for the calm guidance I could have had from my mother, and suddenly I knew that I could never be happy in this schoolhouse without her. There were too many memories. Everywhere I turned I could picture her so clearly.

I wanted to get away. Yes, the Comte was right, I would face the truth. The thought of going to France, of standing by Margot until her child was born, and then going to live in the Comte's household excited me, drew me away from my sense of loss and grief more surely than I had thought anything could do.

No wonder I could not sleep.

All through the day I was absent-minded as I taught my classes. It had been so much easier when the pupils were divided between my mother and myself. She had taken the older ones and I could cope easily with the younger. Before I had taken on the rôle of teacher she had managed quite well, but even she had said what a boon it was to have two of us. She had been a born teacher. I was something less than that.

All through the day I thought of the opportunity which was being offered to me, and it began to seem like an adventure which could restore my interest in life.

When school was over Margot called. She threw herself into my arms and hugged me.

"Oh, Minelle, you are coming with me then! It does not seem half as bad if you are going to be there. Papa told me. He said: 'Mademoiselle Maddox will take care of you. She is thinking about it but I have no doubt that she will come.' I felt happier than I have for a long time."

"It's by no means settled," I told her. "I have not yet made up my mind."

"But you will come, won't you? Oh, Minelle, if you say no, what shall I do?"

"I am not really necessary to the plan. You will go away quietly into the country where your child will be born and put out to foster parents. From there you will go to your father's household and carry on from there. It is not an uncommon story in families like yours, I believe."

"Oh, so cool! So precise! You are just what I need. But Minelle, dear *dear* Minelle, I shall have to go through life with this dark, *dark* secret. I shall need support. I shall need *you*. Papa says you are to be my cousin. Cousine Minelle! Does that not sound just right? And after this horrible business is over we shall be together. You are the only reason I like it here."

"What about James Wedder?"

"Oh, that was fun for a while, but look what it brought me to. It is not as bad as I feared it might be. I mean Papa . . . he was thunderous at first . . . despising me . . . and it was not for having an *affaire*, you know. It was because I had been so foolish as to become pregnant. He said he might have known I had a touch of the wanton in me. But if you will only come with me, Minelle, it will be all right. I know it will. You will come . . . you *must.*"

She had got to her knees and folded her hands together as in prayer. "Please, *please* God, make Minelle come with me."

"Get up and don't be so silly," I said. "This is not the time for histrionics."

She went into peals of laughter, which was, I commented, scarcely becoming to a fallen woman.

"I need you, Minelle," she cried. "You make me laugh. So *sérieuse* . . . and yet not really so. I know you, Minelle. You try to play the schoolmistress, but you could never be a real one. That's what I always believed. Joel was a fool. My father said he is stuffed with sawdust . . . not good red blood."

"Why should he say that about Joel?"

"Because he went away when Papa Derringham said he must. Papa sneers at that."

"Does he sneer at you for going where he sends you?"

"That is different. Joel was not pregnant." The laughter bubbled up again. I could not make up my mind whether this was hysteria or sheer fecklessness. But I felt my spirits lifted by her inconsequential conversation. Moreover, when she implored me to go with her, there was real panic in her eyes.

"I can bear it all if you are there," she said more seriously. "It will be fun . . . almost. I'll be the young married lady whose husband has died suddenly. My staid cousin— English, but still a cousin due to a *mésalliance* years ago— is with me to look after me. She is just the right one to do it because she is so calm and cool and a little severe. Oh, Minelle, you will come. You must."

"Margot, I still have to think. It is a big undertaking and I have not yet made up my mind."

"Papa will be furious if you refuse."

"His feelings are no concern of mine."

"But they are of mine. At the moment he is making light of the matter. That is because he has a solution and you are part of it. You will come, Minelle. I know you will. If you don't, I shall die of despair."

She chattered on, her eyes sparkling. She was not a bit afraid, she said, if I would come with her. She talked as though we were about to embark on some wonderful holiday together. It was foolish, but I began to catch her excitement.

I knew—perhaps I had known all along—that I was going to accept this challenge. I must escape from this house, become so gloomy with the light of my mother's presence removed from it; I must get away from the vaguely menacing shadow of poverty which was beginning to encroach. But it was like taking a step into the unknown.

I dreamed again that night that I was standing outside the schoolhouse, but it was not the familiar scene I saw there. Ahead of me lay a wood . . . the trees thick together. I believed it was an enchanted wood and I was going to walk through it. Then I saw the Comte. He was beckoning to me.

I awoke. Certainly I had made up my mind.

THE SOJOURN AT
PETIT MONTLYS

1

Petit Montlys was a charming small town some hundred miles south of Paris, sheltering in the shadow of its bigger sister town known as Grand Montlys. It was the end of April when we arrived. I had sold my furniture with the help of Sir John and had taken Jenny over to the Mansers', asking them to look after her. Sir John himself paid me a good price for Dower and promised that if I returned to England he would sell her back to me for the price my mother had paid for her. I was to receive a salary from the Comte which was handsome by any standards and only when the burden was lifted from my shoulders did I realize how anxious I had been about my financial situation.

Mrs. Manser shook her head over my decision. Clearly she disapproved. She did not know, of course, that Margot was pregnant, but thought I was taking a post as her companion in the Comte's household, which was the story the Derringhams put about.

"You'll be back," she prophesied. "I give you no more than a couple of months. There'll be a room for you here. Then I reckon you'll know which side your bread is buttered."

I kissed her and thanked her. "You were always such a good friend to me and my mother," I told her.

"I don't like to see a sensible woman take the wrong turning," she said. "I know what it is though. It's all that upset over Joel Derringham. It's clear what that was worth and I do see that you want to get away for a while."

I left it at that, letting her think she was right. I did not want to show her how exhilarated I felt.

We traveled by post chaise to the coast and there took ship for France. We were lucky to have a fair crossing and when we reached the other side were met by a middle-aged couple—evidently loyal servants of the Comte's—who were to be our chaperones throughout the journey.

We did not go through Paris but stayed in small inns and after several days finally arrived at Petit Montlys and there were taken to the home of Madame Grémond, who was to be our landlady for the next few months.

She received us warmly and commiserated with Margot, who had become Madame le Brun, on the exigencies of such a journey for a woman in her condition. I was glad to be able to retain my own name.

I cannot but say how Margot seemed to be enjoying her rôle. She had always liked play acting and this must surely be the most important part she had ever played. The story was that her husband, Pierre le Brun, who had managed a large estate for a very important nobleman, had been drowned while trying to save his master's wolfhound during a flood in northern France. His wife had found that she was to have a child and, because her husband's death had so distressed her, her cousin had, on the advice of her doctor, brought her right away from the scene of the tragedy, that she might remain tranquil until after the birth of her baby.

Margot threw herself so wholeheartedly into her rôle and talked fondly of Pierre, shedding tears over his death and even endowing the wolfhound with life. "Dear faithful Chon Chon. He was devoted to my dear Pierre," she said. "Who would have thought that one day Chon Chon would be the cause of my darling's death."

Then she would talk of how tragic it was that Pierre would never see his child. I wondered whether she was thinking of James Wedder then.

The journey had indeed been exhausting and it was good that we had taken it when we did. A few weeks later and it would have been very trying for Margot.

Madame Grémond turned out to be the most discreet of women and I was to wonder, during the next few months, whether she was aware of the truth. She was a handsome woman and in her youth must have been extremely attractive. She must now be in her mid-forties and the thought occurred to me that she might be doing what she was for an old friend—the Comte of course. If I was right, she was a woman whom he would trust; and of course the thought had occurred to me that she might well have been one of the numerous mistresses I was sure he had had.

The house was pleasant—not large, but set in a garden and approached by a drive. Although it was in the town, it seemed isolated because of the trees which surrounded it.

Margot and I were given rooms side by side at the back of the house overlooking the gardens. These rooms, though not luxurious, were adequately furnished. There were two maids in the house, Jeanne and Émilie Dupont, whose duty it was to wait on us. Jeanne was inclined to be talkative, while Émilie was almost morose and scarcely said a word unless she was spoken to. Jeanne was very interested in us; her little dark eyes were like a monkey's, I thought—alive with curiosity. She hovered about Margot, fussing over her, so eager was she for her comfort. Margot, who loved to be the center of attention, soon grew quite fond of her. I would often find them chattering together.

"Be careful," I warned. "You could easily betray something."

"I shall betray nothing," she protested. "Do you know, sometimes I awake in the night and almost weep for poor Pierre, which shows you how deep I am in my part. It really does seem that he *was* my husband."

"I expect he looks rather like James Wedder."

"Exactly. I thought that was the best way to play it . . . as near to the truth as possible. After all, James is the baby's father and I did lose him suddenly—only by a different method."

"Quite a different kind of exit," I commented wryly.

But I was pleased to see how she was recovering from the first shock of her experience. Now she was gay, actually reveling in the situation, which would have been difficult to understand if one had not been aware of Margot's temperament.

She had one characteristic which was a help to her. She could live completely in the present, no matter how threatening the future might seem. I confess there were times when I was influenced by her and when what was happening seemed like a merry adventure instead of the serious matter it was.

The weather was perfect. All through June we enjoyed the sunshine. We would sit under the sycamore tree and talk as we sewed. We took a great delight in making baby garments though neither of us, I must admit, were exactly geniuses with our needles; and Margot would often tire of a garment before she had finished it. Émilie, it seemed, was an expert needlewoman and more than once she came to the rescue and finished off some little thing, decorating it with the most exquisite feather-stitching, at which she excelled. She would take the garment away and we would find it finished and neatly folded in one of our rooms. When we thanked her she would seem quite embarrassed. I found communication with her very difficult.

"It's due to Jeanne's being so much prettier," Margot told me. "Poor Émilie, she's scarcely a beauty, is she?"

"She's a good worker."

"Maybe, but will that get her a husband? Jeanne plans to marry Gaston the gardener in due course. She told me all about it. Madame Grémond has promised them one of the outhouses which they can turn into a cottage. Gaston is clever with his hands."

Again I repeated my warning: "Do you think you gossip too much with Jeanne?"

"Why should I not talk to her? It passes the time."

"We shall have Madame Grémond complaining that she chats with you instead of working."

"Madame Grémond is anxious to make us comfortable, I think."

"I wonder why we have been sent to her."

"My father arranged it."

"Do you think she is—or might have been—a friend of his?"

Margot lifted her shoulders. "That may be. He has many friends."

I used to wake to the sunshine in the morning and pull up the blinds, which were at all the windows, for the sun could be fierce. I would look out onto the garden, the smooth lawn, the wicker seats under the sycamore tree, the pond in which the birds bathed. It was a scene of utter peace.

During the first weeks we often took a walk through the town where we would shop for what we wanted. We became known as Madame le Brun, the very young widow who had suffered a great tragedy when she had lost the husband who would never see his child, and the English cousin. I knew they gossiped about us; sometimes they would barely wait for us to leave the shop. Of course, our coming was an event in the quietness of Petit Montlys, and I sometimes doubted the Comte's wisdom in sending us here. Whereas we might have been lost in a larger town, here we were the focus of attention.

Sometimes we did a little shopping for Madame Grémond, and I enjoyed buying the hot loaves, which came straight from the glowing oven set in the wall. The baker drew them out with his long tongs and displayed them for us to select those which most appealed to us. Slack-baked, well-baked, medium-baked, you took your choice. And what delicious bread it was!

Then we would stroll through the market which took place every Wednesday, and on those days the peasants would come in from the surrounding country, their produce laden on donkeys, and set up in the market square. The housewives of Petit Montlys drove a hard bargain with them and I liked to listen to the haggling. We so much enjoyed the market that we asked Madame Grémond to let us shop for her there too. Sometimes Jeanne or Émilie would come with us because she said the peasants put up prices when they saw the sad widow and her English cousin.

By the end of June we both felt that we had been in Petit Montlys for months. Sometimes the strangeness of it all would strike me, for my life had changed so drastically. Only this time last year my mother had been alive and I had had no idea that I would ever do anything but continue with the teaching career she had planned for me.

Each day seemed very like the last and there was nothing like this peaceful, pleasant monotony to make the time slip by unheeded.

Margot's condition was now noticeable. We made full loose garments for her and she would laugh at her reflection.

"Who would ever have believed *I* could look like this?"

"Who would have believed you could have allowed yourself to," I countered.

"Trust the prim and proper English cousin to point *that* out. Oh, Minelle, I do love you, you know. I love that astringent way of yours . . . taking me down when I need it. It has not the slightest effect on me, but I love it."

"Margot," I said, "sometimes I think you should be a little more serious."

Her face puckered suddenly. "No, please don't ask me to. It's the baby, Minelle. Now that it's moving, it seems to be real. It seems to be alive."

"It is real. It is alive. It always has been."

"I know. But now it's a person. What will happen when it's born?"

"Your father explained. It will be sent away. It will have a foster mother."

"And I shall never see it again."

"You know that is what is intended."

"It seemed an easy solution then, but lately . . . Well, Minelle, I'm beginning to want it . . . to love it . . ."

"You will have to be brave, Margot."

"I know."

She said no more, but I could see she was brooding. My

featherbrained little Margot was realizing that she was about to become a mother. I was anxious and in a way would have preferred her to behave in her featherbrained, inconsequential manner, for if she were going to grieve for the child she would be very unhappy.

One day there was a rather unpleasant incident in the town which upset the pleasant tenor of the days. Margot did not often accompany me now, as she was getting too unwieldy and preferred to take exercise in the garden. I had bought ribbons to trim a gown for the baby and, as I emerged from the shop, a carriage came clattering by. It was an elegant vehicle drawn by two magnificent white horses. A young man stood at the back resplendent in livery the color of peacock's feathers trimmed with gold braid.

A group of boys standing at the street corner jeered at the young man and one of them threw a stone at him. He took no notice and the carriage went on.

The boys were chattering excitedly together. I heard the word "aristocrats" spat out contemptuously and remembered my talks with Joel Derringham.

Several people had come out of their shop doors and were shouting to each other.

"Did you see the fine carriage?"

"Yes, I saw it. And the haughty ones inside. Looking down their noses at us, eh? Did you see that?"

"I saw. But it will not always be so."

"Down with them. Why should they live in luxury while we starve."

I had seen no evidence of starvation in Petit Montlys, but I did know that those who farmed a little land had difficulty in making a living.

The incident did not end there. Unfortunately the occupants of the carriage decided that they needed some of the cheeses which they must have glimpsed in one of the shops, and the young footman was sent to purchase them.

The sight of him, in his gorgeous uniform, was too much for the children. They ran after him shouting, trying to pull off the braid on his jacket.

He hurried into the cheese shop and the children stayed outside. Monsieur Jourdain, the grocer, would be angry with them if they disturbed his customers, particularly those who could be expected to pay special prices. I was close by so I saw exactly what happened.

When the young man emerged from the shop about six boys leaped on him. They snatched the cheeses from his hands and tore at his coat. In desperation he hit out at them and one boy went sprawling on the cobbles. There was blood on his cheek.

A cry of rage went up and the footman, who must have seen that he was hopelessly outnumbered, pushed his way through the *mêlée* of shouting children and ran.

I went quickly along the street and saw that the carriage was in the square. The young man shouted to the coachman and leaped onto the back of it. In a very short time it was clattering out of the square, but not before several people had run out of their houses shouting abuse for the aristocrats. Stones were flung after the retreating carriage and I was glad when it was out of sight.

The baker had seen me. He must have left his baking to come and look.

"You are all right, Mademoiselle?" he asked.

"Yes, thank you."

"You look distrait."

"That was rather horrible."

"Oh yes. It happens. Wise people should not drive their carriages about the countryside."

"How can they go otherwise?"

"The poor go on foot, Mademoiselle."

"But if one has a carriage . . ."

"It is sad that some should have carriages while others walk."

"It has always been so."

"It is not to say it always will be. The people are tired of the differences. The rich are too rich . . . the poor too poor. The rich care nothing for the poor, but soon, Mademoiselle, they will be made to care."

"And the carriage . . . whose was that?"

"Some lord, I don't doubt. Let him enjoy his carriage . . . while he can."

I went back thoughtfully to the house. As I came into the cool hall I met Madame Grémond.

"Madame le Brun is resting?" she asked.

"Yes. She is beginning to feel the need to. I was glad she was not with me this afternoon. Something unpleasant happened."

"Come into my *salon* and tell me," she said.

It was cool in the room—blinds drawn to shut out the sun. A little old-fashioned, I thought it, and very discreet, with thick blue curtains and some beautiful Sèvres china in the glass cabinet. There was an ornate ormolu clock on the wall. She had some fine objects, I realized. Gifts, I thought, from a lover—the Comte perhaps?

I told her about the incident.

"It happens often nowadays," she said. "If a carriage appears, it is like a red rag to a bull. A fine carriage symbolizes wealth. I have not used mine for six months. It is foolish, but I fancy the people don't like it." She looked round the room and shivered. "In the old days I would not have thought this possible. Times have changed and are changing fast."

"Is it safe for us to go into the town?"

"They wouldn't harm you. It is the aristocrats they are against. France is not a happy country. There is much unrest."

"We have troubles in England."

"Ah, it is a changing world. Those who have had, may not have in the future. There is too much poverty in France. It breeds envy. Many of our rich people do much good, but many are idle and do great harm. There is a growing anger and envy throughout the country. I believe it is even more evident in Paris. What you saw this afternoon is a commonplace."

"I hope I don't see it again. There was murder in the air. I believe they would have killed that innocent young footman."

"They would say he should not be working for the rich and that there was a good reason to attack him because he is an enemy of the people."

"This is dangerous talk."

"There is danger in the air, Mademoiselle. Coming so recently from England, you do not know of these matters. It must have been very different there. Did you live in the country?"

"Yes."

"And you have left your family . . . your friends . . . to be with your cousin?"

"Yes, yes. She needed someone with her."

Madame Grémond nodded sympathetically. I felt she was trying to probe, so I rose quickly. "I must go to Madame le Brun. She will be wondering what has become of me."

In her room Margot was lying on her bed and Jeanne was folding up baby garments, which Margot clearly had been showing her.

Margot was saying: "Everywhere Pierre went there was Chon Chon. Pierre would stride out with his gun and the dog at his heels. It was a large estate. One of the largest in the country."

"It must have belonged to a very rich gentleman."

"Very rich. Pierre was his right-hand man."

"A Duke, Madame? A Count?"

I said: "Hello, how are you?"

"Ah, my dear cousin, how I have missed you!"

I took the baby garments from Jeanne and put them in a drawer. "Thank you, Jeanne," I said and nodded, implying that I wished her to leave us. She curtsied and went out.

"You talk too much, Margot," I said.

"What am I to do? Sit and mope?"

"You will say something you should not."

I had a feeling then that someone was behind the door listening. I went to it swiftly and opened it. No one was there, but I fancied I heard the sound of running footsteps. I was sure Jeanne had intended to listen. I felt very uneasy.

What I had seen that afternoon in the town had set alarm bells ringing through my mind. The trouble in the country did not affect our private one. Yet the apprehension continued.

Margot's time was getting near. The baby was due at the end of August and it was now July. Madame Legère, the midwife, had been sent for. She was a cosy-looking woman, like a cottage loaf in shape, dressed in deep black—the color favored by most of the women—and which somehow made her cheeks look rosier than they actually were. She had keen dark eyes and a faint line of hair about her mouth.

She declared Margot in a good state, carrying the baby just as she should. "It'll be a boy," she said and added, "like as not. I'm promising nothing. It's just the way you're carrying it."

She called once a week and confided to me that she knew my cousin was a very special lady, by which I gathered that she had been paid rather more than she usually was to attend to her.

I felt then that a mystery was being created about us and I supposed that was inevitable. I was growing increasingly aware of the curious looks.

I did not mention that afternoon's incident to Margot. I thought it better for her not to know. I remembered how hurriedly her father had left England on the night of the *soirée*. Since then I had learned something about that *cause célèbre*, Queen Marie Antoinette's necklace, that fabulous piece of jewelry made up of the finest diamonds in the world. I knew that Cardinal de Rohan, who had been duped into thinking that if he helped Marie Antoinette to procure the necklace she would become his mistress, had been arrested and then acquitted and that his acquittal was an implication that the Queen was guilty.

I had heard the Queen discussed slightingly everywhere in France. She was contemptuously called the Austrian Woman, and the country's troubles were blamed on her. I did not need to be told that the affair of the necklace had not added one jot to the peace of the country. In fact, it was almost like a match to dry wood.

It was a strange life—tensions in the streets, as I had seen when the carriage had rumbled past, and Margot and I living our strange shut-away lives during those months while we awaited the birth of her child.

Once when we were sitting in the garden she said: "Sometimes, Minelle, I can't think beyond this place . . . and the baby's coming. After that we are going to my home. It will be to either the country *château* or the *hôtel* in Paris. I shall be light and willowy again. The baby will be gone. It will be as though this never happened."

"It can never be like that," I said. "We shall always remember. Particularly you."

"I shall see my baby sometimes, Minelle. We must visit him . . . you and I."

"It will be forbidden, I am sure."

"Oh, it will be forbidden. My father said, 'When the child is born, it will be given into the care of some good people. I shall arrange that and you will never see it again. You will have to forget this ever happened. Never speak of it, but at the same time regard it as a lesson. Never let this happen again.'"

"He has gone to a great deal of trouble to help you."

"Not to save me but to save my name from dishonor. It makes me laugh sometimes. I am not the only member of the family to have a bastard child. One does not have to look very far for others."

"You must be sensible, Margot. What your father plans is without doubt best for you."

"And never see my child again!"

"You should have thought of that before . . ."

"What do you know of these matters? Do you think that when you are in love, when someone has his arms about you, you think about a nonexistent child?"

"I should have thought the possibility of that nonexistent child's actually existing might have occurred to you."

"Wait, Minelle, wait until you are in love."

I made an impatient movement and she laughed. Then she moved awkwardly in her chair and went on: "It's peaceful here. Do you find it so? It will be different at the *château* and in Paris. My father has the most luxurious residences, they contain many treasures, but being here with you I realize they lack the best thing of all. Peace."

"Peace of mind," I agreed. "It is what wise people always wish for. Tell me about your life in your father's mansions."

"I have rarely been in Paris. When they went there I was often left in the country and spent most of my life there. The *château* was built in the thirteenth century. The great tower—the keep—is what you see first. In the old days there used to be a 'Watch' in the tower, which meant that there was always a man there and it was his duty to give warning when an enemy approached. Even now we have a man there and he gives a warning when guests are arriving by ringing a bell. It is one of the musicians, and to pass the time he sings and composes songs. At night he descends and often sings for us those *chansons de guette*, which you will know, of course, are watchman's songs. It's an old custom and my father clings to old customs as much as possible. I sometimes think he was born too late. He hates this new attitude of the people which we are beginning to see springing up everywhere. He says the serfs are becoming insolent to their masters."

I was silent, thinking of the recent incident in the town.

"Quite a number of castles are of a much later date than ours," went on Margot. "François Premier built the *châteaux* of the Loire a good two hundred years after ours was set up. Of course, ours has been restored and added to. There is the great staircase, which is as old as any part of the building. This leads up to the part of the castle which we occupy. Right at the top of the staircase is a platform. Years ago the lords of the castle used to administer justice from the platform. My father still uses it, and if there is a dispute among any of the people on the estate they are summoned to the platform and my father passes judgment. It is exactly as it used to be done. At the foot of the staircase is a great courtyard and it is there they used to joust and tilt. Now we hold plays there in the summer and if there is a festival or something of that nature it takes place there. Oh, talking of it brings it all back so clearly and, Minelle, I'm frightened. I'm frightened of what is going to happen when we leave here."

"We'll face it when it comes," I said. "Tell me about the people who live in the castle."

"My parents you know. Poor Maman is very often ill or pretends to be. My father hates illness. He doesn't believe in it. He thinks it's something people fancy. Poor Maman is very unhappy. It is something to do with having me instead of a boy and then not being able to have any more."

"It must have been a disappointment to a man like the Comte not to have a son."

"Isn't it maddening, Minelle, the way they want boys . . . always boys. In our country a girl cannot come to the throne. You in England don't go as far as that."

"No, as I have always taught you, two of the greatest periods of English history were when queens were on the throne. Elizabeth and Anne."

"Yes, it's one of the few things I remember from your history lessons. You always looked so fierce when you said that. Waving the flag for our sex."

"Of course, both of them were blessed with clever ministers."

"Well, do you want to give a history lesson or hear about my family?"

"I shall be interested to hear about your family."

"I have told you about my father and mother and you know how ill-assorted they are. It was an arranged marriage when my mother was sixteen and my father seventeen. They saw very little of each other before the wedding. That's how things are arranged in families like ours, and it was considered a most suitable match. Of course, it was as unsuitable as it possibly could be. Poor Maman! She is the one I am sorry for. My father would naturally find consolation elsewhere."

"And that is what he did?"

"Naturally. He had had his adventures before marriage. I wonder why he can be so shocked over me. Not that he really was. As I said, it wasn't what I had done but that I had been found out. It's all right for serving girls and members of the lower classes generally to have a bastard or two (in fact it is often their duty if the lord of the castle takes a fancy to them) but not, oh certainly not, for the daughter of the great family. So you see, there is one law for the rich and one for the poor—and this time it works against us."

"Be serious, Margot. I want to learn something about the people at the castle before I go there."

"Very well. I'm leading up to that. I was going to tell you about Étienne—the crop of my father's earliest wild oats. Étienne lives at the *château*. He is my father's son."

"I thought you said there was no son."

"Minelle, you are being obtuse. He is my father's illegitimate son. Papa was only sixteen when Étienne was born. How he can dare stand in judgment on me I don't know. Not only is there one law for the rich and one for the poor, but one for men and one for women. I was born a year after my parents' marriage. My mother suffered terribly and nearly died. However, both she and I managed to survive the ordeal of my getting born, but the result was that to have another child would endanger her life. So there was my father—who had had everything he wanted in life up to that time—at the age of eighteen, head of a noble house, faced with the fact that he would never have a son. And of course what every man wants—especially one who has a great name to preserve—is a son, and not only one, for he must be doubly sure."

"That must have been a great blow."

"It was not as though he loved my mother. I always thought that if she had stood up to him a little he might have thought more of her. She never did, though. She always avoided him and they saw very little of each other. She spends most of her time in her rooms waited on by Nou Nou, her old nurse, who defends her like a dragon breathing fire, and even daring to stand up to Papa. But I must tell you about Étienne."

"Yes, do tell me about Étienne."

"Naturally I wasn't there at the time, but I have heard servants talk. It was considered amusing that my father should have shown his virility at such an early age. Étienne came into the world to a flourish of trumpets—metaphorically speaking—and has had a very high opinion of himself ever since. He is cast in the same mold as my father—which is not surprising since he is his son. Well, when it was known that my mother could have no more children and the hopes of a legitimate son were no more, my father brought Étienne to the *château* and he was treated like a legitimate son. He has been educated as such and is often with my father. Everyone knows that he is a bastard and that infuriates him, but he hopes to inherit the estates, if not the title. He can be very moody and has outbursts of temper which terrify people. If my mother died and my father married again I don't know what Étienne would do."

"I can see how unfair he would consider that."

"Poor Étienne! He is my father all over again . . . but not quite. You know how it is with people who are not quite what they wish to be. Étienne flouts his nobility, if you know what I mean. I have seen him whip a young boy who called him the Bastard. But he is very attractive. The girls in the servants' quarters will verify that. Étienne is a Comte in all ways except that his mother was not married to his father and he is so determined that no one shall remember that, that he can't forget it himself. Oh and then . . . Léon."

"Another man?"

"Léon's case is very different. Léon has no need to whip small boys. He is no bastard. He was born in Holy Wedlock. His parents were peasants and it would be no use his trying to pretend otherwise, even if he wanted to, for everyone knows it. Léon, though, has received the same education as Étienne and no one would guess he was the son of peasants if they did not know it. Léon, therefore, has an air of nobility which sits easily on him and he would laugh if anyone called him Peasant. To see Léon in his fine velvet jacket and buckskin breeches you would say he was an aristocrat. Which proves, of course, that where a man is brought up can have far more effect on him than who his parents were."

"I have always been inclined to believe that. But tell me more of Léon. Why is he at the *château?*"

"It is rather a romantic story. He came to the *château* when he was six. I was too young to remember. Actually it was soon after I was born and my father had just realized that my mother could have no more children. He was very angry . . . bitter against a fate which had married him to a woman who had become barren after the birth of her first child . . . a daughter . . . and then had had the temerity to go on living."

"Margot!"

"Dear Minelle, are we speaking the truth or not? If my mother had died when I was born, my father would have married again at a suitable interval and I might have had numerous half sisters—and, what is all-important, brothers. Then my little peccadillo might not have been so important. But Maman went on living . . . most inconsiderate of her . . . and Papa was a prisoner of a kind . . . caught by a cruel fate, trapped, married to a woman who could be no use to him."

"This is no way to talk of your parents."

"Very well. I will tell you they are devoted to each other. He never leaves her side. All his thoughts are for her. Is that what you want?"

"Don't be silly, Margot. Naturally I want the truth, but tempered with respect."

"How amusing you are! It is not a matter of respect, but to tell you how things stand. That's what you asked for, did you not? Do you want to hear, or don't you?"

"I want to know as much as possible about the *château* before I go there."

"Then don't expect to hear fairy tales. My father is no charming prince, I do assure you. When he knew that he was saddled with a barren wife he was so angry that he took his horse and rode it till it dropped with exhaustion. Riding madly like that seemed to be the way he gave an outlet to his fury. The household was glad to get him out of the way, for woe betide any of them who angered him. The people used to call him the Devil on Horseback and, when they saw him, kept out of the way."

I was startled, because that was the name I had given him when I had first seen him. It fitted him absolutely.

"Sometimes," went on Margot, "Papa traveled in his *cabriolet,* which he drove himself, using the most spirited horses in his stables. This was more dangerous than when he rode his horse, and one day he was riding in this wild and reckless fashion through the village of Lapine, which was about ten kilos from the *château,* when he ran over a child and killed it."

"How dreadful!"

"I think he was sorry."

"I should hope he was."

"It brought him to his senses, I think. But let me tell you about Léon. He is the twin brother of the boy who was killed. The mother was nearly demented. She so far forgot what she owed her overlord that she came to the castle and tried to stab him. He overpowered her easily. He could have had her executed for attempted murder but he didn't."

"How good of him!" I said with sarcasm. "I suppose he realized that she was merely attempting to do to him what he did to her child."

"Exactly. However, he talked to her. He told her he

deeply regretted his action and he understood her desire for revenge. He would try to atone. The dead boy had a twin brother. And she had . . . how many children was it? I forget. About ten. He would recompense her for the loss of the child by giving her a purse which would be commensurate with what her son would have earned for her had he lived for sixty years. That was not all. He would take the boy's twin and he should be brought up in the *château* as a member of the household. Thus the terrible accident could be turned into a stroke of good fortune for the family."

"I don't see how anything could make up for the loss of the child."

"You do not know these peasants. Their children mean so much money to them. They have so many that they can spare one without too much regret . . . particularly when his loss is going to bring great rewards."

"I am unconvinced."

"Then, dear Minelle, you must remain so. The fact is that, besides Étienne the Bastard, we have Léon the Peasant, and let me tell you this: If I had not explained the situation, you would never have guessed the origins of either."

"It is an unusual household."

That made Margot laugh. "Until I came to England and saw the orderly manners of Derringham Hall and how that which is unpleasant is never mentioned and therefore presumed not to exist . . . until I had a peep into your schoolhouse where life seemed so simple and so easy, I did not understand what an unusual household I had come from."

"You saw only the surface. We all have our problems. In that easy-to-live-in schoolhouse there was often the question of whether we should be able to pay our way and that question became acute during my last weeks there."

"I know, and to that very state of affairs perhaps I owe your presence here, so does it not show that there is always good in everything that happens? If the school had been flourishing, you would not have left it and I should be alone. But for my father's youthful indiscretion Étienne would not be at the *château*, and if he had not ridden in fury through Lapine, Léon would have been trying to grub a living out of the earth and often going to bed hungry. Isn't that a comforting thought?"

"Your philosophy is a lesson to us all, Margot." I was pleased to see her in such good spirits, but talking of the *château* had tired her and I insisted that she drink her bedtime milk and talk no more that night.

2

At the beginning of August Madame Legère moved in. She occupied a small room close to Margot's and her coming reminded both Margot and me vividly that the interlude was nearing its end. I think neither of us wanted it to be over. This was a strange feeling, but those waiting months had been important to us both. We had, as was to be expected, grown closer together; and I think she was pleased, as I was, that when this was over we were not going to part. How she would react to giving up her baby I could not imagine, for as its birth became imminent she had taken a great interest in it and, I was afraid, was beginning to be stirred by maternal love. It was natural enough, but since she was to give up the child, rather sad.

During those waiting months I had looked back over the past and yearned to be able to talk of the future with my mother. When I contemplated what my life would have been if I had stayed in the schoolhouse, I could feel no regret for what I had done. I could see myself becoming more and more uneasy and perhaps in desperation turning to the Mansers and marrying Jim. At the same time I felt I had plunged into a dark passage and was heading towards a future which I could not envisage. Adventure lay before me—the *château*, the Comte and his unusual household. I could only look forward to that with a tingling excitement while I was glad of the waiting period.

Madame Legère had taken Margot over completely. She was always with her and even when we endeavored to be alone for a brief respite it would not be long before the plump little creature would come bustling in wanting to know what *"Petite Maman"* was doing.

"Petite Maman" was amused at first by the appellation, but after a few days she declared she would scream if Madame Legère did not stop it. But Madame Legère went her own way. She made it clear that she was in charge, for if she were not how could we be sure that Baby would make an

easy entrance into the world and *"Petite Maman"* come through without disaster?

It was obvious that we had to endure Madame Legère.

She liked a glass of brandy and kept a bottle handy. I suspected she had frequent nips, but as she was never the worse for it, that seemed nothing to worry about.

"If I had as many bottles of brandy as I've brought babies into the world," she said, "I'd be a rich woman."

"Or a wine merchant or a dipsomaniac," I could not help adding.

She was unsure of me. I had heard her refer to me as the English Cousin, as though I were an enemy.

I would sit in my room sometimes trying to read, but I could always hear Madame Legère's penetrating voice and, having by this time grown accustomed to the accent of the neighborhood, I could follow conversations with ease.

Jeanne was always in attendance and she and Madame Legère vied with each other in talking, although Madame Legère was very often the winner, in view I imagined of her superior position in the household. I told Margot that she should send them away, but she said their chatter amused her.

It was a hot afternoon. August was drawing near to its end. It could not be long now. I was constantly trying to remember what had been happening this time last year. Now I started to imagine what would be taking place a year hence. Hazy pictures filled my mind . . . the great *château*, the wide stone staircase leading to the family's apartments, the household, Margot, Étienne, Léon, the Comte.

I was pulled up sharply in my reverie by the rather shrill tones of Madame Legère.

"I've had some queer cases in my time. There's some, you know, that's *quite* secret. Ladies and gentlemen . . . ha! ha! Don't tell me they're all they're made out to be. They're fond of a bit of love, now and then . . . and not always in the right quarters. I can tell you. All's well and good as long as there's no consequences. But should I complain of consequences? It's these little consequences that make good business for me, bless 'em. And the more scandalous the better the business. I've been paid very well for some of my jobs, I can tell you. I had one lady once . . . oh, very important she was . . . but all wrapped up in secret. I wouldn't like to tell you who *she* was, but I can guess."

"Oh, Madame Legère," squealed Jeanne, "do tell."

"If I was to tell, I'd be breaking my trust, wouldn't I? It

was to keep secrets that I got my little nest egg together . . . as well as for bringing the little darlings into the world. It wasn't an easy birth, that one . . . not the sort I like. But of course I was there and I used to say to her: 'You'll be all right, *Petite Maman*, with old Legère beside you.' That was a comfort to her, that was. Well, when the baby was born, a carriage comes and there's a woman in it who takes the child. Poor *Petite Maman*, she nearly died. Would have, if I hadn't been there to take care of her. Then I had my orders. Tell her the baby died, and that was what she was told. She was heartbroken, but I reckon it was better that way."

"And what happened to the baby?" asked Margot.

"You needn't have any fear about that. It was well cared for, you can be sure. There was money, you see. Lots of it. And all they wanted was for *Petite Maman* to be sent back to them, slender as a virgin, which was what she would have to pass herself off to be."

"Did she believe the baby was dead?" asked Jeanne.

"She believed it. I reckon she's a great lady now, married to a rich lord of a husband, with lots of children running about the grand house . . . only she wouldn't see much of *them*. They'd be with nurses."

"It doesn't seem right," said Jeanne.

"Of course it's not right, but it's what *is*."

"But I would like to know what happened to the baby," put in Margot.

"You set your mind at rest on that," replied Madame Legère soothingly. "Babies born like this are always put in good households. After all, they've got this blue blood in them and these aristocrats think a lot of that sort of blood."

"Their blood's no different from ours," said Jeanne. "My Gaston says that one day the people will have proof of that."

"You'd better not let Madame Grémond hear you talk like that," warned Madame Legère.

"Oh no. She thinks she's one of them. But the time will come when she will have to show whose side she's on."

"What's the matter with you, Jeanne?" asked Margot. "You're getting fierce."

"Oh, she has been listening to Gaston, that's what. Tell Gaston he'd better be careful. People who talk too much might find themselves in trouble. What's wrong with aristocrats? They have bonny babies. Some of my best babies were aristocrats. I remember once . . ."

I had lost interest. I could not stop thinking of the story of the baby which had been born to the aristocratic lady and taken away at birth. I wondered how much she knew of this case. She was certainly probing. And how much had she guessed? Then there were Jeanne's comments to ponder on. It seemed the theme of life here was one of rumbling discontent.

3

It was about a week after that when I was awakened by noises in the adjoining room. I could hear Madame Legère giving orders to Jeanne.

Margot's child was about to be born.

Her labor was neither long nor arduous. She was very lucky in that and by midmorning her son was born.

I went to see her soon afterwards. She was lying back in bed very sleepy, exhausted, yet in a way triumphant, and looking very young.

The baby was wrapped up in red flannel and lying in a cot.

"It's over, Minelle," said Margot wanly. "It's a boy . . . a lovely boy."

I nodded, feeling too moved to speak.

"*Petite Maman* should rest now," said Madame Legère. "I've got some beautiful broth for her when she awakes . . . but sleep first."

Margot closed her eyes. I was very uneasy, wondering how she would feel when the time came to part with the baby, as she surely must.

Jeanne followed me into my room.

'You'll be going away soon now, Mademoiselle," she said.

I nodded. I always felt I must beware of those inquisitive eyes.

"Will you be staying with Madame and the baby?"

"For a while," I replied shortly.

"He'll be such a comfort to her, that little one. After all she's gone through. Has she got a mother and father?"

I wanted to say that I had no time to talk, but I was a little afraid of appearing abrupt which might arouse suspicion.

"Oh yes, she has."

"You'd have thought . . ."

"Thought what?"

"You'd have thought they'd have wanted her to go to them."

"We wanted to get her right away," I said. "Now, Jeanne, I have things to do."

"She mentioned them once . . . It sort of slipped out. It seemed she was a bit afraid of her father like. He seemed a very fine gentleman."

"I am sure you have given yourself the wrong impression."

I went into my room and shut the door, but as I had turned away from her I had caught the fleeting expression on her face—the downward turn of the lips, something which was almost a smirk.

She suspected something and, like Madame Legère, was eager to probe.

Margot had been indiscreet. She had gossiped too freely. When I considered our coming here, it did seem rather odd. Of course, it would have been natural for a young widow to go to her parents to have her child and not come to some remote spot with a cousin who was not even of her own nationality.

Well, we should soon be on our way. But I did wonder what Margot was going to do when the time came for her to part with her baby.

Two weeks passed. Madame Legère stayed with us. Margot would not allow her baby to be swaddled and she loved to wash him and care for him herself. She said she would call him Charles and he became Charlot.

"I have named him after my father," she said. "He is Charles-Auguste Fontaine Delibes. Little Charlot has a lot of his grandfather in him."

"I fail to see it," I replied.

"Oh, but you do not know my father very well, do you? He is a man it is not easy to understand. I wonder if little Charlot will grow up like him. It will be fun to see . . ."

She stopped and her face puckered. I knew that she refused to believe that her baby was going to be taken right away from her.

I was young and inexperienced and I did not know how to treat her. Sometimes I let her run on as though she would keep the baby and we should stay here forever.

I knew what was going to happen. Before long the man and woman who had brought us here would arrive to take us away. Then after a journey, the baby would be delivered to its foster parents and Margot and I would continue our journey to the *château*.

Sometimes I felt impelled to remind her of this.

"I shan't lose him completely," she cried. "I shall go back to him. How could I leave my little Charlot? I must be sure that the people who have him, love him, mustn't I?"

I would try to soothe her but I dreaded the day when the parting must come.

I sensed the tension in the house. Everyone was waiting for the day we should leave. It did not make it easy that we ourselves were unsure.

When I went into the town, shopkeepers asked after Madame—the poor little one who had tragically lost her husband. But now she had her baby to comfort her. And a boy! They knew that was exactly what she had wanted.

I wondered how much they knew of us. I had seen Jeanne gossiping in shops now and then. We were the talk of the little town and again it occurred to me that the Comte had made an error of judgment in sending us to such a small place, where the coming of two women like ourselves was a major event.

During the first week of September our guardians arrived. We were to prepare to leave the following day.

It was over. The carriage was outside our door. Monsieur and Madame Bellegarde—another cousin and his wife—were to take us home. That was the story.

"Such good kind cousins you have, Madame," said Madame Legère. "They will take you home and how his grandparents will love little Charlot!"

They stood grouped at the door of the house—Madame Grémond, Madame Legère, with Jeanne and Émilie standing behind them.

That group made an indelible mark on my memory and often during the months to come I could see them in my mind's eyes, just as they were then.

Margot held the baby and I could see that the tears were slowly running down her cheeks.

"I can't let him go, Minelle, I can't," she whispered.

But of course she must, and in her heart she knew it.

We stayed the first night at an inn. Margot and I shared

a room and we had the baby with us. We scarcely slept at all. Margot talked for most of the night.

She had the wildest ideas. She wanted us to run away and keep the baby. I went along with her, to soothe her, but in the morning I spoke to her sensibly and told her to stop romancing.

"If you had not wanted to part with your baby you should have waited until you were married before you had one."

"There could never be another like my little Charlot," she cried.

She really did love her baby. How much? I wondered. Her emotions were ephemeral, but none the less she did feel deeply at the time, and I supposed that never had she been so involved with another human being as she was with her child.

I was glad of the cool, aloof manner of the Bellegardes—servants of the Comte. They had been sent to do a job and they were going to do it.

Margot said to me: "I shall see Charlot's foster parents and I shall come back and see Charlot. How can they think anything would keep me away from my baby!"

But the separation had been subtly arranged.

We had come to an inn on the previous night and, tired by the long day's traveling, we retired early to bed and were asleep almost immediately.

When we awoke in the morning, Charlot had disappeared.

Margot looked blank and helpless. She had not imagined it would be like that.

She went to the Bellegardes, who told her gently that the child's foster parents had come to the inn last night and taken him away. She need have no fear for him. He had gone to a very good home and would be well cared for throughout his life. Now we must leave. The Comte was expecting us to arrive at the *château* within the next few days.

AT THE
CHÂTEAU SILVAINE

1

Margot was stunned. When I spoke to her, she did not answer. I knew that nothing I said could comfort her, so I remained silent.

As we passed through the country, I knew that she was making mental notes of the places, promising herself that she would come back and find Charlot.

Poor Margot, this was the first time she realized that what had happened was not some sort of high adventure. It had had its terrifying moments, of course, such as when she had discovered she was going to have a child, but even then the excitement had carried her along. Now the abject misery of losing her child enveloped her and she knew what real unhappiness meant.

I shall never forget my first sight of the Château Silvaine. It was built on a slight eminence, and its lofty tower could be seen from several miles away. A great fortress with pepper-pot-shaped towers at its four corners and in the center the great Watch Tower, it looked formidable, menacing—which was what I supposed it was meant to be, for in the thirteenth century it would have been a fortress rather than a home.

As we approached its magnificence increased.

We must have been observed by the minstrel in the Watch Tower, for the grooms were waiting for us as we came into the precincts of the castle.

We were in a big flagged courtyard and ahead of us rose the gray marble staircase of which Margot had told me.

Margot said, "Good day," to the grooms and one replied: "Welcome back to the *château,* Mademoiselle. I am happy to see you."

"Thank you, Jacques," she said. "Is my father expecting us?"

"Oh yes, Mademoiselle, he has given orders, that as soon as you and the English Mademoiselle arrive you are to go to the red *salon* and he is to be told of your arrival."

Margot nodded. "This is my English cousin, Mademoiselle Maddox."

"Mademoiselle," murmured Jacques, bowing.

I inclined my head in acknowledgment and Margot said: "We should go at once to the red *salon*. Then we can go to our rooms."

"Would it not be better to wash and change?" I suggested. "We are rather dusty from the journey."

"He said to the red *salon* first," replied Margot; and I realized, of course, that his word was law.

"We won't mount the great staircase," said Margot. "That is one way to that part of the castle which we use, but there is another. It was the only approach in medieval days, but much of the castle has been altered to provide greater comfort and we can go this way."

"Monsieur, Madame," said Jacques to the Bellegardes, "you will step this way."

Margot led me across the courtyard to a door which we went through. We were in a hall not unlike that at Derringham Manor, but the furniture here was more elaborate and although gilded and intricately decorated gave an impression of delicacy.

There was a beautifully curved staircase leading from the hall and Margot and I ascended this. We went along a corridor and she opened a door. This was the red *salon*. I had never seen such beautiful furnishings and it was elegant in the extreme. The curtains were of red silk edged with gold. There were two or three settees and several gilded chairs. I particularly noticed a cabinet containing glass goblets and decanters. The only thing the room lacked was comfort. Everything in it seemed either too elaborate or fragile to have been put there for use.

I was very conscious of my travel-stained appearance and thought it typical of the Comte not to give us a chance to make ourselves fit for the meeting. I had already started to feel antagonistic towards him and I was sure that he had acted in this way to make us feel at a disadvantage.

When he came in, my heart started to beat fast in spite of my inward resolve not to be browbeaten. He was plainly dressed but everything he wore proclaimed that it was of the best. The wool jacket was perfectly cut, the buttons certainly pure gold; the lace at his wrists and throat dazzlingly white.

He stood, legs apart, arms folded behind his back, looking from one to the other of us, a faint smile of satisfaction settling on his lips.

"So . . . our little *affaire* is over," he said.

Margot curtsied while he looked at her half-amused, half-impatient.

Then his eyes were on me.

"Mademoiselle Maddox, this is a pleasure."

I inclined my head. "I have to thank you," he said, "for helping us out of this unfortunate contretemps. I believe it has been conducted as well as we could have hoped."

"I trust so," I said.

"Pray be seated. You too, Marguerite."

He indicated two chairs and himself took a chair by the window—his back to it so that his face was in shadow and the light fell full on us. I was immediately aware of my less than immaculate appearance.

"Now let us talk of what lies ahead. That little matter is over and we shall never speak of it again. It is as though it never happened. Mademoiselle Maddox is on a visit to us. I think she might remain a distant cousin. We discovered the connection when I was in England. Marguerite has been indisposed and her English cousin had just lost her mother. They comforted each other, and out of the goodness of her heart Mademoiselle Maddox agreed to accompany Marguerite on a little vacation. They have been resting for a month or two in a quiet village in the south and they are employing their time teaching each the other's language. It will be seen how successfully. Mademoiselle, I compliment you on your grasp of our tongue. If I may say so, your accent and intonation have improved since we last met. Your grammar of course was always impeccable, but while many can write our language, few can speak. You are an exception."

"Thank you," I said.

"And since you are my cousin—although such a distant one—I think it inappropriate for me to call you Mademoiselle Maddox. I shall call you Cousin Minelle and you shall call me Cousin Charles. Why, you look horrified!"

"I shall find it difficult," I said with some embarrassment.

"Such a little matter! I had the impression that you were a woman of great resource, capable of mastering the most difficult obstacles—and you balk at a name!"

"I merely find it difficult to regard myself as related to . . ." I waved a hand and finished: "such grandeur."

"I am enchanted that you see it as such. Then you will be happy to be part of a family such as ours."

"I have such a spurious claim."

"But one which is freely given by me." He rose and came

towards us, then, placing his hands on my shoulders, kissed me solemnly on the brow. "Cousin Minelle," he said, "I welcome you into the bosom of the family."

I flushed uneasily, aware of Margot regarding me in some astonishment. He resumed his seat.

"Sealed and settled," he said. "The kiss of welcome—as binding as my seal on a document. We are grateful to you, Cousin, are we not, Marguerite?"

"I don't know what I should have done without Minelle," she answered fervently.

"So . . ." He gesticulated. "We shall entertain here in the *château*," he went on, "and as my cousin you will join with us."

"I had not expected that," I replied. "I shall not really be equipped to join such company."

"Equipped, dear Cousin? Do you mean mentally or sartorially?"

"I certainly did not mean mentally," I retorted tartly.

"I was teasing, for I did not for one moment think you did. Oh, this tiresome matter of clothing ourselves! We have dressmakers in the castle. I'll swear, Cousin, that you have a good sense of dress. I can picture you"—again that gesture—"most excellently garbed. So you see, there is nothing more to be settled."

"I think there is a great deal," I protested. "I came here to act as Margot's companion while she needed me. I thought I was to be employed . . ."

"You are employed. But as a cousin instead of a companion."

"A sort of poor relation?"

"That sounds sad. A relation, yes, and perhaps not so well endowed with riches as some of us . . . but we shall all be too well mannered to remind you of that."

Margot, who had been quietly listening to this conversation, suddenly burst out: "I must see Charlot some time."

"Charlot?" said the Comte coldly. "And who might Charlot be?"

"He is my baby," said Margot quietly.

The Comte's face hardened. Now he looked cruel. *Le Diable* indeed, I thought.

"Have I not made it clear that that matter is over and not to be mentioned again?"

"Do you think I can stop thinking of my little baby?"

"You can certainly stop talking of it."

"You say 'it.' *It* . . . as though he is a . . . *thing* . . .

nothing of importance, to be pushed aside because he has caused inconvenience."

"It . . . or he, as you prefer to call it, has done just that."

"Not to me. I want him. I love him."

He looked from Margot to me, his expression one of exasperation. "Perhaps I have been premature in congratulating you on the manner in which this unfortunate affair has been conducted."

"I must see him sometimes," said Margot sullenly.

"Did you not hear me say that the matter is ended? Cousin Minelle, take Marguerite to her room. She will show you yours. I believe they have put you next to her. I wish to hear no more of this folly."

"Papa." She ran to him and caught his hand. He threw her off impatiently.

"Did you not hear me? Go. Take your cousin and show her her room and get over your foolishness out of my sight."

In that moment I hated him. He had brought his own illegitimate son into his household but he had no sympathy for poor Margot. I went to her and put my arm about her. "Come, Margot," I said, "we will go and rest. We are tired from our journey."

"Charlot . . ." she murmured.

"Charlot is in good hands, Margot," I said gently.

"Cousin Minelle," said the Comte, "I have given orders that the child's name is not to be mentioned. Pray remember that."

Suddenly my feelings were too much for me. I was tired from the journey and he had begun by making me feel at a disadvantage by not allowing me to wash and change; and coming face to face with him and seeing him even more overpowering, even more menacing than he had been in my thoughts, was too much for me.

I burst out: "Have you no human feelings! This is a mother. She has recently borne a child who has been snatched from her."

"Snatched! I did not know it had been snatched. My orders were that it should be quietly taken."

"You know very well what I mean."

"Oh," he said, "melodrama! 'Snatched' sounds so much more effective than 'quietly taken.' You make it sound as though there had been a tug of war over this . . . bastard. I am surprised at you, Cousin. I had thought the English were restrained. Perhaps I have much to learn of them."

"You will learn that this one hates cruelty."

"And would you like to see my daughter's hopes for the future ended because of a youthful folly? Let me tell you, I have gone to great trouble and expense to extricate her from this absurd affair. I employed you because I thought you were possessed of good sense. I am afraid you will have to let me see a little more of that necessary qualification if you are to remain in my service."

"I am sure you will find me most unsuitable. In which case, I had better leave your employ without delay, for if you expect me to silently stand by and condone your cruelty and injustice, I shall not please you, I assure you."

"Hasty! Disobedient! Sentimental! None of these is a quality I admire."

"I did not think I could possibly win your admiration. I shall leave as soon as it is possible. But you must allow me one night's shelter, which in the circumstances you owe me."

"I agree to your night's shelter most certainly. How is it that these auras are built around nations? English *sang-froid*. It is notorious. What a misrepresentation . . . unless, of course, you are not typical of your race."

Margot clung to me crying: "Minelle, you are not going to leave me. I won't let you go. Papa, she must stay with me." She turned to me. "We'll go away together. We'll find Charlot." Then she was back to her father, pulling at his sleeve. "You shall not rob me of my baby. I will not let him go." Her crying had turned to wild laughter and I was alarmed for her.

Then suddenly he struck her across the face.

For a moment there was a tense silence. Time seemed to stand still in the red *salon* and even the plump half-naked ladies who frolicked on the tapestry seemed to be waiting.

The Comte broke the silence. "Cruel, you say," he said, looking at me. "To strike my daughter! I believe it to be the treatment for this sort of hysteria. See, it has quietened her. Go now. Talk to her. Explain to her why it has to happen this way. I rely on you, Cousin Minelle. We shall have much to say to each other in the next few weeks."

There was a singing in my ears. He was canceling our conversation; he was ignoring my threat to leave.

But what I must think of now was Margot.

I took her arm and said: "Come, Margot, let us go. Show me your room . . . and mine."

She was lying on her bed recovering from the scene. I was in my room washing in the cool water which I found in what I knew to be from my studies a *ruelle*, a sort of alcove behind curtains where one could wash and dress away from the bedroom.

My bedroom was as elegant as, I was sure, was every room in the castle. The curtains were of a deep blue as were the bed hangings on the four-poster bed. An Aubusson carpet was on the floor. The furniture was delicate in the style of the last century when Louis XIV had encouraged such elegance and the influence of this had appeared throughout France. There was a beautiful dressing table with gilded cupids on either side of a mirror, holding candles; and a stool with a soft brocade seat—pale blue with deep blue velvet stripes. I could have reveled in such exquisite surroundings if I did not feel so apprehensive, and my apprehension was entirely due to the lord of the castle. I had a growing conviction that he had some ulterior motive in bringing me here, and that it was dishonorable I had no doubt.

The French were realists. They were far more cynical than we were. In England, of course, men took their mistresses and there were scandals now and then, but those were deplored, or there was a pretense that they were. Hypocrisy in a way, and yet this very quality did produce a more moral society. The Kings of France had taken their mistresses openly and *maîtresse en titre,* the title given to the chief of them, was considered honorable. In England that could never be acceptable. The present King of France had no mistresses, not because it would be considered wrong for him to take them, but because he had no inclination to do so. Even his flighty and frivolous wife, Marie Antoinette, took no lovers openly. There were whispers, of course, but who could say whether those were founded on fact or mere rumor? But this was because the King and Queen were different from those who had gone before. Noblemen of France still took mistresses as naturally as wives and none thought the worse of them.

I was well aware that the Comte had a special interest in me and I could see only one reason for it.

How I wished my mother were here. I could imagine her eyes sparkling at the luxury of the *château,* but she would be horrified by the attitude of the Comte and I was sure would whisk me away with all possible speed. I could almost hear her voice coming back to me over the void of our separation: "You must leave, Minella. As soon as you can do so . . . without panic . . . leave."

She is right, I thought. That is what I must do.

If only I could honestly say I was indifferent to him it would be a challenge. I should have enjoyed doing battle with him. But the alarming fact had been brought home to me that I was not. When he had kissed me on the forehead— a cousinly kiss—I had been aware of that excitement. No one else had aroused that in me. I thought of Joel Derringham, pleasant, charming Joel. I had enjoyed being with him; his conversation had been intriguing; he was interested in so many subjects. But there was no excitement there. When he had meekly obeyed his father and gone away, I had not been by any means heartbroken, merely disappointed in him.

And now I was here.

I washed and changed into one of the gowns my mother had ordered from the dressmaker in the hope of making me look a suitable companion for Joel Derringham. It had seemed grand in the schoolhouse. It was scarcely adequate here.

Then I went into Margot's room.

She was still lying on her bed staring blankly up at the ornate ceiling on which cupids sported.

"Oh Minelle," she cried, "how am I going to bear it?"

"It will grow better as time passes," I assured her.

"He is so cruel . . ."

I defended him. "He is thinking of your future."

"You know what they will try to do, don't you? Marry me off to someone. It will be a terrible secret. He will not be told about Charlot."

"Cheer up, Margot. I am sure that when you have other children you will be reconciled."

"You talk exactly as they do, Minelle."

"Because it's the truth."

"Minelle, don't go away."

"You heard what your father said. He doesn't approve of me."

"I think he quite likes you."

"But you heard what he said."

"Yes, but you mustn't go. Think of me here without you. I wouldn't stay. Minelle, don't go. We'll make plans."

"What plans?"

"For finding Charlot. We'll retrace our journey. We'll search everywhere . . . until we find him."

I did not speak. I could see that she needed to indulge in one of her fantasies. For the time being that would provide a crutch for her to lean on . . . or a rope to drag her out of the slough of misery. Poor Margot!

So I bathed her face and helped her to dress while we made plans to go off in search of Charlot—plans which I felt certain would never materialize.

A servant conducted me to the apartments of Madame la Comtesse, who had expressed a wish to see me. I found her lying on a chaise longue, and I was immediately reminded of the first and only time I had seen her in the same position at Derringham Manor.

Here were the same exquisite furnishings of the previous century, with especially delicate colors as though to fit in with the Comtesse's frail state of health.

She was very pale and very slim; in fact, she resembled a china doll and looked as though she might break if roughly handled. Her gown was of clinging chiffon in pale lavender; her dark hair hung in loose curls about her shoulders and her dark eyes were large and long-lashed. Beside her couch was a table laden with bottles and a glass or two.

As I entered the room, a big woman dressed entirely in black came hurrying toward me. Nou Nou, I thought. She certainly looked formidable; her amber-colored eyes reminded me of those of a lioness, and indeed she gave the impression of one defending her cub—if one could apply such a term to the delicate piece of china on the chaise longue. Nou Nou's skin was sallow, her lips tight; I learned later that they could soften in tenderness to the Comtesse and to her only.

"You'll be Mademoiselle Maddox," she said to me. "The Comtesse wished to see you. Don't tire her. She tires easily." She went to her mistress. "Here is the young lady," she said.

A frail hand was held out to me. I took it and bowed over it as seemed to be the custom.

"Bring a chair for my cousin," she said.

Nou Nou did so and whispered to me: "Don't forget. She tires easily."

"You can leave us now, Nouny dear," said the Comtesse.

"I was going to. I've things to do, remember."

She went out, bristling a little I fancied. I imagined she resented anyone's taking the attention of her beloved mistress.

"The Comte has told me about the part you have played," she said. "I wanted to thank you. He has said you are to be our cousin."

"Yes," I answered.

"I was desolate when I heard what had happened to Marguerite."

"It was a sad affair," I agreed.

"But it is settled now . . . most satisfactorily I believe."

"Not so satisfactory to your daughter. She has lost her child."

"Poor Marguerite. It was rather wicked of her. I fear she inherits her father's nature. I trust she will have no more such adventures. I believe you are here to look after her. I am to call you Cousin Minelle and I am to be Cousin Ursule to you."

"Cousin Ursule," I repeated. It was the first time I had heard her name.

"It will be difficult at first," she said, "but a slip or two will not be important. I am in my room most of the time. You need not worry about Nou Nou's hearing. She knows everything that happens in the family. She always has. She disapproves of this." The Comtesse's lips curved momentarily in a smile. "She would have liked to have a baby here. Nou Nou loves babies. She would have liked me to have a dozen."

"Nurses are like that, I believe."

"Nou Nou is. She came with me when I married." Her face puckered a little as though she were remembering something unpleasant. "That was many years ago. I have been ill almost ever since."

The little animation there had been in her face had disappeared. She looked at the table beside her. "I'll take a little of the cordial. Will you pour it for me? It tires me even to lift my arm."

I went to the table and selected the bottle she indicated. She was watching me closely and it occurred to me that she had asked me to pour the cordial that I might come closer to her and give her a chance to study me.

"Just a little, please," she said. "Nou Nou makes it. She is very clever with her concoctions. They are all made from herbs which she grows. This one contains angelica. It's good for headaches. I am tortured by headaches . . . I am a martyr to them. Do you know any good medicines, Cousin Minelle . . . any cures?"

"Absolutely none. I have fortunately never had the need of them."

"Nou Nou has studied them since I became so ill. That was about seventeen years ago . . ."

She paused and I knew she was referring to the birth of

Margot, which had robbed her of her good health and strength.

"Nou Nou shows me the plants she uses. I always remember angelica. The old doctors used to call it the Root of the Holy Ghost because it has such healing properties. Do you find that interesting, Mademoiselle . . . Cousin Minelle?"

"Yes. I find all information interesting."

She nodded. "Basil is good for headaches. Nou Nou uses that too. When I need soothing she gives me a dose of it. It has a wonderful effect. She has a little still room close by where she uses her herbs. She cooks for me, too." The Comtesse looked a little furtive as she glanced over her shoulder. "Nou Nou will not allow anyone but herself to prepare my meals."

I wondered what that meant, and for a moment I thought she was hinting that the Comte was trying to be rid of her. Is this conversation meant to convey some warning? I asked myself.

"She is clearly devoted to you," I said.

"It is good to have someone who is devoted," she answered. Then she seemed to draw her attention away from her ailments with some difficulty. She said: "You have seen the Comte since you arrived?"

I told her I had.

"Has he mentioned Marguerite's marriage to you?"

"No," I replied with some alarm.

"He will give her a little time to recover. It will be a good match. The bridegroom comes from one of the highest families in France. He will have titles and estates one day."

"Is Marguerite to be told?"

"Not yet. Will you try to reconcile her to it? The Comte says you have influence with her. He will insist on obedience but it would be more comfortable if she could be persuaded that it is for the best."

"Madame, she has just had a child and has lost him."

"You must call me Cousin Ursule, by the way. But hasn't the Comte told you that the matter is to be treated as though it never took place?"

"Yes, Cousin Ursule, but . . ."

"I think we should remember it. The Comte does not like his wishes to be ignored. Margot must be brought round to this . . . gradually perhaps . . . but not too gradually. The Comte can be very impatient and he particularly wants to see Marguerite married before long."

"I do not think it would be wise to broach the subject at this stage."

She shrugged her shoulders and half-closed her eyes. "I feel faint," she said. "Call Nou Nou."

Nou Nou came immediately. I fancied she had been not far off, listening to our conversation.

She clucked impatiently and looked towards me. "You've tired her. There, *mignonne*, Nouny's here. I'll give you a little Water of the Queen of Hungary, eh? That never fails to put you right. I made it this morning and it's beautifully fresh."

I went back to my room, considering the Comtesse and her devoted Nou Nou and wondering what other strange people I should find in this household.

By the evening Margot had recovered a little and she came to my room while I was doing my hair.

"We shall be supping in one of the small dining rooms tonight," she said. "There is only the family. My father was anxious for it to be so tonight."

"I am very glad of that. You know, Margot, I am not equipped for life on such a scale. When I agreed to come here, I thought it was as companion to you. I did not know I was to be raised to the rank of cousin and mingle."

"Forget it. We shall get some clothes for you in time. What you are wearing is all right for tonight."

All right! It was the grandest gown I possessed. My mother had been right after all when she had thought I should need some fine garments.

Margot conducted me to the intimate *salle à manger* . . . small but delightful and as exquisitely furnished as the other rooms I had seen in the house. The Comte was already there and there were two young men with him.

"Ah," he said, "my Cousin Minelle. Is it not great good fortune that my sojourn in England was rewarded with a cousin? Étienne, Léon, come and meet my Cousin Minelle."

The two young men bowed and the Comte took my arm. His fingers caressed my arm affectionately and reassuringly.

"This, Cousin, is Étienne. He is my son. Do you see a resemblance?"

Étienne seemed to be waiting eagerly for my reply. "There is an undoubted resemblance," I said, and he smiled at me.

"And this is Léon, whom I adopted when he was six."

I liked Léon from the first. There was something which appealed to me in those laughing eyes. I only discovered when I saw them in daylight that they were deep blue—almost violet. He had very dark hair, rather crinkly, and he wore no wig. He was well but not elaborately dressed. Different from Étienne, whose coat sported lapis lazuli buttons and who had a diamond or two in his cravat.

"I had thought," said the Comte, "that as this is Cousin Minelle's first night with us we should sup *en famille*. Do you think that is a good idea, Cousin?"

I said I thought it was an excellent idea.

"And here is Marguerite. You look better, my dear. The holiday has done you some good. Let us be seated. They are ready to serve. Cousin, you here beside me. Marguerite on my other side."

We sat obediently.

"Now," said the Comte, "we can talk among ourselves. It is rarely that we are without guests, Cousin. But as it is our first evening I thought it would be easier for you to get to know us all . . . like this."

I felt I was dreaming. What was the implication? He was treating me like an honored guest.

"This, my dear Cousin, is one of the most ancient castles in the country," he told me. "You can easily lose yourself in the labyrinth of rooms and passages. Is that not so, Étienne, Léon?"

"It is, Monsieur le Comte," said Étienne.

"They have all been here for many years," explained the Comte, "so it does not strike them."

The servant brought round the highly spiced food, which I did not really care for. In any case I was not hungry.

Léon was regarding me with interest across the table. His smile was warm and I found it comforting. His attitude was different from that of Étienne who, I fancied, was a little suspicious of me. I wondered how much they knew of what had happened. They both seemed colorful personalities to me I suppose because I already knew of their origins, which Margot had explained. Étienne seemed more in awe of the Comte than Léon about whom there was something bold and carefree.

The Comte talked of the castle, the old part of which was only used on ceremonial occasions.

"One of you must show Cousin Minelle over the castle tomorrow."

"Certainly," said Étienne.

"I claim that honor," put in Léon.

"Thank you," I replied, smiling at him.

Étienne asked questions about England and I answered as best I could while the Comte listened attentively.

"You should speak English to our cousin," he said. "It would be courteous to do so. Come now, we shall speak in English."

This curtailed the conversation considerably, for neither Étienne nor Léon had a good command of the language.

"You are silent, Marguerite," said the Comte critically. "I want to see what an adept you have become at our cousin's language."

"Margot can speak English fluently," I said.

"But with a French accent! Why is it that of all the world our two countries find it most difficult to speak each other's language? Can you tell me that?"

"It is the way in which we move our mouths when we speak. The French have developed facial muscles which the English never use and vice versa."

"I am sure, Cousin, that you have an answer for everything."

"I would say that was true," said Margot.

"So the gift of speech has been restored to you."

Margot flushed a little and I asked myself why when I was beginning to like the Comte he had to spoil it with some unkind thrust.

"I don't think she ever lost it," I said with some asperity. "Like most of us Margot feels less inclined for conversation sometimes than others."

"You have a champion, Marguerite. You are very lucky."

"I have always known I was lucky to have Minelle for a friend."

"Very lucky," said the Comte, looking at me.

Léon asked in halting English where we spent our holiday.

There was a brief pause, then the Comte told him in French that it was some little place near Cannes. "About fifteen miles inland," he added, and I was shocked at the glib manner in which he lied.

"I do not know that part well," said Léon, "but I have passed through it. I wonder if I know the place." He turned to me. "What was the name of it?"

I had not expected to find myself in a difficult position so quickly, but I saw that this could be the first of many.

Before I could have spoken the Comte came to the rescue. "It was Framercy . . . was it not, Cousin? I confess I had never heard of it before."

I did not answer but Étienne said:: "It must be a small hamlet."

"There are thousands of such places dotted all over the country," said the Comte. "In any case they had a quiet time, which was what Marguerite needed after her indisposition."

"It is rare that one can find a peaceful spot in France these days," said Étienne, dropping back into French. "In Paris they are talking of nothing but the deficit."

"I am sorry," said the Comte, addressing me, "that you have to come to France at a time when the country is in a sad plight. How different it would have been fifteen . . . twenty years ago. It is astonishing how quickly the clouds can gather. First just a faint shadow on the horizon and the sky starts to grow dark. It has been gradual, but some of us have seen it coming for a long time. Each month it grows a little more menacing." He shrugged his shoulders. "What is France heading for? Who shall say? All we know is that it will come."

"It could be avoided perhaps," suggested Étienne.

"If it is not too late," murmured the Comte.

"I believe it *is* too late." Léon's eyes flashed suddenly. "There has been too much inefficiency, too much poverty in the country, too many taxes, and high food prices have meant starvation for many."

"There have always been rich and poor," the Comte reminded him.

"And now there are some who are saying that it will not always be so."

"They may say it but what can they do about it?"

"Some of the hotheads think they can do something. They are not only getting together in Paris but throughout the country."

"A ragged band," said the Comte. "A mob . . . nothing more. While the army remained loyal they wouldn't have a chance." He frowned and turned to me. "All through the centuries there has been unrest. We had a great King last century, Louis XIV, the Sun King, the supreme monarch, and none dared question his power. Under him France led the world. In science, in art, in war, none could compare with us. The people did not raise their voices then. Then came his grandson Louis XV . . . a man of great charm, but he did not understand the people. When he was young he was known as Louis the Well Beloved, for he was most handsome. But in time his extravagances, his recklessness, his indifference to the will of the people, made him one of the most hated monarchs France has ever known. There was a time when he dared not ride through Paris and had a road built that he might avoid doing so. It was then that the monarchy became insecure. Now we have a good and noble King but, alas, a weak one. Good men are not always good rulers. You know well, Cousin, that virtue and strength make odd bedfellows."

"I would question that," I said. "Would you deny that the saints, who have died for their religion—often painfully—lack strength to set beside their undoubted virtue?"

There was a moment's silence at the table. Margot was looking worried. I realized then that it was not usual to interrupt the Comte in his discourse—particularly to contradict him.

"Fanaticism," he retorted. "When they die they believe they are going to glory. What are a few hours of torment beside an eternity of bliss . . . or whatever they think they are going to? To rule effectively one must be strong, and sometimes it is necessary to practice expediency, which could offend some moral codes. The essential quality of leadership is strength."

"I would say justice."

"My dear Cousin, you have learned your history from books."

"How, pray, do others learn?"

"Through experience."

"No one can live long enough. Are we never to judge any act we have not experienced?"

"If we are wise we shall temper our judgment with caution. I was telling you of our King. He is not a kingly figure and unfortunately his wife has been of little help to him."

"Have you heard what they are calling the Queen now?" asked Étienne. "Madame Deficit."

"They blame her for the deficit," said Léon, "and perhaps rightly so. It is said that her dressmaker's bills are enormous. Her gowns, her hats, her extravagant head adornments, her entertainment at the Petit Trianon, her so-called country life at Le Hameau, where she milks the cows in Sèvres bowls . . . are being talked of everywhere."

"Why should she not have what she wants?" demanded Margot. "She did not ask to come to France. She was forced to marry Louis. She had never seen him before the marriage."

"My dear Margot," the Comte interrupted icily, "naturally a daughter of Maria Theresa should think herself honored to marry a Dauphin of France. She was received here with the utmost respect. The late King was charmed with her."

"Trust him to be charmed with a pretty young girl," said Léon. "We all know what a fancy he had for them . . . the younger the better. That's well known through the scandal of the Parc aux Cerfs."

Étienne said: "Not a suitable subject for the family supper table, Léon."

The Comte put in: "Our cousin is a woman of the world. She understands such matters." Again he turned to me. "Our late King as he grew older had a not unusual partiality for young girls whom his pander was obliged to procure for him. He kept them in a mansion surrounded by a deer park—hence the Parc aux Cerfs."

"I am not surprised that he ceased to be Louis the Well Beloved," I said.

"He was a charming man." The Comte smiled at me challengingly.

"Perhaps my notion of charm is not the same as yours."

"Dear Cousin, these girls were taken from poverty. It must be so. He could not have taken the daughters of noblemen. They were not forced, nor coerced even. They came of their free will. Sometimes their parents brought them. Midinettes from the streets of Paris . . . girls who had little hope of earning an honest living. Many might have been condemned to lead lewd and evil lives; some might have worked if they could have found work until they died of diseases of the lungs or lost their sight through too close needlework. Their only asset was their beauty . . . roses somehow growing on a dung heap. They were seen, picked, and taught to amuse the King."

"And when he tired of them?" I asked.

"He was a grateful man. He gave them a handsome dowry; the pander found husbands for them and they lived happily ever after. Now, Cousin, my dear advocate of virtue, tell me this: Was it better for those girls to wilt and die on their dung heap or, in exchange for a brief lapse from virtue, win for themselves a life of ease and comfort and perhaps good works?"

"It depends on what store they set on virtue."

"You evade the issue. Should they sell their bodies to a sweatshop or a royal master?"

"I can only say that it is an evil system which enables you to pose such a question."

108

"It is a system which exists, not only in France." He looked at me earnestly. "It is this system against which the people are now murmuring."

"It will come right," said Étienne. "Turgot and Necker have gone. We shall see what Monsieur Calonne can do for us."

"Do we bore Mademoiselle Maddox with our politics?" asked Léon.

"Indeed no. I find it interesting. I want to know what is happening."

"Whatever happens," said Léon, "we shall adjust ourselves. That is my feeling. If change is inevitable we must grow accustomed to change."

"I should not care to see a change which brought the mob into the *château*," growled Étienne.

Léon shrugged and Étienne said angrily: "It might be easier for you. You might fit better than some into a peasant's hovel."

There was a silence at the table. The Comte glanced from Étienne to Léon with an expression of amused tolerance on his face. Étienne's was distorted with anger, Léon's nonchalant.

"Certainly I should," said Léon easily. "I remember the days of my extreme youth. I was not unhappy, crawling in the mire. I am sure I could revert without a great deal of difficulty. I am fortunate to know two worlds."

Étienne was silent. I wondered how often there was conflict between these two. It occurred to me that Étienne, so anxious to maintain his relationship with the Comte, was a little resentful of Léon's intrusion and that Léon, being aware of this, cared little.

The Comte changed the subject, and I realized that he was accustomed to lead the conversation at the table and I wondered whether he liked to stir up such storms and watch the effect they had.

"We shall be giving Cousin Minelle a poor view of our country," he said. "Let us talk of those things of which we can be justly proud. You will, I hope, enjoy Paris, Cousin—a great city of culture which I can say without boasting is unequaled in the world. I have a house there. It is called an *hôtel*—but that is what we called our great houses in the past, so it is not an *hôtel* in the sense which you would use the word. It has been in the family for nearly three hundred years. Yes, it was built in the reign of François Premier when some of the finest architecture in the world was set up in France.

109

You will visit some of our beautiful castles of the Loire, I trust; and we shall enjoy introducing you to Paris."

He went on to talk about the contrast of life in the country and the great city—and so passed the rest of the meal.

I had found the conversation unexpected and I knew that my mother would have considered it extremely shocking—not the sort we should have heard at the Derringham table when ladies were present. But it had stimulated me.

After dinner we went to another of the *salons* and there the Comte drank brandy. He insisted on my trying it. It burned my throat and I was afraid to take more than a few sips, which I knew secretly amused him.

When the ormolu clock struck ten he said that he thought it was time Marguerite was in bed. We must not forget that she was suffering from an indisposition. He wanted her to regain her health as quickly as possible. So we said good night and Margot and I went to our rooms.

Margot said: "Minelle, I don't know how I am going to bear it. You know what's going to happen, don't you? They are going to find a husband for me."

"Not yet," I soothed. "You are too young."

"Too young. At seventeen one is old enough."

"You have proved that, I suppose."

"It was the way my father looked at me when he was talking about the Queen and the King and how she was brought here to marry. It was a warning, I know."

"I thought the conversation was a little unusual."

"You mean *risqué*. All that about the Parc aux Cerfs. It was done with a purpose, I think. My father was telling me that I was no longer an innocent virgin and he wanted no nonsense from me. I would have to do as I was told and it would be for my own good . . . like those girls in the Parc."

"Is the conversation always like that when ladies are present?"

Margot was silent and my uneasiness increased.

"Come," I said, "tell me what you are thinking."

"My father has clearly taken a fancy to you, Minelle."

"He certainly made a point of welcoming me . . . and he seems to call me Cousin with relish. But I thought it odd that he should have let the conversation go the way it did."

"He did it purposely."

"I wonder why."

Margot shook her head and I felt a strong desire to be alone with my thoughts, so I said good night and went into my own room.

The candles had been lighted by the maid and it looked charming in their light. I had never known such luxury. I kept thinking of those girls taken from the mean streets and transported to a place like this. How had they felt?

I sat down at the mirror and took the pins from my hair so that it fell about my shoulders. Candlelight is notoriously flattering and I looked almost beautiful. My eyes were bright with excitement, which was the more intense because it was tinged with fear; there was a faint flush under my skin.

I looked over my shoulder at the door. To my relief I saw that there was a key. I went to it at once in order to lock it but before I could do so I heard the murmur of voices. I stood, my hand on the key ready to turn it. The footsteps passed my door, and I could not resist the temptation to open it slightly and peep through. I saw the backs of Étienne and Léon. Moreover, I heard their words.

"But who is she?" Léon was saying.

"Cousin!" That was Étienne. "That's a new idea. She's the new mistress, I suppose."

"Somehow I fancy not yet."

"But she will be . . . and that before long. It's a new way . . . bringing them into the *château*."

I shut the door and locked it with trembling fingers. Then I went and sat down at the mirror. I stared at my reflection in horror for some moments. Then I said aloud: "You must leave as soon as possible."

I slept little that night. What I had overheard had shocked me so deeply that I was trying to convince myself that I had misconstrued the men's meaning. But knowing what I did of the Comte I could see that their conclusions could be logical enough. What should I do? I had burned my boats, having sold the furniture of the schoolhouse and given it up. Quite clearly I should never have left England; I should have realized why the Comte was interested in me. I knew well enough the kind of man he was. Yet when he had suggested I go with Margot the proposition had seemed reasonable. Margot had needed someone to look after her and help her through her ordeal and I seemed to fall naturally into the part. I had believed that when I came to the *château* I should be a companion to her, living as I had heard companions and governesses did in their own quarters somewhere between those of the servants and those of their employers. I had imagined that in a year or so, after Margot married, I should have saved enough money and gained in poise and experience to return to England, open a school and specialize in teaching French.

Perhaps by that time, I had thought, Joel Derringham would have made a suitable marriage and Sir John and Lady Derringham, having realized that what they would think of as that "little bit of folly" was over, would send me pupils.

But the attitude of the Comte and the comments I had overheard made it very clear that I must get away.

When I heard the house stirring I arose and unlocked my door, and in due course a servant appeared with hot water. I washed and dressed in the *ruelle* and then went to Margot's room.

She looked refreshed and much calmer and because of this I thought it better to come straight to the point.

"Margot," I said, "I think my position here is somewhat anomalous."

"What?" she cried.

"I mean it is irregular."

"What do you mean? What *is* your position here?"

"That is what I must ascertain. I thought I was coming here to take a position. I am being paid to be your companion and help you through this difficult time and teach you English. But I find myself a cousin and treated like a guest."

"Well, there had to be this cousin fiction, and I would always treat you as a friend, you know that."

"But the rest of the household . . ."

"You mean my father. Oh, he is known to be eccentric. It amuses him at the moment to make you a cousin. Tomorrow he might decide you are his daughter's companion and treat you as such."

"But I am not prepared to be taken up and set down in this way. You must realize, Margot, that I am not equipped to appear in this sort of society."

"You're thinking of clothes. We'll soon settle that. You can have some of mine . . . or new ones. We'll go to Paris soon, I dare say, and there we'll buy materials."

"I lack the means to do this."

"They will be charged to the account. That's how its done."

"For you, yes . . . and Étienne and Léon perhaps. You are part of the family. I am not. I must go back to England and I want you to understand why."

Her eyes had grown black with fear. "Minelle, please, I beg of you, don't leave me. If you go, I'm alone . . . Can't you see."

"I can't stay here in this position, Margot. It's degrading."

"I don't understand you. Explain."

But I could not bring myself to say: "Your father is planning to make me his mistress." It sounded so dramatic and absurd, and I might have misconstrued the situation. That the two young men had been discussing me was obvious, but they could have been entirely wrong.

Margot had seized my hands. I was afraid she was going to have another of those hysterical bouts. They frightened me, for she really looked wild when they took possession of her.

"Minelle, promise me . . . promise me . . . I can't lose you *and* Charlot. Besides, we're going to find him. I never could do without you. Promise me. I won't let you go until you do."

"I won't go without telling you certainly." I added weakly: "I'll wait a bit. I'll see what happens."

She was satisfied.

"Léon is going to show me the castle," I said. I glanced at the clock. "He will soon be waiting for me in the library."

"It is close to the *salon* where we dined last night."

"Margot," I said, "what do you think of Étienne and Léon?"

"What do I think of them? Well, as brothers, I suppose. They have always been around."

"You are fond of them, I dare say."

"Yes . . . in a way. Léon was always a dreadful tease and Étienne had such a high opinion of himself. Étienne is jealous of anyone Papa takes notice of. Léon simply does not care. That amuses Papa in a way. Once when he was angry with Léon he shouted, 'You can go back to your peasant's hovel!' And Léon prepared to go. That was when he was about fifteen. I remember it well. There was a terrible scene. My father beat him and locked him in his room. But I think he admired Léon for it. You see, when he killed Léon's twin brother he swore he would give Léon a good education and treat him like a member of his family and if Léon went back, Papa would not have carried out his vow. So Léon had to stay."

"But he wanted to, of course."

"Of course he did. He would hate to go back to poverty. In fact, he takes food and money to his family and they depend on him a good deal."

"I'm glad he hasn't turned his back on them."

"He never would. Of course Étienne is quite different. He is delighted to be here and have Papa recognize him as his son. The only thing that irks him is his illegitimacy. I think

113

Papa regrets that too. Étienne is always hoping that he will be legitimatized."

"Is that possible?"

"Something can be done, I believe. Étienne would love to be the future Comte and inherit everything. I think Papa *would* make him his heir, but at the back of his mind is the thought that if Maman died he'd marry again. He's not too old. He was married to my mother when he was seventeen. I'm sure he's hoping to get a legitimate son one day."

"How awful for your mother!"

"She hates him and he despises her. I think she would be afraid if it wasn't for Nou Nou. Nou Nou distrusts my father. She always has. Naturally she wouldn't think anyone was good enough for her *mignonne* Ursule. Nou Nou was her nurse when she was a baby and you know how doting nurses get. She was my nurse too, but my mother was always the one for her; and when my mother became an invalid she didn't really want anything to interfere with her care of her. It's rather embarrassing for my father, for Nou Nou insists on cooking everything my mother eats."

"What a dreadful implication! I wonder he doesn't tell her to go."

"He's amused and he always seems to respect people who amuse him and stand up to him."

"I wonder you don't all do that then."

"We mean to, but somehow when you face him and see him angry, looking like the devil himself, your courage fails you. Mine does. So does Étienne's. I'm not sure of Léon's. He's stood up to him once or twice. Nou Nou is determined to defend my mother and she'd die doing it if necessary."

"But this implies that he is plotting murder."

"He killed Léon's brother."

"That was an accident."

"Yes, but he killed him nevertheless."

I shivered. I felt more strongly than ever that I ought to go home.

It was time for me to go to the library to meet Léon, so I went down. It was disconcerting to find the Comte there. He was seated in an armchair reading a book.

The library was impressive with its great chandelier and the book-lined walls, the painted ceiling, the long windows with their velvet drapes. But in that moment I was aware of nothing but the Comte.

"Good morning, Cousin," he said rising. He came to me

and taking my hand kissed it. "You look as fresh as the morning and as beautiful. I trust you slept well."

I hesitated. "As well as can be expected in a strange bed, thank you."

"Ah. I have slept in so many strange beds that such a thing would never affect me."

"I have come to meet Léon, who is showing me the castle."

"I dismissed him and told him I would take his place."

"Oh!" I was startled.

"I trust you are not displeased. I thought I should be the one to show you my castle. I'm rather proud of it, you know."

"Naturally you must be."

"It has been in my family for five hundred years. That is a long time, eh, Cousin?"

"A very long time. Do you think it necessary to continue this farce of cousinship when we are alone?"

"To tell the truth, I rather like to think of you as my cousin. Do you share my feelings?"

"As a matter of fact, I think the relationship is so absurd that I never consider it seriously. It was in order while Margot and I were . . ."

He raised a hand. "Remember, I have forbidden that matter to be mentioned."

"It is absurd not to when it is the very reason for my being here."

"It is merely a beginning . . . an opening gambit. Do you play chess, Cousin? I am sure you do. If not, I shall teach you."

I said that my mother and I had played together. She had learned from my father, but I was sure my game would not match up to his.

"I am sure it will. I look forward to evenings when we pit our wits over the board. But let us start our tour of exploration. We will go and mount the great staircase. Then we shall enter the really ancient part of the castle."

"I should like that," I said.

"I shall be a better guide than Léon. After all, it has not been in his family for centuries, has it? And although his present affluence appears to sit lightly in him, he never forgets where it came from. Étienne is the same. There are things in life which should be forgotten and those which should be remembered. It is a wise man who can sort out which, for then he will be happy, and is not happiness the goal of us all? The wisest man is the happiest man. Do you agree, Cousin?"

"Yes, I think I do."

"How delighted I am. At last we have found a matter on which we can agree. I hope it won't happen too often, though. I shall enjoy crossing swords with you."

We had come to a great courtyard where, he told me, as Margot already had, the jousts and tilting used to be held. "Look at these steps. They are impressive, are they not? See how the stones have worn away with the tread of thousands of feet over the centuries. Guests of the household used to promenade up and down the staircase. It was a way of taking the air, and when the tournaments were in progress they would use the steps as seats to watch the show. Here on the platform at the top of the staircase my family would sit surrounded by important guests and watch from here. On this very platform they would hold court like kings and mete out justice to malefactors, who would be brought to them and maybe sentenced to a spell in the dungeons from which many of them never emerged. Those were cruel days, Cousin."

"Let us hope there is less cruelty in the world today," I said.

He put a hand on my shoulders and answered: "I am not sure of that. Let us hope the holocaust will be avoided, for God knows what could happen to us if it should come."

He was silent for a while and then he told me how the beggars used to take up their stand by the vaults which supported the great staircase, and they reaped rich rewards on those days when the Comtes of Silvaine gave their tournaments.

"From the platform one reaches the principal apartments of the old castle. Come, Cousin, here is the hall."

"It's vast," I said.

"It needed to be. Here they used to live their public lives. Here the lord of the castle received his messengers, judged those who had misbehaved, summoned his serfs, and gathered together his fiefs when he was going to war."

I shuddered.

"You are cold, Cousin?" He touched my arm lightly and, as I tried to move away as unobtrusively as I could, he noticed and smiled faintly.

"No thanks," I said. "I was just thinking of all the events

116

which must have taken place over the centuries. It is almost as though they have left something behind."

"You are imaginative. I am glad. You will find plenty to catch your fancy here in the castle."

"It will be interesting . . ." Something made me add, ". . . during my brief stay."

"Your stay, dear Cousin, I hope will not be brief."

"I have decided I must go as soon as Marguerite has recovered."

"Perhaps we shall find another reason for holding you here."

"I very much doubt that. I have come to the conclusion that my place is in England . . . teaching school. It is what I was trained for."

"If I may say so, you don't fit the part."

"You may certainly say it, but your opinion will make no difference to my intentions."

"I think you are too wise to act rashly. The school did not pay. Did you not leave it for that reason? That lily-livered creature Joel had put you out of favor with his family and departed. *I* can only despise such an act."

"It was not like that at all."

He raised his eyebrows. "I know he was attracted by you and that is something I can fully understand, but when Papa cracked the whip and said, 'Go,' he went."

"Sir John, like other parents, expected obedience from his offspring, I suppose."

"Your gallant Joel was not a child. One would have expected him to make a stand. But no. I cannot admire a laggard in love."

"There was no question of love. We were good friends. And this is a subject which I find distasteful. Do you mind if we continue exploring the castle?"

He bowed his head. "It is my great wish to please you," he said. "Through the hall here is the chamber which is a sort of *salon*. This and the bedchamber were the chief apartments of the lord and his lady. It was built as a fortress, you see. Creature comforts were not as important as the fortifications."

"The chamber is as large as the hall."

"Yes, here they entertained their guests. They set up tables on trestles and on the dais there was another table— the high table. At this sat the lord, his lady, and the chief guests. After feasting, the tables were removed and the guests sat round the great fire . . . here in the center of the room . . . an open fire."

"I can picture them, sitting round telling stories . . ."

"And singing their songs. The minstrels were constant visitors. They used to roam the countryside calling at castles and great houses where they would sing for their supper. They worked hard, poor devils, and often were badly served, for they would sometimes be refused payment after they had performed."

"I trust never in this castle."

"I trust not. My ancestors were wild and lawless, but although I have heard stories of their wickedness it did not include meanness. We were lavish spenders, reckless in all things, but I never heard of a refusal to pay those who served us well. The high table you see over there looked over the low tables, so that we could keep an eye on our lesser guests. We have kept this part of the *château* as it was and we only use it on ceremonial occasions. I like to be reminded of how my ancestors lived. We don't cover the floor with rushes, of course. What an unsavory custom that was! *Empimenter* was often necessary. Ah, Cousin, you are puzzled. You do not know *empimenter?* Confess. At last I have triumphed."

"Triumphed?" I said. "I cannot understand why you should think I am under the impression that I know everything."

"It is because you are so knowledgeable that I constantly feel that every challenge ends in victory for you."

"Why should there be this . . . unarmed combat?" I demanded with asperity.

"It seems the nature of our relationship."

"Our relationship is that of employer and employed. It is my duty to give satisfaction, not to joust, tilt, or . . ."

"Only once have I disconcerted you, Cousin. That was in the days before our cousinship when you crept into my bedchamber and were caught. Then you looked like a naughty child and I will confess that from that moment you enchanted me."

"I think you should understand . . ."

"Oh, I do understand. I understand perfectly. I know I must tread with care. I know that you are poised for flight. What a tragedy that would be . . . for me . . . and perhaps for you. Don't be afraid, little Cousin. I told you that I come from a line of reckless men, but I am only rash when the occasion demands it."

"This seems an unusual conversation to have grown out of my ignorance regarding the word . . . was it *empimenter?*"

"It is hardly likely that you would know this word, for fortunately it is little used now. It means to perfume by burning juniper wood or Eastern perfumes, and this had to be done when the stench of the rushes was unendurable."

"Surely it would have been simpler to remove the rushes."

"They were replaced now and then but so odiferous were they that they left their aroma behind. See these coffers. In them our treasures were kept . . . gold and silver vessels and furs of course . . . sables, ermines, vair, and miniver. Then when shut, you see, they could be used as seats, for there was not enough seating space for our guests in these seats cut out of the walls. Many of them would have squatted on the floor, round the fires in winter most likely. Through the chamber we pass into the bedchamber. Here many of my ancestors were born."

Our footsteps clattered over the stone floor. There was no bed in the room, only a few pieces of heavy furniture, which I imagined had been used before the rest of the castle had been built.

From this room we passed into several smaller rooms, all sparsely furnished, stone-walled and stone-floored.

"The home of a medieval nobleman," said the Comte. "It is small wonder that as time passed we had to build ourselves more elegant living quarters. We were very proud of our castles, I can tell you. In the reign of François Premier building flourished. We followed the King, you see. He was a great lover of the arts. He once remarked that men could make a King, but only God could make an artist. He was interested in architecture, so it was fashionable for his friends to be interested too and we vied with each other to build beautiful mansions. We built partly to flaunt our wealth and partly to indulge in secret pursuits. Thus we had hidden rooms, secret passages, and we were determined that none but ourselves should know of them, but perhaps I will show you ours one day. One great lady had her architect's head cut off so that she could be sure that he never passed on the secret plans of her house."

"It seemed a drastic measure."

"But you must admit foolproof. Oh dear Cousin, how I enjoy shocking you!"

"I'm afraid I shall have to mar your pleasure by telling you I don't believe the story."

"Why should you not? The lord of the castle—and that means his entire estate which is vast—is supreme. His actions cannot be questioned by his underlings."

"Then I hope you do not contemplate using *your* powers in such a manner."

"It might depend on how tempted I was."

"I suppose a great many people lived in the castle," I said, changing the subject, which I believed was something which was frowned on, as only the Comte decided whether a topic was exhausted.

He raised his eyebrows and I thought he was about to remind me of this but he changed his mind. "A great many," he said. "There were the squires, as they were called. They were in charge of various household departments. There was the squire of the table, of the chamber, of the wine cellar, and so on. Many of them came from noble families and were being prepared to take the order of chivalry. So it was a large household. Of course, the stables were an important part of the castle. There were no carriages in those days but there were horses of all kinds—draft horses, palfreys, and the finest steads for the use of the lord of the castle. In exchange for the services he received, the lord of the castle would educate his squires, and his riches and importance would be judged by the number of squires he supported."

"A custom which no longer exists, though I suppose Étienne and Léon are in some measure the squires of today."

"You could call them that. They receive the education of noblemen and the training that goes to make up breeding. And they are here because I owe a debt to their parents. Yes, you could say it is similar. Ah, here is one other chamber which I must show you. The Chambre des Pucelles—the Maidens' chamber."

I looked into the large room. A spinning wheel stood in one corner and the walls were hung with tapestry.

"Worked by the maidens," said the Comte. "You see it is a light room. Imagine them all, heads bent over their work, plying their needles. The maidens were received at the castle too. They must be of good birth and excel at their needle. To excel at the needle was considered necessary to good breeding. And you, Cousin, how are you with the needle?"

"Completely lacking in breeding, I fear. I sew only when necessary."

"I'm glad of that. Too much bending over embroidery is bad for the eyes and the posture. I can think of many occupations in which a woman can be better employed."

"What do the tapestries represent?"

"Some war between the French and an enemy . . . the English, I suppose. It usually was."

"And the French, I presume, are victorious?"

"Naturally. This was made by Frenchwomen. Countries make their tapestries as they make their history books. It is amazing how the right words—or pictures—can change defeat into victory."

"*I* was taught that the English were driven out of France and no attempt was ever made to deny this. My mother and I taught *our* pupils the same."

"You are a very wise teacher, Cousin."

I believed he was mocking me, but I was enjoying this. I so much liked to listen to his voice, to watch the emotions play across his face, the lift of those finely drawn brows, the quirk of the lips. I enjoyed showing him that, although he might command the rest of the household, he would not command me. I felt alive, as I rarely had before, and all the time I knew that I was being reckless and that, according to everything I had been taught, I should be making plans to get away.

"The governess would sit with the maidens in their chamber," he went on. "I could see *you* in the rôle. That golden hair falling loose, perhaps plaited, though, and one plait falling over your shoulder. You would look very severe when they made a bad stitch or talked too much and too frivolously, but you would have liked their gossip, which would be all about the misdeeds which took place in the castle . . . in high places, perhaps. You would reprimand them but you would be hoping they would go on, for you can be deceitful, Cousin, I believe."

"Why should you believe that?"

"Because I have discovered it. You are planning to go back, you say, when all the time you know you are going to stay. You look at me with disapproval, but I wonder how much you disapprove."

He had shaken me. Could it be true that I was deceiving myself? Since I had known him I seemed to have become unsure of everything and most of all myself. Every instinct was telling me that I would be wise to get away before I became more involved; and yet . . . Perhaps he was right. I *was* deceitful. I was telling myself I was planning to leave when I knew I wanted to stay.

I said sharply: "It is not for me to approve or disapprove."

"I have a notion that you enjoy my company. You sparkle, you bristle, you like to banter . . . in fact, I have the effect on you that you have on me, and that is something we should rejoice in . . . not fight against."

"Monsieur le Comte, you are quite wrong."

"And you are wrong to deny the truth and call me Monsieur le Comte when I have clearly commanded you to call me Charles."

"I did not think that was an order I must necessarily obey."

"All orders are for obeying."

"But I am not one of your squires. I can leave tomorrow. There is nothing to hold me here."

"There is your affection for my daughter. That girl is in a sad state. I did not like that fit of hysteria yesterday. It makes me very uneasy. *You* can calm my daughter. You can make her see reason. Soon she will have to marry. On that I am determined. I want you to stay with her . . . until she is safely married. If you will do that, then you could consider leaving us. During that time I will pay sums of money into an account so that you will have enough to start a school . . . perhaps in Paris, where you could teach English. I could send many people to you as Sir John did in England. It will not be long before this marriage takes place. Marguerite has proved that she is ready for marriage. I know you are a very reasonable young woman. This is not much to ask, is it?"

"I should have to see how everything worked out," I said cautiously. "I could make no promises."

"At least you will consider our poor Marguerite."

I replied that of course I would.

We passed through the old part of the *château* to that which was constructed three hundred years later. Here the elegance of the sixteenth and seventeenth centuries prevailed.

"This you will discover gradually as we live here," he said. "It is the ancient part I wanted to show you myself."

The tour was over. His mood seemed to have changed. He had become a little morose. I wondered why; and although I had enjoyed his company I was relieved to be alone that I might think over what had been said, for I was sure there had been frequent innuendoes behind our conversation.

2

Margot had suffered not only mental but physical strain after her ordeal. She was easily tired and still fretting for her baby. I had no doubt that she needed me. I was sorry for her because it was clear to me that she felt a little lost among her own family. With such parents it did not surprise me, and I was even more grateful for the love and wisdom of my own mother—a greater gift than that which had been bestowed on poor Margot for all her noble lineage and family wealth. As for Étienne and Léon, although they had been brought up in the household, they were scarcely like brothers.

Nou Nou understood Margot's state, for she was one of the few people who were in on the secret. She prescribed a stay in bed for a few days on a diet of her choosing which contained some of her potions and these seemed to make Margot sleep a good deal. I was sure this was necessary, as she seemed refreshed and in better spirits when she awakened from her rests.

This gave me time on my own and both Étienne and Léon seemed determined to be friendly. I took a ride with each of them and, when I looked back, what happened during these rides seemed significant.

On the afternoon of that day when the Comte had taken me round the old part of the castle, Étienne asked me if I would care to ride with him. He would like to show me the countryside, he said.

I had always enjoyed riding—even on poor little Jenny—and I had thought of Dower with longing since I had left her. So I accepted with alacrity. Moreover, I had my rather elegant riding habit which my mother had bought for me to impress Joel Derringham, so I was well equipped.

The only question was, which horse to ride, but Étienne assured me that there would be just the right mount for me in the castle stables.

He was right. There was a lovely strawberry roan.

"Not too frisky," said Étienne. "Oh, I know you are an excellent horsewoman, but just at first . . ."

"How you could have learned such a thing I've no idea,"
I replied. "In fact, I'm just a horsewoman . . . not a good
one."

"You are too modest, Cousin."

I noticed the word "cousin" and smiled inwardly. If I was
the Comte's cousin, Étienne would want me to be his. I was
beginning to understand Étienne.

His manners were impeccable. He helped me to mount and
complimented me on my outfit. "Most elegant," he called it.

"I thought so at home," I told him, "but I am not so sure
here. It's strange how clothes can change in different environ-
ments."

"You would look charming in any environment," said
Étienne gallantly.

The countryside was beautiful, for the leaves of the trees
were now being touched with autumn tints. We cantered and
galloped and I was glad of the practice I had had on Dower.
I was touched by Étienne's care for me, for I noticed how
watchful he was and if he thought I was out of my depth—
which he did once or twice—he would be beside me ready
to make sure that I was all right.

As we were returning to the *château*—I think we must
have been about two miles from it—we came to a house in a
hollow. It was charming, in gray stone over which several
kinds of creeper had spread itself. As the leaves were beginning to turn reddish brown, the effect was delightful.

A woman was standing at the gate as though watching for
someone. I was struck immediately by her rather flamboyant
beauty. She had thick red hair and green eyes; she was tall,
inclined to plumpness, and very elegant.

"I must present you to Madame LeGrand," said Étienne.

"She must be the *château*'s nearest neighbor."

"You are right. She is," replied Étienne.

Madame LeGrand had opened the gate. We dismounted,
Étienne holding my horse while I did so, then tethering both
horses to the post set there for that purpose.

"This is Mademoiselle Maddox," said Étienne.

Madame LeGrand came towards me. She wore a green
gown which became her well and matched her eyes. Beneath
the skirt was a hoop which accentuated the smallness of her
waist, and panniers of rich material draped over it to fall to
the ground disclosing, as it fell apart, a satin petticoat of a
slightly darker shade of green. Her hair was elaborately
dressed—high, according to the fashion prevalent in France
which had been set by the Queen who needed height on

account of her high forehead. The bodice of the green gown was cut low to disclose the whiteness of neck and the beginnings of a well-formed if ample bosom. She was a strikingly beautiful woman.

"I had heard that you were at the *château*, Mademoiselle," she told me, "and I was eager to meet you. I hope you will honor me by taking a glass of wine."

I said I should be delighted to do so.

"Come into the *salon*," she said.

We stepped into a cool hall in which had been arranged leaves of varying greens. Green was evidently her favorite color. It suited her. I saw how attractive were those green eyes with their thick black lashes, particularly in contrast with the burnished reddish hair.

The *salon* was small, but perhaps it seemed so because I had already become accustomed to the rooms at the *château*. Compared with those of the schoolhouse, it would be called big. The furniture was as elegant as that in the castle and there were beautiful rugs on the floor. The pale green of the drapes toned perfectly with that of the cushions. It was indeed a gracious room.

The wine was brought and she asked me how I was enjoying my stay at my cousin's *château*.

I hesitated. In spite of everything I could not think of myself as the Comte's cousin. I replied that I was finding everything very interesting.

"How strange that you should come across the Comte and Marguerite after all those years. You must have been aware of the relationship though. You must have known that you had these connections."

Both she and Étienne seemed to be watching me intently.

"No," I said. "It was a surprise."

"How interesting! And how *did* you come across each other?"

The Comte had said that when you were acting a part it was wise to keep as near the truth as possible. "It was when the Comte and his family were staying at the home of Sir John Derringham in England."

"So you were staying there too?"

"No. I lived there. My mother had a school."

"A school? How odd!"

"Mademoiselle Maddox is a highly educated young lady," said Étienne.

"It was not in the least odd," I retorted. "My mother became a widow and had to support herself and her daughter. As she was well equipped to teach, she did so."

"And the Comte discovered the school," prompted Étienne. "His daughter was a pupil there."

"Ah I see," said Madame LeGrand. "And then he discovered that you were related to him."

"Yes . . . it was like that."

"You must find it strange to come from a school . . . to this." She waved her hand to indicate the *château*.

"It was. I was very happy in the school. When my mother was alive we were content."

"I am sorry. That is sad. And then you came to France?"

"Marguerite needed a holiday. She was unwell. So I came with her."

"And the school?"

"It is finished."

"So you intend to stay here . . . indefinitely?"

It occurred to me that she was asking too many questions for politeness and I was being foolish in thinking I must answer them.

I said coolly: "Madame, I have made no definite plans so therefore I am unable to discuss them with you."

"Mademoiselle Maddox speaks French very well, does she not, Étienne?"

Étienne smiled at me. "I have rarely heard an English person speak so well."

"Only the faintest trace of accent."

"But that is charming," Étienne added.

Madame nodded and I thought it was time I started the questioning. "You have a delightful house here, Madame. Have you lived here long?"

"For some nineteen years."

"It must be the nearest house to the *château*."

"It is less than two miles away."

"And you must be happy to own such a delightful residence."

"I am happy to be here, but I don't own it. Like everything else on this estate it belongs to the Comte Fontaine Delibes. Mademoiselle, have you often visited France?"

"I had never been here before I arrived with Marguerite."

"How very interesting."

I changed the subject and we talked about the beauties of the countryside, the similarities and the differences when compared with that of England; and the conversation stayed in more conventional channels.

After a while we rose to go and she took my hands in hers and expressed the wish that I should find time to call on her again.

"Étienne frequently calls, I'm glad to say. You must bring Mademoiselle again, Étienne, or if you come alone, Mademoiselle, I shall be delighted."

I thanked her for her hospitality while Étienne untethered our horses.

As we mounted and rode away I said: "What a beautiful woman."

"I think so too," he answered. "Perhaps I am prejudiced."

I looked at him in astonishment. He smiled and, keeping his eyes on my face as though intent on my reaction, he added: "Did you realize that she is my mother?"

I felt shaken, thinking immediately of her relationship with the Comte. I wondered whether they had deliberately kept her identity from me so that Étienne might surprise me thus.

I was thankful that I could remain calm, remembering my mother's remarks that an English lady never showed her feelings, particularly in times of stress. Was this stress? It was certainly startling.

I said: "You must be very proud to have such a beautiful mother."

"Yes," he said, "I am."

Was she still his mistress? I wondered. She lived in a house close to the *château* . . . his house. Did he visit her there? Did she come to the *château*?

It was no affair of mine, I told myself grimly.

It was on the following day that I took my ride with Léon. I found him easier to talk to than Étienne. He was more relaxed, more natural. He saw no reason to hide the fact that he was the son of peasants and I liked him for it.

If he lacked Étienne's dark good looks, he had been more lavishly endowed with charm. Those dark blue eyes were arresting in his brown face. His dark crinkly hair, worn short, fitted his head caplike. His clothes were well cut but serviceable and they completely lacked the dash and elegance of Étienne's.

He rode his horse well, as though he and the animal were one. I was on the strawberry roan, which I had ridden on the previous day. I felt a little easier with her, and I was sure she did with me.

Léon was gayer by nature than Étienne—more light-hearted, I fancied, but, like Étienne, he complimented me on my riding habit and we talked about horses for a while. I told him about Dower and how I regretted leaving her behind and how before I had acquired her I trundled round on Jenny.

I found myself telling him about my mother and it was a relief to be able to talk of her easily and with the certainty that he would understand, though why I should have thought so after so short an acquaintance, I was not sure. It was simply that his naturalness appealed to me. He was frank and open and I could be the same.

"What would your mother think if she knew you were here?" he asked.

I hesitated. That she would heartily disapprove of the Comte I was well aware. But she would have enjoyed seeing me treated as a guest in the castle.

I replied: "I think she would agree that I was wise to leave the school when I did . . . before I was in real difficulty with it."

"And I suppose she would think it was *comme il faut* to stay with your cousins?"

"I think Marguerite was glad to have me with her," I said evasively.

He smiled wryly. "And the Comte is equally glad. He makes that clear."

"He is merely being a kind host."

After our previous frankness, the reference to what must be a secret made a momentary barrier between us.

Then he said: "I hear you visited Gabrielle LeGrand yesterday."

"Oh yes."

"She is a very great friend of the Comte, as you no doubt gathered."

"I learned she is Étienne's mother."

"Yes. She and the Comte have been friends for years."

"I understand," I said.

I remembered the words I had heard him exchange with Étienne and I believed he was warning me. They did not believe in the cousinship—and I was not surprised. I could see that Léon had worked out that the Comte had met me in England, had liked me, had plans for me, and had brought me to France in order that he might carry them out. He must have a poor opinion of me. But how could I tell him that I had come solely because Marguerite needed me.

"I suppose," he said conversationally, "that life in England is very different from what it is here."

"Naturally . . . and yet perhaps fundamentally the same."

"Your Sir John Derringham, would he have his mistress living nearby quite blatantly? And what would his wife say?"

I was startled but tried not to show it. "No. That would not be acceptable. Sir John, in any case, would never behave in such a way."

"It is commonplace enough here. Some of our kings have set the example."

"We have had kings who behaved similarly. Charles II for one."

"He had a French mother."

"You seem determined to prove your countrymen light in their morals."

"I think we have different standards."

"What you are thinking of exists in England, most certainly, but it is less openly done. Whether there is a virtue in secrecy I am not sure. But I believe it makes life easier for the people concerned."

"Some of them."

"The wife in such cases. It can't be very pleasant to have a husband's infidelities flaunted in one's face. On the other hand, for the husband and his mistress to meet openly saves *them* a great deal of subterfuge."

"I see you are a realist, Mademoiselle, and much too honest and charming ever to be embroiled in these sordid matters."

Oh yes, it was clearly a warning. I might have been offended, but there was real concern in his eyes and I could not help but be drawn to him.

"You may be sure that I never would be," I said firmly.

He looked very pleased and, reading his thoughts, I realized that he believed the Comte had discovered his cousin—or if the relationship had been invented it had been without my knowledge—had invited her here with his daughter as her companion and that she, having been brought up in a prim English community, had no idea of his intentions.

He was wrong on every point, but I liked him for his concern and assessment.

He seemed to cast aside his anxieties on my account and prepare to enjoy our ride. He began by talking about himself with a frankness I found delightful.

It was a strange fate when everything depended on one incident—like the Comte's killing of his twin brother. "Just think," he said, "but for that my life would have been completely different. Poor little Jean-Pierre. I often wonder if he looks down on me and says: 'There! You owe it all to me.' "

"It was a terrible thing, and yet, as you say, it brought good to you."

"When I go to my old home, I know how good—not only for me but for them all. I am able to help them, you see. The Comte knows of this and is pleased. There is also an allowance for them from him. They have the best house in the village and several acres. They can make a living and are envied by their neighbors. I have heard many of them say that God smiled on them that day when Jean-Pierre was run over."

I shivered slightly.

"Realism, Mademoiselle. It is the strongest characteristic of the French. Had Jean-Pierre not run into the road at that precise moment and under the Comte's horses, he would have lived wretchedly with his family, who would have been in a similar plight. You understand their conclusions."

"I think of your mother. What are her feelings?"

"With a mother it is different. She takes flowers every week to his grave and she grows evergreen bushes there to tell everyone that his memory remains green in her heart."

"But at least she rejoices when she sees you."

"Yes, but it reminds her of my twin brother, of course. People are talking of it now as much as they did when it happened. They blame the Comte more and forget what he has done for our family. It is the rising wave of anger against the aristocracy. Anything that can be brought against them is brought."

"I have been aware of that since I came to France, and I heard of it even before."

"Yes, there are changes coming. I hear of what is brewing when I visit my family. They can be more frank with me than with any who were not of them, as it were. It is a growing tide of resentment. Sometimes there is little reason in it—but God knows at others there is. There are so many injustices in the country. The people are dissatisfied with their rulers. Sometimes I wonder how long it can last. Now it is not safe to travel alone through the villages unless one is dressed as a peasant. Never in my lifetime have I known that before."

"What will be the end of it?"

"Ah, my dear Mademoiselle, for that we must wait and see."

As we were nearing the *château* we heard the sound of horses' hoofs and a man came riding towards us. He was tall, rather soberly dressed, and wore no wig over his plentiful reddish hair.

"It's Lucien Dubois," cried Léon. "Lucien, my dear fellow, it is good to see you."

The man pulled up and took off his hat when he saw me. Léon introduced me. Mademoiselle Maddox, a cousin of the Comte's now visiting the castle.

Lucien Dubois said he was enchanted to meet me and asked if I was staying long.

"So much depends on circumstances," I told him.

"Mademoiselle is English but she speaks our language like a native," said Léon.

"Not quite, I'm afraid," I replied.

"But most excellently," said Monsieur Dubois.

"You will be going to your sister," said Léon. "I hope you are going to stay for a while."

"Like Mademoiselle, I will say that so much depends on the circumstances."

"You have already met Madame LeGrand," said Léon to me. "Monsieur Dubois is her brother."

I thought there was a resemblance—the flamboyant good looks, the distinctive coloring, although the man's eyes were not as green as his sister's—but perhaps he had not the art of accentuating their color.

I wondered what he thought of his sister's relationship with the Comte. Perhaps as a Frenchman he accepted it. I thought cynically that the Comte's nobility probably made the situation tolerable. To be a King's mistress was an honorable position; to be a poor man's, a shameful one. I would not accept the distinction, and if it was due to my immaturity and lack of realism, I was glad of them.

"Well, we shall be seeing you before long, I don't doubt," said Léon.

"If I am not honored with an invitation to the castle, you must come to my sister's house," said Monsieur Dubois. Then, bowing to us, he rode on.

"There you see a man who is disgruntled with life," Léon told me.

"Why?"

"Because he thinks it has not dealt him what he deserves. The plaint of many, you may say. All the failures of the world blame fate."

"The fault is not in our stars, but in ourselves, as our national poet put it."

"There are a lot of them about, Mademoiselle. Envy is the most common emotion in the world. It's the basic ingredient of every deadly sin. Poor Lucien! He has a grievance. I think he has never forgiven the family of Fontaine Delibes."

"What did they do to him?"

"It is not what they did to him but what was done to his father. Jean-Christophe Dubois was incarcerated in the Bastille and died there."

"For what reason?"

"Because the Comte—the present one's father—wanted Jean-Christophe's wife—that was the mother of Lucien and Gabrielle. She was a beautiful woman. Gabrielle has inherited her looks. There is such a thing called a *lettre de cachet*. This could be acquired by influential people and through it they could have their enemies imprisoned. The victims would never know the reason for their detention. The *lettre* was enough to put them there. It is an iniquitous practice. The very words *lettre de cachet* can strike terror into the heart of any man. There is no redress against it. Of course, the Comtes Fontaine Delibes had always had a foot in Court circles and those of the Parlement. Their influence and their power was—and is—great. The present Comte's father wanted this woman, her husband objected and was preparing to take her away. Then one night a messenger arrived at his home. He carried a *lettre de cachet*. Jean-Christophe was never seen again."

"How cruel!"

"The times are cruel. It is for that reason that the people are determined to change them."

"Then it is time they did."

"It takes more than a few weeks to set right the errors of centuries. Jean-Christophe had a son and daughter. The Comte died three years after he had taken Jean-Christophe's wife and there was a new Comte, Charles-Auguste, the present one. Gabrielle was a young widow of eighteen years. She came to plead for her father. Charles-Auguste was struck by her beauty and elegance. He was very young then and impressionable. It was too late. Jean-Christophe died in prison before his release could be brought about. However, Charles-Auguste had fallen in love with Gabrielle and a year after their meeting Étienne was born."

"I am amazed by the drama which seemed to surround the castle."

"Where the Comtes Fontaine Delibes are, there will always be drama."

"Gabrielle at least forgave the injury done to her father."

"Yes, but I fancy it may be different with Lucien. I often think he harbors resentment."

As we rode on to the *château* I could not stop thinking of the poor man who had been ruthlessly condemned to spend the last years of his life in a prison because another wished him out of the way, and it seemed to me that intrigue and drama which would previously have been beyond my conception was building up around me.

Margot called me to her room. She looked radiant and I marveled at the manner in which she could change from depression to excitement.

On her bed were several rolls of material. "Come and look at these, Minelle," she cried.

I examined them. There was a velvet roll of the fashionable puce color and gold lace and another in a beautiful shade of blue with silver lace.

"You are going to have some fine dresses," I commented.

"I am going to have one. The other will be for you. I chose the blue for you and the silver goes with it perfectly. There is going to be a ball and my father's instructions are that I look my best."

I fingered the blue velvet and said: "I cannot accept such a gift."

"Don't be silly, Minelle. How can you go to the ball in what you have brought with you?"

"I obviously can't. But there is an alternative. I shall stay away."

Margot stamped her foot impatiently. "You will not be allowed to. You are to go. It is for this reason that you are to have the dress."

"I did not know when I accepted this post that I was to be a . . . bogus cousin. I came as companion to you."

Margot burst out laughing. "You must be the first person in any post who has complained of being treated too well. Of course you must go to the ball. I need a chaperone, don't I?"

"You talk foolishly. How could you need a chaperone at a ball which your parents will be giving."

"One parent. I don't suppose Mama will be present. She will, as Papa says, have the vapors ready for such an occasion."

"That is not a kind remark, Margot."

"Oh, stop being the prim old schoolmistress. You're not that any more." She picked up the puce-colored velvet and, draping it round her, paraded in front of the mirror. "Is it not magnificent? What a color! It's just right for me. Don't you agree, Minelle? And are you not pleased to see me happier?"

"I am amazed that you can change so quickly."

"I haven't really changed. I still mourn in my heart for Charlot. There is a sadness down here." She pointed to her breast. "But I can't be sad all the time, and loving a ball and a new gown does not make me love my baby any less."

She threw her arms about me and for a few moments we clung together. I think in that moment, for all my air of worldliness, I was as bewildered as she was.

"I don't think I can accept the gown, Margot," I said at length.

"Why not? It's wages, surely."

"I have my wages. This is different."

"Papa will be furious and he has been so good-tempered lately. He personally told me I must choose for us both and then he went on to suggest the colors, which is typical of him. I am sure he would be most displeased if I had 'chosen' anything but what he suggested."

"I think it would be quite wrong for me to accept this."

"Annette, our dressmaker, is coming this afternoon to start work."

I decided that I must see the Comte and also prepare myself to leave. I had discovered too much about him and his way of life to feel happy in his household. I could not throw off the upbringing of a lifetime in a few short months. Moreover, I was sure that my mother's principles of life had more to recommend them than those which I had discovered prevailed at the *château*.

I learned that at this hour the Comte was generally in the library where he did not like to be disturbed. But I decided to brave his displeasure, for if he were displeased with me it would be easier to arrange my departure.

But he seemed far from displeased to see me. He rose immediately and, taking both my hands, drew me into the room. He held out a chair for me. I sat and he sat also but not before bringing his chair closer to mine.

"To what," he said, "do I owe this pleasure?"

"I think it is time there was an understanding," I began, but although I had felt bold and determined before I entered the room my self-possession was fast waning.

"There is nothing I should welcome more. I am sure that one as perceptive as you must be aware of my feelings towards you."

"Before you say any more, let me tell you that I cannot accept a ball dress from you."

"Why not?"

"Because I do not consider it . . ."

"Right and proper!" He raised his eyebrows and I saw the mocking light in his eyes. "You must explain to me. I am most ignorant on these matters. Tell me what it is right to accept and what not right."

"I accept my salary because I earn it as a companion to your daughter, for which post I was engaged."

"Oh, but you became a cousin . . . a connection of the family. Surely one member of the family can give another a gift . . . and how much better to give something which is needed rather than some useless bauble."

"Please, when we are alone let us drop this farce."

"Yes, let us. The truth is that I am falling in love with you. You know it. So why pretend otherwise."

I rose to my feet. He was beside me, his arms about me.

"Please let me go," I said firmly.

"First tell me that you can love me also."

"I do not find this amusing."

"Oddly enough, although my emotions are so deeply stirred, I do. You both amuse and enchant me. I think that is why I am so excited by you. You are different from anyone I have ever known."

"Will you grant me one thing?"

"It shall be my pleasure to give you all you ask."

"Then will you please return to your seat and let me tell you of *my* feelings."

"Your request is naturally granted."

He sat down and I did the same. I felt I must, for my legs were trembling and I was fearful that he might notice how alarmed I was. I clasped my hands firmly and said: "I am not of your circle, Monsieur le Comte."

"Charles," he reproved.

"I cannot call you naturally by your Christian name. You are the Comte to me and always will be. I have been brought up to accept a different code of behavior, a different set of morals. My outlook is quite opposed to yours. You would find me excessively boring, I am sure."

"It delights me that we can never agree on anything. That is just an added charm."

"You are suggesting that I become your mistress. I know that you have had many and that to you this is a natural way of life. Can you understand that it is something I could never accept, and for that reason I have decided to return to England. I had thought I would wait until Margot was settled, but I see now that that is impossible. What you have implied has made it so. I wish to make preparations to leave immediately."

"I am afraid I cannot agree to that. You have been engaged to look after my daughter and I expect you to honor your bond."

"Bond! What bond?"

"What is it? A gentleman's agreement? Only this time it is between two of the opposing sexes. You could not leave Marguerite now!"

"She would understand."

"Would she? You saw that display the other night. But why are we talking of her? Let us talk of ourselves. You would overcome your prejudices. I would show you how. You should have an establishment of your own . . . anything you wished for should be yours."

"Do you think you could tempt me with establishments?"

"Not with establishments, perhaps."

I lowered my eyes before his bold and passionate gaze. I was afraid of him—or perhaps more truthfully of myself.

"Tell me one thing," he said. "If I were in a position to offer you marriage, and did, would you accept?"

I hesitated just too long. Then I said: "Monsieur, I do not know you well enough . . ."

"And what you have heard, I'll warrant, has not always been to my advantage."

"I do not presume to judge."

"Which is exactly what you are doing."

"No, I am trying to say that our lives are far apart. I should go back."

"To what?"

"Does that matter?"

"It is going to matter a great deal to you. What will you do, tell me that. Will you go back to your schoolhouse? With Master Joel likely to come home at any time. Not likely."

"I have a little money . . ."

"Not enough, my brave darling. I see I have been too rash.

I have spoken too soon. You came and caught me off my guard. God knows, I have curbed myself long enough. What do you think I am made of, ice maiden? You were meant for me. I knew it from the moment you came into my bedchamber and when I saw the rose color creep up from your neck to your forehead. I like to embarrass you, for then I put you at a disadvantage. I like to quarrel with you. I like our battles of words. There should be a rich climax to our quarrels. I often think of that. Since I have known you, I have no fancy for anyone else."

"I hope that has not inconvenienced your mistresses."

"A little, as you can imagine," he said with a smile.

"Then it is time I went and equilibrium was restored."

He burst into laughter. "Dearest Minelle, I often think what a fool young Joel was. He could have offered you marriage. Would to God I could. If I could take your hand now and say, 'Be my wife,' I should be the happiest man in France."

"Meanwhile, you congratulate yourself on your inability to do so and save yourself from an act of such folly."

"You and I together . . . what joy we'd have. I know it. I know women . . ."

"You do not have to assure me of that."

"I sense those hidden depths. Oh Minelle, my love, we would have sons, you and I. You are made to bear sons. Come down from that pedestal and be happy. Let us take the next best thing."

"I cannot remain to listen to more of this. I find it offensive. Your invalid wife is under this very roof."

"Much she cares. All she wants is to lie on her bed and complain of her countless ailments to her doting nurse who encourages her."

"I see you are of a very sympathetic nature!"

"Minelle . . ."

I went to the door and he did not attempt to stop me. I was half-glad, half-sorry. I was terrified that he would take me firmly into his arms, for when he did I could not but be aware of that potent attractiveness, and could almost imagine myself casting away the teachings of a lifetime. It was alarming. It was the real reason why I knew I must get away.

I ran to my room, shut the door, and sat down at the mirror. I hardly recognized myself. My cheeks were flaming red and my hair disheveled. I could almost see my mother's disapproving look and hear her admonition: "I should start packing right away. You are in acute danger. You cannot leave this house too soon."

She was right, of course. By her standards I had been insulted. The Comte Fontaine Delibes was suggesting that I become his mistress. I would never have believed such a thing possible. Nor could I have believed I should feel this wild temptation. It was that which told me I must get away.

I started to take out my clothes and fold them.

"Where will you go?" asked my practical self.

"I don't know. I'll get a home somewhere. I'll take a post. I have a little money. Perhaps I could go back to Derringham and try to open a school, and start again. I am more experienced of life now. I might make a success of it."

Then I sat down and covered my face with my hands. It was as though desolation was closing in around me.

There was a tap on my door. Before I could answer, Margot burst in, her face distorted in horror as she flung herself at me.

"Minelle, we've got to run away. I won't stay here. I can't do it. I won't."

"What do you mean? What has happened?"

"My father has just told me."

I looked at her in amazement. He must have sent for her as soon as I had left him.

"The Vicomte de Grasseville has asked for my hand. He is a family equal to our own, and Papa has accepted him for me. At this ball we shall be affianced and married within a month. I won't have it. I am so miserable, Minelle. The only thing that consoles me is that you are here."

"I shall not be staying here long."

"No. You will come with me. You will, won't you? It's the only way I would consider it."

"Margot, I have to tell you. I am planning to leave."

"What, leave here! Why?"

"Because I feel I must get back."

"You mean you would leave *me!*"

"It's better for me to go, Margot."

"Oh!" She let out a long wail and started to weep. Her sobs shook her and she made no effort to restrain them. "I'm so unhappy, Minelle. If you're here I can bear it. We can laugh together. You can't go. I won't let you." She looked at me apppealingly. "We're going to get Charlot back together. We're going to think of a plan. You promised . . . you *promised.* *Everything* can't go wrong. If I've got to marry this Grasseville, then you'll be with me." She started to laugh and that always frightened me; the mingling of tears and laughter could be terrifying.

"Stop it, Margot," I cried. "Stop it."

"I can't help it. It's funny . . . funny . . ."

I took her by the shoulders and shook her.

"Tragically funny," she said, but she was quieter. She leaned against me and went on: "You won't go yet, Minelle. Promise me, oh promise me . . . not yet."

To soothe her I said not yet. Then I was committed to stay for a little while.

I wondered then whether he had broken the news to her because he knew what her reception of it would be. He was diabolically clever, I knew, and adept at getting his own way. That was what frightened me, and yet in an odd way—in which neither I nor my mother could approve—it exhilarated me.

The dressmaker came, but I refused to accept the blue material and said that I would not have it made up. Margot was frantic. "You *must* come to the ball," she cried. "How can you fail me. I shall be forced to accept this Robert de Grasseville and I know I shall hate him. What shall I do? I can only bear it if you come."

"I have not a suitable gown," I said firmly, "and I am determined not to accept such a gift from your father."

She paced up and down, talking of her yearning for Charlot, telling me that life was cruel. *I* was cruel. I knew how wretched she was and I wouldn't help her.

I assured her that I would do anything to help her.

"Anything?" she demanded dramatically.

"Anything that is honorably possible."

She had an idea. As I was so proud she would sell me one of her old gowns. We could have it changed and add to it. I could buy some ribbons and laces and make a new gown of it and have the satisfaction of paying for it.

She was immediately gay contemplating it. "Imagine Papa's face when he sees you. Oh Minelle, we'll do it. It'll be such fun!"

I gave way to please her. No, that's not true. To please myself. I too should like to see his face. He thought he had won a temporary victory, but I should show him that he had not. I would take nothing from him; I was determined to show him that his suggestion was repulsive to me and that I deeply resented it. He must know that I was only staying on Margot's account. As soon as she was married to her Vicomte I should go.

I did want to attend the ball, though. I knew that it would be more grand than anything I had ever conceived. I wanted to see the Comte among his guests. He would probably not deign to notice me in spite of his protestations. I wondered whether Gabrielle LeGrand would be present.

I entered into the conspiracy of the dress, I must admit, with enthusiasm. At least it kept Margot happy. While she was laughing over the matter and going through her wardrobe, making me try on this and that and laughing at the effect of some, she was not thinking of her future.

We found a simple blue silk. "Just your color," she said. The under gown was of gauze dotted with gold and silver knots which gave it a starry look. It was low-cut and diaphanous.

"It never suited me," declared Margot. "I fancy that with a little refurbishing it could just get by. It'll be a little simple for a ball dress. Let's call in Annette and see what she can do."

Annette came in, studied me in the dress and knelt on the floor, her mouth full of pins. She shook her head. "Too large in the waist, too short in the length . . ." was her verdict.

"You can do it, Annette. You can do it," cried Margot, clasping her hands together.

Annette shook her head. "I do not think it is possible."

"Annette-Pas-Possible!" shouted Margot. "That's what we always called her. She always says it's not possible and goes on to make it gloriously possible."

"But this, Mademoiselle . . ." Annette's face was full of woe.

"Take it off the shoulders, Annette," commanded Margot. "Mademoiselle Maddox has good shoulders . . . they slope nicely. So feminine. We must show them. And can you get some more of this starry stuff? We could do with yards and yards more of that."

"I do not think that would be possible," said Annette.

"Nonsense. I'll swear you have some of the very stuff tucked away somewhere. You know you always keep the remnants."

And so it went on, with Annette growing more and more lugubrious and Margot more certain that the dress would be a success.

And it was. I was amazed when it was ready—a froth of gauze and blue silk, expertly pressed and adorned with delicate lace. I had a ball dress, and if it was proved—which I knew it would be—very simple in comparison with others, at least it was adequate and would enable me to go to the ball at very little cost to my purse and none to my pride.

The ball was to be held in the ancient hall and the Comte would receive his guests at the top of the great marble staircase. It would be grand even by castle standards, as it was to announce and celebrate the betrothal of his daughter.

I was sorry for Margot. The idea of being presented with a man for the first time and told: 'This is your future husband!' If this was the way of aristocrats, I was glad I was not one of them.

The day before the ball there was a disturbance in the night. It must have been early morning when I heard voices on the stairs. I opened my door and looked out.

The noise was coming from the Comtesse's apartments. I heard the Comte's voice, rather weary, I thought: "My dear Nou Nou, we have had this before. You know it is only her nerves."

"Not so, Monsieur le Comte. Not so. She has been in pain. I soothed her with a draught, but it cannot last. This is real pain and I want the doctors to see her."

"You know you have only to send for them."

"Then I shall do so without delay."

"Nou Nou, you upset yourself unnecessarily. You know you do. And to awaken me at this hour . . ."

"I know my girl. If others upset themselves a little more now and then it might be better."

"There is no reason why the entire household should share in this *crise de nerfs*."

"It is more than that."

"Now, Nou Nou. You know that my daughter's ball takes place the day after tomorrow. So does her mother. She wants to call attention to herself."

"You are a hard man, Monsieur le Comte."

"In the circumstances I have to be. If you showed a little more firmness on these occasions perhaps there would not be the need for them."

"I shall send for the doctors then."

"Do so by all means."

I realized that I was eavesdropping and went back into my room somewhat ashamed.

Poor Comtesse! She was neglected and sad and perhaps sought to call attention to herself through her delicate constitution. She was using the wrong tactics if she hoped to attract her husband. She should show some spirit . . . as I had done . . .

I pulled myself up sharply. What was I thinking? I was being drawn more and more into the affairs of this household. With a man such as the Comte who had married a woman such as the Comtesse that could be an alarming involvement. I knew this and yet I was allowing myself to be more and more caught up in their lives.

I saw the doctors arrive that day. Nou Nou was waiting for them and took them immediately to her mistress. The Comte was not in the castle but they waited to see him.

Margot and I spent the evening together. She was less exuberant now that the excitement of the dress was over.

"I wonder what Robert will be like," she kept saying.

"It seems strange that you have never seen him."

"I think I may have done when we were children. His family's estates are north of Paris. I believe he visited us when we were in Paris once. He was a horrible boy who ate all the *gâteau* and then took the piece of cream I was saving until the last."

"Not a very auspicious beginning to a lifetime's union," I said, but added: "People change as they grow up. The most awful children become the most charming."

"He'll be fat with spots, I know."

"It's not a bad idea to build up an unpleasant picture. Then you'll be agreeably surprised."

She was laughing again. "You are good for me. You are . . . what is it . . . astringent? That is what Papa likes in you. He does like you a great deal, you know."

"As I shall be leaving here when you marry, it doesn't matter very much what he thinks of me, does it?"

"You will come with me, won't you?"

"Until I have made my plans. But I can't spend all my life in this sort of situation. You must realize that."

"I have plans. When I'm married I'm going to get Charlot with me."

"How?"

"That's for you to work out."

"I should have no idea how to begin."

"Now you sound like Annette-Pas-Possible. *Everything* is possible . . . if you set about it in the right way. And one thing I'm going to do is have Charlot with me. I think of him all the time . . . well, almost all the time. How do I know what sort of people have him? Think of it . . . he will be growing up . . . talking . . ."

"Hardly yet."

"He will be calling someone else Maman."

I could see she was working herself up into another fit of hysteria and this was exactly what I wanted to avoid. So I soothed her by making ridiculous plans as to how we should find Charlot. We would go to the inn where he had been taken from us; we would question people and find the trail which led to him.

This was the sort of game she so much enjoyed and we played it for a long time and went into such detail that she really thought it was possible and derived a great deal of comfort from our planning.

Yes, I could see that she needed me.

3

He looked magnificent standing there at the top of the staircase receiving his guests. Margot was beside him—flushed and very attractive in her puce velvet. When he saw me his eyes kindled. His glance took in my gown. I had been right in thinking it would be very simple in comparison with others. What I had failed to realize was that its very simplicity made it conspicuous.

In my bedroom, I had looked, as I thought, quite beautiful. I had brushed my hair until it shone, and it certainly was, as my mother would have said, my crowning glory. It made a frame about my face and I had dressed it high, padding it a little to make it stand up in accordance with the fashion, with one curl coming forward to hang over my shoulder. I knew I looked my best and Margot had insisted that I wear a tiny black patch—which she provided—at the side of my temple. "It makes your eyes look bigger and bluer," she said. "Besides, it's the fashion."

I could scarcely recognize my reflection as myself.

What a grand assembly it was! The great hall must have seen many such, but I believed it could never have seen a grander one. Flowers had been brought in from the castle hothouses. There were great pots of them on the high table and urns stood on pedestals, fragrant and colorful. I felt a little bewildered by so much elegance. Never had I seen such magnificent apparel as that worn by the women and men. There must have been a fortune in jewels in the castle that night. Musicians were grouped round the high table and the dancing was most elegant and slightly different from that which we did at home.

In my altered gown, adorned only by the cameo brooch which my mother had treasured and worn about twice in her lifetime, I must have looked like a little moth who had somehow become trapped among gorgeous dragonflies.

If you had accepted the Comte's gift you could have competed with them, I admonished myself. But of course that would have been out of the question. If I did look like a drab little moth, at least I was a proud one.

Léon discovered me and asked what I thought of the ball.

"I think that I should never have come. I don't fit in."

"Why not?"

I looked down at my dress. "It's charming," he assured me. "So many of the people look alike. Blindly they follow the fashion. You can scarcely tell one from the other. You are different. You have a style of your own. I find that pleasant."

"You are determined to be kind to me."

"Why should I be otherwise? Shall we join the dancers?"

"I taught dancing at school and my mother taught me. But this is somewhat different."

"Then we'll go in and dance our own dance, shall we?"

We did and he fitted his steps to mine. I had always enjoyed dancing and I began to forget the inadequacy of my costume.

"Have you met the prospective bridegroom?" I asked.

"Robert de Grasseville. Yes. He is a pleasant boy."

"Is he very young?"

"Eighteen or so."

"I do hope Margot will like him."

"It's a good marriage from both families' point of view. What I mean is she'll take a good dowry and he'll give her a good settlement. It's supposed to be very desirable when these rich families unite. It makes them bigger and stronger than ever. It will be the marriage of the year. Marguerite is of course the important member of the family. We're waiting now to see who will be produced for Étienne."

"He'll get a grand marriage too, I suppose."

"Quite grand . . . but perhaps there'll be reservations. There is the bar sinister, remember. I think his marriage is a cause of some contention between his mother and the Comte. It may be that her brother Lucien is here now to discuss just that. What they're after is to get him legitimized, which the Comte would certainly arrange if he thought he was not going to get a legitimate son."

"Well, how can he?"

"He's waiting for the Comtesse to die."

I shivered.

"Yes," he went on, "it does sound callous, but as I have mentioned to you before we're realists. We face the facts . . . and you can be sure the Comte does. What he would like is to be rid of the Comtesse and marry a healthy young girl and get sons."

"It's distasteful to talk like that of the Comtesse while she lies here in the castle."

"Creaking doors go on creaking for a long time. The very fact that they creak means that they get the best attention and so they go on longer than the strong, who aren't so well looked after."

I could not bear to talk of the Comtesse, so I changed the subject and said: "So soon there will be a bride for Étienne."

"Oh yes . . . but no de Grassevilles for him. Unless he is legitimized, of course. If he were acknowledged as the Comte's heir it would be a very different matter. You see why his marriage hangs fire. We used to think that the Comte would have married Gabrielle if he had been free and that would have made things a lot easier. So meanwhile Étienne waits. He would not want a bride with no great prospects and after the marriage find himself heir to a great name and all that goes with it and realize that he had married beneath him."

"You are cynical. What of yourself?"

"I, Mademoiselle, am a free man. I could choose whom I wished—providing she would have me—and none would care very much . . . unless I chose a lady of a great house and she accepted me. Then there would be trouble from her family. I am sure the Comte would be highly amused. But everyone knows my origins. The lucky peasant. No one will want to marry me but for love."

I laughed. "The same would apply to me. Do you know, I think we are indeed the lucky ones."

There was a touch on my shoulder. I looked around. The Comte was standing beside us.

"Thank you for looking after my cousin, Léon," he said. "I will take a turn with her myself now."

It was dismissal. Léon bowed and left me.

The Comte took my hand, surveying my dress while a smile touched his lips.

"I see you, dearest Cousin, attired in your pride," he said.

"I am sorry if you do not like my dress," I replied, "and if you consider my presence here unsuitable and therefore unwelcome . . ."

"It is not like you to ask for compliments. You know there is not a guest more suitable in my eyes or more welcome. The only thing that disappoints me is that we must waste time when there is so little left to us."

"You speak in enigmas."

"Which you interpret correctly, and with the utmost ease. Think. We might be together and yet we must indulge in this . . . courtship, would you call it?"

"I certainly would not."

"What then?"

"Pointless pursuit of which I have no doubt you will soon tire."

"I assure you I am the tireless hunter. I never give up until I have my prey."

"There must come a time in the life of every hunter when he suffers his first defeat. This is that occasion for you."

"Shall we wager on it?"

"I never wager."

"I should love to see you in a glittering gown which I shall have made for you. That is one of Marguerite's. I recognize it. So you can take from her what you cannot take from me?"

"I bought the dress from her."

He laughed aloud and I was aware that several people were watching us. I could imagine the comments. "Cousin? Who is this cousin?" They would speculate about me in the way I had heard Léon and Étienne doing.

"It was good of you to come to the ball," he said. "I'll warrant Marguerite persuaded you."

"I told her I should shortly be leaving."

"And she made you change your mind. Good girl."

"I shall choose the first opportunity to go."

"I believe you plan to go with her when she marries."

"She has asked me to, but I think I should return to England."

"Is that gracious after the way we have done everything to try to make you like us?"

"It is you who have made it impossible for me to stay here."

"Oh cruel Cousin!" he murmured. Then he said: "You must meet Robert. Come."

I was eager to do so and when I was presented to a fresh-faced young man with a pleasant smile I was agreeably surprised. Marguerite's description of the greedy little boy had led me to expect a plump self-indulgent young man. Nothing of the sort. Robert de Grasseville was tall and elegant and what pleased me most was the kindly expression on his youthful face.

It occurred to me that he was as apprehensive as Margot and I warmed to him. He talked to me for a while about horses mainly and the countryside; and Margot was brought to us by her partner in the dance.

She said: "So you have met our cousin, Monsieur de Grasseville?"

It seemed a formal mode of address when they were to be married shortly, but it appeared to be correct. He replied that meeting me had been a great pleasure.

The Comte whispered: "I regret I must leave you now. I shall see you later."

"Let us go in to supper," suggested Margot. She turned to me. "The announcement will be made during it. Minelle, you must come with us. You and Robert *must* be friends."

I was relieved because I could see that she was accepting Robert and prepared to get to know him. I could not, of course, say that they had fallen in love with each other at first sight—that would have been too much to expect—but at least they had not made up their minds to dislike each other.

People were moving towards the new hall, where the buffet was laid out, and the elegance of the display again surprised me. I had never seen food so artistically arranged. There was an abundance of everything and the butlers and footmen in the colored livery of the Fontaine Delibes household looked as if they were part of the scene.

There was wine, which I knew came from the Comte's own vineyards; and I remembered the hungry peasants who were not far away and was relieved that they could not see that table. I looked round for Léon for I wondered whether the same thought had occurred to him, but I could not see him. I did see Gabrielle, though, with her brother. She looked very handsome in a sparkling gown, too flamboyant for my liking, but becoming to her bold good looks. I think Étienne, who was with her, was proud of her.

We sat down at one of the tables near a window. There

was Robert, Margot, and another young man, a friend of Robert's.

Conversation was light and easy and I noticed with another rush of relief that Marguerite was not unhappy. Once she had grown accustomed to the idea that a husband would be chosen for her—which she had been brought up to know she must accept—she could not have envisaged a young man more charming than Robert de Grasseville.

During supper the Comte made the announcement. It was received with applause and Margot and Robert went to stand beside him and receive congratulations. I remained at the table talking to my companion, and it was only a few minutes later that a noise behind me made me turn. I was very close to the window and I saw a face there . . . looking in.

I thought it was Léon's.

The face disappeared and I was still looking out of the window when a heavy stone struck the glass, shattering it, and came hurtling into the room.

There was a brief silence, then cries of dismay and the sound of breaking glass and crockery.

I stood back horrified. The Comte had rushed to the window and was looking out. Then he shouted to the footmen: "Have the grounds searched. Get out the dogs."

There was a babel of talk for a few seconds. Then the Comte spoke again: "It's apparently nothing much. Some mischievous person at his tricks. Let us carry on as though this tiresome incident has not occurred."

It was like a command and I was amazed at the manner in which people such as these seemed to obey him without question.

I sat back in my chair. It was the recurring theme, I knew. The dissatisfaction of those who lacked the means to live comfortably, the anger and envy against those who indulged in extravagances.

What was disturbing me more than anything was the memory of the brief glimpse of a face. It couldn't have been Léon's.

My companion was saying: "They're making a practice of it. It happened only last week at the DeCourcys'. I was dining there and a stone came right through the window. But that was Paris."

I saw Léon coming towards me and I felt my heart begin to beat furiously.

"A nasty incident," he said, taking the chair opposite me.

I glanced at his shoes. They were immaculate. It seemed

impossible that a few minutes ago he could have been outside. It had been raining during the day and the grass was still wet, so surely there would have been some sign.

"I hope you were not frightened," he said to me.

"It happened so quickly."

"But you were very near the window. In the first line of fire."

"Who could have done it?" I demanded, looking full at him. "What good could it do?"

"A few years ago one would have said some maniac. Now it is not so. It's just another expression of the people's disapproval. Let us go back to the old hall. They are dancing there."

I said goodbye to my companion at the table and we went up to the old hall. I felt relieved. I had been mistaken. It could not have been Léon.

I was glad because I was beginning to like him a good deal.

I had retired to my room. My dress lay on the bed and my hair was loose about my shoulders when there was a knock on my door.

I sprang to my feet, thinking for a fearful moment that it might be the Comte.

Margot came in.

"Oh, you are undressed," she said. "I had to talk to you, though. I must. I shall never sleep tonight."

She sat on my bed.

"What did you think of him, Minelle?"

"Robert? Oh, I thought him charming."

"So did I. It was fun, wasn't it? I thought he was going to be awful. You're right . . . but of course you are always right, aren't you? At least, *you* think so. But if you built up a horrible picture you can be agreeably surprised. But I should have liked him anyway. When I was dancing with him I wished . . . oh how I wished . . . that I had never fallen in love with James Wedder."

"It's no use wishing that. It's done and you have to forget it."

"Do you think I can?"

"Not for ever. It will come back to you sometimes, I suppose."

"If you've made a false step you've made it for ever."

"But it doesn't do to brood on it."

"Do you know, Minelle, I think I could forget I had ever

seen James Wedder . . . if it wasn't for Charlot. What should I do, Minelle? Should I tell Robert?"

I was silent. How could I advise on such a matter? How could I know which would be best for her and Robert's happiness?

I compromised. "You should do nothing yet, I think. Wait awhile. In time you and Robert will come to understand each other. Friendship, love, tolerance, all those will grow up between you and when the right time comes to tell, perhaps you will know."

"And Charlot?"

"He is well cared for. I am sure of that."

"But how can I know? If only I could see him."

"Well, that's impossible."

"You talk like Annette. *Nothing* is impossible. I shall go to Paris soon. Yes, I shall. I'm going to stay at Papa's house there and we shall entertain the Grassevilles and then I shall come back here and we'll be married. You will come to Paris with me. There could be an opportunity then."

"What are you thinking of?"

"I mean an opportunity of finding Charlot. If I could be convinced that he is well and happy and people are kind to him it would be different."

"But how could you? You don't know where he is."

"We could find out. You and I . . . we'll do it, Minelle. Yes, we will. We will go on a visit to someone . . . dear old Yvette who used to help Nou Nou in the nursery. I could go and see her and you could come with me."

"We should never be allowed to go alone."

"I have a plan. I have been thinking of it. We could take my maid Mimi and Bessell the groom. Mimi and Bessell are lovers and plan to marry. I have promised them that when I go to Grasseville they shall come and they can marry then. They will be so absorbed in each other . . . that they won't notice much. In any case they would do anything for me."

I thought it was a wild plan, but as I had done before, I allowed Margot to go along with her dream. It was on occasions such as this that she could become hysterical and when she did I had noticed that it was almost always where Charlot was concerned.

I would never have suspected Margot of having deep maternal feelings, but she was always unpredictable; and I supposed that even those who would on the surface seem to make the most unlikely mothers change once a child is born to them.

So eagerly did she discuss the plan that she scarcely mentioned the stone through the window.

"Oh that," she said eventually. "It's happening all over the country. People take little notice of it."

At last she went. I felt tired but unable to sleep and when I did I dreamed vague and ugly dreams, out of which Léon's face, distorted with hatred, kept coming towards me.

The household was now dominated by plans for Margot's wedding. Annette declared herself to be distracted. She would never, never finish in time, she declared. Materials were not the right colors, nothing fitted as it should, and Margot's wardrobe would be a disaster. Meanwhile, beautiful garments continued to be turned out.

Margot was gleeful parading for me in them. She wanted to give me some of her old garments which Annette could "tone up," as she called it. I bought a few and under Annette's tuition made some alterations myself.

"You will need some clothes when we go to Paris," said Margot, and whenever she mentioned the trip her eyes would sparkle and I knew she was thinking of what she called "the plan."

We rode a good deal. She, Léon, Étienne, and I. Sometimes the Comte joined us and when he did he always contrived to lose the others so that he and I were alone. They were aware of his intentions and as usual tried to please him. Against four of them I was helpless, so I often found myself alone with him.

"And so we go on," he said to me one day. "We do not progress very fast, do we?"

"In what way?"

"Towards the blissful end which awaits us both."

"You are in a mocking mood, I see."

"I am always in an excellent mood when I am with you. That is a good augury for the future."

"It certainly shows that you can be good-humored when you wish."

"No, only when I am happy, and that is not always for me to decide."

"I should have thought a man such as you could control his moods."

"It is something I have never learned to do. Perhaps you will teach me, because you control yours admirably. Were you disturbed on the night of the ball when the stone came through the window?"

"I was horrified."

"Some wretched peasant."

"Have you any idea who?"

"It could have been anyone from the neighboring villages."

"Your own vassals."

"What an expression! Yes, it might well have been one of my own vassals. In fact, I'd wager that it was."

"And it disturbs you."

"A broken window is a bagatelle. It is the implication behind it which disturbs. Sometimes I feel as though the entire structure of society is slipping."

"Can you not do something to make it steady?"

He shook his head. "Something should have been done fifty years ago. Perhaps we shall come through this. God knows, my country has been buffeted enough over the centuries . . . yours too. Your people are different. Less fiery. It may well be that they would pause long enough to ask themselves what the consequences of revolution would be. We are more impulsive. You see the difference in our natures . . . reflected in you and me. You are calm; you hide the tumult within. You are adept at it. I'll warrant your mother taught you that it was ill-bred to show your feelings. Oh, Minelle, I would give a great deal to go off with you . . . alone . . . to some remote spot . . . out of France . . . perhaps to an island somewhere in the middle of a blue tropical sea where you and I would be together . . . alone. So much to do . . . so much to talk of . . . There we could live and love in peace."

I was deeply touched by his serious mood, but he was right. I *had* been taught to hide my feelings when my judgment told me it would be wise to do so. I said: "I am sure you would be weary of your island in less than a week. In fact I hardly think you would give it as long."

"Let us try it and see if you are right. Shall we?"

"Such a question does not need an answer. You must know that I am going to leave here. I am staying only until Margot is happily settled. Then I shall go back to England."

"And penury."

"I may be fortunate. I am not without qualifications."

"No. I am sure you would make a success of whatever you set your mind to. You would have continued with the school but for that stupid oaf Joel. What a fool! Perhaps one day he will realize what he has missed and come back to try again. There is one question I want to ask you, Minelle, and I want a serious answer. I know that you disapprove of my way of life. Believe me, it is a matter of upbringing. I live as my ancestors have lived. It is the custom of the *régime*. You have been brought up differently. To you I seem excessively wicked . . . immoral and ruthless. Admit it."

"I admit it," I said.

"And yet, tell the truth, Minelle, you are not without some regard for me?"

I paused and he went on: "Come. You are not afraid to tell the truth, are you?"

"I believe," I replied, "that when a man expresses admiration for a woman, he so appeals to her vanity that it is hard for her not to feel favorably towards one whom—if she is honest—she must admire for his good taste. For there is none who, in her heart, despises herself."

He laughed again. "Enchanting as ever, my dearest Minelle," he said. "So in admiring you I have won a little of your approval. You know the extent of my admiration so I deserve a great deal of your esteem."

"I could never trust you," I said seriously. "You have loved many women."

"Experience is always valuable—no matter in what field— and mine teaches me that I have never loved anyone as I love you."

"The current one is always the most loved," I said.

"You have become a cynic."

"No. I am learning to be a realist."

"Sometimes—life being what it is—it's the same thing. But you still do not answer my question. I have a wife. I am not free to marry therefore. If I were . . ."

"But you are not free . . ."

"I may be . . . some day. I am asking you to tell me what your answer would be if I came to you with an honorable proposal of marriage."

"Which you would not offer if you were free to because you must see that a marriage between us would be highly unsuitable."

"I think it would be the most suitable that was ever made."

"What! The noble Count and the failed schoolmistress."

"He is in great need of the tuition she will give him."

"You are laughing at me."

"No," he said seriously. "I want you to teach me how to be humble and human, how to enjoy what is best in life. I want you to show me how to be happy."

"You have a high opinion of my qualifications."

"But I am sure I assess them correctly. You see how I dote

153

on you. Do your feelings for me increase as you discover what mine are for you?"

"I am suspicious. I know that you are adept at getting what you want from women. It must be interesting to discover various ways of wooing them."

"You misjudge me. Moreover, I suspect you of evading the question. You do not dislike me?"

"You must know that I do not."

"I believe you enjoy these encounters, these verbal fireworks. Do you?"

"Yes, I do."

"Ah. I have wrung an admission from you. I have the impression that you continually seek to evade me, which can only be because I am not free to make an honorable proposal of marriage to you and your upbringing would not allow you to accept any other. That's true, is it not?"

Once more I hesitated too long.

He said: "You have answered me."

We cantered back to the castle side by side.

4

"Cousin!"

The voice floated down to me, light, scarcely audible in the evening air. I had taken a short walk out of doors in the castle gardens. Looking up, I saw the Comtesse stretched out on a chaise longue on the balcony above me.

"Madame?" I said, standing still and gazing up.

Her pale face looked down at me. "Could I interrupt your walk? I should like to speak to you."

"Certainly."

"Come up. The steps will lead you right up to the terrace."

I did as she bid me, feeling a little disturbed, which was understandable considering the attitude her husband had taken towards me.

I mounted the stone steps. She was right. They did take me to her terrace, which jutted out from her bedchamber. This was, of course, not the medieval part of the castle but part of the comfortable luxurious later addition.

"It has been warm today," she said. "I thought a little air would be good for me." She smiled at me. "It must seem odd to someone as healthy as you are to hear people speak continually of their health. Do sit down."

I sat. "I suppose when one has good health one is inclined to take it for granted and forget about it," I answered.

"Exactly. How fortunate not to have to worry all the time what effect things are going to have on you. It is easy to see you enjoy good health, Cousin. Tell me, how are you getting on here? Does it seem strange to you after your school? I am grateful for what you are doing for my daughter."

"It is what I am paid to do, Madame."

"But may I say you are doing it very well indeed." She shifted on her couch. "I think the air has given me a headache. I shall have to ask Nou Nou to prepare a poultice to lay across my forehead. She has an excellent one made from Jupiter's Beard. You look puzzled. You are wondering what that is. One can't live with Nou Nou without learning about these things. It's one of her special plants and like so many of them it is said to be a talisman against evil spells. I can see, Cousin, that you are skeptical. Do you not believe in evil spells?"

"I don't think I do."

"It doesn't necessarily mean that a witch is involved with weird incantations and so on. Evil spells can come about in the most natural ways. There are some people who never bring good to anyone. They could be said to give out evil."

"I suppose that could be true."

"It is always well to avoid such people. Don't you agree, Cousin?"

I wished she would not call me "Cousin." She did it with a certain irony. There was something behind it, something behind her desire to see me.

"Certainly it would be," I agreed.

"I knew you shared my view. You are such a sensible young woman. Margot talks a great deal about you. She thinks you are the fount of wisdom. I . . . er . . . gather that my husband has quite a good opinion of your capabilities."

"I was unaware of that," I said.

"Unaware of my husband's opinion? Is that really so?"

"I . . . I did not know his opinion of me."

She smiled slowly. "I felt sure he had made it clear that he finds your company interesting. He does like the society of women . . . if they are young, handsome, and not without some intelligence. They become flattered and forget his position and that with him it is but a fleeting interest."

"I could never forget the Comte's position . . . nor my own," I said sharply.

She looked down at her delicate hands. "He is my husband after all," she said. "That is something he cannot forget though others might."

"*I* should never forget that, Madame," I retorted. I was uncomfortable. embarrassed, and angry. I wanted to convey that her husband was perfectly safe from me.

"I can see you are sensible," she commented.

"Thank you. I shall shortly be returning to England."

"Ah!" It was a long drawn-out sigh. "I think that is very wise of you." She was silent for a few moments and I had the impression that she regretted having spoken so frankly. She went on conversationally: "From what Margot tells me, it is rather different in England."

"Yes, indeed."

"I scarcely move from here," she went on. "With my husband it is different, of course. It is rarely that I have known him stay in the *château* for such a long time. He is restless. Moreover, it is necessary for him to spend a great deal of time in Paris . . . while I stay here with Nou Nou."

"Who, I know, is a great comfort to you."

"I can't think what I should do without her. She is my friend, my companion, my watchdog." She waved her hand. "When darkness falls I feel afraid. I always did in the dark. Do you, Cousin?"

"No," I replied.

"You are brave. I knew you would be. I have often watched you in the garden . . . you and Margot together. And I have seen you come in from riding with my husband. Well, Margot will soon be married and you will go back to England. That is the best, Cousin. I am glad you see it so. I should like your adventure in my country to bring you happy memories when you go back to England." She was looking at me steadily. A moment ago she had been warning me to keep away from her husband as any jealous wife might. That was reasonable. After all he was her husband. Now her warning was of a different kind. What had she meant about Nou Nou's being her watchdog? The Comte is a dangerous man, she was telling me. Be wary of him.

She had no need to tell me that.

"Yes," she repeated, "you should go back to your own country. There is nothing good for you here. Oh dear!" She put her hand to her head. "My head throbs so. Go into the room and find Nou Nou. Ask her to make up the Jupiter's Beard poultice, will you?"

It was dismissal. I went through the glass doors into the room. Nou Nou came bustling in and I gave the order.

She tut-tutted. "Called you up, did she? She knows it tires her to talk. And she would go out. I knew it was not good for her. Headache, is it? My Jupiter's Beard will soon put paid to that. You came up by the garden stairs, I suppose?"

"Yes," I answered.

"Well, you can go back that way if you like. Tell her I'll have her poultice in next to no time, and first I'm going to bring her in."

I went out onto the terrace. The Comtesse was lying back with her eyes closed. It was an indication that she had nothing more to say to me and I was dismissed.

I was still smoldering with anger and humiliation. When I was with her I had not realized the enormity of what she was hinting. First, she had warned me to keep away from her husband because he was married to her and not free to dally with me. How insulting! As if I were not aware of that! Then she had changed her mood and warned me against him, which had seemed quite sinister, as though there were some dark forces in him of which I was unaware.

It was very disconcerting and brought home to me more forcibly than ever that I must prepare to go.

I thought a good deal about the Comtesse. If I were uneasy about her, she certainly was about me. Perhaps some gossip had reached her. It must have since she had seen fit to give me her twofold warning.

She was certainly right. I ought to get away. In fact I should not have stayed so long. Nor could I have done, I justified myself, if Margot had not been so unhappy every time I suggested leaving.

I did not want to talk to Margot. I was afraid she would bring up the subject. Not that it was difficult to avoid it. Margot was too full of her own affairs to want to discuss anyone else's.

Nevertheless, I had taken to going out, usually in the garden, and finding some quiet spot where I could be alone to think.

When I had been with the Comtesse I had felt guilty. Yet I had done nothing to attract the Comte. Nou Nou had a way of looking at me from under her bushy brows as though

I were Jezebel herself. She made me feel that I should get away without delay, even before Margot's wedding.

It was an impossible situation and had it been presented to me as someone else's problem a year ago I should have said: "The woman is doing wrong by staying. Any decent person would leave at once."

Of course, it was what I should do. My interview with the Comtesse had brought that home more vividly than before.

I had walked beyond the castle precincts and found myself close to Gabrielle's house. His mistress! And she lived near the *château* so that they could meet conveniently. I flushed with shame. And this was the man whom I had allowed to take possession of my thoughts!

I was startled by the sound of horse's hoofs. I went close to the hedge as a rider passed by. There was something familiar about him, although I could not think what.

Gabrielle's house came into view. The man was tethering his horse to the block at her gate. As I came along he turned and we looked full at each other. He looked a little startled and in that flash it was obvious that we were both thinking that we had seen each other somewhere before.

He opened the gate and went up the path to the house. I walked on. Then my heart started to thump with apprehension. I had remembered who the man was.

He was Gaston—the lover of Jeanne, the servant at Madame Grémond's.

I did not mention to Margot the fact that I had seen Gaston. It could only disturb her. I even tried to convince myself that I had been mistaken. After all, I had not seen a great deal of the man when we were at Madame Grémond's. This could have been someone who bore a resemblance to him. There was no real distinguishing feature about him. What should he have been doing at Madame LeGrand's? Taking letters from his mistress? Was it possible then that Madame Grémond and Madame LeGrand knew each other? Of course it was possible. Their connecting link would be the Comte. Two discarded mistresses condoling with each other. Or perhaps not discarded? It was becoming more and more sordid every day.

But I could not, of course, be sure of this and I preferred to think I had made a mistake.

While I was pondering this, Étienne came to me and told me that his mother had expressed the wish that I should call on her again and he wondered whether I would allow him to take me to her.

I said I should be delighted to call, and a few days later, one afternoon I rode with him to her house.

I was taken into the ornate *salon,* where she was waiting to receive me, very elegant but slightly overdressed in pale blue silk and lace.

"Mademoiselle Maddox," she cried warmly, "how enchanted I am to see you. It was good of you to call."

"I am pleased to be asked," I replied, glad as I had often been of my well-cut riding habit which my mother had had made for me. The fact that I had ridden over meant that it was quite right for me to be wearing it.

Étienne left us and I realized that this was going to be a *tête-à-tête.*

She said we should have *le thé* because she knew how the English loved it.

"Have you noticed how we in France are imitating the English more and more? It is a form of flattery. But you would not have noticed it here. It is in Paris that it is obvious. In the shops there are signs 'English spoken here' and the lemonade sellers sell *le Punch.* That is English, as you know. The young men swagger round in English coats with capes. The women are wearing English hats and even the race course at Vincennes tries to be like your Newmarket."

"I did not know this."

"There is much you have yet to learn of France, I feel sure. Then there are those tall vehicles they call 'whiskies.' I can tell you we are becoming more and more English every day."

"That is very interesting."

"You will see this when you go to Paris. You are going, I believe, with Marguerite."

"Yes, that is so."

"Such a good marriage this. The Comte tells me that he is delighted with it. An alliance between Fontaine Delibes and Grasseville. Little could be better."

The tea was brought in by one of the lackeys whose livery was very like the *château* colors—slightly more muted, slightly less grand, with silver buttons instead of gold. I could not help but be amused by the fine distinction.

"Mademoiselle smiles. The tea is to your liking?"

"It is excellent, Madame." And so it was, served in little dishes of Sèvres china, though somewhat unlike our home brew.

Small pastries were served with it. They had delicious fillings of some cream concoction.

"I thought we should become better acquainted," said Gabrielle LeGrand. "I saw you at the ball, of course, but one cannot really talk to people on such occasions. Was it not disgraceful . . . the stone through the window? I would not care to be in the culprit's shoes if he were discovered. The Comte would have little mercy on him and he can be a stern man."

"Do you think they will find him?"

Léon's face swam before me and I admonished myself: Don't be silly. It was an illusion. Of course it wasn't Léon. How could it have been? He could not have been in the ballroom so soon after, looking so fresh. I seemed to be developing a bent for imagining I saw people when it could hardly be likely that I had.

"I doubt it now. Unless one of his enemies betrays him. That sort of thing is happening all over the country. I don't know what things are coming to. Are you staying in France, Mademoiselle?"

"I shall be with Marguerite for a while and when she marries return to England."

She could not hide her relief. She said quickly: "How interesting it must have been to discover your connection with the Comte's family . . . however remote."

I did not answer and she went on: "Do tell me who exactly it was who married into the family. All the time I have known the Fontaine Delibeses I have never before heard there was an English connection."

"You must ask the Comte," I said.

"I see less of him nowadays." She sighed. "There was a time . . . It was a great mistake he made in his marriage. You have met the Comtesse, of course."

"Yes," I answered coolly. I felt she was extremely tactless to mention the Comte's marriage in this way.

"I ask," she said, "because I know she lives a life of retirement. I gather she sees few people. Poor Ursule! Anyone should have known how disastrous that would be. He used to confide in me . . . a great deal. There is no point in attempting to hide the truth of our relationship when it is obvious for all to see. We have a fine son . . . our Étienne. And from her there was simply Marguerite. I will tell you in confidence that he has never ceased to regret that he did not marry me."

"Why did he not?" I asked coldly.

160

"My family was a good one but of course not to be compared with his. I was a widow." She shrugged her shoulders. "He was young then . . . very young. We both were. I shall never forget those days. How much in love we were!" She laughed. "I see you are a little shocked. The English do not talk as freely of these matters as we do. Ah, it was a tragic mistake and he was to realize that again and again."

"These cakes are delicious, Madame. You must have an excellent cook."

"I am glad you like them. They are favorites of the Comte. But one can never be sure how long he will like something. He is fickle in his tastes."

"They are so light," I said. "They make one quite greedy."

"Then do have some more. Étienne is fond of them. We are planning a marriage for him, but he is in no hurry."

"It is never wise to hurry when important matters are planned."

"One of these days . . . who knows . . . Étienne has been brought up in the *château,* you know."

"Yes, I did know."

"The Comte is proud of him. He is a good-looking young man, do you not think so?"

"Indeed I do. He is very handsome."

"One day who shall say what his future will be?"

"That is something none of us can see . . . the future."

I found a certain mischievous pleasure in thwarting her by keeping the conversation on general lines when I knew she was trying to make it personal. I understood her motive well. Like the Comtesse, she was warning me. But her motive was rather different. I believed that the Comtesse was a little concerned for me, while Gabrielle was concerned for herself.

"But we can predict," she said. "If one has known someone for a very long time one knows how that person will act in certain circumstances. Don't you agree?"

I said I thought one could hazard a guess, but as so many people were unpredictable one could never be entirely sure.

She nodded. "It has been a strange life. I met the Comte when I was a very young widow. I came to plead for my father, who had been imprisoned by his. The Comte could not do enough for me. My father had died in prison accused of . . . I know not what—nor did he."

"Yes," I said. "I have heard of those fearful *lettres de cachet.*"

"I think one of the reasons the Comte regrets not marrying me is that it would have done something towards righting the wrong his father did to mine. He once said that he wished he could have the opportunity over again and if ever he did . . ."

I nodded. "It was a terrible injustice which was done to your father."

"He is a strange man . . . Charles-Auguste. He has these flashes of conscience. Look at Léon. He has certainly benefited from the harm done to his family. I suppose we shall go on as before. Étienne will, I know, be legitimized. That has been more or less promised . . . providing of course Charles-Auguste doesn't marry and get a legitimate son. But he can't do that while he has a wife, can he?"

"It is certainly a very complicated matter," I said. "And who shall say how it will end."

"And you will soon be leaving us and forgetting all about us and our problems." Her eyes glittered, seeming to look into my mind. It was almost as though she were commanding me to go.

Then she insisted on showing me her treasures, chief among them a beautiful clock of gold and ivory made in the shape of a castle. It was very elaborate but quite beautiful.

"A gift from the Comte when Étienne was born," she explained. Then she showed me other treasures—all gifts from the Comte.

"A very generous man," she commented, "to those for whom he feels deeply. Mind you, there have been some whose reign has been brief . . . very brief. Those have been quickly dismissed and forgotten."

"How sad for them," I said wryly, "unless they were glad to depart."

She looked at me in some puzzlement. I could see she did not understand me.

I was relieved when Étienne arrived to accompany me back to the castle.

He said: "I will take you by a way I am sure you have not yet discovered. It is a very private short cut to the castle from the house. The Comte had it made eighteen years ago."

The pathway led from the garden through a wood and I was astonished how quickly we reached the castle.

"Why is it so little used?" I asked.

"When it was first made the Comte let it be known that it was for his use and my mother's only. Consequently people kept away. And it has become the rule."

We had arrived at the castle wall. There was a door

through which we went and we were in a courtyard. I had never entered the castle that way before.

It was late afternoon when Nou Nou came to my room. She gave a sharp peremptory knock on the door and without waiting for permission to enter, did so.

"The Comtesse wishes to see you," she said, looking at me in a scornful way which was calculated to make me feel uncomfortable and certainly did.

I stood up.

"Not now. At eight o'clock this evening. She has something she wants to say to you."

I said I would present myself at that time.

"Don't be late. I like to get her settled down for the night before nine o'clock."

"I shall not be late," I promised.

She nodded and left me.

Strange old woman, I thought. A little mad, as all people with obsessions were. In her case, though, it was a selfless obsession. I fell to thinking of poor Nou Nou, who had lost her husband and child and turned to Ursule for comfort. There was no doubt that she had found it to a certain extent.

I wondered about Ursule's childhood before she had become an invalid and how she could be content to live the life she did shut away from the world. It was as though she embraced this life with relish simply because it meant that in doing so she had escaped from her husband. How she must hate him! Perhaps it was fear more than hatred. What had he done to inspire such terror? Nou Nou seemed as though she knew something. I had no doubt that Ursule confided in her. That he would neglect her if she did not interest him, I knew. That he would feel cheated because she could not provide the essential son, I could understand. That he took his mistresses openly and even had one living a stone's throw from the *château* was a fact. But should this make her *fear* him?

There was so much I wanted to know about Ursule.

A few minutes before eight o'clock I made my way to her room. It was a little early and, knowing what a stickler for time Nou Nou was, I hung back in the corridor looking out of the window waiting for those few moments to pass.

Eight o'clock precisely.

I went to the door which was slightly ajar. I pushed it open and looked in. There was a draft from the door which opened onto the terrace. I was just in time to catch a glimpse of the back of the Comte as he disappeared.

I was relieved that I had not come earlier when I should have met him in his wife's room. That could have been embarrassing.

I tiptoed to the bed.

"Madame," I began. Then I paused. The Comtesse was lying back on her pillows, her eyes half-closed. She was clearly very drowsy.

"You wanted to see me, Madame?"

Her eyes were completely closed now. She seemed to be asleep.

I felt uneasy and wondered why she had not canceled our appointment if she was too tired to see me. On the table beside the bed was the usual array of bottles. A glass stood there. I picked it up and smelt it, for there were the dregs of something in the bottom of the glass. Clearly the Comtesse had taken her sleeping draught, which she probably did when she was about to retire. But she must have known how long it took to work, and how strange that she should have taken it in time to send her to sleep when she had asked me to come and see her.

As I stood there I heard a movement behind me. Nou Nou came in. She looked at the glass in my hand.

"I was to see Madame at eight," I said, replacing the glass on the table.

Nou Nou gazed at the sleeping woman and the change in her expression was marked. "Poor lamb," she said. "She was tired out. He has been in. I suppose he tired her . . . as he always does. She must have dropped off to sleep . . . suddenly."

"You will tell her when she awakes that I came, will you?" Nou Nou nodded.

"Perhaps she will say if she wants to see me tomorrow."

Nou Nou said: "We shall see how she feels."

"Good night," I said, and went out.

The next day lived vividly in my memory.

I awoke as usual when one of the serving maids brought in my hot water and put it into the *ruelle*. I washed and took the coffee and *brioche* which was brought to my room.

Margot came, as she often did, bringing her tray with her, and we took our *petit déjeuner* together.

We talked of the proposed trip to Paris and I was glad that she did not mention Charlot. It was comforting to know that her coming marriage had helped her when I had so much feared it would have the reverse effect.

While we were chatting together the door opened and the Comte entered. I had never seen him distraught before, but he certainly was then.

He looked from one to the other of us and then he said: "Marguerite, your mother is dead."

I felt a cold horror grip me. I began to tremble and was afraid it would be noticed.

"She must have died during the night," he said. "Nou Nou has just discovered this."

He did not meet my eyes and I was terribly afraid.

There was tension throughout the castle. The servants were whispering together. I wondered what they were saying. The relationship which existed between the Comte and his wife was well known to them and they must all have been aware of the fact that he wished he were free of her.

Margot came to me.

"I must talk to you, Minelle," she said. "It is terrible. She is dead. It has suddenly struck me. She was my mother . . . but I scarcely knew her. She never seemed to want me with her. I always believed, when I was little, that I was the cause of her illness. Nou Nou seemed to think so too. Poor Nou Nou! She is just sitting beside her rocking to and fro. She mutters to herself and then throws her apron over her face. All I can hear is 'Ursule *mignonne*.' "

"Margot," I said, "how did it happen?"

"She has been delicate for a long time, hasn't she?" Margot replied almost defensively, and I wondered what she was thinking.

"Perhaps," she went on, "she was more ill than we thought. We believed really that she *fancied* she was ill all the time."

The doctors came during the day. They were with the Comte in the chamber of death for a long time.

The Comte asked me to join him in the library and I went full of foreboding.

"Please sit, Minelle," he said. "This is an unexpected shock."

Those words brought me an immense relief.

"I have always suspected that the Comtesse's illness was imaginary," he went on. "It seems I did her an injustice. She was really ill."

"What was her illness?"

He shook his head. "The doctors are bewildered. They are not certain what caused her death. Nou Nou is too distrait to talk. She has been with her since her birth and was completely devoted to her. I'm afraid this shock is going to be too much for her."

I waited for him to go on but for once he seemed at a loss for words.

Then he said slowly: "There will be an autopsy."

I looked at him in astonishment.

"It is the custom," he said, "when the cause of death is uncertain. The doctors have formed the opinion, though, that she died of something she had taken."

"It can't be!" I cried.

"She looks peaceful," he said. "Of one thing we can be certain. She did not die painfully. It seems she went off in a peaceful sleep from which she has not awakened."

"Was it a draught to make her sleep, do you think?"

"It may be so. Nou Nou is too upset to speak to us yet. Tomorrow she will have recovered a little and may be able to help. I believe Ursule was in the habit of taking some draught at bedtime." His eyes did not leave my face. They glittered brightly and I avoided looking directly at him. The fear was strong in me.

"It is going to be rather a difficult time," he said. "This sort of thing can be very unpleasant. There will be a great deal of speculation. There always is when anyone dies suddenly. And the circumstances . . ."

I nodded. "Nou Nou will know whether she took a sleeping draught."

"Nou Nou would prepare it for her. I am sure when she is able to talk we may understand how this happened."

"Do you think that the Comtesse . . ."

"That she did it deliberately? No, I don't think so. I think there has been some terrible mistake. But we can reach no conclusions through conjecture. This may be unpleasant, as I said, and I should prefer you and Marguerite not to be here. Make your preparations to leave for Paris. I think you should go immediately after the autopsy." He paused, then went on briskly: "Now, I do not think you should remain here with me long." He smiled at me wryly, and I knew what was in his mind. His wife had died suddenly and his interest in me was obvious. I could see that we should both be under suspicion. "Send Marguerite to me," he added. "I will warn her that she must be ready to leave for Paris fairly soon."

That was a week of nightmare. Suspicion was rife and I was at the heart of it. I wondered what would happen if the Comte was accused of murder . . . or I was. I could hear accusing voices asking me about my relationship with the Comte. I was his cousin, was I? Would I please explain.

The Comte was less disturbed than I. He was confident that there would be some explanation. There was a distressing scene with Nou Nou, who came to my room one night when I was preparing for bed.

She looked terribly ill. I was sure she had not slept since the death of the Comtesse. She was hollow-eyed and had not brushed or combed her hair; it hung, half up half down, in straggling gray strands about her face. Clutching a bed-gown about her, she looked like a specter.

She said to me: "You do well to look guilty, Mademoiselle."

I replied: "Guilty. I neither look nor feel guilty. You must know that, Nou Nou."

"It was her bedtime dose," she said. "I used to give it to her when she couldn't sleep. I knew just how much was needed to send her off. That night she had had a treble dose. It should have taken an hour to have effect . . . but she was sleeping when I came in . . . You were there that night. He was there too. The two of you . . ."

"She was asleep when I came in. You know that. It was just eight o'clock."

"I didn't know enough of what was going on. There was her dose there by the bed. Well, someone added to it, didn't they? Someone who crept in . . ."

"I tell you she was asleep when I came . . ."

"I came out and found you with the glass in your hand."

"This is absurd. I had only just come into the room."

"There was somebody else there, wasn't there. You know that."

I felt the blood rushing into my cheeks.

"What . . . are you suggesting?"

"Doses don't get into glasses without being put there, do they? Someone did it . . . someone in this house."

For a moment I was too stunned to reply. I kept thinking of that moment when I had seen the Comte slipping out through the French window onto the terrace. How long had he been with her? Long enough to give her the dose . . . to wait while she drank it? Oh no, I told myself, I won't believe it.

I stammered: "You don't know the cause of her death. It has not yet been proved."

Her eyes glittered and she looked at me steadily. "I know," she said. She came close to me and, laying a hand on my arm, peered into my face. "If she'd never married, she'd be alive today. She'd be her bonny self just as she used to be before the wedding. I remember the night before that wedding. I couldn't comfort her. Oh, these marriages. Why can't they let children be children till they know what life's about!"

In spite of the horrible fear which would not leave me, in spite of the shock of realizing how deeply involved I was, I felt sorry for Nou Nou. It seemed that the death of her beloved charge had unhinged her mind. Something had gone out of her. The fierce dragon guarding her treasure had become a sad creature only wanting to crawl into a corner and die. She was looking round to blame someone. She hated the Comte and her venom was directed mainly against him, but because it was known that he had a fondness for me, she let it fall on me too.

"Oh Nou Nou," I said, the compassion I felt for her obvious in my voice, "I am so sorry this has happened."

She looked at me slyly. "Perhaps you think it makes it easier for you, eh? Perhaps you think that now she is out of the way . . ."

"Nou Nou!" I cried sharply. "Stop that wicked talk."

"You'll have a shock." She began to laugh; it was horrible laughter, at times like the cackle of a hen. Then she stopped suddenly. "You and he plot together . . ."

"You must not say such things. That are absolutely false. Let me take you back to your room. You need rest. This has been a terrible shock for you."

Suddenly she started to cry—silently, the tears streaming down her face.

"She was everything to me," she said. "My little lamb, my darling baby. All I'd got. I never took to any other. It was always my little *mignonne*."

"I know," I said.

"But I've lost her. She's not there any more."

"Come, Nou Nou." I took her arm and led her back to her room.

When we were there she broke away from me.

"I shall go to her," she said; and she went into that room where the body of the Comtesse lay.

They were difficult days to live through. I saw little of the Comte. He avoided me, which was wise, because there were whispers about him and it was likely that my name was being linked with his.

I rode out with Marguerite, Étienne, and Léon and as we passed close to a village a stone was thrown at us. It hit Étienne on the arm, but I think it was meant for me.

"Murderess!" shouted a voice.

We saw a group of young men and we knew the missile had come from them. Étienne was for giving chase but Léon deterred him.

"Better be careful," Léon advised. "This could start a riot. Ignore it."

"They need to be taught a lesson."

"We must take care," said Léon, "that they do not attempt to teach us one."

After that I felt reluctant to go out.

We could not leave the *château* until after the autopsy and because of the Comte's position this aroused a good deal of attention. I was terribly afraid because I knew it had already been decided that he had murdered his wife.

I was greatly relieved to hear that I should not be expected to appear. I feared a probing into the reason why I had come to France and what would happen if Marguerite's indiscretion came to light. How would Robert de Grasseville react? Would he want to marry her then? I sometimes felt it would have been better for her to make a complete confession to him—but on the other hand I did not consider myself sufficiently worldly to know whether this would be wise.

The Comte returned in due course. The affair was over and the verdict was that the cause of death was an overdose of a sleeping draught which contained opium in excessive quantities. The Comtesse was discovered to have suffered from a disease of the lungs—a disease from which it was recalled her mother had died. Doctors had visited her recently and had expressed their certainty that she was suffering from this disease in its early stages. If the Comtesse had known of this she would also have known that later she would have to endure great pain. The most likely verdict was that, knowing this, she had taken her own life by drinking a large quantity of the sleeping draught which she had been taking in small doses for some time, and which when taken thus could produce gentle sleep and be quite harmless.

The day he returned Nou Nou paid one of her visits to my bedroom. She seemed to take a delight in my discomfiture.

"So," she said, "you think this is the end of the matter, do you, Mademoiselle?"

"The law is satisfied," I said.

"The law! Who is the law? Who has always been the law? He has . . . he and his kind. One law for the rich . . . one for the poor. That's what the trouble's about. He has his friends . . . all over the place." She stepped nearer to me. "He came to me and he threatened me. He said: 'Stop your scandalous gossip, Nou Nou. If you don't, you can get out. And where would you go then, tell me that? Do you want to be sent away . . . away from the rooms where she lived . . . away from her tomb, where you can weep and revel in your mourning?' Yes, that's what he said. I said to him: 'You were there. You came into the room. You were with her. And then that woman came, didn't she? Did she come to see if you'd done what you planned together? . . .' "

"Stop it, Nou Nou," I said. "You know I came because she said she wanted to see me. You yourself brought the message. She was already asleep when he left."

"You saw him go, didn't you? You came in . . . just as he was going. Oh, it's a strange business, I'd say."

"It's not strange at all, Nou Nou," I said firmly. "And you know it."

She looked startled. "What is it you're so sure of?"

"I know this," I replied. "The verdict has been given. I believe it because it is the only possible one."

She started to laugh wildly. I took her arm and shook it.

"Nou Nou, go back to your room. Try to rest. Try to be calm. This is a terrible tragedy, but it is over and no good can come by dwelling on it."

"It's over for some," she said mournfully. *"Life* is over for some . . . for *mignonne* and her old Nou Nou. Others think it is just beginning for them, perhaps."

I shook my head angrily and she sat down suddenly and covered her face with her hands.

After a while she allowed me to take her back to her room.

It was I who found the stone with the paper attached to it. It was lying in the corridor outside my bedroom. I saw first that the window had been smashed, and there on the floor was this object.

I picked it up. It was a heavy stone and stuck on it was the piece of paper. On this was written in uneven script: "Aristocrat. You murdered your wife but it is one law for the rich, one for the poor. Take heed. Your time will come."

I stood there for some horrified seconds with the paper in my hand.

Perhaps it was wrong of me, but I always made quick decisions, though not always the right ones. I decided then that no one in the castle would see that paper.

I put the stone back on the floor and took the paper into my bedchamber. I spread it out and studied it. The writing was uneven but I had a notion that an attempt had been made to convey the impression of near illiteracy. I felt the paper. It was strong, stout stuff. Not the kind which poor people would use to write their letters on, even if they could write. It was of a shade of blue so pale as to be almost white.

There was a bureau in my bedroom and in this were sheets of notepaper headed with the address of the castle on it in elegant gold letters. The paper was of the same texture as the notepaper used in the castle. It could have been torn off from a piece of this.

There must be something significant in this. Could it be possible that someone in the castle was the Comte's bitter enemy?

I thought, as I always did at times like this, of my mother. I could almost hear her saying to me: "Get out. There's danger all around you. You have already become embroiled in this household and it must stop without delay. Go back to England. Take a post as companion . . . governess . . . or, better still, open a school . . ."

She is right, I thought, I am becoming too much affected by the Comte. He has cast a spell on me in some way. I was trying not to believe that he had slipped the fatal dose into the Comtesse's glass, but I could not with honesty say that I did not doubt him.

Margot was at the door.

"Another stone has been thrown through a window," she announced. "It's just outside here."

I rose and went to look at it.

Margot shrugged her shoulders. "Stupid people. What do they think they are going to achieve by that?"

She was not deeply affected. This sort of thing was becoming a commonplace.

The Comte sent for Margot and me. He looked older, sterner than he had before his wife's death.

"I want you to leave for Paris tomorrow," he said. "I think that would be best. I have had a note from the Grassevilles. They would like you to visit them, but I think it better that you stay in my Paris residence. You are in mourning. The Grassevilles will visit you there. You can shop for what you need." He turned to me suddenly. "I rely on you to look after Marguerite."

I wondered whether I should tell him of the note which had come through the window attached to the stone, but I felt it would only add to his anxieties and I did not care to mention it before Margot. I hoped to see him alone before I left, but I realized that he was aware how closely we were watched. He would know too that it was being said he had escaped justice because he had friends in high places.

I went to my room to make my preparations. I took the piece of paper from the drawer and looked at it, wondering what I should do. I could not leave it and yet what if I took it with me and mislaid it? I made one of my sudden decisions. I tore it into scraps and taking it down to the hall where a fire was burning, I threw it in. I watched the flames curl about the blackened edges. It seemed to form itself into a malevolent face and I was immediately reminded of that one I had seen outside the window on the night of the ball.

Léon! And the paper which might have come from the castle!

It was quite impossible. Léon would never be a traitor to the man who had done so much for him. I was so upset by recent events that my imagination was getting out of hand.

We left early—soon after dawn.

The Comte came down to the courtyard to see us off. He held my hand firmly in his and said: "Take care of my daughter . . . and yourself." Then he added: "Be patient."

I knew what he meant and that remark filled me with excitement, apprehension, and foreboding.

THE
WAITING CITY

1

Paris! What a city of enchantment. If I could have been there in other circumstances, how I should have loved it. My mother and I used to talk of the various places in the world we should like to visit and high on our list had been Paris.

It was a queen of cities, full of beauty and ugliness living side by side. When I studied the maps I thought that the island in the Seine on which the city stood was like a cradle in shape and when I pointed this out to Margot she was only mildly interested.

"A cradle," I said. "It's significant. In this cradle, beauty was reared. François Premier with his love of fine buildings, with his devotion to literature, music, and artists, laid the foundations of the most intellectual court of Europe."

"Trust you to make it sound like a history lesson!" retorted Margot. "Well now, revolution is being reared in your cradle."

I was startled. It was unlike her to talk seriously.

"Those stones which were thrown at the *château*," she went on, "I keep thinking of them. Ten years ago they wouldn't have dared . . . and now *we* dare do nothing about it. Change is coming, Minelle. You can feel it all around you."

I could feel it. In those streets where the crowds jostled, where the vendors shouted their wares—I had the feeling of a waiting city.

The Comte's residence was in the Faubourg Saint Honoré among those of other members of the nobility. They stood, these houses, where they had for two to three hundred years, aloof and elegant. Not far away, I was to discover, was that labyrinth of little streets into which one dared not venture unless accompanied by several strong men—evil-smelling, narrow, cobbled, where lurked those who regarded any stranger as a victim.

We went into them on one occasion accompanied by Bessell and another manservant. Margot had insisted. There was the street of the women who sat at the doors, their faces ludicrously painted, their low-cut dresses deliberately revealing. I remembered the names of the streets, Rue aux Fèves, Rue de la Jouverie, Rue de la Colandre, Rue des Marmousets. They were the streets of the women and the dyers and outside many of the houses stood great tubs in which the dyes were mixed; red, blue, and green dye flowed down the gutters like miniature rivers.

My room in the Comte's *hôtel* was even more elegant than that which I had occupied in the *château*. It overlooked beautiful gardens which were tended by a host of gardeners. There were greenhouses in which exotic blooms flourished and these were used to decorate the rooms.

Margot's room was next to mine. "I arranged it," she told me. "And Mimi is in the anteroom. Bessell is with the grooms."

I had forgotten till then our plan which involved these two. In fact, I had never really taken it seriously and she did not mention it until we had been in Paris two or three days.

The Comte and Comtesse de Grasseville called on our first day. Margot, as the hostess, did the honors very graciously, I thought. She walked in the gardens with them and they were all very solemn. As the Comte had reminded us, we were in mourning.

I wondered then whether this meant a postponement of the wedding and came to the conclusion that this must be so.

I was presented to the Comte and Comtesse. Their manner was a little aloof and I wondered if they had heard rumors about my position in the Comte's household.

I spoke to Margot about this later.

She said she had noticed nothing and they had spoken very kindly of me. "We talked about the wedding," she said, "and by rights we should wait a year. I don't know whether we shall. But I shall go on as though there will be no postponement."

There was shopping to be done. Mimi always accompanied us with Bessell and if we went in the carriage there would be a footman as well. Sometimes we went on foot and that I enjoyed most. We all dressed very quietly for these expeditions, though none of us mentioned this.

I shall never forget the smell of Paris. There seemed to be more mud there than in any other city. It was black mud and there were metal fragments in it. If one of these touched one's garments it would make a hole. I remembered that the old Roman name for Paris was Lutetia, which meant Mud Town, and I was not surprised it had been so called. In the streets boys stood around with brooms to sweep a crossing for those pedestrians who were ready to pay a sou for the service.

I liked to see the way in which the city came alive as it did each morning at seven o'clock when the clerks, neatly dressed, would be going to work, and one or two gardeners could be seen wheeling their barrows into the markets. Gradually the town would put on its bustling and exciting vitality. I told Margot it reminded me of the dawn chorus of the birds. A little stirring, then a little more, and so on adding up to the full song.

She was a little impatient of my enthusiasm. After all, she had known Paris for so long and as with many things that are familiar one ceases to be aware of them.

But how thrilling it was to see the various trades waking up to the day. The barbers, covered in flour with which they powdered the wigs, the lemonade shops opening their doors while the waiters came out with their trays of hot coffee and rolls to be served to those in the surrounding houses who had ordered them the night before. Later, members of the legal profession appeared like black crows in their flapping robes on their way to the Châtelet and the other courts.

Dinner was at three o'clock in fashionable circles and it amused me to see the dandies and the ladies—some in carriages but some on foot—picking their careful way through the mud on their way to their hosts. Then the streets were full of noise and clamor, which died down during the dinner interval to awaken again about five o'clock, when the leisured crowd was making its way to the playhouses or the pleasure gardens.

I wanted to see everything, which Margot thought very childish. She did not know that the need to overlay my anxiety about what might be happening back at the *château* was at the heart of my determination to learn all I could about this stimulating, wonderful city.

Looking back, how glad I was that I saw it then. It was never to be quite the same again.

We shopped. What an array of good things there were in those shops! Their windows were dazzling. Gowns, ready-made, materials for sale, mantles, pelisses, muffs, ribbons, laces. They were a joy to behold. The hats were perhaps the most striking of all. Following the fashions set by the Queen, they were both extravagant and outrageous. Rose Bertin, her dressmaker, made for a few favored people. She graciously consented to make something for the daughter of the Comte Fontaine Delibes.

"I should go to someone who is more eager to serve you," I said.

"You don't understand, Minelle. It means something to be dressed by Rose Bertin."

So we went to her for Margot's fitting. She kept us waiting for an hour and then sent a message to the effect that we must return the next day.

As we came out I noticed a little group of people standing on the corner. They muttered and watched us sullenly as we got into the carriage.

Yes, Paris was certainly an uneasy city. But I was too bemused by its beauty and too stunned by what had happened at the *château* to notice as I otherwise would—and Margot's thoughts were elsewhere.

I was gratified to see that England appeared to be held in great respect. It was as Gabrielle LeGrand had said. The shops were full of clothes proclaiming to be made of English cloth. Signs announced that English was spoken within. In the windows of the shops was written *Le Punch Anglais,* and in all the cafés it was possible to take *le thé.* Even the tall vehicles were called whiskies and an imitation of those used in England.

I was amused and, I must say, somewhat flattered. And in the shops I made no attempt to disguise the fact that, like so many of their products, I came from across the Channel.

We were buying some beautiful satin one day which was to be made into a dress for Margot's trousseau when the man who was serving us leaned across the counter and looking at me earnestly said: "Mademoiselle is from England?"

I agreed that this was so.

"Mademoiselle should go home," he said. "Lose no time."

I looked at him in surprise and he went on: "Any day the storm will break. Today, tomorrow, next week, next year. And when it comes none will be spared. You should go while there is time."

Cold fear touched me then. There had been so many pointers, I could see that everyone around me was trying not to see them, but there had to be uncomfortable moments when they could not be avoided.

This was indeed a waiting city.

We walked out into the sunshine and our steps led us to the Cour du Mai. I could not forget the shopman's warning,

177

and as I walked it seemed to me that a terrible foreboding of the future came to me.

I was to remember it there in the Cour du Mai later on.

Margot came to my room. There was a sparkle in her eyes and she was very flushed.

"It's all arranged," she said. "We are going to see Yvette."

"Who is Yvette?"

"Don't be deliberately obstructive, Minelle. I have told you about Yvette. She used to work with Nou Nou in the nursery. She lives in the country—not so very far from where I lost Charlot."

"My dear Margot, you are not still thinking of looking for him."

"Of course I am. Do you think I would let him go and never know what has happened to him? I must content myself that he is well and happy . . . and not missing me."

"As he was only a few weeks old when you parted from him, he could hardly be expected to know you."

"Of course he'll know me. I'm his mother."

"Oh Margot, you must not be so foolish. You must put that unfortunate episode behind you. You have been lucky. You have a fiancé whom you like very well. He will be kind and good to you."

"Oh don't set yourself up as an oracle. You're not the schoolmistress now, you know. You promised we would go to find him. Are you a breaker of promises?"

I was silent. It was true I had promised when I thought she was on the verge of hysteria, but I had never really taken the plan seriously.

"I have it all worked out," she explained. "I shall go to visit my old nurse Yvette. I want to tell her that I am betrothed to Robert. Mimi and Bessell will accompany us, and we shall take the carriage. We shall stay at inns and travel a little each day and as we are going back to that neighborhood I shall become Madame le Brun. It will be a sort of masquerade. I have told Mimi that it is better not to travel as my father's daughter because of the recent scandal about my mother's death and the mood of the people. She is pleased. She thinks that will be safe. Why don't you say something? You just sit there looking disapproving. I think it's a wonderful plan."

"I only hope you don't do anything foolish."

"Why do you always think I am going to do something foolish?" she demanded.

"Because you often do," I retaliated.

But I could see that she was really set on the plan and there was no withholding her.

Perhaps, I thought, it is not such a bad idea, for if she saw for herself that her child was well cared for she might cease to fret about him. But how could we hope to find him?

She had decided that we should make our way to Petit Montlys but we should not of course call on Madame Grémond. Even she realized what folly that would be.

"What we must do," she said, "is to find the inn where we stayed when Charlot was taken from us and make inquiries in that area."

I said: "It's a wild goose chase."

"Wild geese are sometimes caught," she retorted. "And I'm going to find Charlot."

We set out on our journey and in three days we covered a good few miles and spent the nights at inns, which Bessell had a gift for finding.

Madame le Brun, her cousin, and her man and maid servant clearly had enough money to pay for what they wanted and for that reason they were very welcome.

It was unfortunate that one of our horses should cast a shoe and we must go to the nearest blacksmith and that this should happen to be not much more than a mile away from the town of Petit Montlys.

We left the carriage at the blacksmith's and went into the village, which I remembered from my stay at Petit Montlys. While we waited we decided to take some refreshment at an inn we discovered, and this we did.

The landlord was rather garrulous. News travels fast in such places and he had already heard that we had come in a carriage and the reason for our delay.

"It gives me a chance to serve you some of my wife's bread straight from the oven with good cheese and our own butter—would you like some hot coffee with it? I can serve *le Punch* here. *Mercier* . . . as good English a drink as sold in Paris."

Margot, Mimi, and I took the coffee and hot rolls. Bessell tried the *mercier* and found it good.

"How is life in Paris?" asked the landlord.

"Very gay, very lively," Bessell told him.

"Ah, it is long since I have been. Mademoiselle, I fancy I have seen you before." He was looking straight at me. "You are English, are you not?"

"Yes."

"Staying with Madame Grémond with your cousin who had suffered a great bereavement, were you?"

I looked at Margot, who burst out: "Yes, that's so. I had suffered a bereavement. I lost my poor husband."

"Madame, I trust you are happier now."

"One grows away from sorrow," said Margot.

I could see that Bessell and Mimi were a little bewildered and I said: "We should not stay too long. We have to get on and the blacksmith should have done his job by now."

We came out into the sunshine. Margot was laughing as though what had happened was something of a joke. I felt less happy.

As we walked towards the blacksmith's shop, a young woman came running towards us.

"It is!" she cried. "Why, it is. It's Madame le Brun and Mademoiselle Maddox."

There was no denying who we were, for the woman who faced us was Jeanne.

"It is good to see you, Madame, Mademoiselle," she said. "We often talk of you. How is the little one?"

"He is well," said Margot quietly.

"Such a bonny baby! Madame Legère said she had never seen a bonnier."

How stupid we were to have come! I might have known that we should run into danger. But what would have been the use of pointing that out to Margot!

"With his nurse, I'll warrant," went on Jeanne. "I heard there was a fine carriage at the blacksmith's. Ladies from Paris, they thought. I never dreamed who it would be."

I laid a hand on Margot's arm. "We must be on our way," I said.

"You are coming to see Madame Grémond?"

"No, I'm afraid not," I replied quickly. "Do give her our best wishes and tell her that this time we are in too much of a hurry. We lost our way and that is why we have arrived here. Then, unfortunately, the horse cast a shoe."

"Where are you making for?" asked Jeanne.

"For Parrefours," I said, inventing a name.

"I've never heard of that. What is the nearest big town?"

"That is what we have to find out," I replied. "We really must get to the carriage. Good day."

"It was a pleasure seeing you," said Jeanne, her little monkey's eyes taking in everything, the livery of Bessell, the neat lady's maid cloak of Mimi. I was glad that the times made it necessary for us to dress simply so that Margot's garments did not proclaim her rank too clearly.

We were subdued as we got into the carriage, which was ready for us. I noticed the speculation in Mimi's eyes, but like the good lady's maid that she was, she made no mention of what had passed. I expected that she and Bessell would discuss it later.

Margot refused to be depressed by the encounter. She would concoct some tale for Mimi later, though whether Mimi believed it would be another matter. What had happened appeared to have been very revealing. It lingered very unpleasantly in my mind.

We found our way to the inn where we had been with Charlot. The landlord remembered us. We must have been conspicuous—partly I supposed because of the foreigner, myself; and of course the fact that Margot had arrived with a baby and left without him did make the conclusion a little obvious.

Margot said she would ask a few discreet questions, but Margot and discretion did not really go together. It was soon clear that she was trying to trace the couple who had taken the baby, which clearly she had had to bear in secrecy—and the reason for that would leave little doubt. But she did glean the information that the couple had taken the road south, towards the little town of Bordereaux.

There were three inns at Bordereaux and we tried them all without success. We studied the signposts and found there were three routes which the couple could have taken.

"We must try them all," said Margot firmly.

How weary we were! What a hopeless chase it was! How could we hope to find the baby? But Margot was determined to.

"We cannot stay away much longer," I pointed out. "Already we have behaved in a very strange way. What do you think Mimi and Bessell think?"

"They are servants," retorted Margot haughtily. "They are not paid to think."

"Only when it is in your interests for them to do so, I suppose! They have some inkling of what all this is about. Do you think it wise, Margot?"

"I don't care if it is wise or not. I'm going to find my baby."

So we went on with our inquiries, which brought us no-where.

At length I said to Margot: "You said that this was to be

a visit to your old nurse Yvette. Don't you think it would be wise to call on her since that is supposed to be the object of the journey?"

She said she did not want to waste time, but finally I persuaded her that it would not be wise not to go. Again I seemed to hear the Comte's voice warning me that if one is going to weave a web of deceit it is better to work in a few strands of truth.

Yvette lived in a pretty little house with a walled garden surrounding it. The gates were wide enough for the carriage to pass through and Yvette herself came to the door.

She was a gentle-faced woman whom I liked immediately, but I was very much aware of her evident dismay when she saw who her visitors were.

Margot ran to her and threw herself into her arms.

"My little one," said Yvette fondly. "But this is a surprise!"

"We were in the neighborhood and could not fail to come and see you," said Margot.

"Oh . . . who were you visiting?" asked Yvette.

"Oh . . . well, we really came to see you. It seemed such a long time since I had. This is Mademoiselle Maddox, my friend . . . and cousin."

"Cousin?" said Yvette. "I did not know you had this cousin. Welcome, Mademoiselle. Please do come in. Oh, do I see Mimi? Welcome, Mimi."

But her uneasiness seemed to have increased.

"José will take care of Mimi and your coachman," she said.

José was her maid—a woman as old as herself. Mimi and Bessell went off with her and Margot and I followed Yvette into the house. It was neat, clean, and very comfortably furnished.

"You are happy here, Yvette?" asked Margot.

"Monsieur le Comte has always been good to those who worked well for him," she said. "When you no longer needed me and I left the *château,* he provided this house for me and an income so that I could afford José to look after me. We live very happily here."

She took us into a pleasant room. "And Mademoiselle Maddox is from England?"

I wondered how she knew for I had not mentioned it and my accent should not have betrayed me, as so far I had said very little. My name? Pronounced as Margot pronounced it, it did not sound really English.

"Sit down, my dear child, and you, Mademoiselle. You

will have some refreshment, and you must stay to dine with me. We have a good chicken and José is a wonderful cook."

She picked up a piece of needlework which was lying on a chair.

"Do you still do the same wonderful embroidery, Yvette?" Margot turned to me. "She used to put it on most of my dresses, didn't you, Yvette?"

"I was always fond of my needle. And I hear you are betrothed?"

"Oh, did you hear that then? Who told you?"

Yvette hesitated. Then she said: "The Comte always wants to know how I am faring and he has called on me now and then."

This was an aspect of his character I had not hitherto suspected. I was delighted to learn of it and the knowledge filled me with elation.

Margot said: "We shall be happy to share in the chicken, shall we not, Minelle?"

Still thinking of the Comte's concern for those whom he considered to be in his care, I nodded happily.

"I must show you Yvette's wonderful work," went on Margot. She was out of her armchair and had taken the piece of needlework on which Yvette had been working and brought it over to me. "See! This light feathery stitch. What is this, Yvette?" She held it up. It was a baby's coat.

Yvette blushed and said: "I am working it for a friend."

Margot's face puckered as it always did when she was reminded of babies. I thought then: She will never get over this until she has another child.

She folded the little coat and laid it on a chair. "It's very pretty," she said.

"How is everything at the *château?*" asked Yvette.

"Much as ever. Oh no . . . We have had stones through the windows, haven't we, Minelle?"

Yvette shook her head sadly. "Sometimes I think the people are going mad. We hear little of it here, but there are tales from Paris." Then she talked of the old days and told little anecdotes about Margot's adventures as a child. It was clear that she had a great fondness for her.

"I heard of your mother's death," she said. "That was a great sadness. Poor lady! Nou Nou must be quite demented. For her there was none but the Comtesse. She had had her as a baby. I can understand that. We do not have babies of our own and our charges take that place in our hearts which we could give to our own. The bond is a strong one. Ah, I am a foolish old woman, but I have always loved little babies. Strange tricks of fate often give them to those who do not want them and withhold them from those who do. Poor, poor Nou Nou. I can imagine her grief."

"She is taking it very badly," said Margot. "What was that?"

We listened.

"I thought I heard a child, crying."

"No, no," said Yvette. "If you will excuse me, I will go to the kitchen to see how José is faring with the children. José and I do the cooking between us."

As she opened the door we heard the unmistakable cry of a child.

Margot was beside her.

"You have a baby here," she said.

Yvette flushed scarlet and stammered. "Well . . . for a while. I am looking after . . ."

Margot was up the stairs. In a few seconds she was standing at the top of them holding a baby in her arms. There was a smile of triumph on her face. I thought: God works in a mysterious way, for I knew before Yvette admitted it that we had found Charlot.

She brought him into the room, her face radiant. She sat down and held him in her lap. He was clucking and kicking and seemed clearly pleased with life in spite of the fact that a few moments before he had been crying.

"Oh, he is beautiful . . . beautiful," breathed Margot; and indeed he was. Plump, well-fed, happy, he was all that a baby should be.

Yvette looked at Margot and shook her head slowly. "You should not have come here, my dear," she said.

"Not to see my beautiful Charlot!" cried Margot. "Oh, I have missed my little pet. And to find him here! Yvette, you deceiver—but you have cared for him well."

"Of course, I have cared for him well. Do you think I wouldn't care well for any baby? And yours is especially dear to me. That is what the Comte said: 'I know you will give him that special care,' he said, 'because he is Marguerite's.' But oh, my dear, you should never have come here now that you are betrothed. You see, it was all for the best that he should come here. I don't know what the Comte will say."

"This is my affair," said Margot.

"Margot," I reminded her, "you must see that the best thing that could happen is for Charlot to remain here."

She would not speak. She could not think of anything but that she had Charlot in her arms. She would not let him go and when he slept and Yvette said he must go into his cot, Margot took him upstairs. I guessed that she wanted to be alone with him and I remained with Yvette.

Yvette said to me: "Mademoiselle, I know that you have looked after Marguerite. The Comte has told me everything. He has spoken very warmly of you. I don't know what he will say when he hears you have been here."

"Margot's feelings are very natural. He must understand that."

She nodded. "There is something else that worries me. Inquiries are being made . . . have been made."

"Inquiries? What sort of inquiries?"

"About the child. José hears a good deal that doesn't reach me. She goes into the town on market days. I chided her in the past for being such a gossip, but sometimes it can be useful. The fact that we have a child here cannot be kept a secret naturally and it is realized that I am looking after it for someone in a high place. The Comte's orders were that the child should have the best of everything, and although I was not poor before, I have become more affluent since the baby has been with me. These things are noticed. José tells me that a gentleman, who tried to disguise himself as a traveling salesman and failed because he was clearly an aristocrat, has been asking questions. He is obviously interested in the child and is trying to find out who he is."

"I wonder," I began and paused. Yvette was a woman whom I instinctively trusted. Moreover, she would have been in the Comte's employ for so many years and had been selected by him to look after the child. I went on: "Could it have been Robert de Grasseville . . . Margot's fiancé?"

"That was what occurred to me. It would not be difficult for someone who was ready to ferret to discover that I had been employed at the *château*. The Comte is a man of great distinction. He has visited me twice since the child was brought here. He is anxious for little Charles's welfare and he likes to assure himself that the boy is well. He comes simply dressed for him, Mademoiselle, but, as you know, it is impossible for such men to hide hundreds of years of breeding. Sometimes I tremble when I think what the future holds."

"I understand well. Thank you for telling me."

"There is something else, Mademoiselle. José hears these things. She came in one day and said that she had heard it said that the Comte was the father of the child."

"Oh no! Surely . . ."

She looked at me searchingly. "You were with Margot when the child was born. You have been at the *château*. You see . . ."

I was flushing, hot and indignant.

"You cannot mean that I . . ."

"These rumors get around. I don't know how this one started . . . But you see how it could be possible."

"Yes," I said, "it could be possible, I suppose. Would the Comte have sent his daughter to be with a woman who was to bear his illegitimate child?"

Yvette lifted her shoulders. "It is so much nonsense. But the baby is here. I was a nurse at the *château* and the Comte has called to ascertain all is well with the child. People add up these things and get the wrong answer."

My head was whirling. There seemed no end to the maze of intrigue which was closing around me.

"I think you should be warned, Mademoiselle. Take care of Margot. She is so impulsive and has always acted without thought. I should so much like to see her happily settled and it seems that here is a chance. The Grassevilles are a very good family . . . I mean, their reputation is high. They treat their people well and are generous to them. The match would be the making of Margot. But there is this matter of the child. How I wish little Charles had been Robert de Grasseville's son and born in wedlock."

"That would have been ideal, and we should not be here now if it were so."

"Mademoiselle, I see that you are a sensible young woman. The Comte has great faith in you. Take care of her. It may be that these inquiries did come from the Grassevilles and that if they know that the child is Margot's they will not want to go on with the marriage. I think you should be prepared for that."

"I believe it would be wise not to mention this to Margot now."

"I have been glad to the opportunity to talk to you alone."

I agreed that it had been beneficial. "We can only wait and see what happens," I said. "If it were Robert who was making inquiries, we shall soon know."

She nodded. "But you will be prepared, Mademoiselle, in case anything should go wrong."

I said I would.

Margot returned to us looking ecstatic.

"He is fast asleep. Oh, he is angelic."

I was apprehensive because I knew how miserable she was going to be when she was obliged to part with him.

We stayed the night at Yvette's house, for Margot said she must have a little time with her baby. She sent Mimi and Bessell to the inn, where they stayed the night, and I must say I was relieved that they were out of the house.

She and I lay awake for a long time talking, for we shared a room.

"What am I going to do?" she demanded.

"The wise thing, I hope," I replied.

"I know what you're going to say. Leave Charlot here."

"He could not be better looked after."

"If I had to engage a nurse I would take Yvette before anyone else."

"He has Yvette now and she has obviously cared well for him. Charlot lacks nothing."

"Except his mother."

"In the circumstances, he is best as he is."

"You, you are heartless, Minelle. Sometimes I could slap you for your cool, precise, and so logical manner. I hate it all the more because I know that most people would say you are right."

"Of course I'm right. You have found him. You have the great satisfaction of knowing that he is in the best possible hands. You can come and see him sometimes. What more could you ask?"

"That I could have him with me all the time."

"Then you should have waited until he could be born in a respectable manner."

"You would not have made me *marry* James Wedder?"

"I think it would have been an unsuitable marriage, but having behaved as you did you should be prepared to take the consequences. Your father has done a good deal for you. Now you must do as he wishes."

"Is it fair to Robert?"

"Tell him then."

"You are bold, all of a sudden. He might discard me."

"If that is the case, perhaps it would be better to be discarded."

"How easy it is to solve other people's problems."

I had to agree with her on that.

So we talked through the night and in the morning she

realized that she must go away and she would go happier than she had come, for now she knew that when the longing for Charlot was intolerable she could come and be with him for a while.

The quest had ended more satisfactorily than I had thought possible. Margot had found Charlot and I had learned that there was another side to the Comte's nature than that which he had flaunted for all the world to see. He had cared about Yvette, had settled her comfortably, and he was determined to protect the child however much he deplored his birth. He was human after all, capable of soft feelings.

I was very happy that night.

2

When we returned to Paris there was an urgent message from the Comte. We were to return to the *château* without delay. As the message had been waiting for us for two days, we lost no time in making our preparations.

When we reached the *château* some two days later, the Comte was clearly not pleased. "I had expected you before," he said coldly. "Did you not get my message?"

I explained that we had taken a trip into the country and had returned to Paris only two days ago, when we had received the command which had been immediately obeyed.

"It was a foolish thing to do," he snapped. "Times being as they are, we do not take pleasure trips."

I wondered what he would say if he knew we had visited Yvette.

Later that day he summoned me to him and all his ill humor had disappeared.

"I missed you," he said simply, and I felt that irrepressible excitement rising in me which he alone could give me. "I was beset by my anxieties. You should know, Cousin, that we are heading fast towards some terrible climax. Only a miracle can save us now."

"Miracles sometimes happen," I said.

"A great deal of human ingenuity is needed to assist divine interference to produce a miracle, I have always thought, and alas, at this time when we need genius in our rulers we have only ineptitude."

"It can't be too late."

"That is our only chance. Don't tell me that we have brought this on ourselves, because I know it. None could know it better. As a class, we have been both selfish and obtuse. In the last reign the King and his mistress said that after them would come the deluge. I can hear it thundering very close now. I fancy that—without the miracle—that deluge will soon envelop us."

"But as this is known, surely it is a warning. Can't it be averted?"

"The King is calling together the States General. He is asking the two wealthiest orders in the land—that is, the clergy and the nobility—to make sacrifices to save the country. It is an explosive situation. I must go to Paris . . . I shall be leaving tomorrow. I don't know how long I shall be there, or how long before I see you again. Minelle, I want you to stay here until I send for you. Take care of yourself. Promise me."

"I will," I said.

"And Marguerite too. Take care of her. Don't do anything foolish like going off to look for Marguerite's child."

I caught my breath. "You knew!"

"My dear Cousin, I have people watching for me. I must know what happens about me and that includes my own household. I know you well. You believe with me that it would have been better for Marguerite not to know where the child was. On the other hand you respect her maternal feelings. I know that you found Yvette. Very well. Marguerite knows. She will visit him from time to time, and one day she will be betrayed and then she will have to answer to her husband. When she is married, that is their affair . . . her husband's and hers. While she is unmarried and my daughter, it is mine."

"It seems to me you are omniscient," I said.

"It is well for you to see me as such." He smiled, and when that smile was tender it transformed his face and moved me deeply. "I have to talk to you seriously now, as it may be some time before we see each other again. I am going to Paris for the meeting of the States General. We must look at this clearly. At any time . . . the people could rise. We might subdue them . . . I do not know. But we are living on a razor's edge, Minelle. That is why I am speaking to you now. You must know the depth of my feelings for you."

"No," I replied, "that is exactly what I do not know. I know that you have been attracted by me, which has surprised me. I know that you brought me here for that reason. I know that you have been similarly attracted to many women. It is precisely the depth of your feelings that I do not know."

"And you attach great importance to that?"

"It is surely of the greatest importance."

"I could not talk to you of this while my wife was alive."

I felt sick with fear. Doubts and suspicions crowded into my mind. I tried to fight off this overwhelming fascination. I was sure that my mother was warning me.

"It is such a short time since she died," I heard myself say. "Perhaps you should wait . . ."

"Wait? Wait for what? Until I am dead? By God, Minelle, do you realize that I might never see you again? You are aware of the mood of the people. You have seen the stones thrown through our windows. Do you realize that if this had happened fifty years ago the culprit would have been discovered, flogged, and sent to prison, where he would have remained for years."

"It is not surprising that the people want change."

"Of course it is not surprising. There should have been justice . . . compassion . . . unselfishness . . . care for the poor. We know that now. But they are not clamoring for those things only. They want revenge. If they succeed, there will not be justice. It will simply be a turning of the tables. They will murder us and demand retribution. But you know all this. The country's affairs weary us. They are dreary, depressing, hopeless, and tragic. Minelle, I want to talk of ourselves . . . you and me. Whatever happens, know this. My feelings go deep. At first I thought it was a lighthearted desire . . . such as I have felt throughout my life for many. While you were in Paris, I feared for you. I knew that if I lost you I should never know a moment's happiness again. I am going to ask you to marry me."

"You must realize that is not possible."

"Why not? Are we not both free now?"

"You have been free such a short time. And the circumstances of your wife's death . . ."

"Do you believe what they are saying of me? Dearest Minelle, any black deed they can pin on us, they do, and make a great noise about it. They accuse me of murdering my wife."

I looked at him pleadingly.

"You too?" he went on. "You believe I killed her! You think I slipped up to her bedroom, that I took Nou Nou's concoctions and filled her glass. Is that what you believe?"

I could not speak. It was almost as though my mother were beside me. There, she was saying, as I who had known her so well knew how she would reason, if you believe he could be a murderer, how can you be in love with him?

But she would never have understood this wild emotion. One did not have to have an ideal to love. One could love no matter what the loved one had done, and whatever he did in the future one would go on loving. Perhaps my kind of love was different from that which my mother had known with my father. He had been an honest, upright man, a brave sea captain who cared only for his family and that he should conduct his life honorably. All men were not like that.

The Comte was watching me quizzically.

"So you do believe it," he said. "I know that I want to marry you, and I want it before it is too late. I am no longer very young. The world which I have always known is crumbling about me. I feel a need, an urgency . . ."

"You are telling me that you killed your wife," I said.

"No, I am not. But I will be honest and say that I wanted her out of the way. I despised her. At times I hated her, but never so much as when she stood between you and me. Vaguely before, I had hoped for remarriage that I might get a son. Now that you are here I want it for other reasons too. I have dreamed often of a peaceful existence here in the *château* . . . our children growing up around us . . . the pleasant life going on and on. I knew that with you it would have to be marriage. Oddly enough, it was what I wanted. Then she died. She took an overdose of that sleeping draught because she knew she was suffering from the disease which killed her mother. It was lingering and painful. Do you believe me now?"

I could not meet his eyes, because I knew he would read my doubts there and that I might see the lies in his. I thought of his riding through the village and a small lively boy playing in his path . . . and the Comte, passing on, leaving nothing but a mangled body. That boy died to suit the Comte's whim. It was true he had taken the boy's brother and tried to recompense his family . . . but what recompense was there for death?

I said slowly: "I understand you well. Your way of life has been that those who are not of your class are of a lesser breed. When I consider that, I feel that change is due."

"You are right. But do not believe all that you hear of me. Rumor attaches to those who arouse the envy of others. You yourself are not immune."

"Who should envy me?"

"Many people. There are some who know of my feelings for you. Strange is it not, they envy you for that. There are whispers about me and they include you."

"I am more convinced than ever that I should return to England."

"What! Run away! Leave the sinking ship?"

"It is not really my ship."

"Let me tell you what they are saying. It is known in some places that there has been a child. I have heard the rumor that it is mine and that you are its mother."

I flushed scarlet and he went on almost mockingly: "There, you see it is not wise to believe all the rumors you hear."

"But such a wicked story . . ."

"Most rumor is wicked. Rumormongers take an element of truth and build round it and because they have that foundation of fact the rumor remains firm. But wise people never believe all they hear. I waste my time. What does it matter what they say? I have to go to Paris. I have to leave you here. Minelle, take care of yourself. Do not act rashly. Be ready to do whatever I say you must. You know it will be for your good."

"Thank you," I said.

Then he drew me to him and kissed me as I had never been kissed before and I wanted to stay in his arms for ever.

"Oh Minelle," he said, "why do you deny your heart?" Then he released me. "Perhaps I would not have it otherwise," he went on. "For then it would not be you. Moreover it is a challenge you know. One day you will cast aside all wisdom and come to me because nothing . . . simply nothing will be strong enough to withstand it. That's what I want. Whatever I am, whatever my sins of the past, you will not care. You will love me . . . *me* . . . not for my virtues, which are nonexistent—but for myself alone. I must leave you. I have much to do, for I must go tomorrow. I shall be gone at dawn before you rise . . . but one day, Minelle . . . one day . . ."

Then he kissed me again, holding me as though he would never let me go. I knew he was right. I was fast reaching that stage when whatever he had done, whatever he was guilty of, would seem insignificant beside my great need of him.

I turned and left him hastily, afraid of those emotions which such a short time ago I should have believed I could never experience.

I spent a sleepless night and at dawn I heard the sounds of his departure and was at my window to see him as he rode away. He turned and saw me there. He lifted his hand in acknowledgment.

I was up early and fully dressed when the maid arrived with my *petit déjeuner*. She brought a letter with her.

"Monsieur le Comte said it was to be given to you," she told me. There was a certain avid curiosity in her eyes.

It was written on his crested notepaper—the same as that which had been attached to the stone which had been thrown through the window.

My dearest,
I had to write a few lines after I left you. I want you to take special care from now on. Be patient. One day we shall be together. I have plans for us. I promise you, all will be well.

Charles-Auguste

I read and reread that letter. Charles-Auguste. Oddly enough, the name seemed strange to me. I thought of him always as the Comte . . . the Devil Comte . . the Devil on Horseback, the name I had given him long ago when I had first seen him. These fitted him. But not Charles-Auguste. I had of course learned a great deal about him since the days when I had thought of him as the Devil on Horseback. He was arrogant, of course. He had been brought up to believe that he and his kind were supreme. It had been so for centuries. They took what they wanted and if anyone stood in the way that person was brushed aside. That was firmly embedded in his nature. Would anything ever change that? Yet there was kindliness in him. Had he not taken Léon and looked after him? He had at least made some reparation for the harm he had done that family. He had cared about little Charlot and had made sure that he was well looked after and had even visited Yvette to assure himself of the child's welfare. And for me? Was that real tenderness I had seen? How deep did it really go? Did he really love me differently from the way in which he had loved others? What if I married him and failed to produce a son, should I one day be given a double dose of some fatal poison? Would they come one morning and find *me* dead?

So I did believe he had killed Ursule. It had been so opportune, hadn't it? She had died at the right moment. Why should she, who had been a peevish invalid all her life, suddenly decide that she was going to take it?

So I thought him capable of murder and still I wanted him. I wanted to make love with him. I might as well face the truth. It was what my mother had always said one should do.

I had always thought of love between men and women as that which my mother had had for my father. A woman should always look up to her husband, admire his good qualities. But if the man who excited one more than any other could possibly do, if the man in whose company one found the utmost pleasure was possibly a murderer, what then?

I should have loved to talk to her of these matters—but had she been alive I should never have been in this situation. She would never have approved of my coming to France in the first place and I knew that if she were here now she would say: "We must leave for England without delay."

While I was brooding thus, Margot came in with her *petit déjeuner*.

I hastily thrust the Comte's letter in a drawer and she was so absorbed in her own thoughts that she did not notice my doing so.

"I have to talk to you, Minelle," she said. "It's been worrying me all night. I've scarcely slept."

I wondered then if she was aware of her father's departure and if she had seen him turn and wave to me. But it was hardly likely. When Margot was wrapped up in her own affairs she never noticed what other people were doing.

"I was so shocked," she said. "I would never have believed it of them."

"Of whom are you talking?"

"Of Mimi and Bessell. Of course, the servants have changed such a lot. You must have noticed. They can be so insolent now. But Bessell . . . and Mimi most of all. Of course, it is Bessell's doing. She would never have done it without him."

"What has happened?" I asked, my heart sinking, for I had thought from the first that it had been unwise to share the secret with them.

"Mimi came to me last night and said that Bessell wanted

to speak to me. It didn't occur to me then what it meant. I thought it was something about the horses. When he came, he was different somehow . . . not a bit like the old Bessell. He stood there with a rather unpleasant look on his face and didn't offer any excuse for coming in like that. He said there was a cottage vacant on the estate and he wanted to have it so that he and Mimi could get married right away."

"Well, I suppose that's a natural request."

"I said I thought he should see the head groom and he said that the head groom was not sympathetic towards him, so he thought he would go over his head to me. He said that he'd heard through a friend of his who worked on the Grasseville estate that they were all looking forward to the wedding and they only hoped nothing happened to stop it."

I caught my breath. "Yes," I said, "what then?"

"He implied that he was very friendly with this man at Grasseville and others there too. They were sorry that the wedding was delayed through my mother's death and they were just hoping that nothing else should happen . . ."

"Oh Margot," I said, "I don't like it."

"Nor did I. It was the way he said it. He thought that after our trip he'd got to thinking that I might be kind enough to speak for him about the cottage because a word from me could settle the matter."

"It's blackmail," I cried. "He's hinting that if you don't get the cottage for him, he'll tell his friend at Grasseville about the trip . . . and this friend of his will see that the gossip reaches the family."

Margot nodded slowly.

"There is only one thing to do," I told her. "You should never submit to blackmail. You must see Robert before he has any chance of hearing of this from anyone else. You must tell him the truth."

"If he knew that I had already had a child he wouldn't want to marry me."

"He would if he loved you."

She shook her head. "He wouldn't. I know he wouldn't."

"Well, then, there would be no marriage."

"But I *want* to marry him!"

"You wanted to marry James Wedder once. You ran away to do just that."

"I was young and foolish. I did not know what I was doing then. It's different now. I'm grown up. I have a child. I have plans for the future . . . and they include Robert. I've fallen in love with Robert."

"All the more reason why you won't want to deceive him."

"You are very hard sometimes, Minelle."

"I'm trying to think what is best for you."

"I can't tell Robert. In any case I have already told Bessell he shall have the cottage. Oh, it's no use your looking shocked. I've said it is for Mimi, who has worked well for me. I shall marry Robert; they will stay here; and I shall never see them again."

"Blackmailers don't usually work that way, Margot. The first demand is rarely the last."

"When I am married to Robert I shall tell him, but not before. Oh, I do wish there was not this delay over the marriage."

I looked at her sadly. I felt that events were closing in around us too quickly and too menacingly.

We never rode out unless we were accompanied by a groom. That was the Comte's orders. But I was beginning to notice that curious looks came my way. At one time I had been aloof from the hatred of the crowds. I was a foreigner and although I was at the castle they had at first thought I was there in some menial capacity. Now they had changed. I wondered whether the rumor that I had had a child by the Comte had spread to them.

As we spent a great deal of time in the castle precincts, I saw more of Léon and Étienne than previously. They both had their duties about the estate and even they did not ride out singly.

It was interesting to talk to them and gather their attitudes towards the situation. Étienne was of the opinion that the old *régime* could not be shaken. He had the utmost contempt for what he called "the rabble." The army would be called out, he said, if they attempted to rise, and the army was firmly behind the King. Léon was of the opposite opinion. They would sit over the table long after a meal was finished, arguing together.

"At the moment the army is with the King," said Léon, "but it could turn and once it did that would be the end."

"Nonsense," said Étienne. "In the first place, the army would never be disloyal, and even if it were, power and money is with the nobility."

"You haven't moved with the times," retorted Léon. "I tell you that at the Palais Royale the Duc d'Orléans has been spreading sedition. He has been giving every encouragement to agitators. Everywhere you go they are screaming for

Liberty, Equality, and Fraternity. They are murmuring against the Queen and even against the King. Étienne, you shut your ears."

"And you are always mingling with the peasants, and attach too much importance to them."

"I believe I give them the importance they deserve."

So they argued and I listened and thus began to get a certain grasp of the situation. That each day it was becoming more dangerous I had no doubt and I wondered constantly what was happening to the Comte in Paris.

Étienne said to me one day: "My mother very much wishes that you would call on her. She has asked me to invite you. She has acquired a piece of porcelain . . . a rather fine vase which is said to be English. She would very much like to have your opinion of it."

"I am not an expert on porcelain, I'm afraid."

"Nevertheless, she would like you to see it. May I take you over there tomorrow?"

"Yes, that would be pleasant."

The next day, I was ready at the appointed time. It was about three-thirty when we set out.

Étienne said: "It is better to take the path I showed you. I believe I told you that the Comte had it made years ago. He could visit the house easily then. It has become a little overgrown. It's rarely used now."

He was right. It was overgrown. The branches met in several places over the path and the undergrowth was thick now that the summer was with us.

Gabrielle was waiting.

"It is so good of you to come," she said. "I am so anxious to show you my acquisition. But first we will take *le thé*. I know how you English love it."

She took me into the elegant room where I had sat with her on another occasion. While we drank tea she asked me if I had enjoyed my trip to Paris.

I told her that I had found it most interesting.

"And did you notice how we are imitating the English?"

"I noticed a great deal that was English in the shops and how so many proclaimed that they spoke the language."

"Ah yes, everyone is taking *le thé* now. It must be gratifying to you, Mademoiselle, to know that you are such a success in our country."

"I think it is just a fashion."

"We are a fickle people, you think?"

"Fashions come and go with us all, do they not?"

"It is like a man with his mistresses. They come and go. The wise ones realize that there is generally nothing permanent. The favorite of today can be the discarded of tomorrow. Is the tea to your taste?"

I assured her that it was.

"Do try one of these little cakes. Étienne loves them. He eats far too many. I am very lucky to have my son visit me so often. My brother comes too. We are a closely knit family. I am a lucky woman. Although I could not marry the Comte, at least I did not lose my son. When the relationship is not so close, men are inclined to bring their illegitimate children up in secrecy. I think that must be rather distressing for the poor mother, don't you?"

I felt my color rising. She had heard the rumor obviously and was she suggesting that I was the unmarried mother of the Comte's son?

"One can imagine without experiencing it that it must be upsetting for the mother," I said coolly. "But then I suppose it would be said that it is a contingency which, had she been wise, she would have considered before she put herself into that unfortunate position."

"All women are not as farseeing, are they?"

"Evidently not. I am looking forward to seeing your vase."

"Yes, and I to showing you."

She seemed to linger over tea and I noticed that on several occasions she glanced at the clock in the shape of the *château*, which on our previous meeting she had told me was a present from the Comte. I believed she did so now to remind me of his fondness for her.

She chattered a great deal about Paris, a city which she clearly loved, and as I had been enchanted by it and felt my visit there had been far too brief, I listened with interest.

She told me that I should have visited Les Halles to see the real Paris and she certainly had vivid powers of description. She made me see the great circular space with the six streets leading to it—and all the stalls piled with produce. Then she told me how secondhand clothes were sold from stalls on Mondays on the Place de Grève. It was called the Fair of the Holy Ghost, for what reason she had no idea.

"Oh, it is amusing to see the women turning over the garments and snatching them from one another," she said. "Skirts, bodices, petticoats, hats . . . they are all there in piles. The women try on the clothes in public, which causes a great deal of noise and amusement."

So she went on chattering of Paris and in due course she

sent for the vase. It was beautiful—a deep shade of blue etched with white figures. I told her I believed it was Wedgwood. She was very proud of it. She said it was a gift from someone who knew how she enjoyed things that were English and I wondered whether she was hinting that the donor was the Comte.

When I said I must go, she delayed me with more chatter and I came to the conclusion that she was not only a jealous woman but a garrulous one.

She became momentarily serious. "Ah," she said, "when one is young . . . inexperienced, one believes all one is told. One has to learn not to attach too much importance to the protestations of a lover. He has one object in mind generally. But I have my son, Mademoiselle, and he is a great comfort to me."

"I am sure he must be," I said.

She was smiling at me. "I know *you*, Mademoiselle, will understand."

Her look was almost conspiratorial. I had a very uneasy feeling that she knew of Charlot's existence, and was she really under the impression that he was my son?

"I feel I can really talk to you," she went on. "I know how perceptive you can be. There has always been an understanding between the Comte and myself. You do believe me?"

"Of course, since you tell me so and naturally in the circumstances there would be."

She added: "When our son was born, he was so proud. He has always been so fond of Étienne. The resemblance is strong, don't you agree? He wishes that he had defied opposition in the first place and married me. He always wanted a male heir. What a tragedy if the title and estates went to a distant cousin. He would never allow that. It was understood between us that if the opportunity arose we would marry."

"You mean," I said coldly, "if the Comtesse died."

She lowered her eyes and nodded. "If she did not, then Étienne would be legitimized. Of course, it would be easier if we married. And now she is dead and . . . it is only a matter of time."

"Is that so?"

"Indeed it is. Mademoiselle, we are women of the world. I know the Comte well. I know his partiality for attractive young women and in your way—a rather unusual way—you are attractive."

"Thank you," I said icily.

"It would not be wise to attach too much importance to

his attentions. Perhaps you think I am being presumptuous, but in view of my relationship with the Comte . . . my knowledge of him which goes back over many years, I feel I should warn you. You are a foreigner and may not realize how life is lived here. I believe you could put yourself in a very unpleasant situation. The death of the Comtesse . . . your presence at the *château* . . . Sometimes I wonder if the Comte arranged it."

"Arranged . . . what!"

She lifted her shoulders. "You will go back to England. It could then be said that you had had your hopes . . ."

I stood up. "Madame," I said, "if you are hinting something, will you please be more explicit."

"Yes. Let us speak plainly. In a year's time—in a respectable period—the Comte and I are to marry. Our son will be made legitimate. An unpleasant rumor about the Comtesse's death will persist."

"It has been settled that she took her life."

"Oh but, Mademoiselle, we have to contend with rumor. You will leave here. That is what the Comte intends. I can assure you that soon he will send for you. You will go with Marguerite . . . or perhaps back to England. People will say an English woman came here for a while. She hoped to marry the Comte and the Comtesse died suddenly . . . while the English Mademoiselle was in the house."

"Are you suggesting that I . . . It . . . it's utterly false."

"Of course. But after all, you did come here. You were friendly with the Comte. It was obvious that you had hopes. You see there is the foundation."

"Madame," I said, "I find this conversation nonsensical and offensive. You must excuse me as I wish to bring it to an immediate end."

"I am sorry. I thought you should know the truth."

"Good day, Madame."

"I understand your indignation. You have been treated unfairly. I'm afraid the Comte is ruthless. He uses people for his own ends."

I shook my head and turned away.

She said: "You must wait for Étienne. He will take you back."

"I am going now. Goodbye."

Shaken and trembling, I went out to the stables. I wanted to put as much distance as possible between that woman and myself. Her insinuations were not only offensive, they were frightening.

How dared she suggest that the Comte had brought me here as a scapegoat, that he had killed his wife in order that he might marry Gabrielle and had done it in such a way that the blame could be attached to me.

It was inconceivable. It was the raving of a jealous woman. How could I doubt his sincerity after those scenes between us? That he was a sinner he had never denied. He had much to answer for, but he could never have deceived me so utterly, treated me so callously, as he would have if what she was suggesting were true.

And yet . . . How suspicious I was! I had been thrust into a world which, brought up as I had been by a God-fearing mother with definite ideas of right and wrong, I could not understand.

How long had her affair with him continued? Was it still going on? Did she still attract him? Ethics, morals were considered so differently in the society from which I had come. Perhaps in high places in England there was a similarity. The King's eldest son, Prince George, was notorious for his amours and so were his brothers. There were scandals among the aristocracy. I was sure that those who lived and thought as my mother had, enjoyed happier lives. Then I began to wonder why simple people were thought to be less clever than the sophisticated ones, when the simple people were often happier, and as everyone sought happiness, the wise must be those who knew how to find it and keep it.

Tortured by my thoughts, I had come some way down the path and had reached the spot where the undergrowth grew thickest.

I did not know what it was that broke into my thoughts, but I was suddenly uneasily aware of being watched. It might have been the cracking of a twig; it might have been a certain premonition. I could not say, but in that moment all my senses were alerted. I had the feeling that I was being watched and trailed . . . and for an evil purpose.

"You must never go out alone." Those were the Comte's injunctions. I had disobeyed them. Well, not exactly. Étienne had accompanied me to his mother and I had expected him to come and take me back, which no doubt he would have done had not I, incensed by his mother's insinuations, left when I did.

Fifine, my mare, had been ambling quietly along, for it was difficult to gallop or canter down this path. It would be dangerous, for she needed to pick her way carefully lest she trip over a gnarled root or a tangle of bracken.

"What is it, Fifine?" I whispered.

She moved forward cautiously.

I looked about me. It seemed dark because of the trees. There was silence and then suddenly a sound . . . a stone being dislodged . . . a presence, close . . . very close.

I was fortunate on that day. I leaned forward to speak to Fifine, to urge her forward, and just as I did so a bullet whistled past that spot where a few seconds before my head had been.

I did not hesitate. I dug in my heels. I said: "Go, Fifine!" She did not need to be told. She was as aware of danger as I was.

Neither of us cared for the unevenness of the path. We had to get away from whoever was trying to kill me.

There could be no doubt that that was the intention, for another shot rang out. This was wider of the mark, but clearly I was the target.

It was with tremendous relief that I came into the stables.

One of the grooms came forward and took Fifine from me. I said nothing to him. I thought it wiser not to. My legs were trembling so much that I could scarcely walk.

I went to my room and threw myself on my bed.

I lay there staring up at the canopy. Someone had tried to kill me. Why? Someone had lain in wait in the undergrowth waiting for me to pass along. Who had known that I had visited Gabrielle? Étienne. Léon, I remembered had been there when Étienne had suggested the visit. I had mentioned it to Margot. Any of the servants might have known.

Had someone lain in wait for me? But for that sudden bending forward to speak to Fifine the chances were that I should now be lying dead in the lane.

Margot put her head round the door. "Minelle, where are you? I heard you come in." Then she saw me. "What's wrong? You look as though you've seen a ghost."

I said, my teeth still chattering: "Someone has just tried to kill me."

She sat on the bed and stared at me.

"What? When? Where?"

"In the path from Gabrielle LeGrand's house to the château. Halfway down the path I felt I was being stalked. It was lucky that I did. I leaned forward to urge Fifine on just as a bullet came whistling past my head."

"It must have been someone shooting birds."

"I think it was someone who wanted to kill me. There was a second shot and it was aimed at me."

She had turned pale.

"So," she said, "they are tired of throwing stones through ur windows. Now they have decided to kill us."

"I believe it was someone who wanted me out of the way."

"That's nonsense. Who would?"

"That," I said unsteadily, "is what I have to find out."

To face an attempt on one's life is an unnerving experience and the shock is greater than one at first realizes.

Margot had spread the news. She was concerned and horrified. We discussed it at table.

Étienne said, as Margot had: "They have substituted guns for stones."

Léon was unconvinced. "They have no weapons. If they rose, theirs would be scythes and pitchforks . . . not guns. Where would they get guns? They haven't enough money to buy bread . . . let alone guns."

"Even so," replied Étienne, "one of them could have got hold of a gun."

"But why Mademoiselle?"

"She is reckoned to be one of us now," answered Étienne.

They went on speculating and I could only believe that Étienne was right. One of them had procured a gun. Why should not one of the servants have stolen it from the gun room? After the behavior of Bessell and Mimi I knew that even those whom we had misguidedly trusted were no friends of ours.

A subtle change had crept over the household. They knew of the attempt on my life and sometimes it seemed as though they regarded it as very significant. It was as though it were a sign of the changing mood. The time when they threw stones was passing; they were ready to take stronger action. There was a brooding tension inside the house which I had not noticed before. That such existed outside, I had been well aware, but now it seemed to be creeping closer.

When I saw Mimi, she would cast down her eyes as though she were ashamed, as well she might be. It was different with Bessell. His manner had become almost truculent. There was the implication: You have to think twice about giving me orders now. I know too much.

I think that perhaps the most distressing of all was Nou Nou. For most of the time she was shut away in the rooms she had occupied with the Comtesse. She would not allow anything to be touched in those apartments and the Comte had said that she was to be humored. The servants said they could hear her talking to the Comtesse as though she were still there; and on those occasions when I saw her she would look at me with wide staring eyes, seeming to see nothing. The Comtesse's death had unbalanced her, it was said.

Léon and Étienne were greatly concerned about what had happened to me.

Étienne blamed himself. "I should have been there to bring you back to the *château*," he said. "I intended to come and half an hour later would have been there. I thought you would stay longer."

I did not wish to explain to him that I had found his mother's insinuations so offensive that I had no alternative but to leave.

I merely said: "The shots might have been fired from the bushes if you had been there."

"I suppose so," he admitted. "Of course, they weren't meant for you personally . . . just anyone who was not a peasant. But if I'd been there I should have been through those bushes and caught the villain. You must be careful. Never go out unattended again."

Léon was equally concerned. He waylaid me once when I was in the garden alone and said quietly: "I want to speak to you, Mademoiselle Minelle."

As we walked away from the *château* together, he went on: "I think you may still be in danger."

"You are thinking of the shots?"

He nodded.

"Étienne thinks they were not meant for me personally. I suppose we are all in danger."

"It's the gun that puzzles me," he said. "Had it been a stone . . . or even a knife thrown at you, I could have understood it more. I don't think it was merely a sign of the times."

"What *do* you think?"

"I think that you should lose no time in getting back to England. I wish I could take you." He looked at me quizzically. "Dear Minelle, you should not be involved in all this." He waved his arms. "It is too . . . unsavory."

"But who would want to kill me? No one here really knows me personally."

He shrugged his shoulders. "There has been a death at the *château* and there are unpleasant rumors."

"Don't you believe that the Comtesse took her own life?"

Again that lifting of the shoulders. "Her death was opportune. The Comte is now free. It is what he has wanted for a

204

long time. We do not know what happened. Perhaps we shall never know, but people talk. I can tell you that they will be talking of the death of the Comtesse in the years to come and there will always be speculation. That is how legend grows up. Do not let it concern you. Go away. Put it all behind you. You do not belong in this decaying society."

"I have promised to stay with Margot."

"She will have her own life. You will have yours. You are being caught up in matters which you do not really understand. You judge people by yourself, but let me tell you—all people are not so honest." He smiled at me frankly. "I would be your friend . . . your very good friend. I have a great admiration for you. I would come to England with you but I am chained here, and here I must remain. But please go. You are in danger here. That is a warning which should not be ignored. Good luck was with you once. It may not be again."

"Tell me what you know. Who would want to kill me?"

"All I know is that you must suspect everyone . . . *everyone,* until you have proved them to be innocent."

"You know something."

"I know this: You are a good and charming young lady whom I admire and wish to see in safety. While you are here you are in danger. Please go back to England. There is still time. Who knows, very soon it may be too late."

I turned to him and looked into his face. There was real concern in those vivid blue eyes and his smile was not jaunty as it usually was. I liked him very much. I wanted to tell him that I was sorry I had once thought I saw his face at the window when the stone had been thrown into the ballroom.

Then a terrible feeling of insecurity came to me. He had said: Trust no one. No one. Not Léon, Étienne, not even the Comte.

He looked at me rather wistfully and said softly: "Perhaps . . . when this is over . . . I will come to see you in England. Then we may talk of . . . many things."

Margot was greatly concerned.

"Just suppose those bullets had killed you. What should *I* have done?"

I couldn't help smiling. That was a typical Margot remark.

But she was anxious on my account as well as her own. I would often find her watching me intently.

"It's frightened you, Minelle," she said. "You look different."

205

"I'll get over it."

"I'll swear you didn't sleep well last night."

"I kept dozing, half-awake, half-dreaming I was back in the lane. Once I thought I saw a face in the bushes."

"Whose face?" she asked eagerly.

"Just a face . . ."

That was not quite true. It was a face I had seen before. The face which I saw on the night of the ball. Léon's face . . . and yet not Léon. It was as though a mischievous artist had sketched a few lines on Léon's face—distorting it with rage, envy, and a desire to harm. It was so unlike the Léon I had known that somehow I could not connect the two. Léon had always been kindly and during our conversation had been deeply concerned. I knew that he was tolerant—more so than Étienne. He saw the people had a case, but while he believed great concessions should be given to them, he did not believe in the destruction of a society. It seemed to me that Léon more than any of them understood what was needed and this was natural enough since he had an opportunity of seeing both sides of the case.

Margot talked a great deal about Charlot and her satisfaction that she had discovered him. She was in a rare euphoric mood. It was well, she said, that she had found out Bessell's true nature. She did not believe Mimi was to blame. She had been influenced by Bessell, but she would be glad to be rid of them both.

"How long is the period of mourning?" she asked.

"It's a year in England, I believe," I replied. "It's probably the same in France."

"A year . . . what a long time!"

"It seems unnecessary to set a time for mourning," I commented sadly. "When one has lost someone who is dear, the mourning goes on through one's life. It is not so intense as it was at first, of course, but I don't believe one ever forgets."

"You're thinking of your mother again. You were lucky to have such a mother, Minelle."

"But if she had not been as she was, if she had been less good and kind and understanding, I shouldn't be missing her so sorely now. Sometimes I think she is still advising me."

"Perhaps she is. Perhaps she told you to duck your head when you did so and saved your life."

"Who knows?"

Margot said: "Minelle, you look exhausted. That's not like you. You always have ten times more energy than the rest of us. You should go to bed and sleep and try not to see faces in the bushes."

I did feel tired, though I doubted whether I should sleep. But I wanted to be alone, so we said good night and she went to her room.

I lay in bed—very tired, yet sleepless. I could not stop myself going over every instant of that afternoon from the moment when I had said goodbye to Gabrielle to the time when I came riding into the castle stables. I felt again the first uneasy tremor when I had fancied I was being watched and the mounting terror when I realized that someone was trying to kill me.

I started up in alarm when I heard a sound at my door. It was a sign of my state that my heart began to hammer against my side as I stared in fearful anticipation at the door.

Margot came in. She was carrying a glass in her hand.

"For you, Minelle," she said, setting it down by the bed. "Nou Nou's special concoction, guaranteed to make you sleep. I got it from her."

I lowered my eyes. I thought of the Comte's going into Ursule's room, taking the bottle from Nou Nou's store. Was that what he had done? Had he given it to her before I saw him leaving by the terrace doors? But surely if he had, she would not have been asleep so quickly, for she was almost asleep when I entered. And Nou Nou could not have been far off. What had they said to each other during that last interview? Had she taken her own life, and should I ever know? Was it possible that he . . . I would not let myself think it. But what did I really know of him? That potent spell which he cast over me lulled my common sense to sleep and I could only make excuses for him.

Margot was looking at me inquiringly. "You're dreaming. Still seeing faces? Drink this up and you'll be all right by morning."

"I'll take it later," I said. "Stay and talk awhile."

"You need sleep," she said firmly and set the glass on the table by my bed. Then she sat down on the chair near my dressing table on which stood three candles, only two of which were alight.

"Only two," she said. "It's gloomy in here."

"One was blown out when you opened the door."

"As long as the three don't go out. That's a sign of death. One of the servants said that on the night my mother died three candles in their room went out . . . one after the other."

"You don't believe such superstition, Margot!"

"None of us believes them until we prove them to be true, do we?"

"Some people are very superstitious."

"It is usually those who have something to fear . . . people like sailors and miners. People who run certain hazards."

"We all run hazards."

"But not such obvious ones. Look, another candle has gone out."

"You blew it."

"I did not."

"Light it again."

"Oh no, that would be unlucky. We have to wait and see if the third goes out."

"There's a draft coming from somewhere."

"You always have to have a logical explanation for everything, don't you!"

"It's not a bad idea."

"And you don't believe in the candle legend?"

"Of course I don't."

There was silence for a few moments, then she said: "I have a feeling that something is going to happen soon. Do you think we can go and visit Charlot?"

"Of course we can't. You have seen what disaster our first visit brought."

"Disaster! When I found my baby! Oh, you're thinking of that horrid Bessell. Well, I've settled him. Mimi is quite ashamed of him. She can't do enough for me."

"I don't like it, Margot."

"If only there wasn't this waiting. It's so silly. I don't mourn my mother any more because my marriage has been postponed. These are not normal times, are they? That's why we have to live dangerously . . . because we never really know how much longer we've got to live. You poor Minelle. You look so tired. I'm going to say good night now. Take your potion and sleep well."

As she left, shutting the door with a bang, the third candle went out. I had laughed at the superstition, but I could not repress a shudder. For a moment I was in complete darkness, but as my eyes grew accustomed to the gloom, familiar objects began to take shape. I looked at the glass beside my bed. I picked it up but I did not put it to my lips.

The Comtesse had died from a draught. Someone had

tried to kill me. But it was Margot who had brought this and I knew she would never harm me.

I got out of bed and, taking the glass with me, went to the window. I threw out the contents. I would not want Margot to think I had been suspicious of a draught she had brought.

Now I was really wide awake. It was true I was very tired. My body needed rest but my mind was in no mood to grant it.

I lay down while thoughts chased themselves round and round in my head. I heard the tower clock strike twelve and one. Still I could not sleep.

Perhaps I should have taken the draught, but it was too late for that now.

I dozed but I did not really sleep. My senses were too alert to allow me to. Then suddenly I was wide awake. I heard footsteps in the corridor—footsteps which paused outside my door. Then my door was slowly opening.

At first I thought it was a ghost—so strange was the figure which came into my room. It was gray in the gloom—hair streaming about the shoulders. A woman.

She came and stood by the bed looking down at me. She took the glass and smelt it. Then she leaned forward and saw that I was watching her.

"Nou Nou," I cried. "What are you doing?"

She blinked and looked puzzled. She said: "What are *you* doing here?"

I rose from the bed and, taking my robe, wrapped it round me.

"Nou Nou," I said gently. "What's wrong? What do you want with me?"

My fingers were trembling as I lighted the three candles.

"She's gone," said Nou Nou. "She'll never come back. Sometimes I think I hear her. I follow her voice. It leads me to odd places . . . but she's never there."

Poor Nou Nou. The death of her beloved charge had indeed unbalanced her.

"You should go back to your bed," I said. "You should take one of your sleeping draughts."

"She died after taking one," she said.

"Because she took too much. You must not brood. She was ill, wasn't she? You know how ill."

"She didn't," cried Nou Nou shrilly. "She didn't know how ill she would become."

"Perhaps she did . . . and that was why . . ."

"He killed her. Right from the time the little girl was born he started to kill her. He wanted her out of the way and she knew it. She hated him . . . and he hated her. I hated him too. There was a lot of hatred in this household . . . and in time it killed her."

"Nou Nou, you can do no good by brooding on this. Perhaps it was best for her . . ."

"Best for her!" Her laughter was a shrill cackle. "Best for him." Then she turned her piercing gaze on me. "And best for you . . . so you think. But don't be too sure. He's the devil, he is. No good can come to you through him."

"You are talking without understanding, Nou Nou," I said. "Please go back to your room."

"You were awake when I came in here," she said suddenly, the wildness dropping from her and being replaced by a certain cunning shrewdness which was more terrifying than her hysteria.

I nodded.

"You ought to have been asleep."

"Then I shouldn't have been able to talk to you."

"I didn't come here to *talk* to you."

"Why did you come here then?"

She didn't answer. Then she said: "I'm looking for her. Where is she? They buried her in the vault, but I don't think she's there."

"She is at peace now, Nou Nou."

She was silent and I saw the tears slowly flowing down her cheeks.

"My little *mignonne,* my little bird."

"Don't fret any more. Try to be reconciled. She was ill. She would have suffered a great deal of pain in time."

"Who told you that?" she demanded, shrewd again.

"It was what I heard."

"His tales . . . his excuses."

"Nou Nou, please go to your bed."

"Three candles," she said, and turning blew them out, one after another. She turned to look at me before she blew out the last and I quailed before the venom in her face.

With that she went to the door holding her hand before her as a sleepwalker does.

The door shut. I was out of bed and saw to my relief that I could lock the door. I did this and immediately felt safe.

Then I lay in bed wondering why she had come to me. If I had taken her draught I should have been asleep. What would have happened then?

Sleep! How I longed for it! How I wanted to escape from

my tortuous thoughts that went round and round in my head reaching no conclusion.

My only inference was: There is danger close—and particularly close to me. From whom does it come? And why?

I lay waiting for the dawn, and only with the comfort of daylight could I rest.

3

Three days later the Comte sent for us. Margot and I were to leave for Paris without delay.

I was not sorry to go. The mounting tension in the *château* was becoming unbearable. I felt I was watched and would find myself looking furtively over my shoulder whenever I was alone. I noticed that the servants regarded me oddly. I felt very unsafe.

Therefore it was a great relief to receive the summons.

It was a hot June day when we set out. There was a stillness in the air which in itself seemed ominous. The weather was sultry and there was thunder about.

The city had lost none of its enchantment, though the heat was almost intolerable after the freshness of the country.

I immediately noticed that there were numerous soldiers in the streets—members of the Swiss and French Guards who formed the King's bodyguard. People stood about at street corners, but not in large numbers. They talked earnestly together. The cafés, from which came the delicious smell of roasting coffee, were crowded. People overflowed into the streets where tables under flowered sunshades were placed for their convenience. They chattered endlessly and excitedly.

In the Faubourg Saint Honoré the Comte was waiting for us with some impatience.

He took my hands and held them firmly.

"I heard what happened," he said. "It was horrifying. I sent for you immediately. You must not return to the *château* until I do."

He seemed then to be aware of Margot.

"I have news for you," he said. "You are to be married next week."

We were both too astounded to speak.

"In view of the state of"—the Comte waved his hands expressively—"everything, the Grassevilles and I have come to the conclusion that the marriage should not be delayed. It will necessarily be a quiet wedding. A priest will officiate here. Then you will go to Grasseville and Minelle will go with you . . . temporarily . . . until something can be arranged."

Margot was delightedly astonished and when we went to our rooms to wash off the stains of the journey she came to me at once.

"At last!" she cried. "There was no point in waiting, was there? It was all so silly. Now we shall leave here. My father will no longer be able to command me."

"Perhaps your husband will do that."

She laughed slyly. "Robert! Never. I think I shall get on very well with Robert. I have plans."

I was a little uneasy. Margot's plans were usually wild and dangerous.

The Comte asked me to go to him and I found him in the library.

He said: "When I heard what had happened I was overcome with anxiety. I had to find some way of bringing you here."

"So you arranged your daughter's marriage?"

"It seemed as good an answer as any."

"You use drastic measures to get your way."

"Oh, come. It is time Margot was married. She is the sort who needs a husband. The Grassevilles are a family who have always been popular with the people . . . though how long that popularity will last, who can say? Henri de Grasseville was a father to his fiefs and for that reason it seems difficult to imagine their turning against him. They might, though, in their present mood. Fidelity is not a noticeable quality among people now. They bear grudges more readily than gratitude. But I should feel happier if you were there."

"It is good of you to be so concerned."

"As usual, I think of my own good," he said soberly. "Tell me exactly what happened in the lane."

I told him and he said: "It was a peasant taking a pot shot at someone from the castle and it happened to be you. It's a step in a new direction for them. And where did they get hold of the gun? That's a mystery. We are making sure that no firearms get into the hands of the rabble. That would be fatal."

"Is the situation deteriorating?" I asked.

"It is always deteriorating. Each day we step a little nearer to disaster." He looked at me earnestly. "I think of you all the time," he said. "I dream of the day when we shall be together. Nothing . . . nothing must stand in the way of that."

"There is so much standing in the way," I said.

"Tell me what."

"I don't really know you," I answered. "Sometimes you seem like a stranger to me. Sometimes you amaze me and yet at others I know exactly how you will act."

"That will make life exciting for you. A voyage of discovery. Now listen to my plans. Marguerite will marry and you will go with her. I shall visit you at Grasseville and in due course you shall be my wife."

I did not answer. I kept thinking of Nou Nou at my bedside, of Gabrielle LeGrand's insinuations. He had murdered Ursule, she had hinted, because he was tired of waiting to marry her, Gabrielle. He wanted a legitimate son. Gabrielle had already given him that son; all that was needed was his legitimization, which would be easy if they married. His idea, according to her, was to lead me along so that I might slip into the rôle of scapegoat. She would probably suggest now that he had arranged that I should be removed from the scene. What if he *had* taken that shot at me . . . or arranged that it should be fired?

How could I believe that? It was absurd. Yet some instinct within me was warning me.

He put his arms about me and said my name with the utmost tenderness. I did not resist. I wanted to stay there in his arms and turn my face away from reason.

It was as though Margot hugged some secret to herself which was too precious to tell even to me.

I was amazed how easily she could throw off her troubles and behave as though they had never existed. I was glad she had the good sense not to bring Mimi with her. Mimi might well have refused to come, as she was now soon to be married, and with Bessell to command her she could well have been truculent. The new maid Louise was middle-aged and glad to step into Mimi's shoes. At the same time, Margot had dismissed the conduct of Bessell and Mimi as though it were of no consequence. I wished that I could think so.

We had a busy week, mostly shopping, and once more I was caught up in the excitement of the city. I would watch from my window at two o'clock each day when the wealthy set out in their carriages to keep their dinner appointments. It was indeed a sight, for the ladies' headdresses were becoming so outrageous as to be almost comical. Some would mince along balancing these confections on their heads which would represent anything from a bird of paradise to a ship in full sail. These were the people who aped the nobility—which was a dangerous thing to do these days. In the Comte's household and others of its kind dinner was at six, which gave time to go to the playhouse or the opera by nine o'clock, the hour when the city took on a different character.

We visited a private playhouse on one occasion to see a very special performance of Beaumarchais' *Le Mariage de Figaro*, a play which the Comte said should never have been shown at this time as it was full of sly references to the decadent society which were a delight to those who wished to destroy it.

He was thoughtful and moody as we returned to the *hôtel*.

He had a great deal on his mind and was often away on court matters. It touched me that, in view of all that was happening, he found time to plan for my safety, although, of course, I did not believe his daughter's marriage had been arranged for that reason.

Robert de Grasseville with his parents and a few of their servants arrived in Paris.

In her excitement Margot looked so beautiful that I could almost believe she really was in love. Even though her emotions might be superficial they were all important to her while she felt them.

The marriage took place in the chapel, which was situated at the top of the house. One left behind the luxury of the apartments, ascended a spiral staircase, and stepped into an entirely different atmosphere.

It was cold there. The floor was of flagged stone and there were six pews placed before an altar on which was a beautifully embroidered cloth and, above it, a statue of the Madonna studded with glittering stones.

The ceremony was soon over and Margot and Robert came out of the chapel together looking radiant.

Immediately afterwards we sat at table. The Comte at the head, his new son-in-law on his right hand and Margot on his left. I sat next to Robert's father, Henri de Grasseville.

It was clear that the two families were delighted with the match. Henri de Grasseville whispered to me that the young pair were undoubtedly in love and how gratifying it was to him that this should be so. "Frequently in families like ours marriages have to be arranged," he said. "It so often happens that the partners are unsuitable. Of course, they often grow together. They are so young when they marry they have much to learn and they learn from each other. This is happy from the start."

I agreed with him that the young couple were happy, but I could not help wondering what he would have felt if he had known of Margot's experience, and I fervently hoped that all would go well, but I did feel uneasy remembering the demands of those two servants whom she had trusted.

"It will be well to leave Paris soon," went on Henri de Grasseville. "We are peaceful at Grasseville. There has been no sign of trouble."

I warmed to him. There could not have been a man less like the Comte. There was something innocent about him. He looked as though he believed the best of everyone. I glanced along the table at the Comte's rather saturnine face. He looked like a man who had gone through life trying all manner of adventures and had come through with his idealism tarnished if not broken. I felt a smile curve my lips and at that moment he looked at me, caught me watching him, and there was a look of quizzical inquiry in his eyes.

When the meal was over, we all gathered in the *salon* and the Comte said he thought it would be wise to lose no time in leaving for Grasseville.

"One can never be sure from one moment to another when the trouble will begin," he said. "It only needs some small pretext to set it off."

"Oh Charles-Auguste," laughed Henri de Grasseville, "surely you exaggerate."

The Comte lifted his shoulders. He was determined to have his way.

He came to me and whispered: "I must see you alone before you leave. Go to the library. I will join you there."

Henri de Grasseville was consulting the clock which hung on the wall. "If we are to go today," he said, "we should leave in an hour. Will that suit everyone?"

"It will," said the Comte, speaking for us all.

I went at once to the library. In a short time he was with me.

"My dearest Minelle," he said, "you wonder why I send you away so soon."

"I understand that we must go."

"Poor Henri! He has little notion of the situation. He remains in the country and thinks that because the lambs still bleat and the cows moo as they ever did, nothing is changed. I hope to God he can go on thinking it."

"His is a comfortable philosophy."

"I see you are in the mood for discussion and you are going to say he is a happy man. He goes on believing that everything is good, God watches over us, and the people are kindly innocents. One day he will have a rough awakening. But, you will say, at least he was happy before it came. I should like to take you up on that, but there is little time left to us. Minelle, you have never said you loved me."

"I do not speak lightly of such emotions as you do, having made love to so many women. I dare say you have told people many times that you loved them when all you felt was a passing fancy."

"So when you do tell me, I may be completely and utterly sure?"

I nodded.

He drew me to him and said: "Oh my God, Minelle, how I long for that day. When . . . Minelle?"

"There is so much I must understand."

"So you don't really love me as I am."

"I have to know what you are before I can love you."

"Tell me this. You like my company. I know that. You do not find me repulsive. You like me near you. You sparkle when you look at me, Minelle. You always did. That was why I knew."

"I have lived such a different life from yours. I have to adjust myself to new standards and I don't know whether I can."

"Minelle, can you hear the warning bells? The tocsins are sounding. All through my life I have heard what happened in this city on the eve of St. Bartholomew's Day. That was two hundred years ago . . . two hundred and seventeen to be exact. There were some who felt that coming. It was in the air for weeks before it broke into fearful slaughter. That is how it is now . . . but before what is to come, the Bartholomew will be considered insignificant. Those bells are saying: Live fully now . . . for tomorrow you may not be able to live at all. Why do you deny me . . . when any night might be my last?"

I was afraid. I found myself clinging to him. Then I thought: This is a trick to make me yield. And that showed me clearly the nature of my feelings for him.

216

I did love him, I supposed, if loving meant wanting to be with someone, to talk to him, to feel his arms about me, to learn how to love and be everything to him. Yes, that was true. But I could not trust him. My mind, in its moments of clarity, told me that Ursule had died too fortuitously. I knew that he was adept at making love and I was a novice. I had everything to learn and surely he, in his vast experience, had learned everything . . . including how to deceive.

I must not be foolish. So far I could congratulate myself on having kept him at arm's length in spite of those occasions when my senses had cried out to me to release them. My stern upbringing, the memory of my beloved mother, had always stood between me and folly.

"So," he was saying tenderly, "you do care for me?"

I drew myself from him. I did not look at him for fear of losing my grip on my good sense.

"I have grown fond of your family," I said. "I have been with you for some time and Margot was always my friend. I do see, though, that we have lived different lives and have responded to different ethics. I have a great deal to consider."

He looked at me through half-closed eyes.

"Yes, it is true that you have been brought up in a different society, but you are an adventurer, Minelle. You do not wish to shut yourself in your little world and never explore others. Your nature was clear when you came peeping into the rooms at Derringham Manor. Now that was not what a well-brought-up little girl should do."

"I have grown up a good deal since then."

"Ah yes. You have changed. You see the world through different eyes. You have learned that men and women are not neatly divided into the good and the bad. Is that true, Minelle?"

"Of course it's true. No one is all good, no one all bad."

"Even I?"

"Even you." I was thinking of how he had looked after Yvette and made sure that Charlot was well cared for.

"Well then?"

"I am unsure," I said.

"*Still* unsure?"

"I need time."

"Time is just what we lack. Anything in the world I will give you but that."

"That is all I want. There is so much I have to understand."

"You are thinking of Ursule."

"If one considers marrying a man who has already had a wife it is difficult not to think of her."

"You need have no jealousy regarding her."

"It was not jealousy I was thinking of."

"Her unfortunate end? Good God, I believe you think I killed her. Do you think me capable of that?"

I looked at him steadily and answered: "Yes."

He stared at me for a moment or two and then burst into laughter. "And even so . . . you would consider marrying me?"

I hesitated and he went on: "But of course you are considering. Why else would you ask for time? Oh Minelle, so clever and so obtuse. But you have to persuade the prim side of your nature that it would somehow be *comme il faut* to marry a murderer! Oh Minelle, my love, my darling, what fun we are going to have with that prim side of yours."

Then he held me against him and I was laughing with him—I could not help it. I returned his kisses in an inexperienced way which I knew delighted him.

The clock on the bureau pinged impatiently as though to warn us of the all important passage of time.

He was aware of it. He took my hands. "At least," he said, "I know. It gives me hope. I have to be in Paris for a while. You understand this. There are dangerous men rising against the King, urging the people to destroy the Monarchy and all it stands for. The most dangerous of them all is the Duc d'Orléans who preaches sedition night after night in the Palais Royale. I must stay here and knowing what I know I can have no peace until you are safe in the country . . . or comparatively safe. Go with Margot. Look after her. She is a wayward child . . . yes, little more than a child. She does not seem to grow up. She has her secret . . ." He shrugged his shoulders. "That may bring drama into her life. Who knows? She will need you to care for her, Minelle. She will need your good sound analytical sense. Take care of her and yourself. Protect her from her own folly . . . and one day I will protect you from yours. I will see that you learn the wisdom of accepting life . . . taking what it offers . . . living and never turning away from the best."

Then he kissed me lingeringly, tenderly; and I left him.

AT THE CHÂTEAU
GRASSEVILLE

~~~~~~~~~~~~~~~~~~~~~~~~~~~~~~~~~~~~~

1

Grasseville was a beautiful *château* north of Paris, dominating a quiet market town. It was true that a peaceful atmosphere did emanate from the place and one was immediately aware of it. It was as though the envy, malice, and hatred which prevailed elsewhere had passed over it.

Here the men touched their caps and the women curtsied as we rode by. I noticed that Henri and Robert de Grasseville called greetings to many of them and asked after members of their families. I could understand why the impending storm seemed far away.

It was true that Henri de Grasseville had agreed that the marriage should take place, although convention demanded a longer period of mourning for the bride, but I supposed it had been the Comte who had insisted and Henri was the kind of man who would be ready to give way to the wishes of others.

Margot was delighted with her marriage. She told me that she was deeply in love with Robert and as they seemed as though they hated to be parted, it was clear that they were lovers. She did, however, find time to come to my room sometimes. Our talks had become so much a part of our lives that I really believed she would have missed them if they ever ceased.

She came in one day and stretched herself in the armchair near the mirror, where she could keep glancing at herself with satisfaction. She certainly looked very pretty.

"It's perfect," she announced. "Robert never dreamed that there was anyone like me. I think I was meant for marriage, Minelle."

"I am sure you were."

"While you were meant to teach. That's your *métier* in life."

"Oh thank you. How very exciting for me!"

She laughed. "Robert is amazed by me. He expected me to shrink and protest and be overcome by modesty."

"Which of course you were not."

"I certainly was not."

"Margot, he didn't guess . . ."

She shook her head. "He is the sweetest innocent ever born. It wouldn't occur to him, would it? No one would believe we had that fantastic adventure." Her face crumpled suddenly. "Of course, I still think of Charlot."

"The best thing is for you to console yourself that he is in Yvette's hands and he could not be in better."

"I know. But he is mine."

She sighed and her exultation was a little dimmed. But she was so delighted with her marriage that I was sure her longing for Charlot had abated a little.

There were no restrictions on riding alone here. No one ever thought of danger. Margot and I went into the little market town to make purchases and we were greeted with the utmost respect in every shop. They all knew, of course, that we came from the *château* and that Margot was the future Comtesse.

It was like an oasis in the midst of the desert. When we were tired we would sit down outside a *pâtisserie* under gaily colored umbrellas and drink coffee with little creamy *gâteaux*, the most delicious I had ever tasted. *Le thé* had not yet come to Grasseville and there was no English spoken—which I supposed was another sign of a lack of change.

The myth of my being the cousin was upheld and I was soon known in the town as Mademoiselle La Cousine Anglaise. My command of the language was marveled at and I would sit and chat even more readily than Margot did, for she was too immersed in her own affairs to feel much interest for those of others.

How I loved the smell of baking bread and hot coffee which filled the streets in early morning! I liked to watch the baker draw the loaves out of the oven with his long tong-like instrument. I loved the market days when the produce was brought on handcarts or carts drawn by aged donkeys—fruit, vegetables, eggs, and squawking chickens. I loved to buy from the stalls—a piece of ribbon, some sweetmeat confection tastefully wrapped and tied with ribbon. I could never resist buying, and how they loved to sell! I was sure that Margot and I and the servants we had brought with us were good business and welcomed for that.

The shops were different from those in the big towns. Purchasing was a lengthy matter and one was expected to consider a good deal before buying even the smallest item.

A hasty transaction would be frowned on and a lot of pleasure denied both vendor and purchaser by such a process.

One of my favorite shops was that of the grocer-druggist who sold so many aromatic goods. There were cinnamon, oil, paint, brandy, herbs of all kinds (hung drying from the beams of the ceiling), preserves, ground pepper, and poisons such as arsenic and aqua fortis; and there was of course the omnipresent garlic. There were tall stools in his shop where one could sit and talk to the owner, who often acted as a doctor and told people what to take for this and that ailment.

What a delightful adventure it seemed during those warm sunny days to go into the town and exchange pleasantries with the people one met—not a cloud in that blue sky, no trace of what was below the horizon. Alas, the horizon was not very far away and inevitably creeping nearer.

Only rarely did a carriage come rattling through the town. They were days to remember. I was sitting in the square one day when one came though. The visitors left their carriage and came into the inn for refreshment. I watched them—nobility by their dress and manners, a little watchful, unsure of their reception. They went into the inn—two men and a woman—and two grooms followed them, keeping close in case there was trouble. The inn sign creaked *Le Roi Soleil*. And there was Louis in all his splendor looking haughtily down on the street.

I sat waiting until they emerged—refreshed with wine and those creamy confections of which I was becoming fond.

They were talking together. Scraps of their conversation came to me.

"What a lovely spot! Like old times . . ."

Their carriage drove away. The dust settled after them. Yes, they had discovered our oasis.

I went thoughtfully back to the castle and I had not been in very long when Margot came to me. Some plan was afoot, I knew by the way in which she scintillated with excitement.

"Something wonderful is going to happen," she announced.

For a moment I thought she was going to tell me she was to have a child. Then I realized it was too early yet. Her next words astonished and alarmed me. "Charlot is coming here."

"What?"

"Don't look so amazed. Isn't it the most natural thing? Shouldn't my baby be with me?"

"You have told Robert and he has agreed . . ."

"Told Robert. Do you think I'm crazy! Of course I haven't told Robert. I've been reading the Bible and then the idea came to me. It was divine assistance. God has shown me the way."

"May I share in this divine secret?"

"You remember Moses in the bulrushes. The *dear* little baby. His mother put him in a cradle and hid him there . . . just as my little Charlot shall be hidden."

"It is nothing like Moses in the bulrushes."

"It gave me the idea anyway. I know that Yvette will help. You have to help me too. *You* are to find him."

"I don't understand what you are talking about, Margot."

"Of course you don't because you keep on interrupting. The plan is . . . and it's *such* a good one . . . it can't fail . . . the plan is that Yvette places the baby . . . not in the bulrushes because we haven't any . . . but outside the castle. He'll be in a basket looking adorable. Someone will find him and I have decided it shall be you. You'll bring him into the castle and say: 'I have found a baby. What are we going to do with him?' I shall seize on him and love him from the moment I set eyes on him. I shall plead with Robert to let me keep him . . . and in his present state he can deny me nothing. So I shall have Charlot."

"You can't do this, Margot."

"Why not? Tell me why not."

"It's bad enough as it is, but this is a double deceit."

"I don't care if it's a hundredth deceit if it brings me Charlot."

I was thoughtful. I could see it happening. It could work. It was simple though ingenious. Margot had forgotten that it was already known to Bessell and Mimi that she had had a child.

I said: "You will be running greater risks."

"Minelle," she said dramatically, "I am a mother."

I closed my eyes and visualized it. I was to be the one to find the child. Someone in the plan must do that. It was too hazardous to be left until the child was found naturally.

"Yvette . . ." I began.

"I have arranged it with Yvette, telling her what I want."

"And she is agreeable?"

"You forget Charlot is *my* baby."

"Yes, but she agreed to keep it away from you. That was what your father ordered."

"For once I don't care what my father ordered. Charlot is my baby and I can't live without him. Besides, the plan doesn't end there. Remember the mother of the baby in the bulrushes."

"Jochebed, I believe."

"She came to the princess and was the baby's nurse. Well, that is what Yvette shall be. I shall have to engage a nurse for the baby and I will think of my own nurse Yvette, who strangely enough is on a visit nearby. She was coming to see me. It is like an act of God."

"A little too much coincidence to ring true."

"Life is full of coincidences and this is only a little one. Yvette comes. She loves the baby on sight and when I say: 'Yvette, you must come and be nurse to this dear little foundling boy whom I have adopted as my son and call Charlot after my father . . .'"

"Perhaps your husband might think he should be called after him."

"I shall refuse. 'No, dear Robert,' I shall say, 'your name is for *our* first-born son.'"

"Margot, you practice deceit with an amazing skill."

"It is a useful gift and carries one through life with a certain ease."

"Honesty would be more commendable."

"Are you suggesting that I should go to Robert and say: 'I took a lover before I knew you. I thought I should marry him and Charlot is the result?' You would not have me so unkind to Robert."

"Margot, you are incorrigible. I can only hope this plan will succeed."

"Of course it will. We will make sure it does. Your part is easy. You just find him."

"When?"

"Tomorrow morning."

"Tomorrow!"

"There is no point in delay. Go down tomorrow morning early. Yvette will not leave him until she sees you. She will be hiding in the shrubbery. You were restless and could not sleep, so you decided to take a breath of fresh air. Then as you walked in the gardens, you heard a baby cry. You found the basket. The adorable Charlot looked up at you and smiled. You lost your heart to him at once and persuaded me to keep him."

"Are you going to need a great deal of persuasion?"

"I shall have to consult with my husband. I might weep a little, but I think he is going to be ready to grant my wishes and that he will agree right away. He'll love Charlot. He longs for us to have a baby."

"Other people's are not always so desirable to a man as his own. And I presume he is not to know it is yours."

"Good heavens, no! And please don't refer to Charlot as 'it.' "

"I am surprised that Yvette has agreed to this after being employed by your father."

"Yvette knows that I'll never be happy without him and if she is here as his nurse . . . you see what I mean?"

"I see absolutely."

"Then let us get on with the plan."

I thought of the plan from all angles and I had to admit that it could work providing everything went according to our schedule.

I began to grow excited about it, although I had considerable misgivings. But then ever since I had known of Charlot's existence—before his birth—I had realized that considerable difficulties would be involved.

Thus, on a bright morning, I rose from my bed a little before six, put on shoes and a wrap and went to the shrubbery. Yvette was there. She was carrying the basket, which at my approach, with infinite care, she placed in the bushes.

As soon as she had put it down I went swiftly to it. It was almost as Margot had described it, for Charlot himself opened his eyes and gave me such a knowing look and a crowing laugh that it was as though he were fully aware of the conspiracy.

I carried the basket into the castle. One of the footmen who was in the hall stared at me in amazement.

I said: "A child has been left in the shrubbery."

He was speechless. He could only stare disbelievingly at Charlot. He put a hand on the shawl which was wrapped round the baby and the rather splendid gold braid on his cuffs immediately attracted Charlot's attention. He put out a plump hand to grasp it but the footman jumped back as though there was a snake in the basket instead of a baby.

"He won't bite," I said, and I realized I had named the child's sex.

Charlot crowed as though with derision for us both.

"Mademoiselle, what will you do with it?"

I said: "I think I must ask Madame. It will be for her to decide."

At that moment Madame herself appeared on the staircase, poised, ready to play her part.

"What is it?" she demanded, a little imperiously I thought. "Cousin, what are you doing up at this hour of the morning disturbing us all?"

As though she did not know and was not completely ready for her rôle in this drama, which was somehow more like a comedy!

"Margot," I said, "I have found a baby."

"Found a what? A baby? What nonsense! Are you playing some game? Where could you find a . . . But it is! What can it mean?"

Her eyes were dancing, her cheeks flushed. She was enjoying this. It was dangerous, but that would only add to her enjoyment.

"A baby!" she cried. "Really, Cousin, how could you find a baby? But what a little darling. Is it not adorable?"

She played her part better than I and I knew what it cost to call Charlot "it."

Margot turned to the footman. "Don't you think this is a *beautiful* child, Jean?" The footman looked blank and she went on impatiently. "*I* never saw a more beautiful child." She leaned over the basket. Charlot regarded her solemnly. "He looks like a Charlot to me. Does he to you, Cousin?"

"That could well be his name," I admitted.

"From now on he is Charlot. I must take him to my husband. How excited he will be to know that we have a baby."

Robert had come down to see what had happened to her. He stood on the stairs and I thought how young he looked, how little aware of the real nature of the girl he had married.

Margot ran to him and slipped her arm through his. He smiled at her. There was no doubt that he was very much in love with her.

"What has happened, my dearest?" he asked.

"Oh Robert, such a marvelous thing. Minelle has found a baby."

The poor young man looked bewildered, as well he might. She babbled on: "Yes, he was in the bushes. He must have been left there. Minelle found him this morning. Isn't he enchanting?"

"We must find his parents," said Robert.

"Oh yes," she interrupted impatiently. "Later . . . perhaps.

Oh look, what a little darling. See how contentedly he comes to me."

She picked him up in her arms while Robert watched them fondly, thinking, no doubt, of the children they would have.

The news was soon spreading through the castle. The Comte and Comtesse came to inspect the child. They were indulgent when they saw Margot's delight in him. Their thoughts were obvious. She will make a good mother, after all, which must have been comforting, for before the arrival of the baby no one would have connected Margot with doting motherhood.

It seemed that the entire *château* revolved round the baby. The Comte said that they would soon find the parents. Some-one must know whose the child was. It was very strange, the Comtesse pointed out, that the baby had obviously been very well cared for. He must be almost a year old. Look at his clothes. They had not come from some poor home.

She was not as sure as the Comte that it would be possible to find his parents.

For several days inquiries were made and the whole of the town knew about the baby up at the *château*. It was the Comte's opinion that someone had had to leave the country suddenly—times being what they were—and they had left the baby near the *château* knowing that the Grassevilles would never allow it to suffer neglect. It was the first time I had heard a suggestion in Grasseville that times were changing. The Comtesse did not agree. She believed that no parents would leave a child behind. In her opinion, some poor mother had stolen the clothes from her employer and left the baby at the *château* in the hope that there would be a good life for him there.

Whatever they thought, Charlot remained and Margot took charge of him, to the amusement of her new family. She was so excited by the presence of the baby, so delighted to look after him, that they were all astonished, and being the kind of people they were the baby began to take charge of them. It might have been that Charlot possessed some special charm, but he very quickly became the darling of the household. He had his mother's imperious ways and his father's adventurous nature. However, the fact remained that Margot persuaded Robert that she could never be really happy again if Charlot were taken away from her and that he must be the first of that big family they had promised themselves.

The nursery was refurbished. We went for forages into the market. In the streets we were stopped and asked how the baby was getting on.

"And the little one is settling in, eh? What a happy little boy to have come to the *château* and Madame."

Charlot may have made an inopportune entry into the world but he was fast taking up an important place in it. Even the Comte was hoping that no one would come to claim the child.

Margot declared that she had never been so happy in her life and it really seemed so. She glowed. She laughed a great deal and only I knew that it was the laughter of triumph and that she was congratulating herself on her cleverness.

"The time has come," she told me, "to put into effect the second part of our plan. I have hinted to Robert that we need a nurse and who better than a trusted woman who knew me as a baby and was actually in my nursery."

It was only a matter of time before Yvette came to Grasseville.

2

I had liked Yvette from the moment I had seen her, but it had not occurred to me that her coming would be so important to me.

When she arrived at the castle Margot embraced her affectionately.

"It is wonderful that you were able to come," she said, for the benefit of the servants. "I have told you what has happened. You will love little Charlot."

In Margot's bedroom the three of us were together.

"It worked!" cried Margot. "It worked magnificently." She added rather patronizingly: "You both played your parts well."

"Not as well as you did," I commented wryly. "Naturally you had the leading part."

"And I was the author of our little play. It was a wonderful idea. You must admit."

"I'll tell you at the end," I said.

"Spoilsport." She put out her tongue at me as she used to when we were in school together. Then she turned to Yvette.

"He grows more adorable every day. I wonder if he'll remember you."

"Let's go and see," said Yvette.

Charlot kicked and crowed with obvious pleasure at the sight of Yvette.

Margot picked him up and hugged him. "Not too pleased, my angel, or you will make me jealous."

Yvette took him from her and laid him back in his cot.

"You overexcite him," she said.

"He loves to be excited. Don't forget he is my own flesh and blood."

"That," said Yvette gently, "is something we must try to forget. You have him now. He is your adopted son. That is very satisfactory."

"Do you think I shall ever forget that he is my very own?"

Yvette shook her head.

Yvette and I were thrown together a good deal. I think it was because life in the *château* was in fact affected by what was happening outside and people no longer visited each other as they once had. The Comte and Comtesse de Grasseville did not care to have extravagant parties when there was so much talk about the poverty in the country. I think he and his Comtesse really preferred the simpler life.

In any case, that was how it was and it meant that Yvette and I often sat or walked together in the gardens, where we could talk more easily without being overheard, and I think we both feared that by a word we might betray the true story of Charlot's arrival at the *château*.

It was not long before Yvette was talking of the past.

The most exciting years of her life had been spent at the Château Silvaine. "I went there when I was fifteen years old," she told me. "It was my first post as nursery maid under Madame Rocher . . . otherwise Nou Nou. She had gone to the Comtesse Ursule when she was born and was always with her. She adored Madame Ursule. Her whole life was concentrated on her. There was a story about it. She was married briefly . . . obviously to a Monsieur Rocher. What he did I never learned, but I did hear that there was some accident before her child was due to be born. He died and she lost the child as well. That was why she went to Ursule, and it was said that Ursule saved her reason and she transferred her affection to her employer's child. It was very sad."

"Poor Nou Nou!"

"She was wet nurse to Ursule and used to say: 'That child is part of me.' She could scarcely bear her out of her sight and if ever Ursule was in trouble she would defend her without question. It was not good for the child. When she was very young, if any of us offended her she would threaten to tell Nou Nou. Nou Nou encouraged her in this and Ursule was quite an unpleasant little girl at that time. But she grew out of it. When she was about six or seven she drew away from Nou Nou . . . but not completely. They were too close for that, but she felt restrained, smothered by too much devotion. It can be like that."

I agreed. "What kind of woman was Ursule?"

"Before her marriage she was quite a normal girl, interested in balls and clothes. It was after her marriage that she changed."

"How long were you with her?"

"Until about six years ago. Margot was growing up then and there was no longer the need to keep a nursery. She had a governess and later she went to England, as you know. It was then that the Comte gave me my house and enough to live on and keep a servant. So I settled down with José and thought to spend the rest of my life there."

"You will go back one day."

"Yes, when Charlot is older, I dare say."

"Do you miss the *château?* Your house with José must be very different."

She was silent and a misty look came in her eyes. "Yes," she said, "I missed the *château*. I had one great friendship in my life. I don't think I should ever want to go back."

I longed to know of her great friendship, though I felt it would be impolite to ask. I waited, and soon it came.

"I know this sounds strange, but our friendship grew up gradually. She was goodhearted but a little imperious. That was due to her upbringing."

"You mean Ursule?"

"Yes. I had done something . . . I forget what now, but it offended her. There was the usual cry of 'I'll tell Nou Nou.' I must have been in a perverse mood, for I retorted: 'All right, you little talebearer, tell her.' She stared at me. I remember now her little face, scarlet with rage. She must have been eight years old . . . yes, she was. I remember exactly. She ran to Nou Nou, who of course came bearing down on me like an angel with a flaming sword to defend her darling. I said, 'I am tired of always giving way to this spoilt child.' 'Then,' said Nou Nou, 'you had better pack your box and get out.' 'All right,' I cried, 'I will,' although I had nowhere to go. Nou Nou knew my plight well. 'And where will you go?' she asked. I replied: 'Anywhere is better than fussing over a silly spoilt child and her besotted old nurse.' 'Get out,' shouted Nou Nou. Nou Nou was the power in the Brousseau nursery. Madame and Monsieur Brousseau doted on their daughter and applauded Nou Nou's adulation, so if Nou Nou said I was to go there could be no appealing to a higher authority.

"As I started putting my few possessions into my tin box, wondering what on earth I was going to do, I saw the hopelessness of my situation and gave way to despair. I put my head among my meager treasures and sobbed in fear and misery. Then suddenly I was aware of being watched and when I lifted my head saw Ursule standing there. I can still see her very clearly as she was at that moment. Brown curls tied with blue ribbons and a white embroidered gown to her little ankles. She was a very pretty child with wide brown eyes and thick straight hair, which Nou Nou lovingly put into curl papers every night.

"I remember even now how she used to sit at Nou Nou's feet while Nou Nou twirled the papers deftly and sang songs of Brittany, where she came from, or told legends and stories in a singsong monotonous voice which used to send us all to sleep. At that moment as Ursule looked at me something passed between us. I realized with a little shock that the child was actually sorry for the storm she had provoked. Previously I had thought her a little minx with no thought for anyone but herself. But no, she had some feeling in her.

"The oddest part about it was, she told me later, that some feeling for me started to grow in her then. She didn't know what it was. All she knew was that she did not want me to go. She said, imperious as ever: 'Don't put any more in your box.' And then, with an amazing gentleness, she took the things out and laid them back in their drawers. Nou Nou came in and, seeing me still kneeling on the floor, looking dazed, said: 'Come on, girl. It's time you have done.' Then my little champion lifted her head in a way she had and said: 'She is not going, Nou Nou. I want her to stay.' 'She's a bad and insolent girl,' said Nou Nou. 'I know,' replied Ursule, 'but I want her to stay.' 'Why, my little darling, she called you a tittletaler.' 'Well, I am, Nou Nou. I do tittletale. I want her to stay.' Poor Nou Nou, she was nonplused, but of course her little darling's word was law."

"So she changed from that day?"

231

"It wasn't so sudden as that. We had our ups and downs. But I never gave way to her as Nou Nou did, and I think she liked that. I was a good deal younger than Nou Nou. I was about fifteen at this time when Ursule was eight. Then it was a big difference. It grew less as we grew older. From that day she took an interest in me. I was in a way her creation because, but for her, I should have been turned away. Although she was still Nou Nou's little pet and was constantly in her company, she would often sneak away to me and she began to confide in me in an astonishing way. Nou Nou was a little jealous at first but she realized that her relationship with her darling was very different from mine and so devoted was she to Ursule that she was ready to accept anything that gave her pleasure.

"I had a flair for clothes—not making them . . . we had the seamstresses for that . . . but adding little touches to them, making suggestions which could lift a dress out of the commonplace. Ursule would have me with her when the seamstresses were fitting her. We used to go into the town together to make purchases for she would insist that I accompany her.

"That was not all. She often asked my advice—although she rarely took it. We became fast friends in a way which was not usual between a servant and the daughter of the house.

"The Brousseau parents, as I said, were indulgent. Yvette is a good girl, they used to say. She looks after Ursule as Nou Nou couldn't. And so we grew together like two sisters."

"And that was the greatest friendship of your life. What made you leave?"

"I offended the Comte. I told Ursule that she should stand up to him and criticized him to his face. He said that Marguerite no longer needed a nurse—for I was looking after her at that time. And he sent me away."

"I wonder Ursule allowed it."

Yvette's lips curled. "Everything had changed very much by then. It did after her marriage. He frightened her from the first moment she saw him."

"So in spite of the fact that he gave you your home and your comfortable retirement you do not like him."

"Like him!" She laughed. "It seems an odd word to use in connection with him. I wonder if anyone *likes* the Comte. People fear him. There's no doubt of that. Many respect his wealth and position. Many more hate him. I suppose those who indulge in passing amours with him might say they loved him. But *like* him!"

"And you are one of those who hate him?"

"I would hate anyone who did what he did to Ursule."

"Was he so cruel to her?"

"If she had never married him she would still be alive today."

"You are not saying that he . . . killed her?"

"My dear Mademoiselle, I am saying just that."

I shook my head and she put her hand over mine.

After that she said nothing more and for that day our *tête-à-tête* was over.

I thought a great deal about what Yvette had said. It was almost as though she had some secret information. If she had, I must discover what it was. That it would be detrimental to the Comte she had implied. I shivered as I recalled vividly the expression on her face when she had talked of his killing her.

If he were there beside me, I would be ready to believe this could not be true; when he was not with me I could assess the facts more calmly. I must talk to Yvette. If I knew more of Ursule's nature I might be able to throw some light on the subject.

Margot asked me to go into the town to buy ribbons for a gown that was being made for Charlot. "You must go, Minelle," she said. "You will choose the right color."

I went alone. There had never been any question of our being escorted by day in Grasseville and it would not be the first time I had gone into the town by myself.

The Château Grasseville—far less grand than that of Silvaine—was rather like a glorified country mansion, scarcely worthy of the name *château*. The family owned another castle forty miles north—much bigger I heard—but this was their favorite. It was gracious enough with its four pepper-pot towers and its gray stone walls rising from the slight incline which enabled it to remain in sight of the town and, standing aloof as it did, to dominate it.

It was midmorning. The sun was beginning to climb. In a few hours it would be very hot.

As I walked into the town, several people called a greeting. One woman seated in a basket asked how the little one was. I told her that Charlot was very well indeed.

"Poor mite! To be left like that. I would wring the neck of a mother, Mademoiselle, who left a little one. Yes, I would as easily as Monsieur Berray wrings the necks of his chickens."

"No one could be better cared for than young Charlot is now, Madame."

"I know it well. And young Madame . . . she is born to be a mother. She has become one quickly, eh? Married but a few weeks . . ." Clinging to her basket she tottered perilously, almost overcome by her own humor.

"Madame has a great fondness for babies," I said.

"God bless her."

I passed on. There was scarcely anyone who did not ask after the baby.

I was some time choosing the ribbon, and when I had done so I decided to have a cup of coffee and one of the delectable little cream cakes before I began to walk back.

I sat at a table under the blue umbrella and the coffee was brought to me by Madame Durand, who chatted awhile about the baby who had had the good fortune to be left at the gates of the *château*.

When she had left me I sat brooding on what Yvette had told me and asking myself why she had conceived such a passionate hatred of the Comte. Nou Nou had felt the same towards him. It could only be because of his treatment of Ursule, as they both had such affection for her. There was much I did not know of her. I had fancied her to be a peevish hypochondriac, but it was not now easy to reconcile that assessment of her character with that of a woman who had inspired such devotion. With Nou Nou, who had lost her own child, it was understandable. Yvette was a different case. Yvette was a woman of good sense and independent spirit and since she had formed a great friendship with her employer's daughter it must mean that there was something unusual about that daughter.

Always when I thought of the Comte and his affairs I was sooner or later in complete bewilderment.

As I sat there shielded from the sunshine by the blue umbrella, sipping my coffee and savoring my *gâteau,* I had the strange feeling that I was being watched.

It was all the more extraordinary that I should feel this on a bright, sunny morning in the heart of the town. Turning as unobtrusively as I could, I noticed a man a few tables away from me. As I turned, his head moved and he was staring straight ahead. I was sure he had been intent on me. Then it suddenly occurred to me that I had seen him before. It was when we were on our way from Paris to Grasseville.

He had been at an inn in which we had stayed the night. It was something about the way his head was set on his shoulders which made him recognizable. His neck was slightly shorter than average, his shoulders faintly rounded. He wore a dark wig and one of the tall hats with a brim which hid part of his face—the type of hat which could be seen everywhere. His jacket and breeches were of the same nondescript brown as the hat. He looked, in fact, like many people one saw in towns and villages and would never have attracted attention by his dress. It was merely the set of his head on his shoulders which made me recognize him.

I must be imagining his interest in me. Why should it be there? Unless he had heard, of course, that I came from the *château* and was the cousin of the new Madame who had recently adopted the baby found at the gates.

Yet for the moment that man had given me a twinge of uneasiness. Ever since that distressing event in the lane when I could so easily have lost my life, I had been on the alert.

I was still thinking about the man in the dark wig when I rose and walked away. It did seem odd that he had been at the inn where we had stayed. But perhaps he lived here. I must make discreet inquiries about him.

I walked back to the ribbon shop, having decided to buy some lace which I had seen there. I came out of the shop and walked past the *pâtisserie*. The man was no longer sitting at the table.

I left the town and began the short walk to the *château*. When I reached the incline I turned and looked back. The man was walking along in the direction I had come, as though following me at a discreet distance.

I went to the *château* still thinking of him.

It was not difficult to lure Yvette to talk of Ursule. I found her sitting in the gardens, some sewing in her hands, and I went to join her.

"We should make the most of this," she said. "It won't last long."

"You mean this peace."

She nodded. "I wonder what's happening in Paris. It must be very hot there. It's strange how heat makes tempers rise. At night people will be out in the streets. They will be gathering at the Palais Royale. There'll be speeches and oaths and threats."

"The government may have a solution. I believe th
Comte is attending meetings of the council there."

Yvette shook her head. "The hatred is too strong . .
tempered with envy. There is little that can be done now. I
the mob were to rise I would not care to be a member of th
aristocracy who fell into its hands."

I shivered, thinking of him, arrogant, dignified, seemin
omnipotent in his own castle. It would be different in th
streets of Paris.

"It is the reckoning," said Yvette. "The Comte Fontain
Delibes has been a despotic ruler. His word was law. It ₤
time they were overthrown."

"Why did Ursule marry him?" I asked.

"Poor child, she had no choice."

"I thought the Brousseaux doted on her."

"So they did, but they wanted the best possible marriag
for her. There could not have been a grander . . . outsid
royalty. They wanted honors for her. Happiness, the
thought, would follow. She would have a fine *château* a
her home, a grand name, a husband who was well know
for the part he played in both Paris and the country. Tha
he was the devil incarnate did not seem of any importance."

"Was he so bad?" I asked almost plaintively, wanting he
to say something good of him.

"When they were married he was not very old . . . only
a year or so older than she was . . . but old in sin. A mar
like that is mature at fourteen. You may look disbelieving
but I can assure you he had had his adventures even then
He was eighteen at the time of his marriage. He already
had an established mistress. You know her."

"Gabrielle LeGrand, yes."

"And she had borne him a son. You know of this, how
Étienne was brought to the *château*. Can you think of anything more cruel than to bring a son by another woman to
flaunt before your wife because she is unable to bear more
children?"

"It is heartless, I agree."

"Heartless indeed. He has no heart. He has never thought
anything of greater importance than the gratification of his
desires."

"I should have thought with such parents, with Nou Nou
and you, Ursule could have refused to marry him."

"You know him." She looked at me obliquely and I
wondered what rumors she had heard about me and the
Comte. Clearly she had heard something, for this was the

reason behind her vehemence. She was warning me. "There is about him a certain charm. It's a sort of devilish allure. It seems irresistible to quite a lot of women. To become involved with him is like stepping onto shifting sands. I believe they can be very beautiful, inviting you to walk on them, but as soon as you take your first step you begin to sink, and unless you have the wit and power to withdraw quickly you are lost."

"Do you really think anyone is entirely evil?"

"I think some people glory in the power they have over others. They see themselves towering above everyone else. Their needs, their desires are all important. They must be satisfied no matter who suffers in the process of gratification."

"He looked after you when you left," I reminded her. "He gave you a home and enabled you to have José and live in comfort."

"I thought it was good of him at the time. Later I began to think he might have a motive."

"What motive could he have had?"

"He might have wanted me out of the way."

"Why?"

"He might have had plans for Ursule."

"You can't mean . . ."

"My dear Mademoiselle, I am surprised that a young woman of your apparent good sense should allow herself to be so deceived. But that has happened to others. My poor little Ursule! I remember well the night they sent for her. She went down to the *salon* and was presented to him. The marriage contracts were already drawn up. Oh, it was to be such a grand match! The Brousseau family is an ancient one, but it had lost some of its wealth through the centuries. His family had retained theirs. Thus the family were gaining a son-in-law of equal nobility and vastly great wealth and importance. They needed money and there was a very good marriage settlement which far exceeded the dowry they had to provide for their daughter. It was a most advantageous marriage—smiled on by both sides."

"And Ursule?"

"He charmed her . . . as he has many. She came to me afterwards . . . she always came to me. She would go to Nou Nou as a child who has hurt itself and wants to be kissed and made better. To me she confided her real problems. She was bemused. 'Yvette,' she said, 'I never saw anyone like him. Of course I haven't. There isn't anyone like him.' She walked about in a sort of dream. She was so innocent. She knew nothing of the world. Life for her then was a romantic dream."

"And when you saw him?"

"I did not know him then. I thought he had all the charm and grace which had attracted her. I had to learn later the sort of life he had led. We thought, both Nou Nou and I, that he was almost worthy of her. How quickly we were disillusioned."

"How quickly?" I persisted.

"They went to one of his country homes for the honeymoon. It was Villers Brabante, a beautiful house, small by *château* standards, but charmingly set in rural surroundings . . . quite peaceful . . . the ideal place for a honeymoon . . . providing of course that one has the ideal husband. He was far from that."

"How did you know?"

"One only had to look at her. We . . . Nou Nou and I . . . had gone on to Silvaine to be ready for them when they came back. It was the first time Nou Nou had been parted from her. She was like a hen who has lost her chick. She was clucking all the time, getting distracted. She would sit up at the watch tower with the watchman looking out for their return. Then they came . . . and one look at her face and we knew. She was bewildered. Poor child, she had been taught nothing of life . . . particularly life lived with a man like that. She was bewildered and frightened. Frightened of him . . . frightened of everything. In two weeks she was quite changed."

"He was young too," I said in his defense.

"Young in years, old in experience. He must have found her very different from the loose women he had known. I think she was probably pregnant when they came back, for soon after it was obvious. That too was a great trial for her. She was terrified of having a child. We were closer than ever then. She turned to me. 'There are things I can't talk of to Nou Nou,' she used to say, and she told me how she had disappointed him, how she wanted to be alone, how marriage was so different from what she had thought it would be. We used to sit together during the waiting months and she told me something of what she called her ordeal. And now another awaited her: the birth of her child. 'There has to be a son, Yvette,' she said. 'If this child is a son I shall never go through it again. If it is a girl . . .' Then she shivered and clung to me trembling. I started to hate him then."

"After all," I said, "it is what one expects of marriage. Perhaps the trouble was that Ursule had not been prepared."

"You find excuses for him. Poor Ursule! How ill she was before Marguerite's birth. Nou Nou was in terror that she would never come through. But we had the best doctors, the best midwife, and at last the day came when the child was born. I shall never forget her face when she was told it was a girl. She was very, very ill and the doctors said that if she had another child she would run such risks that could well cost her her life. 'She must make no more attempts to have children,' said the doctors. You would have thought she was a Queen being crowned. Nou Nou and I cried together in our relief. It was as though our darling was restored to us."

"The Comte must have been a very disappointed man."

"He was mad with rage. He used to go out riding or driving and they said he was like a madman. He was in a dilemma. They said he cursed the day he had married. He had an invalid wife . . . one daughter and no son. You must have heard that he killed a boy."

"Yes. Léon's twin brother."

"It was nothing short of murder."

"It was not done purposely. It was an accident. And he compensated the family. I have heard he was very good to them. We know what he did for Léon."

"It cost him nothing. That is the sort of man he is . . . ruthless. Then he brought Étienne to the *château* . . . his bastard son . . . to show her that if she could not give him sons others could. It was a cruel thing to do."

"Was she hurt?"

"She said to me once: 'I don't care, Yvette, as long as I do not have to submit. He may have twenty bastard sons here as long as I don't have to try to give him a legal one.' You see how ruthless he is. He cares so little for his wife's feelings that he brings Étienne here. Étienne's hopes are raised; so are those of his mother. They are hoping that Étienne will be legitimized and made the Comte's heir, but he keeps them on tenterhooks. It amuses him."

"One can only feel sorry for everyone concerned," I said.

She looked at me sharply and shook her head as though in despair.

I went on: "At least Ursule had her daughter."

"She never cared greatly for Marguerite. I think the child reminded her of her birth and all she had suffered."

"It was not Marguerite's fault," I said sharply. "I should have thought it would have been natural for a mother to care for her child."

"Marguerite soon showed herself well able to look after herself. Nou Nou was not very interested in the child either. Her care fell mostly to me. I was very drawn to her. She was such a gay little thing, vivacious, very wayward, impulsive . . . well, she has not changed much."

"I am surprised that Ursule was indifferent to her."

"She was always listless at this time. Soon after Marguerite's birth she suffered another shock. Her mother died. She had been very fond of her mother and her death was a great blow to her."

"So it was unexpected."

Yvette was silent for a while, then she said: "Her mother took her own life."

I was startled.

"Yes," went on Yvette. "It was a great shock to us all. We did not know that she was ill. She had been suffering some internal pains but she had not mentioned this for some time. But when the pain increased she could keep it secret no longer. When she heard that nothing could be done for it, she took an overdose of a sleeping draught."

"Like . . . Ursule," I murmured.

"No," said Yvette firmly. "Not like Ursule. Ursule would never have taken her own life. I know she wouldn't. We talked of this again and again. Ursule was deeply religious. She believed fervently in an afterlife. She used to say to me: 'No matter what one suffers here, Yvette, it is all fleeting. That's what I tell myself. We must endure it and the greater the suffering the more rejoicing there will be when one comes to rest. My mother suffered pain and would have suffered more and she could not endure it. Oh, if only she had waited.' Then she turned to me and gripped my hands and said: 'If only I had known. If only I could have talked to her . . .'"

"And yet when something similar happened to her . . ."

"She was not in great pain then. I know."

"You were not at the *château*," I reminded her.

"When I left the *château*, we wrote to each other. We wrote every week. She wanted to know every detail of my life and she gave me every detail of hers. She opened her heart to me. She kept nothing back. When I left we had made this pact. Later she wrote that our letters were more revealing than our daily contacts. She said that we had become even closer through the pen than we had been before because it was so much easier to say exactly what one meant on paper. That was why I learned so much about her . . . when I was away from her, more than when I was with her. That is why I know that she would never have killed herself."

"How then did she die?"

"Someone murdered her," she said.

I went to my room and stayed there. I did not want to talk of Ursule's death. I would not believe what Yvette was suggesting. That Yvette believed the Comte had killed his wife was without question.

And I knew that the intention of these conversations was to warn me. In her mind she had put me with those women who had become fascinated by him and were picked up and made much of for a while before they were cast off . . . minor *affaires* in a long stream of such, some of greater importance than others, like the one which had brought him Étienne.

In spite of everything, I would not believe this of him. That he had had adventures I knew—indeed, when had he ever made a secret of that?—but that our relationship was different, I was certain.

At times I believed I would be ready to forget everything that had gone before. Everything? Murder? But I would not believe he had killed his wife. He had killed Léon's brother, but that was different—a reckless, thoughtless act which had ended in tragedy but which was quite different from premeditated murder.

While I was brooding there the door opened and Margot looked in. She was not quite her exuberant self.

"Is something wrong?" I cried, raising myself on my arm, for I was lying on my bed.

She sat on the chair near the mirror and looked at me frowning.

She nodded slowly.

"What's happened? Charlot . . . ?"

"Is as beautiful and bonny as ever."

"Then what?"

"It's a note I've had. Armand said a woman had given it to him and it was to be delivered either to me or to you."

"A note? Armand?"

"Please don't repeat everything I say, Minelle. It maddens me."

"Why should a woman give a note to Armand?"

"Because she must have known he comes from the *château*."

Armand was a groom we had brought with us from the Château Silvaine. Étienne had said he was a good man and had recommended us to bring him with us.

"Where's the note?" I asked.

She held out a piece of paper. I took it and read:

It would be well for one of you to come to the Café des Fleurs at ten o'clock on Tuesday morning. You will be sorry if you fail. I know about the baby.

I stared at her. "Who on earth could it be . . .?"

She shook her head impatiently. "Oh, Minelle, what are we going to do? It's worse than Bessell and Mimi."

"It looks to me," I said, "as if it's the same thing as Bessell and Mimi."

"But here . . . in Grasseville. I'm frightened, Minelle."

"It's someone trying to blackmail you," I said.

"How can you be sure?"

"The tone of the note. 'You'll be sorry . . .' It's someone who has found out and wants to make something out of it."

"Whatever shall I do?"

"Could you tell Robert the truth?"

"Are you mad? I never could . . . at least not yet. He thinks I'm so perfect, Minelle."

"He'll have to discover his error sooner or later. Why not sooner?"

"You can be so hard."

"Then why not try someone else?"

"Someone else! You're in this. It says 'one of you.' That means you as well."

"I think you should go."

"I can't. Robert is taking me for a ride."

"Well, cancel it."

"What excuse could I make? I have to go. It would look so odd. He'd only want to know why . . ."

I hesitated. I flattered myself that this was a delicate situation which I could handle better than Margot. After all, I *was* involved. I had been with her during that fateful period. My mind ranged over who it could possibly be. Madame Grémond . . . someone from the house . . . perhaps to whom Bessell and Mimi had talked, someone who had seen them favored and hoped to reap similar benefits.

When at length I said I would go, she threw her arms round me. She knew she could rely on me to settle everything, she declared.

I said: "Listen. This is not settled. It has only just begun. I think you will have to consider telling Robert. That would scatter the blackmailers. You can never know when Bessell and Mimi are coming back with more demands."

"Oh, Minelle, I'm so *frightened*. But you will go and you'll know how to deal with them."

"There is only one wise way in dealing with blackmailers and that is to tell them to do their worst."

She shook her head, real fear in her eyes. I was very fond of her and it was gratifying to see how happy she and Robert were together and I often laughed to think how ingeniously she had brought her baby into the family. But of course it was an uneasy situation and while she kept such a secret, which was inevitably shared by others, dangers could arise.

I was rather touched, too, by the manner in which she could shift everything onto my shoulders. I was sure she would be blithely happy during her morning with Robert. She could always live in the moment, which was perhaps a blessing in some ways, but it did sometimes leave the future to be cared for.

At five minutes to ten I arrived at the Café des Fleurs. I ordered my coffee and the usual *gâteau*, although I had no appetite for it, but I thought Madame would be surprised if I did not and I wanted this to be an ordinary morning. I received a little shock to see the man with the dark wig and the high shoulders walk over. He is the blackmailer, I thought. He *has* been watching me! But he took a seat some distance off and although he glanced my way he did not appear to be really looking at me.

A woman was coming towards me. Émilie! Madame Grémond's maid, the quiet sister of the garrulous Jeanne. I might have known. I had always mistrusted those thin lips, those pale eyes which had never really looked straight at me.

"Mademoiselle is surprised?" she asked with an unpleasant smirk.

"Not entirely," I replied. "What is it you have to say? Please say it quickly and go."

"I'll go in my own time, Mademoiselle. It is not you

who calls the tune now, remember. It won't take long to settle. I know now that the mother of the child was not Madame le Brun but Madame de Grasseville, at that time Mademoiselle Fontaine Delibes, daughter of the great Comte."

"You have worked very hard," I said caustically. "It's a pity it was not in a more worthy cause."

"It wasn't difficult," she said, with an air of modesty. "We all knew that once Madame Grémond had been a great friend of the Comte Fontaine Delibes. She was very proud of it. He came to see her. Then all this happened. We thought Madame le Brun was one of his mistresses and the baby was his. Then Gaston took letters to Madame LeGrand . . . because she and Madame Grémond had kept in touch with each other. Ladies of misfortune . . . not altogether cast off." She sniggered and how I hated her whey-colored face! "Gaston saw you and hung about and caught a glimpse of Madame de Grasseville. He heard how she was going to get married, and then the cat was out of the bag, so as to speak. Gaston and Jeanne want a little something to set up home with and I'd like a bit for my old age. We'd like a thousand francs each to start with, and if we don't get it I shall go to the *château* and tell Madame's husband the whole story."

"You are an unscrupulous and wicked woman."

"Who in my position would not be unscrupulous for three thousand francs?"

"Do you make a practice of this sort of thing?"

"Such good fortune does not often come my way, Mademoiselle. Madame de Grasseville, as she now is . . . talked too much. She gave clues. My sister listened and we talked it over with Gaston. If she had been the Comte's mistress we wouldn't have dared. But, you see, this is different. We don't have to deal with the Comte, do we . . . but with Monsieur de Grasseville."

"I shall see that Madame Grémond knows the sort of people she employs."

"When we have our fortune, what shall we care? Madame Grémond has to be careful of herself. Times are not good for such as she is . . . and for such as you. You will have to be careful how you treat the people now. Come. Bring the francs tomorrow and all will be well."

"Until the next demand?"

"Perhaps there will be no more demands."

"The perpetual promise of the blackmailer, and made to be broken, of course."

Monsieur de Grasseville. You can tell him what you know of his wife. You will get short shrift from him for information that he already knows."

"I don't believe it."

"Nevertheless it is true."

"It's not the story I heard."

"Do you think you are in a position to hear what takes place between a wife and her husband?"

She looked deflated. "You're lying, of course."

"It is not a habit of mine to do so."

"Maybe not, but I reckon you side-step now and then. You managed very well when you were with us. Madame le Brun . . . a husband who was dead . . . drowned, wasn't it? A fine story. You could lie then and you're lying now."

"There is one way of proving it. Go to the *château* and ask for Monsieur de Grasseville. I am sure he would grant you an interview. But you might find someone waiting for you whom you do not expect. Now get out of here while you can safely do so."

"Do not imagine, Mademoiselle, that I shall let this pass. I shall discover the truth and when I have done so I shall know how to act."

"And if you are not careful, so shall we. There is nothing more despicable than a blackmailer. Goodbye. Take warning and never show your face here again."

Émilie, looking sickly pale, rose and, giving me a venomous look, said: "One day it will be different. One day we shall have our revenge on such as you. It has been too easy for you. Those days are over. The time is coming when there'll be change. I'll see the likes of you hanging on the lanterns before long."

She walked away, her head high. Her words had sent a shiver of dismay down my spine. My triumph in victory was gone. So absorbed was I that I forgot to see if the man in the dark wig had followed me.

3

The atmosphere of the household had changed, as I suppose was inevitable after Margot's revelation. She tried to be as gay as before, but she was apprehensive and Robert was subdued. Clearly this had been a shock for him.

Margot was excessively affectionate towards him and he appreciated that, but I caught him looking at Charlot with a kind of wondering amazement, as though he could not really believe the story of his birth.

"He'll get used to it," said Yvette, "and with so many unscrupulous people aware of it, he would certainly have discovered in time. It is best that he knows through her. He is a good young man and she is fortunate to have such a husband. Different from her mother . . ."

That brought us back to Ursule, and as that was a subject which I found irresistible, I encouraged more disclosures.

"She stayed in her room a great deal, I know," I said. "What did people think? I suppose there was a good deal of entertaining at the *château*?"

"There was, and at first she would put in an appearance. They made a show of being a loving couple at first, but after a while she began to plead illness. Of course she did feel weak after Marguerite's birth and she never really regained her health and strength."

"Invalidism became a sort of cult, didn't it?"

"It did. She was childish sometimes. When there was an engagement which she wanted to avoid she would say: 'Oh, I have such a headache.' And Nou Nou would reply: 'I'll get you some spirit of balm or my marjoram juice.' And Ursule would shake her head and say: 'No, Nouny. I don't want any of your herb drinks. I really want to be with you and then my headache will go.' Of course Nou Nou loved that. She liked to think that her little girl could be made well simply by being with her. Then I began to realize that Ursule's illnesses were mostly of the mind. They were excuses. We both hated him so much that we always rushed to her rescue and we would tell him that she was not well enough to be with him."

"It's a dangerous practice," I said, "to feign illness. It's like rough justice. You pretend to be ill in order to escape something and before you realize it you *are* ill."

"It seems so. As the years passed, she became an invalid, although there was rarely anything specifically wrong with her. He despised that in her. He thought her a malingerer, which she was in a way. Yet it seemed to me that her illnesses were real, only they weren't what she said they were. So she became very much the invalid wife. She did not seem to want to go far from her room. She took shelter from him on her couch and chaise longue."

"Can you blame him for looking elsewhere?"

"I do blame him," said Yvette fiercely. "I tell you, I know more than you do."

We were silent for a while and then she said: "One of these days . . ." I waited, but she added: "Never mind."

"But what were you going to say? What is going to happen one of these days?"

"I have her letters," she said. "I've kept every one of them. She wrote to me regularly once a week . . . all those letters over six years. Writing to me was an outlet for her feelings. She just set her thoughts down on paper. It was like talking to her. Sometimes I would have several letters at a time. She used to number them so that I read them in order." Her next words startled me. "I knew of you through her letters. She told me you had come to the *château* . . . and the effect you had on him . . . and he on you . . ."

"I did not know that she was so much aware of me."

"Although she stayed in her room she knew what was happening in the *château*."

"And what did she say of me?"

Yvette was silent.

A messenger from the Comte arrived at Grasseville. He had letters for the Comte de Grasseville, for Margot, and there was one for me.

I took it to my bedroom that I might be alone to read it.

My dearest,

It gives me great satisfaction to know that you are at Grasseville. I want you to remain there until I come for you or send for you. I do not know when that will be, but you may be sure I shall lose no time and it will be as soon as it is possible. The situation in Paris is deteriorating fast. There have been riots and the shopkeepers are barricading their shops. People are marching through the streets wearing the tricolor. The heroes at the moment are Necker and the Duc d'Orléans . . . but that could change tomorrow. There is a feeling that anything can change at any moment. Sometimes I would like to see a confrontation between the King and the nobility on one side and Danton, Desmoulins, and the rest on the other. What Orléans is doing with them I can't imagine. I think he may imagine they will set him up as King. My opinion is that if they dispense with the monarchy there will be no crown. But a crowned King is a King until he dies.

My dear Minelle, how I wish you were here that I might talk of these matters with you. There is one hope that sustains me in this dismal world: One day you and I will be together.

Charles-Auguste

I read his letter over and over again. I glowed with happiness. When I held in my hand a letter he had written to me, nothing I heard of him could alter my feelings for him.

I had retired early that night. Supper had been a somewhat silent meal. The Grassevilles *mère* and *père* were clearly disturbed by the news from Paris. There were times when even Grasseville had to be invaded by the unpleasant truth. Robert, of course, was less exuberant. One could not expect him to be overjoyed by the news that his wife had had a child by someone else before her marriage to him; and he was taking a little time to assimilate the devastating revelation. Margot could always be affected by her father. I wondered what he had said to her.

As I sat at my dressing table brushing my hair, there was a knock on my door and, when I called, "Come in," Yvette entered. She carried a packet of papers in her hand.

"I hope I don't disturb you," she said.

"No, of course not."

"I want to show you something. I have been wrestling with myself for some time and I really think I should."

I knew what she was holding in her hand before she told me.

"Her letters," I said.

"The last I received," she answered. "She must have written them a few days before she died. In fact, they were actually delivered to me on that day. The messenger came with them and neither of us knew what had happened."

"Why do you want to show them to me?"

"Because I think there will be something in them that you ought to know."

I lowered my eyes. She would have known that letters from the Comte had arrived this day and there was one among them for me, which was significant.

"If you are sure you wish me to read them . . ." I began.

"I think it is important that you do." She laid the packet on the dressing table. "Good night," she added and left me.

I lighted the three candles of the candelabrum by my bedside and got into bed. Propped up by pillows, I untied the letters. They were numbers one, two, and three.

The handwriting was firm and I felt reluctant to unfold them and read them, for they had not been intended for me and I felt I was prying on something private. Curious as I was to learn about Ursule, I was very reluctant to read her letters, and if I were honest I would admit that that reluctance was caused by the fear of what I should find rather than a sense of correct behavior. I was afraid of what I should read about the Comte.

I opened the first of the letters.

My dear Yvette,

How good it is to write to you. Our letters are, as you know, a source of great comfort to me. Writing them is like talking to you and you know how I always liked to tell you everything.

Life goes on as before. Nouny with my *petit déjeuner*, drawing the curtains, making sure the sun doesn't bother me and that I am wrapped up against drafts. Not that she would allow any in my room. Marguerite is back now after her long sojourn abroad. There is someone with her called a cousin . . . a fiction if ever there was. It is a new gambit with him. He has never called them cousins before. This one is English. Marguerite knew her during her stay in England. She has been presented to me. A tall good-looking girl with rather beautiful hair—masses of it—and blue eyes of a deep and unusual shade. She seems to have a good conceit of herself, an air of independence, and is not in the least frivolous. In fact, I was surprised, for she is not his type at all. I watch her in the gardens with Marguerite. One always learns so much about people when they are unaware of one's observation. There is a change in him. It has suddenly struck me that this time he may be serious.

I had an uncomfortable pain yesterday afternoon. Nouny made a great fuss about it and insisted on my taking her mistletoe cure. She went on and on about her herbs and plants, as you know she is fond of doing. I have already heard about six hundred times that the druids called it that plant that cures all ills, and it is said to produce immortality. Anyway, Nouny's draught soothed me and I slept most of the afternoon.

I haven't seen him for a week. I dare say he will come in to pay his duty call. It amazes me that he bothers to. I dread his visits and I fancy it would be no deprivation to him to dispense with them.

But what I wanted to tell you was that this time he was different. Usually he sits in the chair and his eyes keep going to the clock. I know he is asking himself how much longer he need stay. He can never hide his contempt. It is there in his eyes, in his voice, and the very way he sits in the chair. He is impatient.

Nouny told him about my pain. You know how she is with him . . . blaming him for everything. If I cut my finger she would find some way of saying it was his fault. And then I fancied I saw something in his eyes . . . speculation.

It is something to do with this girl. She is the most unlikely one you could imagine. She was a schoolteacher. I remember hearing something of her when I was in England not long ago. What a dreadful time that was! But he insisted on my going because we had to see Marguerite. I felt ill all the time, as you know, and I hated to be separated from Nouny. She was frantic until I came back and then started dosing me with all sorts of concoctions to purge me of the contamination of foreign parts!

But the girl . . . He must have seen her then, for Marguerite was at a school run by the girl's mother. She speaks French very well indeed.

I saw him in the gardens with her once. I couldn't see them very clearly, of course, but there was something in his gestures, his attitude . . . I don't think she is his mistress . . . yet. I laughed so much when I saw them in the gardens that Nouny thought I was going into hysterics. I was thinking about Gabrielle LeGrand.

Ours is a very strange household. Well, what can one expect with such a man at the head of it!

It is always good writing to you, Yvette. I should be desolate without our letters. I feel so tired sometimes. Like someone outside life looking in on it. I rather like it that way.

I look forward to hearing your news, dear Yvette, and you must not think I do not love all the details. The fact that José burned the *potage* and birds have ruined the plum crop interests me greatly. I like to know that there is another side of life. Here I feel we live high drama all the time. That makes the quiet life seem very sweet. Perhaps it is what I am trying to escape to.

So write, dear Yvette.

Good night. Ursule

I finished the first letter and folded it. My heart was beating uncomfortably fast. I could see that those letters were going to be revealing. Already I had seen myself through other eyes and I knew that I had been observed when I had not known it.

I opened the second letter.

My dear Yvette,

I have had a further dose of the mistletoe cure. Nouny is going round grunting like a grampus with a kind of mingling disapproval and satisfaction—disapproval for the pain, satisfaction for the cure.

She has spoken to *him* about me and said she wants the doctors. It is fussing of her. I know what's in her mind. She is thinking of my mother. I never really heard the truth of that. They hushed it up and kept a lot from me. She took her own life, I knew, because she was afraid of the future. It was that painful illness which was going to be worse and kill her eventually. No matter what they try to keep from one, there is always gossip to be heard. I have often pretended to be asleep when I was lying there listening to the servants. I have a gift, as you know, for seeming to take in nothing when I am taking in everything. I think they were afraid for me to know too much in case I—who am also ill—might do the same. If Nouny knows me at all, she knows that I would never take my own life. I feel very strongly about this. I have always felt it. Remember how we used to talk about it? I still believe that one must work out one's rôle on earth, however uncomfortable. It's part of a pattern. Nouny gets terribly worked up about what's going to happen to me. She's always saying: "What's going to happen to you when I'm gone?" "Gone where, Nouny?" I ask teasingly. "To Heaven," she says. I laugh at her and she gets so upset I have to cosset her and tell her how important she is to me just to placate her. I agreed to see the doctors and she is talking to *him* about it. I am sure he says: "More malingering." But what do I care?

I am certain that his feelings for the schoolmistress girl are different from usual. This one appears not to be just a woman but *the* woman. For how long, is another matter, but he is certainly obsessed at the time. Nouny is very angry. She hates the girl. Marguerite is very fond of her, though. They are together a good deal. They keep up the myth of cousin. It is a good way of keeping her at the *château* without too much comment. Of course, the girl's presence here is causing a lot of heartburning in some quarters, as you can guess.

When I think of Gabrielle LeGrand brooding in that house of hers like a great spider waiting to catch her fly, I laugh so much that Nouny gets out the Lady's Bedstraw. That's the cure for hysteria, in case you've forgotten. I have learned quite a lot about these things. Living with Nouny, how could one help it? I wonder what Gabrielle thinks of our young lady. Well, while I'm here, what does it matter? Gabrielle comforts herself that I am the invalid and must eventually succumb to my ailments. And she has the stalwart Étienne to offer. A son . . . the hope of the house. Oh, Yvette, what an insult to our sex! We are the unwanted ones. If Marguerite had been a boy, who knows how different our lives might have been. How many women in the world have been cast out for the only reason that they cannot get a son. What a commentary on our society. But I was fortunate. Many have to endure years and years of childbearing . . . daughter, daughter all the time . . . and often miscarriages. I escaped that. I never want those early experiences to happen again. I was not meant for that. I knew it at once and so did he . . . that was why he hated me. You know the sort of man he is. Women are as necessary to him as air. He cannot live without them. It was so from the beginning of his manhood. It will be so to the end. That is why the affair of the schoolmistress is so strange. Of course that could not last . . . that obsession for one. But it is strange that it should exist at all.

Nouny won't admit it, but she appears to be quite a pleasant creature. She has a natural dignity and doesn't give herself airs. She has been strictly brought up and is holding him off, I suspect, because her upbringing would not allow her to indulge in a light love affair with him. Well, we shall see.

The doctors came today. They prodded me and asked

endless questions. Then there was a long conference with Nouny. He was not there, which they must have thought strange. He thought the whole thing was a farce. So it was. It was just to placate Nouny. She went about looking grave and making me rest and asking if I felt any pain. I pretended a bit because that was what she wanted, and it gave her a chance to get out the mistletoe cure.

Good night. I am going to sleep now.

Ursule

There was one more letter. I was beginning to see Ursule as quite a different person from the one I had imagined. She was not the peevish invalid. What she had hated was her marriage. I believed she would have hated marriage with anyone. She was without passion, without maternal instincts. But she could have affection. She clearly had that for Nou Nou and Yvette. She did not want to take part in life. She wanted to spend her days in her room, observing the conduct of those about her. Instead of being aloof, though, she was enormously interested in what was going on. She was like the audience at a play; she wanted to see how they acted while she herself took no part.

I picked up the last letter.

My dear Yvette,

I have suddenly become aware of the drama all about me. It is as though they have all sprung to life. We are on the verge of a revolution, I believe. I have been reading the papers. I know things are very much more grave than we have allowed ourselves to believe. I wonder what will happen to us. I chatted to one of the maids who came in to clean. Nouny was having a nap, so she could talk freely to me, which she wouldn't dare do if Nouny was around. Anything unpleasant, as you know, has to be kept from me. I learned from the girl that there have been riots in various places all over the country and that the people are going to rise and demand their rights. Spoken, I must say, with a certain satisfaction. She looked at my négligé as she talked as though at the given moment she would have that as her share. It is very distressing and I started to wonder what would happen to *me* if there was this turnabout. I cannot imagine anyone's trying to take *his château* from him, can you? He would subdue them with a look.

All this going on, and our not being aware of it, makes me see that there are things happening under my very nose, as it were, which I have not been looking at squarely.

He is still longing for the school lady and she remains aloof. Perhaps she knows it is the way to increase his ardor. But I am not sure. I think she is rather wise. From the little I have gathered from Marguerite she is the fount of all wisdom. It is always Minelle this . . . and Minelle that. Minelle is our school lady. I think that is Marguerite's version of her name. It sounds French, but the lady is as English as it is possible for anyone to be. Our tongue sounds a little incongruous on her lips, though she speaks it perfectly.

He wants me out of the way. Of course he has been wanting that for a long time but never as fervently as now. When I say out of the way, I do not mean just out of sight, but off the earth. I suddenly realized this with a shock, because as you know he is a man who, when he wants, wants fiercely and does not rest until he has it.

I, who have lived thus all these years—which is scarcely living at all—suddenly find myself in the midst of intrigue. You see, Yvette, there are several people who wish me out of the way . . . not mildly but desperately. First, there is my dear husband. How he would love to be rid of me! Then he could go to his schoolmistress and offer her honorable marriage. I believe that is what he wants to do.

And what of Gabrielle . . . all those years patiently waiting for me to die . . . and yet at the same time wanting me to live. If I died he might marry again, but would it be Gabrielle? Gabrielle has proved that she can bear a son. There is that six feet of Fontaine Delibes manhood to prove it. Étienne! And who could doubt that the Comte is his father? Poor Gabrielle, what a quandary for her! The Comte could marry her if he were free, but would he? I know she has been a faithful mistress to him for many years, but it is a tradition that when a man is free to marry it is not his ageing mistress whom he chooses as his wife. He turns and finds a young girl. So there sits our patient Gabrielle. What does she feel to see this young schoolmistress enslaving her lover? And Étienne, what of him?

Then there is Léon. I discovered something about

Léon. It was on the night of the ball. I know so much more than people think. I have always had food, clothes, and even money sent to Léon's family. I felt a certain responsibility, as it was because I did not produce a son that my husband drove so wildly that day there was this terrible accident. I send Édouard, one of my grooms, to Léon's family once a month. He brings me back news of them. He talks to them and comes back and tells me little things about them. Then on the night of the ball . . . this happened. And Léon is aware of it. I am too tired to tell you about it now. It's a long story . . . so next time. But Léon is afraid of what I might do.

There is so much drama in this household, Yvette. I often wonder where it will all end. But it does make life exciting and it could easily be so dull for me. I can't wait to know what will happen next.

I have always been interested in people. It's odd that I should wish to be merely a looker-on. But it's true. I don't want to go down there in the arena. Marriage and all it entails is particularly distasteful to me. I suppose there are people like that. They turn up occasionally.

There are moments of enjoyment in my life . . . writing to you . . . discovering what people are doing. And now suddenly it has all become tremendously exciting.

I can't wait for what will happen next. I shall write to you tomorrow more fully. I'm just a little tired now and I like to be fresh for my letters.

Good night.

Ursule

The letter fell from my hand. I looked at the date. It was written the night before she died.

I now knew why Yvette had decided to show me the letters. She was telling me that Ursule could not possibly have taken her own life.

There was little sleep for me that night. I lay awake brooding on what I had read.

I took the first opportunity of returning the letters to Yvette.

"You've read them?" she asked.

I nodded.

"Did you realize when the last one was written?"

"Yes, the night before she died. She must have written it just before she took the fatal dose."

"Do you think that is the letter of a woman contemplating suicide?"

"No."

"There is only one solution. He killed her."

I was silent and she went on: "He wanted her out of the way. She knew that. She actually said it in the letter."

"I don't believe it. At the autopsy . . ."

"My dear Minelle, you do not know the Comte's power. It has always been so. The doctors would say what he commanded them to."

"Surely they would have more integrity."

"You do not know how things can happen. Someone offends a person in a high place. A little later he receives a *lettre de cachet*. Nothing more is heard of him."

I was silent and she came to me and laid a hand on my arm. "If you are wise," she said, "you will return to England without delay and forget you ever met him."

"Where should I go?"

"Where would you go now if there were trouble?"

"I suppose I should stay with Margot . . . here . . . with you all."

"And if Comte comes for you, what then?" I was silent and she went on: "He might offer to marry you. Would you marry a murderer?"

"There is no proof . . ."

"Didn't you find that in the letter? You read what she had written before she died. The doctors had been. He had sent for them that they might diagnose some imaginary disease."

"It was Nou Nou who sent for them."

"Nou Nou constantly wants to send for them. It would only have been a matter of waiting until she asked for them again."

"If he wanted to be rid of her why did he not do so long ago?"

"Because you were not there."

"But he always wanted to remarry. He wanted a son."

"There was no particular woman before. He was ready to leave it to fate and, if necessary, settle for Étienne."

"You are conjecturing too much."

"Oh, isn't it clear to you, or are you willfully blind?"

I was willfully blind, I knew. The evidence was clear

enough in the letters. She had declared her wish to live only the night before she died.

I had never been so wretched in the whole of my life.

One hot day followed another. When I awoke each morning my first thoughts were of the Comte. I could not shut from my mind the picture of his going into her bedroom and opening Nou Nou's cupboard. All the remedies were neatly labeled in Nou Nou's handwriting. He would tip the fluid into the glass . . . the double . . . or treble dose . . . that meant death.

What could I do? If I asked him for the truth, he would not give it. He was adept at lying. Or would he tell me the truth and try to make me believe that whatever he had done would make no difference to us? Was he right? Could I stand the test? Wasn't it cowardly to run away from it?

But that was what I should do. In the first heat of my passion for him I might forget, but later how should I feel, living with a murderer?

In my dreams my mother returned to me. She pleaded with me. Then in the dream she changed to Yvette and said: "Go home. Don't delay any more."

A strange thing happened a week after I had read those letters. I could almost believe that my mother had arranged it with divine assistance.

I was in my room turning over the question of what I should do when Margot rushed in.

"A visitor," she cried. "Come down at once. You will be surprised."

I immediately thought of the Comte. "Who?" I demanded.

"I'm not telling. Come and see. It's a surprise."

I doubted whether the arrival of the Comte would be such a great surprise, and surely he would not have aroused this reaction in Margot. I looked at myself in the mirror.

"You look all right," Margot assured me. "And there is no time to change or anything like that. Do come now."

So I went with her and, to my utter astonishment, discovered that the visitor was Joel Derringham. I looked at him in amazement and he took my hands in his.

"You look surprised to see me," he said.

"I am completely taken aback."

"I had come to the south of France from Italy and I heard from home that you had gone to France. I thought it would be a good idea to call on the Comte and his family. I went to the *château* and was informed of Marguerite's marriage and that you had accompanied her to Grasseville. So here I am."

"You will stay awhile, I trust," said Margot, very much the *châtelaine*.

"It is delightful of you to offer hospitality and I should be very pleased to take advantage of it."

"Minelle," said Margot imperiously, "you will entertain our guest while I make arrangements for his room to be prepared. What of refreshment, Joel? We dine at six."

"I have had something at an inn and shall be quite happy until six, thank you."

We sat down and when we were alone he looked at me steadily. "It is good to see you again," he said.

"Much has happened since our last meeting," I replied rather tritely.

"A great deal. I was sorry to leave so abruptly."

"Oh, I understand."

"How did you come to leave England?"

"My mother died, as you know, and the school did not prosper without her. It seemed a solution to come with Margot when the opportunity was offered to me."

He nodded. "You have changed little, Minella. Your mother's death was a great blow to you, I know."

"The greatest I ever suffered."

He winced slightly and I realized I had told him that his abrupt departure had not affected me so much.

"She was a wonderful woman," he said. "My father was always talking of her."

But not so wonderful, I thought, that her daughter could be considered worthy of his son. Not that I would have taken him, I assured myself haughtily. But how pleased my dear mother would have been had that union been possible.

"Have you enjoyed your tour?" I asked.

"It is not yet over."

"I thought you were on your way home."

"By no means. It was simply that I heard you were in France and I very much wanted to see you. This country is a boiling caldron of discontent."

"I know. One can't live here without being aware of it."

"It is not the safest place in the world for a young Englishwoman."

"That's true enough."

"You should not stay here. I cannot understand why the Comte has not arranged for your return to England."

I said nothing.

Margot returned. "I will show you your room. I am sure you will wish to wash and perhaps change. You have brought a manservant with you, I see. He is being looked after. I am so pleased you have come. I am sure Minelle is too."

She looked at me a little mischievously and then she took him to his room.

I went to my own. I was really quite shaken by my encounter with him. It brought back memories of home. I could see my mother clearly, her eyes dancing with excitement as she showed me the handsome riding kit spread out on the bed.

It was not long before Margot appeared. She sat in her favorite chair facing the mirror so that she could admire her reflection as she talked.

"He is more handsome than ever," she cried. "Did you not think so?"

"He was always considered to be good-looking."

"He is a very pleasant young man. I have a special interest in him because at one time they had decided that I might marry him."

"You are glad you didn't?"

"I wonder what *he* would have said about Charlot? I don't think he would been quite as lenient as Robert, do you?"

"I have no idea."

"Oh, haughty! The fact was, if I remember rightly, that he was quite interested in *you*. Wasn't that the reason why he was sent off in a hurry?"

"That's all in the past."

"But the past is revived, Minelle. He has revived it by putting in an appearance. I like him. I am sure Robert will be jealous when he hears I was once meant for him. But then I shall tell him where Joel's true fancy lies. I believe he has come here just to see you."

"Nonsense."

"Very unconvincingly said. I thought you always prided yourself on your adherence to the truth and logic. Of *course* he has come to see you." She was serious suddenly. "Oh, Minelle, it's the right thing, it is really. If he wants to take you home to England, you should go."

"Do you want to be rid of me?"

"What a *cruel* thing to say. You know I'd hate you to go. I'm not thinking of myself."

"A novel experience for you."

"Stop this silly bantering. It's serious. Things are bad here. There's going to be an explosion at any minute. What do you think is happening? What of my father? I know how he feels about you . . . and you about him. You're a fool, Minelle. You don't know him. I told you from the first he's got the devil in him. He's no good to any woman."

"Margot, stop it."

"I won't. I'm worried about you. We have been through the Charlot affair together. I'm fond of you. I want you to be happy . . . as I am. I want you to know what it means to marry a *good* man. If you marry Joel Derringham, you'll have a good life. You know you will."

"Shouldn't we wait until he asks me? He hasn't, you know, and he showed clearly not so long ago that as people were thinking along those lines it would be well for him to get away."

"That was his people. Silly ideas they have."

"But he must have agreed to go."

"He did it because he'd always obeyed them. Now he's grown up he's changed his mind."

"You do run on, Margot. You always did. He is merely paying a visit to old friends. Let's leave it at that, shall we?"

She came to me and took my hand. Then she kissed me gently on the cheek.

"I know I'm a selfish butterfly, but there are people I love. Charlot, Robert, and you, Minelle. I want you to be happy. I'll come to England and your children and mine shall play together in the gardens of Derringham Manor. You'll come to Grasseville and when we're old we'll talk about these days and we'll laugh and laugh and live them again in our memories. That's how I want it to be. That's the best way. In your heart you know it. Oh, I am so glad he has come."

Then she kissed me swiftly on the cheek and ran from the room.

We rode together, Joel and I. We talked of old times. How it brought it all back! It filled me with a bittersweet nostalgia. Those happy days when a new ribbon for a dress was so important, and my mother and I used to sit on our little patch of lawn and talk about the future.

"I know how you miss her," Joel said. "You were wise to get away, although it is unfortunate that you should come to this country at this time. But to have stayed in the schoolhouse would have meant you kept your sad memories with you."

"When are you returning home?"

"Any time now . . . perhaps sooner than I had thought."

"Your family will not wish you to be in France just now, I am sure."

"No. As a matter of fact, several people I know are making hasty plans to leave. Here in this rather remote country spot you have no idea how quickly the situation has been changing, and for the worse. I believe the Court is rapidly diminishing. People are finding excuses for leaving Versailles."

"It sounds ominous."

"Indeed yes. Minella, you must come back to England."

"Where should I go?"

"You could come with me."

I raised my eyebrows and said: "Where to?"

"I have been thinking about this ever since I left. I was a fool to go. I don't know why I did. I kept asking myself that for months. Then I promised myself that I would break right away and make new interests, but I couldn't. The fact is, Minella, I have been thinking of you every day since I last saw you. I know now that I shall go on doing that. I want you to marry me."

"What of your family?"

"They will come round. My father has never been a harsh man. Nor my mother. Before anything, they want my happiness."

I shook my head. "It wouldn't be wise. There would be opposition. I should not be accepted."

"My dear Minella, we'd overcome all that in a week."

"I shouldn't want to be accepted on sufferance."

"Is that the only reason why you hesitate . . ."

"It is not," I replied.

"Then why . . . ?"

"In a case like ours, where the marriage would be considered unsuitable . . ."

"Unsuitable! That's nonsense!"

"Your parents did not seem to think so. Let's face it, Joel. We should go back to the small community in which I lived for some years as the schoolmistress's daughter. I was even teacher to the children of your friends and neighbors. Don't let us shut our eyes to that. In a small community it persists forever. I am better educated than your sisters—simply because I was able to assimilate knowledge better than they were—but that doesn't count. They are the daughters of Sir John Derringham, Baronet, Squire of the Manor. I am the daughter of the schoolmistress. In a society like that, it is an unbridgeable gulf."

"Do you mean to tell me that a woman of your spirit would allow such a silly convention to deter her from what she wanted?"

"If she wanted it enough it wouldn't, of course."

"You mean that you don't love me."

"You make it sound unfriendly. I like you very much. It's a great pleasure to see you again, but marriage is a serious matter . . . a lifelong affair. I think you are rushing into this. You see me as a damsel in distress. I am stranded here and revolution creeps nearer. Where can I go? You would rescue me like a medieval knight. It's very commendable, but not enough to build a marriage on."

"You can't forget that I went away. If I had stayed . . . defied my parents . . . it would have been different."

"Who can say? So much has happened since then."

"You were sorry when I went?"

"Yes, I was sorry. I was a little hurt, but it was not a deep wound."

"I am going to suggest that you and I are married here now . . . in France. Then we shall go back to England . . . husband and wife."

"That's very bold of you, Joel. How would you face your parents?"

"You are trying to hurt me. I understand. I hurt you when I went away. But believe me, I regretted it. I regretted it deeply. Look at it my way, Minella. I had lived with my parents all my life, except when I was at the university. We are an amicable family. We always try to please each other and consider what the others want. It is second nature to us. When my father implored me to go away and consider for a while, I naturally obeyed him, even though my deepest inclination was to stay. When you know my father, you will understand. Now when I take you back as my wife he will welcome you, because that is what will make me happy. He already admires you. He will learn to love you, Minella, please don't let the past influence you. Forgive me for what I did. You think it is weakness . . . and so it is, but what happened has made me sure of what I want now and I know that without you I can never be really happy again. There are things in my life which you will find irritating. I am cautious . . . overcautious. I rarely act without thinking. It's my nature. So when I fall in love, because it is the first time—and it will be the last—I am unsure of my emotions. It was only when I went away and communed with myself that I understood. Now I know that more than anything I want to marry you. I want to take you back to Derringham, I want us to be together there for the rest of our lives."

While he was speaking, it was as though my mother had come to stand beside him. I could almost see the joy in her eyes, the tears falling down her cheeks.

"Well, Minella?" he asked gently.

"It can't be," I said. "It's too late."

"What do you mean . . . too late?"

"I mean that it is not the same as it was."

"If I had asked you before I left . . . it would have been different, you mean?"

"Life is not static, is it? I have grown away from Derringham. A few days ago I had no idea that I should ever see you again. Then you come back and say, 'Marry me.' You ask me to decide to change my life in a few minutes."

"I see," he said. "I should have waited. I should have let you become accustomed to seeing me again. All right, Minella, we'll wait. Take a few days. Think of all it would mean. Remember those walks and rides we had together and all the things we talked of. Do you recall them?"

"Yes, they were good times."

"There will be many good times, my dear. We'll go back where we both belong. We'll be together. We'll watch the seasons come and go and each year we'll grow closer to each other. Do you remember how we got along right from the first? Our minds fitted, didn't they? I've never been so stimulated by anyone as I was during our walks together. Minella, it is what your mother would have liked more than anything."

I was deeply moved at that moment. He was right. She, who had always wanted the best for me, had wanted this desperately. I thought of her plundering the Dower Chest to buy clothes for me. I could almost hear her gleeful whisper: "It was not in vain after all."

For her sake, I should consider this.

He could see that I was hesitating and he cried triumphantly: "Yes, Minella, we must have time to think of this. But, my dearest, don't be too long. We are on the edge of a volcano here. I shall not feel safe until we are aboard the packet and alight on English soil."

I was relieved that I had not to give an immediate answer. I wanted to be alone to think.

I was not in love with Joel. I liked him, respected him, trusted him, understood him, and could see ahead of me to the kind of life I would have with him. He was eminently eligible. He was the man my mother would have chosen for me.

And the Comte? Did I love him? I didn't know. All I did know was that I was more excited by him than I had ever been in my life. Did I trust and respect him? How could I trust and respect a man whom I suspected of murdering his wife? Did I understand him? How could I know what was going on in that devious mind? And the life I might have with him? I thought of his wife's words. He had an obsession for me, but how long would it last? I thought of his mistress waiting like a spider to catch her fly. And the background of our lives—this tortured country where the holocaust was likely to break forth at any moment. And then what would happen to people like the Comte and his family?

I thought of the peaceful green meadows of England, the woods where in early summer the bluebells were a blue mist under the trees. I thought of the primroses and violets in the hedges and gathering cobnuts in the autumn, and a wave of nostalgia came over me. I thought of picking pussy willows and filling vases with them, and how I had taken the pupils for rambles in the country so that they might have a lesson in simple botany.

Joel was bringing back those memories and it seemed to me that my mother was with me more vividly than ever.

Joel pressed my hand. "Dear Minella, think about it. Think what it would mean to us both."

I looked at him and saw the kindliness in his face, and I thought how like his father he was. I knew then that if he took me home as his wife, Sir John and Lady Derringham would not let the fact that I was not the bride they would have chosen for him stand in the way of their welcome. I knew that I would have the power to win their love and that I could without much difficulty overcome all the obstacles between myself and the happy life my mother had longed for me to have.

There was, of course, the Comte.

If I had never known him, there could have been no hesitation. But having known him, nothing could ever be the same again.

For the next two days I was constantly in Joel's company. He did not speak of marriage—he was the most tactful of men. We walked a good deal together; we talked of all sorts of subjects of which he was knowledgeable: the illness of the King of England; the wildness of his son, the Prince of Wales; the dissatisfaction of the English with the royal family; the difference between the discontent at home and in France.

"We are of a different temperament," he said. "I don't think it could come to revolution in England. There are the differences between rich and poor; there are the resentments; there are the occasional riots . . . but the atmosphere is quite different. It's coming here, Minella. You can feel it . . . right overhead . . . about to break."

He knew a great deal about the situation, and it was ironical that I should learn more from him than from anyone else. He was the looker-on who saw the best of the game. Moreover, he was astute, politically minded, and shrewd.

"Louis is the worst kind of King for his times," he said. "It's sad, because he is a good man. But he's weak. He wants to be good. He sympathizes with the people, but he is too lethargic. He believes all men are as well meaning as himself. Alas for France! And the Queen, poor Marie Antoinette. She was too young to have so much thrust upon her. Oh, she has been guilty of great extravagance. But she was only a child. Imagine her coming from the stern rigid rule of her indomitable mother to be the petted darling of the dissolute Court of France. Naturally it went to her head, and she was too featherbrained to understand what damage she was doing. What is coming is inevitable, and it will bring no good to France. The mob will have the head of every aristocrat it can lay its hands on—no matter whether they are its enemies or not. There has been injustice and that should be abolished, but the greatest passion in the world is envy and soon the rabble in its rags will be on the march against the nobleman in his castle."

It was uncomfortable hearing, and all the time I was thinking of the Comte.

Joel liked to walk with me after dark so that he could

show me the stars in the sky—the luster of Arcturus and Capella twinkling there, and when he pointed to Mars, conspicuously red on the horizon, it seemed ominous.

I recaptured the pleasure of being with him. He was never dull. We could discuss and disagree with the utmost amity.

THE
REIGN OF TERROR

1

It was afternoon, just after the midday meal. The household was always sleepy at this time. Most took a siesta, a habit I had never fallen into.

There was a tap on my door, for I was in my bedroom, and when I opened it Armand the groom stood there.

"Mademoiselle," he said, "I have received a message from my master."

His master? The Comte, of course. Hadn't Armand come with us from the *château?*

"Yes, Armand?"

"Monsieur le Comte wants you to meet him, and I am to take you to him."

"When?"

"Now, Mademoiselle. He wants us to leave as quietly as possible. He does not want anyone to know that he is in the neighborhood."

"He is in Grasseville?"

"Just beyond the town, Mademoiselle. He is waiting for you there. I have saddled your horse and she is ready in the stables."

"Give me a moment then, and I will change into my riding habit."

"Yes, Mademoiselle, but I beg of you be quick and let no one know where you are going. These are the Comte's orders."

"You can rely on me," I said, excitement rising within me.

He went. I locked the door and changed hastily. I was lucky and saw no one on the way down to the stables.

Armand looked relieved when he saw me. "I trust, Mademoiselle . . ."

"It's all right," I said. "I saw no one."

"That is well."

He helped me into the saddle and very soon we were riding out together.

We skirted the town. I scarcely noticed the way we were going, so excited was I at the prospect of seeing the Comte.

All my probing into the future of the last few days was being turned topsy-turvy just at the prospect of being with him. How could I possibly contemplate marrying one man when the thought of another set my mind whirling in excitement?

We rode on. I had never been in this direction before. The nature of the countryside had changed. It was hilly and we made our way through rough woodland. Once or twice Armand pulled up sharply. I stopped with him.

He appeared to be listening. There was no sound in the wood but the gentle trickle of a stream somewhere near and the sudden buzz of a bee as it flew past.

Armand nodded, appearing satisfied, and prodded his horse.

We came to a small house in the wood. Its stone walls were covered in creeper, and the garden about it was a jungle of overgrown weeds and bushes.

"Is this our destination?" I asked in surprise.

Armand said it was.

"Follow me, Mademoiselle. We'll take the horses to the back of the house and tether them there."

We went round to the back. Whoever lived here could not have tended the garden for more than a year. I looked about for the Comte's horse, for it must be here since he had chosen it for a rendezvous, but I could see nothing.

It was a gloomy spot and instinctively I shrank from alighting.

"Why," I asked, "did the Comte choose such a place?"

Armand lifted his shoulders as though to say it was not for him to question the Comte's commands, only to obey them.

He tethered his horse and came to help me alight. I felt a sudden inclination to spur my horse and gallop away from this place. There was something evil about it. Was it because for the last days I had been thinking about the peace of Derringham?

Armand was tying my horse beside his.

"Armand," I said, "you will come in there with me?"

"But certainly, Mademoiselle."

"It's such an . . . unpleasant little place."

"It is because the overgrown bushes and shrubs make it dark. It is different inside."

"Whose house is it?"

"It belongs to the Comte Fontaine Delibes, Mademoiselle."

"How strange that he should own a house here. It is not on his estate."

"It was a hunting lodge at one time. He has such places all over the country."

I looked away to the right, where a mound of earth rose up from the ground. "Someone has been digging here recently," I said.

"I do not know, Mademoiselle."

"But . . . look."

"Oh, it would seem so. Let us go inside."

"But I want to see this. Look, there's a hole. It looks"—a cold shiver seized me—"it looks like a grave."

"Perhaps someone wanted to bury a dog."

"It is rather big for a dog," I said.

Armand had taken my arm and drew me to the door. He took a key from his pocket and opening the door gave me a gentle push. I was standing in a hall which was dark and a terrible foreboding came to me.

The door shut and I said: "Armand, surely the Comte would not come to a place like this. Where was his horse? If he is already here . . . "

"It may be that he has not arrived yet."

I turned to look at him sharply. A subtle change had come over him. I had never taken much notice of Armand before. He had merely been the groom who had come with us from the *château*. Now he looked uneasy . . . furtive, even. Nonsense! I thought quickly. Imagination! He had been in the Comte's service for many years. It had once been said in Margot's presence and she had not denied it. He was the Comte's good servant. It was the atmosphere of this place which was doing something to my imagination. Then that hole outside which had looked like a grave. Someone had been here recently to dig it.

Armand had gripped my arm as though he feared I would try to escape. It was a strange way for a groom to behave.

He pushed me ahead of him. I thought I heard a sound in the house. I looked up. There seemed to be a film of dust everywhere. It looked like a house in which no one lived. Then who had dug the hole in the garden?

I was aware of Armand's heavy breathing, and suddenly a fearful premonition came to me. I had been brought here to die. The grave in the garden was for me. I had been led into a trap and willingly I had stepped into it. What thoughts can pass through the mind in the space of a few seconds! The Comte had sent one of his servants to bring me here. Why?

To kill me? To bury me in that grave in the garden . . . to leave me there . . . forgotten. Why? He loved me. He had said so. Did he? How could one know? He had the devil in him, how often had I heard that said of him. He wanted Ursule out of the way and he had killed her. He wanted to marry Gabrielle, who had already given him a son. Then what of me? I was to be the scapegoat. If I disappeared it would be said that it was I who had put the fatal dose in Ursule's glass. Nou Nou would support that theory. The Comte would be free of suspicion. Oh, nonsense, nonsense! But he had sent for me and I was here in this fearful place, where every instinct was telling me that I was staring death in the face.

I turned, looking for escape. Then suddenly a door opened. For a moment my eyes would not look. I did not want to see him. I could not bear that my dream world should come tumbling about my ears. If I was going to die I wanted to die in ignorance, refusing to believe that of which so many people had tried to warn me.

Armand was immediately behind me. I lifted my eyes. Standing in the doorway was a figure . . . strangely familiar. I just had time to recognize the short neck, the hat with the brim, the dark wig before he sprang forward and seized me. There was a blinding flash and I was lying on the floor. There was an excruciating pain somewhere . . . I was not sure where . . . for everything was ebbing away, the evil house, the sinister man who had watched me for so long, my frightening speculation, my own consciousness.

When I opened my eyes I was lying in my old bedroom in the Hôtel Delibes. There was cramping pain in my arm, which I realized was bandaged. I tried to struggle up but was immediately giddy and sank back on the pillows.

"Lie still," said a voice. "It is better so."

I did not know the voice, but it was soothing.

There was a parched feeling in my throat and almost immediately a cup was put to my lips. I drank something that was sweet and soothing.

"That's better," said the voice. "Now lie quietly. It might be painful if you move."

"What happened to me?" I asked.

"Try to sleep," was the answer; and so listless did I feel that I obeyed.

When I awoke I saw a woman at my bedside.

"Do you feel better?" It was the same voice as before.

"Yes, thanks. How did I get here?"

"The Comte will explain. He said he was to be called when you awoke."

"He is here then?" I felt suddenly joyous.

He was at my bedside. He took my free hand and kissed it. "Thank God I set Périgot to watch over you. He did a good job."

"What was it all about?"

"You came near to death, my darling. That villain would have killed you . . . and we should never have known what happened. He would have shot you through the heart or the head, which was what he planned to do, and then bury you in that godforsaken place. Why did you go?"

"With Armand, you mean? Why shouldn't I, when he said he was taking me to you?"

"Oh my God, I wish I could get my hands on him. But I will, I promise you."

"But Armand has been in your service for . . . "

"In Étienne's service, I believe. To think that a son of mine . . . What people will do for lands, title, money . . . If I never have a son at all, he'll get nothing now."

"Do you mean that Armand took me there to kill me on Étienne's orders?"

"It could only be so. Armand has disappeared. When he realized that someone was in the house to foil his attempt he made off with all speed."

"And this Périgot?"

"A good man. He has been watchful of you."

"A man with a short neck and a dark wig?"

"I don't know about his wig, but I suppose, now you mention it, he has a short neck."

"So you sent him to guard me?"

"Naturally I sent someone to guard you. I didn't like what had happened on that day when you were fired at in the lane. Périgot did his work well. He followed Armand to the house, saw him dig the grave and guessed what was happening. When he saw you leave Grasseville with him he made sure he was at the house waiting for you when you arrived. Armand was ready to kill you and would have done so if Périgot had not been ready. So the bullet entered your arm instead of your body. Périgot is upset because he did not overpower Armand before the shot was fired, but he was waiting in the house and could only do what he did. If ever we get back to normal, Périgot shall have lands and wealth for what he has done for me."

"Armand!" I murmured. "Why Armand?"

274

"He must work for Étienne. He was always Étienne's groom. They were more than master and servant. It was Étienne—maybe with his mother's connivance, and this I shall discover—who arranged for your little adventure in the lane, I am sure. At least, that put me on the alert. I was determined to take every precaution. I knew that if I could trust anyone I could trust Périgot. I am going to send for him so that you can thank him personally for saving your life."

He came into the room. He looked different without his tall hat and wig, much younger, and the short neck was less noticeable.

He bowed and I said: "Thank you for saving my life."

"Mademoiselle," he replied, "I regret I did not save you completely. I fear that you became aware of me, which showed that I did not make myself unobtrusive enough."

"I couldn't help but be aware of you when you were always there. And how could you have looked after me so expertly if you had not been?"

The Comte said: "We are both grateful to you, Périgot. Your service to us will not be forgotten."

"It is my duty and pleasure to serve you, Monsieur le Comte," he said. "I trust it will be so for very many years."

The Comte was deeply moved and I felt all my fears dropping from me. I wondered why I had ever doubted him—but of course that was the effect his presence always had on me.

When Périgot had gone the Comte sat by my bed and we talked. He said what had happened was clear. Étienne had always hoped to be legitimized and made heir to the estate and title. And so he would have been if there had been no legitimate son. "Of course," he said, "they know of my feelings for you and he began to be afraid. He guessed rightly that I intend to marry you and if you and I had a son—which we fully intend to do, do we not?—his hopes would be completely blighted. Therefore you presented the threat. It's clear, isn't it?"

"Where is Étienne?"

"He was at the *château* looking after estate duties. Armand will have gone to him to tell him of the failure of their plan. I doubt he is at the *château* now, for he will know that I am fully aware of what he has done. He will never dare show his face to me again. It is the end for Étienne. And now there is only one thing to be done. You and I shall marry without delay."

I cried out in protest. I thought of my conversations with Joel. Though I had not promised to marry him, I had not completely refused him. How could I go straight to another man and marry him? Besides, when I thought of marriage, fears and doubts raised their heads once more. The Comte was horrified at Étienne's attempt to murder me, but what of the death of Ursule? Had she not died because she stood in the way of what he wanted, just as I had seemed to stand in Étienne's way?

"Why not?" he demanded fiercely.

"I am not ready," I replied.

"What nonsense is this?"

"Not nonsense, sound good sense. I have to be sure."

"Sure? You mean you are not sure?"

"I think I am, but there is much to consider. There must be in such a serious undertaking as marriage."

"My dearest Minelle, there is only one thing to consider in marriage and that is whether two people love each other. I love you. Have you any doubts of that?"

"It may well be that we do not mean the same thing by love. I know you want to be with me, make love with me . . . but I am not sure that is being in love."

"What is, then?"

"Sharing a lifetime together, mutual respect, understanding. That is important, not the excitement of the moment. Desire, by its very nature, is transient. Before I married I should want to be sure that the man I married was the right father for the children I should have, that he was a man who would share my moral code, a man I could look up to and whom I could trust to be a good father to my children."

"You set a high standard," he said. "I believe the schoolmistress cannot resist setting her suitors an examination."

"It may be so. And perhaps the schoolmistress is not the right wife for a man with a roving eye and a love of adventure."

"My opinion is that she is just the right wife for him. Let us have an end to this nonsense. I will get a priest to marry us within a few days."

"I must have time," I insisted.

"You disappoint me, Minelle. I thought you were adventurous too."

"You see, I am right. I disappoint you already."

"I would rather be disappointed by you than pleased by any other woman."

"That is ridiculous."

"Is that the way to talk to your lord and master?"

"I can see that my proud spirit would never succumb. Oh, how wise I am to consider these things before rushing headlong into a marriage which could be disastrous."

"It would be exciting disaster."

"I would give up the excitement to avoid the disaster."

"You enchant me . . . you always do."

"I can't think why, when I never agree with you."

"Too many people have agreed with me . . . or pretended to. It becomes monotonous."

"I prophesy that disagreement would become equally monotonous and less pleasing to you."

"Try me. Please, Minelle, try me. Listen, my love. Perhaps even now it is too late. The *faubourgs* are preparing to rise. They are coming against us. Let us enjoy life while we can."

"Whoever comes against you, I must have time," I insisted.

He sat by my bed for a long time. We did not speak much but he was silently pleading, I knew. I wavered. So much I wanted to say: "Yes, let us marry. Let us have a little happiness together," but I could not forget walking with Joel, talking with Joel, and perhaps most of all the memory of my mother.

I said suddenly: "Was a message sent to Grasseville to tell them where I was?"

He said that had been taken care of.

"Thank you. They would have been anxious."

I closed my eyes, feigning sleep. I wanted to think, but of course my thoughts led me nowhere but back to the perpetual question.

It was the fourteenth of July—a date in France no one will ever forget. My arm was still bandaged but I was otherwise quite well and it was merely a matter of waiting for the wound to heal.

During the previous day there had been a hush over the city. The weather was hot and sultry and I had the impression that a great beast was crouching, ready to spring.

My own state of mind was tense. In a short time two attempts had been made on my life. One cannot pass through such ordeals unscathed.

I wanted to get away and be alone for a while. In such a mood I put on a light cloak and went out. As I passed through the narrow streets I was aware that furtive glances came my way. Members of the King's guards walked about uneasily. In the distance I could hear the sound of singing.

Someone caught my arm. "Minelle, are you mad?"

It was the Comte. He was soberly dressed in a brown cloak and a tall hat with a brim such as that which had been worn by Périgot. People now took the precaution of never being conspicuously well dressed in the streets.

"You should never have come out. I have been looking for you. I understood you had come in this direction of the Pont Neuf by the Quai de l'Horloge. We must go back at once."

He drew me close to the wall as a party of young men—possibly students—came running past. Their words made me shiver: *"À bas les aristocrates. À la lanterne."*

We walked swiftly past. I was trembling, not for myself but for him. I knew that however homespun his garments, he could never disguise his origins and none would mistake him long for anything but the man he was.

"We will go back at once," he said.

Before we reached the Faubourg Saint Honoré, pandemonium had broken forth and the whole of Paris seemed to have gone mad. There was shouting and screaming in the streets. People were rushing backwards and forwards, joining mobs, chanting, shouting: *"À la Bastille."*

"They are going to the prison," said the Comte. "My God, it has begun."

We reached the Faubourg Saint Honoré in safety.

"You must leave Paris without delay," he said. "It will be unsafe to stay here. Change your clothes as quickly as you can and come down to the stables."

I obeyed him. He was waiting impatiently for me there. He had given orders that those who could should leave the house, but not in a body, gradually. It must not be noticed that they were leaving.

He and I rode south in the direction of the *château*. It was night when we arrived.

As we stood in the hall he turned to me sadly and said: "You left it too late, you see. The revolution has begun. You must leave for England at once. For God's sake do not speak French, for you do it so well that the uneducated might mistake you for a Frenchwoman and you carry yourself in such a way that they would regard you as an enemy of the people."

"What of you? You will escape to England?"

He shook his head. "This is but the beginning. Who knows, there may yet be time to save the crumbling *régime*. It is not for me to leave the sinking ship, Minelle. There is work for me here. I shall return to Paris. I shall go to see the King and his ministers. It may be that all is not lost. But you must go at once. That is my first concern."

"You mean . . . leave you?"

For one moment there was such tenderness in his face that I scarcely recognized him as the man I knew. He held me close to him and kissed my hair. "Foolish Minelle," he said. "Procrastinating Minelle. Now we must say goodbye. You must go and I must stay here."

"I will stay," I said.

He shook his head. "I forbid it."

"So you will send me away?"

He hesitated for a moment and I saw the emotions battling with each other. He believed now that if I stayed we should become lovers, because that was what happened to people in desperate situations when death could be close at hand. They clutched at what life had to offer. But if I stayed, I should be in danger.

He said firmly: "I shall make immediate arrangements for you to leave. Périgot has proved that he can be trusted. He will take you to Calais and you will leave tonight. There must be no delay."

So this was how it had ended. I had been unable to decide for myself and the revolution had decided for me.

Darkness had fallen. I was preparing to leave. In the stables my horse was ready. The Comte had said my departure must be as quiet as possible.

"I shall have no peace while you are here," he said. "You stand a good chance of escape with Périgot to guide you. Don't forget, do not speak French unless it is necessary. Stress your nationality. It will carry you through. The people have no quarrel with foreigners. This is a war between Frenchmen and Frenchmen."

I argued with him. I wanted to stay. Twice I had come near to death. I was ready to risk it again. Anything rather than leave him.

He was moved but adamant.

"Ironical," he said, "when there was no danger, you hesitated. You wanted to be sure, didn't you? You didn't trust me. Nothing has happened to establish that trust . . . and yet you are ready to risk your life to stay with me. Oh, perverse Minelle!"

I could only plead with him. "Let me stay. Let me take a

chance. Or come with me. Why should you not come to England?"

He shook his head. "I am too involved here. I could not desert my colleagues. France is my country. She is about to be torn asunder. I must stay and fight for what I believe to be right. Listen, Minelle, when it is over I will come for you."

I shook my head sadly.

"You do not believe that? You think I will have forgotten you? I tell you this: Whatever happens in the future . . . whatever has happened in the past, I love you. You are the only one for me . . . and although you do not know it yet . . . I am the one for you. How different our lives have been! We have lived by different codes. You have been brought up as a good Christian woman. I . . . well, I have lived in a decadent society. It never occurred to me to consider whether I had a right to behave as I did. Not until I killed a child did I begin to take a little stock of myself, and then my environment was too strong for me. When you came, I changed. I wanted a different life. You made me see everything in a new light. You showed me how to see life through your eyes. I want more lessons, little schoolmistress, and only you can teach me."

"Then I will stay. I will marry you and stay with you."

"If I married you now you would become the Comtesse Fontaine Delibes. That would not be a very good name to have in this new France. God knows what they will do to us, but it will be revenge . . . bitter and cruel. That I am sure of. The last thing that must happen to you just now is that you become one of us. There is only one course open to you now. You must go. It is too late for anything else. Come, we are wasting precious time. Goodbye, my dearest. No, *au revoir*. We shall meet again."

I clung to him. Now I was sure. I belonged with him. I never wanted to leave him. I did not know whether he had killed his wife or not and in that moment I knew I could not have changed my feelings towards him even if he were guilty.

"Périgot is waiting in the stables. There must be no delay."

He put his arm about me and we went out into the hot night air.

As soon as we approached the stables I knew that something was wrong. I was aware of watching eyes, a movement, the sound of heavy breathing. He was aware of it too. His grip on my arm tightened as he drew me hastily towards the stables. Then suddenly there was a shout.

"He's here. Take him now."

As the Comte pushed me from him a torch flared up suddenly. I saw the mob then . . . twenty . . . thirty of them crowding in on us, eyes alight with brutal excitement. They were inflamed with the desire for revenge on any member of that class which had oppressed them for hundreds of years.

"Get into the stables," he muttered to me.

I did not move. I could not leave him.

Then I saw a sight which sickened me. At their head was a face I knew. Léon's.

I only just recognized him in the light from the flare, so distorted was his expression. I had never thought Léon could look like that. His eyes were wild with hatred, his mouth distorted. How different from the suave and kindly man I had known!

"Hang him!" shouted a voice.

"Hang him? That's too nice."

Then they marched on him. I saw him fall . . . and Léon was there.

I could not hear what Léon said, but he was commanding them.

They took him away. I saw him attempt to fight them off, but even he could do nothing against so many. I felt sick with fear and horror. I was shaking with misery.

Oh God, I thought. He is right. It is too late.

2

Périgot was beside me. "Mademoiselle, we should go . . . quickly."

"No," I said, "I shall not go."

"There is nothing that can be done."

"What will they do to him?"

"They are killing his kind all over the country, Mademoiselle. His wish was that you should leave at once for England. This is no place for you."

I shook my head.

"I shall not go until I know what has happened to him."

Périgot said sadly: "Mademoiselle, there is nothing we can do. His wish must be obeyed."

"I shall stay here until I know," I said firmly.

I went into the *château* and to my room. I sat down wearily, my thoughts with him. What would they do to him? What punishment would they inflict for what they called centuries of injustice? His crime was that he belonged to the oppressors. It was now the turn of others to oppress.

He had tried so hard to save me. His thoughts had been all for me. If he had not returned with me to the *château*, he would have been in Paris now. Not that there was safety there, but he would have been with his colleagues at the Court and surely they would have made some stand.

What could I do now? What was there to do? Nothing but wait.

Where had they taken him? Where was he now?

I dared not think.

Léon was the traitor. I had been fond of Léon. It was hard to believe that he would have been the one to lead the mob to the Comte. Nearly all his life he had been nurtured in the *château*—fed, clothed, and educated. And all the time he had nursed such resentment that at the first opportunity he had turned against his benefactor. But his twin brother had been killed . . . by the Comte; and that was something which had never been forgiven.

But the Comte had tried to recompense them. He had taken Léon into his household. Léon had looked after his family. Ursule had helped them. But they could not forgive. All those years they must have been waiting for revenge, and Léon had so carefully concealed his true feelings as to deceive us all.

It *was* Léon whom I had seen on the night of the ball. That should have warned me. But I could not believe it then and had convinced myself that I was mistaken.

But what was the use of brooding on these matters now? There was only one thing that mattered. What was happening to the man I loved?

I stood at the window peering out. I could see the light of a flare in the distance. I strained my eyes. Was he there now? They would kill him. It was murder I had seen in their eyes . . . the hatred for those who had been born to riches and possessed that which they coveted.

I believed that something died in me at that moment. Nothing I could ever do would be the same again. Life had shown me an opportunity—to love, to live excitingly, dangerously perhaps—and I had passed it by. My puritanical up-bringing had not allowed me to accept what life was offering me. I wanted to make sure . . . and so I lost my chance.

This would have come. This was inevitable. But at least we might have had some life together.

Someone had come into my room. I turned sharply and saw Nou Nou.

"So they have taken him," she said. "They have taken the Comte . . ."

I nodded.

"God help him. They are in no mood to be gentle."

I said passionately: "They are madmen. They look like savages. And these are his own people . . . the people who have lived on his estate, benefited from his bounty . . ."

"That could be dangerous talk," she said.

"It's true," I cried. "Nou Nou, what will happen to him?"

"They'll hang him most likely," she said dispassionately.

"No!"

"It's what they're doing. Hanging them on the lanterns. That's what I heard. They've taken the Bastille. It's the start. There is no chance for the Comte and his kind. I am glad my Ursule went when she did. This would have been terrible for her. They won't spare the women, you know."

I could not bear to look at her. She was so calm and almost gloating.

"Oh yes," she went on, "it was right she should go when she did. It wouldn't have done for her to live through this."

I did not want to look at Nou Nou, nor to listen to her; I wanted to be alone with my sorrow.

But she came to me and sat beside me; she laid a cold hand over mine.

"You will never be with him now, will you?" she said. "You will never lie beside him and exult in what she so dreaded. Her mother was the same. Some women are like that. They should never marry. It's not fair to them. But they are reared in ignorance . . . as it is right they should be . . . and then suddenly they come to knowledge and they find it unendurable. Such was my little Ursule. Such a happy girl she was . . . playing with her dolls. She loved her dolls. They used to call her the Little Mother. And then . . . they married her to him. *Anyone* else would have been better. She was so like her mother . . . in every way . . . yes, in every way."

I wished she would go. I could think of nothing but him. What were they doing to him? He would suffer from indignity more than physical pain, I knew. I kept thinking of him as he had been the first time I had seen him, when I had called him the Devil on Horseback. So proud, so formidable, invincible.

"I can tell the truth now," Nou Nou was saying. "It's like a burden dropping from you. I always felt the need to tell the truth. I've been on the point of doing it many times. You suspected him, didn't you? Everyone suspected him—you too. Yes, some thought you'd had a hand in it. He had a motive, didn't he? He was tied to her . . . and she couldn't give him a son and there was a young, healthy woman . . . you, Mademoiselle. It was easy to see how he felt about you. They were all waiting, weren't they? I laughed, I did, to think of Gabrielle LeGrand. What a blow for her, although she might have known it wouldn't be her . . . even if he were free. But they go on hoping, don't they? Such opinions they have of themselves. It was easy to see she had long been a habit with him."

"Please, Nou Nou," I said, "I am very tired."

"Yes, you're tired and they've taken him, haven't they? They'll show no mercy on him. He wasn't much of a one for showing mercy himself, was he? He'll be swinging from a lantern by now. Perhaps they'll hang him from one of his own."

"Stop it, Nou Nou."

"I hated him," she said fiercely. "I hated him for what he did to my Ursule. She dreaded his coming to her."

"You've admitted it would have been the same with any man."

"Some might have been kinder."

"Nou Nou, will you please leave me alone."

"Not till I've told you. You must listen to me. It's best to know the truth. It can do little good now. Perhaps that's why I'm telling you. I knew her mother well. She was good to me. She took me in when I had my trouble . . . when I lost my man and my little one. She put Ursule into my arms and she said: 'Here is your baby now, Nou Nou.' And then there was something to live for. She *was* my baby. My little love. And I stopped thinking so bitterly about my own sweet baby. Her mother was a sick woman. She was like Ursule . . . listless . . . never wanting to do much, turning away from her food, and then the pains started. They flared up. She suffered terribly. She was mad with pain and then she took her own life because she could not endure it any more. It was going to happen to Ursule. She was so like her mother. I knew, didn't I? Who could know better? She had the pains . . . only mildly—as her mother had had them at first—and I had the doctors to her. They said she was suffering from that which had killed her mother. I knew what it was going to be like . . ."

She had my attention now. I was staring at her in amazed horror.

"Yes," said Nou Nou, "she would have suffered if she had lived. And she would never have taken her own life. She had strong feelings against that. She'd talked of them often. 'We're here to fulfill a purpose, Nou Nou,' she used to say. 'It's no use giving up halfway. If you do, you'll have to come back and do it all again.' I couldn't bear to think of her suffering . . . not my little Ursule. So I saw to it that she didn't . . ."

"*You,* Nou Nou. *You* killed her."

"To save her pain," said Nou Nou simply. "There! I'm a murderess, you're thinking. You're thinking that they should take me and hang me on a lantern or send me to the guillotine."

"I know you did it for love," I said.

"Yes, I did it for love. My life is empty now she has gone. But I know this: she is suffering no pain where she is now. That's how I console myself."

"But you let it be thought . . ."

Sly lights came into her eyes. "That *he* had killed her. Yes, I did. He had killed her . . . a thousand times in his thoughts. He wanted her out of the way, but he didn't kill her. I, who longed to have her with me forever, did that."

She covered her face with her hands and began to cry.

"My little one. She looked so peaceful lying there. She would just slip away, I knew. No pain . . . never again. All her fears of him were over. She is happy now, my baby. She is with that other baby . . . my two darlings together."

"Oh Nou Nou," I said, and tried to put an arm about her.

She threw me off. "You'll never have him now," she said malevolently. "It's all over."

Then she rose and glided towards the door. She stopped there and looked back at me.

"You should go home," she said. "Forget this happened . . . if you can." She took a step back into the room and fixed her wild eyes on me. "*You* are in danger too.

They let you go tonight, but you are one of them, remember." Her lips twisted into a grim smile. "The cousin . . . the same family. Now you will see what it means to belong to such a family. They were after the big fish tonight. But all fishes are sweet, as is the blood of aristocrats to them. They want to see it flow . . . the sons', the daughters', the nieces', the nephews', the *cousins'* . . ."

"Nou Nou," I began, but she had turned away and as she went she muttered: "They will come, I tell you. They will come for you."

Then she went out and left me.

I felt stunned by her revelation. I had misjudged him, and I might never have a chance to ask his pardon.

What was happening to him now? Desperately I tried to curb my imagination. I could not shut out of my mind the memory of those distorted faces, crazy with blood lust, determined on revenge.

They had taken him. Nou Nou's voice kept echoing in my ears: "They will come for you."

I sat at the window waiting for the morning. What I should do then I did not know. Where had they taken him? What had happened to him? Perhaps already . . .

I would not allow myself to believe that. I found myself making bargains with God. "Let me see him . . . only once. Let me tell him that I know now how I misjudged him. Let me tell him that I love him . . . that I have always loved him, but that I was too inexperienced, too bound by convention, to know it. Once . . . let me see him once."

He would have said I should not be there. I should have gone off with Périgot while there was a chance. How could I? I could think of nothing but him. My own safety seemed of no importance. If they were going to kill him they could kill me with him.

In the distance I heard shouting. I was immediately at the window looking out. There were lights among the trees . . . torches coming nearer to the *château* as I watched.

Now I could hear their voices. Did I imagine it or could I hear the word: "Cousine."

They were chanting something.

Footsteps outside my door. Light running footsteps.

Voices were whispering. It was the servants. "They are coming for the cousin . . . now."

I went back to the window. I heard it distinctly: *"À bas la cousine. À la lanterne."*

My throat was dry. So it had come, then. I was to be taken by the mob as he had been. This was the price I was to pay. I had allowed myself to be drawn into subterfuge. I had pretended to be Margot's cousin for her sake and afterwards I had allowed the deception to be continued. Now this very pretense could cost my life.

I did not want to die. I wanted so much to live, to be with my love, to grow old with him. There was so much I had to learn about him . . . about life. I had so much to live for . . . if he could be with me.

The noise from below was horrific. I shut my eyes and it was as though those faces made hideous by greed, envy, hatred, and malice were closing in on me.

The light from the torches illumined my room. In the mirror I caught a glimpse of a wild-eyed woman whom I scarcely recognized as myself.

At any moment now . . .

There was a hammering on my door. I went to it and leaned against it.

"Open . . . quickly." It was Périgot.

I turned the key. He seized my arm and dragged me into the corridor. He ran pulling me with him. We mounted a spiral staircase which went on and on.

We had reached the watch tower. There he touched a panel and the wood slid back, disclosing a cavity.

"Get in," he said. "You could be safe here. They will search the *château* but few could know of this place. I will come back when they have gone."

The panel shut on me. I was in complete darkness.

I heard them come into the watch tower. I heard their laughter and their ugly threats as to what they would do when they found me.

Again and again I heard the word "Cousine" and my thoughts went back to the peaceful days of my life when my mother had been alive and it would have seemed impossible that I should ever become a victim of a revolution in France. Cousin . . . That was when it had begun. It was when I had agreed to come to France with Margot and pose as her cousin. If I had not done so . . .

No, I told myself, even with danger and the prospect of violent death close to me, I would do it again. I regret nothing . . . except my doubts of the Comte. "The Devil on Horseback." I used it tenderly now. *My* Devil. But I wanted nothing else from life but to be with him, and I would risk anything for the time I had spent with him. He loved me and I loved him, and I would give my life for that.

At any moment I was expecting the wall to open. They would find the secret sliding panel. Perhaps they would tear the walls down. I crouched, waiting in horror.

Then I realized that the noise had died away. Was I safe then?

It seemed like hours that I waited there in the quiet darkness and then . . . Périgot came.

He had brought rugs and candles.

"You will have to stay here for a while," he said. "The mob was murderous. They have ransacked the *château* and taken away some of the valuables. Thank God, they did not set it on fire. I have convinced them that you escaped when they took the Comte. Some of them have taken horses from the stables and gone off in pursuit. It will die down in a day or so. They have taken others with whom to occupy themselves. You must stay here until I can take you away. As soon as it is possible I will take you to Grasseville."

"Périgot," I said, "it is the second time I have owed my life to you."

"The Comte would never forgive me if I allowed you to come to any harm."

"You talk of him as though . . ."

"Mademoiselle," he said seriously, "the Comte was always one to extricate himself from trouble. He will do it again."

"Oh Périgot, how is that possible?"

"Only God . . . and the Comte . . . will know, Mademoiselle. But it must be. It *will* be."

And Périgot's words did more to lighten the darkness of my hiding place than his candles could ever do.

I passed through that night somehow in my candlelit prison. I lay on my rugs and I thought of the Comte. Périgot was right. He would find some way out.

Périgot came early next morning. He brought food, which I could not eat.

He said that he would have two horses ready in the stables. Thank God, the mob had not taken them all. We must slip down after dark for he did not know whom he could trust. I must try to eat something and be ready when the moment came.

It was the following night when Périgot came again to the tower. I knew that he could not make many journeys to me during the day for fear of arousing suspicion.

"You are leaving immediately," he whispered. "Be careful. Don't speak. We have to get down to the stables undetected."

I stepped out of my hiding place and stood in the watch tower.

Périgot shut the panel and turned to me. "Now we must descend the spiral staircase. I shall go first. Follow me carefully."

I nodded and was about to speak when he put his fingers to his lips.

Then he started down the staircase.

In the main part of the *château* we had to be especially careful, for I understood that we could not know who in the household might betray me. Carefully he went while I followed. It seemed a long journey, but finally we were out of the castle and the cool night air seemed intoxicating after my prison in the hole behind the walls of the watch tower.

Then . . . my heart leaped in terror, for as we entered the stables a man came towards us.

This is the end, I thought. Then I saw who it was.

"Joel!" I cried.

"Hush," whispered Périgot. "All is ready."

"Come, Minella," said Joel, and helped me into the saddle.

Périgot came close. "Your English friend will take you to safety, Mademoiselle," he said. "I have news of the Comte. They did not kill him."

"Oh . . . Périgot! Is that true? You know . . ."

He nodded. "They have taken him to Paris. He is in the Conciergerie."

"Where they go . . . to await death."

"The Comte is not yet dead, Mademoiselle."

"Thank God. Thank you. Périgot, how can I ever . . ."

"Go quickly," said Périgot. "Keep in good heart."

Joel said again: "Come, Minella."

We came out of the stables, and then I was riding, side by side with Joel, away from the *château*.

Through the night we rode until Joel suggested that we give the horses a rest. It was not quite dawn when we came to a wood and we took the horses to a stream to drink. Then Joel tethered them and we leaned against a tree trunk and talked.

He told me how worried he had been when I disappeared and how relieved when a message came from the Comte to tell them that I was in Paris. Joel had gone to the house in Paris and learned where I was.

When he came to the *château* his object was to take me back to Grasseville, for Margot had decided to leave for England with her husband and Charlot. She would not go without me and he agreed wholeheartedly with her that we must leave as soon as possible.

Arriving at the *château,* he had heard what happened and Périgot and he had agreed that it was like an act of Providence that he had come just at that time. He had arranged with Périgot that he and I should leave at once.

"Paris is terrifying," he said. "They are talking of what they will do to certain people when they have them in their hands."

"Was . . . the Comte's name mentioned?"

"It is a well-known name."

I shivered. "And they have him," I murmured. "They came and took him. Léon, that wicked traitor, led them to him."

"Thank God, they did not get you."

"It was Périgot who saved me . . . as he did before."

"He is a devoted servant."

"Oh, Joel," I cried, "they have him there in the Conciergerie. The prison they call the anteroom of death."

"But he is alive," Joel reminded me. "Étienne is in there also. I heard he had been taken in with Armand."

"So they will be there together. I was afraid the mob had killed the Comte."

"No. Périgot told me he is too big a prize for an insignificant death. The mob was persuaded to take him to Paris."

I felt sick with fear. They had taken him to the Conciergerie, the waiting room of death. They would make a great show of his journey to his execution. He was to represent the symbol of their power. Through him they would show that there would be no mercy on those aristocrats who fell into the hands of the people. The tables had been viciously turned. Yet at the same time my spirits were lifted a little because he still lived.

"I must go to Paris," I said to Joel.

"No, Minella. We are going to Grasseville. We must leave this country without delay."

"You must go, Joel, but I shall stay in Paris. While he lives I want to be near him."

"It is madness," said Joel.

"Perhaps, but it is what I shall do."

How patient Joel was with me! How clearly he understood. If I could not leave Paris, then nor would he. He spared himself nothing. He faced a hundred dangers for my sake. He had a friend in the Rue Saint Jacques and we stayed in his house there. It was an unobtrusive dwelling among the booksellers and the seventeenth-century houses. Many students lived there and in the somber clothes which Joel had acquired for us we were inconspicuous.

To be in that city—once so proud and beautiful—and to see it brought low as only mob rule can bring a city, was to suffer deeply, but to know that the man I loved was in the hands of those who would show no mercy was so profound a sorrow that I did not think I could ever recover from it. The shrieking mob roamed the streets in their red caps. The nights were the most terrible. I used to lie in my bed shivering, for I knew that in the morning, if we ventured out, we should see the lifeless corpses dangling from the lanterns . . . sometimes hideously mutilated.

"We should go now," Joel was constantly telling me. "There is nothing more we can do."

"But I could not go . . . not until I knew he was dead."

I would haunt the Cour du Mai and watch the tumbrils go by. I stood there among that morbidly fascinated crowd and listened to the jeers as some nobleman rode by, wigless, head shaved, aloof, disdainful.

I was there when Étienne went by. Haughty, showing no fear, proud of the fact right to the end that he was of noble blood, to establish which he had tried to kill me.

I thought: It is Étienne today. Will it be his father tomorrow?

It was night . . . hideous night. From my window I could hear the shouts of the people.

There was a sudden banging on the front door. I threw a robe about me and went onto the landing. Joel was already at the top of the stairs.

"Stay where you are," he commanded.

I obeyed while he descended the stairs. Then I heard

someone talking to him and a man came up the stairs with him. He wore a cloak and a hat pulled over his eyes.

He took off the hat when he saw me.

"Léon!" I cried, and such waves of anger swept over me that I was speechless. I could only stare at him.

"You are surprised to see me?" he said.

Then I found my voice. "I wonder you dare come here! You, who betrayed him! He brought you to the *château*, gave you education, standing . . ."

Léon held up a hand. "You misjudge me," he said. "I have come to try to save him."

I laughed bitterly. "I saw you on the night they took him."

"I think," said Joel, "we should go somewhere where we can talk. Come into my room."

I shook my head. "I do not want to talk to this man," I said. "Go away. He has come to trick us, Joel. He doesn't want his revenge to stop with the Comte."

Joel had led us into his room. There was a table there with a few chairs. "Come and sit down," he said to me tenderly.

I sat down, Joel beside me. Léon sat opposite. He was looking at me earnestly. "I want to help you," he said. "I always had a great regard for you." He smiled rather one-sidedly. "Why, at one time I thought of offering myself. But I knew how things were. I want you to know that I would be ready to do a great deal for you. I shall run great risks if I do this, but then this is a time of risks. Those who are alive one day are dead the next."

"I want nothing to do with you," I said. "I know you for what you are. I saw you throw the stone through the window on the night of the ball, but I could not believe my eyes and thought I had imagined it. I know now how wrong I was . . . for you were there when they took him. You were at their head. You led them to him. I saw the cruelty and hatred in your eyes and there was no mistaking you then."

"But you were mistaken. I see I must convince you of my loyalty to the Comte."

"You will never do that if you talk all night." I turned to Joel. "Send him away. He is a traitor."

"There is little time left to us," said Léon. "Will you give me a few moments to explain, because if you are going to save the Comte you need my help, and anything I can do will be of no use unless you are ready."

Joel was looking at me. "I saw him," I said. "There can be no doubt."

"You did not see me," said Léon. "You saw my twin brother."

I laughed. "It won't do. We know he died. He was killed by the Comte's horses and this is the reason why you were brought to the *château*."

"My brother was injured . . . badly. It was thought he would never recover. They all thought he was dying. The Comte took me as recompense. But my brother did not die."

"I don't believe it," I said.

"Nevertheless, it's true."

"But where was he all those years?"

"When they knew he was going to recover, my parents believed that if he did all the benefits which came from the *château* would cease. I should be sent from the *château* and one of the great joys of my parents' life was to have an educated son . . . a '*château* boy,' they called me. The thought of losing that was intolerable to them. They loved their children. Oh, they were good parents. That was the main reason why they did what they did. They arranged for my brother to 'die' . . . to appear to be dead, you see. They had a coffin made for him and he lay in it and when the time for burial came—my uncle was the coffinmaker, which simplified matters—it was nailed down and my brother smuggled out of the village to another, fifty miles away, where he was brought up with my cousins."

"It's an incredible story," I said suspiciously.

"Nevertheless, it's true. We were identical twins. It is possible to tell the difference between us if you see us side by side . . . but we could easily be mistaken one for the other. My brother was less able to forgive the Comte than the rest of the family were. He bears the scars of his accident to this day. He walks with a limp. The present situation has given him the chance he has waited for all his life. In his early teens he was fomenting discontent among the peasants. He is clever, though without education. He is shrewd, daring, capable of anything that will bring revenge on a class which he hates, and there is one he hates above all others."

He was so earnest, he told his story so plausibly, that I was beginning to be won over. I glanced at Joel, who was watching Léon intently.

"Let us hear your plan," he said.

"My brother is recognized as one of the leaders of the people. He was responsible for the capture of the Comte and bringing him to Paris. The Comte is well known throughout the country as an aristocrat of aristocrats. It will be a great triumph for them when they can show him in the streets in his tumbril. There will be crowds at the guillotine that day."

I said quickly: "What plan is this?"

"I would try to bring him out of the Conciergerie."

"Impossible," cried Joel.

"Almost," replied Léon. "But perhaps with a great deal of care, cunning, and daring . . . it could be done, but you know to attempt it we should all be risking our lives."

"We are all risking our lives here," I said impatiently.

"This would be a rather greater risk. You may not wish to undertake it. To be caught would not mean only death . . . but horrible death. The people's rage could send them into a frenzy against you."

"I would do anything to save him," I said. Then I looked at Joel. "Joel," I added, "you must not take part in this."

"I'm afraid," Léon pointed out, "I was counting on your help."

"If you are in it, Minella, of course I shall be with you," said Joel firmly. "Let us hear what is expected of us."

"As I said," went on Léon, "my brother is one of the leaders of the revolution. He is known and respected by the people throughout France. Some are afraid of him for his ruthlessness and he would spare none who worked against the revolution. You did not know the difference between us when you saw him in the mob. You thought you saw me on the night of the ball when he was the one you saw. If my brother went to the Conciergerie and demanded to see the prisoner, if he walked out with him to take him to another prison, he could do so."

I began to see what he was leading to.

"Are you saying you would go to the Conciergerie and impersonate your brother?"

"I could attempt it. I know his mannerisms, his walk, his voice. I can imitate them. Whether I should succeed is another matter. If we are caught, I warn you we should be taken by the mob and torn to pieces. It would not be a pleasant ending to our adventure."

"Why are you proposing to do this?" I asked.

He shrugged his shoulders. "Today, one lives dangerously. You see me . . . between two worlds. I am of the people, but by the nature of my upbringing I am on the other side. I am trusted by neither . . . as you have shown me. I have to come down on one side or the other and I have always had a weakness for lost causes. I am a man of some feeling. The Comte was as a father to me . . . oh, a remote sort of father . . . far, far above me, rarely deigning to notice me. But I was proud to be his protégé. I looked up to him. I used to promise myself that I would be like him. He is the sort of man I should most like to be. I cannot bear to think of such talents being severed by the guillotine. My motives are mixed. All my life I have been told: 'Do this, do that. It is the wish of the Comte.' Now I shall have the opportunity of going to the Comte and saying: 'Do this. I, Léon, your peasant protégé have it in my power to save your life.' Think of the satisfaction. There is another point—I have a fondness for him . . . and for you, Mademoiselle Minelle. I suspected Étienne and I cursed myself for not being there to save you. But here is my opportunity."

"Are you quite sure you want to take it?"

"I am completely sure. Listen. I shall go into the prison. I shall wear a cloak as my brother wears. I shall sport the red cap. I shall talk in his voice, imitate his limp, which I can do so that none knows the difference between us. I shall say that the day for the execution of the Comte is fixed and it is to be a day of great rejoicing. We shall make it symbolic of the revolution. For this reason, the Comte is to be paraded through Paris. He will go to another prison—as yet to be secret—and it will be the task of Jean-Pierre Bourron—my brother—to take him to that secret place. I shall have my *cabriolet* waiting outside." He turned to Joel. "You will be my driver. As soon as we are in it you will drive with all speed. You, Minella, will be waiting at the Quai de la Mégisserie, where we can pick you up and then ride on as quickly as we can. On the edge of the city I shall have arranged for a *fiacre* with fresh horses. Then you will ride on to Grasseville, where you can continue your journey to the coast."

"It sounds as though it might work," said Joel. "It will need very careful planning."

"You may rest assured that I have given my deepest thought to this. Are you prepared to join me?"

I looked at Joel. What were we asking of him? He had come to France to take me home, to offer me marriage, and now we were suggesting that he should risk his life—and perhaps face a terrible death—in order that I might find a future with another man.

But he was Joel and he did not hesitate, as I knew he would not. I could almost hear my mother: "You see how right I was. He would be such a good husband to you."

"Of course we must save the Comte," said Joel. And I loved him for his calm reconciliation to whatever fate had to offer him. He was admirable, I knew, as the Comte could never be. But how perverse are our emotions!

"Then," said Léon, "let us get down to the details. If this is to work, everything must go right all the way through. Not until you are on English soil will you be safe."

All that night we were together . . . the three of us. Every detail was discussed over and over again. Léon reminded us once more of the risks we were running and impressed on us that only if we were prepared to consider the terrible cost of failure should we undertake this task.

Could it succeed?

I had watched them leave in the *cabriolet*, Joel disguised as the driver, Léon wrapped in the kind of clothes his brother favored, the red cap on his head.

When they had left, I went to take up my place at the Quai de la Mégisserie.

There were many people in the streets as night came, but we dared not attempt our rescue by day. I had tried to look like an old woman. My hair was completely hidden by my hood and I bent my back as I shuffled along the streets. They were terrifying, those streets by night. One could never be sure when one would be confronted by some horrible sight. The shops were barricaded. Many of them had been looted. Fires would spring up anywhere at any time. One would meet gangs of children singing "*Ça Ira.*"

Paris was the last place one should be in if one did not belong to it.

Perhaps this would be my last night here. It must be. I refused to contemplate failure.

How long the waiting seemed! I must be ready. I had been told to be there to step immediately into the *cabriolet* as it came along beside me. If it did not come in an hour, I was to make my way to our lodging in the Rue Saint Jacques and wait there. If I heard nothing by the morning, I was to leave Paris and make my way to Grasseville, where Margot and Robert would be waiting for me to leave for England.

Never, never can I forget those fearful moments when I

stood there in the heart of revolutionary Paris. I could smell the blood in the streets and the bodies in the river. I heard a clock strike nine and I knew that if they had succeeded, they must be on their way.

How cruel is the imagination! I was tormented by my own speculations. I visualized a thousand horrors and it seemed to me as I stood there that our plan could not succeed. It was certain to be discovered. It was too wild. It was too dangerous.

I waited and waited. If they did not come soon I must make my way back to the Rue Saint Jacques.

A leering man accosted me. I hurried away, but feared to go far. A crowd of students came marching down the road. If the *cabriolet* came now they might try to impede its progress.

"Oh God," I prayed, "let this succeed. I would give anything I have to see his face again."

The sound of wheels. It was the *cabriolet*, driving furiously towards me.

Léon stepped out and helped me in.

I looked at my love. His hands were manacled. His face was pale and there was a streak of blood on his left cheek. But he was smiling at me. That was enough.

I felt I had never been so happy in my life—nor ever could be more so—than I was at that moment on the Quai de la Mégisserie.

AND AFTER

We made our escape. Léon left us once we were out of the city. He drove the *cabriolet* back into Paris.

Joel, the Comte, and I went on to Grasseville where Robert and Margot were waiting for us. We were in England within a few days, where I became the Comtesse Fontaine Delibes. My husband was very ill and it was some weeks before I nursed him back to health. The Derringhams were very good friends to us.

Charles-Auguste—it seemed odd at first to use that name and I never really became accustomed to calling him anything but the Comte in my thoughts—was no longer a rich and powerful man, but he was not penniless. He had money in various parts of the world and we could live comfortably enough, which we did on a small estate not far from the Derringhams. My husband was born to be a squire and it was not long before the estate began to prosper. By the time our first child was born—a son—we had added considerably to our land.

He had changed very little. He was still arrogant, overbearing, unpredictable, but after all, that was the man with whom I had fallen in love, so I would not have had him change. Life was not easy with him. I had not expected it to be. He used to talk vehemently of the rabble and I could see that his life in prison had left an indelible mark on him. He was bitter; he would never be completely content until he was back in France and had regained his estates. France was in his blood and he loved his native land with an abiding passion. We quarreled in a lighthearted way comparing our two countries; and he was always determined that one day we should go back.

Margot had another son, and I was so glad that she could give Robert the reward he wanted most. The Comte had always been amused at the way in which she had brought Charlot into the household. She was undoubtedly his daughter, he said, not without pride, I think. Robert's parents never

new the truth. After all, said Margot, it would only disturb
them.

Charlot was growing into a strong, healthy boy. I often
wondered about his father and I heard later from one of the
servants that he had gone north and done very well up there.

Joel never married. I felt conscience-stricken about Joel.
He was so good and kind, and without him we could never
have brought my husband out of the Conciergerie. I wished
that he would marry and be very happy. He deserved the best.

We were very sad on the day the King of France was
executed, and when he was shortly followed by the Queen,
that seemed the end of the old way of life. "They will never
prosper, these murderers," said Charles-Auguste. "They will
fail just as we failed. Then we shall go back to France and
start again."

I have changed a good deal, I believe. Charles-Auguste
says: "The schoolmistress has receded, but she is ready to
pop out now and then. She will keep us in good order, I
don't doubt, until the end of our days."

I am content, I have known great ecstasy and great fear,
great joy and great sorrow. I suppose that is what life is about.

My marriage has not been a bed of roses, as they say. We
have quarreled a great deal. Charles-Auguste has an indomitable will and hates to be crossed; and I am a woman who
could never suppress her own opinions if she thinks them to
be right. It is inevitable that our lives should be stormy. It is
what we both expect. But perhaps neither of us seeks the
peaceful way, the essence of which is its uneventful tenor. It
was the sort of life I should have had at Derringham and
which my mother wanted for me.

When Charles-Auguste went back to France for a brief
visit to see what had happened to his estates, I did everything
in my power to prevent his going. When he was adamant, I
was determined to go with him. This he forbade, but I went
all the same. I followed him, crossed on the same packet,
and when he came to the inn where he was to stay he found
me there.

His fury was great. How violently we quarreled! He had
refused to take me with him because it might be dangerous.
I had refused to stay for the same reason. That clash of
wills!—how often was it exercised. Sometimes he was the
victor, sometimes I.

I remember how we made love in that old inn at Calais
after we had somehow laughed at our fury.

There could be no doubt that we were made for each other
So the years passed.

The revolution was over, and those who had escaped
started coming back. Léon distinguished himself in Napoleon'
army.

The new *régime* was no more successful than the old
There would always be men without possessions who wanted
those of others, and envy, hatred, malice, indifference to other
would prevail forever, it seemed.

We went back to the *château*, which was miraculously un
scathed. What a thrill it was to mount those steps to the plat
form and look back . . . and back . . .

Margot and Robert and their three children returned with
Charles-Auguste, myself, and our two sons. And so life went
on . . . uneasily sometimes. There was conflict between our
two countries, for when the new France had risen from the
ashes, she had sought to conquer the world under the Corsican
adventurer. We used to discuss, argue, rarely agreeing. I was
for my country, he was for his.

Once he said to me: "Do you know, you ought to have
married Joel Derringham. You would have agreed about
everything. Just imagine how easy life would have been."

"Do you really think I should have?" I asked.

He shook his head and looked at me in the mocking way
which was so familiar to me now and which I had first seen
when I had opened his bedroom door and was caught peering
in.

"It would have been too dull for one of your temperament,
too easy. You would have become like hundreds of other
ladies. You would have shrunk instead of expanding. You
would have been charming and pleasant and inwardly bored.
Have you ever been bored since you married me? Come, tell
the truth."

"No. But I have been exasperated. I have been furiously
angry. I have asked myself why I stay with you."

"And what was the answer to that all important question?"

"The answer was that I only stayed with you because I
should have been the most miserable woman on earth if ever
I left you."

He laughed, but as he drew me to him and held me fast
he was suddenly tender.

"Rejoice," he cried. "At last we are in agreement."

A-3